To my dear friend Michele, thanx for all your help

With the Voice of Angels

and God bless your Gracier family

*The heart's immortal thirst is to be
completely known and all forgiven*

— Henry van Dyke —

*Your Opera/author
Buddy*

Brady Harvin

ISBN: 978-1-935188-07-0

Library of Congress Control Number: 2009941643

Edited by Janet Elaine Smith
Cover by T.C. McMullen
Interior design by Alicia McMullen

A Star Publish LLC Publication
www.starpublishllc.com
Published in 2009
Printed in the United States of America

With the Voice of Angels

Brad Garvin

A Star Publish LLC Book

Il Prologo

"OPERA IS DEAD." Chicago's leading newspaper, *The Herald*, rang the death knell to the nation and the world's performing arts communities. Like an icy slash from the infamous Chicago wind, the cut was deep and chilling, but not unexpected. Opera was now a thing of the past in the nation's heartland, yet only ten years earlier its future in the Windy City had seemed brighter than the very stage lights that had gleamed on many a famous soprano's face.

The Chicago Grande Opera was conceived in the ashes of the Great Chicago Fire of 1872. The people of Chicago were left exhausted but undaunted by the destruction that ravaged their city.

"Tonight our city lay in a twisted heap of ash and soot," bellowed the mayor of the time: Thomas Stanton. "The destruction rained from heaven is beyond that of comprehension.

"Fire has brought many fine and eloquent societies to an end, blazing and engulfing without regret or remorse. Our city has now felt the molten rain that showered from Vesuvius, destroying the classic beauty and nobility of Pompeii. We have been singed by the self-same demon that brought the great Roman Empire to its knees, as the great and awful Nero watched with contempt. We have been visited by the unquenchable tongue that devoured Sodom and Gomorra ages ago. We are charred and choked, we are battered and bruised, but we, the Great City of Chicago, shall press on.

"For, my friend, we shall blaze a new trail. History shall not repeat itself. Discouragement shall not prevail. Comrade, we shall not succumb to the tragic fate that vanquished those of yore.

"For in this city, fire will no longer be seen as destroyer, but—for we proud few by this great lake—it shall be known as purifier. The earth below our feet has been cleansed. The ground upon which we stand has been dedicated, and once again is prepared for our use.

"To those who have lost tonight, this fire is no longer consumer, but redeemer. We are changed in the sight of the world. We are liberated from the weight and filth of the past. We are set free to reinvent these environs.

"And finally, to myself, fire has become 'Resolve.' Yes, my brother, Resolve! From tonight and forward I resolve, *let us* resolve to honor those we have lost, rebuilding this vast heartland, and making for ourselves a home of virtue, blessed by God, built of His wisdom and upon our backs, and seen by the world as the lifeblood of our vast Nation. Fire has now purified us, fire has redeemed us from our mediocrity, and fire has resolved our intentions.

"The ashes around us mourn for what is gone, but let us take these ashes of despair, douse them in our lake's glory, and set to work to build our new...great...home."

After the fire, the reconstruction of the city began. Chicago would not be built of wood and nails this time; it would be a city of stone and brick. It would be built as a lasting monument to man's indomitable spirit, and as a city that would rival the most beautiful in the world. It would become the working man's home.

In a groundswell of public gratitude, city leaders introduced a series of community restoration projects that included the formation of Grant Park, Symphony Hall, the Lincoln Park Zoo and Harbor area, and a vast museum complex, including the Art Institute, the Field Museum of Natural History, and the John G. Shedd Aquarium, the largest non-oceanic aquarium in the world.

But the Chicago Grande Opera was to be the city's artistic center. It would fill this great city, this great home, with song. It would be where the greatest voices of all time would come to sing the soaring, cresting melodies that give opera its life. The Chicago Grande Opera was to be the eye around which the city's performing arts community revolved, and the musical soul of the Midwest.

This mission—the Chicago Grande Opera's mission—went undiminished for over one hundred years.

In 1982, the Chicago Grande Opera, after two decades of little growth, took a major step. Borrowing from Mayor Stanton's famous speech, the CGO announced an ambitious expansion program: "Resolve 2001: Chicago Grande Opera, Now to the Millennium." This enormous project would amplify the company's season from twenty weeks, mid-September to mid-January, to thirty-two weeks, ending in April. This undertaking would create a theatre complex to rival the best in the world. The Metropolitan Opera,

The Vienna Staatsoper, La Scala, Covent Garden—these great opera houses would no longer have a poor brother in the Chicago Grande Opera.

Patron and corporate sponsorship was plentiful. The best firms in theatrical construction were hired and the expansion began. Rolling wagons were installed to accommodate grandiose sets. A stage turntable was installed to accommodate complex circular stagings and scenery shifts. Supertitles, projected simultaneous translations, were employed to bring the great words of Shakespeare, sung through the music of Verdi, to the steelworker from Calumet City.

The artistic community was enthralled. Both singer and musician were exuberant about the work at the world's new great opera house.

For five years, critical acclaim was matched only by financial success. The opera world began noticing the young upstart Chicago Grande Opera with its ambitious directors, artists, and schedule of contemporary opera. American directors found a sympathetic home at the CGO. Gifted young opera composers were granted major projects, ranging from subjects on the Holocaust to lighter works that would have had Rossini chuckling. Lost gloves, broken hearts and tragic death are milk to be suckled by the ardent fan, and the CGO was supplying them in abundance.

Mayor Stanton's speech had come to be seen as prophecy at the Illinois State Theatre, the Chicago Grande Opera's home. "Resolve 2001" was met with unmitigated praise and seen the world round as a classical music triumph and model for opera companies the world over.

But just as Richard Wagner's *Ring des Nibelungen* spins a tale of destruction through jealousy and greed, the Chicago Grande Opera fell prey to these same hideous sins.

The late 1980's crash of the Stock Market had squeezed Chicago's corporate charity, but the CGO would still be financially sound with its myriad private donors and strong public support, along with the bit of governmental "encouragement" it received.

However, a reactionary trend arose throughout the nation in response to some very disturbing government-funded arts projects. A government bandwagon of anti-art sentiment was aroused to seek out and destroy any art not deemed acceptable by certain elected officials. This threat was carried out through the restriction of public funds. Financial assistance was contingent upon the ignorant artistic attitudes of several obese congressmen.

The Chicago Grande Opera found itself at the center of this controversy when it produced and performed a new opera by a young composer named Marian Thomas. Her opera, *Awakening Constance*, was a biographical piece that centered around the love affair between a teenage girl and a married woman.

Awakening Constance was indeed a disturbing story, no matter in what guise it was realized. The use of a teenage girl as the title character, her explicit rape scene by an uncle, and consequent rape by an older woman, brought immediate and universal condemnation. The art community, critics, and even gay and lesbian activists spoke out against the opera. Several United States' senators moved to suspend National Endowment of the Arts funding to the CGO, pending an assessment of its grant guidelines. Valhalla, Wagner's great and glorious heaven, had begun to crumble.

The government "assessment" of the CGO found several disturbing items. First, Ms. Thomas had received the outlandish sum of two million dollars for her opera, with total production costs at 10.1 million dollars. The CGO also paid the librettist, the opera's wordsmith, two million dollars. This amount was completely absurd. The sheer dollar amount for the libretto was completely preposterous, and this fee was made more suspect by the fact that the librettist, Penelope Ambrose, also happened to be Ms. Thomas's lover. The CGO had made the two women quite rich.

Then there was a final question: What happened to the remaining 6.1 million dollars in production costs? There were special lighting effects and a second full orchestra, accounting for about two million dollars, but the opera's sets were small and intimate. The money had seemed to vanish.

Investigators discovered that three million dollars was marked as "overtime" expenses—overtime Ms. Thomas used to orchestrate her opera, and later, to fund night-long orgies with cast and crew. Operatic decadence is well documented, but these drunken and drug-enhanced escapades turned scornful eyes towards the hiring practices of the CGO.

The crack in Valhalla's foundation then became a chasm. Although the National Endowment of the Arts had contributed less than five percent of the annual operating budget for the CGO, the significance of the government's disapproval rang through corporate halls as well.

In the fall of 1990, the Tri-Cor Oil Corporation, the opera's biggest donor, lost billions of dollars in the Middle East with the onset of the Persian Gulf War and had to end its financial support of the opera, the finale to a fifty-three year relationship.

Government funding had ceased, artists were canceling contracts, the Opera's largest donor had fully withdrawn support due to catastrophe, and ticket sales, the smallest portion of the CGO's budget, were in the midst of a decrescendo.

The fire of January 17, 1992 that destroyed the company's warehouse of sets, props, and costumes blazed brighter in the eyes of the city's art community than the Great Fire had some 120 years earlier. With nothing left to salvage but an under-financed insurance check, the CGO Board Meeting of February 19, 1992 was anti-climactic. All operations at the Chicago Grande Opera, artistic and financial, would be suspended indefinitely.

The Chicago Grande Opera had become the Challenger disaster of the entire opera—yea, performing arts world. *The Herald*'s proclamation was correct; opera in Chicago was indeed dead.

March 23, 1992
Lobby, Illinois State Theatre, 4:00 p.m.

We are just as astounded as you gentlemen are," announced the Metropolitan Chicago Arts Council Chairman Jon Bishop. "An anonymous donor has earmarked the Chicago Grande Opera as the sole recipient of their will and estate, and I have been authorized by the Council to grant permission for these funds to be transferred to the Opera. All continued transactions with the estate will take place solely between the estate and the CGO Board."

The Metropolitan Chicago Arts Council had received 100 million dollars to be donated to the Chicago Grande Opera.

Lightning—sudden, unexpected, and blazing—had struck. Fire from heaven had been ignited in Chicago's operatic wasteland. The passionate and engulfing love of song had seared the heart of an anonymous donor. Opera's torch, ignited in the embers of the city's tragedy a century ago, had been reignited by the public, who now refused to let their operatic inferno be quenched.

The donation, rumored to be the will of a famous Chicago patron, was the largest ever to be granted by a single individual to a Chicago arts organization. One hundred million dollars would stoke the furnace at the CGO for several seasons, with the total amount of the donor's estate believed to be four or five times that size.

"I am happy to announce the end of the CGO's 'suspended operations.' Ladies and gentlemen," stuttered the chairman, "The Chicago Grande Opera will begin preparations for its new and revised season immediately." A cheer from the depths of the art community erupted in the conference room.

"If you woulda asked me a month ago if dis day would *ever* occur, I woulda slugged ya," said the chairman in true Chicago-ese. With relief in his voice, Mr. Bishop continued. "In fact, I honestly believed dat the Opera would never open again. I would just like to thank our anonymous donor, who wishes *her*, or, um, uh, rather *their* estate to remain anonymous." Mr. Bishop recovered and removed his foot from his mouth.

"I have contacted William Burrows, the general manager of the CGO. He believes that the opera will be able to open this fall, as originally scheduled. Mr. Burrows has been talking to the newly formed Mexico City Opera Theatre in hopes of collaborating on future projects so as to defray expenses, and as of noon today, their Board of Directors, led by Señor Umberto Juarez, is making plans to send their new, widely acclaimed productions of Puccini's *Tosca*, Wagner's *Der Fliegende Höllander*, and Verdi's *La Traviata* to us as soon as possible." A roar of approval filtered throughout the State Theatre's lobby.

"So the Chicago Grande Opera season will begin on Saturday, September 24, with Puccini's masterpiece, *Tosca*, and, Mr. Burrows and the CGO Board are proud to announce the engagement of the world famous tenor Enzo Santi, who will sing the role of Mario Cavaradossi."

Once again fire, ignited in the heart of one devoted patron, had brought new operatic life to Chicago. The stage where Maria Callas received a twenty minute standing ovation before singing a note, where Jon Vickers tore apart the set as *Peter Grimes*, where Pavarotti and Sutherland charmed the world with their *Daughter of the Regiment*, where the likes of Caruso, Melchior, Albanese, and Flagstad reigned as supreme opera gods, this stage would once again be lit ablaze with the consuming passionate fire of lost love, of treacherous villains, and of supreme tragedy. Opera in Chicago was back, and the man to fuel the flame was himself a torrent of passion, Enzo Santi.

"Ladies and gentlemen," the chairman bubbled with enthusiasm, "the Chicago Grande Opera is back!"

Allegro con fuoco:

Cacciare:
subito e violento

Music is the universal language of mankind
— Longfellow —

One

"That meal was incredible. I'm stuffed. If we don't get to the opera house soon I'm in serious trouble. I should have gone with a size 10," bubbled Sandy Denning, yanking her snug dress down by the hem of her skirt. "For some reason double digits really scare me."

"Opera people certainly know how to eat, don't they? It's what they do with their spare time on the road," laughed Gwen. "That's why so many of them are heavy. Bubbles Sills said Pavarotti misses his family so much that he stays in his apartment and cooks. I guess he's quite the gourmet."

"Back on the 'Stair Bastard' tomorrow for these thighs. Gwen, did you see Stormin' Norman Schwarzkopf?" questioned Sandy. "I can't believe that the CGO would fly him in."

"You know he's a real fan. The Met had him as a special guest and lecturer right after the Gulf War for their opening night," Gwen informed her friend. "He's really a brilliant man. He knows as much about opera as he does about war. He's a true 'Renaissance Man.'"

Sandra Denning and Gwendolyn Silva had roomed together in college. Sandy now lived in Chicago and worked for the multi-billion dollar Amcel Computer Corporation, one of the many corporate deserters in the CGO's crisis of the previous year. Her friend Gwen Silva was the wife of Mr. Enzo Santi, the evening's star tenor. Gwen had decided to give up a minor career in opera to be with the man she loved. It was no real sacrifice. She loved Enzo passionately, and with his instrument, the only management needed consisted of what fee to ask for, and which opera to perform.

Her voice was dark and supple in timbre, with quite an agile proclivity, but was only one voice in a thousand. Her husband's heroic tenor was rare, and one in a million.

"Chicago Grande is pulling out all the stops for this season," Gwen explained. "After everything that went wrong in the last couple of years, they have to recover a lot of things they lost—most importantly, the city's trust.

"That's why the donation last spring was such a godsend," she said, pulling Sandy closer. "It's like an endowment. With a cool hundred 'mil' in the bank, and more to come, you can get the best of everything: the best singers, the best impresarios, the best conductors, and thus, the best opera. Impress the patrons again, kiss up to the politicians, get my husband to shake the rafters with a few high 'C's, and the money moves in the CGO's direction. I bet that hundred doubles in a couple years, and even if it doesn't, the CGO still has cash in the bank to rely on."

"I guess that little feast we just gorged on adds to the piggy banks too," Sandy suggested. "God knows, for food like that I'd do almost anything."

Gwen flashed a *Mona Lisa* smile at Sandy.

"I said *almost* anything," Sandy said, straightening her blouse. "I do have some standards." Both women giggled.

Gwendolyn Silva had been married to Enzo Santi for 13 years. She was an attractive blonde singer who fell in love with this fiery Latino and wanted to be with her husband for the rest of her life. Few marriages in the opera world survive the rigors of travel and the stress of separation, but the Santis wanted to be an exception. And with Enzo's *subito crescendo* in the opera world and its financial rewards, togetherness was possible.

The couple had met in graduate school at Indiana University, where they both honed their operatic art.

Enzo was an Argentinean who came to study with the world famous tenor James Koenig, now teaching after an illustrious 35-year operatic career in Europe and the United States.

Enzo was a natural on stage; Gwen struggled. Gwen was a natural in the classroom; Enzo struggled. However, audiences pay to hear high notes, and Enzo could sing a high 'C' with ease. Not small Mozart-Rossini high notes, but big, round, warm high notes. These notes gave Verdi and Puccini their emotional life. These notes could turn mediocre graduate students into world class opera singers.

Enzo was at his operatic and *tenor*al infancy at 38, and was already being compared to the greatest tenors of all time.

The only physical concern the couple had involved their taxing travel schedule. Many a tenor had succumbed to the hectic jet-propelled opera world and burned out in five or ten years. The Santis aimed for a slowly expanding rise in Enzo's career, one that would last them a lifetime.

Where books failed him, his keen vocal insight placed him well beyond his contemporaries. God had placed in him the very impulse of sound—rich, full, and resonant. He could move audiences to weep with his legato or have them rise to their feet with joy as he sang the triumphant "Nessun Dorma" from Puccini's *Turandot*.

Never pushed, swallowed or forced, his sound moved; it flowed. It caressed and danced in and out of the aisles. It made the light of chandeliers glisten the way snow shimmers in the streetlights. He could draw the public to himself with the furrow of his brow. Then again, this innate actor could revile the throng as he strangled "Desdemona" in a fit of "Otello's" jealous rage. He was envied, worshipped, and emulated, but deep down, while he enjoyed the limelight, the handsome, athletic young man knew this voice was not his own. God had granted this gift, and *he* must be its faithful steward.

This confidence in who he was and for whom he sang also allowed him to take dramatic and vocal risks that all the more thrilled those in attendance. He was never reckless or careless, but aggressive and calculating. The little shake at the climax of an aria, the quick motion of an arm, the almost spoken declamation in the great Wagner operas, all this must be perfected for the operatic art to be what it should. His art, his voice…this gift demanded perfect attention to detail.

Still, with all his love of singing and theatrical motive, his wife was the one thing in all the world that he truly wanted at all costs. She was the heart of his world, and the light of his soul. Gwendolyn Silva had stolen his heart, held it in her delicate hands, and placed it on the wings of song.

The women's long black stretch limousine pulled around the corner onto Wacker Drive where the Illinois State Theatre was located. It was 7:20 p.m., and the opera, *Tosca*, would start at 7:30.

"Will we see your 'divo' before the opera?" inquired the friend.

"Not tonight. E said the interviews this afternoon were exhausting. He needs the time to be quiet and rest his voice. He does have to sing 'Mario' tonight." Gwen liked to call her husband "E." "Besides Sandy, I thought your size eight needed to be adjusted before we find our seats."

"Yeah, it does, but you know me. I am so fickle, I don't want to miss anything, especially with all that has gone on the last few months. This whole thing is so exciting. The limo, the pre-opera dinner, the gala bash tonight, *and* the world's most handsome tenor singing in *Tosca*. Ugh, if I don't shut up I'll never make it into the opera house." She paused a moment. "When will limos come equipped with toilets?" inquired the impetuous red-head.

The car wove around the double-parked opera crowd and along the length of the fifty-year-old theatre, where finally, at the south end of the complex, an usher motioned the limousine driver to pull to the entrance of the thirty-five hundred seat auditorium.

"My God! Look at this place, Gwen," gasped Sandy.

Huge thirty-foot long banners hung from the great archways of the theatre and billowed in Chicago's brisk autumnal air. They pronounced the return of the glorious art to the city. They read "Chicago Grande Opera: From Now to Forever." Others shouted in their purple, black and gold, "CGO: Reborn of Fire."

The car stopped and another usher opened the limousine door for the honored guests. Being the wife of a great opera singer had its privileges. The two friends climbed out of the limousine and stepped onto the thick red carpet that led into the foyer of the Illinois State Theatre. The wind clapped the banners together with the force of a cymbal crash. Gwen emerged from the limo first, adjusted her silk shawl and gazed up and down the columned building.

"Wow!"

Sandy slipped out of the car and continued the wrestling match with the hem of her skirt.

Ushers whisked the two women through the phalanx of reporters, paparazzi, and opera enthusiasts, discreetly pushed to the side by well-placed barricades.

The outer entrance of the opera house was a refurbished majestic monolith to the beauty of the theatrical arts. Similarly styled banners draped either side of the limestone facade and every bit of bronze and copper glittered under a host of television lights.

The women moved through the Grand Entrance onto the foyer's black Italian marble floor. They glanced from side to side with eyes wide in astonishment. Flowers were everywhere, bedecking the aisleways, the entrance and every conceivable crevice that could hold a vase or bouquet.

Standing in majestic power, two white marble statues greeted the public as they entered the building. Apollo, the god of music, stood to the right, and his cohort in harmony, Dionysus, peered at him from the left. They asked the great throng to enter and enjoy this, their most glorious gift to mankind.

The lobby was awash in the requisite sequins, furs, pumps and tuxedos.

The city's mayor, Richard George, stood with the general director of the Chicago Grande Opera, William Burrows, at an elaborately decorated platform directly across from the main entrance to the auditorium. On either side of the two men were their wives, Felicity George, who was active in the city's children's outreach programs, and Janine Burrows, an aging soprano who threw herself into her husband's work as much as he did. The foursome was in appropriately gaudy opera attire, champagne glasses at the ready. Gwen and Sandy moved near the entrance of the auditorium and found a clear view of the platform.

"Gwen, who is that?" Sandy whispered, as a fifth person slowly walked onto the platform, escorted by Emil Walker, assistant to the general director.

"I'll tell you in a minute. I want to hear what Bill Burrows has to say."

William Burrows grabbed a cordless microphone from the base of a five-foot wreath of red roses as the mystery guest approached him and shed her escort. The general director spoke.

"Ladies and gentlemen, may I please have your attention. Tonight it is my honor and truly unexpected privilege to join you in opening the one hundred and tenth season of the Chicago Grande Opera."

Hearing their cue, waiters scurried from the backstage entrance to the auditorium and, carrying hundreds of glasses of champagne, invited those in attendance to join in the approaching toast.

"As everyone here is well aware, the Chicago Grande Opera has had tremendous financial and artistic difficulties of late. We—the board, myself, and our artistic director, Maestro Matthew de Carlo—have made unwise decisions which have cost this great opera company to lose prominence in the performing arts world. I...we apologize to you, Mr. Mayor," nodding to Richard George, "for the detriment these actions have caused this great city by the Lake. We apologize to our corporate supporters, who withstood the critics and our failures for several years and supported the CGO as long as possible. And finally, I apologize to our patrons, our fans, our public. As Mayor Stanton proclaimed so long ago, you, the people of Chicago, are the ones for whom this great opera house was constructed. When the CGO Board and I became more concerned with controversy than quality, more infatuated with money than with music, we doomed this company to disgrace and defeat."

The crowd stood, stunned, searching for the breath that had left the great hall. William Burrows pulled the microphone away from his mouth for a moment, took his handkerchief from his pocket and dabbed the corners of his parched mouth.

"Knowing apology is insufficient, I ask for your mercy. We, the board, ask for your grace and forgiveness.

"Through no merit of our own, but because of the generous donation of late," Burrows nodding to his unnamed stage partner, "the CGO is now able to experience a rebirth, rebirth to the artistic excellence that has defined this opera house from its inception, a rebirth and cleansing to the integrity that ruled this company for three-quarters of a century, and a rebirth to once again lead this great city into the forefront of the artistic world."

A spontaneous shout of "Bravo" arose from the crowd and a wave of applause rolled through the entrance hall, reverberating up and around the great dual staircase, in and out of the stone pillars, and finally, bouncing down off of the sixty-foot rose ornamented ceiling.

"To assure these goals and help fulfill these promises, the CGO Board has retained the services of several reputable independent accounting firms. These fine gentlemen have only the Chicago Grande Opera's best interests at heart. They have promised to keep close attention to this company's financial and artistic actions. All this has been done to safeguard the public's interest in this opera house. I can honestly say I am enjoying their input, which has already aided the CGO.

"I look forward to continuing to build this relationship so that you, our audience, shall never have to traverse the artistic desert in which we, your employees, have so recently indulged."

The general director's contrition left the crowd speechless. The stolen breath had returned to the crowd, which now felt compassion for the humbled speaker. Never before had the head of any organization, let alone an artistic group, laid their soul and their faults open to their constituents in such a public and personal way.

However, the address seemed the only solution if William Burrows was to continue in the capacity of general director. It also was the only way the Chicago artistic community would allow someone who had nearly brought its ruin back into the fold. The penance paid seemed appropriate and heartfelt to the predominantly Catholic Chicagoans.

"He just ate an entire flock of crows," Gwen uttered. "I didn't think there were that many birds in all of Chicago." William Burrows then continued.

"Despite our loss of direction, one patron stood by us, even in her death." Burrows paused and motioned to the mystery woman standing to his right.

"At this time, I would like to toast Mrs. Gloria Brook Filmore, the daughter of the late Mrs. Phyllis Brook, for the support her mother and family have given this opera company throughout the years. Mrs. Filmore, we stand by you in the recent loss of your mother, and thank you for your generosity to this company, even in times of trouble." With an upward sweep of his arm that did not disturb a single drop of champagne, Burrows toasted this generous patron.

"To Phyllis Brook, Mrs. Gloria Brook Filmore, and the entire Brook Family, the Chicago Grande Opera extends our eternal gratitude!"

The entire crowd voiced their approval, glasses were raised and supped, and a thunderous ovation rolled over the marble floor.

Bill Burrows stepped back so that Mrs. Filmore might be the focus of the applause, and leaned over to his wife.

"Where were these bastard patrons when I needed them eight months ago?" Burrows moaned through clinched teeth. "If these sycophants would have applauded a year ago we would never had been in so much trouble"

"Try to remain dignified, Bill, no matter how difficult you find it," murmured Janine. "After all, you'll be presiding over the resurgence of the CGO, and, you now have a nice little cushion in the bank."

The applause finally echoed its last. Burrows moved to speak again.

"Now, ladies and gentlemen, The Chicago Grande Opera is proud to invite you into the theatre to see our new production of Puccini's *Tosca*. The Mexico City Opera Theatre gave this production its world premiere one year ago, and we are proud to present it in its American premiere. It is astounding in its scope, detail, and beauty."

William Burrows kept company with the likes of Winston Churchill when it came to oratory skill, and this particular evening his wit would have to be sharp and genuine. He continued.

"Now once again, I ask you to raise your glasses and join me in toasting the revitalized Chicago Grande Opera: Long live this great city! Long live this great company! And long live this glorious marriage of theatre and music we call 'opera.' Here, here!"

Gwen and Sandy made their way through the auditorium doors and down the main aisle of the hall. The opera would begin a few minutes late to accommodate the prestigious opening night audience. People scurried to and fro, looking for seats, spouses, and famous faces who might be sharing the same area of the theatre.

The two women wove their way into the auditorium in a great procession reminiscent of the "Triumphal March" from *Aida*. The balcony hung over their heads for thirty feet, covering the orchestra section like a great umbrella. Finally, slowly, emerging from the overhang, the full splendor of the renovated theatre swept over the pair of women.

The theatre had been entirely refurbished. Its intricate interior reflected the great halls of the early part of the century when craftsmen were allowed to hone their skills under less restrictive budgets.

The auditorium was ringed with six-foot bronze busts of the great opera composers. Verdi and Wagner, who would never be caught near each other in life, were now permanent neighbors at the center of the Auditorium's "Ring of Passion." Puccini, Rossini, and Donizetti stood to the left of Verdi, forming an Italianate half circle, while the right was balanced by Mozart, Richard Strauss, and a recent addition, Benjamin Britten, whose twentieth century operas demanded recognition. Certainly, there were omissions in this circle, but these men were the masters of the art. The busts, freshly polished, gleamed more brightly and seemed more proud than ever. In honor of this evening's operatic offering, Puccini's bust was softly illuminated, following the theatre's tradition.

New carpet had been laid, the wine color highlighted by small golden flecks, reflecting the scalloped walls of the house. The seats, which had always been a point of disdain among the patrons, had been replaced by the finest, lumbar-supporting, firmly cushioned auditorium chair available. Now many a husband, dragged to the CGO by his wife, could get a good evening's sleep in these luxurious silently folding chairs.

The management, following the lead of prominent New York opera houses, had installed supertitles along the backs of the new chairs. Instantly, the text of each opera would be translated into the viewer's choice of five languages. A small button to one side of the LED screen allowed the viewer to press and find their appropriate language, or shut off the device completely and be undisturbed during the performance. Gone were the days of craning necks, looking for the projected titles above the proscenium.

The great central chandelier, a gift from the Italian government upon the theatre's inauguration, freshly cleaned and polished, shot bolts of warm radiant light in every direction. Ten thousand individual pieces of crystal gave the house an ethereal aura.

The women, after gasping at the changes, finally seated themselves in the fourth row, just to the right of center stage. In a few moments, the amazing young American conductor, David Franciosi, would step into the orchestra pit, ascend his podium, eye-level with the audience, and open this gala evening.

Gwen preferred seats close to the action as opposed to the Parterre Boxes with the general director and his entourage. The Parterre was located on the first level of the balcony, and was considered the "skybox" of the opera world. Drinks were served, seats movable and adjustable, and any visiting dignitary was sure to be at the side of the general director in his reserved spot. The Parterre was where you bought tickets if *you* wanted to be seen, the orchestra seats were where you bought tickets if you wanted to *see*, and the proud wife wanted to see every glance and every sigh from her husband.

"So she's the daughter of the candy heiress," Sandy commented, referring to the ceremony outside. "Good God, she looks great. How old do you think she is?"

"About sixty. Her mother founded the Brook Candy Company in her own kitchen in the 20s. Supposedly, mommy was worth over 500 million dollars when she died last January. Lucky for the CGO that the 'Candy Lady' was sweet on opera," said Gwen.

The orchestra began to tune. The concertmaster, the first chair, first violin, stepped to the podium and motioned the first oboe to play the 'A' that would begin the night's theatrical events. The audience was still humming after the ceremony in the lobby.

"You know, though," said Sandy, "William Burrows never actually said Mrs. Brook was the lady who donated the money."

"Sure, Sandy, some other old gazillionairess croaked since the CGO flopped last year and left all her inheritance to the opera," replied Gwen a bit sardonically.

"All I said was that Mr. Burrows was not specific. My God, after his self-immolation back there, the least he could have done was kiss her feet."

"If I had that much money to dole around I wouldn't want too many folks knowing what I did with it. There are too many greedy s.o.b.'s who want a piece of the pie. I'd be pretty unassuming too."

"I wish I had a bit of the interest on that gazillion she has. I'd buy part interest in Joe Montana. Not the whole man, just particular portions."

"Sandy, stop it." Both women giggled.

The great interwoven gold curtain prepared to open the opera season. Its heavy intertwined silks and satins folded, rippling along the front of the stage, tempting the onlooker with what stood behind it. The great curtain stood grand; it stood majestic, and it stood immovable, until the one man, the Maestro, stepped to his podium, prepared his orchestra, and threw the opera's opening cue.

Backstage
Illinois State Theatre

The gradual hush that fell over the events in front of the curtain was in complete contrast to the organized chaos behind. Crew members placed the final props in their positions and scurried away. Stage hands, wearing their wireless headsets, made their final lighting adjustments to the statue of the Madonna that graced the inside of the church where the evening's drama was to take place.

"Cavaradossi and Sacristan to the stage, this is your final call. Mr. Santi to stage left, please. Mr. Santi to stage left please. House lights are going to black, Maestro to the pit," announced the veteran stage manager, Gary Moore, to the legions of backstage crews, dressers, and technicians that allowed the audience to see seamless, near perfect opera. The lights of the Illinois State Theatre's Francis Mackay Auditorium dimmed to black, precisely on cue. A collective gasp ran up and down each aisle, in and out of each cushion of each chair as the auditorium darkened.

"Spotlight on the Maestro, ready curtain, ready light cue 4," barked Gary. "Go!"

The gallery was the first to see Maestro David Franciosi wind his way through the slim aisle created in the orchestra. A smattering of applause greeted the Maestro. First he walked past the enormous double basses, then along the cellos, sidestepping the first violins, then took three steps up, to the side of the podium, displaying his balding head and slim shoulders to the entire opera house.

Then, as the spark of applause spread though the theatre, the young American took one final step onto the top of the podium, motioned for the entire orchestra to join him in receiving the ovation, and ceremoniously shook the concertmaster's hand. The brilliant young musician then turned to the congregants and bowed.

As the applause faded, the orchestra sat and waited, eyes honed on the conductor's baton...silence...silence...the calm before the musical storm. The conductor loved this moment of deafening, silent anticipation, and he loved to prolong it.

His arms now slowly extended, chest high, became motionless as his eyes searched the orchestra. David Franciosi, in a broad, sweeping gesture, threw the preparation beat to the orchestra, and then...

In a myriad of breath, motion and control, the instruments, led by the timpani and low brass, bathed each ear in the powerful richness of its timbre.

The opening three chords of *Tosca* ignited the evening with the appropriate blast. The curtain parted, revealing the interior of the church, Sant'Andrea della Valle, where Mario would sing of his love for Tosca. The spell had been cast, every listener was entranced.

"Mr. Santi to the stage for your entrance; Mr. Santi to the stage."

The athletic young Argentinean strode through the hall from the artist dressing rooms and pushed through the door that led to the back portion of the stage. Lights flashing "Performance in Progress" reflected on his white open-collared shirt.

Tonight he was the painter, revolutionary, and fugitive Mario Cavaradossi. His mind and vocal cords were clear and focused, even while several butterflies fluttered in his abdomen. Several deep, low, energizing "singer" breaths let him know that his pipes were hot and ready to work.

Enzo Santi had been an apprentice at the CGO in the late seventies, when Chicago had become his second home. Sure, the wind could blow you over, and the winter cold could smack you senseless, but the people were genuine, hearty, and loving. Gwen and he planned to raise a family here in a few years, to raise a tribe away from the cynicism, the frenzy of the East, raise his children where they could play in parks, build snowmen in the backyard, and drink hot chocolate after a cold, snowy school day, raise them in a place where he could teach his children to love soccer as he did.

He and Gwen had experienced all these charms when they came to Carl Sandberg's "City of Big Shoulders." This city and her friends had supported this young couple in their days of hot dogs and macaroni. This city and her friends had supported the young married couple as they grieved the loss of their first child, and later when they buried Gwen's father. This city had rallied round them and made them her own. Enzo and Gwen loved their Chicago, and planned to let this community of strength anchor the rest of their lives.

So, there was no question when the CGO called late last spring and made their plea for his services. Enzo could not refuse. He was heartbroken when he had heard of the opera's demise last January. But now, he wanted to be present when the city hoisted her opera company back from ruin, up onto its mythical shoulders. He slowed as he neared his stage-left entrance doors.

"How do you feel, Enzo?" asked Sam Wheaton, the CGO's reigning "queen" of the supernumeraries, the opera extras. Sam was standing backstage, watching the on-stage action, and waiting for his entrance in the first act finale.

"Great, Sam," replied Enzo in a resonant, focused tone. Enzo knew Sam from his apprentice days. "This is old hat for you, isn't it? How many of these opening nights have you been involved in? Didn't I hear that you've been here since 1952?"

"Actually," taking the stage of the tenor's attention, "I arrived half way through the '51-'52 season, but the '52 season was my first opening night. I was one of Turandot's slaves. I wore a hideous green and gold sequined jump suit thing, with a huge feathered head dress—made me look like a goddamn peacock. I'll tell you, *La Cage aux Folles* had nothing on that ugly old production."

Walking a bit further, Sam politely took the arm of the young tenor, changed tone and addressed his friend.

"Listen, my boy, in all seriousness, I want to tell you, you sound fabulous." The certainty of forty years in the opera business gave meaning to each of Sam's words. "I'm really proud to know you."

"Thanks, Sam, that means a lot," said Enzo, acknowledging the sincerity, but focusing on the task at hand.

The tenor arrived at his backstage entrance and waited for his musical cue and prompt from the assistant stage manager.

"*In bocca al lupo!*" Sam whispered, opera-ese for "break a leg."

"*Crepe lupo,*" E mouthed back in the standard Italian reply.

The door opened and Mario Cavaradossi, via the voice and talent of Enzo Santi, walked into the chapel Sant'Andrea and greeted the Sacristan.

"*Recondit armonia, chi bellezze di strege, e bruna Flora, ardente il confessor*"- Puccini's painter and subversive sang the praise of the woman he loved, Floria Tosca, the soaring vocal line wedded in eternal bliss to the poetry.

Enzo filled each moment of time with movement, with vocal line. He moved from nuance to crescendo, from delicate whisper to triumphant exclamation. Puccini put quill to sheet, but the singer gives breath, gives life, and Mr. Enzo Santi was infusing the night with rapture. Those in attendance, whether dresser, makeup artist, electrician, or thousand-dollar ticket holder, gasped as they beheld a voice truly born of God.

"Pay attention, gentlemen," uttered Gary Moore to his stage-right companions, "because you are seeing and hearing the next great tenor. He was good ten years ago, but since then he has become a god."

It was true. The last ten years had molded the young tenor into an artist for the ages. It was a night to be remembered. A night to be compared with the great Caruso's *Pagliacci*, with Leontyne Price's *Aida*, or with George London's "Wotan" in Wagner's *Ring*.

The passion of the voice, the sheer beauty, the ability to rise from almost spoken delicacy to tumultuous power, left the press, the patrons, all present, awe-struck. A smile swept through the face of his proud wife. She beamed at the beauty that emanated from her husband's voice, and from his life. The audience struggled to stay in their seats after Enzo's first aria. Gwen whispered to herself, "E—I love you so much."

"*Oh Scarpia, avanti a Dio*"—"Scarpia, we shall meet before God" sang Tosca in defiance, as she threw herself over the castle wall to her death.

The orchestra responded with huge brass and percussion claps as the curtain fell with the tragically conflicted heroine.

The audience, bursting into applause, demanded repeated bows from the artists for a full half hour. Enzo, his leading lady, Valencia Domingo, and Scarpia, the villain of the evening, portrayed by the baritone Ildebrando Bruscatti, returned to the stage time and time again to receive the tumult of appreciation.

After the outpouring of ovation and the exuberance of the performance, the crowd made their way to the exits, while many admiring fans moved backstage to make personal appearances with the performers.

"Follow me," shouted Gwen to Sandy over the roar. The two women made their way through the crowd and passed the backstage security desk, where guards kept the fanatics at bay. Gwen waived at one of the many security personnel she had come to know ten years earlier.

"Can we sneak back now?" asked Gwen.

"Of course, Mrs. Santi, go right ahead." The guard leaned over to her a bit, to ensure her ear. "Your husband was great tonight. He took my breath away," said the young thirty-something officer and admirer.

"He took mine too," Sandy chimed in as the women smiled and passed the man. A surge of admirers thrust forward, but was held at bay.

"I'm with the Santis," remarked a female fan with program and pen, ready to pounce at the sight of Enzo.

"Sure you are, and I'm Mayor Daly come back to life," remarked the guard. "Don't worry, you'll get your chance in a few minutes."

The wife and friend made their way down the hall, along a row of lockers, and turned left, following the hall to the Artist Performing Area.

Several dressers said "hello" to Gwen, but scurried about removing costumes, boxing shoes, and collecting the wigs and facial hair needed in order for the operatic illusion to be complete. The small waiting area smelled of basil and garlic. A table to the left held the remains of the dressers' and makeup artists' own little opening night party, replete with pasta, rolls, pizza, salad, and just a bit of champagne. The crumbling remains of a huge chocolate sheet cake still stood as testament to the carnage. Jeff Mallory, head dresser, quickly vanquished the cake crumbs to the refuse and wiped the table clean. He had to get the costumes out of the area before the crush of fans was allowed in.

Gwen knocked politely on the "*Primo Tenore*" door. A black and white plastic placard with "Enzo Santi" engraved on it met the women's eyes.

The star's wife swung the door of the dressing room open and slowly entered. Louis Calabrese, the CGO's chief makeup artist, was just leaving Enzo's dressing room. He smiled at Gwen and slipped out the door.

Gwen peeked around the corner of the five-foot entrance hall to the room. Enzo slowly spun around in his swivel makeup chair, looked his wife in the eyes with his warm, grinning face.

"Did I do good?" asked the exhausted Argentinean, knowing the answer.

Enraptured, Gwen leapt to him as he rose out of his chair. The handsome young couple embraced, slowly looked at each other and met lips. He pulled her close and spoke with his slight Latino accent.

"I only need think of you, and the evening is a success," Enzo said. Gwen, hands laced through her husband's dark black tresses, pulled his face back to hers, and she pressed her mouth again to his, lingering in the rapture of their love and their bond. The pair could have stayed entwined in each other for the entire evening.

Sandy cleared her throat softly to let the lovers know they were not entirely alone. She smiled at their affection.

"I'll just leave you two alone for a while, although I think there will be a riot if the women outside see you two like this."

"Sorry, Sandy," chuckled E once more.

"Don't be sorry, silly." The couple unwound and Sandy crossed the room and kissed Enzo on the cheek. "I'm just not too sure how those crazed women will react if they see 'Mario' having sex right here in the dressing room without Tosca."

"How long do you think you'll be?" Gwen asked her love.

"Sweetheart, it could be a long time tonight," E breathed disappointedly, moving to the makeup table to begin peeling away the veil of grease paint. "Stage management said the autograph hounds were out in full force. You saw them out there, didn't you? And I want to see Frank really quickly before I get to the party."

"So, about an hour?" asked Gwen.

"Better count on two," Enzo said. "Okay?" Gwen nodded her approval.

"But won't you miss the party?" Gwen asked. "I want to personally show you off to the bigshots."

"I'll do the best I can. Promise. I'll tell you this, though, this party is gonna be some kind of blowout. Stage management told me they killed a herd of fatted calves for this gala tonight."

"So much for the new frugal version of Bill Burrows," quipped Sandy. "Maybe his new 'watchdog' accounting firm is full of compulsive overeaters."

"I'll be there sooner than you think," Enzo finished, as he wiped a bit of shading from his cheek, and turned to face the women.

Another kiss between the lovers and the women were out the dressing room door. Within three minutes, the dressers whisked the racks of eighteenth century Tosca costumes out the Artist Area door and up one of the three backstage elevators to safety. One minute later, Jeff Mallory gave an "O.K." sign.

"Release the hounds," was the non-too-subtle cue from the Artist Area Security Guard, Avo Ramirez, to his comrades forty feet away, keeping the crowd at bay.

The hordes of autograph mavens descended and quickly fell into polite but antsy lines. The queue seemed endless, but the tenor would never turn down a seeker. There were people who had paid fifteen bucks for the nosebleed seats and came to every single performance of the season, ardent novices who were developing their operatic ear, and patrons who wanted to be seen with someone important, especially the world's hot new tenor. The courteous singer did not want to disappoint anyone who, being moved by the performance, had taken the time to walk back stage and offer their congratulations.

He also knew that a momentary slip could ruin the entire theatrical event for someone. Life was too short to be cruel or careless. Besides, these were the people who propelled him to perform, who energized his stage persona. He would be patient and attend to everyone. The wide-eyed child, the aspiring young singer, and the overly zealous fan would each receive a glance from his kind open face.

12:00 Midnight

After a cool shower, the tenor roped himself into his tuxedo and headed downstairs to find his friend Frank Stanza, the head of the Properties Department.

The two had met when Enzo was an apprentice at the CGO, the same year Frank joined the company. In the company cafeteria they became friends and shared a passion for sport. Frank lived and died by every Chicago team, but especially the gridiron fellows. Enzo was tutored at Frank's side on the intricacies of American football. Enzo responded by instilling in Frank a healthy appreciation for soccer, the world's version of football. They made fast and devoted friends.

The props department was on the "C" level, the third and lowest level of the house. Enzo had wandered up and down the corridors of this historic building for three years, so he knew his way around. He knew the quickest exits, the fastest elevators, and he even knew where the archives were.

The Illinois State Theatre was a great historic building, but a mess of a structure to navigate. Enzo followed the dimly lit hall that paralleled the loading dock and walked through the door that opened to the stairwell and down to the Props Department. Quickly skipping down, he opened the stairwell exit door to see the light from the hard-working Italian's desk.

"Hey, buddy, what's you doin' down here at dis hour a night?" spoke Enzo, in his best Midwestern Italian accent.

Frank jumped off his stool positioned behind the Props desk and grabbed a two-foot length of pipe, his personal "billy club."

"You silly son of a bitch. I've worked here thirteen years, make dick next to what you opera slobs make, wait on you hand and foot, and still can't find peace away from you bastards, even late at night." Frank settled from his fright, leaned back onto his stool, and placed the pipe in its leather storage pouch to his left.

Frank grinned at his friend. He rose to greet the star of the evening. The two men shook hands and threw their arms around each other. Frank was a funny, raunchy, middle-aged man who found joy in keeping his department spotless and efficient. His father had worked in the theatre as an electrician. Little Frankie would watch his dad at work and had been enthralled with the stage ever since. He did not care if he was paid minimum wage or a million dollars; he wanted to be in the theatre. His passion for the sights and sounds of opera developed as he became a fixture at the State Theatre.

"So, Frank, what did you think?" asked Enzo with a proud, mocking manner the burly man would enjoy.

"You missed that high 'B' in the second act 'Vittoria,' didn't you?" joked Frank. "Not quite your best stuff there." Enzo's mouth fell open, laughing at the sarcasm.

"And you called me a *son of a bitch*!" replied E.

"You know I'm just playin'," Frank said as he poked at Enzo's body. "But ya know, Enzo, when you were here in the early '80's, you were good, but since then, something has happened to your voice. *Cojones* really isn't the right word. I don't know, maybe passion." Frank thought another moment and continued with his unexpected insight.

"I think the good Lord's givin' you something that lets the sufferin' you experience be released from your body—you know, when you sing." Frank emphasized the point with a bob of his head.

Enzo stood silent. Frank continued nonchalantly, turning back to his desk and the sheets he had been filling out.

"Like when your father-in-law died, you got some kind of charisma or somethin' to help your wife through his death." He paused. "Then after that experience, your voice had a heroic edge that you never had before.

Then, when Gwenny miscarried, it was almost as if God said, 'O.K., he experienced sorrow. I'll give him a sympathetic voice now.'" Frank looked up from his pad to his tazered tenor friend and sighed.

"Maybe I'm full of shit, but that's what I noticed tonight. Your voice touches people at the point of their pain," he said and paused, "and then soothes it."

Enzo was mute. His mind raced at the thought of Frank's proposition. Could it be true? The miscarriage of their child had brought the grief he spoke of, and the prolonged death of his godly father-in-law, with its elongated anguish and wear on Gwen—these both gave credence to Frank's conclusion. Tragedy had brought an intangible ingredient to his art, and it was just as the prop man said. This rather simple, good-hearted friend had just laid the singer's vocal life in perspective. Unaware of his insight, Frank continued their exchange.

"How's Gwendolyn doin'? Connie and she talked a bit ago, I think." Constance was Frank's wife.

Finally managing another breath, the Argentinean smiled and spoke. "She's wonderful. I just need to be on the road more this year and neither of us likes the traveling life too much. We are both more of the homebody type, you know."

"Yeah, this travel stuff is tough on the singers. All that movin' around would drive me crazy if I was a singer. Of course Connie tells me I don't even sing good in the shower." Frank laughed to himself. "But then again, when she's in the shower with me, I ain't thinkin' about singin'." Both men laughed.

Enzo moved around the side of Frank's desk and peeked into the room where the props were stored.

"You've been a busy boy lately, haven't you? All this new stuff coming in from Mexico City."

"You wouldn't believe the hassle all these new guys are creating. They won't let me get at the stuff until they look at it first, and now they're makin' me log everything." With the dramatic air of Olivier, Frank continued. "Now E, you know I'm an organized guy, but I've never kept a log in my life. And I certainly don't want to start now, especially for these pricks."

"It can't be that bad, can it?" questioned Enzo.

"E, these guys come in here last March and start changing things, telling us when and where we can go, and what we can and can't do. I just don't like it. Then, a couple of these guys came down real hard on one of my new kids. He was just tryin' to start the fuckin' log books for the *Ballo* later this year and they say he's got to wait. Wait? Wait for what? Wait for these guys to unload everything. They even locked the loading dock doors on us. We were here 'til midnight cleaning up after those guys,"

"Sounds like overtime heaven to me," joked Enzo. "If things are so bad, why not complain to the Union. They have always treated you guys right."

"It doesn't do any good. Besides, they keep the Union rules. It's just, when I can have a three hour job done at 6:00 and then go home to my wife, I don't want to be here doin' nothin' for three hours, then spend the next three logging for their damn books, and get home at eleven o'clock. Sure, I'm getting rich on O.T., but it's a needless pain in the ass."

"That 'hundred mil' sure seems to have made people around here crazy," concluded Enzo.

"I hope that's it," shrugged Frank. "Maybe once they spend it all they'll unpucker their tight..."

"Frank, stop," he said, cutting off his friend's rich palette of words and shaking his head. Changing the subject, Enzo spoke up. "So how is the collection coming along?"

Frank had long boasted about his extensive collection of opera paraphernalia. Nostalgia is strong in opera, where money and flamboyance run well ahead of the rest of the performing arts world.

"These packers from Mexico may be jerks, but they sure do make some incredible set pieces. I've never seen this kind of quality on stage before, E." Frank calmed and his vocal inflection lowered.

"If this new money has done anything, it's kicked the quality of the shows up a notch. As I do their damn prop logs," whispered Frank, "I've been fondling the knives and whips. You know, it gives me practice for when I get home," he said, allowing his raunchy side to emerge again.

Over the years Frank had accumulated a storehouse of opera antiquities. He would take some minuscule prop, a set piece that was easily replaceable, even cut off a small portion of the set that was not visible from the audience, and add it to his treasure trove. He was not stealing; he was gathering historical evidence. Some of his most prized pieces included the white silk scarf that Pavarotti used during his recital at the State Theatre in 1987, the knife Renata Scotto used to kill Sherrill Milnes' Scarpia in the CGO's *Tosca* of 1976, and the net Jon Vickers wrenched as he sang the mad scene in *Peter Grimes*. Frank even "liberated" one of the decapitated, molded prosthetic heads of John the Baptist from an old production of *Salome*.

Of course, a good collector was never caught "collecting."

"Those *Tosca* sets were pretty cool. I wanted to take that red embroidered chair from the second act home with me," mentioned the tenor.

"They even sent a real fireplace for that act, but we had to change it for the fire code here," Frank mentioned. E countered Frank's earlier diatribe.

"So something good *has* come from the partnership with the Mexico City Opera Theatre and the CGO's new found riches."

"I guess so," Frank concluded, conceding the point to Enzo.

"Can I take a look at some of the new stuff in the back?" asked E.

"Sure, help yourself. You know where to look. The new stuff is on the shelves to the right. I have to finish up some stuff here for a few more minutes, so take your time. Oh, yeah," Frank spoke as Enzo walked into the room, "check out the things the company salvaged from the fire at the warehouse last spring. It's right next to the new stuff. Maybe you could add to *your* wimpy little collection," mocked Frank. Enzo was an amateur in the field of opera collecting, mainly because he did not feel free to abide by Frank's "five-fingered" collector's discount.

"I won't be long. I have to go to the shindig," mentioned E.

He made his way down the ten-foot corridor and past the fire doors, wedged open by a door stop. He slipped into the vast dark room that held the props for the Chicago Grande Opera. The room was forty by sixty, with the doors and corridor leading into a side aisle that gave access to the entire room. Metal and wooden shelves leaned and sagged throughout the front half of the storage area.

Lost scarves, lighters, torches, cigarette cases, and sabers were the tools of great tragedy and high humor on stage, and for the CGO, it was all in this cramped space. Boxes of properly labeled small items lined the mix of wooden and metal supports, while larger pieces sat in the open. Figaro's lute hung on the wall next to Mephistofele's goblet. Lenski and Onegin's pistols sat side by side, ridiculing the ill-fated friends.

At the far end of the room was an open area filled with larger set pieces. The freight elevator was at the very back corner, in close proximity to the grander set pieces. Turandot's golden shoulder carriage was set against the far wall, the gambling table from *La Traviata* was tipped on its side to increase floor space, and the foam ghosts used in Verdi's *Macbeth* were stacked in the corner. The shimmering phosphorescent mannequin of the deceased Countessa from Tchaikovsky's *Queen of Spades* was hanging from the fifteen-foot ceiling. It had greeted and startled many a late night visitor to these dark reaches. During his apprentice years Enzo had felt his blood curdle at her visage in an ill-advised attempt to frighten Frank, late after a performance of Giordano's *Andrea Chenier*.

Frank continued his log entries as Enzo turned right, walked down the first aisle of the room and milled through the stacks and boxes. Out of view of his friend and struggling a bit with the darkness, Enzo finally found a box labeled "FIRE," pulled it off the shelf and opened the top. Pushing aside a prop scroll or two to make room, he set the box down and began to remove the contents of last spring's tragic warehouse fire.

Enzo found several pieces of paper, the kind of thick antique paper used on stage. Enzo knew these were props because of the words inscribed on them. As long as a document looked official, no one cared what was actually written on it, so the backstage pranksters would try to break a singer's concentration with a witticism or two. Enzo chuckled to himself as he read the bogus documents.

Outside the storage room, E heard the "C Level" stairwell door shut, and then the slow scrape of leather soles on the concrete floor of the props office. He heard Frank and another person at the desk begin to chat. The faint voices were indecipherable, and besides, the prospect of a new addition to his antiquities had his full attention.

The bottom of Enzo's box was filled with bits of string and tar paper from the collapsed roof of the warehouse. Enzo stuck his hand into the musty box.

Pain ran through his index finger like that of a pin prick. He jerked his hand back and examined the injured digit. A bit of blood appeared. Undaunted by the fear of another encounter with the unknown assailant, the heroic tenor slowly removed the peripheral items and found a piece of metal that looked like a toggle switch, the rocking mechanism common to light switches. Several wires protruded from the piece. The spliced wire was the culprit in the attack. Enzo lifted the piece and smelled it. The switch smelled of charcoal. It was obviously at the scene of the inferno that had ended the Chicago Grande Opera's operations for a month.

Enzo examined the piece and decided it would make a nice momento of the tragic events and subsequent rebirth of the CGO. He slid the switch into the pocket of his jacket, and continued his searching.

The two men at the desk were not on equal footing. Frank knew the man by sight only. The six-foot, hulking visitor was assured and deliberate. He knew Frank very well, as he did all the props crew. It was his job to know these things, and he did his job very, very well. He knew he had the upper hand. He would dictate the terms of the conversation.

"So, Frank, how you doin'?" was the not-so-friendly salutation.

"Fine, how 'bout you?" Frank went along with the jabber while his mind raced to remember the angular face. "Sort of late to still be in this dump, isn't it?"

"Come on, Frank, I can go anywhere in this house at any time I want. You know that." He sneered. "Or you *should* know that."

"Bullshit!" Frank shrugged, speaking his mind. "This place shuts down at one o'clock and nobody but security is allowed in unless there's an emergency."

"The security guards are my friends, Frank." The confident, tuxedoed intruder strolled about, looking casually around the open office and hall.

Frank did not like this sort of cocky demeanor, except in himself, especially late at night when there was work to be done and a wife waiting at home.

"What the hell do you want?" Frank exclaimed, finally losing patience and becoming a bit agitated. "I'm pretty busy and I want to get out of here."

The tuxedoed man arrived in front of the desk, noticed the properties books Frank was attending to, and leaned an elbow on the properties desk, almost nose-to-nose with the Chicagoan.

"How are your logs coming, Frank?" he asked with a snarl that intended threat. "You been a good boy and keeping real accurate logs?" Frank leaned back a bit to avoid the cigarette-tainted breath.

"What do you want, buddy? Come down here late at night, not supposed to be here, and start fuckin' with me. Just get the hell out, would you?" Frank was quite nervous now, and he tried to get back to his work.

"Frankie, what you doin' snoopin' around the new stuff that comes in?" asked the man, squinting his eyes

Now quite enraged, Frank threw his hands on the top of the paper strewn desk.

"That's my goddamn job!" The tuxedo backed up a bit with Frank's outburst, but he still looked Frank right in the eye.

"I've got twelve operas to get ready, ten years worth of burned stuff sittin' around here causing another fire hazard, and all this fucking log shit that the new management wants me to do. When those bastards at the dock won't let me at the new shit, it drives me crazy. I've got directors on my ass wanting this and that piece of crap and I can't give it to them 'cause you guys are screwin' around with the trucks."

In a flash of recognition, Frank now remembered the face of this tuxedoed man. This guy was one of the half dozen men that kept his props' crew at bay while they inspected the sets from Mexico City. He did not know his name, but the face was enough.

"Frank," grunted the man, "don't screw with me." In a low voice, with his dark wide-set eyes intent on the Props Master, he continued. "See, I'm in charge of the transfer between Mexico and Chicago, so, that makes *me* your *fucking* boss," he menaced. "Personally, I think you've been doing more work than fits your job description. Poking around, seeing a lot of things you shouldn't, and I can't have that any more.

"Now I understand that you think what you do will make or break the opera. It won't. Personally, I wouldn't give you a dime for Pavarotti's balls on a platter, *but* you will not be on the dock when I am—or you are history." Frank quickly processed the situation as best he could.

With his left arm, the man grabbed Frank's lapel and clenched his fist. He pulled the prop manager again into his tainted breath.

"So Frankie, be a nice little opera fag and don't mess with me...."

As his words piqued with emphasis, the tuxedoed man thrust the sharpened tip of a pencil from Frank's desk into the flesh between Frank's left thumb and index finger. Frank violently pulled his hand back in pain, breaking the pencil in two. The paper beneath the attack was scrawled with blood, and the gray graphite of the piercing instrument. An inch of the splintered, broken pencil protruded from the top of Frank's left hand. He clutched the injury with his right hand, but Frank could not move because the tuxedo's left arm had moved up and was now wrapped around his neck. He spoke directly into Frank's right ear.

"Or—Frank, my friend, you'll become your own tragedy, right here in your own little opera house."

The left arm released the head of its captive. Frank bent his head to his injured hand and pulled the leaden knife from his flesh. A gusher of crimson poured forth. The grimace on his face revealed the pain involved in the attack.

The assailant pulled back a step and felt a rush of adrenaline at the sight of his prey's anguish. His eyes opened wide and he took a short, spastic breath. The inhaled air was cold, and felt cold all the way into his chest. He chuckled.

"What the hell!" He moved quickly and deliberately behind the desk.

Having finished his search in the property room, Enzo slowly walked down the prop room aisle to the room's main hallway and exit.

He had heard the paper shuffling in the background and heard the voices, but his attention was focused on his search for artifacts. Besides, Frank had been known to throw a paper or two in frustration.

The tenor walked around the corner into the long exit aisle at the south end of the room and there saw a tuxedoed visitor directly behind his friend, both men with their backs to him. He looked down for a moment and reached into his pocket for the switch.

In a flash, the tuxedoed intruder took both arms, grabbed the neck of Enzo's long-time friend and wrenched leftwards. The explosion of sound from his friend's shattering neck hit Enzo in the gut so hard, bile filled his throat.

The tenor's mouth opened, but no sound came forth. His eyes looked from side to side, back and forth, searching for he knew not what.

The hands and arms of the assailant flew up and out as they wrenched life out of the victim. As the lifeless body of Frank Stanza slid down the torso of the assailant, Enzo's knees buckled in sympathetic motion. He grabbed for support from the wall to his left, but found only a staff— "Wotan's" staff—precariously leaned against the end of the shelving.

Enzo clutched at the very staff that restored life to Wotan's disobedient daughter in Wagner's *Die Walküre*; however, Enzo knew that no mythical resurrection would follow this death.

As Enzo's hand grasped the pole, the pole rumbled along the ground, stirring the killer who had knelt near his handiwork. The athletic Argentinean swallowed hard and, turning his back on the murder scene, slid unnoticed, back from whence he came, into the first perpendicular aisle of the properties' room. He moved up the aisle to the room's north end hall, where he had found his treasures. He turned left and hurried past the shelving, arriving at the open end of the room. There he stood, trapped, facing the glowing ghost of the Countessa, still hanging from the ceiling. He squeezed Wotan's staff, still locked in his left hand. The beads of perspiration on his face soaked in the red exit light next to the elevator.

Adrenaline surged through his body, ignited by the ghastly death of his friend and the horror of his own witness. The rush also gave him a familiar alertness, reminiscent of the athletic contests of his youth.

Enzo knew there was an elevator at the end of the room, but it was a freight, and extremely slow. It would also be on the stage level in preparation for tomorrow's stage work. He hid himself as best he could amongst the foam Macbeth ghosts, his mind scrambling to find his *deus ex machina* amid this closed room.

The tuxedoed man rose from Frank's body, which still convulsed in death. The man cautiously made his way down the darkened Props' Room entranceway corridor. His nine-millimeter handgun, now removed from its shoulder strap, made its first appearance of the evening.

His body pressed along the near side of the corridor wall so as to be seen only at the last possible moment, the tuxedo squinted to try and force his eyes to adjust to the unlit room. He kicked the stop from the fire doors to seal the room, enclosing the space, and thus letting him know if anyone passed through the doors and out of the room.

The man spun to his right and looked as best he could down the first aisle. Sequins and jeweled daggers sparkled in the faint red light of the exit sign, confusing the predator. He shook his head and peered, unsure of the occupancy of the passage. He took a few steps further into the room along the south hallway and looked north up the second aisle.

The second aisle was clearer and obviously empty; his eyes finally adapting to the dark. He wondered what had made the sound. Could it have been the elevator motors cooling down, or maybe the building creaking? He wished this to be the explanation, but he must check. He had to be certain that his work was without witness.

Enzo snuggled into the foam ghosts as best he could, but they were situated at the south side of the room. The killer came steadily towards him. Again, the red light of the exit sign reflected, but this time it reflected off the metal object in the killer's hand. Enzo knew it was a gun.

The purge of the room moved quickly now, and the tuxedo, ready, if necessary, for another kill, took long, pressed strides.

A noise in the northernmost corner of the huge room perked the killer's ears and the man turned right, running up the sixth perpendicular aisle of shelves from whence the noise emanated.

In a flurry of arms and legs, the tuxedo found himself sprawling headlong into the shelving on the north wall of the room. The trip was hard and loud, causing prop boxes, candelabras, and jewelry cases to tumble upon the man. Wotan's staff had given Enzo the moment of opportunity he needed. Having wedged the staff foot level between the rows of boxes, Enzo had found the few seconds he believed he needed to escape.

From the end of the room, Enzo leapt from behind the ghostly visages of Macbeth's doom and ran the sixty feet of the corridor as fast as his Edmund Allen's would allow.

The assailant scrambled in the property carnage to find his lost weapon. It was wrapped in faux jewels that had a moment earlier fallen upon him. A quick check of his person found no permanent damage. As he stood, he saw the Contessa coming at him with her phosphorescent glow. He pulled back a moment, startled at the ghostly woman, and set off after the footsteps that had just passed behind him.

The fire door flew open and Enzo slammed it behind him. He could not waste the few seconds of life he had bought himself in front of the killer. He sped to the prop desk and hesitated at the body of his dead friend.

Frank's body lay on its left shoulder, the mangled neck swollen and bruised. Frank's head looked blankly into the prop room, completely over his left shoulder as no living human could do. His mouth was slightly open and the thick tongue of his lifeless friend filled the gap. A small stream of blood dabbed his nostril.

The surreal nature of the situation played in Enzo's mind like a high speed camera, observing the scene perfectly and entirely in an instant. No butterflies fluttered in his stomach now. The sight of his friend, lifeless on the floor, was equal to a punch in the stomach.

As he bent over to compensate for his gut, he threw the tattered wooden stool that Frank had used since his first day at the CGO at the Prop Storage Room door. The stool might buy him another second, and he had to hurry now, for the rumbling in the Props Room had stopped. The man was probably finding his way out of the room.

The tenor bolted through the "C" Level stairwell door, up the four steps in two leaps, to the small landing that sent the case up in the opposite direction. Enzo now heard the opening crash of the props room doors, and then the sound of someone falling. Several obscenities followed the tumult. The stool had bought another second.

His shoes tapped and scraped on each step. The sound was loud enough for him to wince, and thus, loud enough for the pursuer to hear. Bounding up the staircase, Enzo exited at "A" level and turned right. The orchestra pit entrance was to his right, ten feet away. It would make an easy, quiet access to the auditorium, but it held few places to hide. The prompter's box could get him onto the stage and then back behind the curtain, but that would be too time-consuming. Enzo flashed down the hallway, towards the back of the building.

The halls were always full during the day, even through 11:30 p.m., but it was 12:30 in the morning and not a soul was around. Opening night was a party for everyone—singers, crews, and administration—so he was unaccompanied in the dim halls, with a killer at his heels.

Running past the cafeteria and up its adjoining stairs to the stage level, he heard footsteps behind him. The long corridor had not precipitated his escape, but, he believed, would reveal himself to the killer.

Don't look back, just haul ass, Enzo thought. If he could just make it to the lighting booths, he could safely hide himself.

The stage level door was open. He flew through it and onto the stage. The stage was already prepared for Monday's rehearsal of *La Traviata*. In a matter of minutes, it had been completely transformed after the final curtain of his *Tosca*.

That final curtain felt an eternity ago.

Enzo ran in and out of the sets and props that had been meticulously placed by Frank and his crew less than an hour ago, and made his way to the stage manager's desk. The stage was seventy feet deep, but Enzo traversed the space in a few seconds, arriving at the small angled station. The stage right exit was just ahead, but it seemed terribly obvious. He scampered forward, up the slanted metal stairs directly behind the stage manager's desk, and up to the lighting corridors.

This part of the house was truly confusing, but he had been there many times as an apprentice. There were several levels to the lighting area, some leading backstage, some across stage, and still others that led straight up to the grid—the steel-slatted level, seven stories above the stage, where the machinery to lift the curtain and the hanging scenery was located. Enzo knew the third level of the lighting booths led out into the theatre.

The Illinois State Theatre was one of the few opera houses to have light trees so far back into the auditorium. In fact, the light trees farthest from the stage ran alongside the first balcony. The stage lighting would be set from these platforms and adjusted every night depending on which opera was to be performed. Large half-circled shades directed the light towards the stage so as not to distract the patrons seated in close proximity to these lights.

Enzo knew he could lock himself in the access corridor, which led to the auditorium light trees, run to the end of the sealed corridor, stand on the ledge next to where the light crew hung their lamps, and step across the open void to the balcony. He would land right next to the balcony exit curtain where, once through the courtesy curtain and doors, his escape would be complete.

The light crews hopped the rail around the shade frequently in order to see the effect their work had on the productions below. If the electric's crew could do it, this agile, young artist could do it too. The twenty-five foot drop to the orchestra level audience seats would not be a consideration.

Up to the third level of rungs to the corridor, E locked the door to the corridor from the inside, pulled it closed behind him and stole down the thin passage lined with wires and electrical conduit. He heard no footsteps behind him. No person pulled at the freshly locked access door.

A sense of some relief settled upon his heaving, sweaty body. He stopped at the end of the passage and stepped onto the small ledge across from his destination—his safety. The auditorium was dimly lit, but fully recognizable. The four-foot gorge would be easier to traverse than any vocal passage that Leoncavallo had written. He would lean his body forward, grab the handrail, and then place his feet on the ornamented balcony façade. The sweat on his face again reflected the red exit lights, only now, they were those of the Francis Mackay Auditorium.

A final glance down the lighting corridor revealed nothing. A quick scan of the stage and orchestra pit—nothing. He turned to the span and carefully placed his feet with the ends of his leather soles just over the lip of the ledge's rippled metal. The chest of the singer expanded in a slow, preparatory breath, and then, Enzo leaned his six-foot-two- inch frame, as if in slow motion, across the expanse.

His arms stretched out in front of his body. His hand-eye coordination was critical now.

"Watch the rail" rang in his head like the familiar "watch the ball" of his soccer practices. The velocity of his body increased exponentially along its trajectory. His hands, slick with moisture, slapped onto the black metal balcony rail. His left foot moved from the ledge and found purchase on one of the façade's rose-shaped ornaments. He held the position and thought a moment. If he could just swing his right leg across and over the railing... The ornaments on the balcony façade were too fragile, he felt, for his entire weight. Ready...and...

An unexpected noise hit his ears. Enzo's head shot up to find the source of the sound. He heard the outer door of the balcony entrance unlatch, and it was now squeaking open. Enzo's hands tightened their grip and went numb. He only had a second to decide his next move. Nothing was visible through the thick red velvet courtesy curtain. It could be a security guard making his rounds in the house, but he had only ten feet worth of time to decide. A jump down the twenty-five feet to the aisle below would surely be discovered and temporarily injure him in the process—permanently if Frank's killer lurked behind the curtain.

With a thrust off of the rose ornament with his left foot and a release of his hands from the balcony bar, Enzo whipped his head back to create the momentum to travel back the four feet, which he had spanned. With both hands he grabbed the enormous shade that ran the length of the pole to steady himself on the lighting corridor ledge, and then whipped his body behind the shade to conceal himself. Only the light pole shade, which arched around the ledge where Enzo stood, separated him from the balcony—and whoever approached.

The brass curtain rod and rings clacked together as the curtain was slowly pushed to one side. Enzo heard the fibers of the new wine colored carpet rub against a pair of shoes.

Someone had entered. There, six feet away, stood someone whom the tenor had never seen and could not now see either. The curve of the light pole's directional shade was the only thing that stood between the two of them.

Enzo held his breath and leaned into the wall of the small corridor. He stared at the shade's edge, and in nervous thought, searched his mind for a solution to his entrapment.

He could bolt down the lighting corridor, back to the ladders and out, but he had locked the door, knowing the only key lay on the stage manager's desk. The lock that had assured his escape only moments ago was now his snare. The conduit-covered walls of the little light corridor seemed to be closing in on him, seemed to become his tomb.

Options...options! None resulted in escape. Even if he ran down the corridor, there was no place to go.

"Stay calm and breathe silently," he told himself, "and don't move."

Years of stage experience had perfected his silent intake and exhalation. He had used this technique during his death scenes, but the young man now found his life entirely dependent upon his art. He prayed that the person would leave quietly and quickly. As long as Enzo did not move and the stranger did not venture to the far side of the balcony, this horrid companion would never see behind the cover.

Sweat roared like a rolling timpani down his face and fell to the floor through the grated walkway of the corridor. The splash made the faintest of concussions. It seemed like a cymbal crash to the tenor.

Eternity would not seem so long.

Enzo now heard the breathing of the person around the corner. As the man exhaled, his chest rumbled. Time after time the guttural exhalation sounded. Time after time Enzo silently fed oxygen to his own body.

Finally, Enzo heard the fabric of the man's jacket rub on the pants of his dark suit. The man swiveled around to check every direction and every means of escape in the theater. He cleared his throat. Then the tenor heard a harsh, elongated "click" and the scraping of two objects of different composition rubbing together. The rumpling of the jacket told the tenor, at least in the picture formed in his mind, that the man's gun had been placed back in its leather holster.

Enzo closed his eyes for an extended moment, opening them at the recurrence of the sound of the curtain being yanked open. The muffled sound of the door opening and footsteps tapping down the theatre staircase brought a full breath and a final release of tension.

The man was finally gone. Enzo was still locked in the corridor, but his exit was now unblocked. He gathered himself after a minute, trying to contain the shaking of his hands, and prepared to make the lunge to the balcony once again.

The simple task would be much more difficult now. The rush of adrenaline and the racing of his mind had rapidly exhausted him. He stepped to the edge of the walkway, leaned his frame over to the handrail and placed his left foot on the very same rose. He took a quick breath and lunged with his right foot, this time deciding to step to the rounded lower frame of the façade. This would give him two strong footholds from which to push up and over the rail.

His foot pushed away from the metal walkway and landed safely where he had planned. Enzo began to pull himself over the balcony edge.

The rail buckled. His feet tore away from the slippery plaster facade and his body slammed against the jagged edges of the balcony front. He winced in pain as his body bounced, and then settled against the roses.

He looked up and saw the rail slowly bending away from the wall. His body bent with the rail.

A leap to the floor below now looked better than before. His arms, his body, was exhausted and a twenty-foot drop could be managed if he picked the right spot in the aisle below.

He looked up at the rail again. His weight had pulled the support screws of the rail from the wall and buckled the rail support just to the left of his hands. The rail bent no farther, but if it collapsed while he tried to pull himself up the uncontrolled fall would kill him.

The aisle below was now the only answer. He searched for a landing spot in the middle of the aisle, as far away from the wall as possible. A final glance up revealed the black paint of the rail cracking at the point of stress. The rail would not hold much longer.

It was time to fall. He reattained his landing spot, took a deep breath and—wait—he heard the auditorium door directly below him open. The tuxedoed man walked into the hall.

The dangling tenor was fifteen feet above the man whom he believed had killed his friend. This sight reengaged his adrenal gland and caused his fists to spasm, locking them to the weakening rail.

Sweat poured off Enzo, dropping to the floor below.

The darkened theatre obscured him from the man's view once again. Once again he could not breathe. Once again he could not move. Once again he could not make a sound. The rail bent further away from the balcony.

The timpani of sweat rolled again, conveying the same life-and-death sentiment. He bobbed his head from side to side to keep the sweat drops on his person. If they fell to the floor below he would be discovered, and he would be dead.

Eternity slowed again. Enzo watched like some flightless seraph as the man looked up and down the orchestra level aisles. The tuxedo walked a step forward, moving into the auditorium.

A drop of perspiration escaped from the tenor's cheek. It fell to the wine-colored carpet in front of the intruder, whose head was looking to the rear of the theatre. The small concussion of sound drew the man a step further forward, directly below where Enzo hung.

Another explosion of water escaped. Enzo was mad with silent panic. The drop landed on the back of the cheap tuxedo, scraping the polyester as it fell.

The sound spun the killer around. Nothing there!

Enzo looked up to keep the sweat from falling, but in so doing he could not see the actions of his would-be assailant. If he looked down, the projectile would reveal him. He leaned back, even as the balcony rail lowered him further down, and eyed the movements of the man as best he could.

A single bead of sweat formed on his forehead. Enzo felt the water roll down his face next to his eyes, already stung by perspiration, and down his regal nose. A simple flick of the head would usually suffice, but he could not move. The man below now stood on the spot where the previous bead had fallen. Enzo's brow creased in panged defeat. The tiny shift in his facial muscles jarred his face just enough.

The bead of perspiration launched in perfect trajectory towards the head of the man below.

Seconds crawled. The tuxedo began his move into the auditorium, to the middle aisle, and towards the back of the theatre. Enzo seized the opportunity and swung his right foot up onto the lower ledge of the balcony façade. The broken rail held as the tenor pulled his body to the right and up, out of the view of the exiting "patron." His left leg followed, disappearing just before the tuxedo turned and made a last survey of the premises.

The killer tensed a moment in self-directed anger, knowing he had allowed a witness to his work. The muscles in his face flexed and his eyebrows lowered. He knew there would have to be a Second Act, an encore to his performance this evening. He turned, disgusted, and left the auditorium.

Enzo collapsed over the rail. His right patent leather shoe was stained with the single drop of sweat that had meant his doom. He had caught the fateful drop of water on his foot. He now truly knew soccer to be the sport superior to any other in the world.

Now kneeling, Enzo listened for the man. Silence. Silence. Wait a bit more… Silence. Wait even longer. Silence.

He was convinced the man was gone, so he stood and walked out of the hall and down the stairs of the auditorium.

He ran to his dressing room, using the hallway to the far south of the building. He closed and locked the dressing room door behind him, collected his things and looked at his watch. It was 12:45 a.m. Not a soul was in the theatre. He wanted to get out of there, but his friend lay in the basement, dead. Everyone at the switchboard was gone so he could not call the police. He did not feel that he could trust the security guards, since the killer had such easy access to the building.

He would go to the party and come back with an entourage of support to view the crime scene. Enzo started toward his dressing room door. He stopped with a jolt at his sudden revelation.

"His face! I never saw his face." Enzo stopped.

Enzo had viewed the murder from the prop room, but he never saw the murderer's face. He had heard his voice only faintly during the prop room argument, but how was he to help the police find the assassin if he did not even see the man's face?

"Did he see *my* face?" Enzo prayed that he was an unidentified witness, at least to the killer, but he could not be sure. The chase in the halls and stairwells was fast and frightening. He did not remember. His mind was a scramble. The tenor touched his moist cheek.

"I never saw his face."

Two

The gala reception for the triumphant night, held at the Conrad Hilton Grand Ballroom, was missing its vital guest of honor. The dinner had to start without the tenor, who was still at the opera house. Gwen was extremely antsy, but Sandy was schmoozing with the rich old men, inhibitions emancipated by the Dom Perignon.

"I'm sorry, Gwen," William Burrows apologized to the absentee's wife, "we had to go ahead without him. We called over to the house and couldn't find him there."

"He went to see Frank in props," the distressed wife pointed out to the general director. "He said he would be right over after that."

"I'll have security check again. Maybe he got caught up in traffic or something," Burrows muttered, realizing how preposterous his statement was. The Hilton was only ten city blocks from the opera house and it was now past midnight. The city had tucked itself in for the night. There certainly were no traffic problems.

"I'll have someone go call and find out what's happening. Excuse me." Politely withdrawing, Burrows walked away and called one of his staff, a bright young man named Emil Walker, to his side.

"Emil, go call the theatre again about Santi. Have security check the entire house, and double check the dressing rooms. If I know tenors, he's probably doing 'vocal exercises' with some chorus woman somewhere. The stupid bastard needs to at least make an appearance before the party shuts down. These rich bitches will have my ass on a skewer if they can't touch the superstar."

Before finishing his vulgarity, Bill Burrows' wife Janine grabbed him.

"Bill, Enzo is outside and frantic about something. Come quick," Janine Burrows said to her husband. "I've already told Gwen. She's outside with him right now. Something is terribly wrong with the poor boy."

The director and his wife made a hasty but dignified exit and found the tenor slouched on a bench in the hallway, just outside the ballroom. Gwen sat next to her husband, hugging him from the side and wiping the sweat from his brow. Her husband shook uncontrollably, the convulsions bending his body in half. His breathing was rapid and shallow, as if hypothermia was his nemesis.

"Enzo! My God, what is the matter?" the stunned director asked.

"I need to talk to you alone," Enzo said, working for every syllable. The reduced man tilted his head up and looked at the director. "I saw something backstage that I need to tell you." The olive-skinned man had gone into shock on the limousine ride to the hotel. He was ashen, he was sweating profusely, and his muscular frame was being racked with violent seizures.

Gwen pulled his tuxedo jacket tighter around him for comfort and warmth. She looked to the director in silent panic, finding only befuddlement. She turned to her husband.

"Honey, slow down. Look at me, it will be all right," she assured him. "Take a minute and catch your breath."

Enzo turned his head, bouncing in spasms, looking into the brown, sympathetic eyes of his wife. He stared at her through his profuse sweating, through his anguish, and clung to her favor.

Gwen had never seen her husband like this before. He had been the tower of strength for her at critical moments, but now she saw him confused and frightened. She wanted to weep for the man she loved, but instead, she held him tightly and began to breathe a slow, deep breath, in rhythm with him, anchoring, stabilizing him, until the unknown terror subsided.

She took her right hand and placed it on her husband's chest over his heart, spreading her fingers to engulf as much of him as possible. Enzo moved his contorting left hand and seized hers, pulling it further into himself.

Her warm fingers cut through the chill of his skin and provided warmth, supplying a center from which to try and regain control. Enzo focused on his wife only—her hand, her face, her breath.

The Burrows watched as the pair embraced and righted themselves. Gwen gave her strength, with and through her breath, to her ailing husband. The weakness of the one gave strength to the pair.

Several minutes passed with the husband and wife wrapped in each other, fighting off the demons of confusion.

The seizures abated. Enzo's breathing was normalizing, coming into rhythm with Gwen's. Finally, after two laden shudders of exhalation, the husband squeezed his wife's right hand and spoke, looking at the general director.

"I need to talk to you, Bill," he said, beginning to stand and address the G.D.

"Enzo, look at me," Gwen finally burst out, keeping her husband seated. "I want to know what's going on."

Exhausted, Enzo looked at his three friends and decided to let them all know of the incident. He had not yet told anyone about the events he witnessed on "C Level" in the props department. He thought it best to get to the Opening Night Gala Reception as quickly as possible and tell Bill Burrows. Bill could control the situation, and then Gwen and he could retreat to the hotel.

Enzo's mind rushed back to all that had happened-his visit with Frank, his curiosity with the props room, the horror of watching his friend killed before his eyes, and then fleeing for his life. The memory made him feel sick. He had to get help. The theatre was deserted as he left the opera house through the stage door. No security personnel were present as he passed the security desk at the stage door. The limousine waiting to take him to the gala was his only refuge. He had collapsed into the car and arrived at the Hilton five minutes later shaking violently. He had found a men's room on his way up to the party and vomited.

Now his intimate audience of three waited for his pronouncement, hushed, more attentive than any concert had ever been. The words stuck in his throat.

"I went to see Frank," Enzo stuttered. "...I...I...I saw Frank murdered."

The audience was stunned.

Enzo took a drink from a glass of water Janine Burrows had gotten for him. His tongue loosened a bit. He elaborated.

"I went to see Frank Stanza. We talked for a while and I went back to look at the new prop stuff from Mexico. We were alone. I thought we were alone, at least. The prop room was dark. I heard Frank arguing with someone at his desk and...as I came around the corner to leave the prop room...I saw a man break his neck."

Horror befell the three listeners.

"Enzo, are you all right?" Gwen asked her spent husband.

"Yes, I think so. I just started shaking," understating the obvious. The tenor looked at Burrows.

"Bill, I didn't know what to do. I figured you would be able to handle things as well as anyone."

"Does security at the house know about it?" asked Burrows.

"I couldn't find anyone around. Frank and I were down there talking for a while after the show. I looked, but I couldn't find anyone. Even the stage door security desk was vacant. The place was really deserted."

"Where was Frank killed?" Burrows asked. "Where did this happen?"

"Where? I told you, right there at his desk, 'C' Level. I was in the storage room in the back when I heard Frank yelling at someone. When I started to walk out of the room, there they stood. The guy had come around to Frank's backside and that's when I saw...I heard...the guy break Frank's neck." Tears trickled down Enzo's cheeks. "I saw Frank's body fall to the ground."

Janine Burrows sat down on the left side of the distraught tenor.

"Enzo, are you sure you are all right?" Burrows asked, crouching down to look more closely at his employee. He knew that if what Enzo said was true, the CGO troubles could start all over again. A murder was a grisly thing, but prop masters can be replaced. Destroyed opera companies cannot. He focused on the tenor—his money man.

"Enzo, you are sure you are not hurt?" Burrows asked.

"I think I'm fine, just...can't stop shaking. I don't think he saw me, at least not my face. I had to run out of the props room, but I finally got away." Enzo knew the statement was a jumble, but he could not help himself. The words erupted from his mouth without the aid of his brain.

"What are you saying, honey?" Gwen stroked her husband's damp hair.

"He chased me through the house, but I don't think he saw me. At least he gave up looking for me."

"Oh my God," shrieked Janine Burrows.

Bill Burrows knew the situation could quickly get too emotional, so he took control.

"Ladies, I want you to get Enzo back to his hotel room and calm him down. I'll call the police and get over to the opera house and get a handle on the situation," said the general director with great authority.

"Bill, I want to go with you," Enzo stammered.

"Enzo, I can take care of everything at the house right now. The police and I may be over later this morning to go over the details of what happened. In fact, I'm sure we will. But right now, young man, you need to settle down and try to get a hold of yourself. Let your wife take you home, get some food in you and rest a bit. Okay? You just let me take care of all this."

Enzo looked up at the gray-haired man, twenty years his senior, took his hand to pull him close, and whispered the confession that tore at his being.

"I didn't see his face."

"What?" inquired the befuddled G.D.

"I didn't see his face," stammered E. "I didn't see the killer's face."

With those very words, Enzo took on himself the responsibility of his friend's murder. Not only was Frank killed as Enzo helplessly watched, but in the tenor's mind, he had failed his friend by not even seeing the face of the killer. Enzo lowered his head.

"Don't worry, my boy, we'll get to the bottom of this," assured Burrows. "Now you get out of here. I'll come by the hotel later and tell you what the police find. All right?"

Nodding consent, the trio—Enzo, Gwen, and Janine Burrows—made their way out of the hotel to Enzo's limousine, then to the Hyatt where the Santi's were staying.

Gwen wrote Sandy Denning a quick note of apology, asking if she might get home on her own, and said she would fill her in later.

Bill Burrows walked back into the reception and called to his assistant, Emil.

"I need to see Charles O'Leary immediately. It's urgent."

"The chief of police?" inquired the young man.

"Yeah. Have him meet me down the hall, at the top of the main staircase."

The young man scurried to the table where the chief of police, Charles O'Leary, was enjoying the festivities at the expense of the Opera. Burrows watched Emil relate the message and saw the chief nod in consent.

As Burrows watched this, he pulled his cellular phone from his tuxedo jacket pocket. He saw O'Leary shoot a cup of java down his throat to clear the abundance of champagne before he could attend to Bill's "urgent" request. The G.D. punched the seven digits and "sent" the call.

"There is a problem at the house that needs to be taken care of immediately. You probably have ten minutes before the chief of police shows up. No, of course I didn't know anything about it. But *now* this whole thing has to look official. Please make it disappear. All right! Tomorrow? No, not tomorrow. Monday!"

Burrows clicked the phone "off." He saw the large chief begin to rouse himself, and he knew he had to address the reception crowd one final time.

"Damn!" He walked to the podium, stepped to the microphone, apologized for his early departure, and bid his patrons farewell.

"I have been called away on some pressing last minute business," he addressed the crowd, "but again, ladies and gentlemen, let me thank you for supporting the Chicago Grande Opera and for joining us this glorious evening in the inauguration of our *recommitment* to artistic excellence. I bid you all a fond 'adieu.'"

The blitzed crowd, full of champagne and caviar, applauded heartily.

Burrows quickly walked out of the ballroom and joined Chief O'Leary at the top of the grand staircase.

"There's been some trouble at the opera house, some bad trouble I think," spoke the G.D.

Emil Walker was at his boss's side. Burrows did not want any more people than necessary knowing about what had happened. He needed Emil around, but he did not tell him any details. The G.D. gently pulled the arm of the chief of police to one side to privatize their conversation.

Burrows explained what had supposedly happened, where, how, and whom. The if's and why's of the predicament would come after the first three items were established positively.

"Chuck, if this thing is really bad, can you help me on it? I mean with the press? This will look horrible for us if what Enzo said is true," said the worried-looking G.D.

"Bill, I'll do my best to keep this thing quiet, but the papers have ears. And you have to do your part too. Keep your kids at the opera house in line," spoke the old Irishman as he loosened his suspenders, already stretched to their limit on the rotund officer. He was no stranger to gala events, or to the cuisine that accompanied them. He continued.

"But my boy, we still have to find our supposed murderer. In fact, we don't even know if there has been a crime committed yet, let alone a murder. We'll just have to take it one step at a time."

O'Leary was methodical, and for once, Burrows was happy about the deliberate pace taken by the veteran cop. They walked down the enormous staircase and out the front entrance to the police chief's limousine, provided, of course, by the Chicago Grande Opera.

Burrows was glad for this little perk he had extended to the man now. It might find him in greater favor with the officer. He had cursed the chief's expected decadence originally.

The limousine retraced its path of the previous hour. Burrows fidgeted on the black leather seats. O'Leary opened the bar and poured himself a scotch and soda.

The opera house felt a thousand miles away. The general director had to get there, but feared what he would find. Why could not the limo just drive straight up Michigan Avenue and plunge into the Chicago River? Why not? Because his soused companion would keep the car afloat, buoyed by his blubber. The chief spilled his drink on his rented tuxedo. Burrows looked over at him with disgust.

Fat, stupid, son of a bitch, he thought to himself. He looked out the tinted windows to see Buckingham Fountain off to his right. Its three tiers, sculptures, and colored lights, bedecked the night, shooting water seventy feet into the air.

Why did this have to happen tonight, when the art world was focused on him? Why on opening night? He had feared this might transpire, and now it had come to pass, on opening night.

Three

E, Gwen, and Janine Burrows made their way up to the Santis' suite. Enzo, having calmed down a bit, excused himself to go the bedroom to take a shower. He hoped that the warmth of the water and the quiet of the bedroom might restore life to his numbed body. Gwen followed his every step until he began to disrobe, protecting her husband from any further shock.

"E, I'm going to order some hot food. I want you to eat something," whispered Gwen. "Did you hear me, honey? I want you to eat something."

"Yeah...thanks. Some soup would be good," mumbled the man. Gwen closed the bedroom door behind her as she walked into the living room area.

"Janine, would you like something?" asked Gwen.

"Just some coffee."

Picking up the phone, Gwen quickly ordered some lentil soup, a roast beef sandwich, and some odds and ends on which to munch in the weary hours that lay ahead of them.

Gwen hung up and walked over to the small little kitchenette in the hotel room. She and her husband both were coffee connoisseurs and needed at least two hot, rich cups in the morning. The hotel served the finest Colombian blends that suited the South American man.

The real-life tragedy of the evening was accompanied by an uncomfortable silence. The murder had turned the triumph of the operatic evening into an emotional torture.

"Gwen," Janine asked, "is there anything I can do for you and Enzo until the police arrive?"

Gwen sighed and poured the water into the coffeemaker.

"I don't think so, Janine, thanks. We just have to hang around, I guess, until the police and your husband decide what's best."

In the bedroom, the women heard the water from the shower hit the tile walls of the shower stall. The rhythm of the water, the white noise that the shower generated, made both women relax. The evening had been extremely long and through their veins had coursed too much adrenaline. Both women headed to the living room couches.

Gwen, having attended to the coffee, walked back into the living room and sat in the large sofa that dominated the middle of the room. She leaned back and let the soft cushions form to her body. Her feet slipped out of their evening's confines and she slid them to the corner of the couch, between two goose-down pillows. Janine sat across from her, a bit more stately, and crossed her legs as her body melted into a highback chair.

"Will your husband be able to sleep after what happened?" questioned the general director's wife.

"I hope so, but I doubt it. Frank and he arrived at the CGO the same year and they are wonderful friends. If Frank has been killed, it's going to hurt for a long time." Gwen's brow creased as she spoke, responding sympathetically to the pain her husband felt. "I'm sure both of us will have quite a few sleepless nights ahead." Gwen rose abruptly from her cuddled position.

"I should call Connie."

"Connie who?" inquired the general director's wife.

"Frank's wife. If something has happened to Frank, she needs to know about it." Gwen swung her feet to the floor and moved to the phone. Janine quickly interrupted.

"Gwen, wait a minute. The police are over at the opera house right now and they'll take care of it. Besides, if nothing has happened, do you want to wake Connie up and frighten her just to find out there has been some misunderstanding?" Gwen was still antsy, but pulled the phone away from her ear. Janine continued.

"My husband and the police will take care of everything, my dear. Let's wait a bit so we can find out the whole story."

"I sure would hate for the police to tell me something was wrong with Enzo. Don't you think it would be better if a friend told her what happened tonight?" Gwen asked.

"Look, honey, Bill said he would let us know what was going on as soon as he found out, so when he finds out, we'll find out. Then if something is wrong, we can tell Connie in person. O.K.?"

Gwen thought a minute and settled down.

"You're right," Gwen conceded. She sighed and moved back to her cuddled position. It was not necessary to frighten her friend if there was no cause. If this horrible thing had happened to Frank, Bill and the police would tell Enzo first. The couple could then console their friend.

The tension remained on her brow.

Janine sensed Gwen's protective instincts, and she leaned across the little coffee table, embracing the worried wife with her eyes.

"Gwen," Janine assured her, "Bill and I don't doubt your husband. We just need to get a handle on the situation at the opera house if something horrible *has* happened. We believe your husband. We just need to calm ourselves and take one step at a time. Once the police find out what has happened and your husband helps them, everything will settle down. I promise."

The women settled back into their comfort zones and breathed deeply for a minute. The white noise of the shower stopped and the clanging from the other room signaled the end of the liquid massage.

Gwen looked into Janine's eyes, let a shallow breath escape and took a quick intake. She formed her words easily.

"When we met back in grad school I thought Enzo was a nice, shy South American boy who had a beautiful voice and a handsome presence. I still find him adorable, but he's not just that. My husband is my life!"

The seriousness of the statement took Janine by surprise.

"When we got married I was really happy. His career began taking off and we were secure financially, but you know, Janine, he tells me every day that none of this means a thing unless I am here to enjoy it with him." She breathed again.

"A few years ago when Enzo was in the Apprenticeship Program and I found out I was pregnant, he took me on a get-away weekend to celebrate up in Door County. We didn't have much money, but he was so awed that our love was creating another life that he insisted we celebrate in high fashion. He sends me notes, flowers, and even makes up gifts to give me when he has to be away. Once he flew home a day early to surprise me, and when I walked in the door there was a note on the dining room table telling me to walk into the bedroom, lie on the massage table that was set up in there, and to prepare for the night of my life. That evening he gave me a massage, a bath, he brushed my hair, and he even ordered one of those gourmet take-out dinners which he fed me. He wanted me to be indulged. He wanted me to be cared for. This silly man wants me to be the happiest person in the world.

"And you know, his selflessness makes me want to return his love all the more. I want him to be the happiest person in the world.

"But the greatest thing about him is that he wants to be with me, even in life's hardships. When I miscarried, he was in London at Covent Garden singing *Romeo and Juliet*. He not only canceled those performances, but he canceled everything for the next three months just so he could be with me—to cry with me, to hold me, to just be there.

"The same thing happened when my father died. Enzo doesn't want any harm to come to me, but he is smart enough to know heartache does come, and I think the most tender thing about him is that he wants to share my pain and trouble, not only our joys and triumphs.

"Seeing me hurt causes him incredible anguish."

Gwen paused, searching for her words.

"How can I say it? He sacrifices his strength for me. That's what Enzo is to me. He is my strength and my power. He would sacrifice his entire life for me. I don't deserve him, but he has given me the love of many lifetimes."

Janine had lost her breath, listening to the love of these two people for each other. Gwen paused and spoke to herself as much as to Janine.

"And now it is my turn to be strong and be there for him."

Janine thought back to the scene outside the party. Gwen held her husband and breathed for him. She gave him her strength so he could recover himself. The self-sacrifice the one had shown for the other was returned instantly. They had not functioned as separate people; they had functioned as a unit, making each individual stronger in the process.

Janine's eyes zeroed in on the beautiful blonde woman as she continued her revelation.

"I have never seen him as shaken as he was tonight, that's why I know something is terribly wrong. I know he's not lying. He would never do something like that. But right now, I just hope Enzo...I hope all of us can get some rest." Gwen turned to her friend.

"You're right, Janine. Bill and the police will let us know what has happened, and we can do what we need to do after that. I just hope the news is better, rather than worse."

The obnoxious hotel room doorbell rang; the victuals had arrived. They might help settle the jangled nerves of the confined trio.

"Janine, could you get the door?" asked Gwen. "I am sure that's the food. I'm gonna check on Enzo."

There was a bit of commotion in the bedroom, signaling the man's exit from the bathroom. The women moved in opposite directions and saw to their tasks.

Gwen gently opened the closed bedroom door. The bedroom was dark, yet a bathroom light cast a soft yellow glow into the room. She peeked around the opening door.

"Enzo," the mezzo whispered, *sotto voce*. "How are you doing, honey?"

It took her eyes a few seconds to adjust to the dark room; the light from the bathroom casting shadows all about. Her eyes and head moved throughout the bedroom in suspended unison, searching to find her husband. The eyes blinked as they panned the right side of the big firm bed.

Enzo sat on the pillow of the still-made bed, a towel around his waist, leaning against the headboard. His wet head and hair were pressed into the wall behind the headboard and he stared out the partially opened blinds of the terrace.

But he had closed his eyes; his lids were tight and his brow terse with distress.

His wife moved to join him. She placed herself on the bed beside him, sliding into the space left by his legs. She pressed her torso against his angled chest and placed her arms on his muscular shoulders. Gwen gazed up at her husband and kissed his cheek with silken lips. His arms descended, touching her lower back. His hands pulled together and clasped.

His great chest heaved, relieved by her presence but anguished by the events of the waning eve. He had wrestled with his felt dichotomy in the limousine that delivered the trio to the hotel, and again while he was in the shower. It was still haunting him.

These two feelings—love and anguish—were coexisting inside of him. Just as Isolde, while holding her dying Tristan, could no longer be content with life, Enzo could not be satisfied in his life after the murder of his friend. With Frank's murder came an agony, expiration to a portion of his own life. His love for his friend was now inexplicably intertwined with death, the death of part of his own personality, the death of their friendship, and the death of a vital and important human being. Death gnawed at his life, clasping with fiendish claws at his love for his friend, salting the fresh wound it had created in Enzo's heart.

Wagner was right. *Liebe*—love, and Tod—death, could simultaneously exist. These two opposing forces, fighting one another for ultimate victory, co-existed now within his own soul.

Enzo had thought in his youth that Richard Wagner was wrong. The two feelings were separate. Love and passion were fulfillment, they were joy. Death, anguish, and pain only occurred in the absence of love. They mocked love through hatred, through selfishness.

But life had been his teacher and it had proven him emphatically wrong: the loss of their child, the loss of Gwen's father, even Enzo's personal beliefs contradicted him.

Love not only existed with pain and death, but love existed partly to fend off death. Love would make the ultimate sacrifice to pain, and then, eventually, death. Love pulled grief and agony to its breast and tried to quench its fury, just as Gwen now pulled the fire of his grief to herself. The memory would linger, but the sacrifice of the one, sharing the other's burden, made it possible for both to survive.

Enzo's arms tightened, pulling Gwen closer. She responded in-kind, pulling herself up, now laying her head on his shoulder.

His great chest heaved again.

"What can I do?" E questioned. Gwen understood the ambiguous question.

"Nothing but wait, honey."

"I didn't think I would respond this way," Enzo said. "My tears have complete control of me."

"E, *you* don't need to be strong," she assured him. "We can be strong together."

Enzo turned his head away. Gwen now became emphatic.

"Honey, look at me!" He obediently responded.

"You and I loved Frank very much. If something terrible has happened, the police will respond," she assured him. "You were strong when you needed to be." Gwen echoed the words of Janine in the other room.

"Sure, I ran and hid like a child," Enzo interrupted her, "after I watched Frank die."

Gwen sat up in the bed, pulling her husband up with her, and looked directly into his eyes.

"*Enzo*, look at me!" There was a firm, committed edge in her voice. "You are alive," she uttered slowly. She spoke to the logical side of his nature. "Did you know what was going to happen?"

"No...but I heard the voices..."

"When did you hear the voices?"

"When I was in the back of the prop room, looking at the stuff from the fire last spring. I heard Frank and the man."

"What did Frank and the man say?" the wife took the role of a sympathetic interrogator.

"I don't know. Their voices were too soft most of the time. I just heard muffled voices, really."

"What did you see when you came out of the prop room?"

"I saw—I saw *it!*" His face tightened. "I came around the corner from the back of the prop room and I froze as I saw—the man's back—and—Frank slump to the ground." Enzo swallowed. "I fell back into the prop room, as if someone had kicked me in the stomach." He paused, then he grimaced. "I saw him killed some twenty feet away and I couldn't do anything to help him."

His wife, controlling her fright but fully realizing her husband's proximity to the killing, narrowed her eyes and took him by the shoulders.

"Enzo, you had no idea Frank was in danger, otherwise you *would have* been there for him, just as you have been there for me every time I have needed you." Her husband listened intently through the stemming tide of tears.

"Honey, you would be dead too if you hadn't escaped." Her own statement scared her. Gwen now realized how close her husband had come to being murdered, and the thought grieved her heart.

"We can be here to grieve with Connie and to help the police find this man and bring him to justice." Enzo's face lightened. He listened.

Gwen was in control now. She released her strength to her husband.

"You've told me that God gave you your voice and that you are responsible to use it, right? Well, maybe God has also given you this chance to bring justice to Frank's death."

Gwen's voice was calm. It soothed the intense emotion of the previous minutes.

"And we can be here for Connie and the kids," Gwen finished. "We can be weak for each other, but let's be strong for Connie

Enzo slowly nodded his consent. He knew there was nothing he could have done, but the pain of his witness was intertwined with regret. He felt acute sorrow at not taking action in his friend's hopeless situation.

Gwen had found the key to his distress, to his gnawing dichotomy. He was guilty of grieving the loss of his friend, but not guilty of negligence. His witness was a burden, but a burden that he could bear, and a burden that would have a proper end, a burden to be relieved through justice and compassion.

The pain of the previous moments melted away. The couple stared at each other for a moment. Enzo pulled Gwen's lips to his and kissed them in intimate thanks. The lovers once again wrapped themselves in each other's arms, undivided by the horrific events of the evening.

They lay down on the bed and caressed each other tenderly, moving closely to each other in a warm embrace.

It was nearly morning. In a few hours the sun would peek above Lake Michigan's blue horizon, sending the Second City hurtling though another day. The couple fell into a deep sleep, exhausted from exertion and exasperation.

Janine had heard the two in muted tones and knew Gwen had brought a measure of peace to her husband. All was well in the bedroom, so Janine curled up amongst the down pillows of the sofa and was also quickly greeted by the sandman. The trio left the roast beef and lentil soup undisturbed.

Four

3:40 a.m.
Sunday, September 24
Properties Desk, "C" Level
Illinois State Theatre

"Either your tenor boy has a screw loose or he is playing some kind of practical joke," snorted the old cop, Charles O'Leary.

"I don't think he was joking, Charles," the general director said. "He was really upset; he almost fainted telling me about it."

Charles O'Leary, the chief of the Chicago Police Department, was a wise old Irishman whose family had been in law enforcement for three generations.

As chief of police, O'Leary ordered a couple of his best detectives, Mark Hanson and Victor Ferrer, over to the opera house as a favor. The chief wanted to make sure a crime had been committed before bringing in the entire forensics team. Emil Walker, Burrow's assistant, also milled around a bit, but kept a safe distance from the men who were searching "C" Level, but when Bill Burrows turned his head, Emil would be at his side in a moment to carry out whatever task the G.D. needed.

The ordered chaos of the prop area appeared relatively undisturbed. There was a bit of blood on the property desk, but it did not seem out of the ordinary. There was a lot of dirt, scuffs from shoes, and a dark smudge directly behind the desk, but nothing that appeared suspicious. A quick walk through the property storage room revealed a fallen pole and some scattered boxes, but this again seemed to be the method of organization and no cause for concern.

There was apparently nothing to be found, and certainly no dead bodies. It was not long before the old cop let his men go back home.

As his detectives started to exit, the chief thanked them and bade them good night. Emil Walker showed the detectives to the stairwell door that led up and out of the opera house. The chief turned to the director, took a step towards him and glanced once again around the area while he spoke.

"As you see, Bill, all we got is a little blood on the desk and some messed up papers. There's nothin' here that looks fishy," said the police chief. "If you like, we could try and run some prints, but with the number of people—cleaning, security, crews, let alone singers from all over the world—I doubt that would show us anything."

The G.D. was standing directly in front of the props desk, head tilted slightly down, looking vacantly into the rickety old barstool that Frank Stanza used for his properties manager's chair. He did not hear the chief's comment. The chief looked at the weary man and spoke again.

"Bill...Bill. Did you hear me?" He stepped towards the man. "Are you all right?"

The G.D.'s temporarily glazed eyes came back into focus and he turned his head to peer at his old friend.

"Yeah, Charles, I'm all right. I'm just tired," he said as he took a deep breath. Burrows recovered. "I'm sorry for dragging you here like this," he apologized. "I think our tenor friend shook me up last night, you know, and I'm fairly exhausted from the last couple of days."

"No need to apologize, you know that. Besides, it's my job. And after the thrill you folks gave this old Irishman last night, it's my pleasure." The cop smiled. "Do you want me to try and call your man's home, see if I can find him?"

"No, no, Charles, I'll tell my crew chief to give him a call. Thanks though." Burrows nodded his head and Emil quickly stepped to the director's side.

"Emil, could you show the chief the easiest way out of these catacombs, please? You'll get an extra jewel in your heavenly crown for spending the night down here, Chuck," waxed Burrows. A hearty belly laugh erupted from the chief's gut.

"Maybe a night down here will get me out of Purgatory quicker." The cop laughed at his own humorousless joke.

Burrows' waxy smile at the chief's statement revealed his true feelings, but the chief was already leaving.

Get the hell out of here, you stupid, old bastard, he thought.

"This way, sir," Emil spoke to Chief O'Leary. Emil motioned to the stairway door. Burrows began to let down his guard. O'Leary turned around unexpectedly.

"Do you want me to talk to your tenor, Bill?" the old cop asked Burrows.

"No, I'll talk to everyone that needs to be talked to," he said dryly, narrowing his eyes. "Thanks again, Charles," he impatiently finished. "Emil, thank you for staying, but you can get out of here too. In fact, take Monday on me."

"You're sure, sir?" Emil politely asked his boss.

Burrows nodded.

"Thank you," Emil said, "but don't hesitate to call if you need me." Burrows nodded again.

The cop and the assistant made their way up the stairs. The stairwell door shut behind them. Burrows could hear the cop whistling as he ascended. Burrows turned back to the desk and its stool, at which he had just been staring.

There was no sarcasm in his eyes now. No contemptuous glances. No thoughts of disdain for those he felt had abandoned him. He was alone, and uncomfortably so.

He hated this place. He hated what it had done to him. He hated the feeling of being naked, without power. He hated the facade.

The muscles in his face flexed as he nervously ground his teeth together. He slowly walked to the prop desk and put his hands on the top of the dinged and dented wood. He felt the Saharan surface drink in the perspiration from his moist hands. His eyes traced the outline of the top of the desk. He noticed the gouges, he noticed the pencil marks, he noticed the coffee rings, he noticed the frayed fibers.

He noticed the brown-black spot half-way across the desktop. He lifted his right hand to touch the spot. With his middle finger he reached out and tenderly felt the stain.

He pulled his manicured nail back to discover what was underneath.

Nothing. It was perfectly dry, just another stain on a desktop replete with stains.

He touched the spot again and tried to rub his own moisture into the once-crimson spot, but the desiccated wood refused to yield its capture. The general director knew what that stain was. He also knew he would never again see the man who had spilt it.

The general director's brow lowered. His head tilted to the side as he pushed his finger harder into the stain.

"Son of a bitch!"

Five

6:30 a.m. Sunday morning

The sun slowly crept down the horizon onto the Chicago skyline. The perfectly clear morning yielded a jogger winding his way through Grant Park, past Soldier's Field, past the Aquarium and the Planetarium on its distant man-made peninsula. The lake had begun its slow advance with the harsh winter and was now thrusting powerful waves upon the breakwaters and beach along Lake Shore Drive. A few final boats bobbed in the turbulent surf.

The infamous wind was consistent with its reputation and whipped along briskly in the forty-degree air. Few cars wound around the gliding paths of the inner and outer drives. It was an ideal morning for slumber, for that extra blanket to make its debut onto the feet of many midwestern beds. Steam rose from the lake, giving it a frosty quality amongst the bubble of the waves.

East, up Congress Parkway, a white limousine emerged from the line of buildings and entered the park. Splitting the two Indian Warriors at the entrance of Grant Park, the Lincoln Stretch turned left at Buckingham Fountain and headed north past the Drury Lane Theater and the Grant Park Band Shell, with only the occasional whip of wind disturbing the car.

The vehicle was minuscule as it approached the giant hotels at the north end of Grant Park. It continued straight up to the Wacker Drive East intersection, turned right and arrived at the front entrance of the Hyatt, with its new and brilliant entrance.

Bill Burrows got out of the car, impatient with his chauffeur. He made a beeline for the hotel doors.

"Good morning, sir," the overly jovial bellhop said. Silence. He headed straight to the reception area, where he received the information he needed with little expenditure of energy, turned left to the bank of elevators, entered and pressed "18." He paced in the elevator as it lifted him effortlessly to his destination.

"Ding." The doors parted. Burrows turned to the left and made his way down the hall to Room 1801. He pressed the suite's doorbell.

"Hurry up, damn it!" he whispered under his breath.

Janine Burrows heard the doorbell on the second ring, but she could not open her eyes until the third. The bedroom door did not open and she did not want the occupants to be aroused, so she pulled her feet out of the warm crevice of the couch, swung around to sit up, then walked to the door, returning her frock to its proper position. The twists of the fitful night had also dampened her coif. She smacked her cheeks as if slapping the sandman, in an attempt to keep him at bay, and finally made it to the door. She peeked through the so-called hole, and she opened the door to her husband.

"Where's Enzo?"

"Asleep, I believe." Her husband rushed past her. "Bill, what did you find?"

Burrows looked around the spacious suite and, seeing that only his wife had stirred, he scanned the hotel room, in nervous agitation.

"He's not up? I guess I should have expected it."

Janine was growing quite impatient.

"Bill, what is going on?"

The bedroom door swung open. The tenor emerged and headed straight to the director. Burrows expelled a disgusted breath and turned again to his wife.

"Just wait, Janine, will you please?" The bark defied the seemingly polite comment.

Janine pulled back abruptly and bristled, straightening her back. Burrows turned to face the tenor as he slowed to hear the news of the night. The question on E's face was obvious, but the G.D. spoke first.

"Enzo, is there anything you want to tell me about last night that you haven't told me so far?"

Enzo expected news, not interrogation. The tenor's confusion was clear. His mouth opened and an audible breath escaped.

"What?" he stammered. "What do you mean?" The jumble of phrases seemed all too familiar. He returned to what he originally wanted to know from the man.

"Did you find Frank? Bill, please tell me...tell me what you found. *Please.*"

Enzo's hands reflected his intensity—pulled up, open and waiting for a word of compassion, or at least one of dreadful confirmation.

The earnestness of his plea broke Janine's heart. She was tired of this game she had seen her husband play far too often. She turned on the man.

"Bill, stop this bullshit and tell us what you found out!" Her voice crescendoed to accent the final syllable.

"All right, but I have to ask one more time, Enzo. Do you want to tell me anything else about last night and your visit downstairs to Frank?"

"No...Yes...Um...What? Yes, last night I saw... Frank murdered, as I said." The tenor could stand it no longer. He grabbed Bill Burrows by the shoulders in desperation and burst out.

"Please Bill, tell me what you found!"

The G.D. looked Enzo in the eyes and searched his face. He found naught of deception. He breathed to speak.

"Nothing, E."

Enzo pulled back and his shoulders fell.

"We found absolutely nothing!"

Six

The picturesque limousine ride down the ten blocks of Wacker Drive, along the Chicago River, past the corncob-like apartment buildings of Marina Towers and the enormous Merchandise Mart, held no appeal to the four occupants.

There was only one thing on the mind of the stentorian tenor: get to the opera house and view the scene of the previous night's horrific events in person, once again.

Earlier, in the hotel, as they had hustled to leave for the opera house, the group of three spectators had asked the general director every possible question.

"Did you find Frank's body?"

"No."

"Did you find Frank, his blood on the papers on the desk?"

"No. No papers, the desk was totally clear."

"Blood on the floor?"

"Nothing but smudges, heels and dirt."

Burrows explained that all the police found were some props dumped onto the floor of the props room, along with a pole thrown to one side, or accidentally fallen.

"But I was there," E pleaded. "I saw Frank killed."

"I'm sorry, Enzo, but we didn't find anything," responded the director. Gwen took her husband's arm and wrapped her own around it, pulling it to her body in unity.

The G.D. continued. "I'm not doubting you were there and saw Frank. All I'm saying is that there is no evidence that Frank fell victim to some foul play. The place looked perfectly normal."

"How would you know?" spouted the tenor sarcastically. "You've never set foot in the props area before last night."

Gwen was taken aback by her husband's rudeness.

"Enzo, that is uncalled for," she scolded her husband.

"Enzo," the G.D. spoke, uncharacteristically restrained, "I just came from the opera house. I believe you. We all believe you. It's just that Chief O'Leary and two of his best detectives didn't find anything that might indicate Frank fell into some bad circumstances. I'm sorry, but that's where it stands right now. Until we hear something about Frank's whereabouts, for good or ill, there is not much we can do."

Enzo's face fell. His searching eyes wandered about the rich carpeted floor of the suite. He thought and thought. What could he do to change things?

"Can I go to the house and look at the props area?" he asked the director.

"Sure, but I don't see the need to examine an empty storage room again," was the reply. "The police checked it out pretty thoroughly, but if my million dollar tenor wants to go, we'll go."

The four people looked at each other blankly for a moment.

"Enzo, we'll find out what happened to Frank, I promise," Janine Burrows finally said.

The tenor looked up at the open, warm face of the woman. Her simple words and his wife's touch reassured him. It was time to search—no more anxious anticipation—to search for the unfound. Burrows looked at his wife, in all of her impotence, and invisibly smirked.

As Enzo smiled a weak smile at Janine, a spark ignited in his mind.

"I have proof," he proudly proclaimed. He pulled away from his wife and rushed into the bedroom.

"What is he talking about?" Burrows asked disgustedly.

"I don't know," said the befuddled wife.

Out of the bedroom jogged the man, with his piece of opera memorabilia—the frayed toggle switch he had found in the "fire" boxes.

"This proves that I was there last night," proclaimed the tenor, feeling a moment of confirmation.

"This shows that…" Enzo stammered, "that…"

Realizing the burnt piece of refuse was proof of nothing, the searching look and sullen shoulders returned to the tenor.

Gwen brought her husband's gaze to her eyes.

"E, let's go to the opera house and look around, then we can put some things to rest."

Three slammed cups of coffee and fifteen minutes later, the quartet arrived at the opera house. A skeleton crew of security was watching the building until rehearsals resumed on Monday.

7:15 a.m.
Sunday, September 24, 1992
Illinois State Theatre

The two sets of spouses entered the stage door. Enzo, Gwen, and Janine whisked by the security desk and made their way down to the props department. Burrows lagged for a moment, asking the guard on duty, as he had the night before, if anything unusual had been found during the guards' nightly rounds. A door or two improperly locked, but nothing unusual. Nothing, again. Burrows hustled to rejoin the other threesome.

Enzo strode ahead, pushing through the stairwell door, anxious to view what he knew to be the scene of a murder. The others followed, cautiously. Enzo walked hastily to the desk front and explained the events of the previous night: his and Frank's conversation, and his own rummage in the prop room.

"I was back here when I heard someone else come to the desk area," explained E as he strode down the entranceway into the enormous storage room, fire doors wedged open. "I was looking through the fire damaged junk in the first aisle."

Enzo pulled the toggle switch from his pocket he had found the previous night, to once again show his rapt audience of three.

"I heard Frank arguing with someone when I found this." Enzo held up the switch.

"O.K." said Burrows, playing along to satisfy the dramatic man. "Then what happened?"

"I started to walk out of the back room."

"How long were you *in* the room?"

"Less than five minutes, just looking around at some of the damaged props. As I started to walk out and turn the corner I looked up and saw this man, about six feet tall, standing right behind Frank."

"Do you know for sure it was Frank?"

"What do you mean? Of course it was Frank!"

"Do you know who the other man was?

"No, but he was directly behind Frank. He lifted his arms, grabbed Frank's head and..." E's stomach tightened as his mind replayed the scene while he narrated. He could not speak. He looked at his wife for assistance.

Gwen stepped forward. Calmly, she took over the questioning.

"Enzo, is there anything you remember about this man that might be distinct? Something that might give him away?"

Enzo breathed deeply and focused his attention on the inquiry, replaying the rest of the surreal scene from the previous night.

"Six feet tall, and he wore a black tuxedo,"

"Well, that sure helps!" mumbled Burrows.

"Dark hair...I think he had a gun. I couldn't see him. When he was on Frank, his back was turned, when I hid back there," he said, pointing to the back corner of the room and walking down the main south aisle. "It was too dark to see his face. I hid amongst the ghosts."

"Then this guy came after you, after what happened to Frank?" asked Janine.

"Yeah, he heard me, but I hid back here. I put the pole between two of the shelves and when he tripped, I ran for the door."

Just then, E knew he had to go to the balcony. The only proof of his dash for life would be the broken railing in the balcony. Nothing else could be substantiated. The night before, at the party, he was barely able to speak, let alone convey the catastrophe he had beheld.

"We have to go to the balcony, stage right," he spoke out. "Last night I broke the rail as I climbed over from the light tree."

Disbelief filled the director, while astonishment welled up in the women.

"All right," said Burrows exasperated. "Let's go to the balcony."

There it was—the conclusive evidence of the evil deed. The four stood in front of the rail that had been roped off to protect the unsuspecting.

The screws pulled from the plaster, the severe arc weakened from the tenor's weight, the warped paint at the point of stress—all these things brought verity to Enzo's convictions, and more deeply, sorrow to his heart. The evidence brought perplexity to the rest of the group.

Gwen believed her husband. He would not have made up such a tale.

Janine believed only what she saw. Many things were apparently out of place. Enzo was a good man, but he may have misinterpreted some very odd circumstances last night. The key for her was to find the prop master, in whatever state that might be.

Burrows was tired of the whole affair, exhausted. He rubbed his forehead, exasperated.

"Let's go to my office and make some calls," said the G.D. as he exhaled heavily.

Seven

No one picked up the extensions the general director dialed, noone except security. The gala of the night before had put the whole company into a deep sleep until Monday morning, where it deserved to be.

The four amateur sleuths entered the general director's spacious office and followed their sleep-deprived bodies to the nearest repose. The office was decorated with a deep cherry wood, and rich, textured walls. Two large brown leather sofas had been placed against the far walls, and two leather upholstered chairs faced directly across from the general director's desk. The desk itself, also cherry, was a huge seven-by-four-foot family heirloom that Burrows had placed diagonally away from the corner of two walls, from which he was able to see the entire room. Bay windows ran the full fifteen feet from ceiling to floor, overlooking the river and the Jackson Boulevard Bridge.

The women made for the couches, while the men went directly to the desk. Enzo sat quietly in one of the two chairs facing the desk, fatigue and hunger sapping his energy. Burrows walked around the desk and sat down in his highback chair. Oddly, its upholstery was a bit worn, in sharp contrast to the office's new appointments. That chair had seen many an opera season, many a performance, and many a drawn-out negotiation. It had served the general director well for fifteen years. He hoped it would last another decade and a half. Burrows picked up the phone, referred to a printed list of four-digit opera extensions and began dialing.

First phone call—the security office. The guard at the front gate picked up and said no one would be in the office full time until Monday. The opera house was secure, but any real business that needed to be discussed with the head of security, Randall Scott, would have to be done Monday.

Second phone call—opera house management. Nicholas Palmero, was the head of all activities in the auditorium: cleaning crews, usage policy, and maintenance. He would have detailed lists of all unusual occurrences. If a light bulb blew, he had to fill out the "event forms," noting when the bulb blew and what needed to be done to correct it. Of course he was only as good as his staff. One pair of eyes was not enough to keep a theatre the size of the Francis Mackay in tip-top shape. There were six rings at the house management office, but no answer.

Third phone call—the ushers' office. If anything had happened in the auditorium last night that affected the audience, the ushers would have to report it and fill out an "incident report." Five rings—no answer. Burrows hung up.

"I'm afraid there is really no one here, Enzo," said the G.D., setting his phone back on its hook. "After opening last night, I didn't expect anyone to be here."

"Yeah, you're right, Bill," spoke the tenor.

Burrows knew that Enzo was too close to Frank to let this whole supposed misunderstanding rest. He had to alleviate the anxiety that the man felt with some positive action.

"Enzo, I tell you what. After every performance, both stage and house crews have to report any unusual incidents. I know that the broken balcony rail will show up on the security reports, but I want to find out when it was first noticed. Maybe someone besides you and the alleged killer were in here. I sure don't know why security was so lax, but I'm gonna get to the bottom of this." The general director suddenly showed quite an enthusiastic bent to figure out what had happened the previous night.

"Let me get an in-house inquiry started. I'll talk to all the department heads and see if there was anything else unusual about last night. I know the police can't really do anything for at least forty-eight hours, so until then, let me ask around. We'll see just what happened down on 'C' Level and up in the balcony last night. I'll even call the Stanza house to see if anything unusual has happened there."

Enzo's head shook as he looked at the general director. Burrows read his mind.

"I will keep the call very simple, Enzo. I won't let on as to why I am calling. I'll just ask to speak to Frank. Maybe his wife can help us out a bit."

"Bill, I know you have doubts, but I swear, what I saw happened, and I won't rest— I can't rest—until Frank's murder is solved."

"I understand, Enzo, but we need to move one step at a time. There won't be anyone here until tomorrow. I'll check around the house. I'll have Emil start asking questions, and by later tomorrow night we can call the police in, officially."

"All right," said the tenor, sighing. Enzo turned to his wife. "Honey maybe we can go talk to Connie, go to dinner with her this evening." Gwen nodded in agreement.

"Remember though, Enzo, she doesn't really know that anything is amiss, so tread lightly and keep her emotions in mind during your visit," admonished the general director. He continued, "Why don't we get out of here and get some sleep?"

Janine was already sprawled out on the deep brown leather couch, her eyelids falling under the spell of Morpheus. Gwen was more intent on the men's conversation, but the incipient intensity of the last day had worn even her reserve vitality.

And Enzo was physically bankrupt. The warm glow of his usually brilliant smile and tan skin had been blanched by the full-throttled expenditures of the last twenty-four hours.

The couples decided it best to dismiss for the day. The gentlemen would continue their query on the morrow, in the hopes that Monday might yield more evidence than a fractured balcony rail.

It was time to replenish, replenish the heart, soul, mind, and body. Moments were needed to recover the spilt essence of humanity.

Their present toil would surrender to repose, but for Enzo, this toil had not yet born its reward.

Eight

Gwen and Enzo retreated to the hotel. The general director let the Santis take his limousine back to the Hyatt. The long black town car reflected their wills—stretched, dark and underpowered.

The ride felt a hundred miles long. What had been a simple mile a few moments ago was now a ride to Door County, without the greenery.

Arriving at the hotel, Enzo and Gwen ate a simple breakfast of fruit and toast at the hotel's restaurant. No coffee, for now was the time to find those lost hours of sleep, hours that had been sacrificed to the opera, and sacrificed to their friend.

The elevator opened and they climbed in. Enzo walked immediately to the glass elevator wall overlooking the restaurant, lounge, and reception areas. His shoulder and arm pressed against the glass. His forehead then met the same glass, crushing some of his curly black hair under its weight. More sighs filled his chest, and Enzo closed his eyes.

Gwen pressed the round, plastic "18" and walked to her husband's side. He rolled his body away from the glass and tilted towards her. She wrapped his left hand in hers, and hugged him from around the back.

Enzo squeezed the dear, delicate hand in his interlocked fingers. He pulled her hand up to his chest and leaned again onto the elevator glass.

Enzo's mind flashed in and out of consciousness. The elevator motors, Gwen's breathing, the lobby noise leaking through the metal seams of the elevator, even the creak of his own bones; all of the surrounding sounds reverberated throughout his head. Even his eyes seemed to creak as they moved in their sockets.

His brain was strobing scenes of recent history. He heard and saw the orchestral breakdown that the conductor, David Franciosi, had to stop and correct during the dress rehearsal four days earlier. His mind flashed to the pleasant dinner cruise he and his wife had enjoyed last Friday night. It flashed to the "Vittoria" section of the second act of *Tosca* when he sang triumphantly as "Mario Cavaradossi" at Napoleon's conquest of Melas.

His mind flashed to the scene in the props department, the hug he had shared with his friend, their sarcastic conversation, and his steps into the dark hall and chamber of the props room.

Flash! His mind and finger once again felt the pain of the toggle switch lancing his finger. *Flash!* His mind froze and framed the scene of Frank's death.

No aghast horror filled Enzo now. Fatigue had stolen his involuntary responses, and his mind scrolled through the past hours in a hunt of reason.

There again was the back of the man, behind Frank, arms raised to accomplish their grotesque deed.

Flash! Freeze! There was something there. What was it? A glint of color, a spark of a form. It was unclear. He must remember it again. If it was what he wanted, it would stick in his mind. Enzo's mind scrolled slowly through the scene once again.

Flash! Freeze! Frank's body fell lifelessly to the floor and the predator's arms and hands flew away from his body in a terrible triumph.

There it was again, a clue to the killer's identity, locked in the simple cells and chemicals of Enzo's mind. Locked there forever.

The elevator bell rang, announcing its arrival at the eighteenth floor. The doors slid open to allow the patrons to go to their suite. Enzo opened his eyes, looked down and saw Gwen's hand wrapped around his. She was still hugging him from behind. He lifted her hand, cupped over his own, and kissed it.

"Gwen, I remembered something I think will help the police." He kissed the back of her hand again and turned the interlocked fingers over to look upon the back of his own. Enzo stared at the back of his own hand. He could not forget it.

"Thank you for helping me remember, my love."

Gwen had disappeared into her husband's back and arose out of her stupor when Enzo kissed her hand.

"What, honey?" she asked, mumbling.

Enzo pulled her hand down, keeping it in his, reached forward and grabbed the closing door of the elevator.

"Come on, Bonita. I have to write something down." Enzo gently led his wife from the elevator and down the hall to Room 1801.

"I will not forget this time," he vowed.

Enzo had unlocked the trapped image in his mind, and now it would not disappear, not this time. The frozen flash of memory he needed had arrived in his exhaustion. He would write a note to himself to insure the memorized detail. He knew replication was useless right now, but this image of evidence might help relieve the regret of last night.

Enzo and Gwen went into the bedroom and prepared to sleep. Their bodies finally gave up, relinquishing their grip of consciousness so they might attain more later.

Enzo found some calmness in his discovery, but all he could do now was wait for Bill Burrows and the police to do their jobs. He would notify them of his discovery as soon as possible.

Gwen closed the venetian blinds, shielding the bright autumn sun from their bedroom. They stripped their bodies of clothing and slipped under the warm woolen blanket, Enzo writing his note before taking the restful plunge. Gwen slid over to snuggle against the barrel of her husband's chest. He slipped his left arm around her head and under her back, pulling her naked ivory body to himself.

Gwen's left arm crossed his chest, and she ran her nails through his sparse chest hair, squeezing her husband affectionately and lightly massaging his chest. She pulled herself up onto one elbow, alongside Enzo, and kissed his closed eyes.

"Sleep, my darling," she whispered through her own lethargy. "My sweet, precious love, sleep the sleep of angels."

She knew her husband's mind would continue to race from the turmoil of the night, but she once again knew her breath would give focus to his worn body. She inhaled slowly and cast her moist, warm breath over her husband's face, her breasts and torso angled up along his ribcage, pressing into him slightly.

He breathed in her scent, her gift of warmth and life. Enzo's brow descended as the venetian blinds had, relaxing under the weight of his eyelids, and under the weight of the darkness.

Enzo brought his right arm up to his wife's shoulder, caressing the nape of her neck, kneading the knots of his wife's tension. His large hands soothed the spot and he ran his fingers up into the blonde strands, scratching her neck as he ascended it.

Gwen let her open mouth and her lips caress Enzo's forehead, his nose, his cheeks, and his ears. She knew every inch of this man, and was enchanted by all of him. She sighed a breath into his mouth, letting her lips moisten his, letting the cool skin of their faces relax in the touch.

His arms and hands descended, slightly scratching her back, enlivening her muscles and sending a chill upwards. She arched her back in respiration, at the same time moving further onto her husband's body. His hands moved lower and caressed her, slipping down to her hips. With the simple stroke and nudge of his hand, Gwen then breathed into her husband, allowing husband and wife to be united in love, in body and in soul. Gwen's arched back unfurled, released, and she rocked forward, descending to her husband's face.

The warm, ardent breath of the two lovers—face to face, flesh to flesh, soul to soul—gave nourishment to their hearts and minds, and harmony to the discord of the hour. They breathed deeply into each other, giving themselves one to the other in perfect, passionate, spiritual union.

Deep, penetrating stillness descended on the room, and somnolence joined the lovers. Union in sacrifice, renewal through surrender, partnered strength in individual weakness, Enzo and Gwen thrived in the thoughts of being totally surrendered to one another.

Nine

A warm southerly flow of air had taken over the city during the course of the day, and Chicago was basking in this glory of autumn. The breeze that blew in from the lake reminded everyone that it would not be long before Arctic air would grip its frozen fingers around the city. But today, there would be a truce between the Old Man of Winter and the brilliance of Mother Nature's summer.

The sun shone in a clear, fresh sky all day long. No smog from the scorched dog days blanketed the city and her environs. That putrescence was stirred from its grasp with the first chilly blast of the season. What remained was clear and clean, purified by the cleansing moisture of Lake Michigan. This touch of water, evaporated from the dew-soaked grass, heightened the clarity of the daylight hours.

Grant Park, like a desert after a storm, was awash in life and activity. Citizens scampered throughout the esplanades, on foot or by pedal, drenched in the rain of light that had been graciously bestowed upon them. Touch football dominated the playing fields, bringing triumph and turmoil at a level similar to the professionals of Soldier's Field. Strollers rolled down footpaths, parent and child allowing nature to shower such a gift upon them. The child, in its innocence, appreciated the moments for its wonder and beauty; the parent missed the spectacle in a last effort at outdoor exercise.

The small peninsula leading from the John G. Shedd Aquarium out to the Planetarium was full of vehicles on the roadway and lovers on the grass. Final fall picnics were the order of the afternoon, and the vendors followed the scent of the famished.

The bustle climaxed after morning Mass for the strongly Catholic Chicago. The chase for prime park real estate was greatest at this time of year. Even Oak Street Beach, located at the north end of Michigan Avenue, was busy with the hoards that coveted one last opportunity to darken their waning summer suntans. The Water Tower, one of a handful of buildings to withstand the Great Fire, and the shopping center which was built across from it were full of revelers, expressing their warm autumnal bliss economically. Horse and carriage proprietors found business brisk, especially those fortunate enough to own open-air models.

The city's foliage of oak, maple, and elm, so meticulously placed and attended to, presented its full regalia to the crowds of the afternoon. Its hearty browns, reds, and ambers complimented the bright blue of the sky and lake, with the white of the waves and clouds adding motion and outline to the three-dimensional landscape.

The shadows, only moments earlier Lilliputian, were quickly growing to Gulliverian proportions. Slowly swinging from due north at the height of the day, they sloped more and more eastward, swallowing the daylight and park acreage once again. The rarest beauty is fleeting, and this Sabbath's fairness fled expeditiously. Families retreated from the ominous gray that fell with the afternoon. Blankets were gathered and folded, placed in baskets and stored in basements for the distant spring. Lovers took a final embracing stroll around the park, watching the ever more forceful waves butt into the shoreline. The boats left in the water, ebbing in the tide, clanked warning of hard freezes and blizzards to come.

Chicago was great because she could change; she would adapt and celebrate in whatever blew her way. The few flakes of the morning had given rise to a mighty splendor in day, and Chicago celebrated in the beauty, but the city would also celebrate in the white pristine elegance those tiny flakes had foretold.

Gwendolyn and Enzo spent the morn and afternoon in repose, in each other and in psychic recovery. They had fallen asleep around 10:30 a.m. and were knocked out for most of the afternoon. The recent weight placed upon their shoulders had been temporarily relieved by one another, and thus had allowed them to visit the land of Nod unabashedly.

In the tangle of blankets, Enzo rolled left towards his wife, only to find her side of the bed empty. His head settled below where her head had been, landing on the coverless white sheet. The cotton was cool from exposure and gave his cheek a chill. Enzo leaned back, pulled his head up and glanced at the digital clock on his wife's nightstand. 5:37p.m. blared the red numbers. He had slept the day away, but he did not care, not one bit.

The burly man flung his left arm up and over his head, pulled his body to a slanted upright position, and leaned on the bed's headboard. The venetian blinds, having been half opened, leaked the remaining dusky afternoon light. The room was full of these warm sunbeams, and the glare from the lighted bathroom fixtures made the entire room glow. Outside, the stealthy raven flew in from the east, rapidly banishing the day.

Enzo prayed for a calm tranquil eve with his wife, one that would juxtapose the sin-concealed chaos of the previous. The bedroom door was half open and Enzo heard his wife out in the living room area.

"Thank you very much. Oh yes, here you go," she cheerfully addressed the bellhop.

Gwen brought her prizes into the little kitchenette, set the items on the counter and headed for the rustling she had heard in the bedroom. As she approached the door she bent her body sideways, leaning into the doorframe head first. Her position reflected her husband's, whom she spied leaning over onto her side of the bed.

The softened sun lent an amber cast to her bright smiling face. Her blonde, shoulder-length hair was pulled back with a decorative comb, yet hung full around her face. Her lips were slightly pursed and her eyes twinkled from within. Her cheeks, rounded from the exuberance of the smile, flowed up into her eyes and lashes. Gwen's whole body smiled when she did, and Enzo's entire body smiled back in the knowledge that this precious vision was his wife.

"Hello, Sleepyhead," spoke the wife through pursed lips. Enzo stretched his arms over his sleepy head and yawned. "Would you like to come out and play?" finished the wife in coy fashion.

With a hand from the raised arm, Enzo motioned for his wife to come into the bedroom. With a dash across the twelve feet from the door to the bed, Gwen leaped, baggy sweater rising with her, and plopped onto her husband and the bed, trampolining the pair into a unified bounce or two.

She laughed and Enzo's lungs exhaled in a bellow that was only half operatic vocalise and half scream. The bounces landed the pair together in a heap, grabbing and groping for balance, finding bed sheets, breasts, legs and torsos banging together.

"My mother warned me that all American girls want is sex," laughed the Argentinean amidst the jumbling torrent. Enzo quickly ran his hand up the front of the billowing sweater his wife wore. Gwen spasmed in pleasure, giggling uncontrollably, and slapped at her husband's chest.

"Your mother was right," crescendoed the mezzo as she grabbed for her husband's crotch. Enzo laughed and pulled his knees to his chest as Gwen snatched his second most prized bodily possession—vocal chords being his first.

The lovers tumbled for a few minutes, tickling and teasing until Gwen had pinned her husband back onto the pillows. Her hair was tousled from activity, and his was lopsided from sleep. They breathed hard to catch up with themselves.

"Before this sex-crazed American woman ravages your helpless South-American body again," Gwen spoke in between breaths, "I want you to get a shower, get dressed, and meet me in the lobby. You have twenty minutes. This is your mission, should you choose to accept it." Gwen thrust forward and kissed her husband full and strong. She flew off the bed and walked towards the door.

"What if I don't show up for this mission, *Bonita?*" he asked, playfully questioning his wife's authority.

"Then I come up here and change the world's greatest tenor into the world's highest soprano," she intimidated through her militaristic veneer. Enzo, like a bolt, stood up on the bed, wearing nothing but high notes.

"Yes, ma'am!" he proclaimed. With his new-found motivation, Enzo leaped forward off the bed, landed directly in front of Gwen, stood up straight, gave a dual salute, and dashed into the shower.

"That's better, tenor," snickered Gwen, walking out of the bedroom.

She hastily moved to the kitchen, fixing her hair on the way. She grabbed her possessions and left the hotel suite, wearing her radiant smile. The warbling from the bathroom and the sound of the shower ceased when she closed the suite door behind her.

The freshly scrubbed husband arrived in the lobby, wearing jeans and a loose-fitting white sweater similar to his wife's. He carried a lightweight jacket, which held a scarf in its pocket. If Gwen wanted to venture out, he needed to protect his throat from possible weather adversities. Enzo loved the cool night air just as he had loved the crisp mountain breezes of his homeland, but a musical life lived above the musical staff demanded a bit of caution when it was spent outdoors.

Enzo did not see Gwen. The lobby was full of people returning from the day of frolicking outside. The outdoor activity had left the revelers famished, and the hotel restaurant was serving its patrons with speed and courtesy. He craned his neck to the right, looking around the elevator bank towards the hotel's reception area.

From behind, Enzo felt two hands grab his buttocks and slide up to the front of his waist, coming together in a clasp at his waistline. Enzo jolted in surprise at his wife's arrival. Latinos are known for their passion, but seldom is public physical affection expressed. Enzo had become accustomed to his wife's public displays, and he had come to enjoy them. He even enjoyed the blush that permeated his face with one of Gwen's spectacles.

Enzo grabbed her arms at his waist and spun in the hoop Gwen had created in her arms.

"What do you have planned, Sarge?" asked the tenor. Enzo leaned down and kissed his wife.

"We're gonna have a nice quiet evening where no one will disturb us," Gwen said. She kissed her husband in response.

Gwen unclasped her hands, leaned down, and picked up the picnic basket she had ordered earlier. She took hold of Enzo's arm and the couple strolled toward the exit of the hotel. They walked out the front revolving doors of the Marriot and turned left, viewing the *Chicago Tribune* building across the Chicago River from them. Gwen swung the basket like a little girl walking off to school. Enzo smiled in the crisp fifty-degree air of dusk, and followed in tow.

The declining sun sparkled intensely off the river, which cut a westward swath throughout the heart of downtown. The diamond glint on the water brightened the shadows cast eastward from Michigan Avenue's great bank of buildings.

The husband and wife turned left and traveled south, walking down a flight of pedestrian stairs to Wacker Drive's lower level. The dark underground was once the most expensive real estate in the world, but it was now a novelty cherished by lovers of the city. The ceiling and roadway were dark from exhaust, casting a claustrophobic tension about them. The opera house, also on Wacker Drive, had a Lower Wacker Drive entrance used for deliveries, just as most of the major buildings along the road did. The behemoth Sears Tower stood alongside the same drive, two blocks south of the opera house, and boasted an extensive underground dock and terminal.

"Well, this is beautiful. Shall we eat smog with our meal?" sarcastically jibed the man.

"This way, silly," Gwen said, slapping her husband on the butt.

As they came to the bottom of the staircase the pair reversed direction, heading south, and walked along the sidewalk of Columbus Drive, the road perpendicular to Wacker.

Columbus Drive was subterranean at this point. Its northern terminus was just across the river, but looking south from Lower Wacker Drive, the great roadway opened into Grant Park. Like a great runway into nature, Columbus Drive emerged from the dark caves of Lower Wacker and fell into the open fields of the Park.

The roadway slowly descended for a quarter of a mile, falling from the rise at the river crossing. Its pathway seemed another branch of the river, feeding life into the greenery and human vitality into the fields and paths that crisscrossed through the grounds. Columbus Drive was the pulmonary vein that fed into Grant Park, which in turn fed life, substance, and focus to the city.

The pair followed the quarter mile Drive. The sun still shone upon the outer section of Lake Shore Drive, and out into the lake. The rest of the park was shadowed, lit by the rays that crossed above it. The Amoco Oil Building, at the northern edge of the Park, had Columbus Drive as its eastern border. The eighty-six-story office complex was thirty-five years old and a shining highlight of the stunning skyline.

The building's outer shell was covered in eight-by-eight-foot sections of white Italian marble. Many a thousand pound slab had fallen to the earth before the proper adhesive and stud combination was found to anchor the polished stone to the building's skeleton.

This magnificent building was another jewel in the city's architectural crown. Ten-foot-wide columns, covered in the white marble, ran up the entire length of the structure, seemingly for eternity. These columns were separated by dark smokey glass, which gave the inner workings of the building its light. Those white marble pillars steadfastly lifted the tower skyward. They paid homage to the great Hellenic and Roman cultures gone by, but also reflected the stability of modern design and strength. The magnificent white marble acted as a fine cornerstone to the power of Grant Park and the people to whom it was dedicated.

Gwen pulled Enzo across Columbus, avoiding the few cars that ventured into the park, and walked along the eastside of the Amoco Building. Enzo had no idea where they were going. He had seen the building many times, but always at a distance. He loved the clean white exterior, but expected the complex to be closed this late on a Sunday evening. They were surely headed into the park.

Gwen led him around the south of the building. There, before him, stood a huge black marble plaza, twenty feet deep and running the width of the building. The plaza was set into the ground, an entire floor below the roadway beside it. The black marble pulled the bright reflective light of the white down into itself. The plaza was not cold and foreboding; it was glowing with the life drawn from above. To the east end of the plaza was a fountain with square sides in symmetry with the edges of the tower. The spray of water was simple and elegant, cascading from the center in a halo of glistening streams.

To the west side of the plaza was a brilliant steel and cable sculpture. The intertwining rods and bands sprang out of the marble base, twisting like a tornado, around a miniature girded skeleton, lifting the viewer's eyes up, out of the plaza and onto the Amoco Building's white surfaces. The entire building grounded itself in this oddly inviting black hole.

Gwen grabbed Enzo's hand and descended into the plaza and over to the fountain, tugging him along. She set the wicker basket on the four-foot-wide fountain base and motioned to her husband to sit down.

The black marble, which had been soaking in the sun's heat all day, was still warm and juxtaposed the cooler dusk air. Gwen opened the basket and pulled out a red and white checkered tablecloth and she spread it out on the black surface. Napkins, dinnerware, wineglasses, a bottle of red wine, and a scrumptious meal followed.

"Gwenny, where did you find all this stuff?" asked the impressed and famished Enzo.

"I woke up about an hour before you did this afternoon, peeked outside at how lovely it was, and decided we needed a treat."

"But where…"

"Part of the mystery and joy of life is being thankful for things that you are baffled by. So, just sit back, relax, and open the wine, silly," she said, handing a corkscrew to her inquisitor. She smiled with pursed lips and tilted her head to her lover in an expression that let him know she was in charge and had taken care of everything.

Enzo took the hand with the corkscrew in it and kissed the skin just between her thumb and pointer finger. He pulled the corkscrew into his hand, and as he did it, licked Gwen's hand as she pulled it away from him. Enzo laughed and tended to his task.

Gwen, enjoying the play, kissed her own hand where her husband had, and pointed at him, shaking her finger.

"I'll get you back, you big slobbery resonance for brains…" Gwen wiped her hand on her jeans and continued pulling the victuals from their storage spot. Enzo smiled an imitative pursed lip, head-tilted expression to his wife. Both grinned widely and set their places for the meal to come.

Enzo poured the wine and sipped it while his wife prepared the meal. It was obvious now to him that the hotel had helped prepare these portions, but that did not diminish the thoughtfulness or preparation of his *Bonita*. Gwen pulled out the china and placed a plate on either side of the dining cloth, while Enzo placed the napkins and silverware in their place.

Out of the basket Gwen pulled a plastic container of potato salad, another of fresh-cut vegetables accompanied by a scrumptious garlic dip, and a final container of mixed lettuce with chopped carrots, nuts, celery, and radishes. The salad was topped with balsamic vinegar and sesame dressing that Gwen knew was her husband's favorite.

The first course of their dinner was served and devoured rapidly. The fresh vegetables and water soaked lettuce cleansed and purified them as it washed through their bodies. It refreshed the pair who had not consumed enough in the past twenty-four hours.

Then out of the basket came the heated foil tins of the main course. Gwen took the first rectangular little container and peeled back the top layer of foil to reveal tender baby asparagus in a rich, creamy butter sauce. Enzo took the tin and divided the portions onto their respective plates, giving a bit more of his wife's favorite veggie to her. Next came a smaller tin of corn, followed by a large piping hot tin of mashed potatoes, mixed with garlic and chives. Enzo gave himself a larger portion of these, since potatoes, especially garlic-enhanced, were his favorite.

The main dish of sliced prime rib, simmered in its thick red wine-enhanced juices, was lifted out of the picnic basket and also distributed. The rolls, kept warm with a warming stone, topped off the meal.

The tastes and textures of the meal were a wonder to the famished supplicants. The smoothness of the potatoes, accentuated by the snap of the asparagus, the supple moistness of the beef, all played a symphony of refreshment in their mouths. The two people craved the nourishment that had arrived, and thus gratefully put all the elements to proper use.

The evening blanket of dusk unfurled over the city. The low buzz of the warming halogens that hung from every street light on the roadway reverberated in the black marble cave. The huge exterior lights of the Amoco Building flickered on, illuminating the great ivory tusk at the north end of the park. The decorative lights of the park lit every gravel path and trail, each originating at Buckingham Fountain.

The couple ate slowly, enjoying the relative quiet dark of the onsetting eve. The sky above them was deep orange. Apollo and his team were in full retreat, and the advancing night slowly cloaked the skyscrapers along Michigan Avenue.

"I called Connie while you were asleep," said Gwen, finishing a bit of prime rib. Enzo looked up at Gwen with clear concern.

"I asked how she was, Enzo. I didn't let on about last night."

"What did she say?"

"She said that she was worried, of course, but that she didn't feel out of sorts. E, Connie told me that Frank has done this before." Gwen was a bit agitated at the thought of a spouse being so thoughtless.

"You mean that he will just leave for a day or two?" Enzo asked.

"That's what she said, that since last spring Frank hasn't really been himself. Working late and upset about how he and his men were being treated. She said that Frank has been working sometimes through the night, and that he will forget to call." Gwen paused a moment. "Do you think he is having an affair?"

"Oh, honey, I think Frank loves Connie very much," said Enzo, defending what he felt to be the truth about his friend. "When we were talking last night…" Enzo paused, realizing how little time had passed, and how much had happened, "he told me how much he still enjoyed being with her.

"He also told me how much work they have had to do with the change-over this summer."

"I just find it odd that Frank wouldn't call if he was going to be out late," Gwen said contemplatively, "or all night, for God's sakes." She thought a moment. "I guess I am just really blessed having a husband who thinks of me so much." Enzo smiled and turned to his wife.

"Gwen, I thank God every day for three things: third—my family, even though they are far off in Argentina, and I don't get to see them. I was blessed with a loving father and mother, and sisters who tormented me. They want the best for me, and most of all, they believe in me and tell me I can achieve anything I set my heart to."

Gwen listened to her husband. She loved to hear him speak. The music of his voice and the sincerity of his words spoke to her soul.

"Second, I thank God for my voice. It is an instrument bestowed on me that not only gives me great pleasure, but I feel it can change people's hearts and minds. This gift is the voice of angels, and I believe it should heal people. At least, I believe if I am faithful with this gift, it has that potential."

Then Enzo looked directly at Gwen.

"But Gwen, first and foremost, I thank God for you. I know you conceived of this beautiful evening so that my head would flee from the horror of last night. I'm afraid I will always, somewhere in the back of my mind, be thinking of what happened at the opera house, but you have soothed the pain. I hope you know that the infirmity my heart feels for Frank has been soothed by you. I will still think of Frank, sweetheart, but you have removed so much of the pain."

Enzo spoke fervently to the woman whom he adored.

"My love, I pray that you know, first and foremost, I am nothing without you. You are the crown of my life. There is nothing I would not relinquish for you, and there is nothing I would not do for you. None of the accolades, none of the awards, nothing this world has to offer means anything if you are not with me, but with you at my side, the simplest earthly joy is the highest heaven.

"I always knew that the *business* of opera would be difficult—you know, the travel, the hassles with directors and agents—but opera brought you to me. Music put your life together with mine. When I went to grad school I thought music was the greatest thing in my life, and at the time it was, but since I fell in love with you music has taken a poor second place.

"I have found my fulfillment in you. I know that doesn't sound very independent or self-actualized, but you, Gwendolyn Silva, are the person in this world that makes me complete. I am so grateful to God for bringing us together, I want to show my appreciation by loving you more completely, more totally than anything else in this world."

Gwen stood up and walked to where Enzo was sitting. She planted herself between her husband's open legs, which hung over the fountain base where he was seated. She wrapped her arms around him and leaned back as he continued to talk.

"You are that treasure I found amidst my work, for which I will sacrifice all my being. You are my pearl of great price. You are my heart, and you have my soul. To hide this passion of mine is inconceivable, for my heart's immortal thirst is to be completely known and all forgiven by you."

Gwen looked deeply into the dark eyes of her husband. She was once again speechless in front of the man that held her heart, and who cherished it above all else. Her utmost self was given to him, and would be given over and over again, utterly safe, perfectly cherished, and ultimately loved. She kissed each cheek of her tenor, kissed his eyes, his forehead, his chin, and finally, passionately, kissed his lips.

She hugged him tightly and stroked his head of thick black hair. She smiled from her heart and engulfed him with her body.

Gwen stood in wonder at this blessing, the gift of their love. So many of their friends had been through separation and divorce, it almost seemed that their perfect union was incorrect, was not righteous, but in her head and heart she knew this to be wrong. This love was theirs as a gift, as an honor. She and Enzo believed this gift to be from the Immortal, and it was their great glory to continue giving love to one another.

Only in losing yourself will you be found. Only in giving of yourself will you be filled. And only in loving will you truly be loved. Enzo came to these mandates as a child, hearing the word from the church, but seeing its verification in the love his parents had for him and his sisters, and for their God. Selfishness had no place; conceit was never tolerated nor an option. Only through giving, the Santi family believed, were you made whole. Gwen had found and learned this from her husband, and in their gifts to each other they were uplifted and sustained.

Enzo pulled back from the deep embrace, and his toned lightened.

"Now you know, my love, we have to find a permanent abode for our hearts, and I think I have just the place."

Lifting up his sweater to reveal his pants waist, Enzo pulled a small photo he had wedged between his undershirt and his pants. The little five-by-seven was a bit crinkled, but clear and a bright vibrant color.

"What is this, Enzo?" asked the puzzled wife.

"What do you think it is?" answering her question with one of his own.

"I think it is a very nice picture of a very nice house."

"Don't you think an estate like that needs a name? I mean, it is sort of big and homey."

Gwen was puzzled, and more than a little confused. She stared at the photo, then looked up. Her full smile had migrated to one eye, squinting in hard thought. She tried to answer Enzo's most recent question.

"Well, if you would name someplace like this, you would have to know something about the people."

"Like what?"

"Well for starters, you would need to know their name. When big estates get named, it usually has something to do with the name of the people. Like the 'Candy Lady's' house out in River Forest. Don't they call it the 'Brook Mansion'?" Gwen referred to Mrs. Phyllis Brook, the CGO's honoree at last night's opening.

"Oh, yeah, I see. Down in Buenos Aires, there is a big agricultural family that has a place west of the city. It is known as the 'Hacienda Hernandez.' I sort of like that. 'Hacienda' sounds sort of nice for a big ranch or plantation."

"It sure would sound funny up here in the heart of America," Gwen responded with a chuckle.

"Yeah, you're right." Enzo took the photo from his wife's hand, stared at it and replied. "The 'Hacienda Santi' would be a little too Latino for white bread Chicago." The tenor looked at his wife with a Cheshire smile. "Would the 'Santi Estate' sound better? How about 'Tavern on the Santis?' I think that sounds too pretentious, don't you?"

Gwen's face was brightening as she realized what her husband was teasingly saying.

"Certainly the name 'Manor of the Lord Santi and the Lady Gwendolyn,'" imitating an English accent, "that would be much too haughty, wouldn't it?" Enzo was trying not to collapse into full laughter.

"I think I like 'The Santi Estate.' What about you, sweetheart?" The tenor fell to the side, chuckling. Gwen was now starting to laugh through her temporary veneer of inquisitiveness.

"You bought this house, didn't you, you big—big—snicklefritz?" Her father had lovingly given her that absurd moniker.

She leaned into her husband, who had rocked his body upright. Gwen leapt off the ground. Enzo laughed out again and caught her as she leapt forward, rolling the pair back onto the four feet of open black marble behind them.

In between giggles Enzo relayed the full meaning of the photo.

"I didn't buy it; I just placed a bid on it. It has a big backyard where we can let our children play. It has four bedrooms where the bambinos can sleep, and a *huge* master bedroom with a *huge* bank of windows, where we can spend long Sunday mornings. It has a finished basement, but most importantly, a big, open-air front porch so we can sit on beautiful summer evenings and watch the sun set."

Gwen purred in approval and cradled the tenor's head in her hands so it would not bang into the marble.

"But Gwen, if you don't want this house, I'll just withdraw the bid I put on it. No one will care; no big deal." He knew the nonchalant statement would draw a spiked reaction from the tactile woman.

"No you won't, not until I get to view this mansion myself." She playfully continued. "If it meets all my standards, then maybe we will pursue this home thing. Where is the Santi Sanitarium? You wonderful man." Enzo laughed at his wife's alliteration.

"It's in the 'Candy Lady's' neighborhood. Great parks, a forest preserve, great schools, lots of grass and trees, and peace and quiet, a bit away from downtown. I think you are gonna like it," enticed the tenor.

Gwen touched Enzo's hand so both of them could look at the photograph.

"I think I am gonna love it, almost as much as I love you." The couple kissed again. "When can we go see it?" A thought jumped into her mind. "Wait a minute here, buster, when did you have time to find this dream home of ours?" Gwen questioned, scintillated and curious as to the answer.

"I had some afternoons free these past two weeks. I wasn't called to rehearsal every afternoon. Just before we came out here I called a realtor out in the 'burbs and told them what I was looking for. As soon as we arrived he started calling with info on houses, and when I had time, I went out and looked around. I saw this one last Wednesday and I thought it would be perfect." Enzo pulled the couple up a bit so they were now sitting side by side. He became serious.

"Gwenny, I know this is a really big decision, to buy a house and all, but I want you to know it is perfectly all right if you don't want to buy this house. I swear, you won't hurt my feelings—really! I just thought it would be fun to go look a bit, and since we have been talking about moving here, I also thought it might be a nice surprise for you." Enzo again reiterated, "but please, if this is not the house you want, it is not the house that I want. I want *our* house to be exactly what *we* want. O.K., sweetheart?"

"O.K., E," she said, then paused, "but I know I am gonna love it."

The couple loved to surprise each other with exciting news and thoughtful gifts, but they also knew that all major decisions had to be made together, and that if one supposedly perfect situation did not pan out, it was all right to back away, but the beauty and love behind the thoughts were what counted, and what lasted. Gwen stood up and coaxed the photo from Enzo's hand. She squinted to see the details of the home.

"I sure do want to get out there and see this place." She walked over to where she had eaten, examining the picture with x-ray eyes. With her teeth, she nibbled the right side of her lip in a nervous excitement. Enzo knew that when he saw the nibbling begin he had struck a nerve, and that his wife was quite engrossed with this thought of settling down and buying a house. He beamed; satisfied with the enjoyment he had given his wife.

"Oh my, I almost forgot,!" Gwen awoke from her real-estate-induced trance. "We've got dessert in this picnic basket."

She put the photo down next to her dinner plate, which sat unmoved, and reached into the basket and pulled out two pieces of black and white chocolate mousse cake. It was Enzo's favorite, and fortunately, the chef at the Hyatt was also expert in post-dinner delights. Gwen took the plastic wrap off the cake and handed a slice to her husband.

"Oh thank you *so* much." Enzo took the slice of mousse cake and groped for his fork. The cake had melted a bit from the heat of the entrees, so the different flavors of the mousse had oozed together more thoroughly than was intended. Enzo did not mind in the least. This fine, delicate, multi-flavored tidbit liquefied in his mouth.

"Can we see the house tomorrow afternoon, E?"

"I have a coaching at 2:00 on the third act of *Otello*, but if you want to go out after that, I'm game. Maybe we can have dinner with Connie while we're out there."

"Good deal," squealed the wife. "When will you be finished?"

"About 3:30 I think. I'll meet you at the stage door and we should be able to get out there just before rush hour."

"Would you want to ask Connie if she would like to see the house with us? It might get her mind off—well, get her mind off what *you* saw.

"I think that's a wonderful idea."

"I'll call her again and let her know we're coming out."

The pair ate the dessert and enjoyed the breeze that swirled around the plaza. The large columns of the Amoco Building pushed the traveling air down its channeled columns, deep into the plaza. The wind was light and refreshing, but the pair knew it was time to depart. Enzo took a big scoop of cake and turned to his wife.

"I've been thinking about calling Demetrius, that is, if nothing turns up about Frank." Demetrius McDiess was a friend Enzo had met when he first came to the CGO as an apprentice. Demetrius' first day as a security guard fell on the same day Enzo started his apprenticeship program. They had met at the security desk. Enzo did not know where to go for his musical coaching, and Demetrius did not know where to send him. They were two lost puppies, looking for a friendly face, which they had found in each other.

"I think that might be a good idea," reassured Gwen. "I think if it will make you feel better about finding out what happened, it's a good idea. And if anyone can find out what is going on, I think Demetrius can."

Gwen smiled reassuringly at Enzo. He smiled back weakly, thinking of his friend. Enzo then looked down at his mousse cake and saw one last bite. He picked it up with his fork, and called his wife's name.

Gwen turned her head only to see that piece of chocolate mousse flying through the air at her head. She screamed in surprise, trying to whip her head out of the trajectory of the oncoming mousse attack. She failed. The ammunition hit her on her left cheek and slid onto her nose, smearing black and white all over the side of her face.

Enzo cackled, looking for more ammunition in his impromptu food fight. Gwen beat him to the shot and hurled her half-full glass of wine at him, dousing Enzo in an alcoholic baptism. Enzo grabbed a handful of water out of the fountain and threw it on his wife. Gwen had grabbed her slice of cake with her right hand and hid it behind her back. She sat at the ready, knowing her husband's retaliation would also be wonderfully physical.

Sure enough, the tenor flung himself across the blanket at his wife. As Enzo grabbed her left arm Gwen attacked with her right and shoved the half piece of cake in her lover's face. The man convulsed in hilarity, opening his mouth wide to try and ward off the attack in which he was currently mismatched.

Enzo wiped the mousse off of his face with his own hand and proceeded to wipe the sugary postri onto his wife's stomach, exposed by the jostling. A bit of tickling followed the chocolate barrage, with Enzo having the advantage. The motion of Enzo's hand on Gwen's sensitive abdomen made both laugh all the harder.

The culinary war slowed, as did the frolicking. They lay back on the marble, covered in sugar, and breathed in unison for several minutes, staring up at the sky. Their embrace never wavered. They were silent. Not a word was spoken—none were needed. They were confident in the thought that their hearts were in each other's loving hands.

After half an hour the couple cleaned up their meal and themselves and walked back to the hotel, hand-in-hand.

Ten

Monday Morning

It was 3:05 a.m., the fulcrum of the night. The residents of the Windy City had long since gone to bed. They were deep in sleep, completely intoxicated by the stimulus of the glorious Sunday. The vast sea of nocturnal revelers had wholly departed their dramshops and found respite for the remainder of the dark hours. Vehicles were scarce, the avenues largely deserted. The few who travailed during these still hours were in the offices, bakeries, print shops, and hospitals, conducting their tasks, pushing the night away with furious activity—activity that, when properly achieved, was outwardly undetectable. Sanitation trucks chugged along the empty streets, squealing to a rolling halt at every city street corner. The blanket of black had closed the eyes of the city and was now preparing it for the work of the week to come.

The rooftop of the Illinois State Theatre hummed with the cycling of its heating units. The flat, white gravel-covered expanse was the site of origin for the climate comforts within. Huge heating and air conditioning units were all that filled the area. It was a lonely, unvisited site. It had been a favorite for pigeons and lake fowl because of its lack of human traffic and its access to the whipping winds along the Chicago River, directly to the west of the building. From their perches on the roof, the birds would glide and dive, searching for food and bombarding pedestrians, that is, until the city nested a pair of falcons there to cull the abundant sky-rat population.

The larger predatory birds had found a fine home on the top of the Illinois State Theatre. Their nest, planted by Illinois State Zoological Society at Lincoln Park Zoo, sat directly on top of one of the huge metal thermal units. Their five-foot cubed wooden birdhouse protected them and their offspring from the elements. The birds' only company was the whine of the large metallic beast that supported their abode. Its three companions were interspersed along their large plateau. Maintenance people were the only true human visitors to this loft, until, that is, the last few months.

The roof access door was slightly ajar, the latch of the door still slightly wedged in the doorframe. Over time, the hinges of the steel door had slagged with the settling building. They now ground the steel edges of the door and its frame together. The door, obeying its heavy hardened closer, would consistently swing back and slam into the edge of the frame, wedging the mates together until someone came to assist the intercourse by lifting the door handle, allowing it to properly fit into the frame.

The interior of the theatre was empty, but the roof had a visitor. Two large black duffel bags sat on the graveled tar along the western edge of the building. The two bags were equidistant from Washington Boulevard to the north and Madison Avenue to the south.

The visitor loved this time of night—the stillness, the acute quiet. He threw his spent cigarette over the edge of the five-foot brick wall that enclosed the roof from the open sky. The butt tumbled, falling the fifteen stories, rappelling into the building several times and splashing into the Chicago River. The dark murky green swallowed the nicotine-laden filter instantly, dragging it to its riverbed resting place.

The man lit another cigarette and puffed it strongly, blowing the white residue and his cigarette-tainted breath into the air. He flipped the collar of his black wool overcoat up around his neck to ward off the cool night breeze. His shrugged shoulders helped to keep his body heat in, or so he believed.

He glanced along the broad western horizon and pondered a bit. For some unknown reason, the skyscrapers of Chicago were concentrated east of the Chicago River. The Sears Tower, the John Hancock Building, the Illinois Center, the Amoco Building, along with dozens of decades-tall monoliths formed an exclusive club inside the river boundaries. The geological bedrock of their support ran out into Nebraska, but the human architects seemed confined by the branches of the Chicago River.

He searched his mind for the reason for the confinement. None came to mind. What did it matter anyway? He loved downtown, but he loved his quaint little home in the suburbs too.

The man leaned his six-foot body over the brick rail and looked down the fifteen stories at the walkway between the Theatre Building and the River. The ten-foot-wide walkway was Theatre property and should be deserted. He had checked it before he came up. It was once again the time for an act without witness.

The assignment was originally to be performed in two parts. First, insure the continued anonymity of his employer's work by quieting uncontrollable elements in the workplace. Second, find and dispose of any bothersome elements.

His work was meant to be anonymous. It had been until last night. The first step in his assignment had not gone as well as expected, so a third was now needed, a step he prided himself in not having to take. He had to find any and all-unintentional repercussions from steps one and two and quell them with whatever means he deemed necessary. And just as his success had its obvious rewards, his failure would have its own "rewards."

Failure in this business would lead to a short life span. In fact, success was not even a guarantee of continued employment, let alone existence. His employer would not tolerate anything less than thoroughness. Perfection was not necessary, but meticulousness was absolutely demanded. Mistakes had to be immediately rectified, and if necessary, extreme measures would be taken to ensure the integrity of the operation.

His second cigarette was spent. Again, the man sucked the last bit of nicotine through the cotton filter, flicked the butt over the side of the building into the Chicago River, and looked at the black duffel bags. It was time to work.

The spiked silence, the solitude of the middle of the night was the domain for step two of his assignment. He walked to the southwest corner of the roof, his shoes crunching the gravel. He retrieved two cinder mason blocks. A pile of several blocks had been abandoned here after the extensive renovation of the Theatre, part of which included the repair of the roof walls. Many of the large masonry bricks had crumbled and were replaced. The leftover bricks were too much of a hassle to retrieve, and thus remained, finding a semi-permanent home on the roof. Their employ was much different now.

He carried the two blocks back to the duffel bags and squatted down beside the nearer of the two. He unzipped the bag along the top. He had lined the inside with plastic to prevent the contents from seeping onto the heavy canvas material of the duffel bag. The duffel bag would be incinerated later during the day, but it was absolutely necessary that the bag's contents be totally concealed until now.

The man pulled the articles from the bag. They were longer and heavier than the contents of the other bag. Each was encased in another bag, a black nylon net bag that easily revealed the contents. The man had made sure this nylon was heavy duty—the best, the strongest. It was never to be seen again, but it needed to remain taut forever.

Taking one of the cinder blocks, he tied a final knot in the top of the net bag, securing the contents, and tied the ends of the excess rope in a firm knot through and around the cinder block.

The contraption was odd, but effective, and besides, the bag and block combination had a homemade touch, but most importantly, it stirred that feeling of adrenaline he had experienced the night before.

As a child, he had thrown dishes off of bridges. The impact, the violence of the explosion upon hitting the rocks of the shallow river, had made him spasm in laughter. As a teenager he had developed the brick and bag combination with a friend's injured feline. He had tied the animal in a bag, found a large masonry block, and thrown the weighted bag, contents and all, off the Route 45 Bridge into the Chicago Sanitary and Shipping Canal. He even pocketed the fifty-dollar euthanasia fee given to him. His adrenal gland worked well that day, pumping furiously at the sound of the wailing cat taking its last gasps of life. He was also particularly proud that day, for with his very first disposal, he had also made a tidy profit.

He still enjoyed the artistry of disposal.

He lifted the block, dragging the black net bag and its contents on the gravel roof. He balanced the block in his left hand, picked up the cold large limb encased in the nylon with his right hand, then held the pair— cinder block and severed leg—chest level for a moment, then cast them over the edge of the building. The thrust sent the block ahead of the nylon bag, pulling it down towards the water.

He cast it far out into the open air. He did his best to throw it towards the middle of the river. The block and net bag contorted in their death plunge. The trajectory of the fall put the set just short of the middle of the river.

He watched in expectant silence. Three and a half tenterhook seconds built the anticipation. The camera click of his mind captured each wrench of the descent. He waited for the thumping of his heart to be drowned out by the concussion of the water impact.

The splashdown was not as orgasmic as he had hoped. The large brick and the weighted bag hit the water parallel to each other, stretched side to side. The block hit the water a fraction before the black net bag, sloshing the surface of the water, cushioning the bag's entry.

The sound of the cracking water echoed up the walls of the buildings along the river canyon to the top of the Illinois State Theatre. The "pop" that sounded seemed a wasted effort on the man's part. The next would be better, more accurate, and with greater effect.

The man cursed to himself, looking again over the brick wall of the roof to the entry spot. He checked to make sure the block had done its job, anchoring the bag to the bottom of the river. The ripples from the site of impact dissipated immediately, swept away by the southward flowing current. The important part of this job was accomplished, but his thirst for pleasure remained unsatisfied.

He wanted the two objects to enter, cinderblock first, slicing a gash into the surface of the water, then the black bag with its sinewy contents to follow directly behind the block. He knew from experience that this aligned entry would cause a loud smack, not only from the objects hitting the water, but also from the aqua "boom" of the rent water filling the violated space.

The man did not really care where this package landed, as long as it found its way into the water. The block would drag the appendage to the bottom of the murky water, never to be seen again. The flesh would decay slowly, exposed to the open water, and disposed of by the carp and lampreys in the channel. The forty feet of murky green water would cloak his secret deed.

He knelt down and retrieved the second severed leg, encased in the black nylon. He followed the same procedure, walking a bit north on the roof in order to space the objects along the river bottom. This time he would throw the cinder block as if it were a javelin. The bag would again be in his right hand, block in his left, but he would heave the set from the right side of his body in a wood-chopping motion.

He again checked the streets and riverbank below. Nothing appeared. All was quiet. He backed up a few feet to simulate the proper Olympic javelin form. With a burst, the leather soles slid on the tiny slick rocks. He strode the fifteen feet he had marched from the edge of the roof and catapulted the block and bag upward.

The long arc of the pair flew to the far side of the one hundred and fifty-foot wide river. The fifteen story fall allowed the set to travel one hundred feet. The man was almost afraid the tandem would hit the far embankment. This caused adrenaline to pump through his icy veins, but when he heard the *smack* and loud *thud* echo up the buildings, he knew that his javelin experiment had succeeded.

"Yes!" he yelled, thrusting his fist in the air, basking in the glory of his gory accomplishment. No lights lit in inquisition, noone awoke at the disturbing sounds. The predominance of office buildings was vacant, and the small number of apartments in the area was too distant or too aloof to respond.

The empty duffel bag was zipped closed, folded into a small cube of material, and placed to the side. One more bag of which to dispose. The water concussion would be less enthralling, not nearly as visceral. The objects were lighter, more compact, and more easily dealt with.

The same type of black net nylon bags were in the second duffel bag. The man decided to tie the two similar objects to their cinder blocks at the same time. The big thrill of the evening had come already, so this was mere busy work. He did check one thing very carefully.

Earlier, when he had prepared for this moment, he decided it was important to remove all tactile possibilities of identification. He had used a sharp paring knife to peel off the tips of the possible identifiers, and burned them in a tiny acid bath. The putrid scent had burned his eyes and nose, but the art of his disposal would be complete.

He took hold of the clammy piece and carefully examined the digits. They were all perfectly prepared and ready for their flight.

He picked up the other. Again, his earlier effort passed his personal inspection, but as he scrutinized the first, second, third, then fourth, he noticed a flash of reflection. He pulled the appendage up closer to his face.

There on the fourth finger was a gold band. The metal was a bit dull, but still glinted from the light that filled the roof expanse.

The man was intrigued. In the haste of preparing for this moment, this small item had escaped his eye. If it were found by some amazing stretch, any inscription could be used to find the owner. This was not acceptable. The ring would have to be removed.

He spread the rigored fingers apart and wedged the ring finger into the palm of his right hand. A rapid snap of his wrist broke the finger backwards. He plied the piece around in a circle, loosening tendon from bone, and tore the lifeless flesh towards himself with a twist. He had no trouble displacing the finger.

There was no blood. There was no scream of pain in reaction to the act. There was only calculation and purpose, as if he had just pulled apart a chicken wing. This was nothing, meant nothing, and would mean even less once it traveled its final descent.

The man pulled the gold ring off the disjunct finger. The beaded edge was distinctly different from other rings he had seen. The ring was misshapen, out-of-round. The owner had handled many heavy objects over the years, and the wear had slowly distorted what was meant to be a perfect circle.

He rubbed the gold band between his first three fingers, rolling the golden wheel up and down the length of his thumb knuckle. He liked it. He would keep it as a momento, as a souvenir of this killing.

He held the ring up to the faint light that had caught the gold a moment ago and angled the inside of the ring towards the dim illumination. There was an inscription, just as he had suspected. It was difficult to read, but with the proper tilt he was able to make out the simple statement.

"F.S. All my love, forever. P.S."

So much for forever, Frankie, thought the man, smirking at the sappy sentiment. He stood up, slid the ring into his left pants pocket, and looked at the detached ring finger in his right hand. He could not throw it off the building; the loose nylon netting of the bags was too open. The digit could break free and land anywhere, possibly revealing details he could not allow. He looked around for a moment and thought.

In a flash of expediency, with a whirl and a whip of his arm, he flung the finger up into the air and onto the top of the twenty-foot tall heating unit twenty feet away, to the north of the rooftop. The finger spun through the air, a perverse projectile, and landed heavily, skidding to a halt some ten feet from the falcon's lair. No one would look for a missing person, or finger, there.

He returned to his work. The next two contraptions worked quite well, splashing down with tremendous *booms*. The closely joined pairs did not have as much difficulty staying in unison on their descent.

One pair was thrown from a point just south of the middle of the roof, and the other was thrown a few feet north of the middle. This set broke the river water about twenty feet from the theatre side embankment. This arrangement spread the evidence along a satisfactory portion of the river bottom for the man.

He retrieved a final cinder block. One last throw was needed, and this could quite possibly be the most explosive.

He dropped the block next to the bag and reached inside to retrieve the final object. The heavy round head was difficult to grab. The black nylon netting had tangled in the hair of the dead man, and the cold, stiff surfaces flopped around in the oversized satchel. The man finally snatched the noosed drawstring and jerked the net bag out of the duffel.

This was a bit too sloppy. The decapitation filled only a small section of the large net bag. The man struggled to conceive a way to create a snug fit around the bowling ball-sized object. He could put the cinder block in the bag and throw the set together. Not possible—the block could easily cut the cords of the pouch with its abrasive concrete edges. There were no other objects near with which to fill the bag. His mind found no invention with which to complete the foul task. Maybe he needed a cigarette.

He stood, pulled the pack from his jacket's left front pocket, grabbed the lighter from his right pants pocket, and lit the slow-motion cancer. For the man, the muted eve roared with the ignition of the rolled tobacco. He dragged long and hard, puffing at the western suburbs. He stepped to the roof wall and leaned his backside against it, turning southeast to view the darkened skyline.

The Sears Tower rose one hundred and ten stories, two blocks due southeast. There were one or two lights dotting the windows of the black structure, and spotlights kindled the two-hundred-foot radio towers. Flashing red beacons signaled the very top of the towers to passing planes and the sprawling environs. With his left hand the man held his cigarette up to the hundred foot towers, and squinting adjustment for his distant perspective, he blocked one of the huge structures from his sight with the tiny glowing stick. When he closed one eye the minuscule cigarette, held close to his face, obliterated the existence of the enormous monolith.

The burning end of the coffin nail cast an orange glow on his face. The light caused him to notice the imbedded paint on the back of his hand. He flexed the paw, looking at the artwork. He blew the hot blue smoke at the back of his hand and put the cigarette into his mouth.

Kneeling down, he grabbed the nylon pouch and twisted the strands so tightly around the head that they cut into the dead flesh. He gathered the two excess feet of sack and opened the noosed neck. Keeping the twisted end tight, he looped the excess back over the head. Still, a foot and a half of excess net bag hung limp. He twisted and brought the nylon over the head again, forming a third overlap. Now the bag tightly surrounded its contents, covering most of the skin and hair.

Proud of his ingenuity, he tied the loose black ends of the bag in and through the cinderblock's crevices. He pulled the bag until it butted up tight to the block, then he tied the rope back to the bag. He still had enough excess rope to thread and tie again. He did it, tying the rope to a second position of the bag. With a slight taut heave, the bag and its contents pulled closer to the block. The second knot mated the two items, cheek to cheek, for the duration of their existence.

Still kneeling, the man saw the fat tongue of the inhabitant protruding through the strands of black polyester. The dead purple tongue breathed no contempt now; its sharp edge had been blunted.

The sight was a pleasure to the assassin.

"Like I said, Frankie, I'm in charge here." He blew the cigarette smoke into the face of the dead, took the hot embered tip of the cigarette and jabbed it at the lifeless tongue. It burned out quickly in a fizz of flesh.

It was a bit unsatisfactory. There were no winces and no screams of pain. That was over with. The pain had come last night, but the pleasure was lasting even now.

He stood, picking up the conjoined pair, and spun his muscular six-foot frame around. In one motion he heaved the set over the edge of the roof.

As he flung, the gravel under his feet gave way, throwing him into a sprawl. The stumble did not divert enough energy to cause the tied cinderblock and head to thud onto the rooftop, but instead the pair scarcely cleared the brick guard wall. It was not going to land in the Chicago River. It was going to crash onto the theatre's river walkway.

The killer scrambled to his feet, pushing off of the gravel roof with his hands, scraping his palms. The tiny stones that embedded into his flesh went unnoticed. He had a greater concern at the moment. He leered over the barricade and strained in the blue light of night to focus on the descendant.

His eyes picked up the tumbling duo as they fell, end over end. From what he could figure of the trajectory, the cinder block and its cargo were going to crash land on the river walkway behind the Illinois State Theatre.

His adrenal gland had never surged like this. The impending chaos of the situation caused the tiny fibrous ganglion to pour into his bloodstream. His heart pounded through his shirt, and perspiration flowed like the river below.

He was helpless, and he did not like it. His inhalation was constrained and his eyes widened for the impending impact on the concrete embankment. He clutched the brick-topped railing of the roof wall and dug his fingernails into the ledge.

He wished to suspend the present damning effect of gravity, for as it worked at this moment he might as well follow the evidence that would condemn him.

He leaned further over the wall as the block approached its landing.

At the last moment the pair, still falling jerkily, veered away from the building, barely past the river embankment.

The cargo hit the water first. The cinderblock, directly behind, crushed into the skull. The dense, concrete water was a wall, and the cinderblock was the hammer, smashing the victim between. Water erupted from the landing twenty feet into the air, dousing the theatre walkway ten feet above.

The distorted cargo released pieces of its integrity as it was pulled to the riverbed by the weight of the block. The jerking of the liquid descent imitated the airborne one, only more so, with one of the conjoined members dismembered.

A breath of thrill filled the chest of the man two hundred feet above. The sound of the cataclysm surpassed all the previous attempts. He seethed with triumph and voracity. Even in what was thought his imminent failure, he had triumphed. He had felt life above and he had felt death below, and death had been more exhilarating.

He faced the heavens and pulled out another cigarette, lit it, and dragged in celebration of his unexpected achievement. He took another long drag and flipped the quarter-smoked cigarette overboard. He stepped back to the edge and leaned over again.

"Tragedy complete, Frankie."

He picked up the black duffel bags, putting one inside of the other, and collapsed them as well as he could. His shoes scraped the gravel as he walked to the wedged access door. He opened it with a jerk, walked through, and slammed the door into the frame behind him, pulling it completely shut with his added force. He took a keyed lock from his left jacket pocket and sealed the door. Holding the only key, he left the building and headed home, satisfied in another job well and completely done.

No one would ever see the submerged cinderblocks and their human cargo again. The only evidence of the entire evening's disposal was atop the twenty-foot-high heating unit. And soon enough this torn and ripped remainder of Francis Anthony Stanza would vanish, desiccated by the sun and decimated by the birds.

Eleven

1:10p.m.
Monday Afternoon
Rehearsal Room 2
Illinois State Theatre

The doors to the rehearsal room were opened and the visitor slipped in, taking a chair at the rear of the room, behind the singers. The musical tempest in the middle of the room continued unabated.

"Michele, duetto, Atto 3, lettera 'C'," barked the lovable old Italian conductor, Maestro Anton Giardini. He threw his hands into the air like a crazed man, instructing the accompanist for the day, Michael Elliott.

The pianist knew exactly what the Maestro wanted, and with the conductor's downbeat, began the beautiful, lyric introduction to the music desired: Verdi's *Otello*. Enzo and Valencia, as Otello and Desdemona, were making a concerted effort at pleasing the man who would conduct them in this monumental masterpiece later in the year.

Michael let the piano glide, creating the colors of the strings, brass, and woodwinds. He supported the singers, giving his energy to the voices, which soared under his full and luxuriant playing. Valencia, the wrongly accused Desdemona began the duet.

Desdamona: *Dio ti giocondi, o sposo dell'alma mia sovrano!*
God bless you, my husband, my soul's sovereign!

Enzo, as the tortured Moor, *Otello,* responded:
Grazie, madonna, datemi la vostra eburnea mano.
Thank you, my lady, give me your ivory hand.

Caldo mador ne irrora la morbida belta.
Warm moistness bedews its soft beauty.

Desdemona: *Essa ancor l'orme ignora del duolo e dell'eta.*
       It yet knows not the imprint of sorrow or of age.

The gentle sweeping address between husband and wife, overlaid by a full, chordal figure, lifted the scene to an intimate plateau. The piano changed, playing a more aggressive scalar sequence as Otello slyly insinuated his wife in wrongdoing.

The conductor's arms swept up in a violent gesture, attacking the music with gusto.

Otello: *Eppur qui annida il demone gentil di mal consiglio,*
       And yet here lurks the plausible devil of ill counsel,

       che il vago avorio allumina del piccioletto artiglio.
       who emblazons the ivory beauty of this little claw-like limb.

       Mollemente alla prece s'atteggia e al pio fervore...
       with soft deceit he poses as prayer and pious fervor...

The conductor spoke as the singers poured forth the confrontational duet between the needlessly jealous husband and the bewildered wife. "Beauty, legato with sarcasm. Enzo, *molto simpatico* very emotional. Sing these words, they are torture for you." The grand Italian spoke above the piano, his arms sweeping in reflection of the music and the passion of the scene. The conductor spoke his Desdemona.

"Sweetly, innocently, Valencia. Desdemona knows no falsehood."

Desdemona: *Eppur con questa mano io v'ho donato il core.*
       And yet with this same hand I gave my heart to you.

The short interlude of piano led to the simple gesture from the Maestro. "Recitativo now. Speak to your husband."

Desdemona: *Ma riparlar ti debbo di Cassio."*
       But I must speak again to you of Cassio.

"Rage, Enzo! *Molto agitato."*
The piano raced at the implication to the Moor, of his wife's plea for mercy and possible infidelity with Cassio.

"Seized in pain, Enzo. Overcome with torment." Giardini looked directly at Enzo, who did not need the music to stir his memory.

Otello: *Ancor l'ambascia del mio morbo m'assale;*
     I have that pain again which assails me;

     tu la fronte mi fascia."
     Wife, bind my forehead.

Desdemona: *A te.*
       Here. (Giving her handkerchief)

Otello: *No, il fazzoletto voglio ch'io ti donai."*
     No, I want the handkerchief that I gave to you.

The accompaniment surrounded the singers in the lush chords and dissonances of the scene and poetry. The harsh invections of Otello and his fear of deceit were punctuated with short interjections. Desdemona, in her innocent and bewildered state, lifted her voice in pleas to heaven through long, fervent legato lines, pulling at the heart of the listener. The Maestro stopped the singers for a moment.

"Now, we sing this interrogation about the lost *fazzoletto*. Enzo remember, as you tell her of the magic spell interwoven in the handkerchief, watch carefully Verdi's marks. Everything is in the score. *Piannissimo*, then gradually into louder articulations, with the *marcato/legato* at the end of each line." The old man jumped with enthusiasm. "Brilliant! Everything is in the score. Look, the word *talismano*. Perfect setting for the dark spell that Otello wants to cast on his wife, and the harmonies underneath pull the soul with their progression." The Maestro whipped his head again to Michael, who was looking directly at him.

"O.K., Michael, here we go."

The short interjection was heeded perfectly. The nuanced attacks, the articulated moments of anger and defiance wrapped Shakespeare's play into another work of incomparable quality.

"Fervent, Valencia!" as the music approached a climax, the conductor threw his moving hands into the air, the piano filling out the moment before repose.

Desdemona feels that her husband is only trying to confuse her, and she returns to her original subject.

Desdemona: *Tu di me ti fai gioco! Storni così l'inchiesta di Cassio;*
       You are making sport of me! That I forget about Cassio;

       astuzia e questa del tuo pensier.
       Your thoughts are cunning.

The give and take of the argument continued until Otello was totally enraged, and screaming.

Otello: *Il fazzoletto!*
    The handkerchief!

Desdemona: *Gran Dio! nella tua voce v'e un grido di minaccia!*
    Oh God! your voice is a full of menace!

    The turbulent piano pulsed in and out of *crescendos.* Maestro Giardini had full contact with his singers. The motion of his hands drew the singers to him, bringing the black scratches of print to musical life in this drama of love and death. Valencia, still a bit sketchy on a few musical passages, grabbed the binding of her score and dug into the opera with the others. Enzo, having sung the duet before, relaxed into the passion of the scene, his voice darkening and broadening to encompass the tragedy. The short bursts of accompaniment under Michael's strong fingers rolled in chromatic, scale-wise passages, tossing and turning with the minds of the characters. The great accompanist swooned and swayed, giving in to the power of the moments and the emotion of the music.

Otello seizes his wife in his arms, forces her to look at him, and asks her,

Otello: *Alza quegl'occhi. Guardami in faccia! Dimmi chi sei!*
    Lift up your eyes. Look in my face! Tell me who you are!

Desdemona: *La sposa fedel d'Otello.*
    The faithful wife of Otello.

Otello: *Giura! giura e ti danna...*
    Swear! Swear it and damn yourself...

Desdemona: *Otello fedel mi crede.*
    Otello, I am faithful, believe me.

Otello: *Impura ti credo.*
    You are unpure, I believe.

Desdemona: *Casta io son!*   Otello: *Giura e ti danna!*
      Chaste I am!   Swear it and be damned!

The sharp movements of Giardini's arms impulsed the sharp exclamations of the singers and the piano. The conductor's impassioned movements, signaling the musical transition, slowed to a long, broad sweep, looking directly at Valencia. The staccato rhythms and exclamations turned to impassioned phrases, luxuriant for her beautifully rich voice. The *cantabile*—singing—section filled with the pleas of the tortured wife.

Desdemona: "*Mi guarda! Il volto e l'anima ti svelo;*
      Look at me! My face, my soul I show you;

      Il core infranto mi scruta, io prego il cielo per te
      My stricken heart search, I pray to heaven for you

      con questo pianto;
      with these tears:

      per te con queste stille concenti aspergo il suol.
      for you with these scalding drops I sprinkle the ground.

      Guarda le prime lagrime che da me spreme il duol.
      Behold the first tears that I shed by suffering.

      Le prime lagrime!
      My first tears!

Enzo could barely speak the horrible words of the Moor after the mournful supplication of his colleague and friend, Valencia, who was portraying his wife, but he knew he must speak; he must harshly denounce the innocent amidst the supremely glorious underlying music.

Otello: *S'or ti scorge il tuo demone, un angelo ti crede e non t'afferra.*
      If Satan saw you, he'd think you an angel and not touch you.

"Sweetly now, Valencia, *dolcissimo*," Giardini spoke.

Desdemona: *Vede l'Eterno la mia fede!*
      The Eternal sees my innocence!

Otello retorted with a scowl, yelling at his wife.

Otello: *No! La vede l'inferno!*
    No ! Hell sees your infamy!

Desdemona: *La tua giustizia impetro, sposo mio!*
    Your justice I implore, my husband!

At the word "husband" the Moor lashed out, devastated at what he believed to have happened, and fled from his wife. Again, a pianistic eruption signified the violent feelings the man tried to withhold, but, unable to quell her husband's suspicions, her emotions were expressed in tears.

"Expressive now, Valencia, pity in your voice, pity the torment of your husband." The old conductor squeezed every bit of passion from the artists.

Desdemona: *Tu pur piangi? E son io l'innocente cagion di tanto pianto!*
    Why do you weep? Am I the innocent cause of these tears!

    Qual e il mio fallo?
    What is my fault?

Otello: *Che? non sei forse una vil cortigiana?*
    What? are you not a vile "courtesan'?

Desdemona: *Ah!...non son ch'io che esprime quella parola orrenda.*
    Ah....I am not the thing that horrid word expresses.

Maestro Giardini spoke over the short musical interlude.

"Read what Verdi said in the score." The words there encapsulated the final moments of the scene between husband and wife. "Suddenly change from anger to the most terrible ironic calm. Otello takes Desdemona's hand and escorts her to the door. You see, Verdi's own words, amazing." The Maestro finished. "Enzo, complete *pathos*—calm, ironic."

Otello: *Datemi ancor l'eburnea mano, vo' fare ammenda.*
    Give me again your hand, I would make amends.

Vi credea (perdonate se il mio pensiero e fello)
I thought you were (pardon if my thoughts wronged you)

Quella vil cortigiana, che e la sposa d'Otello!
that cunning *whore* who is the wife of Otello!

Enzo soared within the vocal line to the most offensive word that Otello could call his wife—*cortigiana*—whore.

The Maestro waved his arms and halted the rehearsal for a moment of rest and comment.

"My, my, we have done our homework, yes? Excellent, everyone. And you, Michael—fabulous. I think you have twelve fingers. Now, just a few things..." and the musician mentioned a few fine points in the music that he wanted a bit different. A bit of *tenuto* for Valencia in one of her pleas, and Enzo had learned a rhythm wrong, so the group fixed it quickly. On the whole, though, the Maestro was extremely happy.

"Good, now just all of us, again, read the page. What Verdi put on the paper is all we need to have a marvelous opera—in my opinion, the greatest opera of all time—but the key to Verdi is the words. Verdi used a term '*parola scenica*.' It means literally, 'word scene.' He could paint whole opera scenes with words. Remember, we have nothing without these words, especially when they in themselves are masterful. First from Shakespeare, then through Boito." The Maestro referred to the librettist for the work. "Here *fazzoletto*—'handkerchief,' and even *cortigiana*—'whore.' They speak to what the scene is really about. Verdi spoke the words, breathed musical life to them, but he also believed that without the text, he could write nothing. Let's try to recreate that sensitivity to the 'Parola.' Just wonderful!" the excited old man burst out.

"Now Enzo, this next monologue is heartbreak, pathos, perfectly set, that turns to rage and then revenge. Just let the music speak the words *through you*." The conductor turned to the accompanist. "Michael, begin two measures before 'M,'" he said, referring to the musical starting point.

The chord rumbled in crescendo, and the tidal wave of fury, through music, crashed from the piano. Michael could play loudly, really loudly, and this was one of his favorite loud moments. It was an accompanying nugget of fourteen measures that blew the piano lid off, as the Moor throws his wife out of his chamber, and confronts the terror of what he believes to be her infidelity. The wave of the piano rolled and settled into a low, descending bass figure that dragged Otello's soul to hell.

Enzo used his voice as the speaker for what Verdi had first heard in his head, one hundred years before. The almost spoken vocal line reflected the humiliation of the once great warrior.

Otello: *Dio, mi potevi scagliar tutti mali della miseria, della vergogna,*
God, you could have rained on me poverty and shame,

far de miei baldi trofei trionfali una maceria, una menzogna...
made my brave triumphal trophies rubble, and a lie...

e avrei portato la croce crudel d'angoscie e d'onte con calma
I would have born the cruel cross of agony, of disgrace with

fronte e rassegnato al volere del ciel.
a calm brow and resigned to the will of heaven.

The tremolo of the orchestration, in unity with the voice now, lent trembling to the tenor as he sang the horrid words of anguish.

Otello: *Ma,-o pianto, o duol!-m'han rapito il miraggio*
But, o grief, o anguish! To rob me of the mirage

dov'io, giulivo, l'anima acqueto.
where I, joyfully, my soul was nourished.

Spento e quel sol, quel sorriso, quel raggio
Quenched is the sun, the smile, the ray

che mi fa vivo che mi fa lieto!
that gives me life, that gives me joy!

The last two phrases repeated, lifting the voice to a high B flat on the word "raggio" (ray), signifying that lost ray of hope he had in his wife. Enzo, Giardini, and Michael all rose to the phrase with plaintive souls, then settled, changing their intent from pity to anger, and finally revenge.

Tu alfin, Clemenza, pio genio immortal dal roseo riso,
You finally, Clemency, sacred immortal genius of rosy laughter,

copri il tuo viso santo coll'orrida larva infernal!
now your holy face is covered with the mask of hell!

The tumult of voice and piano rose to fury through the music and the words. Perspiration poured from the conductor and the singer as the climax of a fateful, decisive vengeance approached, both musically and dramatically.

> *Ah! Dannazione! Pria confessi il delitto e poscia muoia!*
> Oh! Damnation! Let her confess the sin and then die!

> *Confession! Confession! La prova!*
> The proof!

Maestro Giardini sang the absent Iago's short injection, *"Cassio e la!"* "Cassio is there!" Otello, via Enzo, finished his masterful monologue.

> *La? Cielo! Oh gioia!! Orror! Supplizi immondi!*
> There, Cassio? Oh heaven! Oh horror! Putrid torture!

The crescendo on *"Oh gioia,"* again rose to the high B flat. The tenor expanded to the heights of the phrase and its visceral power moved the Maestro. He began yelling.

"Yes, glorious, yes, my son, excellent." The waving, conductor arms of the small man ceased, and the waving, triumphant fan walked over to hold the cheeks of the tenor. "Si, si, this is my Otello." Michael slowly faded out as the conductor gesticulated with enthusiasm. The conductor looked over the singers' shoulders and spoke to someone behind the group.

"Am I correct, *Signor*? We have a new great 'Otello' on our hands, yes?"

The singers turned and to their surprise saw William Burrows, the general director, seated in the back corner of the huge room. Burrows had snuck in during the tumultuous musical excerpt that had transpired.

He smiled a polite smile and nodded his head to the conductor. He was here on business, not as a musical consultant. The enthused conductor continued.

"Oh my, I think we need a break, yes?" was the rhetorical question. "Bravo, all of you. When we start again, we continue on with the trio. Michael, do we have a Cassio?" asked the man of his accompanist.

"I believe so, but even if we don't, you can fill in, Maestro. If you sing everything as well as that Iago line, you'll be an operatic double threat."

"What is a double 'treat'?" The conductor laughed and asked, not knowing how to pronounce the word properly. Michael took the man's arm.

"I'll tell you over coffee," Michael said.

The conductor turned to the group as he walked out of the rehearsal room.

"Fifteen minutes, everyone, yes?" The group nodded in agreement. Valencia grabbed her purse and made for the door after the conductor. Enzo closed his score, reached into his pocket for his own *fazzoletto*, wiped his face and turned to look at the general director. Burrows had risen and was walking towards him.

"Sounds great. I guess I didn't know you were tackling this role yet."

"It will be the first time on stage. I have done scenes of it before, but I want to be careful. 'Otello' can eat tenors alive. It's such glorious music, though, I couldn't put it off any longer. And with the Maestro, it will be wonderful."

A moment of silence passed, each man feeling a bit uncomfortable with the other. Burrows finally spoke.

"Enzo, I checked with everyone in the Opera House today—the house manager, security, and I personally checked the Performance Incident sheets that have to be filled out," Burrows said. Enzo's head was bowed, knowing the news was to be unhelpful.

"And…" weakly asked the tenor.

"There was nothing in the logs to signify anything unusual. It was supposedly a quiet night here in the House."

"What about the broken railing?" asked Enzo, raising his head defiantly.

"Nick Palermo told me a patron leaned on the rail and caused it to collapse. His usher's Incident Report said exactly the same thing. Security records show that it was roped off at 1:30 a.m."

Enzo's face turned to disbelief. None of that could be true. He had lived the night. His chest was still sore from his crash into the rosettes on the balcony facade.

"It's all a lie, you know," said the tenor matter-of-factly. "All of it. It all happened to me, Bill. I don't know why all this is happening, but those people are lying, because I am *not!*" The pointed statement borrowed from the rage of the rehearsal he had just been singing. He continued in his exasperated tone.

"Bill, everything I said, everything I told you last Saturday night…*it's all true*. And now, someone is changing the facts to make it look like it never happened." Enzo's face began to turn red, and for the first time, anger swelled within him. He had grown impatient with the deceit he knew was being perpetrated.

"We have to call the police again and get them over here. This tiptoeing around, not letting anyone know about what happened…I am sick of it. *I want Frank's killer found!*"

The general director knew the tenor was exasperated. He knew the man was to be believed, but he also knew it was time for him to vent his own rage.

"Now listen here, my boy," he began. "I have done everything you have asked since this supposed murder took place." His voice pinched through his clinched teeth. "I spent the night looking around the basement with a bunch of powdered-sugar coated cops. I brought you over here to search—*again*—for a broken railing that just happened to be wrecked by an idiot audience member. I just finished talking to my security chief and my house manager, who have been here for over twenty years each, trying to track down absolutely what, if anything, happened the other night. And you know what I found? *Not shit!*" He erupted in the tenor's face, a vein emerging from his forehead, throbbing with his accelerating pulse. His semi-controlled wrath would not be held at bay any longer.

"If you want me to ignore the employees, whom I have grown to trust over the years, forget it," he blurted. "They have no reason to lie. Why would they make up what happened?" Enzo stood his ground, silently.

The general director knew Enzo was on the ropes, and he continued to pound him with the scarcity of evidence surrounding his claims.

"Why the hell hasn't anyone reported Frank missing? Why hasn't his wife called to find out why he is supposedly dead? You know why, Enzo? Because he's not dead, that's why!" Burrows slowed the pace of his diatribe to catch a breath, then set his mind into organizing his closing flourish.

"Enzo, there is not one solitary thing in this building that would say Frank Stanza was murdered. All we have is a broken balcony railing that some clumsy bastard broke," he methodically spoke. Burrows looked directly into Enzo's eyes to deliver a series of knockout blows.

"But if Frank is dead—if he *was* killed here, in this opera house—his death is on *your* head." Enzo pulled back in shock, feeling the pain of the words in his gut.

"Because, when he needed you, you ran and hid." Enzo reeled from the statement, groping behind him for the chair he had used at the rehearsal.

"In fact, it's so ironic," Burrows sneered. "If Frank really is dead, you can't even identify the killer."

It was true, and Enzo knew it. He had suffered this torment on the hotel bed the night of the killing, but Gwen was not now here to comfort him. And now Bill Burrows, exasperated at Enzo's seeming ingratitude, was plunging the knife of remembrance back into its still fresh wounds. He shook his head in shock, lowering himself to sit in the chair he had located.

"I don't even believe he is dead, Enzo. Hell, he could be down in props right now, for all I know, working his ass off. You know why? Because I've checked every other goddamn place in this building," screamed the director.

"So if this is some sick joke, Enzo Santi, you can go fuck yourself, because it's not funny, and it never was funny. But if Frank Stanza is really dead, it is on your head, because thanks to you, we'll never find his killer."

Burrows turned and briskly walked towards the double doors of the rehearsal room, his face still red with anger. Enzo sat on the black cushioned chair, his head falling to his knees, elbows firmly planted on his thighs, his hands laced together in front of his face. Dejection consumed him, until in an instant he remembered last evening in the elevator. Enzo called out to the general director.

"The killer had a tattoo on the back of his left hand. I saw it," spoke E, "and I won't forget it, Bill, not until we find him."

Burrows approached the doors, pushed the left one open, and turned back to Enzo.

"You can find your *killer* yourself."

Enzo sat alone in the large, echoing rehearsal hall. His head hung low.

Twelve

Monday Evening

The yellow light of dusk streamed into the deck of bay windows. The imperfections in the glass refracted a shimmer, bending the rays into a mirage of movement. The saffron cast grew darker as the full-length blinds were twisted to their assigned position.

The man who adjusted the blinds was a bit weary. The droop of his eyelids brought a reminding sting of sleep deprivation. The past night's moments of adrenaline had heightened his ecstasy, but now accentuated his fatigue.

The cool air of the previous night had also seized his throat in a bit of twinge. The pour of gold from the distant orb warmed his face, enlivened his body, and gnawed at his contracting eyes.

The large autumnal sun dipped to the horizon. The man pulled a blind to one side and peered onto Upper Wacker Drive and to the masses filtering out of the city. The trenches below were dark, shadowed by the buildings, with its tiny occupants scurrying to their abodes.

The man turned into the room and stepped down the three steps from his elevated position. The stacks of books on the adjacent wall soaked in the cloaked light, capturing and absorbing it, sucking the tinted illumination through the room. He walked along the line of light that angled slightly, permeating the blinds, down the steps to attend to his employer. The three steps found him crossing from pale light into darkness, traversing into the south end of the room.

The large room, bedecked in oak furnishings, had been a meeting room—a boardroom. The long central table had been replaced with a gargantuan oak desk that sat at the south end to the room, just behind the peering gaze of the sun and the windows. The elegance of the space spoke of great knowledge and great power.

The man sitting behind the desk was peering out the south glass exposure. He had spun his black leather chair around, away from the brightness of the inner part of the room. The bright light was not what he liked. The cool shades of evening were more to his taste, and they were well on their way.

"Close the south blinds too," the seated man declared. The assistant walked alongside the huge desk to the south wall of windows. He pulled the nylon cord that brought the blinds into place from their hideaway to the side, then tugged a second cord, tilting the cloth panels into their job of obstruction. The assistant then turned left to the wall and flipped a switch. The tall hunter drapes shuffled electronically out of their lair and into their joined position in just a few moments. The drapes sealed the south end of the room from the view of the outside.

The man who was seated loved his desk's position. It was perfect. It sat just behind the stream of sunlight that spilled into the room. Whoever sat in the chairs on the far side of his desk was hampered by the light cast upon them. Their secrets, their lies, and their confessions were all exposed by the glare just beyond that tiny line drawn by the sun. He, however, was shielded by the darkness, assessing and judging. Whether right or wrong, the decisions ultimately did not matter; his word was law within these corridors.

Whoever sat in those chairs found themselves at a great disadvantage. That was the purpose; that was the point. Whoever came through the great ten-foot double doors, seventy feet behind him, would know their world ended as they crossed the threshold, and that only one man ruled this kingdom.

The man sipped the vodka and tonic cradled in his right hand, gasping at each intake of his chosen poison. The cigars that he dearly loved had to be sparingly enjoyed now. His left hand fidgeted, wishing for an expensive Cuban version, but his health came to his mind more than he wished.

Business and family were the only truly important things in life, and it was necessity that the two be carefully managed.

"What time is he scheduled to show up?" intoned the seated man.

"Just a few minutes," breathed the cigarette-tainted breath. "He is a very prompt person, and I know he doesn't want to disappoint *you*," came the comment, a smirk on his face.

"I want to get out of here." He knew that a single cigar awaited him at home, the reward for a good day's work. "My grandson has a soccer game, and I don't want to miss it." He continued with the business side of matters, relying on his personal assistant.

"There haven't been any problems, have there? Everything is going smoothly?"

"There were a few *persistent* difficulties, but the last of those was handled the other night," the assistant responded confidently. "Everything from this point forward should be as smooth as your drink," he said, referring to the vodka and tonic.

"Let's hope our little operation runs more smoothly than that," he gasped as he finished the last swig. "We also need to keep the people down south happy." He paused, realizing that he had never tried to keep anyone else content. "Well, at least they need to be kept in line."

"Yes, sir," was the sycophantic reply. The man in the chair slowly spun the seat around to face his desk and noticed the large box of special Havana cigars he had received for his birthday. His mouth watered, longing for that simple, yet extremely expensive pleasure. He also noticed his assistant eyeing the sacred cigar box. The two men's eyes met, the lesser feeling caught in the humidor.

"Go ahead and take one; just promise not to smoke it around me. If I smell that incense around here, I'll go nuts." The assistant took one of the stogies and placed it in his suit coat pocket.

He knew this was no small gift. This cigar represented a bond and a friendship between the two men. He had served this man through long and difficult times. He had done the dirty work necessary for the business to progress unimpeded. He knew this man seated before him had done the same, years before. Both men knew the risks were tremendously great, but the lure of the rewards was greater still.

The respect signified by this simple gift filled the assistant with strength. It was not only recognition for service, but a strong vote of confidence within the ranks of this "quiet" business. His fatigued eyes grew wide through the burn of sleeplessness, and he looked at the seated man.

"Thank you very much, sir." He knew that someday he could very well occupy that chair. Some day the man before him would be gone, and he would take this seat of power. This was what he wanted, what he had strived for, what he had killed for. Adrenaline pumped into his bloodstream as he inhaled through his nostrils. *This*, he thought, *will be so.*

Five quiet minutes and another vodka and tonic passed. Finally, a soft knock at the two large entrance doors drew the assistant. Another lackey in a long string of lackeys informed the assistant that the expected guest had arrived.

"Send him in."

After a moment more, the double doors swung open completely. William Burrows walked through, nodded an uncomfortable acknowledgment to the assistant, and made his way into the enormous room.

He looked to his right, saw the amber glow that sparkled about the room, but paced directly towards the desk and the two chairs on the near side of it.

"How are you doing today?" solemnly questioned the G.D. to the older man across the expanse. He continued to stand until one of the two men in the room gave him permission to sit. This was one of the many rules by which he must abide.

"I'm doing just fine, young man," was the flat response. The old man could afford to be kind. His watchdogs would always take care of him, watch his back; however, he did not care for the nonchalance that this newcomer exhibited. From the moment these men had begun dealing with each other, the arrogance and superiority displayed by the lesser did not sit well with him. The boss had taught a few lessons before. When underlings stepped out of line he would crash down upon them like Atlantis into the sea. It might be necessary in this case. The general director was on very thin ice. One misstep and there would be some measure of "discipline" meted out to the unsuspecting Opera Man.

The assistant had followed the G.D. up to the desk, and was now standing behind him, over the left shoulder of Burrows. He, like his boss, was also unhappy with the general director. No one spoke to his employer without first being spoken to *by* his employer. This was also a rule in the present game, and this disrespect made the assistant extremely angry.

The slight also made him anxious—anxious to inflict discomfort. He knew that if he was patient he might receive an opportunity to relieve his anxiety, maybe in this very place.

The old man in the chair raised his right hand and simultaneously told Burrows to sit in one of the two leather chairs. Burrows sat in the high-backed chair to the boss's right. The assistant positioned himself over the left shoulder of the general director, out of Burrows' sight but directly in his boss's. He would jump at the moment he was needed. The old man spoke.

"Congratulations on a fine opening night. Your reviews should soon have you back at the top of *your* opera world." The condescension was not lost on the general manager. He squirmed in the soft leather chair. "My assistant says that your box office can't keep up with the ticket orders since the re-opening of the great Chicago Grande Opera."

The G.D. was nervous and agitated, especially after his confrontation with Enzo earlier. He knew, despite his loathing for this human company, that he had to stay in control, either that or risk some great difficulties. He politely responded.

"It was a great evening for opera," he said as he fidgeted, "on the whole. The performance was nothing short of spectacular, but..." He was cut off by the man across from him.

"You have quite a tenor there, don't you?" asked the boss. He picked up the *Chicago Herald* that sat folded on his desk, folded to the Arts Section and the review of the Saturday night spectacle. "The next—Caruso?" questioned the man, squinting to read the small type. He pulled back and said to the room and the arrogant director, "How many *next Carusos* have there been?"

The general director had heard all these tired old opera accusations before, and there was nothing new coming from the formidable man across from him, but he still kept his head, using the diplomacy that had worked for him on many a negotiating table. The G.D. nodded his head as the man continued.

"For my money, nobody could sing like Corelli. Now there was a tenor with rock-hard balls. Or even Del Monaco. I just can't get excited about these modern singers, Dick," the boss said, looking to the G.D. The man standing behind the general director smirked to himself. "Lots of publicity for a few years, then you don't hear from them ever again." The boss slugged into the chair. "Maybe these hot young singers are all hype in the first place, huh, Dick?"

The boss looked over to the general director, knowing he had called him a pseudonym. It was a small test of the G.D.'s *cojones*. It was an insult meant to measure the meat of the man—the heart and the soul of one who was distrusted. Burrows summoned all his tact and ventured forth into what he knew would be a strenuous conversation, and not about the CGO's successful opening. He folded his hands onto his lap and breathed deeply to calm his inner antagonism.

"Sir," he said honestly, "first, you know my name is William, not Richard," he said with a coy smile on his face, as if playing to the humor of the old man, "and secondly, I fully understand your point. It seems to me, many young, promising singers, who also happen to be very attractive, are rushed into heavy singing schedules before they are physically able to handle such rigors. Thus, they quickly blow out their voices." He paused to make his third point. "There are also those 'so-called' singers who never really had the voice to begin with. Some conductor becomes enamored with some young woman—or man—and pushes their career as much as is within their power. Then, after a few years of critical exposure, these 'great' young talents end up on history's expansive list of has-beens and frauds. Because, Sir," the G.D. intoned, "operatic singing is truly not for the weak-voiced or the weak-willed. Frauds will always be found out and destroyed, whether by the public or by their own hand—or voice, in this case."

The man behind the desk sank deep into the soft leather upholstery as the G.D. prattled. He appeared interested on the surface. Burrows talked of the frauds in the world of singing, but the boss knew Burrows to be fraudulent himself. He appeared the calm, cool steward of the people's opera. In reality, he was a manipulator, a Shylock, full of greed and avarice. The tarnish from his operatic covetousness of previous years had barely been rubbed away, and he was once again, six months later, soiling himself.

The old man could understand the wanton avarice of the slick individual at whom he stared. Every industry is laced with corruption and gluttony. Greed had been considered righteous, considered honorable. Greed had its place within the machinations of his very own business. As long as greed was tempered by loyalty, diligence, and, honesty to those who were your superiors, greed was even beneficial.

But what the corpulent boss could not accept was greed coupled with cowardice, and he believed William Burrows to be a coward.

Cowardice was slave to only one master: expediency. The itching gnaw of cowardice could overwhelm loyalty, honor, and even family. Cowardice would betray and defile while in search of its own protection. Whoever or whatever happened to be the most present ruler, the most proximate envoy, this new leader would capture a coward's fancy.

Cowardice had turned triumph into tragedy, success into slaughter, and victory into vanquish. The boss knew that William Burrows was indeed a coward. He was a coward amongst loyal, honorable men. That made him seethe.

He also realized this piggish man before him created instability, which meant he created work. It was true that Burrows was a conduit for his business operations, but not a completely necessary link. Other methods could be found to achieve the same goal. Burrows was the convenient and immediate opportunity. He held a position that presented not only quick rewards, but possibly long-term solutions.

Still, he would have to be watched. He would have to be monitored so that any buckle in his temporary shield of loyalty could be hammered back into submission immediately. If such a crack were to ripple, shattering the entire veneer of loyalty, exposing the true nature of this man, disposal might be the only option. After all, the two men's relationship depended more on Burrows' acceptance of the boss's leadership, and thus, the greater of the two businesses, than on William Burrows' supply of operatic convenience.

The boss mulled Burrows' last statement over in his thick mind. The general director was correct about one thing; frauds certainly would be found, and they would be destroyed.

The boss smoothly took up where the G.D. had left off, and just as effectively made his point.

"Our business is not for the weak-willed either, Richard," snarled the boss. Burrows sat up sharply, not expecting such a change in mood. The assistant behind Burrows stiffened his back at the bite he heard in his boss's voice. It was time for business.

The boss continued. "My assistant here tells me that some of your people are not responding to the new management on the loading docks the way we had hoped," Burrows said, butting in to the boss's statement.

"Sir, all I asked for was a bit more time. There were really no hostile elements on the docks." Burrows began an earnest plea. "I'm sure you have a good idea what flack Unions can put up, and the stage crew and properties unions wanted clarification on the overtime stipulations. We had men working twenty hours straight, and the Union will not allow that."

The boss lowered his dark snake eyes and honed in on Burrows as he spoke.

"I have dealt with unions all my life. Hell, I helped organize half of 'em in this damn city back in the forties and fifties." The man spoke methodically and with experience. "Unions will do what you want as long as you apply the right pressure, whether that means a pansy-assed bribe that you call a negotiation, or it means bustin' a few heads. What I have to deal with is more important than what you need. *I—hope—that—is—perfectly—clear!*" The insistence of that statement was not what Burrows wanted to hear. He tried another tactic in pleading his case.

"I understand. There is no question in my mind who and what is most important to you and your business. I'm just asking for a bit of ..." the G.D. fumbled with his stuck tongue, "...a bit of 'artistic tolerance.'" He was not happy with his choice of words, and grimaced. "Now that opening night is over, the house will settle in for the season, the hawks from the press will back off a bit, and the whole operation will smooth out. I know it will." Burrows attempted to convince himself of the unknown.

The boss slid his empty glass up onto the desk and motioned for the assistant behind Burrows to collect it. The assistant quickly snatched it with his right hand and pulled back again to his position of surveillance.

"It better start running more smoothly, Dick, or we won't be doin' business for long." The boss spun his chair to the right a bit and glanced up at the assistant. The boss nodded to him. Burrows began again.

"Things will be much smoother than before, I know." Burrows segued into a topic he wanted to bring up with these gentlemen. "One of our main provocateurs down on the docks is—missing."

"Is that so? Now who would that be, Dick?"

Burrows did not want to play this game, but he had commenced it and he now felt obliged. Acting innocent had saved many a guilty man, but he knew any acting in this room would be a mockery. Burrows spoke solemnly.

"His name was Frank Stanza. He had a wife and three children. He didn't need to be..." he paused, "to disappear." The entire room knew where his incomplete statement had led.

The boss nodded, his gaze fixed upon Burrows. Burrows noticed something small flash by his eyes and onto his lap. The small object hit his suit jacket with a tiny "thump" and slid into the valley of jacket material that lay between his legs. He looked down. There in his lap was a band, a gold band. It appeared to be a wedding band—a man's band, wide and small, still brilliantly shining. He let it sit in his lap a moment, pulling his arms up and to his sides.

"Go ahead, Dick," said the boss. "It's a nice momento."

Burrows' brow pulsed with venal pressure. He cautiously picked up the band with his left hand and rolled it along his thumb and index finger. He angled it side to side, catching the glare of the outside light. He examined the item for a moment or two and noticed the inner side of the band. He pulled the ring back from his middle-aged eyes to focus on the inscription.

"F.S.- All my love, forever, P.S."

His fingers began to shake, beads of perspiration clustered at his hairline. His breathing became burdensome. The name he had just mentioned to these two scoundrels, Frank Stanza, now came to life in the small yellow band that slipped in his clammy palm.

He bit his lower lip and realized his suspicions had been confirmed. Denial seemed a silly farce at this point, but he had dealt its lobotomizing hand all too often in the last eight months. Burrows lapsed into ignorance, ignorant of the boss's statement and ignorant of the evidence in his hand.

"Thank you," he said and cleared his obstructed throat. As he stretched out his left hand to place the ring on the right front of the boss's desk, he lied and said, "but I...um...cannot accept it. I don't know whose it is."

Burrows' left hand delicately placed the ring on the grand wooden desk.

"Here's a reminder," bit the voice of the man behind him. In duo with his statement, the assistant, cupping the boss's heavy drinking glass in his right hand, smashed the glass down onto Burrows' exposed left hand. Burrows screamed in pain as the glass tore into his hand. The downward force from the assistant and the heavy, thick glass shattered the tumbler, along with all the bones in the top of the general director's hand. The gold ring Burrows had tried to place on the desk shot across the desk from the impact and flew onto the floor beside the boss's swivel chair.

The shattering glass gouged deep along the top surface of Burrows' hand, tearing the skin, cutting entirely the web of flesh between the left hand's ring and third finger. The assailant pulled back to his assigned position, just over Burrows' left shoulder. After his infliction, he was silent.

Between his first two screams, Burrows pulled his mangled hand back to his body, cupping it in his right, trying to stem the flow of blood. He pulled his handkerchief from his inner breast pocket. The white cotton was soon completely drenched.

The two other men in the room watched silently as the general director writhed in the fine leather chair. The involuntary contraction of his body circled the injured member, protecting it from further harm. No more harm was to come.

He supported one hand with the other at the wrist. Still crying out in anguish, he saw the forty-five degree upward angle the back of his hand created. The broken vessels beneath the undamaged skin swelled the hand, throbbing with Burrows' accelerating heartbeat. He grimaced, peering up at the boss, sitting silently across the desk from him. Tears came to his eyes. In those few short seconds, perspiration flooded his body. Through his body's sympathetic throbbing, Burrows peered up from over his mangled hand.

"Why? What was that? What did I do?" he cried out to the one who ordered the 'hit.'

The boss veered to the right as before, leaned down and picked up the ring that had flown his way in the moment of violence. He methodically sat back up, not looking at the retrieved item, and waited for the adrenaline to dull the pain Burrows was experiencing. Burrows looked back down to his hand, now covered in the red-stained white sheath of a napkin and waited for a response.

He waited. The bobbing of his torso slowed. Endorphins filled the wound and his body. The pain was intense, but he settled in, slowed his breathing, and tried to relax. Burrows pulled himself up straight and leaned back into the chair again, raising his left hand, still supported by the right, from the elbow. The elevation eased the scorch of the lava cruising through the affliction.

The stare from the boss was broken by a heavy breath.

"Bill, if I need to address certain problem elements at the opera house, I'll do it." He paused. "*My way*. No questions. No discussion. Your job is to inform me of any possible difficulties that may arise in how our two enterprises intermingle." He paused again. "Understood?"

Burrows nodded his head in affirmation.

"I don't want to hear about some operatic bellyaching, but if there is some rat-assed little bastard peeking into my affairs, I want to know about it, and I want to know *now*." There was another momentary silence. "Understood?"

Burrows nodded his head in affirmation.

"Good. There was a misunderstanding the other night that my friend here had to address, and so he did. I have felt a bit of misunderstanding between us, and I don't want that. And," he slowed, "I don't think you want that either."

"No, I don't," Burrows responded between convulsed respiration,

"Now, William, listen up." The boss pushed back and rocked slowly in his recliner. "Your little gift, there," referring to the broken hand, "is your reward for two minute missteps. First, I don't want you to use your cell phone like you did Saturday night. Get your ass to a landline. I don't want this whole operation in the shithouse due to some fucking snoop with a scanner." The boss licked his lips, longing for a cigar.

"Second, its time to quit messing with your Unions. Give them what they want; I don't care. We are too big to give a shit about a few dollars thrown at some beer-jockeys that want a raise. Just get your damn Unions off those docks when we need to be there. Understood?"

Burrows nodded again, preferring not to speak.

The boss breathed deeply and settled into his feeling of accomplishment. He finally looked at the ring he had been holding in his right hand. He flipped it in his hand a few times, then looking at his assistant and flung the ring at him. Burrows ducked to the right to stay away from the projectile that had caused his newly inflicted pain. The assistant caught the ring in his left hand, keeping his right hand cupped to his side, and slid the golden piece into his lapel pocket.

"I think this has been a productive little chat, Bill. I think things are clear now, with what is expected, don't you?" Another nod. The boss turned momentarily almost fatherly.

"Now, go get that looked after. We can't have our general director missing out on the new season with an injury, can we?" he said sarcastically, bringing a smile to both him and his assistant. "By the way, my wife would like season tickets. She's a big fan of your new tenor." Another nod followed.

Burrows climbed out of the chair and turned to his left. He stared at the man who had inflicted his injury. He looked down at his left hand, curled at his side, deformed and numb, and thought of Enzo's final statement to him this afternoon. He glanced quickly at the left hand of his assailant.

There it was, the tattoo to which Enzo had referred. The deep blue and black stood out; it was unmistakable. He looked up again and caught the searing eye of the assistant.

Dilemma filled Burrows' body just as the endorphins did. No one but he and Enzo knew about the assistant's tattoo, nor where he had been the other night. If he kept silent, no one would care, and no one would believe Enzo. He could even tip the police to the Frank Stanza killing and they, the police, could attend to this predator's societal dismissal. Should he tell these two men, whom he loathed, to whom he was both indebted and subjugated, what his tenor had witnessed?

He slowly strode past the assistant, head tilted down, away from the desk and out of the immense room. He felt their eyes at his back, the assistant walking just behind him to show him out of the room.

He slowed, stopped, and turned around to face the two men again. He spoke across the distance, past the assistant, to the boss. Burrows decided to remain a coward.

"Enzo Santi saw what happened the other night after the opera. He didn't see the man's face, but he did see the tattoo on his left hand."

The boss got up out of his chair and looked to the assistant, who now clenched his fists. The assistant gave a slight nod to the boss.

"What else did he see?" The boss asked.

"Nothing. Not a single thing! He only knows the height of the man who...and that he had a tattoo on his left hand."

"Is he a threat to us? Any kind of threat?"

"I don't think so," the G.D. said, pondering a moment. "Not at all," he said definitely. "He has no resources, and right now he is overwhelmed with guilt at his impotence at the time of the event." The boss looked down, contemplating the dilemma for a moment.

Burrows turned to the assistant and spoke so the boss could not hear him.

"How are those knees feeling after your tumble in the props room the other night?" The assistant bristled at the cutting tone of the weakling he had just tortured. Burrows had another moment to speak. "Do you feel bad about letting an opera fag get the best of you? Some tough guy you are." Sarcasm dripped from the soaked statement.

Burrows' tongue seemed his only defense, his only weapon. If he could inflict a measure of psychic revenge, it might pay dividends later. The assistant did not really scare him. Even though he had inflicted the injury, he was emasculated without the boss's orders, and Burrows believed the boss did not know the whole story of the bungled and amateurish killing.

The assistant grunted loathfully at the G.D., but he stood still. The boss walked out from behind the desk and up to the two men.

Burrows switched on a very safe bit of charm and talked directly to the approaching boss now, while the assistant's hands shook in rage. Blood began to drip from the assistant's right hand. Burrows took inventory of the boss's Santi dilemma.

"I am in very close contact with Santi. He's closely tied to the opera house and our new success. There is no evidence of wrongdoing in the props department from the other night, and the police don't know anything, except maybe the ingredients for the donuts in our cafeteria," Burrows dispelled with his little smirk before the other two noticed it.

The boss was deadly serious as he walked up to Burrows and said intently. "This Santi better not be a problem. If he turns into one, I want to know. Understood?" Burrows nodded to the boss. "Go on." The boss whipped his head up, motioning Burrows to leave. The assistant stayed right there, perpendicular to the boss. Burrows turned to his left, looked up at the assistant while the boss was in thought, and winked at the assistant with his left eye, camouflaged from the boss, and walked out. The assistant bristled again, but he had to contain his fury.

Burrows strode to the door, cradling his injury, and pushed his back into the right side of the double doors.

"Son of a bitch," he whispered under his breath at the two men he left behind.

The great door closed.

The two men stood silent for a moment, looking at the door in thought. The elder thought on business matters and what would need to be done to protect their trade. The younger longed for a greater taste of adrenaline, for another visit with the man whose hand he had just shattered, who had just insulted him, and possibly jeopardized his own future.

"Your work Saturday night may have been a mistake," the boss waxed philosophically, "but I don't think it will cost us. Remember, my boy, you can twist the living to your will," advised the elder, referring to Burrows, "but the dead tell tales that will kill you." The boss walked back to his desk and resumed his chair.

"Watch him very closely. He can't afford any wrong moves, but neither can we." The assistant nodded "yes" while still looking at the door through which Burrows left.

"Put someone on Santi too. If things get too dicey, we may need to tie up those loose ends too." The assistant finally looked at the boss.

"And look at me," speaking sternly to the protégé, "get over this 'high' you get from the jobs you do. This is business! Feelings and addictions should never get in the way of that. Understand?"

The assistant, still standing in the same place, nodded his head. The boss returned to his desk.

"Get me another drink." The assistant walked to the bar, and raised his right hand to look into his palm. His cupped hand was pooled with his own blood. In his attack on Burrows, an errant shard of glass had plunged deep into his palm. He breathed in sharply, and with his left hand he pulled the imbedded glass out of his hand. The pull was slow; the pain was what he wanted. He threw the shard behind the bar and licked his palm. The iron and salt stung his tongue. The bitter taste remained in his mouth.

Molto vivace:

accelerando, furioso

*In music the dignity of art seems
to find supreme expression*
— Goethe —

Thirteen

9:00 a.m.
Wednesday Morning
Carson's Limousine Service
4939 W. Lake Street

"What a beautiful car," proclaimed Albert "Bill" Hutchinson, standing in front of the immaculate new Lincoln Town Car stretch limousine. "Dis is de car my dreams is made of," whispered the lifelong Chicagoan. He held his stubby arms out to the side, embracing the sensuous curves of the gleaming white, chrome-trimmed vehicle. He drank in the smell of the fresh exterior.

Bill was a limousine driver for the Carson Limousine Service. He had driven all his life. He had loved cars all his life. He wanted to be around them, to touch them, and to smell them.

Having attended Lincoln Technical High School on the city's Near North Side, he had hoped to develop his boyhood love into a position with one of the big three out of Detroit. He had wanted to design these great American cars. Big, powerful, and sleek; built for the American family, for the American man.

However, he did not have the mental prowess to pursue his dream, but found work as a self-taught and high school-trained mechanic, and now as a limousine driver. It was a living, comfortable enough to buy a nice little home in Cicero, find a wife, and raise three daughters.

Now he drove for the pleasure really. He was semi-retired. His wife had scrimped and saved all of their lives, so the couple had a nice little nest egg with which to spoil grandchildren, all of whom lived in the Far Western suburbs. Bill raised his hands to his head and stroked his close-cropped hair.

"I sure like dese newer town cars. Dee older ones were too boxy for me. Dese rounded corners seem more elegant dan dose older models. Hey, Mick, how big is da engine?" Bill called to the maintenance and rental operator, Michael Fitzgerald.

"Five liter V-8, I think."

"Not a V-10? I think the eight cylinder's a little too small for dese land yachts."

"I'm not sure. You're the car buff. I just get the drivers out the door in them. Pop the hood and check her out."

"Oh, boy," moaned the stocky German-American as he walked to the driver's door, opened it and popped the hood. He walked around the front of the car again, feeling under the middle of the hood for the latch. A quick push to the left and the gas cylinders on either side of the hood pulled the huge expanse skyward, exposing the power behind the elegance.

"Definitely a V-10," proclaimed Bill. "I bet dis baby can fly." Bill was never a lover of speed, but the knowledge of capability always excited him. "Bet it gets about 12 miles to da gallon." Bill stuck his head in under the cushioned inner section of the hood. He admired the aluminum engine block and the spangling inner workings of the unused vehicle. With Bill as the driver of this car, Micky knew that the inner workings would stay as perfect and clean as the outer appearance.

Micky spoke up. "All I know is that its got one of them satellite alarm systems on it." Micky walked to the office to get the paper work on Bill's destination and duties for the day. "After gettin' those three Towncars stolen last month, we either got ta alarm every car, or move."

The city's West Side was a tough neighborhood. Auto thieves worked in perfect tandem with storefront chop shops to dismantle, rearrange, and "recycle" vehicles from all over the Chicago area. Cars had been stolen from the Carson fleet before, but Micky wanted to stop this epidemic from spreading. This new satellite tracking system guaranteed that his vehicles would now be watched, even from the heavens.

Michael Fitzgerald had thirty vehicles, plus the big new limo and two new standard-sized Town Cars. Each car had a chart and position on the outer wall of his office. Daily assignments, destinations, vehicle license numbers, and special instructions were posted on this wall. This was where the driver found his work.

Micky always gave Bill the good assignments. He was driving for the enjoyment of it, and best of all, he was unwaveringly honest and hard working. No extra rides, no gypsy-cabbing to and from the airport, and no illegal activity was ever allowed in a car driven by Mr. Hutchinson. He was an honest man, working for a few extra bucks, in the cutthroat business of personnel transportation. Micky wished he had more men like him.

Bill poked his head out the side from under the hood and called to his youthful boss. "By the way, Mick, who am I taking down to Bloomington anyway?"

Micky pulled the chart off the wall's upper left-hand side, number one position, and started to walk back to the enormous white car. When Micky took over as rental operator, he quickly pursued a few large corporate accounts to solidify a core of rental business. The CGO became a client, due to Mickey's competitive prices and his reputation as being fair and honest. If some portion of a rental was incorrect or fouled up, Micky took full responsibility and would rectify the problem immediately.

"You, my good man," he said, faking an air of sophistication, "are working for the Chicago Grande Opera today." Bill played along and bowed to the operator as he approached.

"Most gracious sir, I tank you for dis opportunity to serve such a fine and upstandin' conglomeration as the esteemed Chicago Grande Opera." Bill accentuated the name of the opera company with an artistic panache. Still in an air of flamboyance, he continued. "Might I be escortin' the fabulous Signor Lucitano Paparazzi, sir?" Bill liked music, but certainly did not know the world of opera very well, as evidenced by his tenoral mispronunciation. Micky came out of his act and spoke more seriously, but with a smile.

"Actually, the CGO was hired through the Indiana University School of Music. You are taking Mr. En-zo San-ti," slowly pronouncing the unfamiliar name, "to sing a recital and teach a master class down in Bloomington."

"Is he a big shot?" asked Bill.

"You got me, Old Man. For all I know, he could be some sort of janitor."

"Wow," joked the driver. "A janitor who gets limo rides. Maybe he won da lottery."

"It does say to be a bit gentle with him. Supposedly, he has had some sort of trouble lately."

"What da heck does dat mean?" asked Bill.

"Don't know," Micky replied. "I do know that the general director called me personally to make that request. I don't know what's wrong with the guy. Just be good to him."

Bill smiled a crooked smile and spoke out of the side of his mouth. "I'll charm him with my rapier wit." He raised his eyebrows in jest and hesitated a moment, then said assuredly, "as I do all my clients." Micky handed Bill the chart with the information he had just read.

"If you do, you know these opera people, don't you?" coyly spoke Micky. Bill knew what he was about to say.

"Big tippers!" the men erupted in unison. Bill continued.

"Baby's gonna eat to-night." Bill clutched the chart under his arm and walked to the front of the car again, carefully placing his palms on the front rounded edge of the hood and pushed down to close the huge white reflector. He yanked a clean cloth from his inside suit jacket pocket and wiped clean a smudge he had created on the front of the hood.

"She's all gassed up, so you're ready to go," Micky hollered as he walked back to the office. Bill glanced down at the chart and saw that the pick-up time for Mr. Santi was at 10:00 a.m., the Hyatt Hotel. It would only take him twenty minutes to get to the assigned hotel.

"Hey, I've got twenty-five minutes ta kill. What do you want me ta do?"

"Get a cup of coffee, or get to the Hyatt early and charge a breakfast to room 1801. That's where your singer is staying."

Bill frowned at the suggestion of impropriety. Micky shrugged back. "I don't know. Go sit in your new car and play with the buttons. Be creative."

Bill perked up at the thought of fondling the Town Car's luxurious passenger compartment. He looked up and to the left, thinking of a twenty-minute agenda.

"First, coffee; second, play in the new car." His eyes lit up.

"*New car*, ooooo!"

Fourteen

Enzo saw the white limousine glide into the circle drive of the Hyatt and stop at the three sets of revolving doors at the front of the hotel. He raised himself from the lobby sofa, sat on its front edge, and picked up the two sixteen-ounce insulated paper cups of chocolate mocha coffee he had set on the lobby end table next to him. He watched the driver exit his vehicle.

The black suited driver revolved through the entranceway and walked to the concierge off to the right of the entrance. Enzo had told the concierge where he would be waiting for the limo when it arrived. It was precisely 10:00 a.m.

The twenty-five year old concierge peeked over the driver's left shoulder and gave a quick nod to the tenor. Enzo saw the moving lips of the men, but he could not hear what they were saying. He lip-read the words, "Mr. Santi is right over there. He has been expecting you," as he looked across the way at the two.

The driver quickly turned over his left shoulder, made eye contact with the tenor, politely thanked the concierge, and strode towards the rising, coffee-laden Argentinean. Enzo stood to meet the man and placed one of the cups of coffee onto the table. He wanted to shake the man's hand.

"Good morning, sir," said the driver. "My name is Albert Hutchinson. People call me Bill. I'm from Carson Limousine Service. I'll be your driver for the day." Bill nodded hello to the younger man. "I believe our trip will fill a good bit of this evening also."

Enzo thrust his right hand out to the round, pudgy-faced native. He knew limo drivers were supposed to be quite deferential, but Enzo preferred making a pleasant acquaintance to establishing an uncomfortable subservience. He smiled widely.

"My name is Enzo, Enzo Santi. It is a pleasure to meet you Mr. Hutchinson. I bought an extra cup of coffee. If you would like, you are more than welcome to it."

"That is very kind of you, sir," said the smiling driver. "Maybe once we get on the road. Do you have any baggage that I can get for you?"

"Not really. I do have this little briefcase with some personal items in it." The black nylon brief case sat on the floor at the base of the sofa where E had been sitting. "If you can get one of the coffees or the bag, I think we can be off."

"I'll get the bag, sir," said Bill Hutchinson, smiling, and with that statement, he reached down and picked up the satchel containing music, reading material, and Enzo's musical score of *Otello*, which was still fresh in his mind from yesterday's rehearsal.

Bill led the way out to the shimmering white "ride" and began to open the passenger compartment at the rear of the vehicle. Enzo spoke up as he saw the man doing his duty.

"If you don't mind, I think I would like to sit up front with you for a while."

"No problem with me, sir. Whatever you would like is fine with me."

"Thanks. I might climb in the passenger area later and catch a bit of a nap, but for right now this coffee is picking me up a little." Bill shut the passenger door with another smile and walked to the front of the twenty-five foot car, performed a quick pirouette, and opened the passenger's side door to the front seat. Enzo walked behind, watching the happy, pleasant man.

"Thanks. I haven't been sleeping too well lately." He bowed his six-foot-two-inch frame into the large blue leather compartment and swung his legs into the vehicle.

The driver shut the door and the two men were off on their adventure to southern Indiana. The Chicago morning was bright and fresh. The sun beamed down on the shining white car as it made its way along the Outer Drive and along the Lake. The traffic of the morning had stilled and the byways were uncrowded. The limo snaked around the park, passing the Museum of Science and Industry, some sixty blocks south of downtown. Tens of bright yellow school buses sat in front of the museum, having poured forth their young cargo earlier that morning. A few late arrivals pulled to the entrance of the museum to allow their charges convenient entrance to their day of exploration.

The automobile windshield magnified the sun's warmth. Enzo liked this bit of heat that splashed onto his body. He also enjoyed the splashes that caressed his throat.

The silence was comfortable. The driver had always believed the guest was in control. If the guests would like to speak amongst themselves, or engage him in conversation, it was their prerogative. He did not want to bother a person who needed peace in the midst of a hectic day.

Enzo was content with the beauty and warmth of the ride. He squinted, watching the apartments to the west of the Drive, and to the east, across the water, the far off factories of Calumet City and Northern Indiana that provided steel for the nation, and the world.

The car made its way onto the Chicago Skyway, the two-dollar short cut to Indiana, and accelerated.

"How long have you been driving, Mr. Hutchinson?"

"Oh, 'bout fifteen years now. It keeps me outta trouble, and outta my wife's hair." Bill smiled to his passenger.

"So you haven't been driving all your life?"

"Nope! I was a mechanic, old-time mechanic. I never really caught on to da computer stuff dey started puttin' in the last twenty years, so I called it quits after that."

"Didn't you like the new technology the car companies used?"

Bill tilted his head a bit and glanced at Enzo.

"Partly, but the real reason was that I didn't have the mind to get everything they wanted. Sure, I could plug the wires into the holes dey wanted, dat wasn't a problem; it was not really knowing a car anymore.

"Back when I was a kid they made some beautiful cars, ya know, with character. Now it's all computer designs and efficiencies," he said, motioning with his right arm, "and heck, I couldn't even fit under the hood anymore, they pack everything in so tightly."

Enzo smiled at the passion of the "Old World" American, but he also understood his meaning. Bill continued.

"No fishtails, no scalloped mirrors, no big whitewalls. It's all a little too sterile for me."

"Is it the foreign cars you don't like, or just the whole state of the industry?" Enzo asked curiously.

"Oh, I love cars, young man. Don't get me wrong. Like this car here. Purrs like a kitten," he said, raising his brows. "I guess what I like is." Bill's limited vocabulary halted his sentence. "...is—oh hell, I don't know."

Enzo tried to complete Bill's sentence for him.

"Uniqueness? Character?"

"I guess 'character' is da best word. I tink it's more den dat though. Everyting is perfect now. Can't even work on your own car now-a-days. Part of da fun of havin' sometin new was tinkerin' wit it..." he hesitated, "at least for me." Bill breathed deeply.

"Ah well, dat's o.k. I've had a good life, I shouldn't complain. Like most of us old folks, we like da way tings used ta be." Bill chuckled to himself.

Enzo knew just what he was trying to convey. Technology had improved Mr. Hutchinson's life immeasurably, but it had isolated him from the very thing that he loved.

"I agree, Mr. Hutchinson," Enzo said as he smiled. "Growing up in Argentina, my family didn't have many material things, but we were happy. Momma and Pappa loved us and took care of us. All we needed was each other. When I came to the States, I was amazed by all the things people had, all the things they owned, but I also noticed that they didn't talk to each other. They went and watched TV or went to a movie. Where I grew up, we didn't have television, but we were happy. Today nobody has meals together, no one cleans the dishes together, we microwave the food, put the meals in the dishwasher and go watch TV. The only talking they do is to complain how there is nothing on television." Enzo shook his head. "People have all the technology they want, but it has broken them apart, not brought them together."

"Dat's one ting my wife and I insisted on," Bill spoke up. "We and our tree daughters always had evening supper together." He backpedaled a bit. "I mean every now and then one of the girls would be in a play or have volleyball practice or sometin, but we always set aside dat time for a meal together." He proudly shook his head. "My wife is wonderful at gettin' our girls to talk about deir days and openin' up about any problems. It helped me, too, to get to know my daughters, ya know, understand dem a little better. I tink that forty-five minutes together helped ease the problems we all had, just by keepin us all together and talkin'." Enzo joined him.

"My family back home always had dinner together too. Pappa got home about seven o'clock and we ate about 8:00. After school we did homework and played soccer. We even took music lessons."

"I know," Bill perked up. "I tink life was more intimate. Dat's da word, *intimate*. I don't mean mushy or sexy or nutin', but people cared more for deir families and deir neighbor. Dey weren't all wrapped up in deir own problems."

Enzo smiled at the older man. Albert "Bill" Hutchinson might not be the most intellectually gifted, or the most eloquent of speech, but he was a very wise man—honest, and dedicated to his family and home. He was the kind of person for which the Midwest was known.

Enzo also showed some sadness in his eyes, even through the smile of agreement at the burly driver's truth. Bill, glancing over to the handsome rider, with the knowledge and experience from raising three girls, realized he had hurt the man in some way.

"Are you all right, sir?" was the polite question. Enzo nodded in silent affirmation. Bill was sure his mouth had gotten himself in a quandary. He had offended this important man.

You dumb-ass, he thought. Bill was also wise enough to know that an apology was not a sign of weakness, but a sign of comfort and of compassion.

"I'm awful sorry if I said sometin out a line, sir,"

"Please call me Enzo, Mr. Hutchinson," Enzo asked the driver, even as he shook his head, telling the man he was not offended.

Bill breathed deeply and squished his cheeks to the side as he pulled his lips tight to his teeth. Even as a child, this was his physical manifestation of tension control and contemplation.

"I agree with everything that you have said, Mr. Hutchinson." Bill expelled the held breath in his lungs, and the tight-lipped expression left his face. Enzo continued. "Life moves faster now than it ever has, and I think that in some ways the speed of life has outpaced our ability to cope with everyday stresses."

"Dat's why so many people are on all dose anti-depressants all the time," Bill replied. "Shoot, I saw a news show dat told about grown people so worried about deir dogs dat dey was puttin deir pets on dese drugs," he uttered in astonishment. "People care more for deir pets den dey do about each other dese days."

Enzo tied their thoughts together.

"Instead of turning to our loved ones for support, people pour themselves either into work or into things in life that meet their needs unconditionally."

"You is more precise dan I am," Albert said.

"And as you said, Mr. Hutchinson, people would rather put energy into their pets, or their work, or their gardens, than to find the relief after a long day of going home to their loved ones." Both men, proud of their discussion, nodded in unison.

"It's just a shame to see kids investin' deir lives in tings dat don't last very long."

The limousine exited the Indiana Toll Road. Bill tossed the thirty-cent fare into the waiting receptacle and merged onto Interstate 65, the men's main thoroughfare for the day's travel.

Bill pushed the tiny lever that forced the driver's side window back into its elevated position. The new motors whisked the window up in a flash. He placed his elbow on the small inner window ledge. His mouth puckered quickly, not in tension, only in thought at this particular instance.

"How long have you been married," he hesitated, "um, ah, Enzo?" He chuckled to himself a bit. The informality on the job was a bit peculiar.

"Eleven years," Enzo quickly responded.

"Happy, huh?"

"Intensely."

"I's been married for forty-six years. I got married when I was twenty. My wife was eighteen. I guess I feel a bit bad for dose people who haven't found someone to love. Either dat, or dey have been taken advantage of some way. One of my daughters married a guy who ran around on her. She loved dat jerk so much. She did all she could to save deir marriage, but he was just a selfish jerk. Now she has trouble trusting men at all." The sorrow in the old German's voice was palpable. "I mean, she still trusts her old man, but when you been hurt bad like dat, I tink it takes a long time to trust somebody wit your life again." Enzo responded.

"My parents use to tell me that love should always be taken very seriously; for once it is given it can bring the greatest joy, the most wonderful exuberance, and the greatest laughter, but," Enzo paused, "when selfishly abused, love can bring the most torturous sorrow."

"I tank the good Lord everyday, 'cause for da most part, I's only seen da positive side of dat equation."

"Thank God I have too."

With her husband off to Indiana for the day, Gwen decided to go on a sightseeing tour, but this particular tour would also be a fact finding mission. It would be an investigation of the house she had only seen by photo, a perusal of the house Enzo had surprised her with, and which may be their future home.

Gwen also felt the day would be a wonderful opportunity to meet Connie Stanza, Frank Stanza's wife. Connie had been on Gwen's mind since the events of the past weekend. Gwen believed this afternoon tour was a wonderful opportunity to take Connie to lunch, take her along on the house tour, and to divert her mind from the torment with which she had to be grappling. To Connie, Frank was missing, nowhere to be found, but Gwen knew the truth about her husband.

She had made the necessary calls that morning, and her plan was working out wonderfully. The real estate agent was free this afternoon at two, and the Stanza kids would be at school all day. Connie was happy to hear from her "out of touch friend," and agreed to the lunch and house tour.

Connie also sounded distracted. She would fill Gwen in on the reasons for the distraction when she picked her up at the train stop about 11:00 that morning.

Mrs. Santi left the Hyatt just after her husband and walked down Wacker Drive towards the elevated train. She had walked this route many times, whether shopping along Michigan Avenue or simple strolling along the banks of the Chicago River. She crossed Wacker to be on the river side of the street. This gorgeous man-made chasm delighted her every time she walked along it. Across the river was the Chicago Herald Building, the city's great newspaper, with its white stone facade, directly faced off with the Wrigley Building, built by the chewing gum family. Further down the river were the Marina Towers—their corncob shape was distinctive and impressive—surrounded on all sides by classic architecture. And far in the distance stood the majestic Merchandise Mart, the second largest building in the United States, surpassed only by the Pentagon. The Mart anchored the north bank of the river, a titanic brick building, sitting at the river's fork, where it split both north and south.

Gwen loved the sound of the river. The deep green flow lapped at the concrete banks. This was nature's blessing, the serene white noise that settled Gwen's spirit amidst the din that encroached on any city of prominence.

She made her way further down Wacker and peered over the twenty-five foot raised walkway ledge to view the fireboats. Firemen scurried to and fro, cleaning, checking, and preparing for the inevitable calls along the double-branched river and its gigantic source just east. The activity was exciting, and the sparkle of the boats bobbing in the river current sparked a smile from the viewer.

Gwen walked over to Wabash, where the train was located high above the street. The shadows elongated as she hid from the morning sunlight, sneaking between the skyscrapers, making her way to the train platform. She scurried up the metal stairs and dug in her purse for the necessary fare. The dollar was produced, and she passed through the turnstile.

The elevated train was a noisy ride out the nine miles to its Oak Park termination, but it was fast and relatively safe. She sat on the sunny side of the car and pulled out the picture her husband had given her of the possible Santi Sanctuary.

River Forest was directly west of Oak Park. They were sister cities, sharing a high school, public works, and an upper-middle class camaraderie that separated them from the more industrial suburbs to the south, and the dicey, dangerous Austin District of the great city to the east. The communities also boasted of their cracker-jack law enforcement divisions.

In some circles, the two cities were known as the home of the great Chicago mob kingpins. Oak Park was known for Sam Giancana and his tell-all daughter, while River Forest had been home to the Chairman of the Chicago Mob, Mr. Anthony Accardo. While now in retirement, Mr. Accardo had first made a name for himself serving as Al Capone's bodyguard. He was also rumored to be one of the triggermen in the St.

Valentine's Day Massacre. In the 1940s he had built a thirty-five-room mansion in River Forest, complete with a two-lane bowling alley, indoor swimming pool, and a black onyx bathtub. While under investigation by the Federal Bureau of Investigation and wanted for questioning, Mr. Accardo showed off his home's other impressive feature: an eight-foot black, wrought iron fence, which also happened to be electrified. The FBI became very polite when they encountered this energized "obstacle."

Ironically, River Forest was known for great schools, great parks, no alcohol, two huge Catholic churches, and practically no crime. The mobsters wanted their children to flourish in safe, beautiful neighborhoods, just like any caring parent would. Besides, the mob glory days were over, and River Forest was still a coveted park-like suburb that was ideal for raising a family.

Gwen looked at the picture of the home for some time, bobbing with the impulse of the train. It was a gorgeous Colonial style home with a nice front yard, lots of big elm trees, and a huge back yard. Perfect for children to play in, free as the wind, and safe from the intrusions of the world, safe from a world that would too soon intrude, despite the efforts of loved ones. The three stories, including a finished attic, provided ample space for the opera couple, and it would seem to the excited wife, room enough for the entire neighborhood.

The train bounced along the tracks, moving west through the outlying districts of the city. They passed the great Chicago Stadium, soon to be rebuilt in favor of the more lucrative luxury boxes. The old building, full of lore and history, was the only indoor building to feature a National Football League Championship Game before the modern era. It now housed the great basketball and hockey franchises.

They passed the enormous public housing projects along the Lake Street elevated train. They passed through the city's Austin District, one of the most dangerous communities in the nation. In the fifties, Austin had been one of the premier living areas for the workers of the city, but since that time, and particularly after the riots surrounding the assassination of Martin Luther King, the area's poor economic stability had left it crime and vandalism-ridden.

The elevated train was safe, but this section could be dicey. The train quickly passed through Austin, over Austin Boulevard, and into the near western suburb of Oak Park. The village of River Forest followed two miles further. The Austin train stop was followed by a stop at Ridgeland Avenue, and then Oak Park Avenue, where Connie was to pick up Gwen.

The train squealed to a halt at the Oak Park station, actually located at Marion Street, two blocks short of the Harlem terminus. Gwen hopped up, dashed down the stairway, and out to the curb.

There stood Connie, leaning against the side of her minivan, sunglasses over her eyes, shielded from bright autumn sun, but wearing a jacket in the chill of the day.

The women hugged and were off to their lunch. They settled on a little bistro in the heart of Oak Park: Winberie's.

They were quickly seated in the restaurant, and Connie removed the dark sunglasses she had been wearing. Gwen's face flashed an obvious start at her friend's appearance. The penetrating sun was not the only reason for the shades. Connie's eyes were swollen and red, the obvious result of hours of tears.

"Connie...honey," Gwen shrieked as she gave her friend another embrace, knowing the torment her friend was experiencing. Connie could hardly hold back the tears.

"Talk to me," Gwen continued. "What is wrong?" Gwen knew the probable answer to her question.

"Frank is gone," the words barely left her mouth when sobs fell and tears streamed down her stained, ruddy cheeks. She tried to continue, but she was unable to. The women sat side by side in the beautiful little bistro, huge bay windows peering out onto the picturesque suburban corner.

"What's happened?" asked Gwen, as she pulled tissues from her purse to help her friend. Connie took a moment to quell the flood, then wiped her sensitive, over-rubbed nose and eyes. Her body convulsed in inhalation. The shudder of air shook her body in its fragile state.

"Frank has not come back home since Saturday night," she finally spoke, stumbling and starting in her words. Gwen sat, listening, absorbing the hurt with her friend. "He's been out working for the opera for a day or two before, but *never* this long. And if he had to stay unusually late at the opera house he always gave me a call. I know that this past weekend was the big 'Re-Opening,' but," she began to well with emotion again, "he hasn't called, or even been in touch, Gwen." The tears flowed again. "I'm so scared."

Gwen comprehended the unspoken. She felt her emotions climb to her own throat as they had last Saturday night. Once again, she held them in check.

Her friend sat there, scared of the unknown, and frightened at the possibility of her husband's loss. Gwen had felt this same fright only a few days earlier. Gwen sat, silent, her face, her heart, and her compassion totally bestowed to her friend. Connie continued.

"If I just knew what was going on! If Frank was safe, if he was at the opera house, if he was...I don't know where, Gwen." She stopped. "If I only knew what has happened, I could do something." Connie slowly pulled her emotions to herself.

"But Gwenny, not knowing what's happened, even if he's run off with some other woman," Connie felt this unfeasible, but needed to say it anyway, "at least I would know." She sat, shaking her head, looking into her lap. "At least the kids would know."

Gwen did not know what to do or say. She felt guilty for her knowledge, as guilty as Enzo had felt by his witness, by his circumstantial impotence. Gwen also knew this moment was improper to inform her friend of her husband's fate.

"Have you talked to the police?" Gwen finally asked.

"Yeah," Connie quickly replied. "I called them Sunday, but they said there had to be at least two days before someone is considered missing. So after two days I called again and had a couple of officers over to talk about what happened," she paused in ignorance, "as if I even know what happened."

"Have they found anything?" Every question Gwen asked sounded false, idiotic. She knew the truth and she wanted to embrace her friend, hold her close in the horrible revelation.

"I was only able to report him missing yesterday morning—so no, I haven't heard anything."

"Connie, dear, I'm just asking these questions to help find out what happened, so please do not be offended."

"Gwen, I understand. It's just good to be with a friend." She then paused, aware of the implied question about the state of the marriage. "I also know what you're getting at, but Frank and I were…" Connie stopped in her past tense statement. She hated the implied termination of the relationship by the verb of finality.

"Frank and I are very happy. If he was upset about something, he never let on. Our sex life has always been very satisfying, for him and me both. He loves the kids," she began weeping softly now. Gwen, sensing through the mother the anxiety the Stanza children were experiencing at the absence of their father. Connie composed herself and continued.

"He hasn't been very happy with all the changes at work lately, and his hours have become horrible, but that seems to be the only thing that has really bothered him lately. Besides that, life has been what it always should be."

Gwen asked more questions about work, in pursuit of possibly aiding Enzo in his search for answers, and his frustration.

"What problems have come up at work?"

"Well, since last spring when the Brook money came through, the opera house has been crazy. The hours have been strange, and the new regime has hired a bunch of men that Frank said didn't know anything about opera, or even the stagecraft that they were supposedly hired for. All they did was unload the trucks."

"Unload the trucks? You mean the old crew couldn't do that work anymore?" Gwen paused in confusion. "That's hard work, but it's the easiest part of putting the opera together." Gwen, while at Indiana University, had worked on some of the student opera crews to earn extra money. She was familiar with the backstage workings of an opera house, both from her bit of performing and from that grueling labor.

"Frank was getting home at all hours of the night. The trucks from Mexico...you know," she leaned knowingly to Gwen, "the new opera sets from Mexico City. The trucks weren't arriving until two in the morning." Connie shook her head. "They made Frank and his crew wait, practically sealed away from the dock, while they unloaded the trucks. Then the props guys had to log everything in these new books they came up with."

"Have the police called the opera house? Do they know anything?" Gwen inquired.

"I've called, the police called," shaking her head again, feeling defeated. "No one has seen him since last Saturday night." The table was silent. Connie finally continued.

"Supposedly, someone saw him Sunday sometime, down in the props area, but that's not certain either. I don't know, Gwen. I'm just so scared, for me and the kids. Bobby..."

"You mean the youngest?" Gwen interrupted her friend with the question.

"Yeah," Connie affirmed with a nod. "He's not sleeping. He comes and jumps in bed with me every night now. And Lisa and Johnny are stressing out too. I just don't know what to do." There were no tears now, only the fracturing of her heart, so in love, so distraught, and so concerned for the welfare of her husband and children.

Teardrops streamed down Gwen's face. Connie looked at her friend, focusing on the compassion that filled Gwen's heart, this heart moved to grief, in concert with her friend's grief.

The lunch shared by the friends remained untouched, unimportant. Hearts poured out, one woman to the other, sharing the pain, halving the harm, and loving the one in distress. They adjourned the bistro and walked to the park across Lake Street. They sat in the warm sun and the cool breeze and talked, long and passionately, but everything circled back to the sin of the weekend and its reverberation throughout the lives of the Stanzas and the Santis.

The real estate agent met the women, hand in hand, and gave them the tour of the beautiful structure, warm with charm and grace. The home was spectacular and immaculate. They wove throughout, inspecting and scrutinizing every nook, every cranny. Up and down, slowly and surely, they made their way through, Gwen inwardly delighted, but still focused on the needs of her friend.

The dining room opened onto the backyard. The agent slid the door open and led them through, onto the back brick terrace. The women followed. Wooden fences lined either side of the yard, and a chain link defined the depth of the lot. A garden to the left snaked its boundary back and forth along the yard's north side fence, and then, thirty feet into the yard, the garden encircled a huge elm tree.

Gwen spotted a statue at the base of the tree and pulled her friend with her. The agent spoke about lot size and depth, about figures and sales. The women paid no heed.

They made their way through the verdant grass to the elm, and the guardian at its base. The previous owner had left the figure, whether in the haste of departure or in blessing, the women did not know. They looked intently on the icon.

The blessed Virgin stood before them, arms outstretched and welcoming, bidding the needy to come, summoning the world-weary to place their pain at her feet, and pleading the destitute give their suffering to her sweet Savior and child Jesus.

Gwen took her friend's hands in her own and began to pray. She softly spoke the petition for her friend. Connie squeezed the soft, compassionate skin surrounding her hands and spoke her own petition, sorrow pouring from her injured heart and tears streaming from her eyes.

Gwen focused solely on her friend, pleading the cessation of pain, the end of torment, and the resolution of this terror.

Connie leaned into Gwen, the pain of her husband's disappearance bending her will with her body. Gwen cradled this precious woman in her arms.

The sun was warm on their backs as their tears fed the grass. Gwen looked to the Virgin and spoke to herself.

"Sweet Mother of Christ, protect us in these hours of torment, and please, dear heavenly Father, protect my sweet Enzo."

Interstate 65 rolled in the northern hills, the dunes of Indiana, gently lifting the men up and down like a slow motion roller coaster. Centuries before the lake had churned this earth, grinding the rock into a fine silt that mounted upon itself, rising a hundred feet above its great glacial mill. With the caustic gales of the water, the sand sloped down, south, into the moist, saturated heart of the land.

The rolling dunes descended into the man-made city of Elkhart. The wave of the hills ceased and the limo settled into the long flat drive to Indianapolis. The rich farm fields bordering the roadway soaked in the weak autumnal rays, mulching the stalks of corn, beans, and wheat, recently harvested, promising the proximate year's abundance.

The men chatted of wives and children, even grandchildren—one view spoken from experience, the other gleaming with hope in the promise of a future family. They spoke about sports and news; they told of music and food. They reminisced about friends and loved ones, and they both thoroughly enjoyed the experience.

Thirty miles south of Elkhart, the sleek white Town Car pulled off at an Interstate rest area. The two decided to stretch their legs, when in actuality, stretched bladders were in need of relief. The roadside hovel was nestled in a mirage of trees, having survived the clear cutting necessary for farming. The oaks surrounding the few public places stood in contrast to the still countryside.

Enzo decided to attempt a nap for the two remaining hours of the four to Bloomington.

"Albert, I'm gonna stretch out in the back for a while, try and catch some shut eye."

"No problem, Mr.—ah—Enzo. Do you have any special way you would like to go? I was told to take Route 37 south to Bloomington."

"Actually, Route 67 is a bit quicker." Many a trip to Chicago had taught Enzo the fastest route to and from the University of Indiana. "Take 465 south, around Indy, and 67 is ten minutes north of the exit for 37, but it cuts right over to Bloomington and saves at least twenty minutes."

Bill slowly wrote the directions on his clipboard. He spelled out the words in his closed mouth, as his hand wrote out the directions.

"If you don't mind, if there is any confusion, I may ask you when we get closer, all right?"

"No problem at all, and don't worry about waking me up. I've been sleeping pretty lightly. Besides, I'll need to be bright and cheery when we arrive at I.U."

"All right, Enzo." Bill continued, "And, um—Enzo, please call me Bill. I haven't been called Albert since I was a baby."

Enzo nodded. Albert "Bill" Hutchinson continued again. "Friends call me Bill."

"O.K., Bill."

The two men crawled into the car, Enzo in the passenger compartment, and "Bill" Hutchinson, at the helm of the cruiser. The electronic partition directly behind the driver, separating the two compartments, was raised along with its clear Plexiglas partition and black cover. A two-way intercom allowed rider and driver to converse if need be. Enzo thought the partition should be down, and so he leaned over to the left side console in the plush leather clad "den" and pulled the tiny silver lever. A minute hum rode in unison with the descending partitions.

Enzo could sleep with the small bit of noise that might emanate from the front. In fact, the white noise would probably lull him to sleep. Bill craned his round face into the three-foot wide, two-foot high opening.

"Are you sure you want the partition down, Mr. Santi?" slipping back into his ever polite demeanor.

"I actually like the bit of noise. It will help me doze a bit better."

"Whatever you want, Mr. Santi," Bill replied.

A voice, in soothing baritonal tones, boomed over the intercom, reverberating throughout the open passenger compartment.

"Mr. Albert "Bill" Hutchinson, this is God, Almighty, the Big Guy. Please call the young man in the back seat by his first name, ENZO!"

The rider heard a deep guttural chuckle come from the man seated eight feet behind him, hidden to the left of the dark blue partition. Enzo heard a tiny click, activating the intercom.

"As you wish, *Mr. God.*"

"Thank you very much, Bill," was the less baritonal intercom response.

The ten cylinders of the limousine were ignited and the car pulled into the merging traffic of the rest stop, and then onto Interstate 65.

Enzo settled in to the elegant leather of the wide seat, kicking off his shoes and throwing his suit coat on the far seat of the limo, facing the rear of the automobile. He swiveled his body, placing his torso on the right side on the seat, and pulled his legs up into a fetal position. The frame of the burly tenor barely squeezed into the traveling ottoman. It would suffice the worn man. Enzo sighed and closed his eyes.

He opened his eyes quickly and sat up abruptly..

"Bill," he called without the intercom. His call went unheeded. He crawled along the depth of the compartment and leaned his elbow through the open compartment hole. His head popped through the partition window.

"Bill, I really don't care how fast you drive, but watch out on Route 67. The cops downstate are ruthless. I was caught speeding by a Camaro."

"Really?" came the unastonished reply.

"The police are using unmarked cars to catch speeders down there, so be careful." Enzo started to pull back, out of the compartment window "Don't worry, young man. I've never been caught speeding, and when I'm on company time I obey the speed limit, so I'm sure we won't have any trouble. Thanks for the tip though."

"No problemo."

The two resumed their duties—one driving, one sleeping. The hundred plus miles to Indianapolis passed quickly, and Enzo's shortcut was found without incident. Bloomington was now just forty-five miles away.

Route 67, as all the roadways south of Indianapolis, was a metamorph. It left the heart of Indy's downtown Circle, low and flat, and traveled slightly southwest. It crept under Interstate 465, the western hub of the city's outer expressway, and scampered south toward the winding hills cut by the Ohio River.

The transformation was gradual, but powerfully felt. The first ten miles of the thoroughfare held the last vestige of the northern plains and fields. Sprawling and vast, farm fields dominated the landscape, only now the kin of the vanquished forests to the north had found a foothold, snuggled against the creek beds and developing hills.

Passing through Mooresville, fifteen minutes down Route 67, undulating countryside dominated the horizon. Bluffs a hundred feet high ran along the highway, holding in its heart the limestone that for a hundred years had been quarry cut to build the great stone buildings throughout the state. Local law still regulated its use in new construction, thus insuring its continued profitability.

Although tremendously expensive, the majesty provided by the limestone, the heart of this land, was undeniably powerful. The campus of Indiana University was full of these structures. Classic in construction and fortified from the earth's core, these great buildings made the Bloomington campus one of the most beautiful in the nation.

Bill swiveled his head from side to side, glancing at the mounting trees and woodland. The automobile transmission down-shifted, transferring power as the car mounted the incline of the rolling hills.

Occasionally, semi-tractors full of gravel pulled from the side roads, from the quarries, and lugged up the hills. The limo driver made his way to the left and past these behemoths on their Sisyphean tasks.

Another fifteen minutes passed and the vehicle rounded one of the myriad hills. State route signs indicated the exit to Route 37/Martinsville, and then, twenty miles away, Bloomington, the final destination. Bill turned left and headed into Martinsville. Fast food and used cars filled the passageway between the two state roads, and found a foothold in the town as well. The access road between 67 and 37 skirted Martinsville to the south. The small town had weathered the recession of the late 1980s poorly. The building boon of the mid 80s had ravaged the local economy, as it had many small towns.

The access road the limousine traveled housed the dashed hopes of many 80's small-time entrepreneurs. Junked cars and an abandoned movie theatre were the last vestiges of the unrealistic hopes that led out of the town.

Enzo awakened from his subtle slumber as the limousine rumbled over a set of railroad tracks in the now distant town. He reamed his foggy eyes with balled fists and yawned operatically, singing a descending *falsetto portamento*, from scary soprano to satisfied baritone. His arms pushed forward as his body enlivened, and his lungs sprang to capacity.

He had asked Bill to waken him in this town. Enzo had glimpsed the dead cinema at the edge of town and remembered the scenery from the familiarity of ten years past. Now the car was ascending the two-mile hill that led directly to Bloomington. The final twenty minutes of the morning trip would be spent on this lofty plateau, this minuscule mountain range that separated Martinsville and Bloomington. As they would approach Bloomington and its sprawling environs, the car would descend a similar two-mile hill. The ride to come, on the plateau, would be like that approaching Martinsville, winding and curvaceous, the inspiration for the famous speedway fifty miles to the north.

Halfway up the ascending slope Enzo heard the car's intercom click.

"Enzo, are you awake?" Bill did not say anything else, but listened for movement. The partition was closed. He had not heard any movement from within. Enzo swung his legs off the leather seat and out into the broad, open compartment. His legs and knees were a bit wobbly in their support as he fumbled for his intercom switch. Bill tried again, a bit more voluminous in this attempt.

"Mr. Santi," he bellowed, knowing the polite salutation would get some kind of response if the volume did not, *"we have just left Martinsville and are*

twenty minutes from Bloomington. "Bill paused again and still no response. Enzo found himself at a loss as to the operation of the intercom.

"Damn, what's wrong with this thing?" the frustrated and temporarily thumby man questioned aloud. Again, the voice from the front compartment spoke, still more firmly.

"*Mr. Santi, you asked me...* " Bill's voice trailed off as the partition was lowered from inside the passenger compartment. The faint mechanical buzz startled the driver. Enzo leaned through the open rectangular hole and confirmed for the driver that he was no longer asleep. Enzo raised his eyebrows at the driver, who looked in the rearview to glimpse the guest.

The mocking air of sophistication was applied to the voice.

"Dear Mr. Hutchinson, be a good chap and address me by my given name." Bill smiled at the obvious air.

"I knew dat would get your goat." Bill paused as he saw the tenor yawn. "I din't know if you was awake or not. I was about to pull over."

"I woke up at those railroad tracks in Martinsville. When you called I lost my ability to operate small machinery. Sorry 'bout that."

"No problem at all. I knew you wanted to be up, so I was doin' my best ta get my job done." Bill again looked in the rearview at the bleary-eyed passenger. "You is a handsome man, don't get me wrong," Enzo was curious as to the content of the driver's statement, "but you may want to look in the mirror before we get to your school."

"Why?" smiled Enzo.

"Just take a look." Bill shook his head as he laughed. "Der's a mirror on your side of the partition, I tink." Indeed there was. Enzo pushed the button and elevated the rectangular partition until it was three-quarters elevated.

"Ooohhh mmyyy goodness, that's terribly ugly." Bill laughed again, this time with Enzo, as Bill heard the tenor discover the remnants of his repose.

Enzo had slept on his right side, and thus, the right side of his thick blue-black hair had been squashed. The hair just above his ear was flattened, pummeled against the blue leather, while the portion above his ear had been forced heavenward. The curly tendrils spiraled up like stalactites erupting from their base. Enzo let out a bit of a shriek as he pulled on the unruly locks, pressing them back to their assigned positions with the palm of his hand. The hair protested and boinged back into its upright position. A grunt and a growl came from the owner of the mane, as he set forth to tame the insolent thatch.

The driver kept on, winding through the foothills, crossing the plateau, the snake-like car obeying his commands. The tenor found his briefcase, opened it and retrieved his antidote, his trump card in the hair game, and began liberally applying the spray to the affected head. The locks soon surrendered, wilting under the grip of glue and wax. Enzo laughed to himself.

"Finally." Many mornings, as a boy, Enzo's hair had made similar protests, and his family had made similar laughter.

In the front of the vehicle Bill gazed at the road before him. A blue light flashed in his side mirror, and he gazed into the oblong reflector with its inset fish-eye lens. A black Camaro was pulling up to his vehicle, flashing blue police lights in its front window. Bill, a bit befuddled, looked at his speedometer and found it to read 55 miles per hour. Relief filled his chest. Obviously the officer would pass him and race to the perpetrator. Bill glanced at the car as it approached, fully expecting it to move to the left and whisk past him.

The distance between the vehicles closed to fifty feet, but the Camaro stayed directly behind the limo.

"What did I do?" questioned the mechanic. He thought that possibly his vehicle had exceeded the legal limit while he and his charge kibitzed over the tenor's mussed mop. Bill doubted this scenario, though. Certainly the car was powerful enough to gain speed rapidly, but the hills through which they drove would have caused the transmission to downshift, revving the engine to accelerate.

The driver wiped his right hand over the thinning crewcut of his head and cursed for the first time all day.

"Well, scheisse," was his foreign language obscenity, approximating its English counterpart. He was comforted by his total ignorance of wrongdoing. If he had sinned against the powers of transportation, he knew not how.

Enzo felt the road become terribly rough, and he looked out the tinted windows. Bill was pulling over to the side of the road. The quarter-opened partition allowed Enzo to question the driver, even as he looked out the car windows.

"Bill, what's going on?"

"We're being pulled over. I guess I din't heed your warning about the Camaro cops around here very well."

"What did you do, Bill?"

"I have no idea, Enzo." Bill paused as the car slowed along the gravel shoulder. "I don't tink I was speeding." Enzo moved to the back seat to look more closely at the police vehicle that slowed in tandem. "Dis is a new car. Maybe da plates are odd, or da vehicle sticker is different dan dey seen before." Bill searched for the reason as to their detainment.

"I apologize for dis, Enzo," muttered the contrite driver. "I's never been stopped on the job before."

"Don't worry about it, Bill," Enzo looked at his watch. "We've plenty of time before we need to be at the Musical Arts Center," the men's destination for the little master class that afternoon, and recital that night.

Both cars halted. The gravel popped under the car's weight, supported by the new, knobby tires. Enzo leaned into the back window, watching as the officer opened his door, climbed out of the modified sports car, his head down, popping his flat-brimmed hat on his head and ambling towards their car. Enzo huffed at the stereotypically egotistical swagger as the officer verified the rear license plate of the car, then peered into the back window. Enzo stared back at the man, not knowing that the officer, scrutinizing the inside of the limo as best he could, saw only his own reflection.

Bill waited impatiently to meet the man, still perplexed as to his atrocity. A flat-bed trailer, loaded with two limestone slabs, ten by twelve feet and two feet thick, freshly cut from a nearby quarry, lurched passed the duo on the embankment and returned to its required right lane position. Bill heard the tractor heave as it strained under the weight of the stones. The officer walked alongside the car, tipping his brim to the semi, glancing south, and then north at the otherwise deserted highway. The officer again attempted to peer into the reflective limo windows on his side of the vehicle. The officer's sunglasses mirrored the similar auto glass, diving deep upon itself into reflective oblivion.

The officer had to deal with the driver first. His boots dug into the tiny stones just behind the driver's side window. He rapped a knuckle on the pane. Bill peered up at the leather brim and black sunglasses. An unkempt mustache obscured the mouth of the bony-faced officer. Bill smirked to himself as he noticed the dangling earring in the man's left ear. He had always thought ordinary men looked like "fairies" with earrings, let alone uniformed cops.

With fist and finger, the officer motioned to open the window. The new motor jarred the driver's window quickly and completely down.

"Good morning, Officer," Bill said and smiled.

"Mornin'," came the grizzled reply. To Bill, this voice had the same crackly pinch as the limo tires on the gravel below. "License and registration please."

"Sir, I'm curious. Could you give me an idea of what I may have done wrong?" Bill knew this inquiry could be misinterpreted as confrontational, so he couched the words with an especially pleasant voice and smiling face, like some gargoyle warding off the demons of government.

"Just need to see your license and registration," was the scraped response.

"Not even a clue?" Bill questioned again as he leaned into the door of the car to retrieve his wallet from his pants' pocket. The wallet held his livery license. As he reached for it, he shrugged his shoulders and raised his eyebrows in a child-like plea.

The officer relented but wanted to get to the task at hand. Bill scrutinized the officer's response.

"The limit is 55 around here, not 65, and your tags are expired."

Bill crumpled his face in disbelief. Having given the officer what he desired, he settled back into his seat. He was certain of his speed. He had never been above 60 since they left the expressways to the north. *Whatever*, he thought.

"The registration is in the glove box," Bill told the officer, whom he noticed had twisted around to his left. He still did not understand the charge against him. O.K., speeding—maybe he slipped since exiting the small town now eight miles behind, but Micky was smooth as silk when it came to running the Carson's Limousine Service. Micky would never let a driver out the door without proper plates, tags, and registration.

Another whispered "Whatever" came out of Bill's mouth as he leaned across the front seat and opened the glove compartment. The plastic satchel containing the needed documents was in plain view, unobscured by paraphernalia that cluttered older, more traveled vehicles.

He thumbed through the papers, holding the satchel in his left hand and investigating with his right. He pulled his ample torso back into its blue leather driver's seat.

"That seems imposs..." Bill had not finished his statement of disbelief when he jerked his head and neck back in pain. He turned his head and saw the officer's hands as they returned to his body. In the officer's right hand, Bill saw a hypodermic needle, still spewing its contents. It had been removed before the entire fluid had been injected.

"Hey, what the he..." again Bill's voice left his thought incomplete, this time involuntarily. Bill grabbed the spot on his lower neck that had been punctured. As he touched the small dab of blood, his back contorted. He felt a searing heat thrust into his arm and torso. The contortion violently arched in his back, slamming his head into the immovable portion of the leather partition directly behind him. He was losing all control of his body. His eyes clenched shut as the full impact of the injection spasmed his burly body. The deep screech, growled from his chords, sounded like an animal that had been caught in the sharp barbs of a snare.

The man's head smeared across the panels behind him. He fought the effects of the liquid clutching him, but the outward battle was the remnant of the yielding within.

Bill tried to grasp something, to anchor himself for the continuing onslaught, but the fire was consuming every inch of him. His left arm, now engulfed in the scalding torrent, started shaking, convulsing wildly, thrashing out of his control.

"Aaahh…Gaahhhd…" he finally blurted as his neck and back again threw his head slamming into the partition. The convulsing man's head and right arm now joined in the seizure. He felt the liquid, like creeping molten lava, crawl to the middle of his chest. He gasped for air, for calm, for life. His diaphragm revolted with all his other muscles, preventing its essential drop, and thus the vacuum that forced air into his lungs.

Darkness descended over his wrenching eyes. His head slammed a final time against the blue leather partition behind his head, his bodily force sliding across the leather towards the passenger seat. He focused for a last moment, barely conscious, his spine arched, as if sacrificing himself, offering his neck to this molecular god.

He looked into the partly opened middle section of partition and, with his last ounce of strength, muttered one word.

"En—zo…"

Bill collapsed, slumping into the car's passenger seat, his body still throbbing in spastic movement. In the final moments of his violent struggle his left hand had locked onto the steering wheel and clamped onto it, vise-like. His left arm held his body angular as his face and neck cradled into the crease of the passenger area.

The man outside the car watched in wonder at the power of the injection, the instantaneous response, and the fluid's utter vanquish of its recipient. The visceral thrill, the power of the deed, found release in a whoop of triumph.

"Damn, that's some stuff," he spoke to himself. He leaned down into the open window again, checking the incapacitation of the driver. He pulled off his sunglasses, searching the cab for signs of life. The slumped driver twitched in anesthetized convulsion. The "officer" looked at the closed partition window and glanced again at the paralyzed man in the front. This sadistic nurse reattached the plastic safety tip of the hypodermic needle, straightened his body, and shoved the needle into his jacket pocket.

It was time to attend to the cargo. He reached inside the driver's window with his left arm and pushed the automatic door lock switch to the open position. He then pulled his Smith and Wesson 38-Special from his right side holster and walked to the back door of the limousine. This would be quick and easy, no mess and no problem.

Enzo gazed down at his new friend. The partially opened partition had hid him from outside view, but allowed him to see the scene in front of him.

Enzo had watched the officer, literally face-to-face, as the officer peered in the back window, then in the side panels. The reflective privacy of the inner sanctum he inhabited allowed his inconspicuous observation. All was normal until Bill broke into the thrashings of a beast.

The vehicle rocked and contorted, responding to the two hundred and thirty pounds of tough German muscle. Enzo peered helplessly through the partially lowered partition and watched as his driver—his friend—jerked and jumped throughout the driver's compartment. The spasms became more violent still, and surely the officer would help the ailing man.

Enzo shifted from his perch behind the partition to the side window, directly behind the officer yet inside the car. His face was wrought with panic. He pressed against the car's left side windows, invisible to the outside world.

It was then that he saw the needle, dripping drops of death from its hollow javelin. Enzo saw the officer mouth his exaltation and stand there, in the gravel, as Bill twisted and writhed in burning anguish.

Enzo sprang back to the partition, sensing the officer's inhumanity. He spied through the blue leather divider as Bill clutched the steering wheel in final defeat. Bill then convulsed, his spine arching, smashing his head into the partition that divided them. Bill's head slowly slid below the opening.

"En—zo..."

The passenger knew he had to do something. *Do not mourn, take action. Think, think. Help Frank. No! Help Bill.* Enzo's mind raced, lungs filled, and his head twitched nervously side to side. Why would this man want "Bill" dead? What was his trespass? He sprang again to the window. What was the man outside doing, and what did he plan to do?

Once again he saw him—the leather brim, the black aviator sunglasses, the brown leather coat. Enzo watched as he squatted by the open window, as he replaced the plastic safety cap, and then placed the set in his coat pocket.

Enzo knew this fake officer had reached inside the driver's compartment, but for what? What did the man need or want from the driver?

Enzo found his answer. The man wanted the keys of the car. They were within easy reach and would disable the vehicle temporarily.

Then Enzo heard a snap, and with its sound, he twisted his head to the back doors of the car. The sharp mechanical move pushed the door locks into their upright and open positions. The passenger compartment was now completely open and accessible from the outside, accessible to the officer. Enzo looked up and outside again. The familiar hand-held object again became familiar.

He's after me!

Bill was the means, and now Enzo realized, he was the end. The comfort of this enormous car was to become his sarcophagus. The scroll of reminiscence rolled through his head. He thought of Gwen, the love of his life, and their future together. He thought of his family down in Argentina.

Then he thought of Frank. He felt as if he had let his friend down, allowed him to be killed. Allowed an unseen assassin to rob him of his life.

Now, in this present danger, another friend, just feet away, lay prostrate, if not dead already. Outside stood a man that defied all that Enzo wanted his life to be. All the love and kindness and compassion in which he believed was being hunted by this mercenary. He had to do something; he must do something.

The evil that had occurred days before would not be repeated in his presence. Alberich would not destroy Valhalla. Scarpia would not triumph in Tosca's death. Tristan and Isolda would live to glory in their love.

This present evil, whatever its origin, had to be stopped. Enzo would not allow this contemptuous bastard to rob him of the fruits and happiness of this life. He would fight with all his might.

First, Enzo had to buy some time. The door locks had just been opened. If they were not shut again, this scene would end in an instant.

Enzo flew to the back of his passenger compartment and quickly pressed the toggle switch, locking the doors. He peered up at the "officer," marching to the back of the limo. The man had not reacted to the sound of the doors relocking, a sound that deafened Enzo like the great cannon blast in *Otello*.

Enzo leaped back to the front of the limo, to the partition where he had been seated during the struggle moments before. The gun was the officer's trump card. Even with the door locked, the evil one could blast open the passenger area. Enzo had to get into the driver's seat.

The officer reached the back doors. Enzo watched as he switched the gun into his left hand so he could open the gleaming white portal. Enzo searched the front section of the limo's passenger compartment for the switch that he needed. As the officer pressed the outside door handle, Enzo pushed the switch, lowering the great blue leather partition, already a quarter of the way down.

The officer pressed the thumb latch on the elegant limousine and pulled at the door. It did not budge. He pressed again, this time with a bit more force.

"What the hell?" yelled the false lawman as he started to get angry. The yanks and jerks became more and more violent.

Obscene exclamations began punctuating his unsuccessful entrance.

The electric buzz of the motor operating the partition rang like an annoying orchestral ratchet. Enzo was certain that the hum could be heard outside the vehicle. He looked back, keeping a watchful eye on the assailant. The partition was nearly completely lowered. Enzo nervously glanced between the two events, the officer and the partition.

Silence, more horrible than the screeching ratchet of the partition motor, erupted from the rear of the limo. Enzo's head spun.

"Fuck this shit!" yelled the man in the rear.

Enzo saw the man's right hand retrieve the gun from his left. The officer took a step back, turned his head to the side, pooched his unkempt mustache forward, and fired the gun at his own reflection in the dark, tinted windows.

Enzo winced in the expectant shattering of the glass. The sound reverberated throughout the car. Enzo jerked away, turning his head into the now completely lowered partition.

A peculiar ping met Enzo's ears. He tipped his head to look at the rear again. The window was unfazed by the bullet. Gunpowder caked the point of attempted entry, but the glass was unfazed.

Internal fire sparked external rage in the man outside the limo.

"Fuck!" the officer screamed louder as he realized his failure. He fired the pistol again at the unbowed window. Again, the peculiar ping of ricochet sounded through the cells of the car.

It was bulletproof. The new immaculate white Town Car limousine was bulletproof. The Carson Limousine Service had purchased an impenetrable car, and on this, its inaugural outing, it was being tested to the limits of its capabilities.

The assassin, now realizing the window was shatterproof, began firing at the door handle and lock. For Enzo, now was the moment. If he could dive into the front seat and raise the driver's side window, still open from the earlier attack, maybe he could drive to safety.

He looked back a final time before the fateful plunge. He saw the man, now holding the gun by its butt, slamming the makeshift hammer into the window. Cracks now appeared, chips of hardened lexan flicking off the noble shield.

Now! Dive! Enzo flattened his torso, and dove into the cab of the limo. *Get the window up, get the window up.* If this deed was not accomplished, the man ten feet behind him would surely end his life.

Enzo's torso, burly and barrel-like, scarcely wedged through the two by three foot opening. His dive slammed his back into the upper portion of the partition, but bounced him down into the cab of the car and upon the limp body of Bill. He hung there, his waist suspended at the partition's edge, grappling for the driver's side door controls, pushing the lifeless body to the right. He grabbed the steering wheel to pull himself more into the cab, then flailed his strong right hand at the control knobs that operated the mechanisms within.

He hit the door lock accidentally, but shoved it in the locked position again, forcing the locks to snap again, keeping them locked and safe.

In between his hammering, the man at the back car door heard the scuffling in the automobile's cab. He spun in the gravel and darted for the front of the long white whale. Enzo heard the gravel kick outside.

"Come on, get it," he said under his breath as he found the top left toggle of the four window switches.

The window sailed up, the new window motors happily responding to their given command.

The officer, seeing the window rapidly rise, leapt for the front of the car. Enzo, keeping his finger on the toggle switch, pulled himself still further into the cab. His thighs and shins scraped along the lower edge of the partition. He tried to avoid pressing into Bill's body below him, but he was unable to achieve this.

Enzo fell onto his right side, his back and shoulder against the steering wheel, on top of Bill's lap. His legs spun with his body and his feet began to come through the partition.

The window, just five inches from the top, closed the gap rapidly.

Through the driver's window, Enzo saw the false officer lunge toward the window. The officer shoved the gun's barrel at the closing gap. The glass bent inward, responding to the pressure, but continued its ascent.

The tip of the gun barrel slid up the rising glass more quickly than the glass itself. The metal wedge of a gun arrived at the top of the doorframe, a hairsbreadth before the rising glass.

Enzo looked at the half-inch opening that the gun barrel had allowed the officer, and saw his end as imminent. The bulletproof lexan window could not protect him now. The window and its strong new motor continued to grind the glass plate upward, but to no avail. The gun barrel was wedged between the window and the doorframe, the stuck window holding the gun barrel rigidly horizontal.

The unkempt mustache outside widened in a sinister smile. The man's nicotine-stained teeth crackled as the man viewed his captive prey.

"Like shootin' fish in a barrel," said the man outside the window, his voice seeping in the half-inch opening and falling on desperate ears.

Enzo looked up at the gun. Its very tip, rounded and smooth, surrounded only by the rectangular housing, had caught and kept open one-half inch of the closing window. The black hollow shaft stuck into the limousine's driver's compartment, sealing Enzo's doom.

Enzo's gaze, seeing the gun unhindered and pointing at him, continued up to heaven, up to a God that seemed too enormously distant, too remote and removed. In defeat, Enzo spoke the words he had learned as a child.

"*Bendito Dios, me has olvidado?*"—Holy God, why have you forsaken me?

Enzo's crumpled body lay there before the man, his hand still on the window switch, the motor grinding.

The man outside pulled his body closer to the car and pulled his face up to the half inch of open window.

"Kiss your ass good-bye, motherf..."

With his words, the officer tilted his gun down to target the round face of the Latino man, crumpled on the other side of the window. As he tilted the gun heavenward, the tip of the gun's barrel pulled backwards. The target was acquired.

Enzo's heart sunk. He peered at the small hole at the end of barrel about to deliver its searing lead. Smoke trickled out the shaft. Burning gunpowder from the previous shots oozed its residual vapors.

Enzo watched the hand, the index finger tighten around the metal trigger.

HMMMM........Bang!

The gun fired. Enzo flinched, expecting pain, heat, and death. But there was nothing. The grinding window motor, whose switch Enzo still pressed, had slammed the clear lexan plate up. The motor had closed the half-inch gap in an instant.

As the gun tilted in finding its target, the bottom tip of the barrel had pulled outside of the windowpane. Physics then aided the window and her new powerful motors. The grinding gears, finally relieved of this obstacle, shot the pane in its upward pursuit. The barrel of the gun immediately pressed up against the driver's window, but it was too late. It had closed. The gun tip slammed against the lexan, but the polished metal proved to be no match for the hardened window, which had pushed the gun barrel out of its intrusive position.

At the same instant of expulsion, the trigger of the gun was pulled. The lexan also defied the flying metal, sending the bullet careening down the highway. The tilt of the executioner's tool had proved the margin between life and death.

The officer flew into a rage, firing several times at the window that had just dismissed him. The pings of the ricochet also sent these bullets flying down the highway.

Enzo had to forcibly remove his finger from the window. He looked at his trembling hand, still thrusting the toggle forwards. He pulled his hand away with a tug greater than ever needed for such a simple task. He pulled, contorted, and slunk himself fully into the driver's seat and grabbed the steering wheel. His feet were still in the air, turned opposite to where they should be. He twisted his torso, leaned on his left elbow, and engaged the gearshift.

The man outside pounded on the window with the butt of his gun, for he had made progress with this at the rear window.

The limousine slid into drive and lurched slowly forward, Enzo clinging to the wheel with both hands. He began untwisting himself and achieving full control of the car.

He had no recourse but to press and mangle Bill's body. The limp man had half fallen into the passenger seat, and Enzo was straddling Bill's torso, while trying to move his own legs to the driver's side floor. Enzo knew that to escape he would have to move where he needed to and push with what he could.

As he ran alongside the accelerating vehicle, the officer continued pounding on the car, his snake skin boots slipping in the loose gravel.

Enzo contorted his left leg, pulling it up over the driver's headrest, and kicked the window that had saved his life. He shoved his left leg down to the floor of the limo and pushed as hard as he could into the far right corner of the driver's footwell. His foot hit Bill's immobile leg and Enzo pushed down further, landing on Bill's foot.

The pedal dropped and fuel rushed to the ten big cylinders. The rear wheels dug in to the loose gravel and spun in their tracks, gradually finding solid ground below the tiny stones.

The officer outside was losing ground on the great white car. He gradually fell back alongside the limo, and then, as the car sped away, he fell behind, sprayed with the flecks of rock, each strike stinging his body. He bolted for his powerful sports car. This bastard was not going to escape. The hunt was on, and his little black Camaro would easily catch the white behemoth that was now traveling down the highway.

Enzo kept the car accelerating as best he could. He had managed to put both legs on the floor of the car now, but he was struggling to keep the limp legs of his friend out of the way. His torso still pressed into Bill's, his buttocks pressed into the door, his body in angular imitation of the motionless man below him.

He pressed his legs down to the floor and stood while accelerating. He grabbed the steering wheel with his left hand, guiding the limo down the hilly highway. He then reached with his right arm behind and around the torso of Bill and heaved with all his might.

Bill's body moved right, sliding on the slick leather seats. One more shove gave Enzo the space he needed to handle the car and flee the evil officer. Bill's head and shoulders slid into the passenger side door, arms crimped to his side, lifeless. Enzo reached down and pulled under the knees of the stricken man and shoved his legs also to the right.

Finally, Enzo had a clear path, space to maneuver this gargantuan vehicle. He reattacked the gas pedal and the car responded with a kick. He looked into the rearview mirror and saw the black Camaro approaching like lightening. He pressed all the harder on the accelerator. The vehicle again responded, but with less enthusiasm than before, the ten cylinders accelerating at their capacity.

Another look at the Camaro, and he could see that he had cut the distance between the two cars in half. The weight of the limousine hindered the men from making a clean escape.

The flat-bed semi-truck that was hauling the huge limestone boulders was just ahead in the right lane. Enzo swerved into the left lane and filled the twelve feet as best he could. If he could manage to keep the semi to the right and move parallel with it, he could at least keep the Camaro behind him.

He pulled even with the flatbed truck with its cumbersome cargo and leveled out the speedometer at 55 miles per hour, matching his mate to the right.

The huge blocks of limestone atop the trailer bounced in mimic with the lunging car, the pale rock contrasting the red cab and trailer.

The black Camaro was right behind the two vehicles, firmly centered in the roadway. The police lights were flashing wildly. Enzo knew this was to intimidate the trucker, but he was determined to keep the black messenger behind them.

The semi began to slow down and pull to the side of the road. Enzo began honking the car horn in hopes of grabbing the trucker's attention. Enzo pulled up to the cab of the truck and leaned into his windshield.

He looked up at the confused face of the Hoosier trucker. Enzo was distraught. How could he communicate his dilemma? Enzo glanced at the slain man to his right.

Enzo peered at the trucker, anguish upon his face, and placed his right hand over his heart in a plea for mercy. He then opened his right hand as if to ask the trucker to wait a moment.

Enzo pointed to Bill's body lying in the passenger side of the limousine, and he once again placed his right hand over his heart.

The still defiant trucker looked out his side window at the object to which Enzo was pointing.

There, in the front seat of the limousine, lay a man, leaned on his side, unconscious. A red smear of blood fell from the back of his neck, dripping to the front. The truck driver glanced to the road before him, more perplexed than before, but keeping his speed constant. He tried to figure out what was going on. He glanced back at the lifeless man in the limo. He was about the same age as the man prostrate below him, completely helpless. He looked back at the young limo driver and shrugged his shoulders with complete incomprehension.

Enzo looked back at the truck driver and opened his hand in pause. Enzo thought, *How can I make him understand?*

Enzo formed his right hand into a gun, index finger forward, thumb straight up in the air, and fired twice, the thumb popping down to indicate the discharge. The truck driver nodded in understanding.

Enzo pointed, and with jabbing motion, pointed behind him at the false officer. Enzo made the gun with his hand again and shot the lifeless body next to him. He then, all the while watching the trucker, took his fleshy pistol and shot himself in the heart. Again, he pointed to the rear, placing blame and accountability on the man behind them. He then turned to the trucker, and once again, placed his open hand over his heart, pleading for assistance.

The Camaro was like a hornet, unable to deliver a blow to its prey. The truck blocked the right lane and shoulder and the limo the left. The officer swerved from side to side, looking for an opening so he could race ahead and dictate the terms of the hunt, but nothing was happening, and he was furious. The car responded to his slightest touch, but he was unable to breach the blockade in front of him.

The trucker looked forward a moment. Did he understand correctly? The officer, if indeed he was an officer, had shot the man now supposedly lifeless? And the officer wanted to shoot this young man in the vehicle alongside him? That was his understanding of the charade just played out in the front seat of this limo.

But why? Were these men criminals? He quickly answered himself.

No, that could not be. Would fugitives be traveling in an elegant white stretch limousine? That certainly did not make sense.

The truck driver came to one conclusion. If he were the man in that passenger seat he would want help, even from a stranger, and so he knew what he had to do.

The surreal scene did not make sense to him, but in that flash of a second, he decided to be a Samaritan to these men in desperate need.

He turned to the Latino man, nodded his assistance, and shrugged as if to say, "How can I help?"

Enzo smiled through despair and pantomimed. He pointed at the trucker, then flattened out his hand, pushing it forward.

"Keep moving," Enzo mouthed. He quickly pointed to the trailing vehicle, swept his arm around in a passing gesture, and then crossed it out.

"Don't let him pass," he said. "Please don't let him pass."

The trucker nodded and shifted his tractor into a higher gear, watching his side rearviews for the movement of the Camaro.

Enzo saw the exit sign for Bloomington's College Avenue, the northern shortcut into town. It was one mile ahead. He would exit there. *Accelerate at the last moment, race in front of the flatbed and exit onto the narrow two-lane road.* The Camaro would never be able to pass him there, and the approach to civilization would help his chances of survival.

The two lengthy vehicles rode, side by side, plowing down the road, now at eighty miles an hour.

The exit was half a mile ahead.

The Camaro accelerated to the side of the limo. Enzo veered the big car over on the tiny black two door. The Camaro braked and slid in the grass of the roadway shoulder.

"You're soooo dead, you son of a bitch." The reign of obscenities within the car was ceaseless. The driver's anger crescendoed with the roar of the engine, only, unlike the vehicle's motor, the depraved man's anger never relented.

The Camaro cut back to the other side of the road.

"Let me through, you cocksucker!" yelled the driver as he tried to pass the truck on the right shoulder. Gravel flew onto the road and into the grassy knoll. "God damn it!"

The trucker slowly steered his truck into the shoulder, cutting the black car off. Again, skids and fishtails ensued.

The right-side exit ramp was just a quarter mile ahead.

The three vehicles tumbled down the steep hill just before the exit. Enzo, needing to overtake the neighboring gentle giant, tromped the accelerator with a quarter mile to the exit. The limo plowed forward, its silver and white grill slowly overtaking the red conventional tractor-trailer.

He shoved harder, desperate to move the car more rapidly. He honked the limo horn. The trucker glanced down at his cohort. Enzo mimed an O.K. with his fingers and pushed his hand back. The trucker slowed down a bit and let the limo take off in front.

Behind, the officer tromped his accelerator and made for the right side of the truck and the broad shoulder. The truck driver's attention was on Enzo. The Camaro, like a black wasp, spun up to the side of the flat bed. The limo was just ahead of the truck and merging into the right lane, when the Camaro swung around the right front of the truck. The truck driver, realizing his mistake, pulled the air horn chord hanging just above his left ear.

Enzo heard the blow of the horn and looked to his right as the limo sliced into the right lane. There was the Camaro, half a car length behind him on the right shoulder.

The exit was two hundred feet away. He would miss the exit ramp and careen into the grass embankment if he did not swerve to the right. He pulled the limo wheel hard to the right. The limo shook in protest, the rigid frame, obeying even as inertia begged it to continue straight.

The Camaro and driver feared impact with the enormous car and cut right also. The gravel spewed as the two cars collided. The officer hit the brakes as hard as he could to counter his car's right-angled skid. The limo pushed ahead, up onto the College Avenue Exit ramp. The Camaro swung back around, skidding left, in opposition to the frantic driver's wheel. It swerved again, this second swerve directing the black sports car sidelong into the trucker's path.

The trucker, having slowed at the sight of the spinning cars, pushed the brake pedal to the floor. He was still going sixty miles an hour. The old man's body hit the back of his seat as he pumped hydraulics into the brake chambers. He turned the wheel of his rig to the left, but the vehicle was traveling too quickly.

The truck immediately jack-knifed. The cab buckled, slamming into the left side of the trailer behind it. The weight of the two great stones on the truck bed forced the trailer sideways, the flatbed swinging perpendicular to the roadway.

The limestone strained against its bolts and chains. The tires no longer rolled; they bounced, screeching sideways long the asphalt, under the great weight and sixty miles-per-hour of inertia.

The force was too great and the red semi-trailer tipped onto its right side wheels. Tremendous destructive power was diverted to the mammoth boulders and they snapped their chains. The huge crafted slabs slid off the trailer, just as the trailer toppled onto its right side.

Like reunified twins, the flying horizontal avalanche joined and tumbled into the black Camaro as it swerved broadside into the highway. The enormous weight of the boulders crumpled the aluminum body of the car, shattering and compacting the slight vehicle. The twin rocks, like the giants Fasold and Fafner, rolled and tumbled down the roadway, each galloping stomp churning the vehicle into miniscule pieces.

On its side, and perpendicular to the roadway, the truck dug into the pavement along the left part of the highway. The release of the great rock slabs sapped most of the trucks destructive energy. The truck driver held the steering wheel with all his might, riding his beast until it nestled to a stop.

Enzo, far up the exit ramp, looked left and witnessed the jackknife of the truck and the horrible, tumbling accident. He drove further up the ramp, which angled over and across the highway.

Enzo cringed at the sight as the small automobile was demolished with each grind of the limestone pair. He watched the truck tip over and slide down the highway, directly behind the black scrap metal.

Enzo stopped the great white car on the exit bridge directly over the roadway.

The energy of the carnage finally dissipated. The black Camaro was no more than a mangled frame. Shards of the black vehicle littered the road. Its occupant was nowhere to be found, crushed in the savagery he himself had begotten.

Enzo opened the limo door and placed one foot out of the car. He peered at the toppled, destroyed truck. He waited for some sign of his angel's survival.

Finally, the truck's driver's side door opened. The door swung up and out, like the hatch of some landlocked submarine. The man inside pulled himself up and stood on the steering wheel he had held in his hands for a dozen years. He lifted his right arm and motioned a great wave, signaling his survival. He then, in their hastily concocted sign language, waved the white car and her two occupants on to safety.

Enzo yelled to the driver in their first verbal encounter.

"Thank you—thank you, sir."

"Go on, get outta here," the trucker yelled back.

Enzo hesitated, then climbed back in the car. He drove as fast as he could down College Avenue to Bloomington Hospital. Perhaps his driver, his friend Bill, could yet be saved.

The truck driver pulled his body further up and sat on the truck's open door. He ran his hand through his hair and reached into the cab to retrieve his citizen's band radio receiver.

"Whoever is out there, this is Charlie Trotter. I've had a little fender bender on Route 46 at College Avenue, southbound exit. This is a real piece of work, and in need of immediate assistance. Copy?"

Response to the call was immediate. Mr. Trotter answered just as rapidly. He put his radio down and leaned on his demolished truck door.

"Godspeed, kid," he said as he looked up College Avenue at the distant white beast. He started to climb out of the toppled cab to inspect the carnage.

"Some little fender bender."

Fifteen

3:00 p.m.
Bloomington Hospital
Cardiac Care

James Koenig strode down the aisleways with all the majesty his six-foot frame and sixty-eight years afforded him. The great heldentenor, heroic tenor, had come to Bloomington to teach at *the* Indiana University School of Music. He had come to implant in these students, in these singers, his love for his art. His passion for song and his flair for drama had to be passed on to the next generation of operatic artist. He had come to Indiana to influence the best and the brightest of opera's future.

This is where he had met young Enzo Santi, the handsome, talented South American, man twelve years ago. Enzo had taken the School of Music and the small Bloomington Opera Community by storm.

The teacher had seen the talent immediately, but he knew the boy was singing on adrenaline alone—on the principle of his cords, instead of the interest. If he were not coached and nurtured properly, he would burn out in a few years, as many a talent had done.

The two men became fast friends, both loving sports, food, and the stage. The teacher worked with the student on the high register of his voice; the student's baritonal middle voice was already quite good. He taught him the importance of allowing the sound—his voice—to find its resonant spots, and avoid muscling the sound into a rigid false resonance. The teacher worked with the student on long, smooth legato lines, caressing the notes and vocal passages with the inflection of the text.

The teacher's dramatic coaching was less than necessary, for the student had an impressive command of the theatrical arts, but his long operatic career found the teacher suggesting a few points of stage craft that only one who had survived the operatic trenches would be wise enough to understand.

Enzo even asked the older man to sing at their wedding. Koenig happily agreed, wishing he had found such a wonderful woman as Gwendolyn Silva. Their friendship never faltered.

Koenig now strode down the Bloomington Hospital corridors, perplexed by the tenor's phone call. He himself had arranged for the little recital in the Musical Arts Center this early evening, and Enzo had been ecstatic at the idea. Now the concert would likely be canceled. Koenig was disappointed, but he knew his student was not one to shirk commitments. Something was obviously wrong.

The teacher turned the corner of the hospital aisle and looked down the remaining twenty feet. He saw his boy. His young friend was seated, elbows on knees, on the Berber cloth couches under a bay window.

Enzo tilted his head at the imposing figure down the hall, traveling towards him. He stood, recognizing the gait of the one approaching.

The light streaming in the bay window surrounded the Argentinean with a mist, a glow of life. The teacher's eyes widened at the radiant countenance of the one he knew possessed many angelic qualities, now beaming with a halo of luminescence.

"Maestro," Enzo spoke the consummate Italian word, not only translated "master," but also counselor, advisor, comrade, and confidante.

The teacher spread his arms in greeting. Enzo achieved a weak smile and fell into the arms of his mentor.

"Tell me what's happened, my boy," he said, taking his student's head in his own hands and looking him square in the eye.

Enzo told his friend of the terrorizing encounter on the highway, the assault on Bill, and the escape, aided by the kind man in the big red truck.

"The limo driver—Bill, is it?" asked the teacher. Enzo nodded affirmatively. "He's still alive, then?"

"Thank God, yes," Enzo explained. "The officer..." Enzo hated using this word for the assailant, for one who embodied the antithesis of the title, "the man injected him with something that caused his heart to stop. The doctors think whatever it was gave him a heart attack." The Maestro, arms now crossed, crumpling his brown sportscoat, shook his head in disbelief.

"Why on earth would this maniac be after you and your limo driver?"

Enzo decided the less those around him knew about the events of the past few days, the better for them. If this were an attempt to silence him, then whoever killed Frank knew that he had witnessed the horrible murder last Saturday night.

No, it would be best to keep those around him in the dark, and out of peril. Bill was completely innocent of any fatal knowledge, and he was on the brink of death, hooked to a respirator just down the hall.

"I wish I could tell you, Mr. Koenig," Enzo said, blurring the line between ignorance and restraint.

"Have you called everyone you need to?" asked Koenig, referring to the accident. "Your wife?"

"I've called the limo service; they're driving Bill's wife down right away. The police have already talked to me. They are outside looking at the limo right now." Koenig had noticed the huge white car as he entered the hospital. "They are also at the accident looking for the syringe in the wreckage of the car. Hopefully, that will help the doctors treat Mr. Hutchinson." The senior friend took Enzo by the arm.

"Enzo, you haven't called Gwen?"

"No," came the timid reply. Enzo knew the anguish Gwen would feel at this second attempt on his life. He would spare her for a bit, until Bill had been cared for, and until he could organize his words.

"No, I haven't called Gwenny yet." He sighed. "We've had a rough couple of days and this will upset her too much. Once things settle a bit I'll call her—later today."

The teacher was perplexed, but understanding. After all, this young man had been married longer than he ever had been.

The two men talked a bit more, catching up on the young man's rise to worldwide acclaim, but the conversation seemed hollow. There was nothing more that Enzo could do for Bill. The doctors suggested he get some rest. The teacher offered his home as a retreat. They would notify the police as to Enzo's location, and retire to the woodlands south of the college town to recover from the ordeal.

Koenig wanted to stop quickly by his office at the School of Music. The men rode east on Atwater Street, and turned left on Jordan, across Third and over to the "A" Reserved University parking lot.

There, the second building to the left, just past the I.U. Education Building, was the enormous Musical Arts Center, or as it was referred to, "the MAC." It had been completed in 1972 for the similarly enormous Indiana University School of Music.

Igor Stravinsky, the compositional titan for most of the twentieth century, had called the Indiana University School of Music "the greatest music school in the world." It was home to six symphony orchestras, three jazz ensembles, five bands, three contemporary music ensembles, seven sixty-voice choirs, and also housed one of the largest ballet departments in the world.

But the featured jewel in the University's artistic crown was the Indiana University School of Music *Opera*. Each and every year the Music School produced eight full productions, employing hundreds students, and not only music students, but young men and women from throughout the campus. Three full-time professional carpenters guided student crews through the intricate process of constructing each year's chosen operas. Designers led student painters in the difficult task of wafting the audiences of southern Indiana to Venice, Rome, or even Paris.

The fifteen-hundred-seat theater, with a stage a mere hundred square feet smaller than the Metropolitan's gargantuan site, provided a home for the musical drama. The school's illustrious voice faculty chose the student participants for this stage via one huge autumnal cattle call audition.

Every regional opera company was envious of the high-profile school, and many world-class houses were jealous of the impressive student voices that flocked here to immerse themselves in song.

The gigantic Picasso-inspired steel Muse, who stood amid the foreground of the MAC, welcomed all who entered her doors. She welcomed them to a night of tragedy, of comedy, or of satire, but always to great music.

This was the school Dean Wilfred Bain built, purposefully centered and focused around opera. Opera gave all the artists in the I.U. community an opportunity to perform. Symphony and singer, ballet and chorus, the entire Music School would participate in the experience of giving life to its opera.

Koenig again turned left, heading down the roadway between the Education Building and the MAC. Enzo looked up at the great monolith, built to the artistry of man, and saw hung in the MAC's great open glass facade a huge white banner. The school colors, cream and crimson, dominated the sign.

"Welcome Home Enzo—Our New Great Tenor"

The sign caught Enzo by surprise. He was humbled that his friends here would do such a kind thing for him. Great singers consistently filled the concert halls of this campus. The old Metropolitan Opera's Touring Company came to Bloomington annually, but for the school to welcome him with this sentiment was wonderful and touching.

The car descended the two hundred feet of the drive. Enzo continued to stare at the MAC. Sleeping bags lined the side of the building, curling around to the front entrance and ticket office. The line of camping gear wound around the south side of the building and down the sidewalk to the stage door entrance. The overnight equipment tapered off as the sidewalk turned left and met the roadway. They pulled across the parking lot to the main music buildings.

The stunned man turned to his teacher.

"What is going on, Maestro?"

Koenig glanced to his protégé, believing the man to have the answer to his very question. He snorted in disbelief, and in pleasure.

"They're fans, Enzo," was the simple reply.

Enzo looked back as the car wound into the parking area.

"Fans? For whom?"

As the words came out of his mouth, he knew the answer. Koenig smiled at Enzo, having just swallowed the canary. The gaping mouth, astonished eyes, and utter silence of the young singer perfectly communicated his disbelief.

"*Me?*" The hum of the engine rumbled through the car, as the men sat silently for a moment.

"Of course, my lad," the gentle old teacher said. "For you."

Sixteen

4:00 p.m.

Enzo was exhausted, again. His teacher's home was warm, even lavish, housing the collected memorabilia, photos, autographs, and posters from the thirty-year singing career of an operatic giant. Still, Enzo did not find comfort, or even an exhausted, fitful rest. He decided to take care of the business created from his terror.

First order was to call Gwen, To fill her in on the major events of the morning. Enzo did not like this idea. After seeing the fear in her eyes at his recount of the opera house chase, Enzo decided this time Gwen would only be informed, or rather underinformed, of the driver's heart seizure. This half-truth would allow Enzo to properly frame what had happened, and thus prevent him from needlessly harming his beloved.

The conversation was short, tender, and full of concern. Gwen was adamant about her husband's safety. The driver was in the hospital under constant care, but not doing well.

"Gwenny, sweetheart," Enzo asked, "remember when I mentioned, the other night about calling Demetrius?" He heard his own words, the same jumble of thoughts and ideas, the same as the other night. His words rolled like a locomotive, smoothly gliding towards a cliff-top oblivion.

"Of course, the other night," Gwen responded. Enzo felt her smile through the telephone line

"You mean, pre-food fight?" She piqued the thought of the rollick. "Why, E?" she questioned. Since Enzo was only to be away for one day, the couple's correspondence book, full of birthdays, addresses, and the needed telephone number, was with Gwen.

"I think I would like to call him—and—have him come help us find out what's happened." Gwen listened closely to her husband. She was not assured of his well being. She was concerned about his stuttered speech, but she listened without revealing an ounce of her anxiety. "Do you think that would be O.K.?"

"Honey," she spoke in dulcet mezzo tones, "I think that would be an excellent idea." Like most wives, she had a keenly refined sixth sense. "Would you like me to call him, sweetheart?"

"Could you please?" he apologized, and swallowed with difficulty, pushing back a flood of saliva. "*I* would, but Demetrius' number is with you in Chicago, and…" he stuttered, "I really want—I want Demetrius to figure out what is going on." His voice began to break. The millstone of knowledge pressed into his shoulders, sapping his will.

"Enzo, I'll call him right now, as soon as we hang up." The phone line was silent. "Enzo, are you all right? Really all right, dear?"

"Yeah," was the stammered reply, "but I'll be better when I get back to you. I love you."

It seemed a hundred years since he had told his wife these simple, but life-consuming words. He had left her just six hours earlier, and yet, he was undone. Gwen—his wife, his passion—had flashed before the stage of his mind as the roadside assassin tipped the horrid weapon and fired.

That moment, that flash of eternity, was unendurable. His life was to end and Gwen would be gone from him. His belief in eternity and its comfort was foundational, but this life, this love, the exquisite joy that this woman brought him, made him long for this earthly vapor. He did not want to let it vanish, buffeted in the turbulence of existence. He wanted life, life with her. A life full of her scent, her sweetness, her blessed soul, and her love.

"I love you with all my life, Gwen." He stumbled as he finished.

"And I love you too, sweetheart." Gwen knew something was affecting Enzo, something besides the limo's driver's heart problems. She also realized that soon enough she would have full knowledge of her husband's distress.

She pulled a deep breath and engaged an ascending tone to her voice. She realized it was necessary to lighten her husband's drowning spirits.

"Enzo, guess what I did this morning while you were off on your adventure?"

Enzo cleared his throat and asked, "What?"

"I took the 'EL' out to River Forest." Enzo's flickering mind caught hold of her thought.

"I—visited the sight of the future *Santi Sanctuary*," she proudly announced.

"Did the house meet with your approval, milady?" Enzo feebly joined his wife's diversion. "I thought it might be a bit small."

"Small?" the wife jumped in. "That house is a palace. And it's gorgeous. I loved the master bedroom. That will be fabulous." She took a dramatic breath. "But Enzo, what are we going to do with five bedrooms, honey?"

"Well, we need to start working on filling them up. A big house like that needs more life than just the two of us."

Gwen glowed at the thought of having a baby. She had dreamed of the day when she and Enzo would bring a new life into the world. She did not want just another infant, to be raised by nannies and day care, but she cherished the thought of a new life, bestowed by God, and sustained by their love.

Enzo, curious as to his wife's silence, broke into her thoughts. "Honey, are you still there?"

"Yeah, I just wish you were here right now, so that we could get to work on those little lives."

"Sweetheart, I was referring to your mother," Enzo said and giggled. "She can come live with us."

"You big butthead," Gwen laughed in delight. "You'd really be in trouble if you were here right now. I'd slap you in your big fat head. When you talk like that, you make my uterus ache."

"I need to go, Gwenny. I'll call when I know for sure when I'll get back. I want to stay and be here for Mr. Hutchinson and his family when they come."

"Of course, E. You'll be back tomorrow some time?"

"Yeah, I'll call to let you know exactly when. I'll be at Koenig's house if you need me."

"I always need you, Enzo."

"And I you."

Seventeen

The three stitches in the palm of his hand made the handling of the phone difficult. The pain was present but tolerable, but the stiffness and crust from his body's healing pinched the most supple portion of his hand. He switched the receiver to his left and undamaged hand. His right index finger pecked out the long distance number. The scab three inches below the digit tore as the tendons running through the injury responded to their orders.

The phone rang only once and was promptly answered.

"Bloomington Police. May I help you?" The inquirer cleared his throat.

"Yes, this is Tom Franklin from the *Indianapolis Star*. I understand that there was an incident on Route 37 this afternoon. I'm wondering if you can give me any details."

"The 'incident' you speak of, sir, I believe, was a two-vehicle accident presently under investigation, so the details are still sketchy."

The inquirer flared his nostrils in perplexity.

"Were there any fatalities?" The question was asked in hope and expectation.

"Yes, but the occupant has yet to be identified."

This answer from the overly pleasant operator only added to the mystery storming through the inquirer's mind.

"I don't understand. Was the body not intact?"

"Oh, no sir," was the chuckle of response. "The limestone slabs completely demolished the black car; it was almost unidentifiable. The officers at the scene believe it was a Camaro."

The inquirer changed tactics and played ignorant.

"I must have been misinformed as to the incident, ma'am." The mystery in his mind spilled into his conversation with the woman in Bloomington.

His eyes narrowed, searching for the answer to his supposedly simple question. He screamed to himself, "Who the fuck died, bitch?" The kind operator offered more information to the phony reporter.

"A flat-bed semi-truck, hauling limestone slabs, lost control at Route 37's College Avenue Exit and spilled its cargo onto a black Camaro, killing the driver of the car."

"Damn it," the inquirer whispered.

"The investigating officers believe the destroyed vehicle was carrying an illegal set of police warning lights," the inquirer's head snapped in disgust, "and a handgun was also found in the wreckage."

The line was silent as the polite woman, proud of her encapsulated recount, waited for another question. She had never before been interviewed by a reporter, and she wanted to sound—informed, even if she had never before heard of the *Indianapolis Star*. The line was silent for a moment.

"Are you still there, Mister Franklin?"

"Um, yes," he bumbled, "and there were no other incidents on Route 37 today?" The caller was powerless and biting the corner of his mouth. A familiar bitter taste met his tongue again.

"Well," the operator slowly responded, "a limousine driver did suffer a heart attack while driving, but his passenger was able to transport the man to Bloomington Hospital." There was silence on the end of the line again. The operator stuttered the finish to the day's mundane story.

"The driver is still in intensive care at Bloomington Hospital..." the phone line went dead, and the familiar buzz filled her ears. She had not bothered to check the caller ID until the rude disconnection, and she only caught the first three digits of the ten-digit telephone number. She leaned back to ask her operator friend a question.

"June," asking her phone partner, "is 312 a new Indianapolis area code?"

"Not that I know of," responded the operator partner. "I think that's a Chicago code, Annie. Why?"

"Ooohh, nothin', really. I just had a strange call. That's all."

Beep-beep, beep-beep. The phone rang again.

"Bloomington Police, may I help you?"

He strode through the great doors and into the long, elegant office. The boss, his only boss, looked out the south side windows, sucking the soft, silken tip of the cigar he longed to smoke.

"Sir?"

"Yeah." The low grunt indicated that this man was not in the mood for bad news.

Either way, the news would have to be delivered. The tuxedo decided to hedge his conversation with the boss. He, not the boss, had ordered the hit on the tenor. If this mishap and deception were discovered, he knew his life would be short, but if he blamed the dead man for bungling his surveillance, and thus getting killed, the reprimand would certainly be less severe. The tuxedo, in his best blue pinstriped suit, began to create his story.

"The man I sent to watch Santi," he stopped. The boss's head jerked around to see the speaker. He scowled at his employee. The tuxedo stammered, "The tenor you wanted watched?"

"I know who he is, Gahd damn it!" the boss yelled. The tuxedo stiffened and stopped again. The boss recognized the stare he was given, and he was in no mood to fix someone's error. He had seen it hundreds of times. One simple job gets screwed up because of laziness or incompetence.

The boss despised careless and incompetent work, and his wrath had fallen on many a man who had been sloppy enough to endanger the business. But what burned him almost as much as the incomplete actions were the messengers, the bearers of the bad news, the tellers of these tales of ineptitude. These heralds, trumpeting the arrival of inadequacy, irked him just slightly less than the former. He had wanted to kill every last one of them. Walking up to him, little junkyard dogs, tails not only between their legs, but up their asses, wearing a shit eatin' grin, pleading for forgiveness. He hated the pleas for understanding and mercy. He despised the contrite hearts that came to him for condolence.

Mercy was for the Church and for the family, not, the business. This job, this life, was for professionals; he demanded no less from himself. And to those incompetent ones, those imperiled by their own misdeeds, mercy would be offered only after punishment had been meted out.

The boss knew the up-and-coming man now before him would not snivel, but take his licks and never ask for mercy. If he were to bungle a job, it would be immediately rectified. No groveling and no whimpering. And if he deserved punishment, he would take it like a man.

The boss turned his body to the lesser and walked around his desk towards his first in command, purposeful and intent.

"Tell me what happened," he grunted.

The lesser's mind had construed the simple lie.

"The man tailing the tenor was killed."

"So, get another fucking man on him."

The lesser's brows lowered just slightly, narrowing his eyes in disgust at the boss. The short, fat boss looked at his man's eyes and saw the betrayal— and the lie.

The boss's huge right hand cocked back and swung out and across his body, slapping the underling on the left cheek and snapping his head wildly to the right. The man received the blow and did not move his feet. His torso tilted slightly from the force of the swipe, but his body returned to the front immediately, soldiering to attention. He popped his head right back to its pre-attack position and looked directly into the boss's eyes. He had seen the slow, fat arm sweeping towards him, and, if this had been an adversary, he would have pummeled him, but this was the boss, his mentor, and he knew he had to take a beating in order to get what he wanted.

"Don't lie to me, young man," the boss growled. "I *will not* tolerate deceit!" The tuxedo's countenance softened, understanding the lesson he was being taught. A red, blood-filled handprint rose to the surface of his cheek, outlining the chubby accoster.

The outburst of rage surprised even the assailant. The boss looked up at his protégé, still furious, blood pressure skyrocketing and ballooning his face into a crimson ball. Perspiration flowed from every pore on his head, while intent filled his voice.

He growled through gritted teeth, like an old dog teaching this young, strong dog a new trick.

"I don't care who was killed or who had his leg cut off or who just fucked your wife. Do you understand me?" The tuxedo stood still. The boss shouted the stillsame question.

"*Do You!?*" A slow nod fell from the student's head.

"Never, and I mean never *lie* to me." The boss's voice decrescendoed and his beet-red face released some of its trapped color.

A soft "Yes, sir," moved from the lips of the student. The lesson continued, still eye-to-eye.

"Listen to me, Robert. If you lie to me I cannot make informed decisions. Correct?" Another slow nod. "The truth, no matter how bad it is or how difficult it is to say, has to be spoken." The boss slowed, clawing for breath through his corpulent mouth and jowls.

"If I am given false information concerning the business, then no matter how good a decision I make, the outcome won't be worth shit." The student took in the wise advice.

"This business is too profitable—and too dangerous to start screwin' around with you bein' cute, especially to me. I know too many people who've been killed for..." the boss hesitated, "for lying. At the heart of the matter is trust and information. The information you give me allows me to make decisions that are profitable, both for me and for you."

"And trust," snorted the old man. "If I don't trust you and I don't believe the information you tell me…" The boss paused. "…you are worthless to me."

The student, face flushed from the crack of discipline, soaked in every last word offered him.

"And," the boss spoke slowly and matter-of-factly, "if you are worthless, you are expendable." The old man gazed into the eyes of his protégé and grabbed the taller man by the shoulders.

"Lies have never brought nothin' but problems," he said, like a parent to a child, "and they will destroy everything you and I try to accomplish. Understand?" This question was asked in the soft, fatherly way that brought shame to the hearer's ears. Never again would he deceive this man. He had too much respect for the boss to jeopardize their friendship, and his own very promising future.

"Yessir," the tuxedo said, shaking his head in quiet affirmation.

The old man patted the right and unassailed cheek of his charge.

"Good man, now get another tail on the tenor." The tuxedo turned to go when the boss spoke again. "And listen to me, do not kill him!"

The boss had seen right through the minuscule lie, right through him, to his adrenalized intentions. The second "yessir" was delivered more confidently. He was walking out of the long office when a final comment from the opposite end of the room met his ears.

"And Robert," the tuxedo turned halfway around and looked at the Boss, "bug the tenor's hotel room and phone line. That will be the easiest way to get the information we need."

"Yessir!" The tuxedo turned and left the awesome room.

Eighteen

Bain Auditorium was electric. The crowd had bolted to their unreserved seats at 7:30, the instant the Musical Arts Center doors were opened. The predominantly student audience was spastic with youthful energy. These young men and women had come to see the new great tenor, the voice of the next century, and one of their own.

The students' excitement could not be kept in check. The enthusiasm of the sixteen hundred strong was manifest in the roar of the voices. The nimble young people shouted to one another, trying to be heard over the collective din and to settle in for the concert. Many had brought banners painted on bedsheets, conveying both their welcome and their pride to the man who was about to sing. Ushers collected the percale greetings as soon as they appeared, but they could not keep up with the proliferation. Eventually, house management ceased their confiscation, after the college audience shouted down an usher attempting to collect an "I.U. loves you, Enzo" banner.

The cusp of riot would be permitted for the evening, in light of the special event and the special guest.

The violet stage curtain had been lifted and the stage had been set with the school's production of *La Traviata*. The opera's young lover, Alfredo, had been Enzo's first role while in school here, and the music faculty thought the first act ballroom would make a lovely backdrop to the recital.

At center stage, seated upon the hydraulically raised orchestra pit, soaking in the bright white concert lights, was the nine-foot Steinway concert grand piano, all twelve thousand one-hundred and sixteen pieces, meticulously constructed in the 1940s and expertly tuned by the university.

The black lacquer sat like a panther in the heat of noonday sun. The lid of the instrument was propped fully open, jaw spread wide like a great whale, prepared to fill the room with the purity of its strains.

At the crook of the magnificent black beauty, on the floor, was a tiny white star, placed on the very spot where the great tenor was to perform. The little sticker, a minuscule tribute from the crew who had prepared for the event, awaited the one for whom it was placed.

But the tiny star, unnoticed by the throng, would stay perfectly white, perfectly placed beneath its Herculean partner, untarnished underfoot, unscuffed by the young man who was too heartsick to sing.

Backstage, Enzo paced in the cavernous backstage right area, between the stage manager's desk and the white cinder block wall thirty feet away. Enzo's accompanist for the evening, I.U.'s head opera coach, Mark Phillips, paced alongside Enzo, unaware until a few moments earlier that a problem had arisen.

At the stage manager's desk, a furious conversation was being waged between James Koenig and the Dean of the School of Music, Charles Webster.

"He can *not* go out on that stage and *not* sing," demanded Dean Webster. "If he goes out there, *he will sing*, or he will never set foot in this theatre again." The dean, normally quite sedate and always quite effeminate, was insistent on the course the evening should take. If the young singer was present and well enough to speak to the audience, he was certainly well enough to give the recital.

"Charles, it's not as if you're paying him a great fee. He's singing this concert for free, so don't pull this bullshit impresario crap on me." Koenig had been in many an opera house fiasco, and he could hold his own. "Enzo just wants to talk to the kids and let them know he hasn't blown them off."

"I'm sorry, James, that's not good enough. We have donors out there." The Dean flung his arm in the direction of the auditorium. "They want to give substantial sums of money to the School of Music, *but* they want to hear him sing." The dean flung his arm in a new gesture, this time towards Enzo. "If he's here and not sick *and will not sing*, then I don't want him here ever again."

The teacher was white hot with rage.

"So this evening isn't about Enzo's commitment to his art or to those students out there, it's about your Goddamn coffers?" the teacher chafed. "You should be grateful he's here at all, after what he went through today."

Enzo heard his teacher's interjection.

"If you only knew, Maestro," Enzo said to himself.

"He's here to encourage these young people, and he can certainly do that without singing," Koenig continued.

"Well then, what will he do? Maybe a little soft shoe? Or maybe a Streisand number?" The dean turned petty. Enzo felt that he should have stayed at the Koenig residence, canceled completely, and let the evening evaporate in solitude. Why had he not let the concert be canceled?

He had thought that by this evening, at his triumphant return, he would be enlivened, sparked by gratitude and pride, both for this place and for these people. These people had helped shape him both as a singer and as a man. Tonight was to be a performance of gratitude, of thanks to his friends, to his teachers, and to his Maestro.

But again, murder most foul had whirled his life into chaos.

James Koenig was furious at the unprofessional and demeaning manor the dean was exhibiting.

"Charles, this whole evening is about money! You little prick!" The teacher's voice was now almost lionesque. "Life is not about money, and life is not about opera," he roared. "This kid is heartbroken, but he is still willing to give his heart to this crowd, and all you're worried about is Goddamn money! Well, you can shove your money up your well-oiled..."

Enzo stepped between the pair, proboscis to proboscis, and interrupted the duel.

"Dean Webster," Enzo swallowed, "I did not know my request would cause such a problem. All I ask is that, just for a moment, I can speak to my friends and promise them my speedy return when I will be able to sing for them, and give my soul to them." The dean nodded his head, but his eyes shined defiance.

"I understand," he replied, interjecting betwixt every few words of Enzo's plea. He did not understand.

"Please, allow me just this courtesy—this night, and I promise you, I will return your kindness many times over."

James Koenig believed the battle had been won. Enzo had made his argument eloquently and convincingly, and he deserved the opportunity to speak for himself, before the faces, before the young voices the university was now training.

Webster peered through slight lids, his tin black eyes searching for the decision.

"Enzo, no," he said firmly. James Koenig threw his arms up in outrage and grunted in disgust. Enzo lowered his gaze to meet the small man and study his eyes.

"I—the University has always held the policy that if the performer is unable to participate in an event due to incapacity, whether physical," Webster paused, "or mental," Koenig shrieked again, "then the event will be terminated." The injured Argentinean felt betrayed by his own, but he also knew to think such a thing was not quite fair. Even though they might disagree, there would be another day in which to greet these Indiana throngs.

"You are really the only one to blame in this whole mess anyway, Enzo." The comment from the dean caught the group—Enzo, Koenig, and Mark Phillips—wholly off guard. "If you had alerted us as soon as you felt 'incapacitated,' then we wouldn't have to send this crowd home emptyhearted." With that comment the dean half-turned away from the group and looked at the note of news he was about to deliver to the crowd around the stage corner.

The contemptuous comment sent James Koenig into the empty back stage wing, writhing in contempt for his educational superior. The two student stage managers skulked in the corner, attempting to become theatre mice, and Mark Phillips covered his gaping mouth with a limp hand.

The hearer allowed the comment to roll off his back. Enzo's heart pained from the bite of the comment, but more so for one so unloved as to speak such bitter gall.

The dean moved to the right-side stage entrance, arms pinned to his sides, in his characteristic unconventional stride and prepared to venture on stage. Koenig came straight to Enzo as the dean disappeared onto the stage.

"Enzo, I'm sorry for this whole mess. The Dean..." Koenig searched for an excuse to the verbal barrage.

"There'll be another time to sing," Enzo calmly voiced. "You told me that just an hour ago." Koenig smiled, remembering his own advice. "I will apologize when I come back, and then we will have a wonderful concert together. Yes?"

"Yes," was the resigned remark from the teacher.

At the appearance of Dean Webster the audience quieted, slowly fathoming the onset of disappointing news. The dean stepped to the stage-right podium, microphone at the ready, and delivered the crushing news. The fans wrestled in their seats, once again shocked into reality by what appeared to be a selfish, egotistical operatic cancellation. The assembly swelled in its clamorous ways. The dean's amplified voice was drowning under the tide of discontent.

"Please, let's stay calm, now. Please," the dean was now getting a bit snappish with the crowd, who delivered their displeasure directly at him.

"Mr. Santi has assured me that he will reschedule this recital very soon, and at his first opportunity will return to our presence."

The cacophony drew Enzo and his teacher close to the side of the stage in wonderment.

"They want you, you know, young man," understated the teacher. "Why don't you just go out there and speak to them a moment?"

Enzo looked at the Maestro, bewildered.

"But Dean Webster's wishes were."

"Enzo," the teacher interrupted, "for him this is all about money. So if you go out there and speak from your heart, *and* come back in a month or two, he'll get two services for the price of one." To Enzo, a move like this would be a great disrespect to the dean, regardless of how he himself had been treated.

"And these people tonight," continued Koenig, "will be more dedicated to you and I.U. than ever before."

Now standing, the audience beginning to chant the young tenor's name. "En-zo, En-zo," rocked the walls of the mauve-colored auditorium. Two young undergraduate voice majors, down front in the orchestra section of the auditorium, noticed exactly opposite them, in the dark of backstage, the handsome Argentinean tenor. The two girls screamed their delight.

"He's here, he's here!" Several of her seatmates searched and found the same. The word spread throughout the house, as the entire orchestra audience leaned and peaked as best they were able. The roar of the crowd now completely engulfed the helpless dean who, standing like a bullied little boy, cowered behind the small wooden podium.

"I don't think you have a choice now, Enzo," proclaimed Koenig to his student. "If you don't go out there, we will have to build a new Musical Arts Center next year." Enzo chuckled at the remark. "And," continued Koenig, "it will be named after the *late* Charles Webster." The teacher howled at the prospect of a student uprising. Enzo smiled broadly, acknowledging the humor, but contemplating what to do. He felt his teacher's arm softly press his lower back.

"Go ahead, son," came the paternal assurance, "everything will be all right." Enzo looked at his Maestro. "I promise."

Enzo slowly strode onto the stage of the Musical Arts Center.

The tumult at the appearance of the tenor swelled to deafening heights. Enzo strode confidently past the dean, now half-turned to him. The pursed-lip scowl went unnoticed by the young singer. The dean, arms stiffly at his sides, wrists in flapping perpetuation, retreated to the safety of backstage.

Enzo, as was his custom when entering the concert stage, met every eye that fell upon him. His head slowly scanned each corner of the theatre, offering a personal welcome to each one in attendance.

The crowd flew to its feet as the man made his way to the front of the great black Steinway. The people knew something was amiss, for no accompanist trailed behind, but that first exhilarating moment of recognition, the premier glimpse of greatness, went undampened.

As Enzo arrived at the small white decal, a broad smile filled his face, dimmed only by the fatigued embers of his eyes. He raised his arms in thanks and voiced the same, under the rolling ovation, then politely motioned the throng to retake their seats. The roar hushed to a purr as the audience regained their places.

Enzo stood, silent. His head gazed at the hundreds of students below him, occupying the first rows of the opera palace. He saw the rosy, cherubic faces of the expectant young musicians, all asmile, enraptured at his presence.

He felt for a moment like Houdini. He built towering expectation, and then flew onto the stage as if he were some sort of operatic Messiah. He could mystify with his ability and his showmanship, and they would worship him. They would adore him, a simple man who could fill a room with song.

He closed his eyes and prayed a simple prayer, in all earnestness, within himself.

"Dear Father, let these good people not see me, but see the love You have given me. And may I represent the goodness, the charity you have bestowed upon me, my wife, and our love."

The prayer caught Enzo himself by surprise. Yes, he wanted what he prayed for, but the last five days of his life had been pandemonium. The irony of thanks amid conflict did not escape him, but it did not deter his gratitude either.

The audience grew uncomfortable at the hush and the meditative man before them. Enzo, opening his eyes in conclusion, saw a young auburn-haired woman in her early twenties looking up at him.

"Are you all right, Enzo?" was the silently mouthed question from the concerned student. Her eyes, round and luminous, brought to his mind the painting of the Madonna his parents kept over the family mantle in Argentina. The care and concern, the affection from her eyes filled the home with warmth and acceptance, just as this young woman did now.

"Thank you," he nodded to the young woman, then looked into the crowd.

"Ladies and gentlemen…" The congregants hushed once again, Enzo's first phrase struck him cold. He addressed those he loved again. "My dear friends, colleagues, and teachers. I want to thank you for coming out this evening. I would like to thank Dean Webster and the Voice Faculty of the School of Music for inviting me, not only to sing, but to show my appreciation for all this School has done for me."

The dean, looking on from backstage, huffed a snort of contempt. James Koenig stood next to the perturbed dean and noticed his little snort.

"Charles, you little bitch," he whispered to himself. The crowd, oblivious to the backstage hissing, was drinking in the plaudits.

"Not only did I receive the finest musical training in the world, but most importantly, I found the love of my life while studying at this great school." Breathless delight and a quick round of applause swept the auditorium as the people acknowledged the young man's gratitude.

"I also want to thank my teacher, Maestro James Koenig. Not only has he been the consummate teacher and mentor, he is a dear friend whom I have grown to love. I consider him my 'American' father." Another small round of applause smacked around the hall.

"I must now ask your indulgence." All was perfectly still. "This afternoon I was involved in an unfortunate incident as I traveled here to sing, and due to this incident, I knew that I would not be able to present a concert with the passion and excitement that you, my friends, deserve."

The audience was stunned. Some were concerned for the well-being of the man before them, while others were disappointed at the impending cancellation. There was yet another group, cynical and sardonic, having witnessed many a supposedly "great" singer enter these halls and prove themselves unworthy, at least in their musically self-righteous minds. This supposedly great singer before them had fully met their contrarian opinions.

Enzo knew he would disappoint those before him, and he tried to console them. He spoke above the growing decibels.

"I do want to promise you that I will return in the near future and do what I am unable to do now, sing for you with all my heart and voice." Enzo was satisfied with this statement and felt those before him would understand his plight. Surely this promise to return would appease the shaken throng.

The effect upon the crowd was a bit different. Several disgusted sighs were wafted to the stage. More than one catcall was sounded from the seated group, and several students voiced dissenting remarks.

The lone man, standing in front of that great and powerful instrument, holding virtually all the musical power in the world, was powerless. Enzo's head bobbed from row to row, in and out of the aisles, searching for condolence, or at least understanding.

"His speaking voice is fine," Enzo heard someone say, "so why can't he sing?" The "hush, dear" was too late to cease the question, and too late to stop the ill effect it had on the object of the inquiry. Enzo, arms now out in pleading, bobbed his head, staving off the knockout blow that could come from any one of the sixteen hundred spectators.

Searching, Enzo found his auburn-haired Madonna. Her smile beamed back, even as her face felt concern. She silently asked Enzo a question.

"Can you sing one song for us?" The young woman's brow and eyes now pleaded with empathy. Enzo's mind was silent. The tornado of dissent swirling around him was completely shut out by the serenity of this tender young woman seated before him. He looked into her eyes and decided the course of the evening.

"Yes." The young woman's eyes blazed and a full smile returned to her lips. She did not move a twitch from her cushioned chair, but peered up at the man.

Mark Phillips seated himself at the sleek black gargantuan instrument and methodically screwed each side of the piano bench, raising it to his desired height. Enzo leaned into the crook towards his accompanist.

"What should I sing, Mark?" Enzo asked. "I feel at a loss."

Mark, another consummate coach/accompanist and operaphile asked his famous friend the simple and penetrating question.

"Enzo, how do you feel?" This was not the frivolous query it appeared to be and the singer knew it. "What do you *feel* you should sing?"

Enzo thought quickly through the evening's planned repertoire. Nothing satisfied him.

"I don't know."

Mark had seen the backstage ugliness, and he knew the ins and outs of his former student's voice, so he jumped in with a suggestion.

"Let's sing *the* crowdpleaser." Both men knew what was to come. The crowd before them rustled disaffectedly.

"Go ahead, Mark. I don't think they will settle down unless I sing."

The accompanist swept into the opening of the familiar aria, and Enzo bowed his head, eyes shut, groping for focus and concentration. The rolling chords brought a hush to the audience.

"*Nessun dorma, nessun dorma.*" The great Italian aria from Puccini's *Turandot*, with its lilt and expansive range, engulfed the house. The call went throughout Peking, searching for the secret of the singer's name, the name that would impose tragedy upon the immaculate princess.

His eyes still sealed, the high lyric melody flowed from the throat of the singer. He, the singer, was the one who sang of his love for the great princess, the one who had brought death to all previous suitors.

She, Turandot, groped for his name, the word that would bring her freedom from this heretic. The name, the identity of the mysterious man who had conquered her riddles and reached into her heart, must be found.

Enzo started. There it was. Through this great operatic aria came the intensity, the identification for his performance.

Just like the mythical Princess, he, Enzo Santi, desperately searched for the name of the one who meant death. Puccini's princess believed death would take her when she would be given to this infidel. Enzo had met Death five days earlier. He bore witness to death's deed. He had felt death's destructive power within him. He had fumbled in death's shadow, but escaped.

But Enzo could not unite Death with its dark human appellation. The tattoo, the tuxedo, and the sound of the gun scraping from its leather holster: Death had wrapped his fingers around these objects, around this man, and tooled them to his ends.

"*Nessun Dorma,,* you shall not know my name," spoke Death to Enzo, the thought tumbling in his head.

Enzo's breath stopped inside him. he gasped, inelegantly forcing the last words of the phrase from his lungs. His warm brown eyes, the traitors of his heart, were kept firmly closed, hiding the agony.

Mark continued playing the aria's small choral section, preparing the final vocal ascent, glancing at his friend, bent forward slightly, pressing his hands and fist into his palm. Mark sang with his fingers, wafting the rapturous melody from the steel bands within the great instrument.

Vincerò, Enzo thought. Puccini's next line within the music, "*vincerò,*" "I shall be victorious!" Enzo's mind hopped forward, past his next music. *I shall be victorious,* he thought. Just as Calaf, Puccini's hero swore victory, Enzo, within his searching, swore to himself, "I shall not allow these horrors to continue and remain unpunished. I cannot. I must find the perpetrators of these crimes." And in those precious moments of musical interlude, seconds where he gathered his instrument for the climatic finale, his mind, forced on thoughts of horror, reached a conclusion.

"This must be so, even if I must sacrifice myself for those I love." And as he anticipated the aria's triumphal conclusion, he spoke to himself, "God help me."

The audience heard the struggle within the performer, believing only in the performance. For them, his temporary anguish was the essence of the great singer. They watched his closed eyes for signs of awakening, disturbed initially at the lack of communication, of detachment from them, but the heart that poured forth from this voice embraced them. The voice caressed them with its anguish and its struggle—not in the production of the sound, but in the consummate tenderness of its delivery. They fell silent, pressed to the back of their chairs in rapture.

The teacher and the dean stood backstage. The dean was finally silent, taken by the moment, cleansed of the bitter rage that had engulfed him earlier. Charles Webster surrendered to the caress of the sweet hymn of love, delivered by a man who had shown him only kindness.

The teacher, in both grimace and ecstasy, smile and sorrow, stood proud of the young man whom he had taught, with whom he had had the privilege to fill his life these remaining years. But Enzo had also taught him. While the teacher coached the music, the student coached him in the joy of loving. Enzo had taught him that music was merely the outward expression of the love and passion in your heart. Koenig had expressed to his student the notes on the page, but Enzo had instructed his teacher in the expression of life.

The glacial moments of musical exquisiteness quenched the disturbed, and calmed the earlier storms of discontent. In acute anguish, closed behind the curtains to his mind, this man lifting his voice before them gave of himself, gave what they could not understand, so that they might experience the rapture of the moment.

"*Vincerò!*" The tenor's high 'B' hung in the air, pulsing with energy, shaking the rafters of the hall, lifting the hearer with the voice, vibrating in their chests, and resonating in their minds.

Finally, as if descending from Olympus, the singer descended with his touch of grace, and finished the victorious word as the piano rumbled its final chord.

There was silence.

The auditorium was utterly hushed. The aria rumbled through the recesses of the audience's mind. At that moment, during those crackling seconds, the faintest whisper would have disturbed the stillness of the fragile moment.

Enzo was also silent. The piano and player sat motionless. The vibration of transcendence fogged the room.

Enzo stood before them, perfectly, outwardly quiet; frantically, inwardly distraught.

Dean Webster stood backstage with his hands over his heart, gasping for breath. The teacher, James Koenig, radiated pride.

He had been known as a singer rich with emotion, but Enzo had embued his voice, knowingly or not, with the very sinews of life, with the essence of emotion. Enzo's heart and his soul traveled to the listener through the strains of opera.

The teacher was too old to be musically jealous, but as he stood and beheld the touch of God, he felt his selfishness cleansed from him. He remained still, with the audience, and rejoiced as he viewed the mistakes of his life washed away. The love of which his student had spoken, finally, truly touched his heart.

The creep of silence broke into crackles of applause. The eruption, attempting to refrain from shattering the pristine landscape of silence, broke slowly, edging through the surface of stillness and igniting the crowd. Then a wave of full ovation broke the layers of serenity, and the Musical Arts Center burst into cascades of overwhelming praise.

The crowd rose to its feet, seats not able to contain their onslaught of jubilation. The same people who had so recently grumbled stood, overwhelmed by the sensation transubstantiated to their hearts, via the voice and passion of their Enzo Santi.

Enzo, withstanding the flow of applause, remained still and thought of the young Madonna, the kind woman who had offered herself to him. This student had given the impetus, the love via her affection, not only to perform, but also to sacrifice himself to these people.

He tilted his head slightly to the left, opening his eyes on the spot where she was seated. The crowd around, flailing in joy, was invisible to him. He wanted only to see his young Madonna.

There she stood, amidst the throng, smiling, looking directly into Enzo's eyes. The singer's heart, lifted by this one, this "holy" one, was full of gratitude. He knew he must sing one more song. He must give this song as a thanks offering to this angel of God who had calmed his fears and who had directed his thoughts in moments of despair.

The tumult in his mind remained, but just as his precious wife and only love had brought him stability in turmoil, this heavenly envoy had focused his heart and mind.

Enzo motioned the crowd to silence. As he acknowledged them, their eruption of applause found new heights, reaching levels of intensity that had never before been found in this place.

Knowing that he would not so quickly silence the onslaught, Enzo let his arms move over his heart, thanking the crowd for their appreciation. The audience settled down and took their places at the further instigation of the singer.

"Ladies and gentlemen, thank you for your kindness and your warm reception. Honestly, I must retire," moans came over the never satisfied public, "but I would like to sing one more song."

"This final song, I would like to dedicate it to a young woman who has helped me very much this evening." The audience tittered with delight. "Thank you so much for your patience, and I look forward to returning to give you a full night of singing." Enzo turned to his accompanist.

"You know, don't you?" asked Enzo of Mark.

"I think so," replied the smiling pianist as he mouthed the title to the aria.

Enzo's head bowed in concentration and Mark flipped his music to the appropriate song. Enzo breathed, almost violently, forcing the breath low and deep, into the small of his back. This little ritual energized his body, tingled his lungs, stretched them to operatic capacity, and prepared him for the feat to be undertaken.

Mark placed his fingers over the ivory keys and pressed into the board, beginning the flow of sound, the low, rumbling introduction to the heart-wrenching aria. Mark's left hand, having filled out the previous chords, took the descending melody and snaked low into the depths of the scale. With his smallest finger he touched the final note of the introduction. Alone and hushed, the low "B" sounded in the silent auditorium, reverberating from the great instrument, and seeped into the floor, into the wood, and into the hearts of the audience members.

Silence.

Kuda, kuda, kuda vi udalilis vesni moyei zlatiye dni?
"Oh where, where have you gone, golden days of my youth?

Enzo sang the first phrase, the simple opening half step *"kuda,"* not with his voice, but with the fiber of his soul. The anguish in his heart and in his head began as a trickle, ebbing through the great Tchaikovsky aria. The plaintive moan of the tragic "Lensky," trapped in his plight, sank into Enzo's heart. The pain of this fictional character, and his impending death, clenched Enzo's voice with its torment, suffocating the man while sensitizing his voice.

Enzo's face wrenched with the thoughts, all now being played out in his own life.

Shto dyen gryadushchi mnye gotovit?
What does the coming day hold for me?

Yevo moi vzor naprasno lovit: V glubokoi mglye tayitsa on!
My gaze searches in vain: All is shrouded in darkness!

Nyet nuzhdi; prav sudbi zakon!
No matter; Fate's law is just!

The words pulled at the great singer, taunting him through each turn of phrase, each moment of musical tension. The pain of the death, the pain of regret, all haunted his heart, in perfect sympathy and perfect harmony with the great composer and his tragic young poet.

Padu li ya strloi pronzyonni, Il mimo proletit ona, V syo blago; bdyeniya
Should I fall, pierced by the arrow, or if it fly wide, tis all one; both

I sna Prikhodit chas opredelyonni! Blagoslovyen I dyen zabot,
Sleeping and waking have their hour! Blessed is the day of care,

blagoslovyen I tmi prikhod! Blesnyot zautra luch dennitsi I zayigrayet
blessed also, the coming of darkness! Early now, the dawn gleams and

yarki dyen, A ya, bit mozhet, ya grobnitsi soidu vtayinstvennuyu syen.
the day brightens, while I, perhaps, will enter the shadow of the grave.

I pamyat yunovo poeta poglotit myedlennaya Lyeta.
And the memory of a poet will be engulfed by Lethe's stream.

Zabudet mir mnya no ti! Ti....ti.....Olga...
The world will forget! But you....you....Olga...

The piano filled the hall with the short interlude, wafting through the sentiment just expressed by the words. Enzo heard the piano finish the florid phrase, and it waited for him to enter again, but he could not sing any more. Enzo could not sing this aria. He simply could not continue.

The words meant too much. Each phrase pounded within his heart. His voice could not suffer the anguish of this song, bathed in his real life sorrow. As he spoke the simple word "Olga," his voice quivered, faltering, as if his mind called to his own love, the woman God had given him, now hundreds of miles away. His head bowed low with the utterance of the woman's name, heard by the audience as the composer intended, but heard to Enzo, as the name of his wife: Gwendolyn.

The piano halted, waiting for the singer's re-entrance. Silence. The singer, head still bowed, did not move. His shoulders heaved slightly, perceptible only to Mark. The accompanist saw sweat fall from the face of his friend, then nothing. Stillness.

The audience grew uncomfortable with the held silence, and with their own tightening chests, straining under held breaths. Stillness.

Mark, seeing his friend in trouble, slowly played the little interlude once again, hoping to give Enzo the extra moment he needed to complete the aria.

Enzo heard the piano play his segue again, but he could not. Tears now fell and stained the wooden floor of the MAC stage, mingling with the perspiration that had fallen from the same cheeks.

Enzo cracked open his eyes, searching for an answer to this moment. He looked to his Madonna, only her, pleading for strength and guidance.

There she was, face bright and round, beautiful, perfect, filled with hope, joy, and love. Not only in her radiant purity did she speak to him, Enzo saw in her, in the very nature of this young woman, the face of his wife. His internal logic knew it to be the student from moments before, but he saw only his wife's face transposed upon this woman.

Again he pleaded to the woman, with his eyes, for solace, and once again she nourished his ailing heart.

She spoke to him, in the tumultuous interlude; she spoke as wife to husband, as lover to loved, and as soul to soul.

In silent understanding, in loving nurture, in that moment, Enzo saw the delicate lips of his wife speak.

"It's all right, Enzo. I love you. I eternally love you, only you."

Enzo felt the breath of his wife on his cheek, he felt the breath of his wife fill his lungs, and he felt the warm breath of his wife fill his heart.

Under loving hypnosis, the singer's lungs drew in the cool auditorium air and the man drew himself up, engulfing the fullness of his wife's essence.

Enzo's voice shimmered forth, almost imperceptibly, in an elegant *pianissimo*, round and full, warm and focused, breathing the next phrase.

Skayzhi, Pridyosh li, dyeva krasoti,
Say, will you come, maid of beauty,

slezu prolit and rannei urnoi I dumat:
to shed a tear on my untimely urn and think:

On menya lyubil! Onmnye yedinoi posvyatil rassvyet pechalni
He loved me! To me alone he devoted the sad dawn of his

zhizni burnoi! Akh Olga, ya tebya lyubil,
storm-tossed life! Oh Olga, I loved you,

tebye yedinoi posvyatil rassvyet pechalni zhizni burnoi,
to you alone I devoted this storm-tossed life,

The words stung the singer. Their complete perception of his life
sapped him of strength. But just as he diminished, the consummate love
he felt, the charity that emanated from this angel of heaven, transferred
this pain from his heart to her own. This divine presence, this surrogate
love filled his heart with glorious power and enlivened his voice with an
essence of passion, lifting him to the climax of the musical phrase.

In turn, Enzo sang to the point of the congregation's pain. He touched
their agony with his voice, and then in sweet, lyric breath, soothed the
hurt, the exquisite ache flowing from his mouth.

The afternoon's simple prayer, offered from the supplicant wife before
the Blessed Virgin, in behalf of the suffering husband, had flown to its
intended, and now met every need as it was expressed.

The overwhelming emotion that poured forth from Enzo washed the
congregants in its saving and uplifting power. The audience submitted to
the thrill, to the passion that they were witnessing. People began sobbing,
others could not catch their own breath, as they watched the breath of
God, this sacrifice of love, douse them in its beauty, all via the voice and
breath of this transfixed singer.

The sensations climaxed with the aria.

Akh Olga, ya tebya lyubil! Serdyechni drug,
O Olga, I loved you! My heart's beloved,

zhelanni drug, Pridi, pridi!
my only desire, come, oh come!

Zhelanni drug, pridi, ya tvoi suprug, pridi, pridi! Ya zhdu tebya,
My desire, come, I am your betrothed, come, come! I wait for you,

zhelanni drug, Pridi, pridi; ya tvoi suprug!
My only desire, Come, come; I am your beloved!

Kuda, kuda, kuda vi udalilis, Zlatiye dni, zlatiye dni moyei vesni?
Where, oh where, where have you gone, golden days of my youth?

The vibration from the tenor, the intensity of sound in the last few
phrases were perfectly countered by the pristine voiced *piano*, sung through
the last notes of the aria.

Enzo knew Gwen to be present, for she was inside of him, breathing love into his broken body. His eyes closed as the turbulent aria came to a close. His chest was raised high, his arms were limp at his side, and his eyes were tightly shut. He had been the recipient of his wife's sacrifice, and that sacrifice had let him survive.

The hall was utterly still, completely hushed. These good people had just heard the articulation of the divine, in its complete power, and in its exquisite tenderness. The palpable intimacy of this music stirred their hearts as never before, and these sacred moments had to remain undisturbed.

Tears poured from his eyes, but only his eyes. His powerful body stood tall and quiet.

The air was charged with holy energy, finally erupting in wave after wave of "bravo." The hall was silent no more, for the joy bestowed upon the audience must be repaid, it must be released in unworthy appreciation.

Enzo stood motionless. He lowered his head to spy his Madonna, his wife. His eyes glanced over the crowd to find the seat from where she had offered her strength. His eyes focused on her place and looked for her there.

The seat was empty. No one was there. She was gone. This auburn-haired cherub was not to be found.

This angel had delivered her message. This lovely one had, through the prayers of the Holy Mother and his immaculate wife, lifted him up in his time of weakness, and was now gone. God had allowed him the opportunity to receive this blessing in his moment of acute brokenness.

As the throng screamed their adoration, this physical tower of a man stood before them, weeping tears of thanks and gratitude.

Andantino misterioso:

parlando animato

*Music is a thing which delighteth all ages,
and beseemeth all states; a thing as seasonable
in grief as in sorrow*
— Richard Hooker —

Nineteen

Enzo dragged his way out of the new black limousine that had been sent for him. He tipped the driver generously, finding it ironic that this man was intact, and finding it tragic that the previous driver was fighting for his life. Enzo had purposefully kept the driver distant, unlike his gregarious nature. He had remained in the passenger compartment. He did not sit in the forward compartment, not for one moment. Enzo did not sleep during the four hour passage. He had attempted to study *Otello* for his upcoming engagement, but his thoughts were not on his work.

Each car that passed the limousine, each police vehicle that sat on the side of the road, every black sports car, every single blare of a honking car horn, each occurrence of the ordinary jolted the irritated nerves of the emotionally sensitized young man.

Unexpectedly, the limousine driver pulled off the side of the expressway. The tenor's heart came out of his chest. Enzo vaulted to the open partition between the two compartments.

"What's happening?" he panicked, shouting to the driver. The driver jumped at the verbal attack and pumped the brakes powerfully, slamming and sliding the stretched car in the gravel of the embankment.

"Mr. Santi, sir!" spasmed the driver.

"What's the matter?" Enzo quickly shot back. "Why are we stopping?"

"The oil light on the dashboard lit up, and I wanted to check the oil," he said loudly, but politely responding to his charge. The driver swallowed the apple that had lodged in his larynx. "If we are low, I need to fill it up." Enzo's brow and pulsing neck veins told the driver that this man was responding to something more than met his eye.

"Sir, we don't have to stop," stuttered the driver, a young man of no more than thirty. "We can keep driving until we come to a rest stop on the highway, sir." The young man, having fully stopped the vehicle and craning over his shoulder at the singer, tried to appease the man. Enzo's head darted from side to side, searching each of the limo's windows. He searched and found naught. He moaned to himself, expelling the putrid, horrified breath. He knew he was on the verge of becoming totally irrational.

"No, I'm sorry," apologized the frazzled Argentinean, gathering himself with a fresh breath. "I'm sorry for scaring you. I thought there was a problem." Enzo slid into the seat that abutted the partition, twisting his body as he rubbed the leather seat.

The driver, knowing of the previous day's "heart attack" reassured the passenger.

"Sir, I promise everything is fine. I'll check the oil and be right back, I promise."

"O.K.," was the weak, elderly response.

In less than two minutes the oil had been checked, filled, and the men were back on their way to the Windy City. The boy driver apologized.

"I'm sorry I didn't alert you to what was happening."

"That is quite all right. I just really want to get back to Chicago."

"Hour and a half more, sir," the driver said cheerfully. "We'll be there, lickitty-split." Enzo climbed back into the rear seat and tried to calm himself. That task was not easily accomplished.

"Thanks very much, sir." The limousine pulled out of the Hyatt's circle drive and headed for home. Enzo arrived at his hotel room directly and opened the door without delay.

Six feet before him, in the doorway, was his wife, his radiant angel. She came to him. Her gaze, her warm, bright almond eyes were draped by golden tendrils wisping from the delicate strands pulled back from her ivory cheeks.

Gwen, having heard the door, had left her guest and run to the apartment entrance. She was expecting her love, and his arrival caused all other activity to cease.

There he was, satchel and briefcase in opposite hands, dropping them as he caught sight of her. She closed the gap and ran into his arms. They embraced, held tight, and rocked in weary motion.

Enzo took Gwen's face in his hands, each palm caressing each cheek, and gazed into each almond eye.

"This has been the longest day and a half in my life, sweetheart," Enzo spoke. "I couldn't wait to get back to you." They kissed and embraced once again.

"Enzo, look at me." The man looked, not having looked away. "Are you all right?"

"Yeah, Gwenny," he reassured, "I'm O.K. I just need to tell you a couple of things later." Gwen pulled Enzo into the living room.

"We have company, sweetheart." Enzo looked up from his wife and saw across the room, down the two steps into the apartment, a tall, black man. His head was shaven and glowed under the lights of the room. His goatee drew his face into an angular point, accentuating his eyes and steely gaze. This gaze, although hardened and tooled by his trade, broke into a broad smile at the tenderness of the couple, and at the entrance of his friend.

Enzo, matching smiles, rushed into the room and greeted the visitor. "Demetrius! Thank God you are here!"

The afternoon among friends passed without the usual frivolity. The normal casual conversation was dispersed with quickly. Everyone was fine; Demetrius's investigative business was thriving, and life was the usual hectic experience it always had been. And besides, the friends had kept tabs on each other after both had left the CGO.

They had met during Enzo's apprentice years and while Demetrius was working security at the Illinois State Theatre. The stage door security desk was one of Demetrius's primary responsibilities, and thus he was responsible for allowing all comers and goers within the opera house. Singers, orchestra members, conductors, chorus, food service, anyone or anything that had business in the opera house entered through the stage door.

The men had become friends over the three years Enzo apprenticed at the Opera Center, and Enzo was the person who encouraged the intelligent young man to higher things.

Anthony Demetrius McDies came from a lower middle-class family, the youngest of three boys in a family of five children. He was a tough, funny kid who was honed under the oppression of his older brothers. This tutelage had toughened the scrawny youngster. Playing catch up to those older than him had taught him a strong work ethic and had instilled in him an unshakable desire to reach his goals.

He loved athletics and was always a player, working twice as hard as the stars, but never reaching their level of natural performance. His grades in school were good, even above average, but not great, again achieved under strict drive, determination, and parental supervision.

He had a stable home with mother and father both present until his late teens. His father had worked security at the opera house for forty years, and his mother worked for a dry cleaner. They supplied their children's needs and showered them in love and attention, while denying themselves in order for the children to have the more.

Demetrius's father died when he was seventeen, a heart attack claiming another middle-aged African-American male. He loved his father and missed him deeply, and had lashed out at others through his loss. He knew it was untrue, but he felt abandoned by his father, and mourned through several years of aimlessness.

Once out of high school, he knew he had to go to work. College was out of the question financially, except for a psyche class and a criminal justice class he had taken at Triton Junior College in the western suburbs. He did not know where to turn, so he again turned to his father for at least a partial answer.

Demetrius began working security at the Illinois State Theatre when he was nineteen. He slugged through six years of the menial tasks before he met Enzo.

The vibrant young singer had been a playful and delightful comrade, but the two men, similar of age, stature, and intelligence, were slow to friendship.

Demetrius had been leery of operatic folks. He had seen the backbiting, the politics, and the self-obsession. He had observed the gross excess of conductors, singers, and musicians, abusing themselves physically, mentally, and sexually, and he had seen the destruction this life reigned on families. He had come to enjoy the music and appreciate the art form, while despising the participants.

So when the young handsome South American tenor showed up, he thought Enzo to be another decadent, egotistical, self-esteem-starved musician. It did not take long for him to notice a marked difference in the Argentinean man.

Enzo had taken time to talk to him, a "lowly security guard." Few singers did this, let alone the "elite" up-and-comers selected for the CGO's Young Artist Program.

Enzo enjoyed the budding friendship, while also noticing the distance that his American friend kept. Sports were always a topic of conversation, but the young singer noticed in this young man a real affinity for investigative work. The classes he had taken at Triton Junior College whetted Demetrius's appetite for this work, and as hobby, he had done his best to keep up with much of the latest surveillance and investigative technologies.

Enzo also saw in his friend a love of learning and of history. At first sight, this security guard seemed shy and retiring, even a bit suspicious, but behind the outer stratum of apprehension lay an unfocused thirst for knowledge.

"Knowledge is the key to success," was one of Demetrius's favorite little phrases. Enzo had heard it many times, and yet Enzo saw a man trapped in a job that did not let him express or cultivate his desires.

Enzo, not great in school but loving the history of his art, prodded his friend to go back and continue his education, however and wherever possible.

"Sure, that's easy for you to say, with all the money you have," was Demetrius's immediate response. Enzo understood the pointed statement on every level it was intended.

"Listen, Demetrius, you are my friend, but you don't really know me, just as I don't really know you. I know you didn't grow up with a lot of stuff. Neither did I. I was a scrawny kid, growing up poor in Argentina, so don't tell me about money and life.

"I know I was given a gift, but I've worked hard at developing my voice. I've been training for fifteen years, learning how to phrase, how to breathe, how to sing." Enzo asked an unexpected question. "You know how long a doctor studies? Eight years—twelve at the most." Demetrius knew he had misspoken, but Enzo continued with his point. "My family didn't have money, but we sacrificed for each other. I knew that I needed to come to the States to train, so I packed up, not knowing a soul, took out thousands of dollars in loans, and worked my butt off to get where I am today." Enzo paused. "And I'm still a struggling artist." Demetrius shrunk back and away. Enzo, ending the assault, stepped towards Demetrius. Demetrius knew Enzo was sympathetic to his situation.

"Listen, my friend, you are very intelligent and very gifted. You just need to go out, get your education, and find out what you love to do. Then go out and do it."

Enzo's words were key in Demetrius's decision to work for a degree, committing to sacrifice his present for a future of vast rewards.

Demetrius continued working at the opera house while taking night classes. Enzo, having a small, stable income at the Opera Center for Young Artists, even co-signed one of Demetrius's student loans. The two men found great humor in the proverbial "blood and turnip" scenario.

Then, after several years of struggle and the toil of nineteen-hour days, the young security guard earned his college degree in criminal justice, with a minor in psychology. Enzo and Gwen were present and conspicuous at the ceremony, and at the all-night celebration with family and friends, for Demetrius was the first of his family to achieve such an honor.

Demetrius thanked his family, and more specifically, his father, who even though absent, had inspired him through the words of his good friends. Enzo loved the little speech.

After several years involved with organized law enforcement, Demetrius invested once again in himself, establishing an investigative business. He was his own boss, his own man, and within these bounds he flourished.

The friends were never distant in each other's minds, despite times of infrequent communication and months of separation.

"When did you arrive, my friend?" Enzo asked, sipping the tea his wife had brought to him. Gwen sat next to her husband, holding his arm.

"I flew in this morning from Minneapolis," was the full, mellow bass response from the friend. "I booked the flight as soon as Gwen called." Demetrius leaned back into his comfortable chair and looked at his friend.

Demetrius could see the weary heart that beat in the chest of Enzo. He saw the face, lined with concern and solicitude, and his shoulders, always held high and strong, sagged under a weight that he could not bear alone. Enzo fidgeted and wrung his hands, unable to quiet the raging emotion behind them.

Enzo was the same man he had come to know and love, blood brothers in life, but the crush of Atlas now tolled upon weakening shoulders.

Enzo jabbered about the ride to Chicago, and about the shortest concert of his life, but he masked what he truly wanted to say. Gwen was puzzled, but attentive to her husband's rambling.

"Enzo," Demetrius firmly interrupted. "Enzo, please!" The hearer stopped, feigning a smile, and looked Demetrius in the eye. As quickly as he spied the dark round orb he looked away.

"Gwenny told me what happened." Demetrius spoke slowly and articulately. "You don't need these histrionics, and you don't need to pretend to be someone other than yourself. I'm here to find out what happened, and to bring Frank's murderer to justice." A weak smile appeared across the singer's fatigued face.

"Now, let me take the burden you've borne, and I'll carry it for a while."

"Thank you, Demetrius," Enzo uttered through tear-filled eyes. The torrent of emotion, the witness to Frank's murder, and the dreadful encore of Albert Hutchinson's attempted and unconfessed murder, all this broke through the wall of stoicism Enzo had built, protecting, he believed, himself and his wife from further harm.

Sobs streamed down the sunken face of the heroic tenor. Gwen, sharing the weight of her husband's knowledge and emotion, wept for the man whom she now cradled in her loving arms. She caressed the dark strands of curls that covered his head. Her sweet voice spoke, over and over again.

"It's O.K., honey. Demetrius is here now. Sssshh, my love, it's all right. Demetrius is here now. I love you...I love you...I love you, Enzo."

Demetrius leaned to the front edge of his chair and witnessed the depth of the sorrow, the engulfing anxiety that Enzo had been enduring, all being released at that moment. His face had spoken of the strain, as did the wringing of his hands and his distracting jabber.

But now, the husband and wife filled each other with assurance, gave each other tender love, bore for each other the anguish, and took from each other the affliction placed upon them.

Demetrius sat, astonished at the comfort bestowed by the couple's compassion for one another, as the onus of evil was purged from their souls through their paired sacrifice.

He sat, watching and waiting, loving the pair for loving one another, and astonished at the power of their union.

Twenty

The reviews from the first round of performances at the *New* Chicago Grande Opera poured in to the opera house. The artistic press had sharpened their mighty quills, ready to report of the miscarriage, waiting for the debacle, for the enormous financial and cultural events to plummet to the ground, under-powered and uninspired. The reporters had hovered, waiting for the fiasco to culminate. The critics—failed artists, singers, players, and teachers themselves—stood at the artistic cusp, anxious to slash the life from a performance that revealed one too many miscues. The fourth artistic estate peered in at the opening of the Chicago Grande Opera's new artistic life as the meat of a brewing scandal, ready to be exposed, revealing all its filth and decay. The world had watched and waited for the reports from journalists who vented their inadequacies upon those who had attained superior performance levels than they themselves had.

The hordes had gone hungry.

The opening weekend and first week's performances hovered like a sweet perfume in the air of the House. Never had a series of opera performances been so touched by the Muses. The enchanted web of orchestrated betrayal and seduction had enraptured even the harshest of critical voices.

Opening night was hailed as one of the ten great artistic nights Chicago had seen this century. From the general director's "*mea culpa*" before the opera, to the final roars of "Bravo" upon Tosca's fatal plunge, the Illinois State Theatre had been under a spell.

Worldwide, the praise rang in unison. No discordant voice was heard amongst the masses. The tenor received an overwhelming tribute.

"Truly the first great Italian tenor of the next Millennium. The supple phrasing, the tender sweetness bathed in beauty, was matched only by the sheer power displayed in the enormous Vittoria midway through Act II. Simply an evening that I will never forget," were the words of Jon Reinisch, the chief Arts critic for the *Chicago Herald*.

"Miss Armiliato's Tosca was outstanding, matching Mr. Santi's intensity, while employing her voice with extreme precision. And Mr. Bruscatti, our Scarpia, snarled an effective and menacing dictator, broadly filling the stage with a voice that found ring on top, and warmth below." Vienna, Milan, New York, London—everyone praised the New CGO, its collaborators, the Mexico City Opera Theatre, and especially General Director William Burrows, who, though crucified a year earlier for his supposed mismanagement, had stayed the course, atoned for his errors, and had given the great people of the Midwest their voice once again. All of Chicago rejoiced, as did lovers of opera the world over.

William Burrows hustled into his office.

"Mr. Burrows," anxiously spoke Brenda De Haan, the G.D.'s office secretary. "More fabulous reviews are in from opening weekend."

"Great," the G.D. grunted flatly, betraying the meaning of the word, picking at the soft cast that surrounded his left hand. The secretary continued, hoping to change the director's foul mood of late.

"New reviews from Paris, Madrid, and Tokyo," she bubbled. "Those Japanese critics sure do love American opera." The attractive, motherly woman could not melt the ice around the man.

"I'll be in my office," Burrows muttered. "Please try and keep things quiet for me today, O.K. Brenda?" The bright smile faded from the rosy cheeks that longed for, and rightfully deserved compliment. The secretary descended from her emotional peak and delivered the news of the morning.

"A priority package came for you about ten minutes ago. It's on your desk." Burrows came to life, pushing his door open with his left elbow.

"Did you open it, Brenda?" accused the director, eyes trained on the soft blues of the woman.

"No sir," recoiled the secretary. "You told me to leave all packages for you to open. I just placed it on your desk." Brenda thought all the good news of the weekend and of opening night would ease the funk her boss had been in for the last several months. She could not figure out what had bedeviled this formerly pleasant, even jolly man. Besides, if his sour attitude continued, her stomach would not be able to take the abuse and accusation it had endured over that span.

"Thank you, then, Brenda," the G.D. returned as he stood in the opened door to his office. "Oh, Brenda, is my Margaret Price C.D. in here, or do you have it?"

"I believe it's in there, sir." The woman paused. "On your compact disc player, I think." The general director disappeared into the office as her statement concluded, and the door shut with a "thud."

Brenda reached for a tissue, perched on the outside right edge of her desk, and wiped the welled tears from her sparkling eyes.

"What is wrong with him?" She blew her nose and returned to the work at hand. Within ten minutes she was again bubbling, telling her friends the welcomed news of the wonderful reviews of the weekend.

The general director searched the compact disc player and its environs for the Margaret Price C.D. There it was, just as Brenda said, on top of the player itself. The man pushed the power "on" for both the stereo receiver and the C.D. player below it, and placed the compact disc in the player's tray. He pushed "play."

The Act IV solo from Verdi's *Otello* had always been one of the general director's favorite opera moments. The sweet and innocent "Desdemona," confused and distraught by her husband's accusations, was perfectly set by the master of Italian opera, amidst the melancholy woodwinds. This aria and its following "Ave Maria" melted the heart of the director every single time he heard it. He believed this morning would be no exception.

As the music played, he walked to his desk and grabbed the express package, return address from Signor Umberto Juarez, General Director of the Mexico City Opera Theatre. He knew what the package held, and he did not want to open it.

The aria played, Margaret Price lifting her voice in the delicate "Salce," or "Willow Song," sung by Shakespeare's heroine.

The song told the story of a young woman named Barbara, who, forsaken by love, is convinced of her impending death. Desdemona sings the song as her own, her voice lifting and lilting around the supple melody, and delicate accompanying English horn, clarinets, and oboes. The office filled with the stunning shimmer of the soprano, pure and precise, yet tender, wrapped around the emotion of the scene and the tragedy of the circumstances.

The man sat at his desk. He set the thick eleven-by-fourteen inch envelope on the open space before him and held it by his fingertips. The director's eyes darkened as they looked at the brightly colored paper container.

"*Salce, salce, salce.*" The "willow" tree, with its lilt and foreboding, embodied the sorrow of the moments Desdemona was enduring. The music continued.

"*Povero Barbara,*" the descending vocal line reflected perfectly the descending spirit of the doomed wife.

The director continued watching the envelope—thinking, wishing he could take back the time and the intimidation, his own and that inflicted upon him. He struggled with his moments of commitment.

Why had life come to this? Why had his ego and his confidence led him to such things? He caressed the package, slipping his fingers from side to side, up and down the edges, cursing the known contents to oblivion, but then, eyes sliding side to side in their sockets, arrogantly, snatching them back from his accursed condemnation.

Desdemona's plea continued. She erupted. The ill-fated woman, with an explosion of vocal and orchestral *fortissimo*, screamed; she pleaded to her maid and friend.

"*O Emilia, Emilia, addio, addio!*" "Oh Emilia, farewell, farewell!"

The director was startled at the outburst of tumultuous emotion visiting his ears once again, this music he had adored since his college days.

He stared at the stereo for a moment, over the right edge of the held object. The beauty he had fallen in love with those many years ago—the expression, the stagecraft, the passion of doomed love, the glory of melody, the orchestra-this transcendent art; it now plunged its knife into his heart, set his funeral pyre ablaze, and poisoned the very draught that had brought all meaning to his life.

His only love had looked at him, at his selfishness, at his sin, and spat upon his visage, upon his deception.

Desdemona sang.

"*Ave Maria, grazia plena,*" Otello's wife sang to the virgin for forgiveness and supplication before her beloved Jesus.

Burrows took the end of the package and pulled the tab, perfectly slicing the sealed, outer lining open, splaying the contents to full view. He quickly grabbed the typed pages and the necessary forms, clipped together from behind.

The letter was a formal congratulation from Señor Juarez in Mexico City on the tremendous re-opening of the Chicago Grande Opera.

Burrows slid the form letter, written months earlier, to the side and viewed the forms. The list compiled all information necessary for the continued collaboration between the two companies. Customs forms, shipping forms, projected weights and projected budgets, they all came in the specially delivered envelope.

The coming operas were also listed, and these operas, produced by the Mexico City Opera Theatre, were all enormous.

New productions of *Aida, Boris Godunov, Don Carlo, Lohengrin, Billy Budd, Jenufa, Rusalka, Faust, La Boheme, Queen of Spades, Rigoletto*; the list continued for several paragraphs, all of them big, elaborate, and expensive sets. Huge set pieces, gargantuan props, desks, chaises, bookcases, would all have to be shipped to Chicago and produced by the Chicago Grande Opera.

With each passing day the director's commitment deepened. He was being sucked permanently in—life, hope, and soul—all being pulled deeper into the quagmire of calamity.

He viewed the forms before him—the coming onslaught—and allowed the papers to cascade upon his lap. He looked to his right, past his bookcase, at the fifteen-foot tall slotted windows and watched the sunlight stream its yellow glow to the room.

The sunlight was jaundiced to the director. It was the yellow of poison and of bile. His eyes burned, as Desdemona's had, from sorrow.

Desdemona, settled from her prayer to the Blessed Virgin, sang her realization and her fate, quietly surrounded by Verdi's exquisite string hush.

"Ed ora della morte," "at the hour of death, my death." Burrows stared at the pain of light, the itch to his eyes, irritating the burn. His throat closed and his mouth was like cotton, enervated by the dilemma that lay in front of him on clean white sheets of paper. In spoken voice he mouthed with Desdemona her excruciating repetition.

"Ed ora della morte!"

Burrows let his head fall back to the repose of the recliner, regret etched upon his face.

Desdemona, given voice through the exquisite singer, sang quietly the conclusion to her prayer.

"Amen." The arpeggiated finale to the wife's prayer floated to heaven. William Burrows sat motionless at his desk, letting the perfect masterpiece fill him. He spoke with the tortured wife.

"Amen."

When would the Moor come to slay him?

Twenty-One

Demetrius and the Santis were to share lunch together at the Hyatt's elegant restaurant, Cafe Paradiso. It would be a late lunch, 2:00 p.m. Demetrius had been awake since eight o'clock and had decided to go to the opera house to greet his old friends, the old security guard buddies, and lay a congenial groundwork for the tough questions and interrogations ahead. He arrived about 10:30 a.m.

He stopped and talked to Randy Scott, head of the opera house security, in the little office he occupied next to the stage door. The security hief hated being called Randy, a moniker from his youth, but some of the fellows around the opera house used it affectionately, so he let it pass.

"How do you guys keep tabs on all the new stuff that is coming in here from Mexico City?" asked Demetrius of his former boss.

"Oh my Gahd, Demetrius," Randy quipped. "It's like freakin' cargo terminal at O'Hare Airport in here." He leaned back, clasping his hands behind his balding head. "New sets and new equipment are overrunnin' da place. We get new cargo in at least once a week. And they deliver at the worst times too. I've had to double the graveyard detail to accommodate the truck's arrival times."

"The trucks from Mexico City?" Demetrius asked.

"Yeah, and dat stuff smells like shit too. Never smelled an opera set like dat before." The security chief laughed out of the side of his mouth and continued. "'Cept, you remember dat fat soprano a couple years back, who would mess her drawers every night when she was singin'? Guess she was pushin' a bit too hard." Demetrius enjoyed a bit of sick humor, but this particular memory was a bit too much for him. He winced, wrinkling his eyes in disdain.

"Dat Faust set smelled like *Aida* when we used to put elephants in it, crappin' all over the stage. I tink dey had to burn dat Faust set after dat soprano got done wit it."

"So," Demetrius recovered from his wince and feigned sensitivity, "the sets from Mexico are a bit too malodorous for your delicate sinuses?"

"Maybe dem Mexicans piss on everyting before dey send it to us, so we knows where to send it back to. Ya know, markin' deir territory." Demetrius heard the disgusting contradiction.

"Well, what is it?" Demetrius asked, superficially joking, but inwardly serious, "Shit or piss? What do those Mexican sets smell like, you old bugger?"

"Definitely piss," Randy said. "If it had been shit, da methane woulda ignited the whole of Lower Wacker Drive by now." Demetrius was satisfied with the final answer of his friend. He continued his camouflaged interrogation.

"What's the CGO doin' with all the old sets? I wouldn't think there would be room, even at the storage yard," commented Demetrius.

"Where da hell were ya, D? Don't ya remember the fire last year?" asked the security head of his former employee. "Most of that stuff got burned up. Dey got ta replace almost everyting."

Demetrius had not forgotten. He wanted to hear the story of the Chicago Grande Opera's demise from one of its more informed employees. He faked his ignorance.

"I heard about the fire, but I didn't think it was that huge."

"You shoulda seen da news photos. The whole building went up, da whole freakin' block. The fire marshal declared it a total loss."

"And they'd let their insurance lapse..."

Randy interrupted the obvious conclusion to the statement with a roar of Chicago verbosity.

"Oohh, Judas Priest, we thought we was all out of jobs. Hey, wait a minute, D." The head of security slid his rolling recliner to the right, towards the gray file cabinet, leaned back further, straining his recliner, and snatched the newspaper from the top of the four metal drawers. "Here, look at dis." The man handed Demetrius a copy of the year-old *Chicago Herald*, front page, which was dominated by a photo of the blaze. "Keep it. I gots half a dozen others at home collectin' dust."

Demetrius took the tarnished paper and glanced at the cover. The grainy photograph spoke the volumes to which words were unable to convey. One square block of old rented warehouses was ablaze—the storage buildings for the Chicago Grande Opera.

Demetrius was consumed by the power represented in the pictures. The inferno was frozen, full force, captured on the wooden page. The sienna fingers lept from the roof, licking the brick walls through windowed mouths, seeping skyward, defying gravity, flying cloudward. Hell was spitting its defiance toward Heaven. The wide-angled photo, taken by helicopter, framed the building, end-to-end, glowing with the consuming heat. Demetrius studied the photos, amazed at the destructive force that raged unchecked. He shook his head and resumed his conversation.

"I guess I don't understand the whole scenario, Randy." Demetrius leaned into the doorjamb, crossing his arms, scrunching the tan leather of his coat. "The CGO had been kicking artistic ass the last couple of years. Why would the management just implode like that?"

Randy curled his index finger twice, motioning Demetrius closer, knowing some of the CGO management could be standing just outside his door. He pulled his body flat over his desk from the overly reclined swayback position in his chair.

"Simple, 'D,'" Randy whispered flatly. "Dey got greedy. Burrows got a big head and thought he could do no wrong. Den dat damn 'lesbo' opera came along and you couldn't even fill the orchestra section of Mackay," he said, referring to the Illinois State Theatre's performing hall. "Damn shame, too. Dey had a great ting goin'," he reminisced, "and dey blew it."

"And the half-billion dollar Brook gift saved the day?" Again, Demetrius feigned ignorance to hear the perspective of his friend's thirty years of opera experience.

"Yeah, her and Mexico City. It seems like dey got as much money as the CGO has now."

"You mean the five hundred mil?" Demetrius reasserted the implied financial security.

"Beautiful stuff dey bring in here. I'll tell ya," the security chief said, shaking his head, "been here over twenty-five years, never seen sets like dat before. Gorgeous!"

"You're just getting soft in your old age," Demetrius poked.

"Nah, kid, it ain't me,." he said, serious as a heart attack. "Dis stuff is incredible." Randy stroked his roughly shaven shadow and looked toward the office ceiling in contemplation. The recliner returned to its comfort zone.

"The desks, the columns...you seen dat statue of the Virgin, Act I? Supposedly dey hired a real sculptor for dat ting, down in Mexico. Da fake books in *Tosca*? Dose damn books are real—hollowed out, but real. Why did dey have to do dat?"

"Doesn't all that 'real' equipment weigh too much?"

"Hell yeah, it does," Randy affirmed. "Dat's why dey need so many trucks rollin' in here all the time. And I'll tell you what, dey all weigh a ton too."

Demetrius soaked in all the information Randy wanted to offer and stored it all in his well-trained brain.

Once satisfied with his chat, Demetrius excused himself politely from his old friend, knowing the security head needed to be busy with his "securing."

Randy had given him a temporary pass, so Demetrius was now able to roam the opera house unhindered. It was already almost eleven and the house would really be humming with the rehearsal day in a few minutes.

The talk Gwen and he had shared yesterday, before Enzo arrived, alerted him to the damaged balcony rail. He wanted to talk to Nicholas Palermo, the head of House Management.

Nick was a wonderful Hispanic man who had also been around the opera house for many years. He was another one of the hundreds of kind, enthusiastic people that worked amongst the arts—behind the scenes, backstage, in the lobby, ushering patrons, giving impromptu tours, and doing the small but important tasks of the opera house.

Demetrius knew Nick from his years of working here, but not as well as he knew Randy. But, there were no worries. Nick was an honest, straightforward man who treated everyone the same, with kindness and respect. He would not lie to cover his own mistakes, but acknowledge and remedy the problem as best he could, and he would certainly know about the balcony rail in question.

Demetrius walked to the concealed corner office, which looked like a broom closet, but opened into a vast three-sectioned area. This office was one of the many hidden alcoves that speckled the Illinois State Theatre.

Demetrius knocked and the round-faced smiling man quickly answered.

"Good morning, young man. Can I help you?"

"Mr. Palermo, my name is Demetrius McDiess. I used to work security here at the opera house."

"Of course." A wider smile filled the cheeks of the house manager. "My mind was racing, trying to place where I had seen you. Of course, Demetrius. Would you like to come in?"

The two men entered the office, chatting about the in-between years. Nick was proud, and genuinely thrilled at the way this young man had pulled himself up from nothing.

"So you worked here and went to school at the same time?" Nick asked. Demetrius affirmed it. "Isn't that just wonderful! You should be very proud of your accomplishments. All your hard work paying off now." Spending time with Nick was very empowering. Nick was one who, like the Santis, took pride in the accomplishments of their friends, who loved the challenge of life, and the intensity of striving for more. There was not a jealous bone in this fine man's body; he simply enjoyed living life and gloried in the good deeds of others, all the while living a committed Christian life, loving others, both in their triumphs and their tragedies.

"Praise the Lord" filled Nick's interjections as Demetrius explained further where life and work had taken him. Demetrius almost felt like the son of this man who stood before him, beaming with pride and joy.

"How has life been around here, Mr. Palermo?" Demetrius smiled at his new number one fan.

"We had a glorious opening night last Saturday, thank God. We sure needed it." Demetrius looked puzzled and cocked his head to the right, thus encouraging the continued elaboration.

"Of course, you know of the difficult last few years."

"Enzo has kept me up-to-date with some of the problems you've had here," Demetrius replied. "I've been in Minneapolis for a little while, so I lost touch with all that was going on."

"Well, praise God, we've had a tremendous opening week. You said you know Enzo? You mean Mr. Santi?"

"While I was here working security he was in the young artist program."

"Wonderful. He seems like such a nice fellow. I haven't been able to know him personally yet, but he sure has given two spectacular performances this past week." Demetrius smiled at the compliment directed toward his friend.

"He's as nice as anyone I know," Demetrius commented. "Both him and his wife. In fact, Enzo was the man who really encouraged me to get the degree I did. I think he wanted me to succeed as much as I wanted to."

"Wonderful. It's a real blessing to have friends that are so like Barnabas." Demetrius did not understand the name used, or its reference. He asked its meaning.

"Oh, well, Barnabas was St. Paul's traveling companion on their early missionary journeys, but the men split up later when Paul got angry with Mark."

"Mark?" asked Demetrius.

"Yes, before he became *Saint* Mark. You see, Mark was just a kid at the time, so he was young, scared and immature, but Barnabas believed in Mark, so he took him under his wing and nurtured him." Nick beamed as he told the Bible story, privileged to share the meaning of his life with another precious soul. "Of course, when Barnabas chose Mark, that meant he and Paul had to part ways. But the miraculous thing is, Mark went on to become a great evangelist, spreading the Gospel, doing great things for the kingdom of God. If Barnabas had listened to Paul, Mark may have been left out in the cold.

"Anyway, because of the way Barnabas nurtured people, sparking their desire and nurturing their commitment, he was know as the 'Son of Encouragement.' He spent his life helping others become greater than they could be on their own." Nick smiled again.

"That's why I called Mr. Santi a 'Barnabas,' a friend who encourages others become greater than they thought possible."

Nick was absolutely correct. Enzo and Gwen were "Sons of Encouragement," taking glory in the accomplishments of their friends. Demetrius smiled and remembered the comparison.

"I believe that would fit you too, Mr. Palermo," complimented Demetrius.

"Please call me Nick," he said and smiled, "and you are very kind, young man. I pray that I can live up to that compliment." The conversation ran a bit dry and Nick had much to do.

"Mr. McDiess, is there something specific that I can help you with?"

"Please call me Demetrius, or D." Nick nodded. "I hope you can help me with something, Nick."

Nick quickly perused the performance reports for the four performances since opening night. He scrutinized opening night. The sheets were clear. One patron who had imbibed a bit too much during the intermission of *Tosca* had to be escorted to a waiting taxi, but nothing was truly out of the ordinary.

"Nothing here looks out of order, Demetrius," commented Nick. "The patrons have been exemplary since opening night." Nick scanned his desk for possible missing forms. He had collated them Monday morning. He looked in the plastic "Performance Reports" tray, where the nightly sheets were returned. There was one report in the tray from the night in question.

"Oh wait, here it is. How did I overlook this thing?" Nick read the sheet and became very disturbed.

"Yeah, the balcony rail was broken. According to this, a patron leaned over it, but the usher was right there and grabbed the person before she tumbled over the ledge. My goodness!" The polite declamation hid the true outrage the house manager felt. Nick shook his head in appropriate anger.

"What's wrong, Nick?"

"The ushers are supposed to tell me about anything major that happens in the house during a performance, that includes up until the time the last patron leaves the auditorium. This young lady should have reported such a major problem to me immediately. She's gonna lose her job over this, I'm afraid." Nick shook his head.

"If you don't mind, can you tell me about the person who worked that particular area?" Demetrius asked.

"Sure." Nick scanned the page, searching for the signature in question, signed by the irresponsible usher. "Saturday night, Leah Goldberg was assigned to Left Front Balcony." Nick looked up from his desk. "I don't understand it. She's a college student studying Spanish Literature at Roosevelt University. She's an excellent usher, honest, never given me any reason to doubt her abilities. She's funny as a crutch too. Really funny."

The prospect of terminating this young lady's job caused Nick much anguish. Demetrius thought through the conflicting stories, believing a patsy had been chosen.

"Oh, Leah, why did you do that to me?" Nick rhetorically asked his absent usher. He looked up at Demetrius again. "She's never given me any reason *not* to trust her—until now." He liked the young woman very much, but this oversight was inexcusable.

"Shoot!" Nick uttered his most offensive vulgarity, in utter disappointment at his usher's sin. There would have to be a price paid for this sin of omission.

"Nick," Demetrius interjected, "can we take a look at the balcony rail along the left of the auditorium?" Nick looked up at Demetrius. "…before you fire the young lady?"

"We sure can. I want to find out exactly what happened Saturday night." Nick referred only to his usher and the broken balcony rail.

"Me too." Demetrius smiled in affirmation.

The balcony rail, the sleek black snake that wound along the edge of the first row of balcony seats, looked to be in perfect condition. The smooth acrylic surface gleamed in the auditorium's working lights. The mounting, mightily secured to the decorated wall, appeared unblemished from the supposed fracture of the previous Saturday night. The supporting bracket, running perpendicular to the horizontal rail, stood at perfect upright attention, anchoring the strength of the rail in the solid front wall of the balcony.

"If this broke, they sure did a wonderful job fixing it," said the house manager. "I don't see a thing wrong with it."

Demetrius knelt down and began a very careful examination of the section of rail in question, the one Gwen had viewed the previous Sunday morning.

The top edge was perfect. The welded joint at the perpendicular support bracket was smooth and slick. Demetrius ran his hand along the top edge of the rail, right to left, from support bracket to wall anchor. Everything looked fine from the top.

Demetrius knelt down to inspect the under side of the rail, again starting at the support bracket.

"Here we go," Demetrius spoke in discovery. Small flecks of unpainted solder, gleaming silver, were imbedded at the underside of the joint between the rail and the bracket. Demetrius also examined the rail's wall anchor.

The anchor, the hole sunk into the wall, was chipped at its base. The round support bracket had cracked away some of the cement that had been poured when the house had put in the walls. In fact, the cracks only appeared at the stage side of the bracket.

Demetrius ran his index finger into the crack. The bit of moisture on the digit lifted some of the dust out of the small hole. He eyed the substance and rubbed it between his thumb and index finger.

He showed the evidence to Nick. Interested, Nick watched the trained investigator snoop out the evidence of the belatedly reported mishap. Down on his knees, Demetrius looked left to the auditorium wall and swiveled to meet the rail's joint. Here, the rail bent downward as it met the wall, leaving a four-inch excess that held two concrete anchors and the bolts that performed the anchoring. This piece of rail also appeared normal under first inspection. Demetrius examined the underside. Nothing. He lifted his knee and crouched, peering at the shining black rail edge pressed into the wall. Nothing on the balcony side.

Demetrius looked over the edge, focusing on the stage side edge where the rail and wall met.

"Here's some more," he said calmly. He had discovered tracks. Two streaks, a curving parallel path, had been dug. This trail, as Demetrius knew, had been created from Enzo's weight pulling the bolts from the wall and then dragging the two sharp daggers from their moorings.

Demetrius stood and showed Nick the confirming evidence. Indeed, the rail had been forcibly pulled from the wall. Nick became increasingly upset with his usher. Demetrius stood silent. The direction of the evidence and the force necessary to damage the rail—these things could only have been applied by a weight from the other side of the rail, from over the retaining wall at the men's feet. No patron could have applied such force. It had to have been caused by Enzo, fleeing for his life and leaping to the rail, hoping his jump would precipitate his safety.

"Thank God no one was hurt," Nick said. "I'm gonna get Leah in here as soon as possible. She's got some serious explaining to do." Demetrius heard the chatter but he remained silent, disturbed by this confirmation of Saturday night's horrible chase.

"She's gonna lose her job for sure," Nick continued.

"Nick," Demetrius asked, "can I talk to her before you do anything?"

"I guess so. Why?" Nick replied.

"I think there is more to this story than we can see." Demetrius looked seriously into Nick's eyes. Nick saw the intent and believed the man, the investigator.

"What do you mean?"

"I just think your usher may be innocent. In fact, would you do me a favor and not terminate her until I can poke around a little more?"

Nick knew Demetrius was trustworthy. He had been an excellent security guard, and seemed to know his business. He could respect a wish like this, but only temporarily.

"I tell you what, Demetrius, I won't fire her for a while, but with this kind of oversight, I can't let her work for a few days. I can't risk the patron's safety if this incident was her responsibility."

"O.K.," Demetrius answered, "but if she is innocent, I want her paid for the days she has gone without work." Nick thought a moment. He could accept that proposition. His budget could afford to reimburse someone who was wrongfully accused.

"Deal! If she is innocent, she'll deserve more than the few nights of salary she'll miss."

The men left the balcony. Demetrius had catalogued what he needed to know for the moment. Both Nicholas Palermo and Randall Scott had provided reams of information that could prove useful in his quest for answers and in his search for a murderer's identification.

On the stage of the Francis Mackay Auditorium stood a man, obfuscated by the left side stage wall, behind the proscenium arch, snuggled in front of the great gold curtain. He had watched the investigation, curious as to the men's intention. He was familiar with the one man—the opera house regular. This simple idiot stood around sucking up to the ticket holders. He was nothing. He was no one, and would be no trouble.

He did not know the other man—the black man, the man who discovered the little mishap. This black man confirmed the unfinished deed from the previous Saturday night.

Cigarette-tainted breath heaved into the narrow passage in which he was cocked. The curtain pressed his body into the rough wall around which he peered.

He was angry and his work was mounting. This new man, this black man, would have to be guarded carefully. He breathed the stale air trapped around the curtain, tinted with upholstery mold and its sprayed retardant.

He slipped out of his cloth enclosure, into the back stage corridor and exited the building.

The hall and passageways on the "C" level of the opera house were quiet, remaining as yet undisturbed by the coming activities of the day. The fluorescent lights were illuminated, snapping to buzzing brightness by a computer several floors away. Not a soul disturbed the silence in the Properties Department. The rough, chipped desktop sat alone, wishing the owner would return and warm its atmosphere. The spotted desktop hid the coffee and tea, the dropped sugar from the cinnamon rolls, the crumbles of sandwiches and snacks that had littered the expanse for the past two decades.

Amidst the splotches and smears, the spots and stains, the crumbs and chips, remained the stigma, the documentation of deeds most foul, covert in its obvious placement. The hidden evidence, sinking deeper into the dry wood, mixed amongst its colleagues, perfectly inconspicuous.

Demetrius slid through the door in speedy silence. He began his examination of the room and outer hall. He had walked these halls before, countless times, but now he searched—he discriminated. His previous assignment was simply security, locking down, and assuring safety. His present task was that of discovery.

He walked from side to side, gazing all around the desk and its office mates. He looked at the desktop, still littered with papers, stacked to one side, properties' log sheets sitting on top of the bundle.

Demetrius ran his hands along the outside edge of the desktop. The cracked wooden sides scraped his callused fingers. He bent over, observing the sides of the desk and the floor surrounding the bureau. There was nothing.

He found himself behind the desk, standing in the very spot he had seen the property's manager stand many times. He picked up the log sheets to the left and leafed through the papers. Most had been filled out completely. Several at the bottom of the pile were unmarked. Two-thirds of the way through the stack one sheet was almost fully completed, yet unfinished.

This page had been obviously crinkled. Demetrius closely examined the page, both sides. The front and printed side had a pattern of creases branching out from an uncreased center point, approximately three inches in diameter. Demetrius turned the page over. There were brown streaks etched along the back of the page, but only directly below the three-inch oval found on the topside of the sheet.

Demetrius took one of the unused forms from his left hand and compared the crinkled piece against the fresh one. He put them both on the desktop and scrutinized the used one. He placed his right hand, palm down, over the three-inch oval at the center of the crumpled pattern, then moved his hand to the fresh paper. He pressed his palm into the paper, and with his fingers pulled the sheet's edges inward. Slowly, he slid his hand over the paper, still pressed along the top of the rough desktop.

He lifted his hand. On the fresh unused paper he had produced the same pattern outlined on the sheet just to the right, only in opposition to it. He had produced a right-hand duplicate of the pattern he found, so, logically, the sheet he found would have been someone's left hand, grasping the paper, palm flat, and sliding the paper across the desk top.

Demetrius picked up both sheets—the original and his copy—and turned them over. Again, the same brown pattern appeared under his palm, lifted from the colored fibers on the desktop.

He looked around for an envelope to claim his evidence, but he found none. He put the two pieces of paper on the stack to the left and continued his search.

He again bent low to the ground, training his eyes on any blemish, on any odd chip or grain that he might find. He squatted even lower and looked under the desk. The shadow prevented close inspection. He whipped out the penlight he kept in his coat pocket and lit the dark area.

Dust bunnies hopped under the desk, along with tiny scraps of paper and a thin layer of grime. The area had been mopped, but the swipes from the cotton strands never reached beneath the firmly planted properties' home.

Demetrius scanned, sweeping the beam of light from left to right, across the miniature ocean of soot. He stopped the beam on a tiny shard. He reached under the six-inch space, and with the tip of the penlight nudged the tiny black morsel towards him.

Demetrius took a piece of blank white paper from the desk top, folded it in half and scooped the piece into the closed side of the folded paper. He rose from his crouch and stood behind the desk, commencing his examination of the tiny spike.

As the little black arrowhead rolled and bobbed down the slotted paper, it left a tiny black trail. The little granular trace slithered down the artificial slope like a sidewinder down a dune.

This sidewinder was the finely sharpened tip of a pencil, broken off and abused, but Demetrius, raising the paper and pencil tip close to his face, thought the carbon funnel a bit curious. He used his penlight again, even in the full fluorescent glow about him, to pour an intense, all-revealing glare on the tiny leaden shard. He noticed a thick brown glaze solidified over the object, encasing the core.

Demetrius gently tapped the penlight against the pencil tip, nestled in the creased paper, and then wiped the tapped point of the light across the white paper he cradled in his hand.

Red smeared across the white surface. The substance seemed like caramelized brown sugar, coating the fiber within. The moisture from Demetrius's breath dappled the dark substance and allowed it to streak across the page. He could not be sure, but it responded as human blood would, as it had in the hundred of other investigations he had performed.

Demetrius folded the white paper, enclosing the evidence, and placed it in his pocket along with his penlight. He was satisfied with his findings, but he knew they did not prove anything. That evidence would need to be more substantial, and a week after the misdeed, that evidence was probably no longer attainable.

The investigator walked into the property's storage room. He strode slowly, through the short entrance hall, under the glowing red "exit" sign, through the double doors and up to the huge shelving. Wotan's staff leaned just to the right, against the shelving. The operatically enchanted staff yearned to tell its true-life story of murder and mayhem, of which it had played the part of savior. But away from the operatic gods, it stood silent.

Demetrius walked up and down each aisle, noticing the props he had seen while working security. There were the huge staffs to his right, and the goblets and the knives, forming every imaginable shape. These objects spoke to the singer, to the performer in his soul. Whereas he was no singer, no opera performer, he had spent his working life in discovery and in drama.

He was the one who solved the puzzles opera plots would scramble. He found the missing person, and discovered the cloaked documentation of crimes and misdemeanors. It was he who solved the mystery behind sordid events, whether covert or in the public domain.

He had come to love the art, the spirit, and even the essence of opera and his investigative work allowed him to feel that same thrill that comes from a performance. By performing tasks thought impossible he lived out his own mysteries and enjoyed his own dramas.

Demetrius saw the ghosts hanging from the ceiling at the far end of the props' room and remembered a quick fright he had experienced backstage late one night. He laughed to himself.

He walked to the north hallway of the room and came upon the boxes labeled "Fire." He pulled one of them out of its alcove and opened the folded top.

A puff of soot billowed out of the makeshift chimney, escaping from the boxed confines. Demetrius picked through the rubble. Very little was salvageable within the first box. Nothing in the second caught his attention either. Half-burnt papers filled most of the boxes. The second to last box was filled with tools—not stage tools, but work tools. He closed each box as he finished with it and made his way to the exit.

He was quite satisfied with his morning in the opera house. He made his way up the stairway and out of the building, but before leaving, he visited the lighting hallway and the grid where Enzo had been trapped.

Demetrius stepped to the very edge his friend had occupied the previous Saturday night, holding the vertical bar around the light curtain for stability. He squatted on the edge of the platform. He scrutinized the facade into which Enzo had slammed. All appeared normal.

Demetrius looked down. The twenty feet were magnified by the lofty position. He looked over the four feet of expanse Enzo had leaped across. He stood, amazed at his friend's effort, and the risk he had taken. Of course impending death had forced Enzo's hand, and his decision to leap had to be made.

Demetrius started to understand the urgency of his friend's predicament. He believed Enzo even more as he stood on the ledge, holding the light pole.

"We'll find him, E," Demetrius said to himself. "I promise."

Twenty-Two

The Santis had a relaxed, slumbersome morning. They crawled out of bed at 10:30 and roused themselves for the coming day. Gwen showered quickly, while Enzo stayed in bed, eyes half open, caught between worlds, conscious and "un," for the fifteen minutes of his wife's bath. He peered into both worlds of consciousness, traveling through the last day's events with great speed, spinning through the catalogue of his mind. Their sleep had been deep and refreshing, truly the brother of death.

The couple had a light breakfast, in expectation of the coming meeting. Enzo knew he had to tell Demetrius and Gwen about everything that had happened, both the events of Saturday night and of the last two days. While the shower's stream of hot water pounded his body, he thought his way through the complexities of the scenes, detaching himself, to clarify the transpirations.

Saturday was frozen in his mind, locked tightly in gray matter. He had a clear picture of the tattoo on the fiend's left hand, and he cleared the cobwebs from his final conversation with Frank.

Wednesday's horror was more easily retrieved. He saw Bill again; he saw his driver-friend's blood stained neck, he heard the shots at the bulletproof limo windows, and he stared at the assassin's gleaming silver gun, wedged in the front window, tilting towards him, ready to end his life. The shower water rained onto his head.

Enzo leaned into the water, his left arm out, pushing against the shower stall, the tile receiving the full weight of the tenor's heart. Enzo shut off the stream, and with it, the feelings he longed to hold, to cleave to his breast, but which he refused to allow as impediment in his search for justice.

The three friends met at the quaint Café Paradiso, nestled in lobby greenery just east of the entrance to the grand hotel. Enzo and Gwen, though both recovered from the previous eve, sat down to replenish their lost energy. Demetrius, having had a very full morning, also ordered quite a substantial portion.

Demetrius shared the news of his morning snoop at the opera house, but he did not reveal all. He did not want his findings to influence the information Enzo would supply. Demetrius wanted the facts solely from the eyes of one murder witness—no embellishment, and no outside enhancement. Motives for the crime would be surmised only as information was compiled and as circumstantial stories were verified.

The three quickly consumed their meals, the green venue brightening their chatter. Finally, Demetrius looked to Enzo.

"Enzo, I want you to think back to Saturday and tell me everything that happened." Enzo opened his mouth and prepared to open the doors to his anguished heart. Demetrius caught him before he uttered a word.

"Enzo, I want you to take some deep breaths, close your eyes, and really give yourself a moment to focus." Enzo obeyed, like a good student, shutting the windows to his soul and opening the window to his memory. Demetrius stopped speaking for a moment. The surrounding noise of the restaurant—its soft words, its clattering dishes, its hum and its vibration— all were heard as white noise, focusing the tenor on his memories.

"E, you are right here amongst friends and loved ones, perfectly safe and secure." Demetrius pulled his pen and note pad from his coat pocket and focused. "Now, think back to the evening of the Chicago Grande Opera's Opening Night...and tell me everything that happened—every step, every word, every action."

Room 1801 was being cleaned. The couple had finally vacated for a while and the crack team of hotel personnel attended to the linens, towels and general maintenance. The kitchen area was wiped down and addressed, the bath and bedroom were whisked spotless, and the living room area was dusted and vacuumed. The fifteen whirlwind minutes sucked all the filth from the room, leaving it without blemish.

The two-woman crew packed up and moved down the hall to their regularly appointed room. The Santis' delay caused their abode to be attended to out of its normal order.

The door was locked and left undisturbed by the women. They hustled into 1808 and began their dance with dirt once again.

A maintenance man came to 1801 as soon as the scurrying women disappeared into their next room. The door was opened with the pass card, and quickly closed. He checked the room for cleanliness. Fine job. He walked from room to room, scouting the work of the women.

Wonderful! A coin would have hit the ceiling if trampolined from the bedspread. And the floors were shiny as a dinner plate.

However, he had not come as the hotel supervisor.

He quickly walked to the telephone next to the bed, pulled on a pair of thin black gloves, unscrewed the receiver, and placed a small electronic device within. The cover was quickly replaced. Every phone in the apartment was cleaned in the same manner.

He pulled a small leather pouch from his jacket, removed one of the tiny black receivers from it, and attached it to the underside of the bedroom nightstand. He placed another receiver at the top of the picture frame that hung over the bed. He never touched the springboard of linen, but leaned his six-and-a-half-foot frame over the king-sized mattress and stuck the device in place.

The living room received the same attention. End table, chairs, light fixtures, all became habitats for the tiny electronic rodents.

As the anti-exterminator finished his task, a faint scratching crawled into his ears from the huge bay windows to the south.

The man walked to the sound. Spinning fibers of wood etched through the ceiling and flittered to the finished floor. A drill bit pushed through and created a half-inch diameter hole.

The man wet his fingers and wiped the debris from the floor, then reached up and found the white fish-eye lens hanging through the ceiling hole. He reached in his left front pants pocket and pulled out a white plastic collar. He slid the collar over the lens to stabilize the device in the ceiling.

The maintenance man heard one tap from the room above. He grabbed the lens by the sides and twisted it slowly to the left. Three taps sounded, signaling the end to his adjustment. The camera was in place.

The cleaner walked back into the bedroom and saw the twirling strands. He quickly grabbed a hand towel and spread it out on the bedspread. The falling debris landed on the towel, keeping the bedspread perfect. The lens collar was attached and the lens focused. There was a camera directly over the suite's huge bed.

One last task and the job would be done. He quickly walked into the kitchen, looking out over the living room, and heard the same scratching. He grabbed a chair, stepped up, and peered above the cabinets. The lens was pulled through the ceiling above the kitchen cabinets. The darkness of this recess allowed a bigger lens, and thus a better view of the living room.

The tapping was accomplished and the lens placed in perfect position. The man jumped off the chair, replaced it, and scanned his work. He thought through each placement, through each device, each moment of commencing surveillance. He was satisfied.

He left and immediately removed his gloves to prevent passing suspicion. Up he went to 1901 and his post. Tedious hours would now pass, in hopes of precious little information.

The Hyatt Hotel's Suite 1801 was a spotless abode, clean from top to bottom, from wall to wall, from ceiling to floor, and yet, it was grossly infested.

Enzo rattled through the events of the previous Saturday night as if speaking from a script. The lids to his eyes never opened. He spoke of the pre-opera meal of pasta and sauce he never failed to eat, he spoke of kissing his wife before heading to the theatre, of the limousine ride over to the house. He whisked through the stage entrance and the detail of the performance night, the accolades, the endless applause, the triumphant third act aria, spun of silken voice, and, via Puccini, of tragic love.

The post-performance dialogue came just as easily. The passionate kiss and embrace of his wife, the dressers scurrying about, the wig mistress hustling to and fro.

Gwen saw, in Enzo's closed eyes, a beautiful calm as he spoke of her, of the tenderness they shared, and the loving pride she had in his performance. Enzo glowed with a light from within, a radiance that filled him as he spoke of her and the few moments they shared after the opening night performance.

"Gwen stepped up to me and threw herself in my arms, pressing herself to me, and I received this beautiful woman." Demetrius's hypnosis had found a willing recipient in the tired singer.

"She leaned into me and kissed me, unworthy as I am. Thank you, my love."

Gwen did not remember hearing the words he spoke now, for Enzo had not spoken them aloud. This memory was how Enzo's mind perceived that moment. These words were not spoken, they were felt; the intimacy of the reminiscence to her husband, the awe with which he beheld his wife, cradled her heart. He was absolutely, completely devoted to her, and in her heart of hearts she echoed the words of her husband.

Enzo scrolled forward to the moment of his encounter with Frank, on "C" level.

"We talked of wives and careers. He felt over-worked and abused now." Demetrius began questioning, to deepen the insight of the conversation.

"How was Frank abused at work, in the opera house?"

"Frank said the new regime was making him and his crew stay up all night, waiting to unload the trucks."

"What trucks, Enzo?"

"The trucks from Mexico City, with all the new sets and costumes from Mexico City."

"Why was Frank upset about what was going on?"

"Frank said that some new guys were in charge of the shipments now and that they insisted nobody touch anything. The new guys had to unload everything first, before the crews could get to them." Demetrius found this curious. Enzo continued. "They even locked the dock. They wouldn't allow anyone on the dock until they had unloaded everything."

Enzo stopped for a moment, and Demetrius tilted his head to the side, jotting down what seemed significant.

"Frank wanted to get home to his wife. He said the overtime was great, but that he didn't want to be at the opera house until eleven at night when his job could have been done at six or so."

"He also said he hated keeping the new log books."

"What books, Enzo?" Demetrius inquired again.

"Frank had never kept a log of all the properties' equipment before, but the new people at the house, from Mexico City, they were making him keep logs of all the new material—the new props that came in from the opera in Mexico. He hated doing it. In fact, that was what he was doing when I went down to 'C' level to see him.

"He did say that he had never seen such great work on props before. He said that they were the finest, most intricate work he had ever seen. Much too good for the opera stage—at least that is what Frank thought."

"Why too good?" Demetrius questioned this seemingly odd statement.

"Because on stage the action has to *look* believable. Knives and trinkets can always be fake, or cut in half to save money. Up close, most stage machinery and props look really shabby, but with lights and with music the theatre is transformed, and the patrons see with their hearts." Enzo stopped a moment, his eyes still closed, deep in thought. "You should know that, Demetrius. You worked there and saw some of those silly props."

Enzo's little jab injected some lightness into the tremendously serious proceedings. Demetrius continued his questioning.

"So, Enzo, was there anything else you can remember from the conversation with Frank that might be significant?"

"After listening to Frank talk of all the problems with the new guys, we talked about our opera collections, and the fire last year."

"Go on."

"He admired the new props, most of which had to be replaced after the fire anyway, and he said I could look in the properties' room to add to my collection. There were several old boxes from the fire, stuff the CGO thought might be salvageable. It ended up being mostly junk, so while Frank finished up I went back into the props' room and searched through the fire damaged boxes."

"And that is when Frank was killed," Demetrius spoke softly, "while you were in the props storage room?" Enzo's back straightened, stiffening with the remembered tension, but remained in his hypnotic concentration.

"I found something interesting in one of the boxes, and took a look at it. I heard the voices at the props' desk, but it was all muffled and unclear, so when I found my prize I started to walk out of the props' room into the hallway. That was when I saw the man, with his back to me, standing behind Frank."

Unnerved by her husband's recount, Gwen worked to calm herself. She felt the pain her husband was in now controlling her own stomach. She breathed and gazed at Enzo, his head tilted downward, his eyes wide shut in hypnotic concentration.

"That was when he killed Frank."

Demetrius knew that the method of execution was not important and he jumped into Enzo's stream of thought.

"Enzo, I want you to relax and concentrate."

"Breathe with me, honey." Gwen took her husband's right hand, setting on the chair's arm, and wrapped her fingers over the top of his.

"Was there anything in those moments that would help identify the assailant? Be patient and run through the scene again. Everything is all right. Just see it as a slow-motion sequence—every detail and every frame."

Enzo scrolled through the murder slowly, in obedience to his friend. He could not see the man's face; he turned his head too fast. Frank was hunched over something on the props' desk. Up went the arms of the man, his hands and fingers flared to grab the hunched body of his friend.

It hurt Enzo to watch it over and over, the pull on the head and the violent snap, but he had to see it, over and over again. Each replay drew into clearer resolution the black and red tattoo on the assassin's left hand.

Pull, snap, and there it was. The left hand was frozen on the side of Frank's broken neck. Crunch, the explosion of Frank's vertebrae sounded in Enzo's head, and there again, the hand, the treacherous tool, stood locked, trapped in the singer's memory.

The conclusion of the scene was obvious, and Enzo did not scroll further. He stayed in his relaxed, focused state for an extended moment.

"The man who killed Frank had a tattoo on his left hand, on the back of his left hand," he uttered. "I know exactly what it looks like. It is black and red and very unique. Other than that, even with the chase through the props room and the opera house, I never saw any part of him again." The two observers sat back into their chairs and relaxed a bit, believing the interrogation was over.

Enzo's eyes opened in conclusion to the interview. He awoke from his hypnotic sleep, from the same nightmare, lived in real time, with real people. At least now he had information, a small bit of identification, so this horrifying work found some reward. And now, with those two dear ones at his side, the spirit of heaviness that had covered him subsided. The black hole of ignorance gave way to a glimmer of hope.

"Gwen, honey," Enzo asked of his wife, "could you go to the room and get that switch I found?"

"Where did you leave it, sweetheart?" asked the obedient wife, pushing her chair from the table to run the errand.

"I believe it's still on the living room desk. If not there, then on the nightstand on my side of the bed." Gwen nodded as she left, confirming the information. She hustled away and up in the elevator.

Enzo, deciding to spare his wife this torment, immediately told Demetrius of the horrifying limousine ride to Bloomington.

"Did this guy look familiar to you?"

"Not at all, 'D.' I'd never seen him before."

"Any similarities between him and the guy from Saturday night? Anything that you can think of?"

"I don't think so. The guy Wednesday was sort of a 'hick.' Bad teeth, crooked nose, very thin. The man Saturday looked bulkier, stocky. I don't think they were the same guy," Enzo concluded.

"The driver is still in the hospital in Bloomington?"

"Yeah," Enzo said and nodded.

"And the Camaro was totally destroyed?" continued Demetrius.

"From what I saw, I don't know how it couldn't have been totally destroyed. The slabs of rock tumbled with it for a long time." Demetrius had been concerned about his friend since the call Gwen made a few days ago, but this recent attempt on his life, made by a police impostor, caused even greater concern.

Demetrius's mind rolled in thought and hypothesis. Who knew of the murder of Frank Stanza besides Enzo, Gwen, the opera power structure, and the cops? The cops were not even interested; there was no body, no evidence, and presently they were just investigating the disappearance of Frank Stanza.

Why would the man hired to save the CGO be in so much peril for the witness of a murder? Enzo's original witness would obviously cause the assailant to hunt for witnesses within the opera house, but a second attempt on his life planned to appear as a roadside murder, in Southern Indiana? Demetrius was bewildered.

What did the murder of Frank Stanza accomplish for the murderer? What information would a "props' master" hold that was worth silencing? What was being hidden in the catacombs of 'C' Level at the Illinois State Theatre?

Was Enzo just the unwitting witness, stumbling upon the covert? What had Enzo unearthed, if anything? Or, what had Frank Stanza discovered that would jeopardize his life?

The investigator wound his way through the questions, only to remain answerless, but he believed he knew where the answers could be found.

"Enzo, I want you to be more aware of your safety from now on," Demetrius stated. Enzo agreed.

"I'm gonna get you a bulletproof vest and I want you to wear it."

"All right," answered again the calm, forthright man. "Demetrius, you know I do not want Gwen to know about Indiana. I will tell her soon enough, but I don't want her to worry over that too."

"That's between you and her, and I'll honor your wishes, but she deserves to know."

"I know," Enzo said sheepishly. "Besides, I can't keep things from her anyway. Her sixth sense is perfectly tuned to my frequency."

Demetrius saw Gwen walking out of the elevator and making her way back to the table. He had a few last things he needed to ask in order to honor Enzo's wish.

"Enzo," Demetrius inquired, "who knew you were going to Bloomington?"

"It wasn't a secret. Obviously, Gwenny knew. I told the rehearsal department that I would be gone for a day or two, but I don't think I ever told them where. And of course the people down in Bloomington knew. I think that's it," added the perplexed man.

Enzo and Demetrius thought the same thing at the same time. The only way someone would have been able to set up such a complex murder attempt would have been to have known before hand of the impending trip, its travel route, its destination, and the spots along the road that would lend themselves to a quiet, concealed double murder. Demetrius knew he had to go back to the source of the information, then track his leads. And William Burrows was his prime candidate.

Gwen was just returning to the table as the men finished their talk, and she handed the switch to Enzo, who in turn gave it to Demetrius.

"Thank you, my love," cooed Enzo. Enzo turned to Demetrius. "Here's the switch I got out of the trash from the warehouse fire."

Demetrius twisted the switch in his hand, rotating the piece for his eyes to scan every corner. He discerned the connections closely, and finally brought the piece to his nose, sniffing the charred plastic and wiring.

"This doesn't look like any toggle switch I've ever seen," commented the detective. "Can I keep this?"

"That's why I had Gwenny get it. It is all yours, 'D.'"

"Smells a bit odd too. I'm gonna have some tests run on it and see what comes back. The tests might destroy the piece, Enzo."

"I don't care. I just want to find out who has caused all this carnage."

"Well, all you two have to do now is sit back and relax. I think I have an idea where to start looking," Demetrius said confidently, "but first, Enzo, I want you to draw me a tattoo."

Twenty-Three

The untrained hand did not know how to proceed. The rough pencil outline had barely been attempted, and the artist was unhappy with his feeble attempts.

He crumbled the white hotel paper into his palm and tossed the offending hack sketch into the waste receptacle. The underlying white sheet, creased under the pressed pencil tip, held no new clues as to the accomplishment of his task.

He sat back in his chair, and rolled his stiffened neck in crackling relief. He closed his eyes and breathed, slowly and surely, expanding the breadth of rib and posterior. The artist allowed the pencil to rest under fingertip, to lay motionless nestled in the valley of finger and thumb.

Behind darkened eyes, his mind projected the picture of composition. The subject had been in motion, but the eyes had caught the shifting object between activities. The sliver of a second lay frozen in his mind.

The light of the actuality was dim, but the original sparkled upon the ivory canvas where it had been burned. The colors were dark and vacant, hollow in depth, shallow in substance. The black outline of the scrawl incompletely confined the angry reds and petulant yellows that dominated the work, while tortured lines flowed into the precise points of daggers.

The subject was frozen, motionless in the mind, but the artist was unable to capture the essence of the piece.

More breath flowed through his lungs and into his bloodstream. The cool air vibrated his nerves. His hand began sweeping in small circles. His head leaned back in the tiny desk chair, mouth agape from the weight of its jaw, air passing down the throat, over relaxed tongue.

He sat up, looked at the continual swirls of his hand, delicately gripping the graphite medium, and began applying gray to white.

The sweeping of the hand brought curve to the sides of the subject, and flowed through the edges. Rises and humps, canyons and mountains, all took on their appropriate scope. The hand listened only to the picture, obeyed only the subject, not allowing the human fragility to disturb the recreation of its intention.

Focus and form filled the page. The framework for color was sketched well and outlined meticulously, the pencil adding dabs of charcoal, shades of black, and untouched spaces of white.

After fifteen minutes Enzo sat back and beheld his creation. The brand upon the hand of Frank's assailant now had essence. The form before him was nigh unto a perfect replication of that which he had seen one week ago, gripped in memory, and locked in the sight of the witness.

But the concentration for which the artist had to subjugate himself, the relaxation, the calmness, and the focus, these all fell as scales from the artist's eyes when the tattoo revealed its content.

The subject was hideous, in form and purpose, for no creature of this sort could intend kind. It was the vision of aggression, violence, and torture.

Enzo began shading with colored pencils, as a child would, the lines and curves and openness of the sketch.

It was the head of some hideous creature. It was the snarling head of a mythical aggressor—part lion, part goat, and part man—appearing capable of the biblical destruction that its form implied.

The beast's head was almost perfectly triangular, pointed downward. This point of the triangle was the jaw of the creature, mouthless, four jagged fangs protruding down, the outer teeth twice the size of the inner. No lower jaw was present, only upper teeth, ready to tear and rip at its prey, unable to devour, capable only of slaughter.

The inner teeth led up into the sunken skull-like nostrils, hollow and dark, flared and full, black chasms of corruption. Between the two empty nostrils, a bone protruded sharply from the brow, separating one from the other.

The top curves of the huge nose holes, sweeping upward, taking intent from below, were the eyes—slanted, deep and dark. The layers of flesh surrounding the eyes pointed into the nose bone, curving up and over the cheek, and once again rising to the sides.

The eyes were crimson, the color of hell, betraying the intent of the heart. The forehead loomed ominous, hanging over the slits that prevented escape. Layer upon layer of flesh seemed to fall into the eyes, finally converging into blackness.

The protruding brow gave rise to two horns, extending from the outside edge of each eye, perfect in slope-symmetry. Their curve rounded out from the side of the head, pulling the cheekbones up and over the sides of the eyes. Never narrowing, the horns rose far above the skull that owned them, and turned into each other until their symmetry found them directly over each eye. There, at the end, they slashed into razor points, directed one toward the other, but purposed, like a tool against all others.

Ridges of bone rolled out of the skull, above the brow, between the horns that were anchored just to the sides. These heavy platelets of crushing ivory protruded, flowing one onto the other, as waves crashing upon themselves. The thick ridges added height and protection to the creature, and menace to the eyes of the beast.

The outer sides of each cheek had behind them four sloping, ridged slats of bone. These slats flared the head, and as a Chinese mask, these ridges gave breadth and intimidation to the beast.

The horrid, angry face was a mass of protrusion and bone, fleshless and aggressive. It was malevolent—flared nostrils, angry eyes, hostile horns above. In its shell of protection it scowled maliciously, massive and murderous, intent on producing pain.

Enzo scribbled an illegible phrase on the bottom slat of the flared mask. He did not know what the words were, but he knew there was writing present, burned into the flesh of the murderer.

He then, within the open area created by the rounded horns, drew two letters. Within the left horn he carved a sweeping capital letter "C." The slope and angle of the letter within the cavity was a perfect reflection of the left horn, matching precisely the attitude of its captor.

The right horn held within its cavity a similarly-styled letter, same in slope and sweep, this symbol, soft and rounded, resembling the letter "Z."

The letters encapsulated within the beast's horns belied the character of the picture. They were clear and elegant, imitating the lines of grandeur in a hideous portrait below. They were captive of the monster, nestled in the brow of the hated creature.

The reds of the tattoo were dark, blood-stained, lining the outer edges. Black line and burnt colors filled the picture, outlining the scarlet. The skull remained its fleshy color, under nicotine-stained yellow hands.

It was complete. The tattoo that leapt out of Enzo's unconscious was now formed and present on paper. The symbol of the beast seemed clear. It was formed to encourage fear—to betray, to inflict evil, to forge an ever-imminent thought of death. The week of horror was summed up in this sketch. The catharsis of expression had removed this demon from Enzo's mind, and now he sought to deliver its vile expression to its owner, to place the hand beneath the brand, and to lock the monster away for all time.

Twenty-Four

"John, I need to ask a favor," requested Demetrius of his old friend. "I need to park a brown van on Lower Wacker Drive for about two weeks, and I don't want anybody messing with it."

Detective John McGrail knew Demetrius McDiess very well. In the detective's uniformed days he was the cop on the opera house beat. Fair-skinned and Irish as a leprechaun, John was present whenever the Illinois State Theatre dealt with the Chicago Police Department. He was the officer on whom the Chicago Grande Opera relied when help was needed. Security in the house could not handle every problem, and so, when the Chicago PD was requested, John was the man.

Demetrius had gotten to know John when the house cracked down on illegal drug use in the late 1980s. Demetrius, being the sleuth himself and a crack security guard at the time, fed information to his officer friend as he became privy to it. Demetrius and John both had a disposition for honesty and loyalty. They were a good pair of good men.

"What yer really askin' is if I'll get you a free parking pass for a couple of weeks, aren't ya, D?" John cracked wisely, leaning back in his standard issue office chair. "What do I get out of this, babe?" he said, with a smirk on his face, of his opera house buddy.

"Dinner?"

"We goin' out or you cookin'?"

"Cookin' in," replied 'D.'

"You or your mom cookin'?" John finally got to the real question, knowing the culinary artistry of Demetrius's mother.

"Probably me."

"No deal! If your mom was cookin' I'd do it, but not for your steamed dog crap." John's smirk grew bigger. "Offer sometin' good or I'll write your dirty-ass van up myself." John liked his sarcastic Irish humor a little more than anyone else liked it. He hesitated a moment then added, "I'll lock dat Denver boot on myself, babe."

"Four White Sox tickets, playin' the A's, box seats." Demetrius knew this offer would be refused by the northsider. John was already shaking his head.

"Fuck you, get me the Cubbies or I'll kick yer ass outta here right now."

Demetrius did not have much to offer his friend, at least not yet. What he did have were future dividends. If he promised John the credit for what might go down at the CGO, that might be worth more than any set of baseball tickets.

He would offer John everything—all the surveillance tapes, all the audio, and all the concrete evidence. If the operation was as big as he thought, Demetrius knew there would be a handsome promotion for his cop friend.

"John, listen to me, no more 'wise,' promise." Demetrius became serious with his friend and leaned onto the front edge of his desk. John removed the smirk and widened his eyes. "I have to do a little surveillance, and if it pans out, important people could go down, and I'll have the 411." John sat up in his chair. "I'll give you the whole game, exclusive, just give me two weeks in the tunnel, unencumbered."

"How big are these people?" inquired the officer.

"Internationals! Probably a lot of important local people too, with, I'd guess, national aspirations."

John's detective mind salivated. His narrow eyes searched his friend's face.

"You'll give me the whole shootin' match, lock to barrel?" whispered the piqued and discerning detective.

"All yours," Demetrius said and nodded.

"You got it, babe," John nodded back. "Two weeks," he pointed vocally. "But if nothin' plays out, you *still* owe me." He paused in greed. "Cubbie tickets; eight box seats, against the Phillies." John thrust his index finger at his friend, reapplying the smirk.

"And something else?" asked Demetrius. John's faded freckles knew he was getting played like a deck of cards. "It all ties in with the same game," Demetrius continued.

"What am I, the damn information desk?"

Demetrius pulled the little piece of paper housing the tiny graphite pencil tip from his coat pocket. The red substance had stained the paper, but the tip was still well-coated with the dried crimson.

John unfolded the paper, creased twice, and opened it to find the contents.

"Careful, John," Demetrius warned. "I don't want to lose that little thing."

"You said one favor when you walked in here, D," commented the taken detective.

"One favor, with many tasks," Demetrius said, half-smiling at his friend.

"Crap!" John knew he was in for a lot of extra work now that Demetrius had sold him on the "big sting." Demetrius sensed his disgust.

"But, John," Demetrius tilted his head in assurance, "there will be boundless rewards."

"Crap!" The City of Chicago detective studied the tiny morsel.

"Looks like a pencil tip," the Irishman said, then paused. "What the hell's on it?"

"That's what I'm hoping your lab will tell me."

"O.K., you big jerk, I'll do this too." McGrail paused. "What else you got?"

Demetrius pulled Enzo's opera find, the oddly configured toggle switch, from his other coat pocket and handed it to the friend across the desk.

"I think it smells funny, physically and figuratively."

"You got a better sniffer dan I do, babe." John sniffed the switch. He sniffed again. "Charcoal to me."

"Run that through the lab too, if you could," John looked up with the switch in his face, eyes leering over the burnt plastic and wiring, eyebrows lowered. "Please?" finished Demetrius.

"Yeah, yeah, I'll do it, but your little operation better get big real quick or you'll be in hock up to your ass with me, man."

"Here's where you can reach me, but I'll come visit you every now and then." Demetrius handed Detective McGrail a business card with his cell phone number. "John," Demetrius said and suddenly turned quite serious, "*really* keep this baby hushed up."

John did not joke now, for he saw the look and sincere gaze of the fine man before him. The switch was lowered from his eyes as he stared back at his friend. He nodded and spoke slowly to match his friend's intensity.

"You got it, babe."

"And John, thanks." Demetrius started to walk out of the tiny cramped office. "And I promise, man, this whole thing will be yours." John, with a smile on his face, nodded to his exiting friend.

"We'll see ya, babe."

The handsome black man whisked out of the office and the detective picked up the phone. He dialed quickly and waited for the phone to ring.

"Yeah. Detective McGrail here. Get me Forensics." A moment passed, and two chirps from the modern Bell device met his ears.

"Yea, Dorothy darlin'," he charmed the pathologist, "I got a favor to ask, babe."

Twenty-Five

5:35 p.m.
Saturday Evening
Downtown Chicago

The clouds dominated the blustery autumn day. The northern storms pushed against the warm southerly flow, bringing dark, moisture-laden skies. The wind whipped all afternoon. Clanging flagpoles warned the few adventurers to beware the coming torrents. The great banners hanging in front of the Illinois State Theatre creased at their bottom edge, slits creeping into the fabric, foretelling the eventual tears that would destroy the fine, regal drapery.

As in any great towering city, the street chasms accelerated the autumnal zephyrs, forcing the gales downward, between narrow passages, shoving the minotaur into its maze of concrete and steel. As the wind ascended, climbing the steep mountains of cities, the torrent grew angrier, wilder, protesting the impediments below and pounding its chest in superiority to the human artifice.

The great towers of Chicago leaned and swayed in the blasts. The pillaresque John Hancock Tower, rising straight and strong for one hundred floors, anchored in bedrock, bowed in reverence to the great gales, swaying twenty-four inches side to side, just less than the force necessary to rip the tower from its pylons and to send it plummeting back to ashes.

The huge bay windows in the enormous suite shook behind the force of the gusts, but the round man facing the panes paid no heed to the beast that blew. His drink was in his right hand, and his lips were wet, ready to moisten the tip of his favorite cigar.

His left hand fidgeted with his pants leg, and finally rested in the pocket. He stood there in the thin maroon cardigan his daughter had bought him just recently, stylishly buttoned to the very top.

Much work would have to be done early next week, but his preparation was done. The weekend could be spent with family, and at Mass, preferably tonight's mass. Saturday evening Mass was always shorter than Sunday's, and with the weekend ritual done a day early, the entire Sabbath could be spent relaxing.

The great twin doors to the suite opened and the assistant entered the room. He saw the boss standing in the bay windows, up the three stairs. He walked directly for him, ready at the boss's bidding to deliver the news. The boss cleared his throat.

"Talk to me, Robert."

"Yes, sir," spoke the reverent underling. "Everything is in place for next week's shipment. They'll be leaving tonight and arriving early Tuesday morning."

"Excellent," the boss responded, never laying eyes on his enforcer and "business manager." "Everything on their end is all right?" he asked over his shoulder to the man a few steps behind.

"Yes, sir. All the payments have been made and accepted, except for one." The boss's head turned towards the underling, tilting his ear to scrutinize the words. "But he was dealt with," finished the assistant.

"Good. There are a couple personal items on this shipment that I want in this office by Wednesday afternoon. You know what they are?"

The underling nodded.

As the evening deepened, the men's reflection appeared in the mirror of the bay windows, the outside darkening, and the inside illuminating the reflective presence of the two men.

The boss sipped his drink and chewed his protruding bottom lip, sucking the moisture off of it.

"You are in charge, Robert," the boss reiterated.

"Yes, sir."

"*Personally*, in charge." The air forced through his jowly cheeks emphasized the statement through an explosive "p."

"Yes, sir." The words were not threats, simply responsibility, and the assistant cherished the tasks.

The boss sipped his drink again, sucking mostly melted ice. The men were silent, watching the wind swirl the clouds above them, and inspecting their now prominent reflections.

As they stood in the window reflection the assistant noticed his mentor. He had never seen the boss look so diminutive. The dark skies outside hid his searching eyes. He stood strong and handsome, able and willing to do whatever it took to ensure success, but beside him stood the boss, feeble, weak, and rotund, yet still honored. The young man knew the time would come—his time for ascendance, and his time for power.

The assistant's eyes left the boss's reflection and lighted upon the back of the mentor's head. It was time for more business.

"Sir, the other matter?"

"Tell me, Robert."

"We are on top of them with both audio and visual. The singer and his wife have been pretty low key since he returned from Indiana." The enforcer nearly slipped, telling the boss of the botched attempt on Enzo's life. The boss had not ordered it, but he also did not know about it, so he would leave the matter alone.

"What about the other one?" the boss asked.

"The nigger." The boss's left hand swung out and missed the face of his underling, the fat man's body tilting off balance. The rotund man stepped to catch his reeling body before he tumbled down the steps behind him. Diluted alcohol and ice flew through the air, out of the glass in the boss's right hand, which was flailing to find support. The liquid wafted in slow motion, hung in even sky, down the steps of the window perch. The assistant, having avoided the weak jab, grabbed the waist of his mentor and steadied him, allowing the boss to regain his balance.

The pair finally stood upright together, the boss panting from the sudden exertion. He pulled himself up straight, his paunch pressed to the firm abdominal muscles of his "number one." His ferocious eyes peered at the underling. The boss quickly put his glass in his left hand, more certain of his right. The previously errant paw swept across the left cheek of the underling, snapping the head of the tanned, suited enforcer. His head received the smack and instantly returned to face forward. The tiger-eyes of the boss, blood-shot, dark and angry, leered into the lesser's.

"Don't you underestimate dis *man*, Robert," accentuated the boss, avoiding the racial epithet. "By your manner and your tongue, you've already screwed up. You've already underestimated him." The scent of alcohol and cigar sprayed into the assistant's face, his cheek again crimson under the pressure of the disciplinary tool.

"You underestimated that props kid, and then you killed him. Now dis black detective comes snoopin' around, stickin' his nose where it don't belong, all because of dat one mistake, dat one miscalculation."

The old man softened his glare and relaxed his stiffened neck.

"You see, son, one...little...misstep, and our whole house comes tumblin' down." The boss turned and walked down the three steps and headed for his desk.

"You have to listen," sighed the old man. "Listen and think. Listen to what people say, and listen more closely to what dey don't say. Then take action, applying pressure to the points of greatest resistance." The apprentice, still attentive, followed the mentor down the steps. He watched the old man bounce unassuredly down the simple three steps. The boss waddled to the desk and turned.

"And when people get in the way of business, just like children, warn 'em once, and if they don't comply after that, you spank 'em, and you spank 'em hard."

The assistant nodded affirmation again, his eyes flat and agitated. He was growing weary of these little "lessons" in business.

"Robert, the only mistake you made was disposing of our props man. If you had applied da bit of pressure I would've, he'd be under our thumb right now, and more scared than a cop out of donuts." The assistant leered at the boss.

"Now, we're not gonna underestimate dis detective fellow, or the damn tenor. Watch 'em close, real close." The boss put on the suit coat that was hanging on the back of his recliner behind his desk. "Dey all have pressure points dat we can push if dey get too close." The coat slid on one arm and hung to his back, his left arm searching for the armhole. "But wait and listen. Now dat dey're bugged, get your information, and move when you need to, but *only* when you need to." The jacket hoisted its way up onto the once-broad shoulders.

"Then when you do move, *crush 'em,* cause..." his fat cheeks exploded with consonance, "cause we can't allow no loose ends, or we're all gonna go down fuckin' hard." The boss walked past the desk and towards the doors. The assistant spun slowly and watched the man walk by him. The aged man grew almost puny with each step he took towards the door. He gazed at the fat man who hobbled to the office exit.

"Call my car," ordered the boss. "I'm going to Mass with my family."

"Yessir." The barely audible reply seeped through contemptuous lips. The phone was picked up and the call made.

The tuxedo leaned on the great dark desk and hung up the phone. He crossed his arms, and watched the double doors swing closed.

I should've let him fall, he thought. *I'd be sitting in the chair, and I'd decide what happens...when, and to whom.* His eyes again narrowed and grew like his mentor's, bloodshot and ferocious. He would not abide this abuse much longer.

If he'd have fallen, I'd be in charge, and no more fucking" lessons." And even if the fall did not kill the bloated mentor immediately, the student would have enjoyed putting this man, the one who had schooled him in the finer points of "business," out of his corpulent misery.

Besides, it was time for new blood, for more aggressive tactics. And the "business" in which these gentlemen were involved was becoming more aggressive and more bloody.

Just a little longer, he thought, *and I'm gonna make a killing*. The memory of past success ignited his excitement. A violent inhalation snapped his spine upright. His hands on his crossed arms clutched the flesh of his biceps.

"Just a little longer…"

Twenty-Six

Demetrius's van was an old brown Dodge that looked as if it should have been condemned years ago. The front bumper, torn off of the driver's side, was held in place by electrical wire. The sides of the vehicle were scarred and scraped, weather-bleached and worn. The passenger side of the brown wonder had been sideswiped several times, and flecks of white, blue, and red slid across the body where these hit-and-run bandits had perpetrated their crime.

Demetrius did not care. The shell of the battered vehicle was the perfect camouflage for the surveillance equipment inside. He had installed a partition behind the driver's compartment to shield the investigative contents of the vehicle from those passing by. The van's engine ran fine, satisfying the detective, but one glance by any pedestrian at the physical appearance of the behemoth would make one suspect the monstrosity was headed straight for the pound.

Demetrius pulled the vehicular eyesore fifty yards north of the opera house's lower Wacker Drive loading dock, into the unused parking lane. This seemed a safe distance from the loading dock for the van to avoid suspicion, but too great a distance for his surveillance equipment. Demetrius looked over his shoulder and backed the van up to a similar location, 10 yards closer to the loading dock. This location satisfied the man.

The ugly brown vehicle fit in perfectly with the scattered debris, the supply trucks, and the skyscraper exhaust vents that lined the once most valuable real estate in the world. The green lights on lower Wacker, designed to best illuminate the subterranean passageway, cast a phantasmal glow, turning the little surveillance van into a tiny shop of unnatural discovery.

2:00 p.m.
Sunday, October 1

Demetrius decided to look again into the property's holding area. He would scrutinize the logbooks Enzo had told him Frank so hated completing. Nothing showed itself. The muscular black investigator dissected every nook and crept through every cranny, but he found nothing. He searched through the giant props' storage room, again leafing through the debris of the inferno that consumed the opera warehouse last January. Nothing appeared to him. Nothing revealed the slightest inkling of culpable information.

"Talk to me, Frank," Demetrius muttered as he strode out of the storage room and stared down at the desk. He walked around the desk slowly. There was nothing on the floor. He walked around again, looking up at the ceiling and the panels above.

He pulled the little flashlight from his pocket and examined shadow and substance, contemplating dark and light, scrutinizing corner and expanse. There was nothing.

He stood behind the desk and pulled up the wooden stool that had been kicked to the wall behind the desk. The logbooks stood stacked to his left. He pulled the top book to the desk in front of him and began leafing through the simple dimestore journal.

The ledgers were clean, neat, unextraordinary. He leafed through every page. The journal was divided into sections, each section given a specific date. Then, each date coincided with those particular props and sets originally received from the Mexico City Opera Theatre.

Demetrius was perplexed. He had not seen this book before now. The date of the most recently entered information was from Friday, September 29th. He decided that while he was poking around the props department two mornings ago, this particular log book was on the opera stage being used, releasing and cataloguing the needed set pieces for the opera being rehearsed.

The duct-taped top of the stool stuck to Demetrius's fine woolen pants. The great bonding agent sought a new partner in union, and grabbed at the delicate fabric as the man shifted in his seat, leaning and lunging to the desk.

The entries appeared in order and complete. A schedule of shipments from the Mexico City Opera Theatre had been taped to the front page of the journal. There were several dates in the summer, August being filled with five arrivals. The next trucks were due to arrive this Tuesday, October 3. The expected time of arrival was 2:00 a.m.

Demetrius found the arrival time unusual, but long-haul trucks were not unknown for such odd schedules, particularly when the equipment being delivered was so specialized.

Penciled in next to the two o'clock arrival time were the words "bullshit." The word was obviously the opinion of the discontented crews, expressed by their sympathetic props crew chief.

At the bottom of the white schedule paper was the word "BUT..."

Some sort of arcane reference from the discontented crews? The odd conjunction leapt out in its curious obscurity.

The taped stool top had clung firmly to the pants legs and now did not want to release its capture.

"Damn it," blurted the frustrated man, sliding his leg away from the eternally sticky bonding strip.

Demetrius stood up quickly, tired of the tug-of-war with the inanimate object. The force of his stand pulled the stool up with him. The tape peeled off, releasing the woolen pants under the weight of the stool.

The stool landed with a thud on its two hind legs and tipped backwards. Demetrius repeated his condemnation and grabbed for the stool. His hand hit only the front edge of the shabby wooden seat, rocketing the seat to the cinderblock behind the desk. The stool top rammed into the white wall, and bounced off of the barrier.

With its singular odd word, "BUT..." on its inner leaf, Demetrius put the logbook down in disgust. He leaned over to grab the stool and to put the wicked little menace back in its proper place. He grabbed the leg support, located midway between seat and leg bottom that connected the stool legs. He pulled the tattered furniture to set it up straight.

As he pulled the stool up, he noticed the underside of the seat. A wad of duct tape had been pushed up onto the seat from the underside. The stiff gray tape would remain there forever if need be, holding and supporting the chair from the underside.

Demetrius thought nothing of the appendage, but then, squinting in the shadows of Sunday's dimmed lighting, he found the outline of something within. He pulled the stool up and onto the props desk and began his dissection.

As he turned the stool over to see the underside more clearly, the tape collapsed under gravity. Gravity had held it suspended, hanging under the stool for hours, even days, but now, the constant force of the earth's rotation pushed down on the bonded area from a different angle. The hollow bulbous center sank under its own weight.

Demetrius reached in and pushed on the sunken area. Indeed, a pocket of tape had been formed around something. Demetrius felt for the edges of the block of tape and picked with his index finger at the corner of goo and fiber, pulling up an edge that both thumb and index finger could remove.

He pulled slowly, not wanting to harm the package inside this odd wrapping. An imperfect square of tape peeled away from the seat's underside. The fleshy side of the tape was exposed along the edges of the patch.

A thin stack of photos was set under the duct taped sarcophagus. The top photo clung to the tacky tape surface. Demetrius pulled the tape over into his palm, and then pulled the patch completely off the stool seat. He reached in with his right hand and retrieved the small stack of pictures.

He pulled five photos from the stool bottom and left the one stuck to the duct tape alone, not wanting to damage the picture. He leafed through the stack: six photos in all.

They were a series of photos taken on the opera house loading dock. A semi-tractor trailer was pulled up to the dock and the grainy photos, taken through a small crack in one of the dock doors, revealed several men unloading packages from the rear of the truck. The first photo was very blurry, but showed three men standing around a piece of scenery, pulled partially out of the truck. One man knelt down and tugged at the backside of some scenery, while the other two steadied the set piece.

The second picture disclosed two of the workers carrying large plastic bags out of the truck, and a third man placing two of the plastic bags in a separate black nylon satchel. The third photo showed four men wheeling a huge urn out into the dock, and the fourth pictured the same men reaching into the urn. This same photo pictured one of the men beside the urn holding what appeared to have been a portion of the contents of the urn. The fifth was a clear picture of two of the men, facing the unknown photographer, taking orders from a third man, whose back was to the camera, his left hand and arm pointing to the dock, out of the picture.

The sixth photo, the duct-taped photo, was the oddest of all. It was not of the men on the dock; it was not of the contents, or even a photo of the truck that had made the deliveries.

This last one was a picture of a garbage can, supposedly sitting on the dock. The surrounding dark cement floor and brick walls were familiar to the former security guard. The dark green garbage can was full of a dark brown powder, finely ground. What was oddest of all, the photographer's own hand was in the picture, reaching around the front of the camera, holding two things, as distant and focused from his eyes as possible, yet within camera range. The hand of the photographer held more of the dark brown powder, and several white pellets, the size of marbles and a bit oblong, but still dominantly round. A little white seam lined the middle of the pellets, matted on the rough pink palm of the photographer.

The ground brown powder looked like coffee, but the white pellets were a definite mystery to Demetrius. He whipped through the photos again, searching and discriminating the unfocused details of the crude surveillance work.

The best of the lot was the fifth photo—the two men facing the camera, with the third pointing to the left, his back to the camera, directing the others.

Demetrius searched the faces and peered at the back of the head of the supposed leader. He scanned the sides and the depth of the photo, seeking detail. The two stocky, dark-haired men facing the lens were unfamiliar to him, but he had been away from the Illinois State Theatre for quite a while. The third man, wearing a black jacket and black pants, head slightly tilted to the left, tracking the lead of his arm, was totally unknown and faceless.

Demetrius followed the arm with the subject of the photo, out to the left, down the arm. His black jacket sleeves ended in his white hand.

There was something on the man's hand. The small photos made it difficult to hone in on the exact nature of the object, but there was color on the hand, with the index finger pointed sternly off camera.

There it was. The hand at the end of this man's arm was painted, colored in the hues that Enzo had described and drawn for him. The backside of this photographed man's hand was tattooed, described exactly by his friend two days before.

The black ink-stained, skull-like figure peered through hollow eyes. The reds of the tattoo gleamed in the fluorescent light of the dock. The ferocious fangs pierced down into the wrist of the man. The swirling horns sloped into the top of the hand, edging the knuckles. Lined in crimson, the beast's flared neck flowed into the chubby thumb and flat of the hand. Even the scrawl on either side of the demon's jaw was visible, yet somehow not completely legible. The yellow nicotine stains, casting the surreal pall on the tattoo, shone through. Some little dime store developer had taken these negatives and pulled out great detail from a second-rate apparatus.

And there he was. The killer, back turned to the camera, identified by the lone remembered distinguishing mark on his body. Finally, his existence had been clarified, and now Demetrius had to find this hideous human being and bring him to justice.

He stared at the photo long and hard, hoping to find anything else, any mark, any mole, any recognizable sign. There was none. The tattoo alone drew his attention, labeling the man who would now be the pursued. The photos went into Demetrius's coat pocket. Demetrius looked again to the logbook, with its cryptic message "BUT..." and looked down to the stool that held his discovery.

"You forgot the second 'T' my friend," said the man, now realizing what the misspelled code signified, "but thank you for the tip, Frank." Demetrius looked around the props room, as if thanking the ghost of the man who had toiled for this opera company, and gave his life, attempting to unravel the chaos within the bowels of this great theatre.

"Now to shake these people up a little bit."

Demetrius replaced the logbooks. He made certain there was no sign of tampering, and then quickly scurried up the three flights of stairs and out of the opera house.

The room was poorly lit and still. The stairwell fire door settled into its closed position with a click and latch. The props area was quiet, having revealed its secret contents to Demetrius, but also to another.

A tiny camera had been recording the fine detective work of the last few minutes. The apparatus was set upon the heat ducts down the hall from the props desk, hugging the ceiling. The miniature movie camera had filmed the entire scene.

Those who would view it knew this behavior could not continue much longer. Tension was piling upon tension, and nerve was fraying nerve. Those people caught in witness of the events of the last days now possessed evidence of the secrets behind the *New* Chicago Grande Opera. These conspirators, spying this witness's discoveries, knew that soon this man and all witnesses would have to be silenced.

3:00 p.m.
Sunday, October 1

The telephone rang only once.

"Hello," spoke the older woman's voice.

"Mrs. Hutchinson?"

"Yes, this is Dorothy Hutchinson."

"Mrs. Hutchinson, this is Enzo Santi." It was the first time Enzo had been able to talk to the wife of Bill, his limousine driver. The valiant driver was still holding on to life, although he was still in intensive care, and deep in a coma.

Carson Limousine Service had taken Mrs. Hutchinson down to Bloomington Hospital as soon as news of the "accident" had been received.

Enzo had prompted the call from the hospital, informing the nurses of the car service's name and location. Michael Fitzgerald, the service's rental operator, had driven Mrs. Hutchinson himself.

"Mrs. Hutchinson, is there anything I can do for you?" asked Enzo, miles north.

"I don't think so, Mr. Santi," responded the weary woman. "The hospital staff has been very kind to us." She paused, "to me," she said, correcting herself. Her weak smile traveled through the phone lines. "And they are taking good care of Bill."

"Have the doctors said anything about how he's doing?"

"They say he's about the same. I just have to wait," responded the woman, "and pray."

"I'm praying with you, Mrs. Hutchinson." Enzo had wanted to stay in Bloomington, at least to see Mrs. Hutchinson, but his teacher, James Koenig, had advised him to get back to his wife and recover from his own ordeal. Of course Koenig did not know the real story of what happened on the trip to Bloomington.

"Have any of your children arrived yet?"

"My youngest came almost immediately. I called her as soon as I got in the limousine to come down here. Michael was very nice to let me use his car phone. She's staying with me."

"Could I speak to her, Mrs. Hutchinson?"

"Of course..."

"Mrs. Hutchinson?"

"Yes, Mr. Santi."

"Please, call me Enzo, ma'am."

"All right."

"I want you to know I'm praying for you and your husband. He's such a kind man. We enjoyed our day together, traveling...down...to Bloomington." Enzo's voice began to shake as he saw Bill's face looking up to him, trapped in the limousine, pleading for relief from the scalding injection that had seized his heart.

"I know, Enzo," spoke the woman. "I'm praying also," her voice soothed his distress. "And I am praying for you, Enzo. May God bless you."

Enzo heard the tenderness and the generosity of this woman. In all her torment, she was bestowing blessings upon him.

"Thank you, Mrs. Hutchinson," Enzo spoke. "He has blessed me."

"Here is my daughter, Enzo. Thank you again for calling."

A moment passed as the phone was given to the daughter. Enzo heard the heart monitor in the background beeping slowly, watching the status of the patient so near at hand.

"Hello?"

"Yes, this is Enzo Santi, Miss Hutchinson."

"It's so nice of you to call, Mr. Santi. What can I do for you?" The thirty-year-old daughter spoke quietly, feeling the same heartache as her mother.

"Have the doctors said anything about what happened?"

"They did say it looked like a heart attack," she answered, "but they are still doing more tests."

"Have you been treated well, Miss?"

"Very well. The hospital has let us use anything we need. We were even given a rental car." The young woman paused. "I think Carson is giving us a rental car, since this has happened while dad was working."

"How nice of them," Enzo responded. "How do you think your father is doing?"

"I think maybe improving a bit. His heart seems stronger than when he came in. It's just a slow process...waiting, you know."

"Yes, I know. Where are you staying?"

"Mom sleeps here quite a bit, but there is a Quality Inn just up from the hospital. I sleep there, and try to get Mom to come too."

"Is your mom getting enough rest?"

"No, but I'm gonna insist she sleep at the hotel tonight. Of course, she doesn't want to leave Dad."

"I'm so sorry I had to leave so quickly. I wanted to stay, but..."

"No apology necessary, Mr. Santi. You have been so kind to call and check up on Dad and us. There wasn't anything you could do to prevent a heart attack."

Enzo felt relieved that these folks, like their husband and father, were so forgiving.

"I won't keep you, Miss Hutchinson, but I'd like to speak to the nurse, if I could?"

"My pleasure, Mr. Santi."

"Call me Enzo, please. I feel like I know you folks from what your father has told me about you all, so please, call me Enzo."

"All right, Enzo. I'll try to transfer you to the nurse, if I can figure out—oh, here we go."

"God bless you, ladies, and God bless Bill."

"Thank you again, Enzo. Good-bye, and hold on."

The phone buzzed and beeped while the transfer took place.

"Intensive Care."

"This is Enzo Santi. I am calling about Albert Hutchinson. I would like to talk to Nurse Greendale."

"Hello, Mr. Santi, this is Nurse Greendale."

"Thank you so much for helping me with the car rental, and the extras for the Hutchinsons."

"No problem. It's much easier using other people's credit cards than my own," kidded the intensive care nurse, "and besides, you have a huge limit."

"My pleasure," Enzo countered, smiling to himself, "but could you do me one more favor?"

"What? You want more flowers and food for the Hutchinsons? The room is a smorgasbord as it is." Her tone was more light-hearted than her words, so Enzo knew all was fine.

"Could you call the Quality Inn, give them my credit card number, and tell them I will pay for the Hutchinson's hotel bill. Everything included, phone, cable, whatever the bill comes to?"

"No problem, Enzo. I'll do it right now," quipped the good humored nurse. "Do you mind if I put that addition on my house with what's left on your limit?"

"Fine by me," smiled the Argentinean. "I owe you more than that for all the help you've been to me."

"Stop it, silly," she said, beaming. "Just get me those signed recordings you promised, and we're all fair and square."

"They're already in the mail, Mrs. Greendale." Enzo had relied on this nurse to supply the needs of those he had left in need. She was a valued helper in his kindness to the Hutchinsons. "Any news about Mr. Hutchinson?"

"The doctor said that it looks like he was injected with potassium."

"Potassium? I thought that was good for you."

"Not if you have too much, Enzo. If you're injected, it goes straight to the heart and clogs everything up. It messes with the receptors. Ya see, your heartbeat is regulated by an exchange of potassium and sodium, and when you're injected with 10cc's of potassium, your heart stops beating. Sends you right into cardiac arrest. Fortunately for Mr. Hutchinson, the doctors don't think he was injected with enough to kill him, but it was awfully close. He's still in pretty bad shape."

"What is the prognosis?"

"Don't know yet. He hasn't responded well to what they've done so far, so we have to wait and see if he can fight through this thing. If his heart was in good shape, he may be o.k. And, if he ate a lot of salt."

"Is it easy to get medical potassium? I mean I've heard of it in bananas, but who could get something like that."

"Anybody in the medical profession can get it. It's fairly common in the hospital, but you have to have medical connections."

"Thank you so much for all your help, Nurse Greendale. You've been a godsend."

"No problem, Enzo, but like I said, those compact discs better be on their way." The nurse feigned toughness.

Enzo had sent four of his opera CDs, all signed, and had also sent a gift certificate for a weekend getaway in Indianapolis for the nurse, for both her and her husband.

"Don't worry," Enzo responded, "they'll be there shortly."

5:00 p.m.
Sunday evening

"Thank you for seeing me, Mrs. Filmore," Demetrius said politely. "I hope I'm not taking you away from anything important."

"Oh no, Mr. McDiess," the regal, well-bred woman responded. "Just a lazy Sunday by the pool." She turned and invited Demetrius into her home. It was an estate befitting the wealth and prominence the Brook family had built in the city. The Brook Candy Company had supplied Chicago with sweet delights for decades, and the benefits of her mother's founding and ownership of that company were on display throughout the Filmore mansion. It was not pretentious, but certainly elegant and perfectly comfortable.

"Would you like something to drink, Mr. McDiess?"

"No thank you, ma'am." The two walked into the living room just to the right of the entrance hall and sat down. The room was dominated by a family portrait, expertly photographed and beautifully lit, highlighting Mrs. Brook Filmore, her husband, who had entered his wife's family business of candy, and their four children, all young adults between the ages of fifteen and twenty-five.

"That's a beautiful portrait, Mrs. Filmore."

"Thank you. Those four are my pride and joy. My oldest is just finishing medical school. He wants to be a pediatrician."

"Any of your children want to go into the family business?" asked Demetrius. The middle-aged woman chuckled to herself and smiled broadly.

"Well, my youngest, Sam, loves sweets, but whether he wants to go into the candy business is up to him. Laura, our second daughter, is actually quite an entrepreneur. She was always selling something as a child, so maybe her destiny is to join the Brook Candy Company."

She smiled as only a proud mother can, recalling the joys and the difficulties of giving your life to the nurture of your child. Unlike many upper-class children who are neglected by absentee parents, these Brook grandchildren had been cared for with love, not money alone.

"So, your family still has control of Brook Candy?" Demetrius was happy at how easily their conversation was progressing.

"Oh yes, my husband has been acting chairman for twenty years. He is the one who helped Brook Candy establish a national name. We had been more of a Midwest specialty company, but he brought us to the rest of the country's attention." Information flowed from her gentle spirit, and her face exuded honesty.

"What are your holdings worth now, especially since your move nationally?"

She leaned back, one arm draped over the back of the chaise on which she leaned, and thought a moment.

"Somewhere around two billion dollars, I guess." She spoke again to clarify, "give or take a little. But that is the company's worth, not our personal worth. I won't tell you those numbers. I'm sure you understand, Mr. McDiess."

"So, if you don't mind me asking, was the gift your mother gave to the Chicago Grande Opera a corporate gift or a personal gift, if you don't mind answering." Demetrius couched his question.

"No, I don't mind," she said affirmingly, "but I don't know."

"You don't know?"

"Well, Mr. McDiess," she pulled her arm down from its lofty position, "if I understand correctly, the gift to the opera was about five hundred million dollars, and as you should know, a two billion dollar company doesn't really have that kind of cash lying around. The two billion is usually invested in equipment and product. Sure, we have cash reserves, but not that much. I doubt our lawyers would allow us to keep that much cash on hand."

"So, your mother must have willed the money to the opera from her personal holdings?"

"Well, I really don't want to talk about my mother's personal will and testament, but yes, she did leave a substantial sum to the Chicago Grande," a broad smile grew across Mrs. Filmore's face.

"But..." Demetrius slowed, trying to get the needed information, "would you characterize that sum to be half a billion dollars?" Mrs. Filmore's smile grew increasingly broad, and the matron started to laugh.

"No, Mr. McDiess. I would characterize my mother's gift as nowhere close to that number." Mrs. Filmore's laughter slowed as she listened to herself. "Oh, what the hell," she said. "My mother gave the CGO about ten million dollars."

"That's very generous of her and her estate," Demetrius complimented.

"It certainly is, Mr. McDiess, but," she paused, "not even close to the half billion she is receiving the credit for, right?"

"Yes, ma'am," Demetrius answered. Mrs. Filmore was a sharp conversationalist, and saw right to Demetrius' point.

"Then why did the CGO honor you at the Opening Night Ceremony?"

"I don't know, Mr. McDiess. I showed up at our family box, and the general director asked me to join him on the podium in the foyer, so I did. I didn't realize what was going on either. Bill just said he wanted to thank my mother for all her help in reviving the CGO, so, as a dutiful daughter who loved her mother, I went and took pleasure in the good deed my mother had done." Demetrius's confusion continued, as did Mrs. Filmore's. She continued.

"Ten million dollars is not chopped liver, you know, young man."

"No, ma'am, I understand that." Demetrius laughed and apologized. She had to acknowledge his confusion, though, which was hers as well.

"But you are right, Mr. McDiess. I don't know who gave the money to the CGO. All I know is that my mother donated a substantial sum to the Chicago Grande Opera, but she's receiving the credit for an astronomical donation." Demetrius nodded in agreement with the helpful matriarch.

"That kind of donation would give Warren Buffet a rash." Mrs. Filmore's sense of humor found itself for the first time this afternoon. "Now, young man, since I have been honest with you, answer a few questions for me." Demetrius smiled, sensing the approaching interrogation.

"I'll do my best, ma'am."

"Fair enough," she replied. "Who wants to give all the credit for this donation to my mother?"

"I don't know," Demetrius replied. Mrs. Filmore squinted her eyes, unsatisfied. "I don't know *yet*, ma'am." She smiled at his correction.

"Why would someone want to hide their donation like that?"

"Why don't you want people to know your business?" Demetrius asked her in return.

"Because it is not any of *their* business," she answered. Demetrius nodded with her as she answered her own question. Mrs. Filmore was still unhappy with her interrogation of Demetrius.

"No, it's really not that, is it? Whoever gave that money to the CGO has actively encouraged this rumor concerning the source of the donation. Right?"

"It appears that way, ma'am."

"So why don't they, whoever *they* are, why don't they want the public to know about the donation?"

Aha! Mrs. Filmore had asked the vital question. The same question that Demetrius was trying to answer, and the question that he felt was at the root of Frank's murder and the attempted murder of Enzo.

"I honestly don't know yet, ma'am," Demetrius slowly extolled. "That's what I'm trying to find out. What is really going on at the Illinois State Theatre?"

Mrs. Filmore smiled, proud of her progress as an amateur detective.

"So that's the question at the CGO," she said. "What is Bill Burrows trying to hide?" She smiled with a grin like that of a Cheshire cat.

Demetrius thought exactly the same thing, only Mrs. Filmore had added the name—Bill Burrows—not just the organization.

William Burrows, General Director, would be privy to all financial transactions within the CGO, and thus might be pressed into divulging some explosive answers.

"You are an excellent detective, Mrs. Filmore. You ask the right questions." Proud of the compliment, Mrs. Filmore leaned back in her chaise and smiled broadly again.

"Thank you, Mr. McDiess. And when you find out what is going on at the CGO, you must tell me," she leaned into the elegant man sitting across from her, "first hand."

"It's a deal, Mrs. Filmore."

Demetrius thanked her for her help and she saw him to the door. There was still a bit of sunlight to encourage play in the pool back behind the house, so she was off. Demetrius put on his black Raybans, shielding his eyes from the descending sun, and walked to his black Dodge Stealth parked in the street.

"What is William Burrows hiding?" He shook his head again. "Excellent question!"

Twenty-Seven

8:30 p.m.
Sunday Evening, October 1

The Santis ate dinner in their suite with their good friend, Demetrius McDiess. The room service was excellent, and the Santis were able to concoct some dishes of their own that beautifully complimented the huge meal of pasta.

Gwen was an expert at whipping up an exquisite Caesar salad, with just the right blend of herbs, spices, and balsamic vinegar. Enzo made the coffee, his only real culinary expertise. Demetrius brought the wine, partly out of kindness, and partly to celebrate what he would tell the couple.

It had been another lazy Sunday for the Santis, restful and quiet. Enzo still believed one day of the week should be focused on nothing but quietness. This was their day, when most of the world's opera houses were dark, and when he and his family could actively worship in the morning and passively worship in the afternoon and evening. Besides, the coming week would be very busy. Several *Otello* rehearsals were scheduled, and Enzo had two Tosca performances, one on Wednesday and another this coming Saturday. He was, after all, the talk of the town with his passionate portrayal of Puccini's tragic hero.

While the offstage life of the tenor had exploded in turbulence, that same violence, that fire, had burned its engulfing flames into the performances that had been given over the last week and a half. He was scorching himself into the annals of opera history with his full-throttle heroic performances, and yet he was oblivious to the accolades. As long as his friend's death was unsolved, and as long as his family was caught up in the turmoil, his art was secondary, even tertiary, in his realm of thinking.

"How was the Santis' Sunday?" asked Demetrius, snatching a corkscrew from the kitchenette to open the wine he had purchased.

"Wonderful," beamed Gwen, as she tossed the Caesar in the large wooden salad bowl. "We didn't do a thing except go to church this morning. I forgot how much I like Fourth Pres.," she said, referring to the huge Presbyterian Church up Michigan Avenue. "But it was restful and quiet."

Having found three wineglasses, Demetrius walked down the kitchenette stairs into the main room towards Enzo.

"It was fabulous," Enzo seconded.

"You haven't told her, have you, E?" whispered the concerned friend of the withholding husband. "She needs to know, Enzo, the sooner the better," then he added, "and the easier."

"I know," Enzo nodded.

Demetrius thumped the chest of the tenor, searching for the protective bulletproof vest he had lent him. There was nothing but flesh.

"Enzo, where is the vest?" Demetrius snarled. The investigator was genuinely perturbed at this oversight.

"In the other room," Enzo calmly answered. "It's too small, Demetrius. It was cutting off my circulation. Besides, we're indoors. Nothing can harm us up here." The tenor was overconfident, having released his burden onto Demetrius. He felt with the tattoo drawn and Demetrius on the case, life would soon return to normal. Enzo believed good was on his side, and he was confident of its triumph. Despite all the operatic evil that had triumphed over him on-stage, Enzo knew that goodness would prevail offstage.

"Enzo, look at me," demanded Demetrius. "Don't get too cocky too soon." Demetrius looked over his shoulder to ensure Gwen's location in the tiny kitchen. "Yes, I've got good news, but this isn't over yet, and I don't think you should take anything for granted.."

Enzo's face fell as he looked at his friend.

"Especially your life." Seeing Enzo look down a moment, Demetrius added, "or your wife's life."

Enzo's eyes bolted back up to those of his friend.

"Could Gwen be in danger?" asked the distraught husband.

"Enzo," softened D, "I'm just saying that these people have tried to kill you twice, and they don't even know what information you have. If we've stumbled onto something this big, these guys will stop at nothing to protect their interests."

Enzo looked down again, ashamed of his arrogance. He would not risk his wife's life or safety for anything.

"I'm sorry, Demetrius."

"I know, Enzo. We just need to be careful—and diligent." The men shared a secure smile and poured the wine. Gwen walked down into the room with the finished salad.

"The vest really is too tight around my chest, though, Demetrius," the tenor stated matter-of-factly.

"Baritones are supposed to be barrel-chested; you tenors are supposed to be fat as pigs." Enzo laughed. Gwen heard the laughter as she descended from the kitchenette.

"I am still in my descending stage." Rubbing his chest and stomach, Enzo pushed his firm stomach out, pretending to show an overweight posture. "My chest is slowly falling into my stomach."

Enzo took a glass of wine and then took the salad from Gwen with his opposite hand.

"By the time I'm fifty I will look like the Michelin man," the Argentinean said and smiled, "just as a good tenor should. Flab helps the high notes," the tenor crooned. He laughed a hearty, tenoral *melisma*.

"If you get fat I'll run your butt off," spoke the approaching wife in jest. "Or make you eat brussel sprouts at every meal."

"Yuck! I guess I will have to stay lean and mean. A sexy high-note machine."

The trio laughed more, Enzo especially, after referring to sex in front of someone other than his wife. The embarrassment of the word caught him off guard.

"Here's your wine, sweetheart," he said, switching the salad to his other hand, ready to place it on the dining table. Enzo leaned into his wife's face and gave her a kiss.

"Mmmm...thank you," she cooed after the kiss. "Do we have everything, guys?" she asked, searching the apartment for any final touches to the meal. The room service cart on the far side of the table held the pasta.

"Mmm, excellent wine, D," commented the hostess.

"Thanks," responded the giver. "I picked it up at the wine shop around the corner, on State. They've got a great selection." The group walked to the three place settings around the comfortable dining table and partook of the bounty.

Gwen spoke a short word of blessing and the three friends dined. They were perfectly comfortable with each other and the evening flew away. The Santis told their friend about the house in the near western suburbs. They chatted of the family that would fill the halls of the home nestled in parks and playgrounds, in preserves and grass. Enzo hoped for two boys and a girl, the daughter to be the baby. The boys would love American football, but be expert at the world version. The future mother and father would teach them and train them, encouraging them in whatever pursuit they chose for their lives.

"What about music?" Demetrius paused. "...opera?"

"We want our children, someday," Gwen smiled at her husband, "to become what they dream, and if music is what they dream, we'll support them in that decision."

"Gwen will be in charge of the musical education," Enzo piped. "I will hone their athletic skills." Enzo sipped his wine, aiding the digestion of his meal.

"But most of all," Enzo stared directly at his wife, "we want our home to be full of love and laughter." The Argentinean paused to take in the love of his life, sitting regally at the end of the table.

Gwen's cheeks were rosy from her bit of imbibing, and her flushed face, spreading throughout her countenance, warmed the room.

Gwen returned the gaze from her lover, allowing her smile to fill her face. Her stare was intent on him. Enzo's eyes touched her cheeks, caressed her arms, stroked her neck, and kissed her mouth.

They did not touch, and they did not speak. They made love one to another, with the giving of their eyes, the sharing of their minds, and the surrender of their hearts. They were one flesh, one soul, and one life, lived out in two fragile, gifted people who cared not for themselves, but only, eternally, intent on giving to the other. Theirs was a perfect love and perfect union—passionate, understanding, selfless, and unconditional.

The wife winked her right eye lightly, affirming the affection her husband gave her. They were wholly lost in one another's love.

Gwen drew her head away from Enzo and pulled out of their momentary intimacy.

"What about you, D. Has anyone kindled your fancy?" she asked.

"Not yet, but there are a couple of prospects up in Minnesota. I talked to my mother a couple of days ago and she has a couple of prospects here too."

"Well, when you decide to settle down, you'll make a wonderful husband." Enzo spoke with complete confidence in his friend.

"I don't know, Enzo," the suddenly timid friend said, backing off. "I think life in general, much less marriage, is a bit too scary right now." Gwen leaned up onto the table, her left elbow supporting her. Enzo swiveled his chair to the right to pay full body attention to Demetrius.

"But look at us," spoke the perfectly contented wife. "We have found the perfect mate in each other. I would give everything for Enzo, and I know he would give up everything for me."

"I realize that, Gwen." Demetrius's face strained a bit. "I don't doubt your love for each other, and I had a wonderful example in my parents too, but..." he paused wanting to choose each syllable carefully, "but today I think most people are too selfish to really give of themselves completely."

"You know, D," Enzo spoke, "I got caught up in all the opera hype when I first came to the States. I was 'the wonder boy from South America,' and Indiana University gave me everything. I had a little spending money, a scholarship, a great teacher, and was given lots of roles at the opera theatre. But I remember, after my first performance, Traviata, I went back stage to visit with my friends, and I felt empty."

"But that usually happens after big performances, doesn't it?" asked the non-performing member of the group.

"No, it wasn't a post-performance let-down," responded Enzo. "This was an emptiness that came from singing my heart out, and not really having anyone to share the success with." Enzo continued quickly, for he had had these thoughts before. "I had been raised to offer myself to others. Give to family, give to the church, and give to your husband and wife. My parents taught me that genuine fulfillment comes from offering you life in this way.

"But all I had done since coming to the States was take. It was the most hollow feeling I've ever felt." Enzo cocked his head to the side, still feeling the shame of that day. "I treated my costume and makeup people horribly. I was rude to the director; I even threatened to quit the production because I thought one of my tempos was too slow." Enzo shook his head in self-disgust. "All this arrogance from a know-nothing kid.

"So, I'm standing in the reception line, having just sung *Alfredo* really well, and no one came up to congratulate me." The room was silent as Enzo rolled the remembrance through his head.

"Here was this long line, two hundred people, waiting to greet their children, their friends, and even their colleagues, but not a soul came up to me, not even to say hello."

"No one?" asked Demetrius.

"One old lady, who I think was the Violetta's grandmother, came up to me and said she enjoyed my singing, but then she said, and I can still remember her actual words. She said, 'I hope you love someone more than yourself before you sing about true love again.'" Enzo sat silent for a moment, as did Gwen and Demetrius.

"Those were her actual words. This tiny woman, in this squeaky little voice, had accused me of being selfish. She burned her eyes into me and accused me of exploiting others, of taking kindness from my friends and then just discarding them.

"Even though I had sung really well, the audience hadn't come to see some dark-skinned Pavarotti; the audience wanted to see a real person give of himself, give of his talents, and to love them through his gifts.

"I went back to my dressing room and cried like a baby. Everything my parents had given me, all my friends' help, and all my teacher's advice, they hadn't meant anything. I was a pit of consumption, sucking up all that

I could, and in return, giving nothing. And that is exactly what I was rewarded with: nothing."

"Enzo and I have found that when you give yourself to others, your generosity returns in abundance. And when you give yourself up in love, the trust and beauty of love is beyond any temporary exhilaration that might come from selfishness. Love only truly works when you are powerless with each other."

"We gave Mother Teresa the Nobel Prize for giving herself to others," Enzo spoke, "and if we all lived our lives like that dear woman did, we'd all be a lot happier."

"All this is what I think I might be afraid of," Demetrius joined in the sentiment. "I watched my parents give that love to each other and to us kids. I watched them give of themselves to achieve a really deep love. But right now," Demetrius spoke with disappointment, "I see most people today just living for themselves, either unwilling or unable to love in total surrender."

"Don't you think the media—you know, movies, TV, and advertisements—that they tell us you have to focus on yourself? Think what would happen if ad agencies told the public to give everything away, and we all started doing that." Gwen smiled. "You know, giving to the poor, helping the needy, no one would need anything and everybody would be contented."

"But big business wouldn't make any money," Enzo spoke. The group chuckled.

"That night at I.U., I was disappointed that, despite growing up in an environment of love and selflessness, I had forsaken it all because I believed I was the most important thing in the world. My parents did not teach me that, but I started believing it. Since that day back at I.U., I asked my friends to forgive me, and decided that life was not for the taking, because I can never have all the things I *want*...but that life, and love," Enzo took the hand of his wife, "is for sharing, giving, and loving. Not just physically, but emotionally, mentally, and spiritually. And thank God, he gave me Gwen, someone who wants what I want, and gives me more love, honor, and humor, than I could ever dare dream or deserve."

"I hope I can find someone like that," Demetrius said, "but if you ever croak, I get first dibs on your widow." He sipped his wine.

"I have already told Gwen that when I die she has to carry my ashes around with her everywhere she goes." The group chuckled again. "Death will not separate me from the love of this woman."

"And an urn will sure put a damper on dating anybody," Gwen spoke over the laughter. "Just picture it; I'm out on a date with some handsome blond man…" Enzo craned his neck toward his wife in mock protest, his raven locks objecting to the humorous slight. "We're having dinner and I pull out of some grocery bag this little genie bottle. 'Hi, my name is Gwen, this is my first husband, Enzo. He's shorter now that he's dead. Say hello, honey.'"

Gwen mimed holding an urn of ashes up to an imaginary courtier and, using her faux urn lid like the mouth of a puppet, spoke in her best Argentinean tenor voice.

"Buenas dias, my name is Enzo. You toucha my wife, I weell keeelllll you."

Gales of laughter streamed from the cords of the dinner guests.

After the guffawing ceased the hostess asked for dessert orders. None were taken; appetites were sated, and so the three poured more wine, started some coffee, and retired to the terrace overlooking Grant Park. October's premier evening, clear and dark blue, raised the skyline to new heights, the starry night expanding above their glorious city. The singer wrapped a scarf around his instrument, while the wife and friend exposed themselves to the cool fall breeze.

"Demetrius, I think I would like to hire a bodyguard."

"That might be a good idea." The detective thought a moment, sipping the warm Colombian coffee he had exchanged for his wine. "Why don't you hire one for when I am not around? We've been together a lot, and I can watch you and Gwen, except when I need to take off."

"Why do we need a bodyguard?" Gwen asked, leaning on the armrest of Enzo's chair. She looked at both men, head darting between the two who were sitting across from one another.

Enzo looked over to his detective friend. Demetrius was nodding his head, waiting for the explanation.

"Gwen," Enzo sighed, "when I went down to Bloomington, a man in a police car tried to kill me."

"Enzo!" Gwen was not as disappointed as she was suddenly afraid. She looked over at Demetrius.

"You knew this?" she asked the friend across from them on the terrace. Demetrius nodded.

"And your driver, Mr. Hutchinson?" She searched Enzo's face.

"The officer pulled us over, and I saw him inject Bill with a syringe of, well, what I now know was potassium."

Enzo continued the tale, telling his uninformed wife a quick overview of the ride. Gwen knew Enzo felt responsible for this man, Mr. Hutchinson, for he had kept in touch with the Hutchinson family at the Bloomington Hospital, and she now knew why he was so concerned for the Hutchinson family. As Gwen was told the tale, she slid off the perch at her husband's arm and knelt at his side. She put her head down as Enzo finished. Enzo felt horrible.

"Gwen, I'm so sorry I waited so long to tell you." Gwen was silent a moment, her head still bowed. "I didn't want to burden you more than you already had been."

"Stop it, Enzo," she said, then she paused a moment before speaking again. "What happens to you happens to me. I knew something was wrong, and I knew you would tell me sometime, but *please*, my love, don't keep these things from me."

"I'm sorry," Enzo apologized, his eyes looking deep into his wife's eyes.

"I forgive you," Gwen smiled, "and I love you. And thank God you are all right."

Happy that the hidden had been revealed, Demetrius thought over the bodyguard issue. He sipped from his cup. Moments of cool passed. Lights dotted the park below, outlining streets, defining paths. Cars traced the dotted lines along the lakefront to the left.

"Enzo, I think a bodyguard is a good idea, but I think you really only need him while you're in here."

"Why's that?"

"For one, you are too important to the opera, so I don't think anyone will touch you, and second, no one knows exactly what you know." Enzo thought about his friend's assessment of the situation. It seemed accurate, but he would rather be safe than sorry in concern for—not only his safety, but even more for his wife's.

"But they," Enzo said to himself, "whoever *they* are, have already tried to kill me twice. And I don't know who knew I was going to Bloomington, at least up here." Enzo shook his head in discovery. He knew someone whom he had told.

"Bill Burrows knew!" Enzo was startled at his apparent accusation. "In fact, he's known everything that I've done." Demetrius looked calmly at his friend and his personal discovery, but the investigator had been piecing that very same exclamation together these past several days. Demetrius had been asking the questions to himself over and over.

Who knew about the attempt on Enzo's life in the opera house opening night? Who had access to the opera house offices and records? Who could alter them without fear of reprisal? Who knew where Enzo was going Wednesday morning, and what route he would be taking, and even what type of automobile he would be traveling in?

The only answer Demetrius could find, and which Enzo now believed, was William Burrows. Burrows was the only person Enzo had confided in about the opening night tragedy, and he was the only person privy to all the information involved in this developing drama. William Burrows was the one man who focused all the dim lights of this whole operatic mess.

"I'm gonna pay Mr. Burrows a visit tomorrow morning," Demetrius said, "and hopefully shake things up a bit."

Enzo did not want to believe his suspicions about this man, one who had guided the Chicago Grande Opera out of hard times and had helped it flourish.

Bill Burrows had helped start Enzo on his professional career, granting him a position in the prized CGO Young Artist Program a decade earlier. He had nurtured Enzo in the business of opera. Still, Enzo could not deny the circumstances and their supposed evidence. Everything pointed to William Burrows, directly and indirectly.

"What are you going to do?" Enzo asked.

"Just ask some very pointed questions, see how Burrows reacts," Demetrius said, "and then see what happens around the opera house."

The October wind, even eighteen floors up, now buffeted the trio on the apartment terrace. It was becoming a bit too much to enjoy, and it was getting a bit too late for an opera singer to be out in the increasing chill. The friends sipped their last coffee and gathered themselves together to head back inside. Enzo left the terrace last and slid the glass doors shut, then locked the panel.

"I think I'll head to bed," Demetrius said, excusing himself. "This week should help explain a lot, and we'll all need our rest." Gwen walked over to Demetrius, took his coffee cup, and gave her friend a kiss on the cheek.

"Thanks for all your help, Demetrius," graced the appreciative woman. "You've brought sanity back to our lives." Demetrius smiled wide, showing the beautiful, yet seldom seen softness that he possessed. He was not an investigator around these friends. He was himself, and he enjoyed the simplicity of being just that.

"I'm glad I can help, Gwen," Demetrius responded. "When my friends are in trouble, I'll do anything I can to solve the problem." Gwen walked to the kitchen with the collected dishes. "Besides, if you keep feeding me like this, I'll have to travel with you guys permanently." Enzo walked up to Demetrius and gave his friend a bear hug.

"She is right, D," Enzo seconded. "You have given me..." He paused. "You've given *us* hope by looking into this—thing," Enzo did not know how to describe the imbroglio. "You've given us back the tranquillity we had lost amongst the evil that had been consuming us."

Demetrius had not thought of his investigation in these terms. The witnessed murder of a friend, the attempt on Enzo's life, and the mounting evidence around the CGO and its general director were indeed daunting, but to think of it as evil struck Demetrius at the core of his childhood beliefs. Indeed, something wicked had come to the Chicago Grande Opera, and Demetrius knew its power was growing. He just prayed that he and his friends had the strength to find it out, and eradicate it.

"It's my pleasure, Enzo," he said. "Oh, yeah, I'll get you another vest, and you call the hotel desk. I think they'll be able to help with recommending a bodyguard." Enzo nodded.

"But let's stay vigilant, Enzo," Demetrius said, walking up the apartment steps and to the door.

"I'll see you all tomorrow." Demetrius looked over at Gwen in the kitchenette and said goodnight. The man walked out the door and headed to his room. He was asleep quickly, relaxed from the meal, and confident in his course for tomorrow.

Enzo and Gwen quickly cleaned up the remains of the meal and rolled the room service cart, full of empty dishes, over to the base of the stairs at the apartment entrance.

It was time for bed; the couple was weary from a full day of rest.

"I'll finish up, honey," Gwen said to her husband, with only a few dishes left.

"Sure?"

"Yeah, head on to bed. I'll be in in a minute." Enzo knew his wife would suggest this to him. He wiped his hands and bolted for the bedroom. Gwen enjoyed the simplicity of washing dishes—the easy cleaning and the quiet solitude involved in the simple, essential task.

The few dishes were quickly dispatched. She wiped her hands and threw the dish-towel over the kitchen faucet. She walked to the apartment door, locked the dead bolt, and headed to the bedroom.

She arrived at the door, and there was her husband, standing in his boxer shorts next to the bed, his hands behind his back. Gwen looked at the bed. It was covered in a huge white sheet and strewn with extra pillows. Over the entire spread were sprinkled the petals of dozens of yellow roses, her favorite.

She knew what her husband had hidden behind his back, and without a word she shed her clothes, pulled the comb from her hair and walked over to her husband, still standing at the side of the bed, waiting. Her invigorated body leaned up into him, and she kissed Enzo deeply and sensually, rubbing herself against him.

"I am all yours, wonderful man," Gwen whispered to her husband. She pulled away, slowly laying herself prone on the bed, her face against the cool linen of the pillows. The petals fell around her, sliding down the crisp, clean sheet, touching her breasts, caressing her sides, and scenting the air.

She breathed deeply and expelled tension with her breath. Enzo climbed onto the bed, straddling her legs. With his left hand, he softly sprinkled more petals upon the back of his wife, allowing their velvety texture to fall between his fingers. The cascade of tenderness fell upon her shoulders, lighted upon her hair, and slid into the small of her naked back.

"Just relax, bonita," Enzo said softly. He poured the oil from his right hand upon his wife's back, the slow drip mixing with petals, moistening her skin, and exciting her mind. He put the oil aside.

Enzo leaned into the small of his wife's back and pressed up, oil lubricating the path up to her shoulder. His fingers kneaded her spine up and down, relaxing the tension built up throughout her back. He reached her shoulders and massaged each side, rubbing her neck up into her head. He pulled down along the outside of her back, engulfing her arms in his hands, forcing anxiety to flee out her fingertips. He caressed her sides, touching the sides of her breasts, massaging them with the oil, and arousing the woman.

Enzo drizzled more oil onto his wife and poured himself into her sole pleasure. He listened to her body and let her dictate his being. He gave everything to her, and gloried in her perfectness—her perfectness for him. He massaged her buttocks, then rubbed her legs, drawing tension to himself and supplying calmness to his love.

"Okay, bonita," Enzo whispered. "It's time." Gwen knew just what to do. She turned and lay on her back, directing this gift of relaxation and tenderness, and guiding his hands for her ultimate pleasure and deep meditation. He stroked her long, lean legs and slowly pressed up her body into her stomach and breasts. She sank into the sheets, soaked in the oil, and drank in the strength and suppleness of her husband.

She was totally relaxed and ebbed toward unconsciousness.

Enzo straddled his wife's stomach, careful to keep pressure from her body. He stroked her breasts, and massaged up to her shoulders. He gently rubbed her neck with his warm hands, finding those particular aches that were unique to this woman he loved, and known only by him. He covered her face in his open palms, the warmth and moisture from his hands filled her lungs with warmth and refreshment.

He slid his hands up her face and gradually massaged her temples, rubbed her cheeks, and allowed his hands to encircle her face. He massaged her hair, pressing her scalp, and delicately squeezed her locks, relaxing her follicles.

The dimly lit bedroom was warm with the husband's offering and with the wife's deep long breath. Perspiration dabbed the bodies of both lovers. With his offering complete, Enzo slid off to the side of his wife and leaned onto his elbow. He took one of the yellow rose petals in his fingers, and gently drew the petal over every inch of his wife's relaxed body.

"Oh, Enzo," Gwen purred with delight at the touch of the petal and he knew that her thoughts, her sensual intent was only from him, the one she adored.

"My sweet love!" Enzo softly whispered to his wife. Gwen turned her head and looked up to him. With her right hand she pulled his face to hers and kissed him. Enzo's hand cupped her face as their lips drank each other in. Gwen cradled Enzo down into the now oily sheet and caressed his body. She shared the massage oil that he had applied, allowing her entire moisturized body to lubricate his.

The couple delighted in the joy of their love, and in the beautiful, erotic pleasure of unrestrained, uninhibited passion. The excited laughter and eager breath that erupted from them drew them deeper into each other and again solidified their commitment and desire to be, only and always, for each other.

The voyeurs in room 1901 enjoyed the show they watched from the couple below. Both men found pornographic delight in what they perceived as mere masturbation. Neither could conceive of the intimacy shared between the lovers, husband and wife, dedicated and longing only for each other.

Watching the events that transpired in 1801 was their job. They had thought the tiny microphones and cameras would reveal the plottings and plannings of the couple and their accomplice, but the evening had turned out a dud. Just…talk…talk…talk about relationships and friendships.

There had been a moment when the gentlemen first spoke that had appeared promising, but the words remained ultimately unimportant to their purposes.

Everything was recorded anyway. The tape and video equipment captured the dinner between friends through fish eyes, but when the group decided to step onto the balcony audio surveillance had been lost. The camera above the kitchen cabinets pictured the three sitting, sipping their beverages, but the great Chicago wind whistled through the glass terrace door, obscuring any voice that may have been recorded.

It was a fruitless evening for the pair of men. Even the porno, which they eyed intently, was sub-par.

"Boy, she is hot," spoke the younger, defiling himself with his lust. "I'd love to get a hold of her for a few minutes." The younger man's statement intended violence and domination. The older man yawned and walked to the queen-sized bed, off to the side of all the equipment.

"I'm gonna get some sleep. Wake me if anything *really* happens."

"Don't you wanta see?" the younger man's eyes turned excited. "It looks like they're fuckin' again."

"Knock yourself out, kid," the older man replied as he lay down in the bed, fully clothed and fully fatigued.

All was quiet in 1901. The surveillance for the night was finished with the onset of sleep by the occupants below. The equipment recorded every toss and every turn of the lovers. The young man, who kept watch, rewound his favorite section and popped the videotape into the one unused video player.

The tape rolled upon the video screen. In bluish-gray light walked Gwen, naked and unafraid before her husband, protector, lover, and friend. The young man rewound the tape again and again. He watched her striptease, the arch of her back as she slid her panties off, and the stretch of her arms as she unhooked her bra, letting it ride down her body, draping across her breasts, and finally falling to the floor. He imagined her walking up to him, seductive, and sultry, and then, forced by his hand into submission and degradation.

His smile grew wide and inflamed. His teeth chattered on edge, and he bit his lip. He watched the scene over and over again. He moaned and cursed through the chattering teeth.

"I gotta have her... *Please*, let me have her."

The intimacy of the two wooed them into tranquillity. They held each other in their sleep, touching and caressing even in their unconsciousness. They had no idea that the touch of love that filled their bedroom, that the tenderness expressed by husband to wife and woman to man, was overseen by the depraved. The evil above them grew greedy and lecherous at the sight of the pure and perfect. It coveted the honest, the sincere, and the blessedly sensual.

Malevolence stood over the tender couple and spat on them, wishing to snatch away this purity, and to drag it to hell.

Twenty-Eight

7:00 a.m.
Monday October 2

Demetrius walked straight to the loading dock of the opera house, having conversed with the security guard at the theatre's backstage entrance. He had ingratiated himself with stories of his years in the house. The unaware guard quickly let the man, who was one of his own, backstage.

He wanted to get in and out of the house quickly and quietly this morning. He was glad the workday in the theatre had not begun.

Crews were due at 8:00, and rehearsals began at 11:00, so he had a very comfortable cushion of time. Fifteen minutes was all he needed. He'd be done by 7:20.

He walked onto the dock, then looked throughout the adjoining corridors to insure vacancy. Not a soul was stirring. He closed the double swinging doors to the dock, quickly taped a sheet of white paper over the one-foot square glass in the doors, and went to work.

The cameras he was using were no bigger than a pen and could be set anywhere, or on anything. The only difficulty would be to place a transmitter somewhere out on the dock to boost the televised signal to his ugly brown van out the dock doors and north on Lower Wacker Drive.

He needed different angles of the dock, cameras pointing to where the trucks arriving from Mexico would unload their cargo.

One camera was placed above the double swinging doors to the south of the dock. The square closing mechanism for the doors would conceal the pen/camera just above it on a tiny ledge created by the door's own frame. Easy, one done. Now to place a camera to view the opposite angles.

This placement was more difficult. Several pillars divided the dock and its two semi-truck bays exactly down the middle. The first camera would see down the length of the dock, but Demetrius wanted one camera on each dock individually.

The drop ceiling provided the answer. He had helped his parents hang one of these nasty fiberglass ceilings in their western Chicago home, and he knew that he could hollow out some fiberglass, poke a hole through the white plastic lower face, and no one would ever know that the cameras were there.

He found a chair to elevate himself at the south end of the dock. Up he climbed, pushing away the fiberglass panel and hollowing out a pen-shaped hole with his finger. He pushed the minute camera though the created hole and shoved the lens through the white plastic lining.

The lens easily punctured the plastic. Demetrius pulled the camera back a bit until the tiny lens was angled exactly toward the rear of where the delivery trucks would stand.

There was one more camera to place. It was 7:25. It was taking a bit longer than he had thought. He grabbed the chair and took off for the northern end of the dock. Up, panel off, camera hole created, punched, and pulled to conceal. Demetrius reached to place the panel back up into the support structure.

"Excuse me," a voice came from the door below him. Demetrius was startled. He quickly recovered.

"Yes," he responded, looking over his shoulder. It was the security guard he had buttered up earlier, leaning through the left swinging door, holding it open as he talked.

"What are you doing up there?" the guard asked in puzzlement.

"Nothing, really. When I walked by this morning I saw this panel hanging down from the ceiling and I thought I should put it back up."

"How did it fall out?" Good question. Demetrius's first lie was convincing enough; he just had to add to the fable.

"Oh, they're always falling out. If a truck goes by out on Wacker, these things will shake free." It sounded good, whether it was true or not. Demetrius had the panel and camera back in place, secure.

"What's up?" he asked the curious guard.

"You're a friend of the tenor, right?"

"Yeah."

"Um, would you mind getting his autograph for me?" The guard was a bit shy.

"No problem." Demetrius was now at ease himself, realizing he was out of danger. "Who should I have him make it out to?"

"To Angie," the guard smiled, "and could he say somethin' about how we are friends?"

"Sure, man." Demetrius quickly scanned the guard's nametag and made a mental note. "For Angie, by way of Dennis. No problem, Dennis."

"Thanks a lot. I thought I had seen you with Mr. Santini," the guard nodded, "and my girlfriend wanted to get his autograph, so I said I would." Demetrius stepped down off the chair.

"I'll have him send a signed photo right over, I promise."

"Thank you, sir. I knew you'd help me out." The guard walked out the door and back to his post. Demetrius laughed at the grandeur people assigned to someone who could sing opera. He knew Enzo to be a caring, loving friend and husband, but the world saw him as an icon.

"One autograph from Mr. Santini." He set out to place the transmitter.

He decided on the underside of the metal stairwell that the truck drivers climbed up to enter the dock area from the street. Only the truck drivers would walk through this area, and the stair steps would conceal the antennas hidden underneath them. The surrounding floor was grimy and sooty. No one would want to linger in this area.

He left, happy with what he had done. His cameras would spy whatever passed through the metal gates of this loading dock, but Tuesday at two in the morning would be the real test. That was when the trucks from Mexico City would roll in and unload their cargo.

The trucks would be carrying the new production of Verdi's *Un Ballo in Maschera* and Mozart's *Don Giovanni*. Frank's log sheet indicated there would be a total of fourteen semi-trucks from the Mexico City Opera Theatre. Intimate opera was not what the collaboration between the two opera companies was about, but neither was it about opera.

Demetrius left the theatre. He affixed one last transmitter to one of the Lower Wacker Drive cement support pillars to boost the signal further.

He drove his rented Intrepid along the Lower Drive and pulled in front of the hideous brown van. He squawked the van's alarm system to "off," or so he thought. The wrong squawk greeted his ears. He had turned the alarm "on." He hit his hand-held button again and definitely turned the alarm "off" this time. He slid open the passenger side door. A potato chip bag spun in the waft of the opening door and fell out of the van.

"Oh, man," Demetrius scolded, "if you're gonna eat this crap, at least clean up after yourself." A small black man wearing wire-rimmed glasses spun around in the metal stool that sat in front of the surveillance monitors.

"You nailed it, D," he said. "Perfect placement on all three cameras. And the signal boosters too. We'll even be able to see into the trucks, I bet."

"Those cameras are simple—just point and shoot. Anybody could place those things, Harris." Harris Barton shoved has mouth full of the greasy fried potatoes he had been devouring and discarding on the van's floor.

"Could you please keep this van clean, man?" Demetrius pleaded. "This equipment is sensitive to dirt. And Harris," spoke the slightly exacerbated detective, "keep the alarm 'on' when you are in this thing, please. I don't want anybody messing with this van." Demetrius slowed his speech to drive home the point.

"Goofiest thing I ever heard of," remarked the little man in the van. "An alarm that you want activated while I'm inside it."

"It's insurance, man," remarked Demetrius. "If you keep the alarm on, then I don't have to worry about thieves kickin' your scrawny little ass and stealin' my property." The friends laughed. "I'd think after what happened to you, you'd alarm your wallet."

Harris Barton was a friend of Demetrius from his old neighborhood. He was a banty rooster of a man, full of energy, thin as a rail, and sharp as a tack. He had started a video production company two years earlier, so he was well acquainted with the surveillance contents of the van. Unfortunately, his company quickly folded when thieves stole most of his uninsured equipment. He had declared bankruptcy and had been working himself out of debt ever since. He always had a steady job, working at Radio Shack for a while and a number of other video and computer outlets, but he was unimpressed by most of them, and most importantly, he longed to be his own boss. He had been saving to enter corporate America, and thus, any extra work that might help fulfill that mission was happily taken.

Demetrius knew Harris would be able to help out with this surveillance. The actual work would not be dangerous, and Harris was a whiz with the equipment. Demetrius was assured of Harris's safety, and he was also confident with the electronics whiz in his employ.

Demetrius picked up the empty chip bags and wadded them up, tossing them out of the van into the dingy Lower Drive green tunnel.

"Come on, Harris, I'll take you to breakfast." Harris turned off the equipment, locked the van, and the men walked towards the rented Intrepid.

"Sweet ride, D."

"Harris," Demetrius stopped walking and looked intently at his friend.

"What?" Harris was unaware of his friend's intention.

"The van," Demetrius cried, "alarm the frickin' van."

"Oh, yeah!" Harris dug in his pocket for the key chain activator, unable to pull it out of his terribly tight black jeans. Demetrius shook his head as his friend hopped around, thrusting his hand into his front jeans pocket.

"Forget it." Demetrius laughed as he grabbed his remote control and squawked the van's alarm into activation.

"Last time I forget, D, I promise," Harris bantered.

"Get in the car, ya butt-head." They climbed in and took off for a leisurely breakfast. Harris could eat twice what Demetius could, and not be a bit fazed.

Twenty-Nine

10:00 a.m.

"Detective John McGrail, please." Demetrius phoned from the restaurant where he and Harris had just devoured their breakfast. Harris, per usual, had two entire meals and could have eaten more, but Demetrius had things to do and people to intimidate.

He was hoping his Chicago police detective friend had found out something about his evidence. He was happy that the van was not being ticketed, but Demetrius also hoped the famously slow Chicago Forensics Unit had treated their friend, Detective McGrail, with expedience. Demetrius wanted the pieces of this investigation to fall into place at the proper time, and Tuesday morning seemed to be the moment of truth.

"McGrail here."

"John, it's Demetrius. How was your weekend?"

"Hey, babe," replied the jovial Irishman, "had a blast. Went over to the Indiana Dunes. Froze my ass off, but the leaves were great. Even got some hunting in."

"Did you bag anything?"

"Couple geese, no big deal." The phone was silent a second, each man expecting the other to speak. Finally John spoke.

"Guess what, babe?"

"Talk to me, John."

"My little forensics sweetheart did a little overtime this weekend for me. You'll never guess what she found."

Demetrius grew antsy. "I think I have an idea. Tell me about the pencil tip first."

"Shit, the boring stuff. O.K., doesn't matter to me. You're the one coming up with Cubbie tickets. Let's see." The detective leafed through the two-page report from his forensics friends. Page two reported on the tiny black object.

"Here ya go, babe." He paused, then read, "The object is a graphite compound, commonly used in pencils. The piece is covered in type 'B' positive blood, and has an unusually high concentration of skin and muscle tissue imbedded into the graphite. The tissue samples are consistent with the blood sample."

"So, the pencil tip is stained with blood and skin from the same guy," Demetrius spoke. "Probably somebody from the props department."

"Yep, that's what it's sayin'. Now the good stuff. You ready 'D?'" Detective McGrail cleared his throat, for the information he found tremendously interesting.

"The plastic galvanized steel switch plate is common to most office and home construction. The switch is still in fairly good condition, charred, appearing to have been in a high heat situation."

"Here's the good part." John read further. "However, the wiring in the switch is not consistent with any known electrical configuration. The wiring, while badly charred as well, reveals in it a complex series of operations that would occur in tandem with the flipping of the toggle. Upon further examination, and discriminating chemical procedures," John stopped again, "she means they tested the damn thing." Demetrius nodded over the phone.

"Read, John!"

"O.K.—discriminating procedures. O.K., gasoline residue was found, covering eighty percent of the device. In examining the remaining twenty percent of the device, a further residue was found that would be consistent with that left by the ignition of semtec."

Demetrius's ears perked up and his mouth repeated, "Semtec? Plastic explosives?"

"Yep. I told you this was the good part. But wait..." John continued with his reading. "Also imbedded in what remained of the wire's plastic insulation were tiny fragments of semtec itself." John leaned back in his standard issue police recliner and smiled widely. "You know what my forensics darlin' is telling you, don't you?" John's broadening smile revealed his small, coffee-stained teeth. He was about to laugh, excited by this significant evidence.

Demetrius had pieced the forensic information together as it was read to him.

"That switch was the trigger for a bomb, wasn't it, John?"

"That's what I read, babe." John threw his arms forward and swung up in his chair, laying the report on the desk before him. He punched his words to his friend, overenunciating each syllable.

"But not only that, 'D,'" the friend pieced the puzzle together more accurately. "You got a plastic explosive ignition that ignites some form of gasoline. Whether the gas was a bomb or just spread throughout the joint, when this little switch was flipped it caused a hell of an explosion."

Demetrius was jotting this information down on his note pad, listening at the same time.

"Demetrius, wherever you got this thing, you got a great case for arson. This would have blown the Water Tower to kingdom come." The detective spoke of one of the city's few survivors of the Great Fire.

Demetrius thought about the origin of the switch. Enzo had said it had been found in the ruins of the Chicago Grande Opera's warehouse fire. A fire that, last January, effectively ended the CGO's operations due to its financial instability. With the company's fiscal difficulties, the warehouse had been tremendously underinsured, and thus, the fire destroyed all real invested property of the CGO. There were no assets, and no way of making enough money to continue the company's operation.

"'D,' you still there?" John listened for his friend to respond.

"Uh, yeah, John," he finally blurted out. "Just thinking."

"Where did you get this thing anyway?"

"You remember the opera warehouse fire last January?" Demetrius responded without hesitation.

"Yeah?" The detective knew about what his friend was talking. "You found this thing in all that shit?" John spoke in astonishment.

"Yep," Demetrius replied. "The scraps had been packed up and sent over to the opera house to see if anything could be salvaged."

John was not an opera fan, but the blaze stood out fresh in his mind. Beat officers had told him of the inferno. It had been a four-alarm mess that had burned for twenty hours. The paper, plaster, and wood construction of the opera sets, stacked one upon the other, had made a tinder box waiting to ignite, and as it did, it had burned itself completely and totally. Mephisto had danced with his flame that fateful winter night, and he had not allowed anyone to douse his conflagration. There had been little for the opera to salvage.

"John, could you look into what the official fire department report said was the cause of the fire?" Demetrius asked. "I'm curious who in that department made this decision. And with what evidence."

"No problem, babe," the cop replied. "And I'll keep it all really quiet, like the forensic stuff over the weekend."

"Thanks, John," Demetrius said. "Thanks again." The simple and firm appreciation was not given lightly, and the officer knew it.

"D?" asked McGrail, "This thing is gettin' bigger than you thought, isn't it?" John heard, as good detectives do, the introspective tone of

Demetrius's voice. Demetrius lowered his head into the black payphone's receiver, almost ducking into the communications booth.

"Yeah, John," Demetrius slowly spoke. "It's getting bigger and meaner every day."

"D," interjected John, "screw me wantin' the credit," the detective said, refuting Demetrius's offer of first discovery in his investigation. "If this thing is gettin' to be overwhelming, babe, call me and I'll come with the fuckin' Chicago Cavalry."

This assurance relieved Demetrius's mind and calmed him considerably. The forensics report into the toggle switch put this investigation into a whole different category. Plastic explosives, gasoline, and an elaborate triggering mechanism was not merely aimed at shutting the CGO down, but also focused upon leaving it destitute, with no means of recovery.

Questions were mounting upon questions, but their answers were held somewhere within the Chicago Grande Opera, and the company was not offering any clues. It was time to initiate some interference.

"John," Demetrius replied to his friend, "believe me, when this hits the fan, you'll be at my side. Talk to you soon."

The men hung up and Demetrius was off with Harris to the Illinois State Theatre for an unexpected meeting.

The symbols kept running through his head: C-4, plastic explosives used to detonate an opera warehouse full of basically useless sets and props. The place could have been torched easily enough with a cigarette lighter and newspapers, but whoever decided the warehouse had to be destroyed, whoever decided Enzo and his driver should be killed, whoever these people were, they had money, they had connections, and they had serious business on their minds, and their business would not stand for any human interference.

Andante sostenuto, Presto orrendo:

a sangue freddo, portare via

Music is the speech of angels
— Thomas Carlyle —

Man is the only animal who causes pain to others with no other object than wanting to do so
— Schopenhauer —

Thirty

Demetrius let Harris off at the van. Harris immediately opened it up and set off the alarm.

"Damn," he giggled. "I'll never remember that alarm."

He dug in his jeans pocket, holding the alarm's switch, hopping and jumping around again on the crumbling pavement on the side of Lower Wacker Drive. He finally retrieved the button, squawked the alarm "off," and climbed into the van.

Demetrius wanted him to jot down some license plate numbers, so Harris grabbed the note pad off the surveillance console. His energetic walk strode him up the Drive's exit ramp and onto the Upper Drive quickly. Harris scoped and studied the area Demetrius wanted him to watch.

He was directly in front of the opera house, walking along the sidewalk. Along Wacker Drive, in front of the theater, were the reserved parking spots for the power brokers within the CGO. The general director had a spot, as did the artistic director. Several of the important crew chiefs also had reserved parking spaces, but Demetrius did not want those license numbers. The more important people, the G.D. and the A.D., had chauffeurs guarding and polishing their vehicles—big black Lincoln Town Cars.

Harris decided he did not need to risk confrontation with these burly drivers, so he kept a distance. He easily wrote down the vehicle license numbers, starting from the least conspicuous. These were directly outside the stage door entrance, the northernmost entrance to the Illinois State Theatre. He simply walked along, writing down the make, model, and numbers that appeared on the red, white, and blue Illinois plates.

He was now up to the two tough numbers, the automobiles with chauffeurs. He finished with the third from last automobile and walked around one of the curbside stone pillars that supported the front edge of the gargantuan opera house. The public sidewalk was canopied by the theatre and its pillared walkway.

He peeked around the side of the pillar and slid his body around to the inside covered walkway. He peeked again, and one of the chauffeurs was staring directly back at him. Harris pulled his head back behind the pillar and breathed a quick sigh. He had been caught. He knew he would never be a detective, but he did love his electronics.

"Hey you," called out the closest man. "What the hell you doin'?"

Harris came around the corner nonchalantly and put on a mask.

"Ya, how you doin', man?" Harris did his best to stay cool. "I need to take down your license plates."

"You do and I'll kick the shit right outta ya."

Harris believed the man. The chauffeur, who was a big Polish Chicagoan, started for the little black man. Harris protested.

"Wait, man," he pleaded, sensing that pain might soon follow this chauffeur's verbal aggression. Harris thought up a lie, and thought it up quickly. "There are some new cops out here walkin' the beat, and they been ticketin' these cars for the opera." The chauffeur kept moving toward Harris.

"What the hell are you talkin' about?" he asked incredulously.

"Some rookie cop has been ticketing all these opera vehicles," Harris continued, "and Robert Burrows wanted me to get the numbers so the opera could stop the harassment from the police." Harris hoped he had gotten the general director's name correct. It sounded good, even if it was wrong, and he had delivered the lie with authority, so he believed the ruse would hold. The man slowed his gate and looked Harris over.

"You sure?" he paused, "I haven't seen any cops taking any license numbers out here."

Harris kept up the lying, and thanks to fortune, he saw a helper across the street.

"Damn, man, look over there." Harris pointed to a meter maid on a three-wheeled scooter on the opposite side of Wacker Drive, traveling northbound. She pulled off to the side. "Maybe she's the overworked type that's wantin' to bust our nuts," Harris said, afraid he was losing his believability, "but somebody's writin' us up." The burly white man, who also posed as a bodyguard, looked over his shoulder and saw the plump woman squeeze herself out of the motorized tricycle. He thought a minute, his face screwed up in disgust.

"Damn cops!" the man exhorted. Harris knew he was gaining ground, so he pushed his luck even more.

"So, if you want me to go back in there empty-handed, fine, I'm happy to get back to my crew. *But,* I was supposed to get your plate number so we could get the PD off our back." His lie was getting a bit too elaborate.

"I'll just tell Richard Burrows that his driver wouldn't let me do my job. That's fine." Harris threw his hands up in the air and spun his waifish form round, as if to leave.

All right," the driver yelled in exacerbation. "Take the damn numbers!"

"Hey, don't blame me, man." Harris spun back to finish his once simple job. "Blame the cops." The cars were obviously Lincoln Town Cars, so Harris quickly jotted down the license plate of the car directly in front of him, and then stepped a foot further south to see the last car's license plate. He spun, finishing the dictation, and left in a flash. "Sorry for the trouble, man." Harris scooted back up Wacker Drive and even walked in the theatre's stage door, standing there for five minutes, insuring his elusiveness to the two chauffeurs.

The chauffeur walked back to his car and leaned on the passenger side front fender, just over the wheel of his auto. The driver from the first car, the general director's car, walked back to talk to his friend.

"What was that all about?" he asked his companion.

"The cops are ticketing the limos for the opera company again. This little guy needed the numbers to give the cops so they won't keep ticketing us." The second driver joined his friend as he leaned on the fender, the two perfectly identical in their suits and manner.

"I didn't know the general director's name was..." the driver thought a moment, confused by the name game in which Harris had just unwittingly involved him. "Wait, the general director—which is it, Richard or Robert Burrows?" The first driver looked to his friend for confirmation.

"Neither, dumbass," the second driver harshly corrected his friend. "It's *William* Burrows."

The first man thought nothing of the name conundrum, but instead, he blamed the little black man.

"Boy, was that guy confused."

10:15 a.m.
General Director's Office
Illinois State Theatre

William Burrows had been in his office since 6:30 in the morning. He had arrived before any of the office staff, entering one dark, unlighted hall after another to arrive at the large doors of his sanctuary. But somehow that word, "sanctuary," was no longer appropriate.

His office had been an elegant, lavish, jubilant room for the last decade. Artists would enter, chat with the well-respected opera leader, bring food, cakes, friends, even poodles, and have a joyous operatic festival at the Chicago Grande Opera. This office had been the center for enjoyment and leisure for some of the world's great musicians. People would come, friends via the party of opera, and share wine, share stories, and share life with the happy and beloved general director of the CGO.

This office had been the sight of life and laughter, of pleasure and frivolity, of business and of art. Now this office was no longer the sight for this *joie de vivre*. His abode was no longer his sanctuary. It was no longer a place of fulfillment in the arts and satisfaction in employment. Evil had stepped through the great doors, and it had defiled this chamber.

This office was now a pagan sanctum, ripe with malice. The foothold of this devilish beast had anchored itself in the director's office and had sunk its talons more deeply with each passing performance.

His own greed had caused his near destruction little more than one year ago, and in attempted survival, he had clutched at the only straw available to him—one offered by the depraved, one seeking to solidify their deeds behind the cloak of opera.

Puccini had written of *Il Tabarro*, the cloak. The veil, of which the great composer had written, concealed the murder of an adulterous lover, seized in the arms of the jealous husband. The cloak Burrows had unfurled, hiding corruption in this great city, reeked of its own death and its own destruction, feasting on the lives of the pure, the honest, and the lovely.

The art form that encompassed all that was beautiful, all that was good and lovely. William Burrows' opera, the Chicago Grande Opera, cloaked the presence of evil within the heart of this great homeland, Chicago.

Burrows turned on his compact disc player, selecting "La mamma morta" from Giordano's *Andrea Chenier*. Maria Callas, singing with the voice of the sweet, injured and hopeless Maddelena, wept in song, her heart breaking at the evil and destruction around her. Her voice soared, lifting the drama to the inevitable tragedy.

Burrows heard this woman, this character, and found in her words perfect identification. He was trapped in hopelessness, and he was caught in the snare that he believed would end in his death. This reflection made him weak, made him scared, as his own transgressions came into sharper focus, magnified in the light of the enormous evil that now dominated this place.

Burrows had found the idea of self-destruction as a tremendously viable option. He was the front for the corruption within the CGO, and if he were no longer available, the corrupt would be forced to flee as the light of investigation fleshed them out of their den.

He rubbed his face with his right hand, having first drawn his left hand up to his face. This was usually the job of his left hand, but the plaster cast healing his injured paw prevented its use. The hand throbbed as blood ran to it, making the cast feel as if it would blow apart, releasing the tension but preventing the injury from healing properly.

Self-destruction would not be a noble thing, but it would heal the wounds he had passively allowed to fester at the CGO. Yes indeed, it was definitely an option.

Burrows heard a knock at the door. He had heard the secretaries arrive about 9:30, but he had ignored their bustle around the outer office, instead focusing on the business of the opera and the job of organizing the transfer of sets and equipment from Mexico City to Chicago for the coming season. He answered the door vocally, raising his voice from behind his desk.

"Yes," he shouted. The door was cracked open, so Brenda De Haan peeked her head through and leaned into the room. She was not quite sure if her boss had arrived or not, but the aria within had solved the mystery.

"Someone would like to speak with you, Mr. Burrows," she said softly. Burrows put down the papers in his hand and responded, "I really don't want to speak to anyone right now." Burrows thought some more and gazed at his appointment book. It was blank. "And he doesn't have an appointment, does he, Brenda?"

"No, sir, he doesn't."

"Tell him to set up something with you."

Brenda stood in the door, needing to deliver the visitor's message, but not wanting to disturb her employer's mood. Burrows again looked at the woman and spoke plaintively. "What is it, Brenda?"

"He says he used to work here," she started, "and that he is aware of some problems on the loading dock."

Like the Border collie Burrows kept at home, his ears shot up at the important information. He felt his face flush and heat surge into his neck. Whoever had sent this woman in knew what would get his attention. Burrows thought some more. It must be his "friends" from the other night, the ones who had inflicted the wound upon his left hand. No one else knew of the treachery beneath the opera house, and so the boss, now his boss too, must need to send him a message.

"Please send him in, Brenda," Burrows' kind response surprised the secretary, but it was intended to prepare the G.D. for the ominous presence about to enter the room. Burrows hoped a lighthearted aura might ease the tension inflicted upon him the other day. The men with whom he was dealing kept grudges, but he wanted them to know he had snapped to attention and would tow the line, at least a while longer.

Brenda opened the door fully to allow the visitor entrance.

"This way, Demetrius," she smiled, as she let the handsome friend of hers from years ago into the general director's office.

The general director was stunned as he stood and heard the guest's name from his secretary's mouth. He was not expecting this man, this man who caught his eye but whom he could not place.

Burrows walked out from behind the desk and went over to greet his visitor. He tried to sound at ease, repeating the name he just heard, trying to jog his memory for the name of this distantly familiar face.

"Demetrius..." the G.D. spoke, remembering the face, but unable to locate the reminiscence.

The black man made his way to the G.D., who had emerged from behind the desk. Demetrius stuck out his hand in greeting.

"Mr. Burrows," spoke Demetrius, introducing himself. "Demetrius McDiess. I used to work with security here at the opera house, and I'm good friends with the Santis."

"Aha," spoke the G.D., discovering the origin of the young man. "I was struggling with where I had seen you before, Demetrius. I didn't think I had seen you recently. What have you been up to since leaving the CGO?"

The men stood beside the great desk in the corner of the office and made with the pleasantries.

"I went to school, got my degree, and started my own detective agency."

"Wow!" Burrows masked his concern under a face of excitement. "That's wonderful. Where do you work? I mean, where is your agency?"

"I work mostly in the Minneapolis area, but I still come to Chicago quite a bit. I grew up on the West Side and most of my family still lives here, so I visit regularly."

Burrows motioned the young detective to the chair in front of his desk and retreated to his tall swivel chair, listening as the man updated his old boss.

"I'm hoping to open an office here, too. Looking into the financing right now."

"You are really moving up, aren't you, young man?" complimented the general director. "Congratulations on all your success."

"Thank you, sir. I have to say that your star was the one who pushed me into pursuing those goals."

"Enzo?" asked the G.D.

"He certainly did. We became friends when he was an apprentice here, and he encouraged me to follow my goals. He even helped out with the loans for college," Burrows' eyebrows raised, "I mean, he co-signed them. Both he and Gwen are really great friends."

Demetrius paused from his recollection, then turned his stare directly to the general director and intently finished. "There isn't anything I wouldn't do for Enzo and Gwen." The statement was true and Demetrius delivered it with several meanings. Burrows received every meaning intended by the young detective and now psychologist. Burrows could play mind games too, and he smiled back at the detective, hiding his growing disdain for the intended threat.

"Isn't that nice." Burrows smiled and nodded his head. His clenched teeth did not escape Demetrius's studious eyes. Demetrius noticed the white cast.

"What happened to your hand, Mr. Burrows?"

"A little accident with some glass, that's all."

Demetrius did not believe the general director.

"That must have been some glass to have broken your hand, and on the top of your hand at that."

"It certainly was." Burrows leaned back into his chair, crossing his hands in front of his chest, setting his right hand over the white plastered left one.

Demetrius continued. "Because with glass, doctors usually just stitch you up and put butterfly bandages over the gash. Don't they usually put casts on when bones are broken?"

Burrows' mind raced with questions. Could this young man know what happened to him the other night? Was he working for the boss and keeping an eye on Enzo for them, or was he truly Enzo's friend? Burrows decided to continue playing along.

"I really have no idea, Demetrius. I just know the doctor wanted a cast on this hand. He felt like it would heal better that way."

Demetrius broke in on the G.D.

"Because I've seen lots of broken hands, and they are always casted on the inside, not the outside. I mean, the break is always on the palm or in the fingers, never on the back side."

The rapid fire was agitating Burrows and Demetrius was happy to accomplish his purpose. If Burrows was flustered and defensive and Demetrius could keep him talking, maybe something would spill from the eloquent lips of the general director. Demetrius asked again about the cause of the cast.

"How did you break it again, Mr. Burrows?"

Burrows took a deep breath, sunk further into his chair and repeated his earlier explanation.

"At home, on some glass," he sighed, "that's all, Demetrius." The G.D. wanted to get him out of the office, but he remained polite.

"Now, Demetrius, what can I do for you?" The general director was relieved to know this stupid little game was over, and that this young man could begin with his real inquiry.

"Mr. Burrows, can you tell me a little about Frank Stanza?"

Aha! played only in Burrows' mind this time. Frank Stanza was the topic of conversation. "Caution" would have to be the word, and "safety" the byword.

"I know that he was an excellent props master, and..." Burrows paused, not wanting to give away anything vital, "that he has been missing since our opening night a week and a half ago."

"You know that Enzo saw Frank killed in the props storage room down on your 'C' Level."

"Demetrius, I believe that since you have talked with Enzo, he also told you that I called the chief of police and his best two detectives over in the middle of the night after our opening, and those gentlemen found nothing suspicious. We were here until the wee hours of the morning, and there was not a trace of any wrong doing."

"So you think Enzo is lying?" Demetrius tried to put words in the general director's mouth.

"Well, Demetrius," Burrows responded, "whatever happened down there, I don't believe that Frank Stanza was killed." Burrows lied. He waited a moment, summoning thoughts to put his lies together as clearly as possible.

"Enzo and Frank were great friends, I know that, but at this point, with no evidence, no motives, and no Frank, how can anyone conclude that he was killed?"

"Then why do you speak of Frank in the past tense, Mr. Burrows?"

"I'm simply speaking of the time Enzo thought he saw the murder, and until something shows up, what I understand from Chief O'Leary, Frank will be classified as a missing person."

Demetrius kept his stare in place, back straight and arms clutching their rests.

"I do have an opera company to run and I can't worry too much about the sordid affairs of our prop master, who in my opinion, and might I add the police's opinion, may be out gallivanting with some girlfriend he found."

The words grew more emphatic as they poured out of his mouth. Burrows was tired of contemplating his culpability in the death of Frank Stanza, but the charade continued to play out in his words and actions. Demetrius kept up the pressure.

"Mr. Burrows, I went and visited Mrs. Gloria Brook Filmore yesterday afternoon. Have you ever been to the Filmore mansion, Mr. Burrows?"

Burrows did not pretend to smile now. His expression was low and dark, his brow sullen, eyes hidden.

"Yes, I have, Mr. McDiess." Burrows was quickly becoming exacerbated. "Many times."

"I was talking with her about the huge donation that you credited her mother with making to the Chicago Grande Opera. I understand the speech you gave on opening night was quite a show."

Demetrius lightened his expression to allow his interrogated to know he was aware of the acting skill employed during the opening night *mea culpa*.

"Mrs. Filmore told me that neither her mother's estate, nor the Brook Candy Company was responsible for the half a billion dollars that will soon be in your coffers."

Burrows grew more and more angry. He spoke through gritted teeth.

"Is there some question, Mr. McDiess, or even some point to this discussion?" Rage built behind the decaying veneer.

"Sure, Mr. Burrows, there are several wonderful questions that scream to be answered." Demetrius was having fun with the now squeamish director.

"First of all, who gave you the half billion dollars, Mr. Burrows, since it was not the Brook Estate?" Demetrius asked, point blank.

Burrows breathed to insult the young visitor, but he was cut short by the caramel-skinned man across from him. Burrows felt like the undersized little boy beat upon by bullies, then beaten again by his parents, for the mere point of humiliation.

Demetrius turned the question/answer discussion into a monologue.

"Since I know you won't answer that question truthfully, I'll just think out loud for a minute or two, if you don't mind, Mr. Burrows." Demetrius leaned to the right side of his chair, onto his elbow, and began his diatribe. "I know that all donations are a matter of public record, and the Brook Estate is credited in the public record with the first hundred million donated last spring to restart the CGO, and my guess would be, that the Brook Estate will also be credited with all future donations. *But* Mrs. Filmore says 'no,' that's not true. The Brooks are not the great generous donors of the half billion. So, who gave the opera all that money? It seems easy to me, especially since someone is obviously trying to obfuscate the source of the donations. It must be criminal. Now, that part is easy, isn't it, Mr. Burrows?"

Demetrius paused and breathed. Burrows had no air in his lungs, and his face became pale.

"But it was convenient that Mrs. Brook died so suddenly last fall, in that she would be the only person who could possibly afford to bail the CGO out of their fiscal nightmare..." Demetrius paused for point, "also created by you, Mr. Burrows." Demetrius returned to his argument.

"Now, I'm a generous man, but if I weren't and I wanted to be a good detective, I might believe that someone in the CGO, or someone wanting to influence the CGO, murdered Mrs. Brook, knowing that if her estate went to the CGO, she would make a great cover to restart the opera.

"But, Mr. Burrows, that theory doesn't work because the money did not come from the Brook Estate...but...if you paid off a lawyer to let the public record reflect the gift, then maybe Mrs. Brook's death could be the devil-send that the CGO needed."

Burrows' eyes darted around the room, his head shifting and bobbing with each targeted statement.

"Now you have a dead Mrs. Brook, so you can hide the influx of money, but if the money did not come from the Brook Estate, where did it come from?"

"You have that one figured out too, I suppose," Burrows said nervously. Sarcasm dripped off each syllable.

"I have some ideas, Mr. Burrows, but it's necessary, in order to figure out everything behind the scenes, to ask the right questions." Demetrius lightened his tone. "I learned that in Criminal Justice Class."

"So who would want to influence a multi-million dollar a year organization, but hide the fact all along?" Demetrius looked across the desk in gleeful condescension. "This one is really easy, Mr. Burrows, so you can answer it if you want."

Burrows shook his head slowly while his right hand picked at his plaster-casted left hand.

"Come on, it's obvious." Demetrius' voice rose to instigate reaction. "O.K., I'll answer. Organized crime. But you still had some assets last fall, so someone burns your assets to the ground, knowing the insurance has not been paid. The CGO is left with nothing except a greedy general director and a public that wants its opera company to live. Organized crime steps in and they have the answer to all your problems. They supply the donation which will get the CGO back onto its feet, and the incoming money will be covered up by some lawyer who says the huge donation is legitimate." Demetrius paused from his sermon for a bit of commentary.

"It's really pretty slick, the way things have worked out since last year when you screwed everyone in Chicago by ruining this company."

Sweat tumbled down the general director's brow and his pulse raced. And Demetrius continued.

"Next question is, why would organized crime want an opera company in the first place? Or what great moneymaking industry is the CGO able to influence? All the money coming in to the opera is accounted for, except of course the half-billion just donated by the mob, and the company has no real assets besides opera sets, a theatre, and a loading dock. But then, Mr. Burrows, all your assets were destroyed in that horrible fire last January at the storage warehouse, weren't they?"

Demetrius spoke as if he was reading from a script. The plot unfolded easily and obviously now, and each statement dragged William Burrows further down the road to suicide. The sermon continued.

"Now you have an opera company with no assets at all, a sudden influx of half a *billion* dollars, and guess what happens. The Mexico City Opera Theatre comes to the rescue and offers to send you all their new sets. Thank God for the Mexico City Opera Theatre! They will supply everything you need: sets, props, even cash if you need it." More sarcasm erupted, this time from Demetrius.

"Of course, being a good detective now, I believe Mexico City supplied the half billion anyway, so it seems logical that they would send up all their huge sets to be used here.

"But we still haven't answered the basic question. Why would the mob be interested in the CGO, and how would they make money on a public enterprise?"

"This one's easy too, but I know you want me to answer." Demetrius smiled a fake grin, and immediately changed tone.

"If the men who are really running this place are also running the Mexico City Opera, and if all the trucks are coming here from Mexico, it seems to me that one way everyone could make money is through transportation.

"O.K., I realize that is the nice word for it, but smuggling would be infinitely easier if two publicly supported companies who found it necessary to move huge amounts of equipment from country to country were in business together. There might be no stopping that kind of enterprise.

"And with the size of all the new sets, you could smuggle anything you want. Damn, I saw those *Tosca* sets, and you could have smuggled an elephant into the country if you wanted. What was it, Mr. Burrows—eight semi-trailers of stuff, just for one opera?

"My guess is that most of what is coming in is narcotics, especially since you," Burrows peered at the detective, hearing the accusation, "since you and the CGO have received such a huge gift in order to keep silent."

Demetrius was finally silent a moment. Burrows was happy the jabber had finally stopped, but the detective started once again.

"It would be a great investment too, when you think about the whole financial side of the dealings. A huge opera production costs, what, Mr. Burrows? At the most, five million dollars? And with the great public thanks shown in support of bringing great art to Chicago, there would be very few questions asked about what is going on here. And shoot," Demetrius leaned to the other side of his chair, "for a narcotics ring to spend five million on an opera set that, when all the false walls, and props, and faux columns are lined with narcotics, would bring in about seventy million in cash. That's a great return on your money, don't you think, Mr. Burrows? And think of all the prestige Chicago gains in the eyes of the world by putting on the best opera in the world.

"Thousands of people come and go every day here in the Illinois State Theatre, you have easy access to the Chicago River, to Upper and Lower Wacker Drive, you have a truck dock, several entrances and exits, and I would guess more than one secret entrance and passageway around here, especially knowing how old this building is. And everything is concealed, hidden within plain view of the city, in the public domain, and right out on Wacker Drive."

Demetrius smiled in true amazement at the complex organizations he outlined for the general director.

"This setup is amazing in its complexity, but it's still based in utter simplicity. It's, in a way, a unique work of art, Mr. Burrows, amongst your unique works of operatic art."

Demetrius shook his head, astounded, not at what he believed to be the truth, but at the act he now put on, hoping for some kind of a reaction. Burrows sat sulking in his plush recliner, his eyes merely slits, darting side to side. Then he realized something this fine young detective had seemed to overlook. He sat up in his chair, ready for his assault.

"All this conjecture is well and good, and it takes an impressive mind to conjure up these fantasies, Mr. McDiess," the general director complimented the detective, but honing in on his target, he tried to raze the well-constructed plot.

"Everything you have mentioned is merely hypothesis, solely conjecture, and in my opinion comes very close to slander, especially if you would be foolish enough to spread these suppositions." Burrows believed he had countered well. "So unless you have some real evidence, Mr. McDiess, or at least some stronger circumstantial evidence, please keep your opinions and your presence out of the Illinois State Theatre."

The trap slammed shut on the general director. Demetrius grinned broadly and reached into his coat pocket.

"You're right, Mr. Burrows. I can't prove anything right now. You may just be smuggling art work, or bearer bonds, but I do believe you are smuggling something." Demetrius took a grand, dramatic pause, "And here is why I think that, Mr. Burrows. I'd like you to take a look at these, Mr. Burrows." Demetrius had hoped the director would take this logical step towards the state of evidence surrounding Demetrius's hypothesis. Demetrius flipped six photographs, or rather copies of photographs, onto the G.D.'s desktop. The director leafed through the photos, eyeing each one carefully.

"What is this supposed to tell me, Mr. McDiess?"

"Mr. Burrows, you surprise me now," sardonic in tone. "Those photos were taken by Frank Stanza." Demetrius lied about the absolute truth in that statement. "They were taken, as you see, at your loading dock, and they identify several men off-loading plastic packages, transferring material from your new sets, into their personal possession."

"And so..." the director weakly retorted.

"And so..." Demetrius took an accusatory tone with the contemptuous one, and, Demetrius now believed, unchangeably corrupt director, "do these men work for you?" Burrows was silent.

"Silence, huh? Well, I'll finish again." Demetrius's voice raised in disdain. "Either you were robbed, or you knowingly allow these men to off-load smuggled merchandise from the trucks that arrive here from Mexico."

"These show nothing, God damn it!" Burrows finally exploded in anger at the young man accusing him. "They don't show one fucking thing." The offensive felt better to the G.D., but he could not dig his way out of the trap sprung upon him. "They're all fuzzy, out of focus, and this last one is some God damn white and brown shit." He turned vile upon the visitor. "Now get the hell out of my office and never set foot in this theatre again."

The director stood, raging and exhilarated from the effort he had just spewed forth. Demetrius was undaunted and stood slowly. He spoke of the clear implications evident in the sixth photograph.

"Mr. Burrows, I *will* leave now, but just for your personal information, the sixth photo you hold in your smashed left hand," Demetrius emphasized to the unaware patsy, "is a picture of Frank Stanza's left hand. Do you know what he's holding?" Demetrius quickly spoke up again. "Of course you don't. Fresh coffee, off-loaded with the plastic packages in the other photos. You see, Mr. Burrows, drug dealers use coffee to throw dogs off the scent of their drugs." Demetrius condescended to the street ignorant snob. "You learn that in the 'hood, not in Criminal Justice Class.

"But, as you said, the white pellets threw me for a minute, too. But you know what those white pellets are? Those are ammonia pellets. You see, if a dog sniffs ammonia, that dog is totally ineffective as a drug detector for at least twenty minutes."

Burrows moved his head to look at the photo again.

"Isn't that interesting, Mr. Burrows? Someone around here felt it necessary to lace your opera sets with fresh coffee and ammonia. Now, the only people I can think of who might want to do that would be drug dealers wanting to supply the nostrils of the Midwest with plenty of stimulation. And you see, if you also grease the palms of our underpaid border patrol, this drug clearinghouse called the Chicago Grande Opera is a money machine, ringing up sales for the Mexico City Opera Theatre and the henchmen who run that operation." Demetrius turned to leave, but before leaving, he took back the photos.

"You add all this circumstantial evidence to the explosive trigger found in your warehouse fire last January, and you have a nice little conspiracy on your hands."

Burrows' face was puzzled. Demetrius seized his next opportunity.

"Oh, yeah, I forgot to tell you about that evidence, Mr. Burrows. I found a complex ignition switch in the rubble of your big warehouse fire. And it was laced with plastic explosives, so the evidence is falling into place, and soon the rats that have burrowed into this place aren't gonna have anywhere else to hide, 'cause the CGO is gonna come falling down around them."

Now Demetrius was ready to make his intended move. He had pummeled the general director with solid and convincing arguments behind what he believed to be the evil of the Chicago Grande Opera, and now that Burrows was weakened by the blows, Demetrius could make an offer of aid. He stepped into the great desk, piercing the comfortable zone of distance between the men.

"You see, Mr. Burrows, I think you're just a pawn in the hands of some evil men who came along when you were in real trouble. In fact, I doubt you were privy to half of what I just told you. You just wanted to run your opera company. While you sleep in your Gold Coast apartment, these men do their business off the back of the trucks. *But, Mr. Burrows, you're just as guilty as any dealer selling crack to the people of this city, selling death to the people I grew up with.*" Demetrius clenched his teeth. "And I guarantee, that you will go down with the rest of 'em if you don't surrender right now."

Demetrius was completely earnest in his threat, but he also knew he had to give this coward a chance to redeem himself.

The two men faced each other, both silent for the first time in fifteen minutes. Burrows swallowed painfully, still picking at his cast, the present evidence of his contract with the devil. Burrows' glance moved from side to side. He looked up into the face of Demetrius and saw a man of conviction, a man of truth, and a man of moral certainty.

"I..." the general director's mouth opened.

Nothing more would come from the desert mouth that hung from his face.

Demetrius spoke slowly to the director, for the first time of the morning without another agenda, but completely in truth and in unwavering justice. Demetrius pleaded with simple words, spoken in sympathy for the man, once so great, yet now so corrupt, helplessly languishing in his own ineptitude.

"Mr. Burrows, you realize that I have to tear all this down, and you'll be engulfed in the collapse, only, unlike Samson, Mr. Burrows, you'll have no redemption waiting for you." Demetrius stared at the man, but he had waited long enough. He threw a card on the desk with his phone number on it, then he walked away.

William Burrows stood behind his desk, motionless, inert, and certain of his doom. Just moments before he had contemplated his unknown demise, and thought suicide was his only release. But then only moments later, as if sent from heaven, was an opportunity to escape, to defy the heinous presence he had introduced to this opera house, and to do right, to end the treachery that was eating away at his soul. But he had passed the opportunity by, unable to free himself from the clutches of self-loathing, and incapable of freeing himself from the stranglehold of contempt. He was doomed—doomed to live under evil's oppression and die at its whim. And he was doomed by virtue, which would judge him traitor, coward, and full of iniquity.

He swallowed heavily again, trying to clear his ego from his throat, and sat down in his chair. He began to breathe again. He had only one decision left to make and one turn left to negotiate.

Callas's voice, sweet and supple, rang in his head. She, too, the great diva, was doomed, doomed with the heroines in her art, and doomed also by the choices she had made in her life.

The tragedy played over and over in the general director's head. He was doomed. Doomed by his art, and doomed to eternal death. And, there was no escape.

Thirty-One

The cassette tape played the conversation between the two men. It was obvious that the one was in complete control of the discussion, dictating the tone, the method, and the timbre of the hour.

"Is that that damn detective?" the boss, seated in his position of power, asked the two underlings.

"Yes, sir," the technician with the player spoke. "We got it just this morning, in Burrows' office."

The recording was slightly fuzzy, an operatic recording being played in the background.

"Didn't the video come out?" demanded the boss.

"It did, sir, but the quality was less than great, and we knew," the technician deferred to the boss's number one, giving a little nod, "that you would want to hear this as soon as possible."

The conversation played on. The boss and the assistant were intent on the content of the detective's monologue. The fifteen minutes were interrupted by the gentlemen's voices only twice. The last two minutes of the tape were unintelligible. The voices were soft and distant.

"Why the hell can't we hear this part?" screamed the boss at the audio technician.

"You see, sir," he tried to explain, "the men moved away from the microphones at the desk, and the detective lowered his voice. The proximity of the men's voices, combined with the music in the background, blurred the surveillance."

The boss was unhappy and looked toward his number one.

"What did the video look like?"

"Bad," was the monotone response from the enforcer. "Grainy and unusable."

"You couldn't read lips off of the video?" inquired the boss.

"No, sir," the two underlings responded in unison.

The tape snapped to a halt and clicked off. The boss looked the technician directly in the eye.

"Listen, young man," he growled, "get those cameras fixed and get it done *now*. I'm not paying you for shit like this. Understand?"

The technician grabbed his tape player and nodded a cowering "yes" to the intimidating leader.

"Now get out of here and get back to work."

The number one walked the technician to the door, closed it and came back for what he knew would be a decision-making discussion. As he walked back to the boss, the man rubbed his hands together, sensing some action— action that he himself would take care of personally. The tattoo on the back of his left hand wiggled under the pressure applied by his expectant grip. He stood at the front and center of the desk, directly opposite from the obese slobbering CEO of their industry. He thought, *I shall attain to power!*

His steely glance met the angry eyes of the boss. The two were unified in their thought. The tape recording had confirmed the need for forceful and decisive action. The dark, heavy brow hung lower and lower on the boss as he addressed his trusted one.

"What about Burrows?" The growls grew in intensity with each syllable.

"He hasn't said a thing." The number one paused. "And he hasn't come to us with this information." The boss's chest filled with hissing air, funneling down blocked passageways. His chest heaved again and again.

"You know what has to be done, don't you, Robert?" The boss's eyes enjoyed the menace he saw in his man. The underling's senses heightened as he watched the anger within his boss grow.

"Yes, sir," he spoke, grinding his vocal chords into obedience.

"First, we have to stop this detective," the boss snarled contemptuously, "before he gets any closer. We have to attack 'em where they're most vulnerable and shut 'em up."

The number one agreed. He had viewed all the tapes, all the surveillance, and had all the information he needed in order to neuter the little band of informants.

"I know just what to do, sir," he said and smiled. "After I take action, that detective won't dare do a thing."

"Good," barked the boss in approval, "and stop the leaks. And when you have them under your thumb," the boss pointed to his trusted one and he paused, "then kill 'em, Robert. Kill 'em all."

"Yes sir."

"Robert, remember too, these are high profile people, this opera singer. They are constantly watched, so you must be discreet."

"I know just what to do, sir." The assistant, after listening to the many recording devices and the information they had gathered, had to ask one more question.

"Sir?"

"Yes, Robert."

"Should we still go ahead with the shipment arriving tomorrow night? If that detective has all the information he says he has, should we delay until he is taken care of?"

"Can you silence him enough for the shipment to go through as planned?"

"Yes I can, sir."

"Then bring it in," the boss stated, "but don't give this McDiess character any room to breathe. Understand?"

"Oh yes, sir."

"Now get going," the boss ordered.

"What about Burrows?" The assistant was not questioning the boss's decision, merely checking for clarification of his duties. Because of their earlier conversations, the underling knew that Burrows was valuable, and might still be twisted into the "model employee."

"Wait on him," the boss responded, grateful that the assistant had asked the question. "He may still work out for us."

"Yes, sir." The assistant moved quickly to the door, needing time to prepare his work, but knowing exactly what plan would silence the infiltrators. It would be a beautiful, operatic tragedy.

"About Burrows, Robert," the boss yelled to the man exiting the room, "you can hurt him a little."

The underling's smile grew and he cackled at the boss's request.

"Yes sir!" The assistant left the room quickly, delighted that his pent-up desires would find release. The door swung shut and the boss was alone. He knew his man would enjoy inflicting punishment upon the insufferable cowardice of William Burrows. The boss saw this order as a toy given to the child restricted to his room on a sunny afternoon. It would alleviate the tension he had felt growing between the two of them, a tension that would one day be resolved, a tension that he knew would end with the younger man's ascension to power.

That was fine by the boss. That was how this business worked and that was how he had attained to his own power, but he knew the impatience of the younger man needed to be shaped if he were to be successful in the further ventures of their industry. A few life and business lessons still needed to be taught to the impetuous, arrogant, violent man, and he, the boss, was the only one who would be able to teach them.

He took a Cuban from his humidor, bit the end, and reached for his lighter. He grunted a laugh, remembering when he had been ordered to act, just as he had ordered today, and recalling the thrill that filled him when he had completed his deeds.

He pulled the warm tobacco smoke into his mouth and fell more deeply into his chair.

"Kill 'em all."

He laughed again and blew the smoke out into the room.

There was a knock on the door, and a young man called to the boss.

"Sir, there is a William Burrows here to see you. He says it is urgent."

More smoke filled the office and the boss looked over the fine fifty-dollar rolled tobacco leaves.

"Send him in."

Burrows walked hastily into the office, sweat pouring off his brow, and sat only when motioned to do so by the boss.

"Demetrius McDiess came to see me this morning." He paused, swallowing. "And he said that he has discovered what's happening at the opera house." The boss nodded.

"Well, Bill, I'm glad you came in."

The lobby information desk was just to the east of the four elevators: three public, and one private. Demetrius sat across from the information desk, shrouded behind his leather coat and dark glasses. He held a tiny camera in his lap and snapped a shot of every person that emerged from the elevator doors.

After his lancing of William Burrows moments before, and with Burrows' refusal to cooperate, he knew the general director would need to relay their conversation to the men in charge of this conspiracy.

He had picked up the limousine license plate numbers from Harris, and then, right on schedule, followed the general director's limousine, Illinois Livery Licensee plate 2B0-R2DI, just south on Wacker Drive, into one of Chicago's unnamed skyscrapers.

Demetrius pulled his Intrepid slowly behind the limo after Burrows exited, and quickly followed the nervous general director into the lobby and to the elevators.

Burrows used the private elevator and fidgeted nervously, picking at his cast, waiting for the electronic doors to open. Demetrius could not enter the private elevator. His inquiry at the lobby information desk revealed only a private party leasing the penthouse.

Unable to enter the elevator and ride up to the conspiracy in the sky, Demetrius decided to wait and watch, seeing who came and went from the private elevator. It did not take long for the cables of the lift to heat up.

Burrows had been gone only a few minutes when several dark-suited men emerged from the elevator. There was one man who led the group. He was about forty-five, with dark hair, stocky, six-feet tall or so. The other three were typical wiseguy wanna-bes, walking tough, dark-suited, with slicked-back hair, and even the requisite pinkie rings. They were almost laughable to the detective. Those three men resembled remnants from the era of Capone, from the times of the Big Tuna, Anthony Accardo, and from the violent days of Chicago mob lore.

But the obvious leader was not this way. He looked tough. He had the dark suit, but there was no pretense about him. His physique bulged through the dark wool, and his fists were clenched. He scanned the lobby as he emerged, completely aware of his surroundings, his eyes honed to mischief, his glance ready for action.

Demetrius had to be careful not to be seen by this one. The other three strode with ambivalence, ignorant of their surroundings, but the one—the man Demetrius identified as the leader—was hawk-like, ready to swoop and attack anything that defied him.

The group was out the lobby doors and gone before Demetrius was able to follow, but he had acquired good, clean shots of the group. Maybe John McGrail could help out with some identifications.

Before leaving, Demetrius jotted down all pertinent information concerning the building. Maybe John could also give him some more info on the penthouse occupants.

Demetrius picked up a deli sandwich and drove down to his surveillance van. He slid the doors open and no alarm sounded. Harris jumped again, hitting his head on the top of the van's metal roof.

"Harris!" Demetrius bellowed.

"Damn, 'D.'" Harris rubbed his head and turned in one motion. "You scared the shit out a me."

"The alarm, Harris!" Harris ignored his friend and began bragging.

"Yo, 'D,' I got the secondary VCR hooked up to the primary one." Demetrius, unimpressed, threw the white deli bag full of lunch at his goofy employee. The bag bounced off of Harris's flat chest and landed in his arms.

"No, 'D,' you don't get it," he tried to explain, caught up in his accomplishment. "Now your surveillance cameras can give two copies immediately." He paused, vibrating with excitement, "and no degradation in quality."

"Great," Demetrius said sarcastically. Harris pushed his falling glasses back up onto the brim of his nose, proud of his work in this game of surveillance and oblivious to the unimpressed response of his friend. He dug into the white bag.

"You get me somethin' good, D?"

"Yeah, I got ya somethin' good," responded 'D,' "but the way you scarf food down, your tongue doesn't get a chance to taste it anyway."

Harris had already unwrapped the barbecued pork sandwich and shoved it into his mouth, seemingly on the verge of starvation. He turned to sit at the surveillance console.

"What about a drink, D?"

Demetrius smiled and shook his head.

"You're a piece of work, Harris."

Thirty-Two

7:30 p.m.
Monday, October 2

Demetrius joined the Santis for dinner again. He walked down from his own luxury suite and saw, posted at the Santis' door, a burly twenty-something guard. He was crew-cut and freshly scrubbed, seated in a folding chair at the suite's entrance.

"Hi, I'm Demetrius McDiess," the friend introduced himself to the guard. "I'm hoping the Santis are here."

"Yes, sir, they are." the polite young man stood to shake hands. He rose to an ominous six-feet five-inch height, "high school defensive end" stamped upon his hulking figure. "They told me you would be coming down. My name is Brick Youngblood."

"How did the Santis find you so quickly, *Brick*?" Demetrius was unsure of the unusual name, and thus emphasized the word.

"I work security here in the Hyatt, sir. I am studying Criminal Justice, and work here part time."

"Are you sure you can handle this job?" Demetrius wanted to verify the young man's metal. "Have you worked as a personal security guard before?"

"Well, sir," the young man answered, assured of himself, "I have worked here several years. I am familiar with the staff, the facilities, and I do have a second degree black belt in karate, so I think I can handle watching the Santis." The clear-skinned smile exuded confidence and assurance. Demetrius was still unsure of this supposedly untried appointee.

"Will you be handling all the shifts here, Brick? You know it's a twenty-four-hour-a-day job."

"Oh no, sir. I'm actually on vacation, but I needed the extra money so I'm sticking around to help the Santis out. Two other hotel guards are doing the same thing. We are running twelve-hour shifts—six-to-six, with twenty-four off in between."

"Do you have any other kind of..." Demetrius looked for the proper discreet word, "protection?" The college kid reached behind his chair and produced an enormous black steel flashlight. It was, in essence, a billy club with a bulb in the end.

"The hotel will not allow its security personnel to carry firearms," the young man, professional and impressive, said, "but this is all that we have ever needed in the Hyatt, sir."

Demetrius smiled and looked at the boy, not knowing what forces he had surrounded himself with, and spoke under his breath.

"I hope you're right." Demetrius decided he could lighten up on the young hunk, and he began to kibitz.

"Criminal Justice, huh? Where you studying, Brick?"

"Northwestern. This is my last year."

The lad relaxed, feeling the official job interview to be over. The questions the Santis had asked were much less invasive and much less probing, but the young guard knew who was paying the bills, and also, who was the experienced professional, the man truly in charge of the couple's protection. Brick knew that Mr. McDiess was just doing his job for the Santis.

Demetrius knocked on the door.

"I studied Criminal Justice at Triton first," Demetrius offered, "and finished at UIC." Demetrius believed the kid from the Big Ten would think his education inferior, but Demetrius knew that becoming a good detective was more about street smarts than about book knowledge. The books would only solidify the evidence. An understanding of human nature and a feel for the human mind would solve most mysteries more quickly than a good degree from a squeaky-clean university.

"I have some friends who go to Triton and love the education they're getting out there." The boy did not seem to condescend. "I understand that they have some excellent professors." He was much more generous than Demetrius had expected.

"What do you want to do when you graduate?" Demetrius asked. The door opened. Gwen was putting her earring on. Enzo walked up the few steps to the door.

"I hope to work for the District Attorney, sir," Brick answered.

"Good, we're gonna be on the same team." Demetrius smiled.

"With as big as Brick is, I don't think I'd want to be on the other team." Gwen heard the two and spoke up. "You'd get squashed awful quick."

The friends greeted each other and left the young man seated at the door. He wished them a pleasant evening.

Enzo had a hankering for sweets, so at Gwen's suggestion the three friends decided to dine at The Cheesecake Corporation, located at the base of the John Hancock Tower. Instead of taking Demetrius's car or a taxi, the glorious fall day demanded a walk up Michigan Avenue to the restaurant eight blocks away. Before they left for the restaurant, Demetrius thumped Enzo on the chest. Under his fingers, Demetrius felt the kevlar mesh that protected the chest of his friend.

"Thank you, Enzo," Demetrius told the tenor. "I know it isn't the most comfortable thing to wear, but I don't think it'll be necessary much longer."

"You're in charge, my friend," responded the tenor. "Besides, it's so tight, I work on expanding my breathing against the resistance it provides." Enzo faked a gasp, unable to stretch the bulletproof material.

"I'll see if I can find one a bit bigger," Demetrius concluded.

Enzo wrapped his scarf around his neck and the trio was off for their autumnal stroll. They kept a quick gait, following Upper Wacker along the Chicago River to the corner of Michigan Avenue. The intersection held within it a line of bronze plaques, outlining a huge square. The golden-dotted outline covered nearly the entire four-way stop.

This was the heart of Chicago, born in Fort Sheridan, the outpost along Lake Michigan, which had stood on this very spot one hundred and fifty years earlier. It had been an outpost for traders and pelts, for Indians and frontiersmen. It was situated along the mighty waters from which sprang the great metropolis of today.

The friends walked north over the Michigan Avenue Bridge and looked to the great newspaper buildings that guarded the historic sight and its legacy. The darkening October eve had signaled the ornamental spotlights of the buildings to brighten the way. The great white stone Herald Tower and its western partner, the Wrigley Building, focused the pedestrian and auto traffic into the great concourse of north Michigan.

The wind was at its best through these caverns of steel and concrete, lifting skirts, jostling hair, and buffeting souls.

West down the river, staring at the waterway's enormous fork, they again admired the Marina Towers and the huge Merchandise Mart.

The three scurried in the breeze and finally left the bridge. As he had been ten years before, Enzo was fascinated by the Herald Tower. Its facade and main entrance incorporated stones from every country of the world in which the great journal was represented. The oddly shaped stones—different colors, sizes, and textures—sparked the entrance with animation, a life which ebbed with respect for the different cultures, peoples, and ideas represented not only upon the building, but throughout this city of immigrants.

Michigan Avenue was lit with thousands of tiny white lights, which had been strung in the trees lining the avenue. The reds, tans, saffrons, and greens whirling in the wind spun into a kaleidoscope of color. The lights were a year-round illumination that delighted all comers. The tiny ornaments danced in the limbs and sparkled with the glow from the shops and businesses, keeping Michigan Avenue moving and thriving.

The immaculately clean, prosperous street was the pride of the city, full of shops and hotels, restaurants and attractions, and just a quarter of a mile ahead, in direct view, apparently splitting the avenue in half, was the Chicago Water Tower. The tawny stone of the monument stood notably in the median of the avenue.

This fine building, having withstood the city's great inferno, stood proud and prominent, lending support to the city that built itself again from the ashes, and in the shadow of the Tower's simple strength. This Tower and its companion Pumping Station had fed the city its water, allowing her to mature into this great city of strength.

The Tower now stood in retirement, the proud grandparent of her offspring, admired the world over.

The three passed the great monument and peered up at the colossal Hancock Tower—black glass and steel, straight up, one hundred floors. The Hancock, The Water Tower's favorite son, stood over the tiny stone building as its guardian.

The plaza in front of the Hancock descended into shops, and to the south side to the Cheesecake Corporation, the party's destination.

The quick walk had invigorated all of them, and they were ready for a sumptuous meal. They were seated just inside, in a splendid panorama looking up and northwest, through the city. Gwen had wanted to sit outside, but the tenor thought the wind might be too much for his throat.

"And the cheesecake is good for your throat?" Gwen jibed.

"Yes," Enzo feigned superiority. "It coats my throat with sugar and energy." Enzo impersonated his best flamboyant Italian tenor.

"Dee weend is my enemee, and weel bareeng dee seeckness to *mia voce*."

Demetrius laughed, as did Gwen. This wee concession, made for Enzo's monstrous, yet delicate instrument, was fine with everyone. Besides, the view from the window table was spectacular.

The eve passed with big meals all around, and even bigger slices of cheesecake. Gwen ate half of everything she was served and saved the rest for later, as did Demetrius. Enzo ordered a feast and devoured the entire thing. Demetrius watched his friend, and knew of only one other person who could eat with such abandon.

"Enzo," asked the detective friend, "you're gonna blimp up if you keep eating like that."

Gwen laughed as her husband tried to speak through the caramel, chocolate chip cheesecake. He grabbed his glass of water and took a swig.

"Don't worry, D, he's working out," spoke Gwen. "We did a bunch of heavy lifting last night."

Enzo blurted out the mixture of water and cheesecake into his plate and burst into laughter, peals of which rivaled the gales outside.

The tenor's face flushed, part embarrassment, part joy, and a great part, delight. Gwen's own remark caught her off-guard and her face reddened as well. Demetrius was a bit unprepared for the lovers' talk, but decided to join in the bit of ribaldry.

"So, Enzo," he began dryly, "you've been practicing your squat thrusts pretty regularly, huh?"

The comment induced the hysterics with which it was intended. The laughter filled the restaurant, emptying after the evening rush, and drew attention to the three wild ones at the window.

None of the three cared. There had been too much concern, too much worry during the past days. This triumvirate gave in to the relaxation found in their laughter.

Demetrius was never insulted by the affection displayed by the devoted couple. In fact, he enjoyed the affection they shared with one another. Their love spilled onto him. The joy they found in each other made them more beautiful people—more tender, more aware, and more lively. The fact that they completely loved each other had fashioned in their union an openness and honesty toward others, and to the sensitivity that caring for others entailed. They were dedicated to each other, and in their perfect dedication, free to share their joy with the world.

Gwen reached under the table and slid her hand up her husband's inner thigh, landing on the most sensitive of his legs. The laughter that racked Enzo's body did not allow his wife's hand to create a sensual feeling, but instead, in the tense state his muscles were in, heightened the uncontrollable roar. Gwen's strong diaphragmatic muscles matched Enzo's tenoral squeals. She poked her husband in the side. He again sent shards of paint-peeling laughter reverberating off the glass. The window bounced the great sound into the main dining room of the Cheesecake Corporation.

Demetrius gave his best impersonation of an operatic guffaw, digging deep into his lungs and pushing out bellowy chuckles.

The trio's waitress covered her ears and walked to the table. Without a word, she motioned the group to tone down slightly. Gwen nodded in recognition and closed her mouth to prevent the majority of sound from escaping.

Enzo, through restrained convulsions, asked for tea, after which he pulled his wife's wooden chair over to his side, Gwen still seated in it, sliding along for the ride. He grabbed her shoulder and caressed her neck. She turned and smiled directly at her husband. Enzo slid his hand down to her side and grabbed her hand. They squeezed in unison, found control of their laughter, and looked out the window in front of them.

Demetrius knew why he was still a bachelor. He had not found a companion with whom he could share the intimacy that he wanted, like that of the Santis. He had dated many wonderful women, but he had not found the one to whom nothing would be hidden, to whom his heart would be lost, and to whom his life would be given.

He watched the couple, his friends, and he fell in love with them.

The walk back to the Hyatt was leisurely, the group opting for the Lake Shore Drive, inner sidewalk. The wind had eased, and the tall apartments along the tree-lined walk protected them from errant blasts. The open water just beyond the three was a playground where the breezes could run about, hiding behind hulls, tugging masts, and creating waves. The flags atop the many moored schooners flapped, the bells upon the boats clapped their delight, feeling the playful youth push and pull in this watery wonderland.

Lights adorned Navy Pier, with its huge ferris wheel. Past the Pier, across the harbor, the Aquarium and Planetarium glowed their partnership with the remarkable retired ship-builder.

The stars in the sky lit the trio's trail, slowly and faintly, through the trees and windows, past the signs and autos, across the glorious river and to the hotel.

Food and exercise had sapped blood from the friends' heads. Yawns and shivers decorated their gate, but comfort and rest welcomed them to their apartment doors. Their young bodyguard stood as they approached, smiled, then sat back down. Brick resumed reading his *Sports Illustrated* while the trio talked.

Gwen offered Demetrius a nightcap, but he refused.

"I've got to relieve Harris in a couple of hours, and I need to get a little sleep," he said in the doorway of 1801.

"Harris?" Gwen questioned, slipping out of her shoes, and cuddling into the chest of her husband, whose arm had wrapped her in warmth during their walk home.

"He's the friend that's helping out with the van." Gwen and Enzo looked puzzled, squinting through the sleepy eyes. The detective had purposefully kept the couple out of the information loop to protect them. He decided to fill them in on the details.

"I've set up a surveillance system at the opera house, and Harris, a childhood buddy, has been helping me out with the watches."

"You think Frank was killed to protect something wrong at the opera house, D?" Enzo inquired softly.

"I'm almost certain," Demetrius said and nodded, "but I think we'll find out for sure tonight."

"Can I help?" asked Enzo, wanting to flesh out the reason for his friend's murder, but Demetrius knew the singer would be a surveillance liability. "Enzo, you've done all that you can do," he assured the tenor. "When we catch these guys, I'll make sure you're there to see Frank's killers locked up." Gwen leaned over to Demetrius and kissed his cheek, gave him a hug, and said goodnight.

"Now go get your sleep," Demetrius mentioned, "or should I say exercise?"

The joke drew a smile and chuckle from the men. Having retreated into the apartment, but having heard the sly remark, Gwen's cackle reverberated through the doorway and into the hall.

"O.K.," Enzo responded. "Goodnight, my friend."

"Goodnight, Brick," Demetrius politely said to the young guard as he passed him.

"Good night, sir," responded the young man.

The door to 1801 was shut and Demetrius retreated to his room for two hours of sleep. He wanted to be at the van no later than 1:00 a.m. The trucks were due at 2 a.m.; that would give him an hour to enter the van and avoid any detection.

Yawns filled the walk to his apartment. The two hours of rest would feel wonderful after this Monday's tense proceedings.

Room 1901 was confused by the conversation at the door below them.

"Surveillance van?" the older of the two wiseguys said in whisper. "Has he mentioned a van before?" The question was directed at his young partner.

"Never!" the young man said. The wiser of the two guys walked to the phone.

"I'm calling Robert," he declared. "If there's a shipment coming in, we can't have any shit like dat goin' on."

The younger guy spun away from his partner who was already making the call, and peered at the video screen. The opera couple was preparing for bed. The younger watched as Gwen threw her clothes onto the bedroom's dresser. Enzo sat at the foot of the bed, his back to the fish-eye lens taking in the scene.

Gwen, in delicate white bra and silken lace panties, walked from the dresser over to her husband. Enzo tenderly hugged her around the waist.

The voyeur raised the volume on the bedroom microphones. Through the bit of static he heard Enzo speak.

"I love you."

The man smiled like a hyena, expelling his rancid breath from a rancid heart.

"I love you too, honey," Gwen replied, the words for only this one in her arms.

But, the one above took the words to his heart and groped the woman with his eyes. The man touched the video screen, pawing at her breasts.

Enzo delicately helped his wife finish disrobing. The one above fondled the blue monitor with each new garment cast away.

Enzo pulled his wife into bed, where they cradled each other, weary and windblown, into the arms of rest.

Disappointment filled the face of the young pervert above. He was disappointed that there was no action, no sex, and most of all, no clear view of her. The tiny camera below showed only the darkened outline of the two wrapped in each other.

"You heard what I said," sounded the voice from across the room, in mid-discussion. "I don't know where, he didn't say. Yes, I have it on tape..."

Nothing disturbed the young one at the screen. His left hand pressed the screen over her body. His right hand fell into his lap and he spoke to himself.

"Oh, baby," he growled. "It won't be long now."

1:30 a.m.
Tuesday, October 3
Lower Wacker Drive

Demetrius and Harris had been talking for the last half an hour, preparing for the arrival of what Demetrius hoped would be concrete evidence to the hypotheses he had drawn. The roadway was quiet; the green glow within Lower Wacker made the scummy brown van appear almost purple.

Demetrius was impressed with Harris's work in the van. He had connected several of the recording devices and interconnected the equipment to allow differing devices to make multiple copies simultaneously. During the afternoon, the energetic friend had even gone out to his home and retrieved a sleeping bag, which was rolled up in the corner. Harris had anticipated long, sleepless hours in this confined, yet thrilling, electronic environment.

Of course the alarm had not been activated, and upon entering the van, Demetrius had frightened his friend again. Harris had locked the vehicle, though, so Demetrius was a little happier with the forgetful technician.

Harris was in his element, adjusting monitors, tweaking receivers, and increasing the portable studio's capacities, but while the equipment was running better than ever, the floor of the van was covered with debris: wrappers, drink containers, sandwich bags, and a box of Twinkies lay strewn on the shag-carpeted floor. Demetrius decided that with all the work and time his friend was giving him, he himself would be responsible for the van's sanitation.

"Did you eat all these things?" Demetrius asked, picking up the Twinkies box and looking directly at Harris.

"Yeah, why?"

"When you die there isn't gonna be blood in your veins, they'll be flowing with corn syrup."

"They sure hit the spot this afternoon." The human garbage can reached into his shirt pocket and pulled out a remaining sugary sponge cake. "I got one last one, D. You want it?" Demetrius looked at the box.

"Twelve individually wrapped sponge cakes per box," he read, shaking his head. "You ate eleven of these things?" Demetrius asked in amazement and disgust.

"Well, you didn't bring much for lunch, and I was hungry." Harris unwrapped the last Twinkie, wadding its plastic wrapper in his palm and throwing it at the trash can behind him. He stuffed the Twinkie down his throat.

"You're not gonna die," Demetrius joked. "The Hostess Corporation is having you preserved, one Twinkie at a time."

"Don't forget my Suzy-Q's," Harris replied. "Gotta have my sweet black Suzy."

Harris puckered his lips, making love to the black devil's food cake and multi-syllabic, preservative-laden "treat." The conversation slowed. Harris stayed at the main console, while Demetrius pulled up a plastic milk crate and sat behind him. The men settled in for their night of discovery.

One hour passed; there was nothing. An hour and a half passed and there was only quiet. Lower Wacker was desolate. All the equipment without and within the van was operating perfectly, yet there was no commotion from within the opera's truck dock. Demetrius was getting fidgety, but Harris sat still, full of sugar, overflowing with energy. All of his energy was focused on the monitors, transmitters, and receivers, and upon their perfect function. Harris also jabbered more and more as he came to believe that tonight was not the designated arrival Demetrius believed it to be.

"Where could they be?" Demetrius questioned out loud.

"The drive from Mexico City is a long one. Could the trucks have gotten hung up somewhere?" Harris mused out loud.

Demetrius thought this logical. If the trucks were simply hauling conventional material they could certainly be delayed, but not if they were smuggling drugs. No delays would be allowed with a cargo that would be so highly valued. Besides, the delays would be factored into the drive time.

"I don't think so, Harris," he spoke softly. "Besides, there isn't any movement inside the opera house either. If they were expecting a delivery, somebody would have been here by now." The blue-screened monitors reflected in the smaller man's glasses. He turned to his friend.

"What went wrong?"

Demetrius pulled his notepad from his jacket pocket. There it was, written exactly as Frank Stanza had written it on his ledger at the Props Desk: 2:00 a.m., Tuesday, October 3.

"What's today, Harris?" asked the detective.

Harris looked at his watch and found the tiny number.

"Well, technically, it's the third of October, but most people would still consider it the second."

"What do you mean?" Demetrius was confused by his friend.

"I don't consider the date to change until I've gone to sleep." Demetrius was still puzzled. Harris saw the confusion and explained.   "Look D, most people, even if they're awake until three in the morning, still think the date is the previous day."

Demetrius listened with almost derisive thoughts.

"See, to me, right now *feels* like Monday, October second, 'cause I haven't gone to bed yet."

Something was making sense to the detective.

"When you fall asleep after your day is complete," Harris pushed his thoughts a bit more forcefully, "*that* is when the calendar changes in your mind. Not at midnight, which is technically the date change."

Demetrius reflected out loud.

"So, if I told you that the trucks were gonna be here at 2:00 a.m., Tuesday, the third of October, when would you expect the trucks?"

It was easier to ask this question than to argue about semantics.

"Well, if it was me, technically," Harris clarified, "I would think you were talking about right now, because, technically, that's what time it is, *and* what date it is." Harris thought and spoke at the same time, "*but* some people might think that 2:00 a.m., October third is..." he paused, not wanting to confuse his obviously frustrated friend, "tomorrow night."

Demetrius bobbed his head in thought. Harris added a clarification.

"Technically, that would be 2:00 a.m., October fourth, but if you haven't finished your day, it would still feel like the third of October."

"So what you're saying is that we're a night early?" Demetrius asked.

Harris, proud of his new-found position of *consigliere*, expanded.

"D, I'm just saying, that's a possible explanation if your trucks don't show tonight."

It made sense to Demetrius, this confusion over arrival times. With the way Harris had set up the equipment, they could record the dock activity tonight, review it in the morning, and stand watch again tomorrow night. Hopefully, that would be the actual intended hour.

"Why don't you go home, Harris?" Demetrius suggested. "You've been here all day, and I think you're right; it's gonna be a quiet night."

"You sure, D?" asked Harris. "I don't mind stayin'."

"No, let's aim for tomorrow night. I'll keep watch the rest of the night and get some sleep tomorrow," he paused, "and hopefully, we won't be disappointed tomorrow night too."

"O.K., D." Harris collected himself and moved to the door. "Feel free to use my sleeping bag, man." The van door slid open. "I'll see ya tomorrow."

Harris heaved his body into the sliding door, sending it shut, but jumped in, halting its slide. "What time you want me here tomorrow, D?"

"'Bout two."

"In the afternoon, right?" Harris's question once again clarified the issue of time, still hanging in the air.

"Yeah." Demetrius moved to the door to aid in its closure. "And Harris, it could be a really late one tomorrow night." Harris' smiled, pushing up his glasses.

"Don't worry D, I'll have the equipment up, runnin,' and ready to snag your bad guys."

The man's infectious smile permeated Demetrius. The door slid shut and Demetrius watched through the van's windshield. The little man bobbed his way to the Lower Wacker Drive off-ramp, up, out of sight and over to the Lake Street Elevated Train.

Demetrius checked the power supply on his equipment, then let the equipment run through the night. He unfurled Harris's sleeping bag and lay down in the open, clean aisle of the van. He partially disrobed and slid his muscular frame into the sleeping bag. The slumber sack only covered his body to his pectoral muscles. The bag was perfect for his friend, but miniature for him. He laughed, grabbing the console seat cushion for a pillow, and tried to snooze.

His shoulders grew cold in the surrounding night air, but he did not mind. He settled in for an uncomfortable night's nap. He thought of how fine a friend he had found in Harris. He was a good man, with excellent technical skills, who had never received a fair shake in his life.

Maybe he could help me start an agency here, Demetrius thought. *He could be the technical man, and I would be the sleuth.* The idea had merit, but it would have to wait for another day. There was too much pressing work to be done, and the coming nights could be very long.

The shag of the floor imprinted his body with its scalloped pattern. Demetrius fell asleep and lay undisturbed the night through.

Thirty-Three

The couple walked through the house together for the first time, and Gwen was just as excited as she had been a week ago. Enzo watched his wife steer him through the rooms of the huge five-bedroom River Forest palace, winding their way and talking about her ideas for each room.

The dining room would stay fairly intact, but the kitchen would need some improvements. It was in dire need of updating, and besides, Gwen hoped that when—or if—they decided to buy this house it would be a spot for family, friends, and for the enjoyment of life. It would be a home to be *lived in,* not just admired. And besides, with a brood of little Santis, the home would have to be serviceable.

"Let's go upstairs, Enzo," the wife bubbled.

The husband ran up the flight of stairs behind his wife. She went into the master bedroom and stood in the doorway. It was spacious, huge, really, and it gave the ambitious wife visions of endless, wonderful warm nights cuddled against her husband's chest.

"Gwenny," Enzo asked, "what do you think? Should we buy this place?"

Gwen turned to her husband standing behind her. She was glowing with a smile.

"Do you *really* like it, Enzo?" She coyly and politely lowered her head, deferring to the love of her life.

"Yes, I like it very much, sweetheart," he responded, "but if it is not what *we* want, let's keep looking."

"I think it's everything that we want, honey," Gwen spoke. "There is space for a music room, a guest room…the kitchen is a wonderful size, it just needs a little work, and," she paused, "there's plenty of room for babies."

Enzo smiled at his wife's maternal grin.

"There certainly is," he agreed.

They stood in the bedroom, silent for a moment, each one searching the other's face. Enzo spoke first.

"Well, why don't we get it?"

The smile on Gwen's mouth exploded onto her face. Her shoulders raised into her neck as she felt the excitement of their future home. Her face flushed and tears came to her eyes. Enzo was confused.

"Sweetheart, are you O.K.?" he asked. "We don't need to get this house if you have seen another you like." Gwen shook her head.

"It's not that, silly," she explained. "These are tears of joy."

She reached into her purse to find a tissue, but instead found a note. She opened it and read. Enzo, seeing her discovery, moved into the bedroom to check the window views.

It was a poem, addressed to her, typed, with a handwritten note at the bottom.

Do I love you more than a day?
Days used to be faint hours to endure.
Now, through our love, I feel each hour
On this spinned world about the sun.
Embodied time, I live creation, through you.
And I love you more than a day.

Do I love you more than the air?
Air used to seem just nothingness.
Through our love, now it seems
No less God's air, airing your life's breath;
Too rich for space; too dear for death.
Through you. And I love you more than the air.
                                        -Jack Larson-

*You, my love, have filled my life with all God's treasures,
for before you, I was nothing. My life, my art, my essence are wound
in and around your being. Without you, the best of this world gives
no pleasure, the exhalted of earth has no substance. It is all a pale
shadow compared to the love that you give to me, freely, abundantly,
and tenderly.*

*Your love gives this feeble man all hope, all beauty, all purity;
all that anyone could hope to feel in this God ordained glimpse of
forever, I find in just the twinkle of your eye.*

Art is nothing without you. Song is lacking, for its vibrance

WITH THE VOICE OF ANGELS

is captured by you. I am hopeless without you, forever devoted to you,
and in all my brokenness, I am given totally unto you.
              Your eternally loving
                    "E"

Gwen walked to her husband, staring out the window. He turned as she approached. She reached up and wrapped her arms around the man who filled her heart. They kissed. Gwen brought her moist cheek to Enzo's ears.

"And I am nothing without you," she whispered, "but I am the most fortunate woman in the world, knowing your love."

They held each other, long and tight, deep in love and lost to the world. Gwen slid down from her husband's neck and took his hand.

"Follow me."

He obediently followed. She led him down the stairs, through the dining room, and out the glass doors into the back yard. The early afternoon sun warmed their backs as Gwen led her husband to her intended destination.

Enzo looked into the small garden and the wonderful elm that dominated the north portion of the yard. He saw why Gwen had led him here. He looked at the Virgin, arms open in comfort and blessing, welcoming the couple to the seat of The Divine.

"When Patty and I came here last week, we prayed on this spot," Gwen spoke softly. The wife pulled her husband's hand close to herself, bringing him to her side.

"As she prayed for her husband, I prayed for you, Enzo, and I know the Virgin heard my prayer, because..." She paused. "I know what happened down there, and the Lord brought you back to me safe."

Enzo felt guilty and knew that he must confess again, fully, the horror of the ride to his wife. He also wanted to tell her of his vision, during the two-aria recital, the vision given to him, helping him in his time of need. He must tell her of this also.

"Enzo, I would like us to pray a prayer of thanks, and of dedication."

Enzo smiled, touched with intimacy, and filled with gratitude.

"Thanks for your safety, for our safety, and a dedication to the love and happiness with which we want our house to be dominated."

Enzo's arms wrapped around Gwen and they bowed their heads before the Madonna. Enzo prayed out loud, reciting the "Hail Mary," infusing it with a thankfulness and sincerity that he had not known until now. He then poured his heart—their hearts—into an offering of thanks: thanks for their love, for their dedication to each other, for Enzo's safety amidst the evil that had oppressed them, and for the work and dedication of their dear friend Demetrius. Enzo then lifted a prayer to the heavens, pleading for wisdom, for guidance, and for blessing upon the home that they were to begin, promised before God, dedicated to His work, filled with His joy, and founded on the love with which He had infused them.

"Grant these petitions from your humble servants, oh great and mighty God, in the name of your Blessed Son and our sweet Savior, Jesus Christ." The couple looked upon each other, and with one heart, soul, mind, and strength, said, "Amen."

The "El" ride back to the Hyatt was quiet, the couple wrapped in each other as teenage lovers would be.

"Gwen," Enzo softly spoke over the clack of the steel train wheels, "I need to tell you again about the trip to Bloomington." She did not say one word, but sat next to her husband, attention undivided, and listened as he purged another of his heartbreaks, one that had ended in near death—for him, and for a good, innocent man.

Enzo found his wife surprisingly calm as he again conveyed the story more completely—the false patrolman, Bill's plea for help, the shots at the limousine window, him eyeing the pistol and contemplating the end of his life, and the godsend—the help from the kindly trucker, offering his life and his livelihood to save these strangers. He had been the light of mercy in the heart of hell's darkness.

Enzo was quiet after telling the tale.

"Thank you, my love, for listening to me," Enzo uttered to his wife. "And Gwen, I am sorry I didn't tell you everything before now," he said, his emotions showing on his face, "but I didn't want to burden you any more."

"What time did this man stop you and Bill?" she asked. Enzo was unprepared for the odd question, but he did his best to comply.

"Um, let me think, sweetheart." Moments ticked away. "It was about 2:30, I guess."

Gwen, radiant, smiled with ease.

"You see, Enzo, I was praying for your safety exactly then," her eyes had become a focus of energy, "in front of the Madonna." Enzo drew those splendid eyes into his own.

"She heard my prayer, and I knew the Lord would keep you safe."

Enzo thought back to his desperate moments in the limousine. In that moment he remembered, in his mind's replay, seeing his wife and believing he would never look upon her visage again.

In that moment, as death stared him in the eye, she, his wife was there. She had given herself to him in mind and thought. Through the power of the mystical, through the self-sacrifice and strength in their unified weakness, and in their reliance on the love that dominated their lives, Gwen felt and sensed his distress and offered herself as a blessed sacrament to combat this evil.

"I know you were there, my love," Enzo said. "I felt you there as that man stared at me," he paused, "and in the face that strengthened me as I sang that night."

Gwen tilted her head, wanting further explanation.

"You see, I had lost control at the concert. I was exhausted, and I didn't think I could recover," spoke the man of strength, "but in that total exhaustion I looked up and saw a young woman. She had the face of the Virgin, the face of the icon I knew from my family's home." Relief filled his voice. "She, this young woman, watched as I struggled on the stage of the Musical Arts Center.

"As I looked to her for strength, she gave it to me. She offered me her strength, and in that moment of failure, she allowed me to infuse my voice with power and with tragedy. It all allowed that performance to triumph."

Grateful astonishment flowed from his words.

"And Gwenny, when I finished with the performance, I looked to find the young woman in the crowd." Enzo shook his head in disbelief. "But she was not there. She was gone."

In a moment of emotion, Enzo crossed himself, a silent thanks for intervention in time of need.

"And now I know," Enzo spoke with determination and discovery, "it was all through your love, there, at our future home, that saved my life that afternoon. And you supplied the angel of my need that evening."

The train clacked, passing over the miles.

Enzo stared at his wife, and Gwen gazed into his big dark eyes. They found solace in their dedication to one another, and in the intercession of love.

The train closed in on the city. The huge skyscrapers rushed forth in giant domination. The lovers were deep inside their thoughts, given over to a hushed communion.

The train rumbled into the State Street Station.

"Thank the good Lord, Demetrius is finishing up with his investigation. It's time for things at the opera house to get back to normal," Enzo said.

The train doors parted and the couple rose to exit.

"Did Demetrius tell you that, sweetheart?" asked the wife.

"Indirectly. Besides, I get the feeling he's about to pounce on the men responsible for Frank's murder." Enzo did not know any of this positively, but he spoke with assurance. Gwen turned the conversation to other matters.

"Let's make sure to call the real estate agent with our bid." Enzo smiled at his wife. "We don't want our dream house getting away," Gwen said.

The couple energized their steps as they left the "El." The quick pace filled them with vibrance, and found their stomachs aching, in need of food. They headed to the vast network of restaurants along Wabash, underneath the elevated train tracks, and began their search for sustenance. They never noticed the young man. He looked like a student, but he had followed them on their little house hunt.

He was also ready for a late lunch, and then to resume his post in the Hyatt Hotel, room 1901.

Thirty-Four

Harris spent the day reviewing the previous night's surveillance tapes. They were black and grainy, simply footage of a security guard walking past every three hours.

He cleaned several of the tape heads and improved the recording quality on each of the video recorders. It was a tedious job, but Harris was excellent at keeping himself busy, and since he had fixed everything else in the van, he could take time to maintain this setup.

There was a knock on the van about nine o'clock that evening, just as he was about to find some food. He peeked through the fiberboard panel that separated the driver's compartment from the guts of the van and saw in the driver's side window one of Chicago's finest.

Damn! he thought, *I thought D got the cops to leave us alone.*

The officer was silently telling the occupant of the van to roll down the driver's window. Harris climbed through the sliding panel and sat sideways in the driver's seat. He rolled the window down.

"Good evening," the polite officer offered. Harris responded the same.

"Can I ask what you are doing here tonight, sir?" The officer was not aggressive, which relieved Harris, but he looked all over the outside of the van, then bobbed his head, trying to see what was inside.

Harris did not know what to say. He did not want to give the operation away, but he knew vehicles could not be left on Lower Wacker unattended and apparently abandoned.

"I am doing some work on my van, sir. I had to pull over to get out of traffic."

"Mechanical difficulties?"

"Sort of, sir. I am in the back working on the wiring." Harris decided this lie was paying off. "I'm a mechanic, and I'm trying to get it started so I can get out of here."

The officer now seemed more distracted than Harris. He peeked along the sides of the van. Harris did not even know if the man in blue had heard his lie.

Harris looked in the rearview mirror and saw a man near the back of the vehicle.

"Sir," asked the confused Harris, "what is that man doing back there?" The officer at the window quickly stepped in front of the outside rearview mirror to obscure Harris's view of the man to the rear.

"He's my partner. He's taking down your license number." Harris had seen the man in the rear and he was wearing street clothes. The officer saw the troubled look on Harris's face.

"Don't worry, sir," the man explained, "he was just checking out the other side of the van. We get quite a few abandoned vehicles down here, and vagrants climb inside them and set up house. Ya know what I mean? We're just being careful. A lot of those people get violent on us, and we didn't know what you were doing here."

"I see," Harris responded, not really understanding. "Why's he in plain clothes?"

"He just got off his shift and he said he'd help me take a look around here. Thank you for your time, sir. Sorry to disturb you."

The officer and his friend walked behind the van and out of sight. Harris watched in the rearview mirror as the men crossed the roadway and disappeared.

The officer cursed as he walked to the rear.

"Did you get it done?" asked the uniformed officer.

"Yeah," the first man said and smiled. "It's done."

Harris was confused by the little encounter.

"Damn, he was more anxious to leave than I was to have him leave." Harris sat in the driver's seat for a moment and breathed deeply, confused by the foot patrolman. His face crumpled down around his glasses as he discerned the odd conversation. It was not worth his while to try and figure out the cops. That was Demetrius's job. He'd fill his detective friend in on the details when he arrived.

"So much for Demetrius's friends on the force." Harris believed Demetrius's contact on the CPD had let them down. The cops were supposed to leave the van alone for a couple of weeks, and now, just a few days into the surveillance, he was already being harassed.

Harris smacked his lips in a fit of oral necessity.

"Time for a Suzy-Q."

He climbed back into the van compartment, unveiled his precious devil's food cake, and resumed work. If the bewitching hour was 2:00 a.m.

he needed everything in order, hot and ready to go. He was almost ready—equipment clean, functioning and warm. He would be ready early, by midnight at least.

"Let's see," he asked himself, "what can I do?"

He threw the Suzy-Q wrapper on the van floor and searched for more work. Demetrius should be arriving within the hour, and then the evening would truly begin.

1:56 a.m.

Harris was frantic. Demetrius had not arrived. He had stopped by the van at ten o'clock and said he would be back before midnight. Two hours of sleep was all he said he needed, then he would be back. Those two hours had passed, and he had not returned.

Harris watched the screens with frantic control. Since 12:30, the truck docks at the theatre had become an ever-agitated beehive. The lights were turned on at 12:15 a.m. and several men began moving boxes and adjusting dock space. The cameras were functioning perfectly. The three angled lenses gave full view of the crawl of men and the dingy truck dock, both inside and into the loading ramp.

At 1:00 a.m. several more men joined those who were preparing the dock. One seemed to be the leader, pointing and instructing the others in the way to proceed. He was tall, muscular, and, even through the silence, menacing. Harris thought that several times he had seen the leader look directly into the lens of the concealed cameras. He would peer up into the ten-foot ceiling of the space and rub his neck, but he never approached the lenses, so Harris believed the supposed discovery was merely his own over-discrimination.

At 1:30 Harris saw a couple of the underlings close the inside access doors to the dock and lock them from within, bolt and chain.

"'D," Harris said, "I wish you were here!"

Harris was meticulous as he jotted down the cassette deck's counter, signaling what he believed to be important moments in the evening's string of events. He was extremely uncomfortable without his tall, strong partner, and after the little encounter with the police, he wanted Demetrius present to attend to any miscues.

At 1:55 Harris's knees began to bounce up and down in nervous agitation. Several very serious guns had been produced within the dock, a couple seeming to be Israeli-made uzis, fully automatic, killing machines.

Harris had noticed that the leader was carrying a large handgun under his left arm, holstered under the slick, black leather jacket.

Great snorts from truck air horns echoed down the concrete corridor. The blast from the trucks terrified the already edgy Harris.

"Damn, I wish he'd given me a phone." Demetrius had neglected to leave a portable phone in the van. "If he's at the hotel I'm gonna kill him."

The huge diesel engines chugged up Wacker Drive and slowed at their intended building. Harris peeked out of the shaded back door windows of the van and saw several long semi-trailers stop at the side of the roadway. The first truck jerked into gear as the outer dock doors were opened.

The camera could not see the entire roadway, but through the van window Harris saw four men walk out into the roadway, under the opening opera house doors. Two men, apparently unarmed, walked out to converse with the truck drivers, while the other two, each strapped with an uzi, stayed more closely hidden in the dock doorway.

The two men, after conversing with the drivers, ran to the north end of Wacker and pulled roadblocks into the street, forcing the minuscule traffic to exit onto the Upper Drive. After the two men had finished blocking the northbound traffic, they ran to the southbound side, and, two blocks south of the theatre's truck dock, placed barricades in the street there also.

Harris pulled his gaze from the window as the two men ran by, oblivious to him and his surveillance gear. Harris clenched his teeth and bit at his fingernails.

"Come on, D, I don't like being here alone."

Harris returned to his monitor. The first truck slowly backed into the dock. The second truck chose the unused opening and backed his truck into the waiting hole.

The dock and two truck trailer doors were now perfectly visible to Harris via his cameras. The nine-foot trailer doors were swung open and pinned to the side of the dock. The underlings began unloading the huge cargo.

Harris craned his neck and drew closer to the screen. The men were bringing out what looked like a huge piece of a sea vessel. Harris did not know for which opera this might be used, but as he looked closely at the backside of the set, the words "Ballo in Maschera" were printed there.

The men on the dock went to work. The leader pulled a sheet of paper from his inside coat pocket and unfolded it. He read from the paper and began pointing to the different pieces of cargo that had already been removed by the henchmen.

The underlings produced their pocketknives and began ripping into the back of the exposed opera set. Harris glanced at the video counter and quickly wrote down the number.

"Oh my god!" Harris spoke as his mouth fell fully open. The men continued their slicing and ripping, tearing apart the back of the opera set.

"Come on D, please—please—please get here."

Harris was desperate. He felt trapped in his little surveillance van. If he emerged the men outside would see him and pursue him. He wanted his detective friend to arrive, but with the roadblocks in place Demetrius would have trouble getting to the van. The men from the opera house had no impediment to their work, and the uzis were meant to halt any unforeseen impediments.

"Shit, D," Harris cursed, his legs bouncing in agitated spasm. "Where the hell are you?"

The van had become his own sado-masochistic hell, full of what he loved, but wrapped in an environment that gave only pain. Harris began to sweat and hyperventilate. He grabbed the console edge to steady himself.

"Relax," he told himself over and over. "They don't know you're here." He continued to watch, every frame adding to his discomfort.

"Relax, Harris," he told himself. "Relax."

2:45 a.m.

The Dodge Intrepid crept its way southbound. The car was in the northbound lanes of Lower Wacker Drive, creeping southbound in reverse. Lower Wacker Drive had been closed off, both directions. All access to the very spot Demetrius wanted to be was shut down. He decided to drive to Randolph Street, two blocks north of the Illinois State Theatre, and drive down the "on" ramp that led to Wacker's northbound lanes. Since the northbound traffic was diverted two blocks south of the theatre, no traffic would impede his entrance. Once he was in the northbound lanes he turned his lights off, put the car into reverse and backed up, into the far eastside, building access lanes. After two city blocks of backing his way along concrete pillars, he stopped in front of his van. He slid to the Intrepid's passenger-side door, and quietly got out of the car. He crept out, barely closing the car door behind him, and crouched as he quickly sprinted to the van's sliding door. As he ran, he saw the trucks lined up along the side of the roadway.

He tried to open the van's side door, edging pressure onto its handle, but it was locked. He pulled out his key and unlocked the door.

"Demetrius?" came the whisper that met his ears.

"It's me, Harris," he whispered in response. He slid the door open, and climbed into the van.

"It's about time, you asshole."

The whisper was angry and aggressive, unlike the affable young man with whom Demetrius had grown up. The outburst also led Demetrius to suspect foul deeds afoot.

"I'm sorry, Harris," he apologized, ashamed to have left his friend in a completely vulnerable position. "The hotel wake-up call never came."

Harris did not respond to the apology.

Demetrius felt horrible. He had asked the hotel to wake him at 11:30 *p.m.* The call never came. He had slept uncomfortably the night before on the van's shag floor, and he would need to be awake all night tonight, but he never imagined he would miss these moments, the moment for which the entire previous week had been building. If he had not circumvented the roadblocks, the whole night's surveillance could have been lost. He apologized again, for the magnitude of the delinquency deserved his remorse.

He felt better upon seeing Harris safe in the van. He drew close to his bespectacled friend.

"D, there is some heavy stuff happening here tonight."

"Talk to me, Harris."

Harris did not say a word. He reached for the secondary video recorder, allowing the other decks to continue taping. Harris scrolled through the tape.

"Just watch," he said, fear and disgust mingling in the tone of his voice. Harris found his note pad. Stop one—the leader and his henchmen pulled their firearms into the open, and locked the dock doors. Demetrius watched as Harris played the tape's first significant moments.

The leader was the man from the building lobby yesterday. The photos Demetrius had taken from the lobby were being developed so Detective McGrail could help him identify some of these men.

"Lots of guns," Harris said, "and lots of bad guys."

"Yea," Demetrius commented, "and with that arsenal, something else must be on their minds too."

"No shit, Sherlock!" Harris scrolled to stop number two on his cassette tape.

The henchmen had pulled out the scenery from the truck trailer and cut into the backside of the big set pieces. With each plunge of their blades, more and more brown powder fell from the expanding wounds.

"There's the coffee," Demetrius said to himself. "See those white pellets, Harris?" Demetrius pointed to the white balls amongst the brown powder.

"Yeah, D."

"Those are ammonia pellets."

"Well, with what's coming up," Harris spoke, "I didn't think they were opening a Starbuck's."

Out of the brown and white powder fell several packages. The square blocks were approximately twelve inches across the front and six inches thick.

Almost as quickly as they hit the floor a henchman would scoop up the bundles and place them in a black nylon satchel. He placed twenty blocks in the first bag, while two other men did the same. There was a pile of forty or fifty black nylon bags visible in the back corner of the dock. One of the bags was filled half-way, and set aside.

"I didn't see the pile of bags the first time," Harris confessed. Demetrius was aghast.

"Oh my god!" Demetrius blurted.

"That's what I said when I saw it for the first time," he whispered, "only I was scared shitless, and alone."

The men gazed at the rolling tape. The live action in the monitors reflected the recorded one almost perfectly.

"Is that what I think it is?" Harris asked.

"I think so, Harris."

"How many trucks are there, D?" Neither man took his eyes off the video screen.

"Eight, I think."

"Eight!" Harris replied, astonished. "How much could they bring in on eight trucks?"

"My guess is," Demetrius looked over to Harris, "a couple of thousand pounds, total." He explained further, correcting himself. "Each truck could fudge a thousand pounds or so, maybe more." Demetrius stopped. "Wait a second, those opera sets are relatively light, so they could pack that truck with whatever they want. I'd say a couple of thousand pounds per truck, at least."

"There's a fortune in every one of those bags," Harris said, shaking his head.

"A fortune in pain, Harris."

Harris hit the fast-forward button and gray streaks crossed the monitor the men were viewing. The other equipment—the live feed—continued capturing the hoodlums on tape.

"Most of the footage is like this, but there are two spots that were different," Harris explained as he scrolled to the taped footage in question. During the break, Demetrius watched the live performance on the dock. Two men began to clean up the mounting debris.

Harris arrived at the spot on the tape. This footage was slightly different. The henchmen cut into the scenery once again, but there was no brown powder and no white pellets. Instead, the slicing produced long, thin bricks, again covered in white plastic, nearly one foot long, but small and rectangular. These chunks were lined up side by side, taped to the inside panel of a fake opera wall.

"If the other stuff is cocaine, or their drug of choice," Harris said, "what's that stuff?"

Demetrius closed in on the monitor. The different-sized packages were placed in separate satchels from the larger blocks.

"I wonder," Demetrius spoke out loud. He pulled his wallet from his pocket, removing a twenty-dollar bill. He held the bill to the monitor where the long rectangular packages were being retrieved. The perspective was askew, but he thought the size of the package similar.

"What do you think, Harris?" he asked his friend for confirmation.

"You think they're smugglin' money?" Harris asked, thinking the idea preposterous.

"If these guys are moving this much cocaine, there has to be millions of dollars in cash coming in every week," Demetrius spoke, "and if the endowment from Mrs. Brook is a forgery, then the people behind the opera company could funnel money directly into that fake endowment."

The complex puzzle was fitting into place.

"There's a hundred million in the bank right now, and supposedly the gift from Mrs. Brook was gonna be more than half a billion dollars."

The numbers were staggering to the two middle-class city kids. Harris pushed his glasses up onto the brim of his nose. It was time for another Suzy-Q; the tension of the evening was sapping his energy. Demetrius continued in his thoughts.

"The CGO has the fake donation it can hide money in, but also an opera company like this has all kinds of soft money around."

"Soft money?" Harris asked, confused.

"Money that comes in from things like the snack bar, the champagne bar, personal gifts...even the gift shop makes big bucks." Harris nodded, understanding.

"Most of what comes in through those little businesses is cash," Demetrius paused, "without any real exchange of goods."

"You mean no one can trace the brownies and liquor people buy?"

"Exactly. Money from those accounts can be manipulated. Funnel this dirty money either into the big donation or into several smaller accounts without traceable assets, and the money gets cleaned. I would think that the actual opera portion here at the State Theatre would have the same set up. It's basically a cash business. Artist fees, backstage materials, instrument maintenance, almost everything that has to do with an opera company can be manipulated to appear as obscure expenditures. Manipulate those numbers, adjust some expenses, and you could launder the cash collected through the drug sales," Demetrius concluded, "and none of that money could be traced. The money ends up in the accounts of legitimate businesses, or in the singers' pockets. Any opera company is tailor made to clean up dirty money."

"But why would the Mexico City Opera Theatre be sending American dollars up here?" Harris hit upon an excellent question.

"My guess would be to fill up the fake endowment. The bosses had to set up the legitimate business of opera in order to manipulate the soft money accounts. Then, if you share productions, your product—both opera and narcotics—is easily portable.

"Enzo told me once that opera fans love a winner. Success breeds success."

"Like when the Bulls won the NBA Championship," Harris added, "everybody becomes a Bulls fan."

"And buys Bulls merchandise," Demetrius finished. "If the CGO is a successful opera company, patron money floods in, so the guys in Mexico create a prestigious opera company, supposedly backed by an influential donor. Then, with that prestige, money comes flooding in from legitimate sources..."

"And the dirty money gets even cleaner?" Harris finished, hoping to have guessed the conclusion.

"Exactly. The muddier the financial waters, the better for those guys." Demetrius pointed at the monitor.

"It was perfect," Demetrius concluded. "The only thing the CGO had left was this building—no assets, no sets, no ticket sales, no help from the government. The Chicago Grande Opera was the perfect set up."

"Damn!" Harris mustered, amazed. "But where did it all start?"

"My guess is that somebody in Mexico started using the opera down there to hide drug money," Demetrius responded. "The CGO opened an opportunity for the drugs to come to the States, and for them to make more money up here."

They continued watching the tape. Piles of drugs and money were put into the black nylon satchels. The bags were filled with either drugs or money, but not both; except for the single black satchel set aside with both items. This satchel was the leader's personal stash, a reward for all his outstanding work.

"One more spot," Harris said. He quickly cued the tape to the last spot.

The same *modus operandi*, but a small jewelbox emerged from the trucks instead. The box was given to the leader, the black leather clad tough, who put the box aside, into the corner. Not one of the other men touched the box.

"I don't know, Harris," Demetrius said, viewing the faux jewel case. "Maybe diamonds, jewels of some sort."

The men were puzzled by the case, untouched and undisturbed. The henchmen went back to their work, filling bags and putting the equipment back into the trucks. Demetrius looked around to the spectacular surveillance setup Harris had created.

"Do you have a copy of what we've seen so far? I want to take it with me, Harris." said the detective.

"You can have this one," responded the techie. "I've been recording all the activity on one of the other tapes. It's technically a copy, but it's first generation." Harris ejected the tape on the machine the men were watching. He put the surveillance video in a cardboard cover and handed it to his friend. Demetrius put the tape into his inner jacket pocket.

"What are you gonna do with it, D?"

"Put it in a secure place, like the hotel safe." Harris turned back to the monitors. The henchmen were resting after some hard work, sitting on the set pieces that stood in the dock area.

"Hey D, look," Harris declared. The leader walked over to the jeweled box, took his pocketknife, and sliced the label off the front panel. The lid was lifted and the man began handing cigars to his workers.

"Cubans?" Harris asked.

Demetrius laughed, proven wrong in his precious gem assumption.

"Anything that's illegal, I guess," he answered, "and Cubans *are* illegal." The friends kept watching their targets. The leader, stogie sitting in the left side of his mouth, reached deep into the box, moved several cigars aside, and pulled out a jeweled necklace.

"I guess I wasn't totally wrong," Demetrius concluded, seeing the jewelry produced. "You could smuggle humans in those trucks, there's so much extra space, but drugs are the most profitable."

Harris had relaxed in the study of the tapes. Demetrius's presence also put him at ease.

"I'm gonna get this to the Hyatt, but I'll be back in ten minutes," Demetrius explained.

"O.K., D, but you better get your black ass back here quick. I don't like being so close to all those guns."

"Ten minutes, Harris, tops!" Demetrius moved to the van's sliding side door.

"Oh, D, I almost forgot," Harris spoke up and spun in the console chair. "Your cop friend didn't do a very good job of keepin' *the man* off our backs."

"What do you mean?"

"Some cop came by and asked me what I was doin' down here." Harris paused. "Actually, a couple of cops showed up."

"I'll give John a call tomorrow morning and make sure we're left alone." Demetrius started to leave, but he was curious as to how his nervous friend had handled the officers.

"Harris, what did you tell 'em you were doin?"

"Fixing the van." Harris smiled, his glasses raising under his cheeky smile. "I said the van broke down and that I was repairing it. They seemed to want to get goin' anyway, so it wasn't a very hard sell."

"Good." Demetrius carefully unlatched the door and slid it open, his hunched frame unfolding into the open roadway.

"Ten minutes, man, no more," Harris whispered affirmingly. Demetrius nodded his head in acknowledgment. The door was closed, softly and tenderly. Harris returned to his monitor. One of the henchmen seemed to be blowing cigar smoke directly into one of the camera lenses. Once again, Harris was frightened, thinking that these men had discovered this little surveillance outfit. He heard a tapping on the windshield of the van. It startled him, but he got up and went to the front, grabbing a Suzy-Q as he moved. He looked through the panels. It was D.

Demetrius made a motion with his hand. Harris was at first confused by the gesture. Demetrius's thumb pressed into his forefinger, over a closed palm. Harris squinted at the hand. He nodded his head, and laughed to himself.

"Damn, I forgot again." The little laugh relaxed him some more, and with a Suzy-Q in his left hand, he began hopping, thrusting his right hand into his too tight jean pocket, searching for the van's alarm button.

Great idea! Harris was unsettled anyway, and the alarm would keep him feeling safe while Demetrius was gone. He never remembered the alarm, but now he was happy to use this extra line of defense.

Demetrius watched his friend hop, fighting with the seal between his body and his jeans. As Harris disappeared out of windshield view and into the van's guts, Demetrius turned, seeing the roadway empty, and walked to his sleek, black Intrepid.

He took a few steps towards his car and heard the familiar "squawk" from the van's alarm system.

A tremendous explosion joined the sound of the activating alarm. In paired chords the thunder crack of the ignition cut the trapped air within the roadway corridor. The deep thrust of destruction was immediately attacked by a cacophony of screaming metal and glass.

The van flew up into the air, fire erupting from within, from around, and from above. The concussion of the detonation pounded Demetrius in the back, throwing him ten feet into the air and slamming him into the east concrete wall of Lower Wacker Drive. Parked in front of the van, the Intrepid's rear tires were thrown into the air. The car was lifted under the power of the blast. The weight of the engine was the only thing that kept the car from becoming completely airborne. As the explosion expanded, the rear end of the car flew higher, pivoting upon its heavy front end, and flew up into the concrete wall, directly towards Demetrius.

Demetrius slid down the wall and crashed to the ground, landing between the wall and the still-ascending rear of the car. If he did not move, he would be crushed under the falling car.

He scrambled to escape. The back bumper of the Intrepid crashed into the wall. The car jolted with the impact. The car's descent slowed as its bumper scraped its way down the concrete, the car's frame contorting under its own weight. Demetrius pushed forward, digging and crawling in the three feet of space still afforded him. The metal bumper screamed as it gouged the concrete wall.

Demetrius pulled himself further towards the front, stationary portion of the Intrepid. He did not look behind him. His ears pained under the shrieking metal as it ripped and fell upon him. The car's bumper dug further into the wall, the vehicle still falling, now in slow motion.

Demetrius's feet could not move fast enough. The particle debris in the roadway would not allow his feet to grip the cement. He pulled with his hands, pebbles imbedding into his palms. He slipped and fell onto his right forearm. The car was upon him. The concrete wall and the car's bumper scarcely held the back end of the vehicle aloft. The bumper disintegrated, ripped apart, trying to support the vehicle's weight. The Intrepid crashed to the earth.

With a final lunge, Demetrius pushed upon his forearm, diving along the wall of Wacker Drive, toward the front of the car. The rear of the car fell with a thud, the broken bumper clanging behind it. The car bounced at its landing, the tires absorbing the shock. Demetrius's back was pinned to the concrete wall. His feet lay under his car, six inches in front of the rear wheel, which still wiggled, dissipating the energy of detonation. The side of the car had grazed his legs as it fell, but his legs were undamaged. His chest and head were eight inches from the body of the car.

Demetrius lay beside the car's front passenger side tire, looking straight at it, but, he was safe, having avoided being crushed by his own rental vehicle.

He slid his torso up from where he was, over the edge of the Intrepid, and looked back at the van. The skyward force of the detonation had rocketted the van into the ceiling of the enclosed drive. As the van blew upward, it buckled just behind the driver's compartment, becoming a wedge, a grotesque rocket, thrusting higher, heaven-bound, toward oblivion. The now jagged metal roof of the van crumpled as it impacted the reinforced upper roadway. Glass expanded, flying and slicing everything that impeded its progress. Chunks of metal fell into the roadway, blown and torn apart.

Flames engulfed every inner portion. The vehicle fell from the concrete roof, crushed horizontally, cut in half, compacted by the immovable object above.

The obscenity, watching this vehicle fall to the ground, utterly annihilated, pulled Demetrius up to the front of the Intrepid. As the van hit the ground, another small explosion ripped apart the outer shell of the cargo compartment.

Standing in front of the hood of the Intrepid, Demetrius watched the thin metal shell of the vehicle melt away, flames feeding on every inch of material. No equipment was intact; there was no semblance of a driver's compartment. The sliding side door had been blown off its hinges and had smashed into the roadway wall to the east. The other doors had been blown open, the windows blown out. Glass was everywhere—sprinkled on the Intrepid, strewn over the roadway. Everything—the van, the tapes, and Harris—everything was gone, blown to eternity with one tap of the car alarm that he, Demetrius, had asked to be activated.

Harris was dead. Realization pumped through Demetrius's body, pounding his insides just as the blast had pounded his back. There was no body to be seen in the rubble. There was no hint of life, no hope of survival.

Bang! Another explosion. A short concussion of cement popped off of the roadside wall to Demetrius's left. He did not hear a gun shot, but the crater in the wall next to him told him differently.

He ducked down, hiding himself along the grill of the Intrepid. Blood flowed from his left elbow, seeping through his jacket and shirt. His arm was full of glass from the explosion. He looked everywhere, his head darting back and forth, but there was no one to be seen.

Who had fired? Who had tried to kill him—again? Harris had shown him the men with the uzis. They were everywhere; on Lower Wacker Drive, within the Opera House truck dock, around the corner ramp, out in the roadway. He also knew that these men, responsible for the murder of Harris and the van's destruction, would have heard the explosion and would be coming to inspect the damage that they had done and to clean up any remaining human ends. He had to get out of there.

A quick glance around the roadway revealed nothing. There was no movement, at least not yet. There were no more shots. He heard yelling from the direction of the truck dock so he decided this was his chance, maybe his only chance.

He ran for the car door and grabbed the handle. It was locked. The yelling was growing louder. He reached in his pocket for the keys. In the sliding and scraping along the concrete wall his pants legs had bunched up, binding his pockets. He jumped up to release the woolen pants legs, and they fell down his leg. He jabbed his hand into his pocket and found the keys. He was off.

In that moment, Demetrius had become Harris, jumping up and down, digging for his keys, trying to fix what was wrong. Only now, Harris was dead, he was no more, obliterated in a flash.

The great Jupiter, king of the gods, had cast his thunderbolt, blowing Apollo's son, Phaethon, out of the sky. The careless child had lost control of the great chariot of fire, singeing the heavens and scorching the earth. Jupiter had no recourse. The young man had come too close to destroying everything. He had to be stopped. And Harris had done the same. He had come too close for safety. He had penetrated the lair of evil and would cast it into light, had he not been engulfed by the overwhelming inferno.

The Intrepid screeched away, out of the side access lane and onto northbound Wacker Drive. There was no traffic on Lower Wacker Drive. There was no noise surrounding Demetrius from building or vehicle, only the hum of the automobile as it carried Demetrius to safety.

He kept checking his rearview mirror for followers. There were none. His mind was racing along with the car, weaving side to side in the green tunnel. He turned east, following the river's edge, and veered right. He had to escape. He had to find safety.

But who would have known about the surveillance van? And who was responsible for Harris's death?

The car careened from side to side as it avoided the Wells Street embankment, protruding into the middle of the roadway. Demetrius held the steering wheel with his left hand, reached into his coat pocket, found his white handkerchief, and pressed it to the blood dripping from his left elbow. The exploded projectile glass cut deeper into his arm as he bent it to drive, ripping skin and causing him pain. Sweat filled his brow, dancing in the flashing yellow caution lights he approached along Lower Wacker. He yelled to himself. "Who knew about the van?" Still louder he repeated the question. "Who knew?"

His mind scrolled through the myriad conversations he had engaged in these past days.

He had told his friend John McGrail. Demetrius knew his secret safe with John. He was not a threat. He was a friend and could be trusted.

His mind scrolled further. He had told Burrows of the investigation and of his suspicions, but certainly not of the van.

Obviously, Harris knew of the van, but he was a relative loner and had no contacts in the opera community or the criminal community. The frustrated detective dug into the depths of his gray matter and could not find his answer. There was one more possibility.

Had he told the Santis about the surveillance setup? He could not remember for sure. They had partaken of much wine Sunday night and they had spoken many times since, but he could not remember.

"Wait," Demetrius now recalled. "Monday night, in front of their suite." He *had* told the Santis. He had mentioned his friend Harris to them, after which he told them about the surveillance van, and the bodyguard was right there also. He could have heard the conversation, but this young man had worked at the hotel too long. He did not seem to be culpable in the treachery just committed. Besides, he was a student, too young to be connected to these criminal enterprises.

That must be it. He had told the Santis in the doorway of their hotel suite. This had been his only transgression. But how could the surveillance van and Harris be destroyed by that little conversation in the doorway of Hyatt room 1801?

There had to be bugs"—listening devices—placed in the apartment. This meant that these men were privy to any information within 1801.

They had killed Frank Stanza for a few pictures. They had tried to kill Enzo twice, not knowing the depth of his knowledge. They had killed Harris and destroyed the van with all of its contents. And, they had tried to kill him.

Demetrius believed his conversation Monday morning with William Burrows had set all these events in motion. But if the destruction of the van was meant to kill both he and Harris, as well as destroy any evidence of these men's wrongdoing, then the conspirators were intent on destroying any and all evidence, suspected or proven, that would compromise their industry.

Demetrius's brows grew dark. Panic gripped his heart. He reached for his cell phone. He dialed the Hyatt Hotel. A recorded voice came on the line.

"Your call cannot be completed from your present location."

"Damn!" Demetrius cursed. The steel and concrete underground of Lower Wacker Drive was obscuring his call. He sped the Intrepid though the lower level Michigan Avenue overpass and blew through the red light.

The Intrepid darted north over the river's bridge, past the Billy Goat Tavern, to escape the confines of the roadway. Time was ticking by and Enzo and Gwen were in danger. It would take too much time to get to the hotel.

He turned left on Grand and headed west. He pulled to the side and placed the call again. The phone rang. Thank God.

The two henchmen ran back to the dock with the news of the blast. The van was totaled. Nothing survived.

"Excellent," the leader snarled. "Both of 'em dead?" The two henchmen looked at each other. One man carried an uzi. He spoke.

"A car drove off," he meekly told the man, "so we think the detective got away."

A scream of violence came from deep within the heart of the leader. "God damn it!"

His eruption ignited the dock. The unarmed man spoke up, over the fury.

"But there is no evidence left. They don't have anything to pin on us."

The leader looked at the two men. He was now quiet, boiling within, pressure seeping through the cracks of his skin. He turned away from the two men, to one of his other accomplices.

"Get me a phone...*Now!*" shrieked the leader. The man bolted, getting one of the group's cell phones. The leader reached under his left arm, and in the same motion turned. His gun erupted in a discharge.

The unarmed man fell to the ground, dead. His armed partner watched the dead body. In that instant his own life came into precise focus. He would be next. He would be dead. In controlled fury, the leader stared at the man still standing, his eyes furious.

"I don't want one more fuckin' screw up! They all have to die." He paused, reddened by hate, then added, "or we're all gonna die." The leader pointed his gun at the armed man, but did not fire. "Understand?" he shouted. The other men watched, not moving. They knew any one of them could be next. They could be slain in a moment, but greed had stolen their senses. Lust had captured their hearts, and they would follow their master to the end. The man who had been sent for the phone returned. He was in obvious distress.

"The cells won't work underground like this, sir," he stammered. The leader snapped his head toward the man. "But the dock office here has an outside line." The man pointed to the tiny office just to the left. The leader turned his body full to the man, his gun now at his side.

The underling was unsure how to proceed. He shook for a moment under the terrible stare, then with a great heave, he kicked the locked office door down. The leader put his gun away and walked to the office. He quickly dialed the seven numbers he needed and spoke.

"Take 'em both, and meet me," he barked at the two underlings stationed at the hotel. "But don't kill 'em. We may need to use 'em as bait." The leader came out of the office.

"Get rid of the body," the leader ordered the henchmen. "No traces. Finish up here and take the goods to the warehouse. I've got to take care of some other things."

The leader left the dock, taking his personal black satchel, half full of cash, half full of drugs, with him. It would be put on the roof of the opera house, his own private stash, in his own private enclave.

Two men grabbed the fallen comrade, pushing the heavy man to the side. They would have to dispose of him later. The collection process on the dock continued further into the night.

"Enzo, I want you to meet me," Demetrius spoke frantically. He could not say actual names. If the room was bugged, the phones would be bugged too.

"Where?" the bleary-eyed tenor said, trying to awake from his night's sleep.

"Bring Gwen, and..." Demetrius paused, "meet me where we used to eat pizza, back when you were an apprentice."

"You mean at..." Demetrius jumped in to halt the statement.

"Don't say the name, Enzo, just go *now*, and bring Gwen."

"All right, Demetrius," was the confused reply.

"And Enzo, take a cab, but travel in a roundabout way. Don't let anyone follow you."

"O.K." Enzo yawned. The phone was hung up. Demetrius raced west on Grand Avenue to their appointed destination.

Enzo roused himself. Gwen turned, still half asleep.

"What was that, honey?" The groggy voice was more aslumber than awake. Enzo cleared his throat.

"That was Demetrius. He wants me to meet him, right now." The tenor reached over and grabbed the pants that had been strewn across the chair next to his bed. He stood to find a shirt. Gwen rolled over to look at her husband.

"Do you want me to come, honey?" She snuggled into the woolen blanket and licked her dry, nighttime lips. Enzo looked down at his wife, angelic and perfect. He squinted the sleep away. Demetrius had asked Gwen to come along, but with the bodyguard outside, Gwen would be safe.

"No, sweetheart," he replied, "you stay here. I'll be back in a bit."

Gwen did not acknowledge her husband's response. She had traveled to a different domain.

Enzo pulled a tee shirt over his head quickly, grabbed his coat, and was out the door.

"Sir," asked Brick, standing, "is everything all right?"

"Yeah," replied the tenor. "Just watch Gwen for me. I'll be back in a little while." Brick sat back down and looked back into his textbook, *Criminal Pathology*. Enzo walked down the hall and disappeared into the elevator.

A taxi swung around and picked up the tenor.

"Carmen's Pizza, please."

"Do you have a street address, sir?" the late night driver asked.

"Western and North Avenues, I believe." Enzo sat back and the taxi was off. "Oh, and could you make sure to take a bit of a crazy route?"

The taxi driver nodded and smelled a big fare.

"If anybody's followin' us, I'll lose 'em, promise," came the thick Chicago reply. The car was gone, swiftly, safely, circuitously carrying Enzo to his appointed destination.

"I'd think Carmen's would be closed at this time of night."

Brick rolled his neck, releasing the strain of the close, quiet quarters. His six-foot-five-inch frame was not accustomed to this much sedentary activity. He stood and stretched his arms. Only a couple of hours left until relief would come. He slapped his face with light hands and looked around the hallways. There was nothing like the quiet of 3:00 a.m. All around him were hotel guests, thousands of people, hushed and locked away, rejuvenating themselves to the strains of the central air conditioner.

The silence was broken from down the hall. An older man staggered to one of the emergency stairwells. The bodyguard looked up and down the halls again. All was silent except for the mumbles of this one inebriated man.

As a bodyguard, his duty was to stay at his post, watching and protecting room 1801. As a security guard, he was supposed to help men like this one reach their hotel rooms without incident.

The man clutched at the exit stairwell handle and slipped, falling to one knee. Brick walked down the hall towards the man. If this patron were to injure himself while he watched, it would not reflect well on his bi-annual assessment.

Brick quickly strode down the hall to the drunken man.

"Sir, can I help you find your room?" asked the polite young man of the drunk.

"It'sss rahhht, here," slurred the man, as he pushed open the emergency stairwell door and walked though.

"No, sir," Brick replied, "I'm sure your room is not in there." The hunk smiled, following the drunk into the stairwell, offering his assistance.

There was a crackle of electricity, a spark of destructive power. A miniature bolt of lightening leapt across the expanse and struck its victim.

Brick's body slammed up against the stairwell's cinderblock wall. He convulsed with the ten thousand volts that passed through his body. The short circuit that collapsed his body sent his eyes up into his head. He was blind, he was racked with pain, and he was helpless. He heard nothing, saw nothing, and his legs could support nothing. His weakened, seizing body drew into a fetal position. The stairwell door jolted closed.

The fake drunk stood up and spoke to his young comrade. "Let's go." The young one began to pull out his gun. The fake drunk, the wiser and more deliberate of the two, grabbed the reaching arm.

"No, no," he said. "We don't need ta do dat. The tazer won't let him remember anyting. Besides, we got someone else to take care of." The other man, over-impulsive, put the gun back in its holster and pulled the stairwell door open. He smiled lustily. The door closed behind him.

They walked out into the hallway, the college kid bodyguard still convulsing from being electrocuted by the hand-held device. The men walked quickly to the door of 1801.

Carmen's Pizza was the most delicious, overlooked pizza joint in Chicago. Demetrius and the Santis had dined regularly at the restaurant ten years ago.

Demetrius had dated the owner's daughter, a beautiful young Hispanic woman named Patricia. Demetrius knew that she could supply a safe hideaway for the night, and help him bandage his arm. This safety would give him time to figure out how to proceed. His misjudgments had already cost Harris his life, but with Enzo and Gwen on their way to the restaurant, he felt that at least *they* would be safe.

This violence must come to an end, either in a court of law, or, he knew, with the trio's deaths. There was too much at stake now. Demetrius had intentionally tipped his hand, hoping to catch the perpetrators in damning action, but the men behind William Burrows had not only called that hand, but had tried to cut it off, to sever the outside intimidation completely. The game was life and death now, and he feared that for him and the Santis this Russian Roulette was being played with five bullets and one empty chamber.

On the drive to Carmen's, Demetrius pulled his fourteen-shot Smith and Wesson from under the Intrepid's front seat and slung it over his left shoulder. He had never wanted to use it, but evil was now unleashed, and the gun might be his only protection.

Patricia lived above the restaurant, in an apartment next to her parents. She had worked for the family for several years, and was now studying nursing. She had fallen for the handsome man, but he was not ready for commitment, at least not the kind of commitment she wanted.

Demetrius woke her, knocking at the second-level back door. She let her ex-lover and present friend into her home. He was quiet, yet frantic, as he explained his predicament.

Patricia remembered Enzo and his wife Gwen. They would soon be here. Demetrius pleaded for her help. She offered it without question.

Patricia was horrified at Demetrius's injury. She took his jacket and bandaged his wounds. They waited. She spent the time pulling glass from the injured elbow. She nursed her friend, rubbing the wounds in alcohol, while Demetrius winced. She salved the area and bound it, then led Demetrius down to the restaurant. They would wait for Enzo and Gwen there. The lights remained off, the shades pulled down.

For a moment, the scene seemed almost funny to the beautiful raven-haired woman. It was something out of Chicago's mobster past—the good guys glancing out the darkened window, waiting for their contact to arrive.

She brought two glasses of water from the kitchen and sat at the table by the window. Demetrius's shadow was large in the shaded street light. Demetrius never looked at her as she sat, offering him a drink.

She knew this was not funny; it was not a game. Demetrius was a light-hearted, giving man, but now he was completely quiet and totally serious. She offered any help that he might need. He thanked her and agreed that he might have to take her up on her offer.

The taxi arrived twenty minutes after Demetrius called. It had taken too long. The detective looked for his two friends, but he saw only one.

Enzo had forgotten Carmen's address, but followed Western north until he found the once familiar restaurant. The taxi rolled up to the darkened pizzeria. No one seemed to be present and no one had followed them. Enzo handed the driver forty dollars, twenty more than the fare, and asked the driver to stay a moment. If Demetrius was not there, Enzo did not want to be stranded.

He climbed out of the car and walked to the simple glass door. The cab purred at the curb, waiting for a signaled "thanks" or a re-engagement. The neighborhood was a bit dingier than he had remembered from ten years ago, but it still had an old-world charm. The enormously wide Western Avenue, the huge north/south artery on the city's near West Side, was vacant, no cars and no people.

The pizzeria door opened and Demetrius stood there in the doorway. Enzo signaled the taxi to depart.

"Are you safe, Enzo?" asked the nervous friend.

"Demetrius?" Enzo whispered, not seeing Demetrius in the shadow.

"Yes, I'm fine." Demetrius looked everywhere for Enzo's companion.

"Where's Gwen, Enzo?" he whispered in frenzy, stepping into the light.

"She's at the hotel." Enzo now saw Demetrius's face—the lines of terror, the sweat pouring down, the stained shirt, and the bloody arm. Demetrius grabbed Enzo by his shoulders, ignoring the pain of the arm.

"I let her sleep. She was exhausted."

"I told you to bring her *with you*, Enzo!"

Enzo became as furious as his friend, but he did not know what was wrong.

"D," Enzo said, searching Demetrius's face, "what's wrong?"

"They blew it up, Enzo. The van—everything. And Harris was in the van. They killed him."

"Your friend?" Demetrius nodded at the question.

"They know everything I've done," Demetrius said.

Enzo now knew why Demetrius had asked Gwen to come along. He read it in his friend's face, but Demetrius spoke the words.

"They're trying to kill all of us." Panic raced through Enzo.

"Gwen!" he screamed.

Demetrius grabbed the man and pulled him in, through the restaurant, to the back alley where the damaged Intrepid was parked. Patricia followed the men as they ran to the car.

"Demetrius," she cried, "remember, it's safe here." Demetrius looked back to Patricia, willing in this crisis, none of which she understood.

"We'll be back, Patrice." The Intrepid squealed its wheels on the pavement, flying back to the Hyatt, hoping that Gwen was still safely asleep. Patricia returned to her apartment and prepared for a long night, unfolding towels and pulling sheets from closets.

"Patricia!" her mother had awoken, hearing the commotion next to her own apartment. "What is going on?" Patricia walked in and out of the light from her little apartment kitchen.

"Mama, you remember Demetrius? He and his friends are in danger." Mama looked indifferent, a smug smile on her face.

"No Mama, *real* danger." Her daughter's face was serious. "They may need our help."

That was all the convincing the old woman needed.

"Dios mio," she said, crossing herself.

Patricia saw her mother and thought the invocation appropriate. She said the same and looked to the small crucifix that adorned her darkened living room, the symbol of agony, of terror, of supplication, and finally, of triumph.

"Keep them safe, Holy Father."

Gwen woke to the sound of the doorbell. She was groggy. Enzo was gone, but she did not know why.

Oh yes, he had to go meet Demetrius. But why in the middle of the night, with an opera to sing this coming evening? The insistent bell rang again and again. She threw the covers off of her body and put a robe over her nighttime chemise. She rubbed her eyes.

"What in the world is going on?" She walked out of the bedroom and stepped up the two steps to the suite door. A voice spoke up from outside. It sounded like Brick.

"Your husband forget his keys, Gwen." She decided not to peek through the door hole, the bodyguard giving her a secure feeling.

"Brick, don't you have a set of keys to our apartment?"

"No, Gwen, I don't," was the response. She found it a bit odd for Brick to call her by her first name. He had been so polite up to now.

The younger of the two men outside of the door waited, thirsty in lust, murmuring.

"Now you're mine."

Gwen opened the door. She spoke.

"You left without your keys, Enz..."

She could not finish her statement.

The Intrepid wheeled to a halt in front of the Hyatt. Both men ran out of the car, Demetrius leaving the auto running. They raced to the elevator and pushed the "up" button and hit number 18. Demetrius held his gun at his side in concealment. Enzo paced back and forth in the elevator, sweat peeling from his brow. Butterflies filled his stomach. They would not leave. Thoughts of his wife crackled through every sinew of his body.

"She has to be in the apartment, she has to be safe. Please, dear God, keep her safe."

Demetrius stepped to the side of the hallway, gun in hand. The hall was empty. He peered down the passage to the door of 1801. There was no one outside the door. The bodyguard was gone. His chair was empty, his magazine, books, and flashlight still under his chair. Demetrius breathed, but he did not like the emptiness of the hallway.

Enzo bolted out in front of him, neglecting his own safety, needing to find his wife.

"Enzo!" cried Demetrius. "Wait." Demetrius bolted after his friend. Enzo grabbed at his keys, oblivious to Brick's absence. Demetrius grabbed Enzo's shaking hands.

"Enzo, let me do this."

The key was found and the frightened tenor handed the detective the door key.

"Stand to the side, Enzo."

Enzo refused. He was going in that door as soon as it would allow him entrance. Demetrius was trying to protect the man from the crimes that may have been perpetrated behind this hotel room door.

Demetrius, almost to the same degree as Enzo, wanted Gwen to be here, safe inside the apartment, but with the events of the evening, he also prayed that if she was here, in this room, that she would be alive.

Demetrius inserted the key. The friction of each ridge and groove pressed against each tumbler, rumbling up Demetrius's right hand. The metal to metal ratchet ripped the air. The only other sound in the hall was the pounding of each man's heart.

Demetrius whispered to Enzo, "One, two, three." With each counted number, Enzo drew more closely to terror, the terror of Gwen being gone, or the terror of her unresponsive presence. His wife must be there. She had to be in the apartment. And she had to be alive.

The whipping door sucked Demetrius into the room. Bursts of energy threw his body side to side, his eyes looking to every corner, every section of the vast living room and kitchen. The gun followed his eyes, followed his body.

In his scan of the apartment, he saw nothing. He jumped down the two entrance steps and rushed to the bedroom, again whipping the door wide, entering like a lion upon the unsuspecting. He searched in and out—

bathroom, bedroom, anywhere in the suite that might accommodate Enzo's wife.

Enzo followed quickly, calling his wife's name, leaving the door flung open.

"Gwen!" he shouted. "Please, honey, where are you?" Demetrius walked back into the living room; Enzo entered the bedroom, still calling his wife's unanswered name. As the inevitable fact seeped into Enzo's mind, his calls became sobs.

"Gwen," he cried, "my wife...where are you, sweetheart?" He walked into the living room, torrents flowing from his eyes, his body shaking. The familiar contortions of torment gripped his body again.

"Oh, dear God, please, no!"

Enzo fell upon the dining table, collapsing in remorse.

"What have I done?" cried the distraught tenor. "I've killed my own wife."

Demetrius scanned the room, hoping to find a note, a package, even a phone message. There was nothing. He ran over to his friend.

"Enzo," he shouted through whispers, "Enzo, look at me. There's still time, we just have to think." Enzo shook his head, looking at his friend through the tears.

"How?"

"They haven't killed me, Enzo," said the detective. "I have information that they need destroyed, but they don't know that *I* know." Enzo choked back the flood washing down his face.

"They won't touch Gwen until they have *us!*" Demetrius said.

"But we have nothing to offer," Enzo said.

He could not make sense of Demetrius's words. Demetrius believed the men who had taken Gwen would still be listening, spying on the apartment through the bugs he believed were hiding in the recesses of the room. He stood up, leaving the tenor at the table, and eyed the far reaches of the apartment. He poked his head under tables, and he inspected the suite.

Demetrius walked back over to Enzo and spoke loudly, so the bugs would hear him. He reached into his jacket pocket and pulled out a videocassette.

"I have a video of what's going on at the opera house, Enzo," he paused, "and we can trade this tape...for Gwen's life."

"So you think she's still alive?"

"I pray she is, Enzo." Demetrius sat at the table with his friend. "I think whoever took Gwen came to kill you and her both. Since you were already gone, they had to take Gwen. She's their insurance."

"Insurance of what?"

"Insurance that we won't go to the police. If Gwen is dead, *we* have nothing to lose by going to the police, but if they've kidnapped her, they can tell *us* what to do, they can dictate the terms."

Enzo listened through the stained eyes of agony. He could not think. She was gone. His life, his hope, and his future had been taken, and he had allowed her capture. These thoughts shouted in his head, drowning out Demetrius's voice.

"We can only fight if *each* side has something the other one wants. We want Gwen and they want the tape." Demetrius paused, intent on relieving the burden from his friend.

"If Gwen is dead," the detective vowed, "the men who did this are all gonna go down. But...if she's alive," he looked into Enzo's eye, "which I think she is...then this is the most valuable thing we have right now." He shook the tape in his hand. "It gives us the power we need to deal with the devil."

"But won't they kill us all anyway..." Enzo thought the horrible. "because we know what's going on?"

Demetrius looked at his friend, sullen and sick. Enzo knew the answer to be "yes."

"We have to take one step at a time, Enzo," Demetrius responded, deflecting the obvious answer. "Our first priority has to be to get Gwen, then we'll deal with saving ourselves."

Demetrius knew these men would never give up Gwen. They would never let Enzo or Gwen, or anyone who could expose them, live. Knowledge was their enemy. It was the one exposure that would cause their own death, and so they would silence anyone that dared speak the truth. And death was the one tool that they could wield against the others in order to prevent their own demise.

"We've got the tape and Frank's photos," Demetrius concluded. "That's all we need." The phone rang, startling both men. Their jangled nerves told their bodies it was time for flight.

Demetrius answered the phone. Enzo stood next to him, his ear to the receiver.

"We have your wife," spoke the garbled, electronically distorted voice.

"Is she all right?" Demetrius asked.

"She will not be harmed if you do as we ask." Demetrius knew this was a lie. She would be harmed. All three of them would be harmed.

"We will contact you tomorrow night, after the opera." Enzo looked at Demetrius, chagrined. "Until then, carry on as normal. If you contact the police, she will die." Enzo's hand raised to his mouth, hearing the word, "if you contact the FBI, she will die. Remember, anything out of the ordinary will result in the very ugly death of a very beautiful woman."

"Where will you contact us?" Demetrius asked.

"You will be contacted at the opera house, in the tenor's dressing room, after the performance." It was time that Demetrius let these men know about his evidence, to make them squirm a little bit.

"I have a video tape of tonight's little delivery." Demetrius waited a moment. The silence on the line indicated their ignorance and discomfort. Demetrius continued with his statement. "Now listen to me. If anything happens to the woman, the tape *will* go to the police immediately. If she remains safe, the tape will disappear." The voice over the phone knew Demetrius was lying.

"Just keep quiet and sing your opera or your wife will die. You'll hear from us tomorrow night, at the opera house." The telephone clicked as the electronic voice disappeared. The line was dead.

"Sing the opera?" Enzo turned to Demetrius. "How can I sing with Gwen gone? I can barely speak without her." Enzo could not fathom the request. Demetrius hung up the receiver.

"Enzo, we've got eighteen hours to figure out what to do. You heard 'em," he paused, then calmly said, "You've got to sing. If you don't...."

There was a stumbling at the open apartment door. Demetrius whirled around, gun drawn, ready to fire.

A hand grabbed the doorframe. There stood Brick, trembling and clutching his chest. Demetrius put his gun away and walked overto the young man.

Brick stumbled further into the room before Demetrius reached him. The detective grabbed his left arm. Brick winced in pain.

"I feel like I've been kicked in the chest by a horse," said the young man, coming to settle in a chair. Demetrius opened the white shirt of the young man to inspect whatever wound burned beneath.

The top three buttons fell open and on the young man's chest were burns. The little bit of hair on his chest had been singed, and two welts were forming, blisters rising on opposite sides of his sternum.

Brick inhaled and exhaled sporadically, still reeling from the impulse that hadsent his body into seizure.

"Brick," Demetrius asked, "do you remember anything that happened? Did you see any faces, any clue to who took Gwen?"

Brick sat up in the chair, responding to the implied fact in the question.

"Mrs. Santi is gone?" he asked, unbelieving. The college kid was heartbroken. He looked at Enzo.

"I'm sorry, sir. I just went down the hall to help a drunk old man."

"It's all right, Brick," Demetrius assured him. "Just help us now. What happened? Who tried to kill you?"

There was not much to tell. The bodyguard had been disabled, only seeing the side of the fake drunk's face. Mrs. Santi must have been taken after that.

"Wait!" Brick said. "There's one thing that we can check." The collegian stood slowly, grunting with the throbbing pain in his chest. Enzo and Demetrius stood to go, following Brick.

"Enzo," said Demetrius, "get whatever things you need now. We are not coming back here."

"There's nothing here I need," Enzo spoke. "Only her."

And, to Enzo, it was truly nothing, it meant nothing. The clothing, the music, the jewelry—it was all worthless. All the jewels of the world were now worthless to this man. The only thing that mattered to him was gone, and he knew right then that he would sacrifice his life for the safe return of his cherished love. His life had ended tonight with her disappearance, and it would not return, it would not hold any meaning, until she was safe in his arms.

The three men left. The door to the suite was closed, but now there was no one to keep in, and no one to keep out. The chair outside the apartment sat empty. The elegant room was deserted.

Room 1801 was quiet. Evil had entered, quickly and overpoweringly. It had taken the life that it wanted, that it needed, and left in its wake only misery.

Thirty-Five

The boss snoozed in his big recliner. With the onslaught of old age, his ability to stay awake long hours had left him. He sat, his drink in front of him, head lowered, snoring with the power of Wagnerian trombones.

His first in charge, his assistant, entered again and again, seeing to the business of the evening. It had been a busy night. Their product had arrived, several tasks had been accomplished, collateral had been seized, and competitors crippled. The final task for the week would be to permanently disable this meddling threat.

He had captured the one thing that these interlopers most dearly cherished, but in that capture, the infidels had found the one thing that could end all this profitable business.

It would appear to be an even trade, each party owning what the other wanted. But there would be no trade. With their hands still on their reclaimed asset, the arbiters would be crushed.

Everything that was to happen this evening had happened. The boss had insisted on overseeing the evening's activities, another slap in the face of his apprentice. The apprentice had to acknowledge the mounting problems within and without the business. He also thought the problems would soon be solved, finally and forthrightly.

He walked into the office and over to the huge desk, which restrained the fat and fatigued leader.

What a sight! He stood over the man, his own body lean, his muscles taut, and his mind sharp. Before him, weak and corpulent, the elder of the community sat, drooling upon himself.

One little act right would bestow all this man's power upon him. He pictured it in his mind. The quick snap of the neck, like the one several weeks ago, one jolt upon the head of this man, and this snoring obesity would be entering the next world.

It would almost be humane. The boss had outgrown his position here. He was unaware of the increased factor of technology, ignorant of the new cutthroat rules in the work of organized crime. The only thing that safeguarded him, the only protection he was afforded, was bestowed upon him by his position. Only his long years of service, his slow ascension, and his survival gave him respect now.

He had been great—crushing, killing, and ruling the city. He was a lion of a man, tearing apart anything that stood in his usurping pathway. He had created distribution networks, discovered legal loopholes, and unified the underground city. He had been great.

But that time was gone. He was now captive to that previous time, lost in a different age. He was not what he had been, nor did he care to be. He could not rule much longer.

He was lost in his mind; it was clouded and feeble. He was lost in ability; his great strength had left him years ago, giving way to atrophy and obesity. He was lost in the ways of the world; his life had been telephone and television, the New World was fax and the Worldwide Web.

Only his position held him in esteem, held him in authority. He was nothing, and would be returned to nothing.

The man looked down upon the boss.

"Soon I will be king!"

The little whisper shook the slumbering boss, and he snorted his way from the unconscious to the conscious. He searched for familiarity, finding it as he looked up to see his number one.

"Robert," he growled. "Tell me."

"The van is destroyed, and the little man operating it has been vaporized."

"Good."

Number one held nothing back. He had no fear of this man now, not of his slap, and not of his "discipline." Even in his unfinished business, he felt perfectly in control. His outburst on the truck dock was merely his own discipline upon his own rank and file.

"What about the detective and the couple?" the old man asked.

"The detective was not in the van when it went up." The boss looked up at his man. "And the tenor was with the detective. So, we took the wife."

"Good." The boss's head swayed back and forth, trying to keep sleep at bay. "Where have you taken her?"

"To the warehouse. She's locked up in one of the storage units." The boss finally shook sleep away and addressed his malignant pupil.

"Keep her safe, Robert. Remember, there are rules we want to play by here. Keep her safe until we can take them all out."

"Yes, sir."

"What about the other two?"

"The detective said he has a tape of tonight's delivery."

"Do you believe him?" asked the boss.

"I don't know," was the honest answer. "He's very smart. He's trying to strengthen his position. But we have the wife. She's the trump card. Besides, with the people we have on the force, if there is a tape, I think I can make it go away."

"What about the FBI?" further inquired the boss.

"Santi and McDiess won't do anything unless we tell them. As long as we imply harm to the wife, they're neutered." There was an evil smile from the horrible man. "We'll contact them tonight," he said, looking directly into the glossy eyes of his mentor, "after the opera."

"What do you have planned, Robert?" The boss was aware of his man's passion for the theatrical.

"Tonight's opera is a tragedy, sir." Robert smirked and the boss laughed. "It's a real tragedy."

Thirty-Six

Brick had recovered from his jolt, and he was hot.

"Give me the damn tape, Jerrod," he demanded. "I need to see what's on the cameras from 2:30 to 3:30."

The fellow security guard was insistent.

"Brick, if I give you the tape, it'll be my job."

Demetrius and Enzo stood in the background, waiting for their friend to attain the security videos.

"Look," Brick yelled, "Gwen Santi has been kidnapped, and I need to see the videos. No one else needs to know. Just play us the tape. We'll shut the hell up, I promise."

"Who's Gwen Santi?" The man monitoring the Hyatt Hotel video room was oblivious as to the "who" and "what" of the situation.

"She's my wife," Enzo spoke from the door of the small room. "She was kidnapped from room 1801, about 2:40 this morning."

"Look, sir," spoke the monitor's night supervisor, "you are not even supposed to be in here, and without authorization, I can't let anyone look at those tapes." Demetrius was getting more and more angry, ready to beat the man into submission. He had not felt this rage for a long time.

"Fine, let's go," Demetrius baited the men. "We'll let Enzo go on national television, declaring the state of folly that Hyatt's security is in." He stared at the ignorant and needlessly difficult man sitting before him. "I'm sure the major networks would love to hear about the Hyatt's lack of cooperation in this investigation." Demetrius hit a home run with his *coup de grace*.

"And I'm sure you'll lose your job when the heads roll, here in the security office." Demetrius took a step toward the door.

Jerrod, the forty-four year old, third-shift security chief, now thoroughly intimidated by the forceful man, backpedaled as fast as he could.

"What do you mean, national television?" Jerrod asked.

"Enzo Santi is the world's greatest opera singer," Demetrius shot back, the declaration sounding a bit empty, "and his wife has been kidnapped, and you won't let the primary investigator see the evidence that may save his wife's life." Demetrius again moved to the door.

"Let's go!" Demetrius shouted.

"Sorry, man," Brick said, supporting the play Demetrius had just made. "Nice knowin' ya."

"Wait, wait!" Jerrod jumped out of his chair. "Just give me a second." The men did not stop moving. "I'll cue it up. Wait, please!"

Enzo, Brick, and Demetrius stopped and walked back into the room. The video man scurried around the room, looking for the appropriate tape. "Just give me a second."

"Seconds count, Jerrod," Brick told his fellow employee. The tactics employed by the college kid impressed Demetrius.

"There's one camera for each floor," Jerrod explained, "and we change the tapes every four hours." The three were getting increasingly antsy. "One more second." The drawer was pulled—floor eighteen, midnight to four—and the videocassette inserted.

Jerrod scrolled through the tape.

"Why does it flash around like that?" asked Enzo.

"The cameras are hooked up to a computer that cycles the different angles every five seconds," Brick explained.

The computerized recorder flashed from angle to angle every five seconds. It showed one section of the hallway, then, five seconds later, flashed to the opposite direction, and then finally, showed the activity in front of the floor's elevator. Each flash down the Santi's hallway showed Brick, sitting there guarding 1801, shifting and fidgeting. The clock counter on the cassette reached the two-hour, twenty-minute mark.

"Slow down," Brick stated. The video player slowed as 2:30 passed.

Then, out the door of suite 1801, at 2:34, Enzo darted down the hallway and disappeared under the camera lens to the elevator, on his way to meet Demetrius. The shifting views caught Enzo as he entered the elevator.

At 2:39, the five seconds in front of 1801 showed Brick, now curious as to some activity down the hall. The five seconds elapsed, and down the other direction the camera showed the fake drunk staggering into the escape stairwell.

The next view of Brick barely showed his moving head pass under the lens. The next supposed shot of the drunk was not of the drunk. Two men walked out of the stairwell door and headed down the hall in the opposite direction of the camera's view. Brick had been disabled in the stairwell, and now, in the following ten seconds, these two bastards were abducting Gwen.

Enzo was reliving the moment of his wife's terror. His face was pure anguish, feeling the fear that his wife never had time to experience.

The camera flashed to the front of the elevator. The feet of the two men walking past the camera were all that was seen.

Finally, after the longest five seconds of Enzo's life, the camera peered back down the hallway to room 1801.

There they were at the door, standing, waiting. One man's arm was raised, pushing the doorbell, rousing the occupant. Five seconds were gone. The camera shifted to the opposite empty hallway, then to the empty elevator doors, and after another ten agonizing seconds, back to the door of 1801.

Enzo moaned in agony, watching the scene. The two men had grabbed the woman. She had fallen limply into their arms. It appeared that she had been drugged. They dragged her a few feet, then the camera flashed to the next scene: the empty hallway. Five seconds ticked away. The camera flashed to the elevator doors. One, two, three—there were footsteps approaching, and the camera closed in on the men. One had picked Gwen up in his arms. As they approached the camera, Gwen's body began to appear. Her fallen arm flopped low, bouncing with the stride of her captor.

Five—the computer again viewed the hallway down to 1801. The men were under the camera, out of sight for ten seconds.

The ten seconds between the security camera's same views ticked away. The first five ticked and the camera showed the opposite hallway. Nothing. One, two, three, four, five...

The camera in front of the elevator was blank; no one was there.

"Where did they go?" asked Brick, leaning on the video console his supervisor was operating.

"I don't know," Jerrod responded. Demetrius blew up.

"You don't know! Where could they have gone as they left the eighteenth floor if they didn't use the elevator?" He stepped in on the man.

"Ah, let's see," Jerrod returned. "If they didn't use the main elevators, they could have used the service elevators."

"Then get the service elevator's tapes!" Demetrius declared. Brick turned to Demetrius, sullen in his look. He then glanced at Jerrod for a moment, then back to his detective companion.

"There are no cameras watching the service elevators," Jerrod said.

"Damn it!" Brick continued. "Everybody who works here has a security pass. And you can't gain access to the service elevators without a security pass."

Jerrod nodded as Brick spoke, happy to have some of the pressure taken off of him.

"The elevators are secured, so only hotel personnel can use them," Jerrod finished, trying to cooperate with the video search. "Unless there's an emergency, like a fire alarm."

"Well, they disappeared," Demetrius shouted, "and I don't think they're still in the building, especially with a hostage."

Brick's mind started churning.

"Obviously they stole an elevator pass, so they must have left via the service exit. Jerrod, what about the security cameras on the dock, at the service entrance?" Jerrod looked to his friend, astonished.

"Yeah," Jerrod exhaled. "There are two cameras down there. They're on the same five-second rotation, but there's one that is constantly on the loading dock."

Jerrod spun in his chair and dug into the video files again. Out came two tapes. He scrolled through the first. He reached 2:40a.m. and halted the machine.

"If we're lucky, we'll catch 'em coming out of the elevator." Again the five-second rotation ticked away. The men viewed the tape as it wandered down the hall of the service area, down the opposite direction, and then there was a five-second view of the service elevator entrance.

The tape clock ran to 2:41. View—five seconds, view—five seconds, view.

"There!" Jerrod jumped. The elevator light flashed in the black and white video, signaling the opening of the elevator doors. The man carrying Gwen slid his body sideways, head and shoulders turned away from the camera, and walked left, away from the view of the video. The second man looked right, gun to his side, as he followed him out of the elevator. Jerrod froze the frame.

"That's the drunk from the hallway," Brick confirmed. Demetrius shook his head, his arms folded, discerning the tape.

"There's not anything we can use. We know he was one of the guys, but it won't help us locate Gwen."

Jerrod scrolled through the next minute of the tape to confirm the absence of any more information. There was nothing. Again, he spun, collected the next tape, and scrolled to 2:40.

The service area was well lit. The surveillance camera had been hung at the far end of the hotel's loading dock, its wide angle lens capturing all activity in the area, twenty-four hours a day.

"There's a car, a black limo... No, just a Town Car, in the corner." Jerrod and Brick eyed every inch of tape.

"It doesn't look occupied," Jerrod finished.

"But it's running," Brick confirmed. "Look at the exhaust pipe."

"What about the plates?" Demetrius asked. "Can you make them out?"

"Not yet," Brick answered, "but when they leave they have to come this way, so we should have a clear shot of the numbers.

2:42—Out came the three people, one being carried. The two men scurried to the black car with their cargo.

Enzo was totally out of the investigation. He could only watch and wonder if his wife was still alive. She lay limp, flopping as a rag doll, convulsing with every step the scoundrel took. Every step these men took carried his wife further away from him.

"My Gilda," Enzo said, "stolen in the night—while I was away."

Enzo watched his wife take part in the same story as Verdi's great tragic character, Rigoletto. Gwen had been captured and lay helpless. Gilda, Rigoletto's dear daughter, had also been taken. Both men, loving father and loving husband, were too late to prevent the kidnapping of their beloved. Enzo felt the operatic tragedy within his heart, within each muscle that moved on his sturdy frame. He felt the insufferable pain of Rigoletto, holding his daughter, dead, just as he, Enzo Santi, watched his wife, lying within the grasp of death.

The kidnappers boarded the vehicle, loading their prize into the passenger compartment with them. The vehicle was off, passing the surveillance camera.

"There!" shouted Jerrod. "We've got it." The license plate flashed by the camera. Jerrod scrolled back; the vehicle reversed itself within the monitor's view. He hit the "pause" button.

"I can scroll through frame by frame now." Jerrod hit the needed button. Inch by inch the car came towards the camera again, the license numbers out of focus. With each frame, the black numbers sharpened under the bright security lighting of the area.

"Black Town Car, number, 2, B, O, Jerrod?" Brick shouted, squinting at the monitor. The sharp-eyed techie finished.

"2, B, O," Jerrod paused, "R, 2, D, 1." Demetrius wrote the numbers down in his notepad as the men spoke.

"D-*I*, Jerrod! Not D-one," Brick corrected his friend.

"Yeah, I think you're right."

"Which?" spoke the detective.

"D-I!" Jerrod and Brick responded in unison.

Demetrius changed the number to the letter with the flick of his pen, and again looked at the frozen Town Car in the screen.

"D-I, D-I?" He thumbed through the earlier pages of his note pad.

There was the number, 2BO-R2DI, right in front of him. Harris had collected the number Monday morning, and he had followed that very license, that very car to the abode of his nemesis.

"That's William Burrows' car!" Demetrius said. Enzo's bowed head raised. "They took Gwen in Burrows' car."

"Those cars are leased to the CGO, Demetrius," Enzo's voice spoke weakly, pinched in heart sickness. "The CGO got me a car for the ride to Bloomington through their service."

"So it's not his car, Enzo?" asked Demetrius, lightening his tone, coaxing further explanation from him.

"It's Burrows' to use, but he doesn't own it. The CGO lets him use it." Enzo thought back to his first meeting with the friend who had driven him to Bloomington: Albert "Bill" Hutchinson. Enzo closed his eyes, temporarily shutting out his wife's image, trying to recall the name. He heard the voice of the now stricken man whispering in his mind. Enzo mouthed the words as he heard them.

"My name is Albert Hutchinson, I work for—I work for the—Carson Limousine Service." Enzo looked out of his imposed trance, up at his friend. "The Carson Limousine Service, Demetrius." Demetrius smiled at his friend.

"That's what we needed, Enzo." The tenor's eyes were worn and frayed; the dark orbs seemed to drip blood. Demetrius again looked to Enzo and fell deep into his horrified eyes.

"We'll find her Enzo, I promise."

Thirty-Seven

Demetrius sent Brick home. There was nothing left to do tonight, but Demetrius would be sure to call him tomorrow. He would need the strong young man again. Brick apologized again for his ineptitude. Demetrius accepted the apology, knowing there was nothing the kid could have done to prevent the kidnapping.

It was 5:00 a.m. when Demetrius and Enzo arrived at their safehouse, the apartment above Carmen's Pizzeria. Demetrius pulled the Intrepid into the alleyway and parked in the one open spot behind the restaurant.

Patricia came to her door, one flight of stairs above the restaurant. She turned on the lights of the apartment and the men came up the stairs. She looked at Enzo, upon his face. He had become an old man. Her dark eyes searched the tenor, his head down, slumping, dragging himself up the stairs. She looked at Demetrius, walking up the stairs behind Enzo. His eyes met hers, and he shook his head slightly.

"They took her?" Patricia mouthed to her former companion.

Demetrius, again, without words, answered. The nod startled the woman. She went to Enzo and offered her arm to him.

Enzo took her arm and continued up the twenty steps of his Mount Everest. The three entered the apartment.

"What can I do?" offered the woman.

"We need to try and rest, Patrice," Demetrius said. Enzo had not spoken, not even a whisper. He was dark and aged as he sat on the couch in the tiny living room past the kitchen. Patricia and Demetrius talked in the kitchen.

"They took her from the hotel, but we got some pictures and a license plate from the car that took her," Demetrius explained, "but we can't do anything 'til morning."

"O.K.," she listened, "but what do *they* want, D? The kidnappers."

"They want this," he held up the videotape from the surveillance van, "and—they want us dead."

Patricia could not believe her ears. She stood, numb at the matter-of-fact statement from her friend.

"That's why they took Gwen. They can control us now, and they want to control what happens to this tape."

"What about the police?" Demetrius explained the situation to the woman. He told her of their options, of the kidnapper's order for Enzo to perform, and of the small hope that the Carson Limo Service might offer a clue to Gwen's whereabouts. There was to be no police, and no interference.

"But if Enzo is gonna get through all of this, he has got to rest," Demetrius concluded, whispering to the fledgling nurse.

"O.K.," she nodded. "I'll be right back." Patricia disappeared into the bedroom and reemerged with a glass of water and something in her hand. She walked over to Enzo and knelt down before him.

"Enzo."

He was not mentally present. He had been lost to despair. In his mind, Enzo heard his wife's voice call to him. His head raised from its bowed position, and there he saw the eyes of his wife in the woman tending to his brokenness.

Patricia offered her eyes to him, the pulse of her soul, a comforting gift to his aching heart. She touched his hand, limp, in his lap.

"I want you to take this."

He nodded his head in affirmation.

"It's nothing, really. It helps me sleep when I'm..." she hesitated, finding no moment in her own life comparable to this. "When I'm...helpless." She offered the tiny pill to him. "You have the same Latin blood that I do, so this should let you rest a bit." He took the tablet and placed it in his mouth. She offered the glass and he drank.

"Come with me." Patricia gave her hand to the man. Enzo rose, and as a child trusts his mother, he followed this woman into the bedroom.

Enzo sat on the bed, expressionless. Patricia became an angel of repose. She pulled the shoes off the man, pulled the clean sheets back for him, and took his shoulders in her hands, pressing him down, into the mattress. He lay there, eyes wide, distress etched upon orb and brow. His head fell into the downy pillow.

She took his hand, feeling the tension, the uncertainty. She took it in her own, and soothed it with the motion of her fingers.

Patricia watched her patient, and for the first time since arriving at this place, Enzo breathed. His body fell into the rhythm of inhalation and exhalation. His face remained in its horror, but his eyes fell shut. Patricia stood up and placed her palm upon his stricken brow.

Enzo felt the warmth of her touch and placed his hand over hers. Drops fell from the sides of his eyes. After a moment his hand fell to his side. Patricia stroked her hand across the man's face and then pressed her hand to his chest. Another moment passed and she pulled her hand away. She returned to the living room, where Demetrius sat on the far end of the couch. Behind her, she pulled the bedroom door to within a crack of closure. She wanted to stay aware of her patient's condition.

"Will he sleep?" Demetrius asked.

"Not much," she replied. She came around from the bedroom door and sat next to her old friend.

"If he were sick, I could treat him. If he had pneumonia, doctors could treat it. If he had the flu, I'd give him chicken soup, but when emotions are added to any condition, dosage gets thrown out the window." Patricia looked to Demetrius and saw that he did not look well either.

"Will you sleep?" she asked.

"Not much," he answered the same. "The mind again," Demetrius said. "My mind is playing out scenarios." Demetrius thought out loud, bouncing thoughts off his lovely former companion.

"What can I do? What will *they* do? Why do they want Enzo to sing? What should I do with the tape?" Demetrius exhaled from exhaustion and slouched into the couch. He even thought of his own remorse.

"Why did I put Harris in harm's way?"

Patricia did not understand the entirety of the evening's events, but she knew Demetrius would not let a friend down.

"There was nothing you could do, D," she said, soothing him. "If you'd have known you would have, but you didn't know," Patrice said emphatically, "and you're lucky you're not dead too."

Patricia took his hand and pulled him up. He needed to rest, he needed to let his mind collapse, and he could not do that in his present state.

She took him out to the back stairs and up one flight, to the roof of the building. There were two aluminum lawn chairs, green plastic criss-crossing the frame as both seat and back. She pushed him into one of the creaky aluminum chaises and sat in the other.

Above them the black night sky was full of white cumulus clouds, the cotton vapors reflecting the city lights, swirling high above in the dark mass of space.

The roof of the restaurant and apartment was tall enough to see over the top of this West Side neighborhood. The creaking chairs adjusted to the couple's weight, digging into the rooftop. Demetrius and Patricia looked eastward.

Sparkling under illumination from the heavens there stood the spectacular skyline of the Windy City. They looked southeast upon the great line of towers and skyscrapers, which cut into the clouds as they passed through the remarkable man-made landscape.

The air was fresh. October was cooling and calming the city, removing the heat and discomfort of the summer. The brisk air did the same for Demetrius, soothing his rampant mind with calming strokes from the eve's slight zephyr.

The first hint of morning appeared on the horizon. A dim orange crawled up the blanket of blue, folding upon the lake and the land. The light reached to the north and to the south, stretching around the city, to take her in the hands of day.

The friends sat quietly, Patricia admiring the city in which she lived, Demetrius looking into the awesome sky above, capped by twinkling stars.

"You bring all your men up here?" he asked.

"No, I never liked anybody enough to let them see this," she said, smiling. Demetrius looked over at Patricia.

"So I'm the first, huh?" He smiled in a bit of sardonic disbelief. Patricia looked over to Demetrius and bestowed her vision upon him.

"You were always the first, Demetrius." Her face gave way to a beautiful smile. She returned to *her* view of *her* city.

Demetrius looked back at his friend, spectacular in affection, tender in heart. He reached out and took her hand.

"Thank you, Patrice."

Under the dark black Chicago night, Demetrius fell into slumber, fitful but restful. The friends shared the sunrise together. Demetrius slept under billowy skies, while Patricia watched her companion, finally safe from the world.

She knew that tomorrow he would have to throw himself into harm's way. She caressed his hand, still in hers, and watched the sun break the blue lake horizon. The day came quickly. Light seeped lower and lower, its powerful source climbing higher and higher.

Patricia could not hold back the day. She thought of her days in parochial school, studying literature. Just as Joshua prayed to the Lord, asking him to hold back the setting sun that he might vanquish Israel's enemies, Patricia wished for the celestial rotation to halt. Only, unlike Joshua, she would pray that the day never come, that the sun would remain below the horizon, keeping these men and the ones they loved safe from danger.

She looked to the east, to the horizon. The sun rose along the vast waters of Michigan. The great star would not hold back. The earth's rotation would not cease, and the day would come. Yellow light filled the receding blackness. Day was upon them, bringing with it uncertainty, jeopardy, and possibly death.

Patricia looked out into the great city.

"Keep them from evil, and keep them safe."

The sun burned into Demetrius's eyes. Lack of sleep had sensitized them, and the bright morning sunlight ate through his eyelids. He stumbled about, remembering where he was. His watch read 8:30 a.m. He had slept for three hours. That would have to be enough for today. He needed to get to work.

Patricia was gone, but the smell of bacon emanated from below, indicating that she was also preparing for the day. Demetrius rose and headed down to the little apartment.

She had dressed and was cooking eggs to go along with the bacon. She smiled as she saw him come through the door.

"Hungry?"

"Yeah."

"Enzo is showering."

"Did he get much sleep?"

"He rustled around for a while after I came down 'bout 6:30, but I don't think very much."

"Did you get any sleep, Patrice?"

"No," she said and smiled again, "but I can sleep later. You guys need to be taken care of right now."

Demetrius wondered why he had stopped pursuing this woman. She was giving, openhearted, funny, and tremendously beautiful, but most importantly, she was loving. She was loving to her family, to her friends, and even to strangers that came in the night, seeking sanctuary.

He walked over to Patricia and kissed her on the cheek.

"You've been a real savior, Patrice," Demetrius said sincerely. "Thank you."

"Eat, D." She smiled. "You're gonna need your strength. I don't want you getting kill..." She did not want to finish the statement. Whether they were a couple or not, she did not want her friend to be hurt.

Demetrius sat at the kitchen table and was served eggs and bacon. The meal filled his empty stomach, filled his muscles with energy, and enlivened his mind to fully grasp the information that he hoped would come his way today, and with that information, decisions would have to be made, decisions that could mean life or death for Gwen, Enzo, and himself.

Enzo came out of the bedroom, his hair wet, wearing the same clothes from the night before. He looked no better than last night. He came to the table.

"Morning," he said as he looked at Patricia and then at Demetrius.

"Enzo, eat," Demetrius demanded. "I need you today, and Gwen needs you tonight." Enzo's eyes were only slightly open, and they were still bloodshot from the night before.

"I can't eat," he mumbled flatly. "I can't sleep. I want Gwen back."

"I do too, Enzo," Demetrius responded, "but if we screw up we'll all die, and I don't want that. You have to eat!"

Enzo looked around and saw some toast pop up from the toaster. He grabbed it and stuffed it in his mouth. The bread never touched his tongue, but was swallowed immediately. He devoured everything that was offered him, quickly and without pleasure, because now life held no pleasure without the one that he loved at his side.

Thirty-Eight

Mildew bittered the air, stinging each breath, constricting each inhalation. The groggy occupant of the filth-ridden container choked and gagged, her lungs acclimating to the rancid stench.

More coughs followed; she was cold. She was still in her chemise, her champagne-hued silk robe smashed to her side. She was disheveled. Her chemise had been pulled at, torn. She steadied herself upon her right elbow and looked upon herself.

She did not remember much—a man at the door, Enzo gone, a stab at her arm, and then collapse. She squinted her eyes, forcing focus, the effects of the drug that had caused her sleep still clawing at her consciousness.

She sat up and tried to find light. Her eyes would adjust more quickly with light. A small sliver pierced each end of whatever chamber she inhabited. A green glow filled the walls, sinking into the dimness from whence the illumination came.

Leaning against the wall of her chamber, she sat fully up. It was rough, cold, and held large ridges. Her back did not enjoy being pressed to the surface of the walls.

She swallowed, gagging on the tasted stench being forced down her throat. Her mouth was completely dehydrated. She forced her tongue unstuck and ordered moisture from her body, commanding her mouth to find some bit of water.

She swallowed again. The pain and taste were less bitter with this attempt.

Her eyes were focusing now. She looked closely at herself, at her predicament, her disheveled state, her nightclothes rumpled and moved. She knew no fall would have tossed her clothing in such a manner.

Her mind was clearing, awakening slowly. Her left arm was sore. She grabbed it and the pain was greater. It ached, like the ache she knew from childhood inoculations.

She noticed that her left breast had fallen out of her chemise. She knew this would not happen on its own. Gwen swallowed again and tucked her breast back within her nightshirt.

Her breast was tremendously sore. It felt bruised, almost ripped from the muscle of her chest. She clutched her heart with open palm, and knew she must inspect her accosted body more fully. She must know if someone had forced themselves on her. She must know if the men at the apartment door had defiled the temple dedicated only to her husband. She reached down and felt her panties.

She did not remember. She thought Brick was outside the door to protect her, and Enzo close to comfort her. She had had no time to scream, no time to call for help. There was a hand over her face, and then the world went black.

She did not feel as though she had been violated. Her body did not feel as though it had been compelled to engage. She closed her eyes and searched for evidence that might prove her wrong. She became nauseous at the thought.

In reaction to the grotesque search she conducted of her body, her mind focused on the warmth of love she had for her husband. The thoughts of divine union pushed the horror of her state aside. In her love, in the thoughts of her love, she was transformed; she became greater than herself.

In spite of that, her physical surroundings overwhelmed her senses, shaking her into the putrid present. The pain, the odor, the cold—they all clawed at her delicate body.

"Please, dear God," she prayed. "No."

Still, there seemed to be no evidence of anyone molesting her. There was no evidence of one forcing her into subjugation. Her breast and clothes had obviously been torn, but at least she felt that they had stopped, content with fondling and groping.

She breathed a sigh of short relief. The stench of the room sent her into fits of coughing. Her eyes had now adjusted to the little light in the room. She laid her head against the wall and coughed a final time. She peered around the room.

She sat on one end of a forty-foot corridor. The walls were about eight feet apart, and the ceiling, ten feet high. She studied the room, up and down, side to side. There were vent holes in the walls, eight feet off the ground, four vents to the length of the room's side. Light rushed in through the vent at the far end of the room, and the eerie green glow became more intense with the passing of time, with the coming of day.

Gwen stood and walked to the end of this corridor, towards the light. She reached up and touched the opening. Her fingers fit through the slit, but nothing else. The green glow was actually the material composing the walls of this Bluebeard's chamber. She scratched at the green material with her fingers, and swirling under her fingernails, bits of worn fiberglass scraped away.

She could only scratch the surface; the walls were thick and hard. This place was not meant for people, but now she was the object that had to be stored. She was being kept by the men who had killed Frank Stanza, the same men who were responsible for the attempts on her husband's life.

Her bare feet were stung by shards of glass that had been left on the floor of the room. She walked back to where she had been placed, the opposite end of the room. She decided day was dawning due to the increasing intensity of the light that filled her chamber. The green glow grew more vibrant. The yellow sunlight through the vent now streamed over her shoulder and onto the opposite end of this place.

At the end of this sarcophagus, near where she had been sealed, was a latch. Whoever had placed her here had set her down just inside the chamber opening. She looked up to the sides and saw the bolts of the swinging door hinges protruding through the green walls.

She made her way to the end of the chamber and started pushing at the thick fiberglass entrance to the enclosure. She breathed deep and shoved at the middle of the closed wall, hoping to crack, and then open the doors.

Her heave again filled her lungs with the abominable fetid air in this place. Her body convulsed in coughs. Over and over, with each diaphragmatic convulsion, Gwen slammed her fists into the green fiberglass doors.

She finally cleared her lungs of the stench, when, in the door upon which she pounded, an eye-level metal window six inches long slid open.

"Hi, Gwenny." She could hear the sneer in the eyes that peered through the opening. "I'm sorry about the accommodations. Not quite what they were at the Hyatt, are they, honey?"

Gwen knew the eyes. The young man who had injected her at the hotel owned those eyes. He had dark hair and a ruddy, scarred complexion. But those eyes were the features that she knew. They leered at her in malicious grandeur.

"Let me outta here, you bastard!" she screamed at the man.

Gwen heard a voice from outside speak. The young man in the metal window turned his head to his growling partner.

"Let her alone, man," the low voice barked, unhappy with his young counterpart. "She's valuable."

"All right," he responded. But he did not obey. The awful eyes returned to Gwen. She had come over directly in front of the sliding metal window.

"I've been watchin' you, Gwen," he groaned, "and I've sure liked what I saw. As soon as Enzo is out of the picture, you an' me, we're gonna have a good time. A real good time."

She spat at the eyes, at the man leering at her. He cackled horribly, his eyes eating into the flesh that he desired.

"I like a little fight, Gwen. It makes the conquest all the more sweet," he breathed through closed teeth. "And you *will* be sweet."

The little metal door inched shut. Gwen stepped to the side of her prison and fell along the side, down the heavy fiberglass wall. She brought her hand to her mouth and began to weep. Her lungs burned as she cried, the stale air sinking deeper into her chest with each convulsive sob.

She sobbed for her plight and in fear for what was to come, but more so, she sobbed for her husband. This man's threat meant that Enzo was in danger, and she knew she was the bait to lure him to his death.

"Please, dear God," Gwen wept bitterly, "keep my husband safe. If you will, take me," she prayed, "but keep my love from evil, and keep him safe."

Her tears stained her silken robe. She sat in her dank dungeon, fighting despair, fending off frustration, and hoping for her salvation.

Thirty-Nine

10:30 a.m.
Wednesday October 4
Carson's Limousine Service

Michael Elliott called Bloomington Hospital every day to check on the health of his best driver, Albert "Bill" Hutchinson. Bill had suffered the heart attack on the job, and Michael not only felt responsible for his well being, but also considered Bill a friend.

He had driven Mrs. Hutchinson down to Bloomington personally as soon as word of the accident came to the office, but Michael had found it necessary to return to Chicago the next morning. He had made himself indispensable at the Carson Limo Service and he now regretted the fact that he felt so obligated to the work.

He only asked for simple things: a personal day or two, a pay raise. After all, he had increased the service's bottom line through cost cutting and through the corporate accounts he had acquired. He also did not want his drivers to come unglued when he decided to take a long weekend now and then.

But now, the relaxing job he pictured would not appear for a long time. His best driver was ill, limos were being stolen off the lot, and gasoline had not returned to its pre-Gulf War price. Costs were tight, and he was in charge. Even the big corporate accounts he had secured were squeezing their wallets as the U.S. recession slowly dissipated.

Now was certainly not the time to make waves or suggest adding to the payroll. Problems would be blamed on him, while the corporate heads would take the credit for any increased profits. Work life right now was tough, but things would get better.

The morning phone call to the Bloomington Hospital had, in fact, cheered the overworked supervisor. The doctors attending to Bill felt that he was out of the woods physically. The relief in Mrs. Hutchinson's voice had lifted his spirits. He had been working at his desk all morning.

Two men—one black man, one Latino man, both large and both disheveled—came straight to the office where he was sitting. They did not hesitate and they did not care to kibitz with the men wandering around the garage.

Here comes a scam, Michael thought, watching the two approach him.

The supervisor had seen every scam imaginable in this neighborhood: donations for his sick sister with leukemia, contributions to the Neighborhood Crime Watch. Michael always responded the same way. The corporation donated as it saw fit, and there was no money on the premises. He always added that the nearest drug rehabilitation center was four blocks to the east. Most of the "donations" these people received found its way up their own noses.

Michael was ready with his speech when the Latino gentleman spoke.

"Michael Elliott?" was the question. Michael nodded. "My name is Enzo Santi."

The name was familiar to Michael. "I was the man whom Bill Hutchinson drove down to Bloomington, when he was nearly killed."

Demetrius closed the office door as Enzo spoke.

"This is my friend Demetrius McDiess, Mr. Elliott."

"Please, call me Mike, Mr. Santi," responded the supervisor. "Please sit down." The three men sat. Michael spoke again.

"I called down to Bloomington this morning. I guess the doctors think Bill is gonna be all right. Mrs. Hutchinson told me herself." A big grin came to Michael's face. It was met by a weak sigh of relief from Mr. Santi.

"That's wonderful, Mr. Elliott, it truly is, but right now I need your help."

Michael looked at the worn face and defeated countenance of Enzo Santi, the great, fragile, opera superstar. He did not look like someone who should be in this neighborhood, let alone dressed like a vagrant.

"Mr. Santi, with what you went through helping Bill out last Wednesday, I'll do anything I can to help ya out."

Enzo looked over to Demetrius, who decided to tell their story to this uninformed man.

"Mr. Elliott," Demetrius began, "the accident last Wednesday was actually an attempt to kill Enzo. Mr. Hutchinson was someone who happened to be in the way."

Michael Elliott fell back into his chair. Disbelief filled his face.

"How can that be? He was just driving you to a concert." Michael spoke his thoughts. "Why would someone want an opera singer dead?

"Enzo saw a man killed," Demetrius explained, "and that man held evidence to a drug conspiracy at the Illinois State Theatre." Demetrius spoke slowly and plainly, not wanting to miss a detail. "You see, the attack on your driver was actually an attempt to silence what Enzo knew about the Chicago Grande Opera."

"Come on, an opera company dealing drugs?" Michael said sardonically.

"Michael," Enzo leaned forward. "I want you to believe *this*. Last night Demetrius caught these men unloading their shipment. Then these men kidnapped my wife." Enzo was now leaning across the desk and becoming increasingly agitated.

"I don't care what you believe happened to Bill. I don't care what you think is happening at the opera house." Enzo stood, his voice a quiet scream. "All I want you to know is that last night they kidnapped my wife because of what's on this video tape." Enzo pointed to Demetrius, who pulled the tape from his pocket. Enzo continued.

"This is the security video from the Hyatt Hotel last night," Enzo lied, but Demetrius played along. Enzo continued.

"Two men loaded my wife, Gwen, into a black Lincoln Town Car with the license plate..." Enzo looked to Demetrius for the numbers.

"2BO-R2DI," the detective said.

"Mr. Elliott," Enzo settled, "I know you're a good man. Bill told me so on the way to Bloomington. But these men are gonna kill my wife..." Enzo paused, "if you don't help us."

Michael was stunned and intimidated. Could all this be true? Why would an opera singer come all the way down here if he was playing some kind of mind game? And was the Chicago Grande Opera really involved in the drug trade?

Then Michael thought of a way to verify the stories Mr. Santi was telling. He picked up the phone and dialed. The phone began to ring.

"Mr. Santi," Michael asked, "if you were there when these people tried to murder Bill, how did they do it?" Enzo sighed confidently.

"Believe it or not, I saw some man dressed like a highway patrolman inject something into his neck."

Michael nodded and returned to his phone call.

"Yes, my name is Michael Elliott, William Hutchinson's employer. For our medical insurance records we need to know the illness Mr. Hutchinson is suffering from." Michael listened as the nurse told of the details of the illness.

"Our records originally showed that he suffered a heart attack." He paused. "So that is *incorrect*? All right. How did this poison get into his body?" Michael listened some more. "All right, thank you very much, ma'am." Michael hung up the phone.

Enzo looked to the cautious supervisor and spoke.

"Potassium, into the left side of the neck."

Michael nodded back at Enzo.

"Do you believe me, Mr. Elliott?" Enzo pleaded.

"Yeah, I believe you, Mr. Santi," Michael responded, suddenly sympathetic to the plight of the man. "I just had to check. So how can I help you?" he asked, pulling closely up to the desk.

"Where is the car with this license plate?" Demetrius began.

"Let me go out to the assignment board." Michael got up from the desk, walked out of the office, to the left, and to the huge assignment board. He posted the daily assignments here. Each car—make, model, license plate number, and keys—each had a position, typed in bold black letters on the board. The names of the drivers were posted under each position, indicating which car they would be driving for the day.

"Do you have a dispatch that you can contact your driver with, or at least have him report his location?"

"Damn," Michael cursed, "I thought so." Enzo and Demetrius searched for further explanation. Michael continued.

"You see, the limo you're talkin about is a full-timer. With that type of contract, the drivers don't check in; they're on a full-time basis. We don't even give 'em radios." The explanation was not sitting well with the two desperate men. "Basically, we supply the car and the CGO uses it however they see fit."

Demetrius was stumped.

"At the end of their season they give the cars back to us, and then we start using them on a daily basis."

"What about the driver? Can you contact him?" Demetrius asked.

"With this deal, they supply their own driver. It's a hand's off contract, and with companies who use this service all the time it ends up being cheaper for them. I came up with the idea. It's basically a lease. We supply the car and they supply the driver, usually part-time, no benefits."

Demetrius scrutinized the assignment board, searching for help in this new quandary.

Indeed, the spot marked for car #5-Lincoln Town Car, License 2BO-R2DI, had not been disturbed. There were no keys, no papers, and no clues.

Demetrius noticed the similarity of the license plate numbers. He found a license that was almost a perfect match to the car used to kidnap Gwen.

"Why are the plates so similar?" he asked.

"Livery plates are given consecutively. We just happened to file most of the paperwork on the cars at the same time." Another hopeless avenue.

Enzo and Demetrius had run into a dead end. The limousine service could not help.

"Wait a second, guys," Michael said. "Maybe we got somethin' here." He bolted into his office. Enzo and Demetrius followed close behind him.

"We just got one of those satellite tracking systems for the cars. We had a bunch of cars stolen this past year. The system holds down our insurance costs, and they guarantee the recovery of any car that has this system." Michael paused. "It uses a special uplink in the car's trunk. I call the satellite company and tell them that the car has been stolen. The satellite company turns the uplink on, and then their satellite tracks the car to exactly where it is, or at least where the uplink is." This was the break Enzo and Demetrius needed.

"Just keep your fingers crossed," Michael said.

"What's the problem?" Demetrius asked.

"That particular car is an older one," Michael told him, "I don't remember if we put the satellite system on it before the CGO took it." He leafed through his paperwork and found the car in question.

"2BO-R2DI, yeah, it's got it. We installed it just before the CGO took it in August." There was a breath of hope in the room.

"I'll call the cops," Michael said, picking up the phone. Demetrius put his finger on the receiver, halting the call.

"We can't do that, Michael," he said. "The men who kidnapped Gwen said that she would be killed if we contacted the cops."

Michael's hands fell helplessly to his sides.

"That's how the satellite system works," Michael explained. "You call the cops, then they go through the satellite company to find the car."

"Can't we go directly to the satellite company?" Demetrius improvised. "Tell them that one of your drivers is joyriding, or drunk, and you need the car?" It sounded plausible, and Demetrius was not going to take no for an answer.

"I'll try, but I don't think they'll go for it." Michael was happy to cooperate, especially if what these men said was true, and so far, everything they claimed proved to be so.

"I'll do my best, Mr. Santi," he vowed, "but this could take a while."

"Like how long?" Enzo asked.

"Maybe all day," Michael responded. "It depends how long I have to haggle with the company, and then how long it takes the satellite to find the uplink." Demetrius reached into his pocket and pulled out a card.

"This is my cell phone number. When you find out where the car is, give me a call."

"As soon as I know, you'll know...I promise."

Enzo reached out to Michael and took his hand.

"Mr. Elliott, thanks for your help."

"I'll stay here all day if I have to, gentlemen."

As they walked out of the office, Demetrius stopped Enzo.

"I want to make a call, Enzo. It's time to clear something up."

The call was made and Enzo and Demetrius walked out of the Carson Limousine Service.

"McGrail, here."

"John, it's Demetrius."

"Hey, how those Cubs tickets comin', babe?" Demetrius had no time to play.

"John, I need a big favor."

"Shoot."

"I need you to run an APB on a Town Car, license number 2BO-R3D1." John repeated the numbers.

"R-three-D-one. Right?"

"Right!"

"Demetrius," the police detective changed the conversation, "I heard there was some trouble on Lower Wacker Drive last night. Somethin' about a van being destroyed."

Demetrius held the phone close to his ear and, as John spoke, he remembered seeing his friend blown to bits.

"Yeah," he confirmed, "that's why I need this Town Car located. It should help me find what I need to find. And John, I need you to meet me at the Illinois State Theatre Stage Door tonight." Demetrius wanted his cop friend to help out as he said he would.

"Is this our little agreement?"

"Yeah."

"What time?"

"After the opera—'bout 11:00."

"I'm there, babe." The detective sounded excited at the prospects of this evening's adventure.

"And John," finished Demetrius, "keep the APB under wraps. The cops are not supposed to know about it." The veteran officer began to add things up.

"Sure D," he answered, "you got it." He knew Demetrius would not ask these things if he were not near to solving his little dilemma.

"Should I come prepared?" the cop asked, implying armed.

"To the teeth. If you can bring something extra for me, I'd appreciate it."

"O.K., babe. That it?"

"Yeah."

"See ya tonight, D. 11:00, at the opera house."

The officer looked at the license number. It seemed odd, not quite right. His pale Irish face screwed up and he looked at the number again.

"He must have written down the wrong number."

Marcia maestoso e tragico:

con passione e sacrifizio

It is a sin peculiar to man to hate his victim
— Tacitus —

*Man is almost always as wicked as
his needs require*
— Leopardi —

Forty

Enzo began the afternoon with a nap. He entered his performance day ritual, but he could not sleep.

The two men returned to Patricia's apartment to find lunch waiting for them. Demetrius ate; Enzo picked at the food sent up from the restaurant below. There was nothing that either of them could do but wait.

While Enzo tried to rest in the bedroom, Demetrius punched the video cassette into Patricia's player and watched the footage Harris had captured of last night's delivery. There was nothing new on the pictures. He only wanted to view the prize that kept Gwen from being killed. This little tape was the only leverage he had. It could destroy the conspiracy at the Chicago Grande Opera, or it could destroy him and his friends.

Presently, the conspiracy held the upper hand, knowing Gwen's life was more valuable to Enzo and him than the tape was to the conspirators.

Demetrius snatched the tape out of the VCR and stuck it into its cardboard case, then set it on top of the television. He browsed through the neatly stacked videos to the side of Patricia's TV, took one of the animated shorts from its spot, and pushed it into the machine. He tried to rest his mind, to turn it off from the harried pace of the last forty-eight hours. Perhaps in these moments of futile repose solutions to this deadly predicament would reveal themselves. He sank onto the couch and stared at the glowing television screen.

The ritual in which Enzo was engaged was just as fruitless as the effort in the main room. Sleep would not come to him. Exhaustion filled him, but his mind would not allow slumber. His body would not relax without the one who gave him comfort. His mind would not recline without the woman who filled him with peace.

Enzo made himself remain in bed for two hours. The bit of food he had eaten did not digest. His stomach was sour. He found no comfort.

He finally sat up, anger filling him. Rage consumed the fibers that had found beauty in worship and in sacrifice. In anger, Enzo prayed, furious with passion, and desperate with hate.

The inevitable "why" found his lips. He silently screamed at a God who now seemed indifferent to the plight of the pure when faced with the power of evil.

"We worship you," he shrieked within his mind, "and you forsake us in our hour of need?"

The bedroom was quiet. To Enzo, the room felt deprived of life, empty of any reason for living.

"Are the innocent to be condemned to live under the heel of the oppressor, spat upon by the depraved?"

Enzo was thrown back onto the bed, his body convulsing in hatred, hatred for the work of men who sought destruction and cherished perversity.

The emotion that he had never wanted to feel, that he had sworn to eradicate from his life, anger raged within his body. He was powerless to help the one whom he loved completely. He was weak in the face of death and ruled by the onslaught of sin.

A noise in the room disturbed him. He heard a voice, distant and muffled. He pulled himself up from the bed. Through the wall behind him he heard the murmur of an old woman, speaking in Spanish.

The old woman next door mumbled over and over again, repeating her supplication with greater and greater fervency. Her voice took on the words of scripture.

"Keep these ones from Satan," she implored, "keep them in thy divine grace," she spoke. She read again. Enzo stood and pulled himself to the thin apartment wall, his heart pounding in his chest. The woman read, using his native tongue.

"For greater love hath no man than this, that he lay down his life for his friends."

The old woman prayed more fervently; the clicking of her rosary beads could be heard through the thin wall.

"Bless them in their hour of need, and may this husband love his wife in her time of need, just as Christ gave himself for His bride, your holy Catholic Church."

Enzo fell away from the wall, stumbled through the darkened room and ran into the main room. His face was washed in emotion.

"Patricia," he asked, "who is in the next room?"

"I'm sorry, is Mama too loud?" Patricia answered apologetically.

"What is she doing?" he asked fervently.

"I suppose she is praying for you and Gwen," she answered. "Last night I told her what happened, so I would guess that she is praying for you."

Enzo collapsed in shame. The two friends rushed to him, Patricia grabbing him first. Enzo's head was down, but as she touched him he looked up and spoke, as if to his own wife.

"I will lay down my life for you. I will give my all for you. If the gift of my life will ensure your safety, I give it freely and forever..."

The tears flowed, purging the anger and the remorse he had felt. The tears purged self-doubt and doused the self-immolation that had consumed him since his wife's kidnapping. The hatred of evil still held to his heart and mind, but it would not engulf him. He would conquer for his wife, even if that conquest meant his own death.

Patricia comforted him, rocking him back and forth in soothing rhythmic strokes. She knew the prayer was directed to the one Enzo loved, but she offered her friendship in tender sympathy to the broken man.

Enzo repeated, time and again: "Take my life, but keep my wife safe. Take my life..."

Forty-One

Enzo wanted to get to the opera house earlier than usual. He arrived at 6:00, a half an hour before he would regularly appear when he had a 7:30 curtain.

Demetrius had phoned Brick earlier in the day and asked him to rent a black Lincoln Town Car for the ride over to the opera house. Brick would be the chauffeur and protector for the entourage of two. Brick found no problem in securing a car, although he could only find a dark blue vehicle. That was fine by Demetrius. The car just had to be dark, very dark. Brick also decided to bring a Louisville slugger from his sixteen-inch softball equipment. He hoped he would not have to use it, but he put it in the trunk anyway.

Demetrius had loaded the trunk of the rental car with everything he had kept in the Intrepid: two handguns, three bulletproof vests, and several bags of photo equipment. The Intrepid was a marked car now. The conspirators would know that car by sight and thus be aware of Demetrius' presence.The two men arrived at the *Primo Tenore* dressing room without incident. Brick was outside with the car, Demetrius with Enzo, and there was security all around the stage door.

Enzo closed his dressing room door and tried to find some peace amongst the operatic trappings.

"I'll be back in ten minutes, Enzo," Demetrius said.

"Where are you going?"

"I'm gonna talk to security. I want them to know that you've been threatened."

"Won't that put Gwen in danger, Demetrius?" Enzo remembered the warning of last night's phone call. Demetrius allayed his fears.

"I trust Randy Scott. I won't really tell him anything, but I'll voice my concern about your safety."

"O.K."

"I'll be back in ten minutes." Demetrius left and Enzo locked the door behind him.

Enzo felt trapped in his own little operatic cocoon. He knew he could trust the people around him, these theatre people he knew from years before, but his mind would not settle.

He began to vocalize, stepping to the piano, finding the appropriate notes, and singing through scales. His attempts at music were completely unsatisfying. His voice was choked off, incomplete and strained. The ears within his head could not actually hear. The pain of his predicament muffled them. Tonight would not be an opera. Tonight's performance would not be acceptable, but Enzo did not care.

He pushed breath to his lungs, forcing the expansion, and violently, in a fit of defiance to his gift, blew out the breath. His vocal chords smacked together, producing tense, pressured tones.

In his mind's ear he was just some screaming operatic wanna-be, shoving and manipulating his puny instrument to poorly reproduce great art.

His voice would not respond. The impetus of his sound was not within his body. The accentuation of his instrument was not within his mind, or even within his grasp. The love of his music and his art was not wrapped up in himself.

The need to sing came from his love, came from his dedication and commitment to his wife, and because she was gone, the great voice would remain hidden, locked away until that sweet moment when they would be reunited, when love would conquer their foes and bind them together once again.

Enzo Santi would sing tonight, but only with his voice, with the shell of his soul. He would not sing with his heart, for it lay in the hands of the one person who gave his life meaning.

The supernumerary dressing room always filled up early. They often had to be on stage before the principles. They were the surrounding characters that gave glory to the opera stars. They were the people, often out of sheer adoration for the art form, who would spend their entire day preparing to stand in a corner, holding a spear or dressing up as henchman to some overweight operatic villain.

The supers were the slaves, the servants, the silent family, and the cupbearers to the opera gods. They were the most overlooked, yet most dedicated performers in the theatre. Their dank little dressing room reflected their importance in the eyes of the company, but in their own hearts they felt they were contributing an integral and necessary addendum to this overly flamboyant performing art.

Sam Wheaton was center stage, weaving another of his operatic tales of hilarity and misfortune.

"So back in '66, I'm standing there as one of the slaves in *Aida*. Remember those old rags we wore for that scene?" Sam asked for confirmation, which was nodded from all corners of the room. "And the 'king,' who's been standing still for the entire scene, starts to wobble. I mean the old Italian boy is on the verge of collapsing." The lisp in Sam's effeminate voice dominated his speech. One of the other older men spoke up.

"Wasn't it Nicola Rossi Lemeni singing that night?"

Sam, insulted at being interrupted, turned pissy.

"Who gives a goddamn who it was?" He hopped back into form and continued.

"Anyway, nobody notices him starting to wobble, and all this is happening during the big parade of the soldiers. My God, there were horses and dogs and camels that year." Sam sidestepped a moment. "If they do *Aida* when the circus is in town, they often use the elephants too, but thank God they didn't that year."

Several of the younger super men started to giggle in anticipation.

"So down the old boy heads, knees locked, stiff as a board." Sam's arm, elbow to wrist, imitated the motion of the fainting singer.

"You mean his *body*, don't you?" a younger man made the rude comment.

"If I'd been with him, he'd have stayed up longer than he did," yelled one of the fellow gay supers to his friend.

"You go, girl!"

"Anyway," Sam finally returned to the bulk of his story, "he falls over, knocking the 'queen' and four or five women over, then..." Sam added the dramatic pause, "he rolled down the stairs of his throne and into the path of the two horses. Well, the horses reared up and nearly stomped him to death."

"Oh Sam," a younger man spoke in disbelief, "you're tellin' tales out of school."

"I swear this is all true." Sam crossed himself and continued the story. "So you've got all these fat chorus women trying to come down the stairs in those tight white Egyptian dresses they wore, and they started tumbling down those narrow stairs. I thought I was at a bowling alley. Two or three women started walking down fine, then this one tripped from the back, and the whole kit'n'caboodle fell right over."

"Did the woman pick up the spare?" added one of the unamused listeners.

Sam, acerbic again, rejoined.

"I'll pick up your spare if you don't shut up." He continued. "So the horses stop rearing, but they're spooked, and the women collect Mr. Rossi-Lemeni, who looks drunk, but happy as a clam to have all these women around him. So he's gettin' up, grabbin' as many boobs as he can, clawing his way back to the top of the stairs, and the horses continue downstage, under the hot lights, now scared completely to death, poor things, and poop this huge load of shit right in front of the prompter's box."

The sporadic giggles now erupted in unified roars of laughter. Sam spoke over his satisfied audience.

"Crap is flying into the prompter's box, into the orchestra pit, it's *everywhere*," Sam craned his neck in accentuation. "Well, by now the audience is screaming with laughter. The conductor has his face in his hands, and the prompter is cleaning herself off. Everybody on stage is trying not to laugh, so we are literally shaking with tension, ya know when you can't laugh, but your body has to. It's horrible.

"Well, the chorus guys are making farting noises and cracking up, and the orchestra is disgusted by the whole thing. So we are all stunned when, out of nowhere, falling from the spotlights above, one of the lighting guys tosses a roll of toilet paper onto the stage." Screams filled the room, and uncontrolled gales of enjoyment surrounded the man telling the tale.

"And I have never seen a roll of toilet paper bounce so far. It hit the steps in front of the king, bounces off the steps and down stage, unrolling and twirling all the way, spun right past the prompter, and then, this Scott's tissue from hell, cascaded into the pit."

The laughter continued for several minutes as the men improvised what each of them would have done. Sam got the best of them all, per usual.

"I know I wasn't the only one that night who peed my pants. I think that show was personally responsible for the development of Depends Undergarments. Oh my God, I've never laughed so much in my life."

Two unknown men had entered the room while the supers were regaling each other in their humor. They were tough looking characters, not the usual type of men who would be seen in the supers' dressing room. Sam, never one to play favorites, walked over and shook hands with the men.

"Hi, I'm Sam Wheaton, one of the long-time supers here. Can I help you?"

The more imposing man spoke, and the other one remained completely quiet.

"Bill Burrows asked us to fill in for a couple of the supers who couldn't make it tonight, but I think we're only on at the end."

"You mean the last scene?" Sam looked for further explanation.

"Uh, yeah."

"Well, come on in. The sign-in sheet is over there," he pointed to the white sheet on the plaque by the door. "Put your name down and check off the day you were here."

Sam became a bit upset at these two men. He walked back to his dressing position—a three-foot section of mirror—and began his evening ritual. He was to be a henchman for Scarpia this evening, and in the third act he would become a soldier, along with these new men.

"What's the matter, Sam?" his mirror neighbor asked.

"That damn Bill Burrows, giving our jobs to whoever wants 'em. I tell you what, the union rep is gonna here about this. My partner has been on the waiting list to be a super for two years, and Burrows just overrides the Union." Sam grew more upset with each word. "We'll just see about that!"

The two new men took their places at the mirror and shook a few more hands. They were obviously not very comfortable. Sam turned and looked at them again. He felt bad. He had not treated them very well. Burrows was the one to blame, not these fellows. He decided to strike up a conversation with them.

"So, gentlemen, we didn't get your names," Sam commented. "Introduce yourselves."

There was obviously more discomfort on their faces now. Again the tougher of the two spoke first.

"I'm Mitch Kuptchak," he said, knowing this group would never recognize the name from the National Basketball Association.

"I'm, uh, I'm...." the other man stuttered.

Sam cut him off, trying to be funny.

"Stutter much, do we?"

"I'm...Allan Stone."

Sam continued his polite, and not so polite, banter.

"Wow, same as the director of Opera Festival Chicago, the little opera company in town?" The second new man did not know how to respond.

"I guess, I've never heard of him. I don't like opera very much."

"Then what the hell are ya doin' here, Allan?" The room tittered at the sarcastic rhetoric. The tough man glared at the second man, telling him to shut up, without saying a word.

Sam saw that the first man, the tougher of the two, seemed more at ease with himself.

"So, Mitch, what did you do to the back of your hand? That's a huge bandage." The fake Mitch looked down, upset at the observant inquiry.

"I got into a fight the other night. If you'll excuse us…" the two new men bolted for the door. "We'll be back before the third act." They were gone, down the hall.

"I hope they fit into the costumes," Sam spoke. "That first guy looked awfully rough." Sam pursed his lips and raised his eyebrows at his gay neighbor.

"He does seem to carry around a big—'package,' doesn't he?" the neighbor spoke.

Sam crossed his arms, raised his left hand to his chin and watched the men walk away from the room, down the hall and out of sight. Sam pulled a lewd opera reference, one of his store of hundreds.

"He can be my 'Masetto' any time." Sam finished. The two older gay men laughed.

"*Batti, Batti, o bel Masetto.*"

Randall Scott was in the security office overseeing the slowly growing activity within the Illinois State Theatre. Demetrius knocked at the door.

"Get in here, D," shouted the man playfully. "What ya doin', and how's your tenor friend?"

"That's exactly what I want to talk to you about, Randy."

Demetrius quickly lied that threats had been made on Enzo's life. Randall perked up and started asking questions.

"Have you called the police?"

"No. We don't want to alarm Gwen."

"What do you want me to do, D?" asked the perplexed chief.

"Can you just alert your guys that there might be somebody trying to interrupt the show, or gain access to the parts of the theatre that the performers are in? Maybe even watch out for guns."

"You got it, man. I'll let 'em know what's up, but tell 'em to be discreet." Demetrius was happy with his friend's response.

"I'll even talk to Nick Palermo. If the ushers see anything suspicious, I'll make sure they let us know."

"Great, Randy. I really appreciate it." Demetrius started out the door.

"Hey, D," said the chief, "you find what you was lookin' for?" Demetrius was confused for a moment.

"What do ya mean, Randy?"

"All dose questions de udder day you asked me, dat wasn't just for personal knowledge, was it?"

Demetrius did not know if he could fully trust the chief of security after everything he had learned. Randall could be completely innocent of what was happening at the Illinois State Theatre, or he might be completely ignorant of what was going on. But with either possibility, Demetrius could not trust someone who was so lax or so unaware in his job as to allow the foul deeds that were taking place within these walls.

Then, a final possibility occurred to Demetrius. Randall Scott could be one of the men involved in this little operation. He could be receiving kickbacks for his silence, and he could be one of the most deadly people he had yet to encounter.

There was no scenario in which Randall Scott could be trusted.

"Just been pokin' around, really. I like being a detective too much not to ask questions." Demetrius paused. "Besides, those pictures of the opera fire really piqued my interest."

"How long you around, D?" asked the security chief.

Paranoia seeped into Demetrius's thoughts. Why would Randall want to know such information?

He shook off his spinning inquisitions.

"Tomorrow! I got to get back to Minneapolis. Too much work up there to have too much fun down here." Demetrius smiled, lifting his hand to wave good-bye. "Talk to ya later, Randy."

Randy Scott smiled back.

"Talk to ya later, Demetrius. Hey, if I don't see ya, have a safe trip back to Minneapolis." The chief nodded his head and watched Demetrius leave his office.

After the young detective left, the chief of security at the Illinois State Theatre picked up his phone and made the necessary phone calls about his friend and the young tenor.

Her hands were tender and bloody from the afternoon's tasks. Gwen had decided that she would not allow her fate to be solely determined by the men outside this plastic tomb. Scraping together the bits of broken plaster, glass, and wood on the floor of her "room," she collected a substantial pile of debris and stored it in the near corner, the end of the room where the swinging doors were located. The debris was set down in the far corner, opposite from where the chamber door would open, out of the view of the sliding window, and thus out of the view of the men outside.

She decided that she must be locked in a semi-truck trailer. This conclusion was reached after much searching and the recollection of past experience.

As a young singer following her husband to his apprenticeship at the CGO, the couple had often shared meals in the State Theatre's cafeteria. She would walk by the opera house loading dock on her way to the cafeteria, where she would pass the stage crew, loading and unloading the sets for the season. These burly fellows were never bothered by the overwhelming smell of mildew that came from within the trailers holding the sets. It always made her nauseous.

It also struck her strange that the trailers were green. One of the stage crew had explained that the trailers were often kept outside, and metal trailers would rust in the weather. Fiberglass would not rust, and thus would keep the sets safe. The mildew was the side effect of leaky fiberglass trailers, soiling the sets and growing unabated for months, sometimes even years at a time. The CGO would spray the sets with mildew retardant, but it seemed to do little good.

So she was trapped, jailed in one of these great semi-trailers, gagging at the smell of mildew and looking for a means of escape. There was none.

The heat of the day's sun, magnified by warehouse windows, had exacerbated the odors of her enclosure. Feeling choked and gagging, she had to make herself relax every now and then, as she felt suffocated by smell. She found cool air at the seams to the doors, but she was too short to take full advantage of the vents, eight feet off the floor of the trailer.

Midway through the day her captors had given her food and water through the sliding door. The older man, the eyes she did not know, had pushed the bottled water and sandwiches through the window. The younger man, the eyes, was always close by, speaking from a hidden position, telling of her impending destiny.

The older man's eyes looked kind, even fatherly. He barked "silence" to the verbose younger one when his comments became offensive, even to him. The stream of graphic remarks would rise again after Gwen would hear footsteps depart from the trailer. The perverted eyes would slide the window open and promise his captive gratification she had never experienced before.

After several comments questioning the younger man's ability as a lover, and hearing the rage that accompanied her provocation, Gwen decided silence was the better form of valor. When the inevitable verbal attacks would come, his eyes touching and fondling hers, she would step to the hidden corner and pray for her swift and safe release.

The pile of debris could be used as a weapon. When they did come to take her, she would not be taken without a fight. As the swinging door of the trailer would open, the men would be hampered by the darkness, unaware of her position in the trailer. The shards of glass and splinters of wood could be driven into the eyes of her tormentors, blinding and surprising them.

She pictured the horrible plan as liberation from her confinement. Throw the cutting debris into the hideous eyes of the men while they were still unaware of her position in the trailer, and with all her might, kick, scratch, and claw a pathway to freedom.

It would be better to fight these men and die in that struggle than to be mutilated in what she now believed to be her ultimate doom. She prayed for strength in death, for freedom in death, and for strength to endure the torture she believed awaited her.

She crouched in the corner, away from the sliding window of the huge door, and prayed for her husband. She prayed for Enzo to her own neglect, for she knew that he was doing the same for her, and no matter what happened here in this life, they would one day be together, unified in love and filled with perfect happiness again.

The window slid open quickly. The young eyes were there, searching for his captive "love."

"Gwenny, where are you?" he sang in falsetto tones, tormenting her. His eyes adjusted to the light and he found her, sitting far down the fiberglass corridor. She remained silent, hunched low, never looking up. She decided to remain in view for now, letting the man expect his sighting. She did not want to reveal her corner hiding place prematurely, and ruin her chance at escape.

"It won't be long now, sweetheart," he said.

The word "sweetheart" had never sounded vile before, but it now seeped with corruption.

"We'll be free of our little problem any time now," he cackled in the window, seeing her down along the wall, knowing she had heard, and craving her voluptuous form. He became excited, watching her chest rise and fall with each breath.

Gwen pulled her knees closer to her chest, wrapping her arms around them, and let her head fall.

"And then you and me can be together."

She could sense the smile on his face and the lust in his heart.

"I can't wait to get my hands all over you." His voice slowed as he intoned his malignant intent. "You're gonna be all mine, baby, after this one little opera."

Gwen did not move but remained still, praying, and thinking only of the one she loved.

Enzo listened as best he could to his jabbering friend, Louis Calabrese, the CGO's head makeup man. Enzo usually found his filthy mouth somewhat humorous, the cosmetic artist combining words and ideas that had never before been uttered, but tonight was different. Enzo wanted to be left alone, to concentrate on his wife and to try to inch his way through this opera. The polite conversation continued.

"My gahd, baby," Louis responded. "Really?"

Enzo again answered the inquiry about the beautiful young female dresser.

"Yes, Lou," he expelled, "she's married."

Louis stepped back, eyeing the blush and light eyeliner he had applied to the mocha-skinned singer.

"The stage crew is gonna be brokenhearted when they hear about that. I saw one of them hittin' on her the other day."

Enzo closed his eyes as the eyebrow pencil was lightly applied. Louis's conversations continued whether there was an audience or not.

"Of course, with the stage crew it doesn't matter if she's married or not. Those guys will stick their weenies through a wedding ring like they're old pros at it." Louis found this idea quite funny, and so he continued on that train of thought.

"And knowing those guys, if men had tits on their backs, they wouldn't be safe from those bastards either."

Louis fell back into laughter and Enzo politely smiled, not ready for the raunch of this overpowering friend. Louis sensed the man's demeanor.

"Sorry, baby," his gravely voice apologized. "I know you got an opera to sing."

"It's not that, Louis." Enzo sighed. "I've got a lot on my mind, and opera is the least of all my thoughts right now."

Louis nodded, unknowing, but still feeling Enzo's discomfort. He grabbed the shoulder of the tenor and gave it a gentle squeeze.

"I'll leave you alone, baby," he said shyly, "and I'll keep a good thought for ya." Louis patted his friend on the cheek as he always did when he finished with a makeup job, and left the tenor to himself.

The artifice, the production, the false faces that surrounded him, the whole of the opera was not welcome tonight. The superficiality of the self-important, the swagger of the conductor, the superiority of the strings, the neurotic woodwinds, the easy-going brass section, they all were distractions.

The friends he loved—Louis, the wig and makeup workers, the chorus, his dresser Jeff Mallory, the security guards—these people were his friends. They were real people who happened to work in opera, but he could not express his pain, he could not release his emotions to them.

Like the devious magician, not allowing the audience to see what was behind the curtain, Enzo hid his heartbreak, silencing himself to the friends that would help, but who could not.

He was sweating profusely and he dabbed his face with the paper towels on the sink before him. Makeup pulled from his face under the abrasive pressure. He stood and paced within his dressing room, still locked from the inside.

"Ten minutes 'til places, please," the opera intercom barked to the performers. Gary Moore said again to those not listening the first time. "Ten minutes to the top of Act I, *Tosca*."

The time was now upon him. The opera was about to begin.

Enzo had grown to love these moments on the cusp of a performance; the excitement in his head, the butterflies in his stomach, the energy of the orchestra, the flurry of the crews putting the final touches on artistic reality. All this was unity in an art form that was seen as selfish and grandiose, when in actuality it was an intricate process involving thousands of different parts. He had always been happy to work with such giving and sharing people.

But tonight was torture. Every word he spoke, every fan he ignored, every movement of his head, every breath he took, it all filled him with pain.

The entirety of the theatre filled his soul with anguish, for the only meaning that the whole spectacle brought into focus was the meaning of his love for Gwendolyn Silva. The emptiness of the orchestra, the sweep of the violins, the majesty of the woodwinds, the power of the brass, the crash of the cymbals, they were all naught, they were all nothing, without her love.

If he sang with the voice of Caruso, if he thrilled with the ring of Corelli, if he uttered the songs of angels, if he sang the greatest songs of mankind, the world would not know the meaning, for he did not have his love. She had been stolen away.

All that surrounded him—this great art, this great hall, this great city, and these great people, all that man would call exalted—it was oblivion in the absence of the one for whom he lived to love.

They were gone. All three cameras Demetrius had hidden on the dock were gone. He moved about, searching for his lenses with great difficulty. The arriving chorus members entered and walked by on their way to their dressing rooms. Their activity made his work more troublesome than it need be.

Every spot he had chosen was empty. The killers had found the cameras and disposed of them. Demetrius felt the shame of his situation. Had he facilitated Harris's death with sloppy detective work? He could never know for sure, but the disappearance of the cameras weighed against him.

The opera house monitor popped on.

"Five minutes to curtain," again sounded Gary Moore's voice. "Five minutes to curtain, *places* for the top of Act I, *Tosca*. Angelotti, the Sacristan, Mario, super men, everyone to places please. We are at five minutes. Thank you."

Demetrius needed to get back to Enzo. He would accompany him to the stage, stay with him in his dressing room, and attend to the needs of his friend. Right now, they must do as they were told in order to keep Gwen alive. Demetrius knew that one slight deviation from the conspirators' orders could result in Gwen's death.

Demetrius was off to the principle dressing rooms and off to protect his friend from any theatrical harm.

"Five minutes, please; Mr. Santi to stage left. Mr. Horton, Mr. Willton, and Mr. Wells, to places please. Orchestra to the pit, this is your final call, orchestra to the pit, please."

On stage the inside of the faux church was immaculate, perfect, better than perfect. It was operatically resplendent. The stage crew hustled back and forth. Several men cranked up the fog machine to blast the stage just before the curtain rose, casting a mystical glow over the proceedings within the fake church. Vast billows of white pumped out of the huge hose, filling the stage. The altars were finally perfect; every cushion, every door, each prop, from the painter's colors to the nuns' rosaries, every last detail had been set to perfection.

The performers walked from the dressing rooms out to the stage. Even backstage, the electric hum from the gathered audience crackled as the performance grew near. The singers dispersed, heading to their appointed entrance positions, finding the props due their character.

Below stage the strings were the last to weave their way into the tight confines of the orchestra pit. The last gust of nicotine was their necessary evil, dragged in the orchestra lounge forty feet away. The brass were warmed up, their lips moist and supple, ready to blast their way into the violent opening chords of the opera. It would be a busy evening for the brass, and they were happy. Puccini was their friend, writing huge tracks of dominating, aggressive music to accompany his *verismo* heroes and villains.

The woodwinds had been in the pit for fifteen minutes, honing their delicate embouchures, whittling away at their reeds, and fighting the never-ending battle to find a reed that would withstand the rigors of opera, and stay in tune. They poked and twisted, adjusting minute bands and finite embers to achieve the warm sound they desired. These were amazing musical craftspeople.

The percussion tapped and patted away at their bound kettles and strapped sticks. The members of their team were all set, their sturdy instruments placed, sticks at the ready, and so the group of five sat back telling jokes, all except for the timpanist, the king of the percussion. The timpanist sat on his swiveling stool, lightly bouncing his mallet off the covered kettle top, blowing into his pitch pipe, and pressing the instrument's pedal, adjusting to the perfect tune, the exact pitch for the opening chords of this bombastic entrance.

The librarian took care of any last minute needs within the ranks of the musicians and then stepped into the aisle at the back of the pit, arms crossed behind his back, scanning the pit for problems. There were none. He left the pit and headed to the conductor's dressing room to call the young phenom to the podium.

The conductor's podium stood tall above the orchestra, directly in the middle of pit. Along the pit's edge, a small decorative wall separated orchestra from pit, performer from audience. Several people in the prestigious first row leaned over the cushioned barrier and peered into the musical heart of the Chicago Grande Opera. The squeaks and squawks, the blows and blips, the sounds and colors that sprang upon the audience from the orchestral preparation sent vibrations into the audience. The flutter within the pit, the impending musical detonation, and the imminent dramatic proceedings gripped the audience of Chicagoans to the core of their passions. Even the opera's outcome, long known and understood, seemed in doubt as the anticipation of the great evening's performance came to its commencement.

"House lights to half," Gary Moore spoke into his microphone, alerting the performers that the time of genesis was upon them.

God had given man music, and God had lent his image in song. He had supplied beauty through portrait and convinced humanity of the infinite and eternal drama by means of the spoken word, but never had the power of music and thought, drama and tragedy, been presented so powerfully as in the union of speech and song, the creation of opera.

Again and again villains would triumph, heroes would fall, lovers would be torn apart, and tragedy would besiege the great and the good, but the divine unification of music and drama had infused the unique outcome with intense power and understanding. Opera spoke to the soul of people. Opera touched the hearts of the lover and the loved alike. It fulfilled the burning desire within man to feel genuine, unmitigated emotion. Opera brought pure love, and ultimately, life, to the greater and more intense understanding of the Midwestern citizenry, fatigued of sapped expectations and feeble existences.

The "A" from the principal oboe sounded. The orchestra, each in turn, found their home pitches, and the theatre lights were brought to black.

Fragile illumination was cast upon the bust of Puccini, high above the stage. The white marble seemed to glow as if from within. The proud composer offered his masterpiece to the people, and trusted that his *drama con la musica* would close their hearts in its grasp.

A collective gasp arose from the audience as the conductor greeted his orchestra. The young conductor, David Franciosi, stepped to the podium, the exuberant crowd offering still greater applause.

The great gold divider, the huge four-story curtain, shimmered under intensifying stage lights.

The conductor received his applause, then turned to his friends and his enemies within the pit, lifting his right arm quietly, white baton growing from his hand, and with the huge uplift of his body and arms the orchestra launched into Scarpia's theme, the unifying element in Puccini's *Tosca*.

The brass took over, punishing the audience with the violent and imposing theme of the night's villain, then off the orchestra flew under the waving arms of the conductor. The *vivacissimo con violenza* introduced the escaped rebel leader, Angelotti, having just fled the clutches of the hated villain.

The Sacristan would soon follow, and then Mario Cavaradossi would enter, finding contentment in his passion for the great singer and his love, Floria Tosca.

Demetrius met Enzo in the artist area just as he was walking out to the stage for his entrance. Enzo looked bad. He was sweating, pale, and he looked as if he was about to collapse into shock.

As he looked at Demetrius, Enzo felt more at ease than he had in the previous hour. His friend had not returned as appointed, and the now inevitable fear of death permeated all his thoughts of friendship and love.

"Where have you been, Demetrius?" asked the distraught friend.

"I'm sorry, Enzo. I've been checking out the house." Demetrius knew the performance was underway, so he walked to the stage with the star tenor. "I'll fill you in later, but I'm all right, and you're gonna be fine. Just relax, Enzo."

The words rumbled in Enzo's ears, but found no resonance in his soul. His head was low, his hands shook, but there were no performance butterflies in his stomach. Still, he had no control of his emotions.

The two men arrived at the backstage entrance for the painter, Mario Cavaradossi. The muffled music filtered through the set pieces, back to the two men and the myriad of supers, choristers, and stage management standing near by.

Sam Wheaton stepped over to his friend Enzo to wish him luck, per usual.

"*In bocca al lupo*, Enzo," he lisped. Enzo looked up to see from where the good luck came. Sam was there, all smiles. But then Sam got a full view of the singer and gasped.

Enzo saw the reaction to his own visage and became sick to his stomach. He flew from his friends, groping for a receptacle to use in his moment of illness. Demetrius watched his friend, frail and struggling for relief. Enzo found a waste can under the stage manager's desk and his body convulsed in expulsion.

The stage management was frantic. Their tenor had run away sick, and his entrance was only a few musical bars away. The Sacristan began to sing the "Angelus" in the production's church, just on stage, seconds before Enzo was to be on stage with him.

"Sort of a Corelli moment," remarked one of the choristers, comparing this tenor to the famously neurotic tenor.

Sympathy filled Demetrius's eyes as he watched the powerful man, the great singer, brought low by fear. He wanted to shout to those mocking the fragile man in his torment. He wanted to declare the bravery and love that this friend was showing in hopes of saving his wife.

Enzo convulsed violently over the trash can, quickly wiped his chin, and rushed to his stage entrance. He knew what he had to do. He had to sing, and no sickness or disability would stop him. If his wife needed him to sing, he would sing only for her.

He was there at his mark, and just as the Sacristan finished his sung prayer, Mario Cavaradossi, via Enzo Santi, entered, gasping, barely able to utter his first line, "*Che fai?*" "What are you doing?" to the stunned priest.

The Sacristan, sung by an old Chicago Grande Opera mainstay, James Court, looked to the young singer, and his eyes turned to saucers. Enzo would have to get used to this reaction.

The catch in Enzo's throat did not immediately clear as he started to sing the opening bars to the famous aria. The Sacristan, James, moved to his usual position, still staring at the obviously sick singer. He began cleaning the paintbrushes the singer/painter/revolutionary would use.

Enzo did not care about his performance. His head was down; drops of perspiration dripped off his face, and his stomach ached. The first line of the aria came, transported by violins sweeping through the gorgeous introduction and transforming the moment. The strings plucked their last few notes in descending *arpeggio*, and the moment to sing came.

Enzo was silent. His voice had been stolen. There was no passion to perform. There was no love to infill his thoughts as he stood before the four thousand-member audience.

Silence filled the Francis Mackay Auditorium, a silence soon vanquished by murmurs. The audience was unsettled and began to rustle in their chairs. The prompter, hidden in her little downstage box, was screaming at Enzo, "*Recondita armonia*," "Mysterious harmony."

But nothing came from the mouth of the tenor. No words emanated from the painter's mouth as he stood before his easel. Puccini was silent in the moment of panic. The prompter stopped speaking to Enzo, knowing more than poetic recollection was the problem.

The maestro, David Franciosi, instructed the orchestra to repeat the opening bars. Maybe Enzo would find himself in the extra moments of music given him.

Demetrius looked on, watching the spectacle. He watched Enzo's life falling apart before his eyes. He watched as his friend blamed himself for the danger his wife was now in, and for his lack of responsibility for his wife's safety. Enzo's pain also ached within Demetrius.

The introduction was upon the tenor again. Enzo remained still. The violins *pizzicatoed* through the final bar of introduction.

Enzo's eyes were closed, the theatre of his mind locked on Gwen. There in his head was the perfect picture of the woman he loved, and for whom he needed to sing, yet in those eternal moments there was no song. There was no Madonna in the audience to save him, and there was no wife near him to send her love.

The old woman's voice, Patricia's mother, filled his ears. "Greater love hath no man than this, that he lay down his life for his love."

"Help me, Gwen," Enzo whispered.

The aria introduction was again over. The stage management began to panic.

"Should I bring in the curtain?" Gary Moore asked no one in particular. "Damn it, he's not gonna sing. What should I do? Should I bring in the curtain?" The scramble backstage flew into a fury in just seconds, oddly opposite to the deadly quiet on stage.

Demetrius looked on, sympathetic and hurting. David Franciosi dropped his baton, arms falling to his side. It was time to close the curtain, call the understudy and start the opera again in fifteen minutes.

James Court stood from his stool, from his brush cleaning, walked over to the frozen man, and whispered into his ear.

"Enzo, its time to sing. Please sing for us."

Gwen's voice filled Enzo's ear. Her soft mezzo caressed his ear and warmed his heart. The tenor heard Gwen through the voice of this operatic priest.

The words echoed in his head again.

"Please save me!"

It would all be for Gwen. No one else mattered.

A great breath coursed through his throat, down into his lungs, and filled his body with her love, all given to him.

Recondita armonia, di bellezza diverse,
"Mysterious union, of diverse beauty,

e bruna Floria l'ardente amante mia.
and my dark-haired Tosca, she is my passionate love.

Huge sound erupted from the heart of Enzo. His eyes were still shut, closed to the audience, but the voice that had been stolen from him, the passion that had fled with the kidnapping of his wife, everything that he needed to perform, flooded back into his being.

And in the flood of real life distress, operatic artifice was washed away. Falsity was dispersed. The line between audience and performer was removed, and Enzo, impassioned in his peril, touched each heart of each audience member with the passion of his message. Enzo sang only for Gwen, but those in attendance were invited to suffer through the horror, invited to share in the immense beauty offered the world with the love of Enzo for his wife.

The conductor quickly roused the orchestra and the great ensemble met the warm luxurious sound of the tenor, stride for stride and note for note.

E te, beltade ignota, cinta di chiome bionda,
you, unknown beauty, crown of golden hair,

Tu azzurro hai l'occhio, Tosca ha l'occhio nero.
You have blue eyes, but Tosca has dark eyes.

Enzo met each vocal challenge with perfect control, but the sound that pulsed through his chords, that rang throughout the opera house, this sound was infused with romance, and in the awesomeness that poured forth there shone through the voice a tenderness. Even through the chandelier-shaking volume produced the exquisite pain Enzo felt invaded the arena. The audience was dumbstruck by the emotions that infused this tenor's singing.

The aria's end approached. Enzo slowly opened his eyes and saw nothing but bright lights. He raised his head, tears dripping, sweat mingling, and looked to the heavens in prayer.

> *Ma nel ritrar costei, il mio solo pensiero,*
> But in painting this other, my only thought,

> *ah, il mio sol pensiero sei tu, Tosca sei tu!*
> Oh, my only thought is of you, Tosca, is of you!

Enzo swept up to the great high B flat, his wife's visage in his mind, and sang the note from the core of his being. Time stopped as the reverberation wafted into the hall.

Enzo's eyes closed again as he sang to his wife, as he sang for his wife. The vibration carried, throbbing into eternity. The huge note, sung from a cannon, settled into conclusion and hung on the thought of devotion and sacrifice.

The wave of applause threw the conductor, David Franciosi, onto the podium, onto the music he had just conducted. He knew in his heart, though, that if this tenor were to sing like this the rest of the evening, he, the orchestra, and the rest of the principles would just be along for a ride of tremendous musical and emotional proportions. He could not take credit for this monumental performance. It was all within the singer before him.

The applause would not die down, and the audience would not be seated. Even the orchestra, indignant at the original foul-up, was now swept into the current of adulation. Roars came from the men and women in the audience, on their feet, servant to the gratitude springing from their trembling bodies.

Five minutes passed and finally the audience was calmed and seated.

The opera continued. Enzo was in a surreal state. His mind thought of nothing but Gwen, but his body was ruled by the emotions in which he was wrapped. Anger, hatred, love, sorrow, vengeance, and desperation filled his fiber and controlled his singing. He was not in command of his stage work right now. The Divine had grabbed him and now spoke through him in his ultimate hour of need.

Yet as he sang, the tremendous irony panged in him. In the moment of greatest despair, and at the instant when opera meant nothing to him, his voice and his art were triumphing, rising to heights never before conceived, even by the all-time great singers.

Opera was nothing, life was nothing in these moments, and so all abandon could be cast upon them, but life and love were found through Gwen, and she would be the one person that dictated all action, even up to his final moments.

The first act continued, with Enzo scaling one vocal height after another, unthinking, undisturbed by difficulty, and unimpaired by what was around him.

The duet between him and Tosca, Valencia Armiliato, was exquisite, the woman rising to the occasion but barely keeping pace with the dispossessed Mario. He was musically perfect, and possessed dramatically.

Valencia was a bit confounded by the awesome thrill of singing with one for whom each moment was surging with passion. Again the audience exploded as Tosca left her Mario and exited the on-stage chapel. Enzo stood still after escorting his friend out and received the applause for both of them. She stood just off stage, looked back to Enzo, and blew him a kiss. He never saw it.

One more quick scene and we're done with Act I, Enzo thought. The scene commenced. Enzo sang his vow with incredible power.

La vita mi costasse, vi salverò!
If it costs my life, I will save you!
Mario vowed aid to his friend, and fugitive Angelotti,
and swore destruction to the villain, Scarpia.

Every fiber of Enzo's body swore this, not to his stage partner, not to the simple drama that took place here in this theatre, but to the one who had captivated his heart long ago, and who now captivated his every thought.

The only empty box in the house was the general director's box. William Burrows had decided he could not abide performances of opera anymore, so he had retreated to his office.

The G.D. had been sitting in his office, studying reports for the coming season, leafing through pages and trying to ignore the beauty that filled the stage by immersing himself in the business at hand.

His left hand bothered him terribly. The healing of his shattered paw had also brought with it discomfort. The itch beneath the plaster gnawed at him all day long. He picked endlessly at the cast, chipping away at the object of pain and humiliation, but he could not fully escape the production presented one hundred yards away. The performance monitor was on, sending the sounds of the opera into his office. He had wanted to hear something else—anything else. He did not want to hear the voice of Enzo Santi. He did not want to hear the voice that, in its perfect clarity and power, stabbed guilt throughout his mind.

The director was uneasy in his chair, tapping his foot, picking at the cast.

His ears perked at the silence that did not disturb the speakers. Enzo should be singing. His aria should be sung at this moment.

He heard the orchestra introduction again. Finally, that voice, the tenor who had come to him ten years ago, the young man who had grown into a great artist, was now offering his everything on the stage.

The purity of sound was too much for the director to endure. He rose and walked to the monitor volume control, its panel sunk into the wall, next to his office door.

The huge climax, the fury of passion, the love and power in the sung moment would not allow Burrows to touch the simple knob.

Burrows remembered his first opera, *Rusalka*. He was ten years old, brought to the opera by his grandmother. He did not want to go. But when the curtain drew back revealing the mystical landscape, he had been captured. He had been hostage to the wonderful beauty and power of opera. And as a ten-year-old boy he remembered feeling ashamed as he wept during the haunting "Hymn to the Moon." The lovely princess offered herself to love, in whatever form it would come. The poetry wafted the vocal line to perfection.

His grandmother assured him that life was full of love and beauty, and that it was wonderful to cry also. To cry when faced with beauty was the only true and real form of gratitude.

Burrows let his head fall to the office wall. His eyes overflowed. Again, as a child, William Burrows beheld the truth. Only now, the one who now sang had allowed truth to fill his life, and this man, Enzo Santi, cherished the joy given him with unending gratitude.

Paid for in cash, signed in his own scrawl, William Burrows' soul had become empty of love and devoid of passion. Even hope had fled from the man, from the hidden villain who had grown heartless in pursuit of power. And love would not, could never, dwell in the presence of power.

Enzo collapsed in his dressing room. Demetrius was with him every step of the way from his exit to now. He searched every area backstage, knowing death could be lurking around any corner.

Enzo fell on the chaise in his dressing room and lay out, exhausted and defeated.

"Is there anything I can do to help you, Enzo?" asked Demetrius.

"Can you get me some pasta from the cafeteria?"

"No problem." Demetrius rushed out of the dressing room, relocked the door and let Enzo have his peace.

The act had tired him. Time had become obsolete. There was no telling how each moment was divided from the next. The evening was long. The final curtain seemed days away. He just wanted to complete this evening and set to the task of finding his wife.

The entire opera house was abuzz with the anticipation generated by the stupendous first act. Enzo had never sung better and hoards of people were flocking to the dressing rooms to talk to the budding superstar.

There was a knock on the door.

"Who is it?" Enzo answered.

"It's Jeff Mallory, Enzo," responded the tenor's dresser. "How ya doin'? Can I get anything for ya?"

Enzo walked to the door and opened it, seeing the head dresser being shoved into the door from behind.

"I'm all set, Jeff," Enzo responded. Enzo turned away to close the door. Jeff squeezed into the room before the door closed.

"Enzo, I wouldn't normally bother you during a performance," Jeff apologized, "but there are several who want to talk to you."

Enzo sat back on the sofa and looked at the young man he had known for ten years.

"Jeff, I don't want to see anybody tonight," he weakly responded.

Jeff saw the fatigue in Enzo's face and acknowledged his request.

"I guess you ate your Wheaties tonight, huh?"

"Somethin' like that," Enzo said. Jeff knew something waswrong with the normally jovial tenor.

"Where's Gwen tonight?" the dresser asked. Enzo put his head down again. What would honesty hurt?

"I don't know, Jeff." The dresser did not know how to take this comment, so he let it pass and left the tenor alone.

"Remember, if you need anything, let me know."

Enzo nodded. The door opened to noisy conversation, all in praise of the once-in-a-lifetime performance taking place.

Enzo lay back on the chaise again. Act II would be easy, no real tough singing. Act II was Scarpia's act, where the villain stated his plans and forced his will upon the innocent, but for the tragic hero, vocally and dramatically, Act II was the easiest of the three.

The final act would be the test of his stamina this evening, and his final aria would be excruciating.

Enzo closed his eyes, and in the theatre of his mind, he saw again his wife. The hubbub outside disturbed his concentration, but he focused solely on her.

"Hey, you can't smoke back here," yelled Gary Moore to the new super. "Get outside if you're gonna smoke."

The dark eyes of the man glared at the stage manager. He threw down his cigarette and stepped on it. He was standing over the stage right prop table, and he rubbed his face with his left hand. The bandage stuck to the top of his hand matched his skin perfectly. It covered what was needed perfectly. It was neither too big nor too small.

He leaned on the table that was holding the props for the coming acts. He reached under the edge of the table, feeling along the front, searching for what he wanted. It was there; the first one was there and the second one just behind the first.

All he had to do was wait another forty minutes. Act II would be over soon enough. His career as supernumerary would begin in Act III, and it would end in those same moments.

He needed another smoke. He checked his watch and decided to catch a drag at his favorite spot. He walked to the grid elevator and rode up. The crews were too busy changing the scenery to notice him. He climbed up the few steps after the elevator ride, pulled his keys from his pocket and unlocked the door that led to the roof.

He could catch an undisturbed nicotine high up amid the horizon. And he could check on the one satchel of the "product" he had stored on the roof in case of emergency. It was always prudent to have a backup plan in case of problems. He smoked on the gravel roof of the Illinois State Theatre, and checked on his black satchel, his own private retirement account.

He had forty minutes before the next act. Then, in those silly soldier costumes, it would be time to work.

As the Second Act began, William Burrows crept into his box seat. There was no one else occupying the general director's parterre box. He stepped to the front of the rectangular area and took his seat. The five other lavish, upholstered chairs stayed unoccupied. He was not entertaining any special guests tonight. There was no million-dollar donor to suck up to, so he sat down to enjoy his production of *Tosca*.

The buzz around him continued, even as the lights were dimmed for the entrance of the conductor. Patrons next to him mumbled.

"I've seen every show here for the last thirty years," spoke an older woman who had indeed seen everything the CGO had to offer over that period of time, "and I'll tell you, this is the greatest performance of anything I have ever seen, *ever!*" She continued. "And that Enzo Santi is not only gorgeous, but does he have a voice? Mark my words, in another twenty years this performance will still be in people's minds."

Burrows picked at his cast, dropping white flecks of plaster upon the wine colored carpeting. Success was what he had strived for all his life, but now, success meant his continued oppression.

The Second Act triumphed as did the first, Enzo again stealing the show. His glorious "Vittoria" startled the audience. The dynamic intensity shook their bodies, providing a rush never before experienced. The tactile pounce that hit the crowd frightened them, and not until they caught their breath did excitement fill their hearts. The onslaught of applause again stopped the proceedings. Tosca and Scarpia stood on-stage in mute duet, the tenor having been hustled off-stage as the stage directions ordered.

The impact of Enzo's sound punished Burrows, throbbing in his head. How could this young man sing with such abandon, with such might? How could he lift this song of victory after all that he had been through?

The director decided he must speak with the young man. He must know from where this strength came. And he must find a way to infuse his own sagging soul with this ultimate force.

The curtain had not fully closed when the general director headed backstage to address Enzo. A trail of white plaster littered his path to the artists' dressing rooms.

Supernumerary Dressing Room

Sam was wired. He was in all his flamboyant glory, chatting and preening on this night of history. His good friend Enzo Santi was stealing the hearts of the nation with this performance, and he, Sam Wheaton, was a personal friend of the one and only tenor.

He danced around the dressing room in his soldier outfit, moving with an unseen partner, ready to guide Enzo through his third act scene.

"Oh my God," he whispered, "this night will go down in the annals, I tell you. It's simply the best night of my operatic life."

One of the wiseacre young men spoke up.

"Don't you mean anals, Sam?" A roar of bawdy humor crackled through the dressing room.

"You read my mind, bitch," Sam playfully answered.

The two new supers were ignoring the others and their gay camaraderie. They were both extremely uncomfortable.

The leader of the two men was having trouble with his leather shoulder straps. They had tangled as he fought to put on his soldier costume. Sam, always willing to help and offer his forty years of experience, galloped over to the initiate.

Sam took both his arms, now drunk with joy, and reached around the struggling man's waist from the rear. The leader did not like this one bit.

"Don't touch me, faggot!" he yelled, spinning and removing Sam's arms.

The old man in his jubilation would not relent. He took the very arms that had thrust him away, and he began dancing with the handsome new super.

The leader ripped his arm away from Sam and grabbed Sam's throat with his right hand, wrenching Sam's opposite arm with his left. The action was so quick and violent, the other men in the dressing room were caught off guard. The new super then slammed Sam into the white cinderblock wall of the dressing room.

Sam gasped for breath, his airway squelched under the grip of this man's fingers. Sam's head was pushed up as it hit the wall. He winced in pain, and several of the other men screamed in horror.

The leader quickly realized that this was not why he was there; he had another job to do.

"Listen to me, asshole," he said as he released pressure from the aged neck, "I don't want any trouble. Now just back off and you won't ever see me again, I promise."

Sam gasped for air, which was now flowing to his lungs, and slid down the wall to the floor. The rest of the men in the dressing room stood their ground, ready to fight this intruder who had threatened their friend.

The men closed in on the two new supers, not longing for a fight, but not willing to back down either. The leader of the two yelled at the room, "Just leave us the fuck alone."

The leader motioned that it was time to go. The two men grabbed the rest of their stage gear and left the supers' dressing room.

Sam lay on the floor in a heap, shaking and frightened, but apparently unhurt. Two of the younger supers looked down the hall, but the two new men had already disappeared.

"Sam, are you all right?" Several supers helped the old man to his feet.

"Eight minutes to Act III; places please," the monitor sounded. Sam shook his head and quickly recovered.

"My God, I don't want to miss my entrance." The man bounced to his feet and dashed off to his assigned operatic post.

Primo Tenore Dressing Room

Enzo roused himself from the couch. This little divan had become his refuge in the night's horrible progression. He walked over to the dressing rack that was built into the rightside door hallway. He grabbed the cloth vest he was to wear during the Third Act.

Demetrius watched Enzo retrieve his vest, but he noticed something else. On the shelf above the closet pole, Demetrius spied Enzo's bulletproof vest.

"Enzo, what are you doing?" Demetrius walked over to the vest and grabbed it from the shelf. "I told you to wear this thing *all* the time. That includes right now." Demetrius scolded the tenor, but the harsh sound did not ring true.

"Demetrius," he barely uttered, "that vest doesn't fit, and besides, I can barely sing as it is. With Gwen gone, there isn't any purpose to any of this. I'm sorry, but I can't wear the vest. It won't fit under my clothes, and I can't breathe with it on." The weary eyes pleaded with his friend. "Please, I can't."

"Wear mine, Enzo." Demetrius started to take off his jacket. Enzo stopped him.

"No, D."

"Well, at least let me try and find a bigger one, maybe in the trunk of the car." Enzo turned to his friend a final time.

"No, Demetrius. Just let me finish this opera, and then let's find Gwen." Demetrius had been overruled, and Enzo would not give in to his wishes.

"All right," Demetrius consented, "but I want you off of that stage as soon as possible."

"Fine."

There was a knock at the door. William Burrows poked his head in to the room. Enzo did not see him, but Demetrius, facing the door, excused himself and went to the door, pushing Burrows back out into the hall.

"Mr. Director, could I speak to you in private?"

Burrows heard the command and knew that the detective was not giving him an option.

"Let's step into one of the empty dressing rooms, Mr. McDiess."

The two men weaved their way, Burrows leading, and entered one of the principle dressing rooms on the woman's side of the artists' area.

The general director walked into the middle of the room and turned around. Demetrius pulled the latch from the propped open door and let the door fall into its frame.

"What can I do for you now, Mr. McDi..."

Demetrius was all over the general director, grabbing his lapels and shoving him into the dressing table. The general director grunted in assault, falling back, his head thrust towards the mirrors hung over the makeup table.

Demetrius thrust his full weight upon Burrows, clutching the G.D.'s coat, pressing the material up into the man's throat. Burrows pushed away as much as he could, but the strength of the detective had overwhelmed him. He was defenseless. His back was arched across the makeup table, his head pressed into the mirror, bright makeup lights framing his crumpled body. Demetrius was furious, and he began his aggressive conversation.

"You son of a bitch," he muttered under his breath. "Where is she?"

The general director was perplexed.

"What are you talking about?" the G.D. screamed, his eyes darting about, fearing more pain and humiliation. Demetrius did not believe the fear.

"You know what I'm talking about," he said, his voice now raised. "Where's Gwen?"

Burrows was still confused, and he was almost in tears.

"I really don't know," he winced, trying to respond, his throat pressed from Demetrius's pressure. "Enzo's Gwen?" Burrows asked.

"Yes! Where is she, you damned bastard?"

Demetrius lifted Burrows from his compromised position on the makeup table, and, throwing and pouncing at once, he cast the general director onto the dressing room chaise. The detective did not care what happened. There were to be no more games. He was going to get information from Burrows this time, whether pain was involved or not.

This evil had to end, and Burrows was the man who had allowed the demon to enter the Illinois State Theatre. He must know where the demon was now lurking.

They slammed together onto the chaise, Demetrius shoving the older man into the short padded couch.

"I'm tired of your lies and bullshit!" Demetrius cursed the coward. "Now you're gonna tell me what you know or I'm gonna beat the shit out of you."

Panic filled the general director. The eyes of the detective raged within his head. The director pushed away with his left hand, his cast crunching and cracking.

"All right, please," the director pleaded to the detective.

Demetrius eased his grip upon the man below him, but kept his dominant position, ready and willing to apply force if needed.

"I honestly didn't know about Gwen," the G.D. said, pushing himself up a bit. "I'm sorry." The general director shook his head and repeated the apology. "I didn't want anyone here to get involved. I thought this thing would be simple. They could have what they wanted, if they just gave us the ability to perform."

"It's all bullshit, isn't it?" Demetrius scornfully spoke to the man.

"No, not everything. The deal with Mexico is for the operas, they *are* helping us out."

"But these men control the opera down there too, don't they?"

"I don't know. I just know they needed the space to transport goods to the U.S., or at least that's what I came to believe." Demetrius's contempt grew by the moment.

"Your transportation is called smuggling, and they're killing people, you son of a bitch," Demetrius screamed, "and that makes you an accessory." Demetrius paused to ask a final time. "Now, why did they ask Enzo to sing tonight, and where are they keeping Gwen?"

"I don't know, really. You have to believe me." Burrows appeared sincere, but he was known for the different faces he could wear. "The only contact I have with them is through an office south of here, on Wacker. I really don't know anything else."

Demetrius needed to figure out what was available to these men.

"They have total access here, right?"

"Yes," Burrows nodded, sweat pouring off his brow.

"What about anything else the CGO has control of?"

"We rented a new warehouse down in Calumet City, on the lakefront. I guess they would have access to that too," Burrows said.

Demetrius, while not fully satisfied with the responses of the general director, knew there was no more to get from this miscreant. He raised himself from the enforced position over the G.D. and straightened his leather coat.

"Be assured, Burrows," Demetrius let his fury rage through a small, spiked voice, "if Gwen is dead, I'm comin' after you. But either way, this whole house is going down." He paused, fully disdaining the grotesque man sitting down in front of him. "You sold out the people that made you who you are, and you've sold death to the kids in this city. If I don't come for you, the people in this town are gonna want your blood." Demetrius walked to the door of the dressing room. "You better pray Gwen's alive."

Demetrius walked out of the room and stood by Enzo's door, waiting for him to emerge for his Third Act.

Burrows sat on the chaise. The heavy metal door slammed into its frame again, sealing the hallway noise away. He was desperate. He had thought he could balance the line between the CGO and the infidels, but, like any traitor, he had been caught proving loyalty to the other side, to the enemy, and now both sides wanted him silenced. He put his head in his hands and searched for answers to save himself. He could not find them.

He thought of the innocence of the woman now being held. The beautiful woman locked away, waiting what he knew to be her death. Where could she be? He asked himself over and over, but he came to no conclusions. These men were too powerful, had too many connections, and could be anywhere. It was hopeless.

Burrows thought more, sliding and shifting in the couch. And why would these men, in all their hatred of life and art, why would they make Enzo sing tonight?

"Enzo?" Demetrius opened the dressing room door and poked his head in. "Are you ready?"

Enzo stood before him, worn and weary, but ready.

"Yeah," he responded. "Is there any news from Carson?"

"No," Demetrius said. "I'm gonna use one of the house phones. The building is screwing up my cell phone."

"I'm gonna head out to the stage."

"Please wait for me, Enzo. I don't want anything to happen to you."

"I'll be all right, Demetrius. There's too many people around. Besides," Enzo said, "I'll just be on-stage."

Demetrius did not like the offer, but he accepted it. He retreated to another empty dressing room and dialed Carson Limousine Service.

Directly outside his dressing room, in the artist reception area, sat Emil Walker, the general director's assistant. He had been relieved of his duties for the evening, but he stayed to see the amazing performance. He was chatting with a few of the dressers who were also seated in the little foyer.

"Emil," Enzo spoke up, "could you come here a minute?"

The young administrator leapt from his chair, honored to help out the amazing singer and kind man.

"What can I do for you, Mr. Santi?" he asked.

"I've been calling you all evening, Mr. McDiess. All I've gotten was that damn 'out of range' signal." Demetrius was upset with himself for letting the limo service slip from his mind.

"I'm sorry, Mr. Elliott. Do you have anything?"

"Yeah, I do. The satellite service was great. They didn't tell the cops, and they activated the signal. I've got the location of the limo. Are you ready, Mr. McDiess?"

Demetrius whipped out his note pad and prepared to write.

"Yeah, I'm all set."

He jotted down the address as Michael quoted it to him.

"Great, Michael. Thank you so much."

"I'm glad I could help."

Demetrius needed to check one more thing.

"Has the vehicle been moving over the last hours, or has it been pretty stationary?"

"The service said that since I called in, it has been at that address, except for an hour early this afternoon."

"Great. Thank you again, Michael."

"Good luck, Mr. McDiess. If there's anything else I can help with, please let me know."

Demetrius was relieved to have finally gotten a break. If Gwen was there, as he suspected, maybe he, Enzo, and his friend, Detective John McGrail, could gain the advantage of surprise.

He closed his notepad and went to the stage of the Chicago Grande Opera.

The elaborate Third Act was in place, both above and below the stage. Gary Moore was speaking over his headset microphone, checking each opera department for their state of readiness.

Everything was in place. Each light had been focused, every prop positioned, each piece of stage machinery working and prepared, the supers lined up and ready stage right, and the singer, Mr. Santi, in position below, ready to begin.

"Maestro to the pit, please. Maestro to the pit." The monitors around the house rang in concert with their approach to the final act of the evening.

The orchestra was tuned, several percussionists took their places off-stage. They grabbed their mallets and stood before their chimes.

Below the stage, Enzo climbed into the prison cell, where he, as Mario Cavaradossi, had been taken to await the opera's dawn.

Demetrius stood backstage left, waiting for the twenty minutes of inspired song to begin. He would stay right where he was, waiting to take Enzo away after the performance—to find his wife. The minutes in this divine act were ticking away too slowly.

The conductor walked to the podium. Unfettered ovations fell into the pit and penetrated the walls backstage. Enzo heard the roar, but he ignored it. His job was before him. This act was tremendously difficult, and he must concentrate. He must sing with abandon, finish the evening, and then find Gwen.

The audience hushed, nervous and excited. Of the great tenor roles, the most beautiful, and most challenging, was the Third Act of Puccini's *Tosca*. Tenors had lived and died by this act. Its combination of glorious majesty, resplendent melodies, and agonizing triumph had ruined many a tenor. But for those who could withstand the difficulty of its challenge, legends were established.

The audience had heard the young Argentinean conquer every obstacle of the evening. Not only had Enzo met each vocal challenge, soaring to tremendous artistic heights, but he had filled the night with passion, pouring his heart into each word, and imbuing every phrase with ardor. His declamation of the text, his body shaking volume, his gorgeous *pianissimos*— his performance had stolen the hearts of the city. This night, buzzing in everyone's mind, would live throughout history as the night of glorious perfection at the Chicago Grande Opera.

The baton dropped and the act began. The horns blasted their majestic opening, setting the theme for the first two pages of music. The recounting of the first act love scene between Tosca and Mario swept the audience in the ultimate love shared between the two.

Flutes danced their way down parallel scales, delighting the early morning setting. In the distance, a young shepherd boy began to sing.

Backstage, one of the CGO coaches sang quietly along with the chorus boy chosen to sing the shepherd. The sweet little melody rang atop the palaces.

The curtain had revealed the roof of the Saint Angelo Castle, the prison where Mario Cavaradossi was being held. The great winged statue dominated the set. The morning light perfectly rose upon the Roman horizon. Soldiers walked about in the morning light, watching the city.

The shepherd's song rang out, greeting those henchmen, prancing about, defying the treachery held within the prison walls. The pure little voice wandered upon the air, penetrating the prison roof.

Io de sospiri, te ne rimanno tanti,
I send you sighs, there are many,

pe' quante foje ne smoveno venti
as many as the leaves blown by the wind

Tu me disprezzi io me ciaccoro;
You despise me, my heart grieves;

lampena d'oro, me fai morir!
lamp of gold, I die for you!

The sweet little melody met Enzo's ears, twenty-five feet below. He knew the words, he knew the meaning, not just in his mind, but within his heart.

"*Me fai morir!*" Enzo spoke.

The beautiful song was finished. The cue from Gary Moore was given. The orchestra moved to tumultuous strains. The strings, dominated by cellos, filled the hall with plaintive wails of love ripped from its lovers. Chimes clanged in the morning air, signaling the onset of a new day.

The great set moved skyward, the winged guardian lifting the roof of the prison. The hydraulics beneath the stage pushed the set up, and opened upon Enzo, sitting in his prison cell.

Again, the plaintive moan from the depths of the orchestra filled the room and every heart in the theatre. It was to be Mario Cavaradossi's last sunrise.

Enzo breathed and filled even the simple recitative with ardor, pleading for a moment alone to give his final farewell. The cellos met Mario in their plea; the string quartet of instruments asked the jailer for a moment of privacy and reflection.

Unico resto di mia ricchezza e questo anel.
Here is the end of my riches, this ring.

Se promettete di consegnale il mio ultimo addio, esso e vostro.
Promise to give Tosca my last farewell, and it is yours.

The jailer relented, taking the ring and leaving the poet alone with his thoughts. Enzo, as Mario, sat at the simple wooden table.

"How can I sing this?" he said to himself. "These words are too much."

Enzo looked up and saw the crowd. Then he saw the conductor leading the glorious orchestra in the introduction of his tremendous aria. Enzo looked down to draw a deep breath.

The clarinets ascended into the aria's lofty melody. The exquisite strains were joined by Enzo; with one breath, one great effort, he forced his voice into activation.

The clarinet played over the words, expressing in music the anguish of the painter, awaiting death.

E lucevan le stelle e oleazzava la terra, stridea l'uscio dell'orto.
Stars were shining, the earth perfumed, the garden gate creaked.

E un passo sfiorava la rena. Entrava ella, fragrante,
Footsteps grazed the path. She entered, all fragrant,

mi cadea fra le braccia.
she fell into my arms.

Enzo's heart fell in his chest with each word, written in passion, given as drama, but transpiring, ripping apart his own life. His only love was in each word, and he wept as he sang.

O dolci baci, o languide carezze,
O sweet kisses, o soft caresses,

The melody rose in unison with the orchestra. Enzo's voice was on the verge of collapse, yet somehow he was able to complete each phrase.

mentr'io fremente le belle forme disciogliea dai veli!
While I trembled, your beautiful form is removed from the veil!

Svani per sempre il sogno mio d'amore—
Gone forever is my dream of love—

L'ora e fuggita e muoio disperata! E muoio disperata!
The hour has fled, and I die despairing! I die despairing!

E non ho amato mai tanto la vita!
And never have I loved life so much!

The aria streamed from Enzo. The despair within his life flooded forth in song. Each breath held back the tears that welled in his eyes. Each phrase was dedicated to his wife. Each moment he lived was because of her, and her love for him.

The last phrase rose. Enzo's tremendous high "A" vibrated through every heart.

Enzo fell into tears as he descended from the devastatingly perfect phrase, falling onto the little table on which he wrote the words to Tosca, but where he pledged his life to his wife, Gwen. Sorrow overcame Enzo's operatic mask of Mario Cavaradossi.

The theatre was silent. There was no applause; there was no "bravo." The only sound came from the tenor. His sobs echoed throughout the great hall. David Franciosi put his baton to his side. The orchestra held their bows, halting their music.

The audience, so captivated by this young man, found themselves choked under the intensity of his emotion, now conveyed to them.

Demetrius stood in the wings, watching his friend completely out of control, completely lost to the love of his wife, and shattered by her disappearance.

No one—no super, no crew worker, no audience member, no orchestra player—no one wanted to shatter the exquisite pain that had been given them this night. Before them lay a man, convulsing in agony, adorning them with his being, with his essence. Those who heard held his offering in their grasp, adoring it.

The Maestro finally cleared his own choked throat and offered Enzo a quiet "bravo." With this permission, the audience flew into a rage, rising from their seats, exalting the tenor. People were weeping, shouting, applauding. An ecstatic electricity filled the arena, engulfing the whole.

The young tenor did not hear the uproar, but simply kept weeping. His eyes would not relent, drops staining his shirt and the table.

The backstage performers could not move. The ecstasy of the moment froze them in their places. Gary Moore stood at the stage manager's desk, his mouth agape, microphone at the ready, but not giving any command.

William Burrows had returned to his box all alone, and he wept. He wept for the performance, he wept for his deeds, and he wept for Enzo, forced to offer his life on the operatic stage.

The foundations of the theatre vibrated from the ovation. The stage manager finally spoke into the microphone.

"Tosca, Ms. Armiliato, to your entrance, please." The evening's Tosca, Enzo's friend Valencia Armiliato, had been ready to walk onto the stage with her "safe conduct" message from Scarpia, but she stood still in the doorway, moved by her colleague's performance.

Enzo stayed at the prison table with his head bowed. He could not celebrate. There was no reason to rejoice.

The applause finally slowed and the operatic clockwork of motion began again. Tosca entered, surprising her Mario, and told her love how she had killed the evil man, Scarpia.

Valencia was fabulous, but Enzo, head still lowered, took each phrase and squeezed every bit of dramatic tension and musical possibility from it.

The supers were lining up stage right, retrieving their rifles for the opera's concluding scene. The two outcasts stayed by themselves, away from the other men.

The leader of the two walked over to the prop table where the soldiers' rifles were lying. He reached with his right hand, picked up one of the rifles, while simultaneously ripping what had been placed under the table from its moorings. He pulled the two items, up in front of him, at the same time. In his right hand, horizontal to the prop's table, was the execution rifle, loaded with a blank round of ammunition. In his left hand, horizontal to the table and directly below the blank rifle, was another rifle. The leader slipped the rifle in his right hand back onto the table. He had the rifle he wanted and was ready for *Tosca's* final scene.

The partner also walked to the props table and manipulated the two rifles. He now also had a rifle that had been pre-set under the props table.

The duet on stage continued. The fervent lovers, ecstatic in their triumph, were prepared to escape the clutches of evil. Tosca explained their means of escape.

Ma prima, ridi amor, prima sarai fucilato per finta,
But first, laugh, my love, first you will be shot

ad armi scariche. Simulato supplizio.
By unloaded arms. A sham execution.

Al colpo, cadi. I soldati sen vanno, e noi siam salvi!
As they fire, fall. The soldiers will leave, and we are saved!

The glorious duet continued; the man and woman, rapt in love, free to escape, sang of their tremendous triumph.

Trionfal,di nova speme l'anima freme in celestial crescente ardor.
Triumphant, with new hope, the soul trembles in heavenly passion.

Ed in armonico vol gia l'anima va all'estasi d'amor
And in harmonious flight, the soul flies to the ecstasy of love.

Enzo, understanding every word, looked up for the first time, fully at the audience, and stared at the director's box. William Burrows watched as the tenor exclaimed the text, clear and true. It was Enzo's declaration of war upon Burrows and his cohorts.

Energy filled the tenor. The opera was almost over. These horrible men would contact him, and then Demetrius and he would end this nightmare and Gwen would be safe.

Enzo's eyes burned into the director, sitting in the box, trembling under the intent conveyed to him by the tenor. William Burrows knew the end was near.

"Platform, go," Gary Moore spoke into the microphone, directing the crew to send the hydraulics back down, lowering the jail cell below stage, and again revealing the roof of the Saint Angelo Castle. The men above were preparing for Mario's fake execution. And in that moment within the opera, Scarpia would have his last revenge.

"Supers ready?" A nod was given to the stage manager as the supers lined up for their firing squad positions. The two new men were last in line; they would be the soldiers farthest down stage, towards the audience.

The leader looked from side to side, put his rifle under his left arm, and ripped the flesh-colored bandage off of the back of his hand.

The tattooed red, black and yellow of the hideous beast were again revealed, only this time its appearance would not mark the beginning of detection; it would mark the end of its only witness.

Enzo and Valencia walked up the jail stairs onto the roof of the set, the roof of the operatic prison, now ready for Mario's falsified "fake" execution.

Demetrius was uneasy, pacing back and forth, thinking what they would do after the opera. They would meet McGrail in a few moments, then they would receive the needed phone call, and at last they would set off to find Gwen.

Demetrius had the address he needed. Michael Elliott had given him what he believed to be Gwen's location. He knew there was not much time. Every minute counted towards Gwen's life.

David Franciosi threw the enormous cue that set Puccini's famous execution march into motion. The percussion and strings initiated the sound in ominous chords, then the flute and woodwinds joined the melody. The forbidding roll of the bass drum accentuated the downbeats, imparting power to the state-ordered assassination.

The soldiers were cued onto the stage. The men slowly marched downstage and circled around to their line of eight. As they circled, the two amateur soldiers stared directly at the audience.

William Burrows looked at these two amateurs, cursing them in their ignorance of the great artistic events that had just been brought forth. Then he noticed the final soldier, glaring back and forth throughout the auditorium.

"They must be new," whispered the woman in the next box. "They sure aren't used to being on stage."

Burrows saw the face of the man, the last soldier in line. Then the man turned away, prepared for his stage task.

Burrows clutched his shattered hand, white plaster cupped in his undamaged one. It could not be him. It could not be the man who had broken his hand. He would not be able to gain access to the opera while it was in progress.

Burrows' aging eyes looked as closely as they could. It appeared to be him. He leaned to the woman in the box next to him.

"Can I use you binoculars just one second? Please," he urgently whispered. They were lent without hesitation.

The G.D. pulled the lenses to his eyes. The orchestra was building to its climax, brass joining the orchestral entourage.

It was him, gun in hand, preparing to fire at Enzo, just as the opera called for. But why was he here, on stage?

Burrows' mind raced frantically, searching for the answer.

Demetrius stared out onto the stage, watching Enzo climb the prison stairs to take his position, just twenty feet away. The detective leaned his frame into the ten feet of space that led directly onto the stage.

Enzo marched, head lowered again. It was an incredible sight—the stage falling into place, the crew members lifting the offstage stairways into place, the extras marching, fulfilling their role, the orchestra roaring its foreboding strains, and the singers lifting their voices to glory.

As they climbed up from the prison cell, Enzo, as Mario, walked to his stage position. His work was over. The opera was finally finished. This last moment would pass quickly and he could be off to find his wife. Fatigue lowered his head as he stood next to the stage left prison wall, waiting Scarpia's fake execution.

Valencia sang now, commenting on the final scene, giving her love, Mario, acting directions. She stood up above the tenor on the castle turret. The platform, five stone steps up, gave the woman a perfect view of the operatic proceedings.

Tosca sang of the mock execution.

Come e lunga l'attesa! Perche indugiano ancor?
How long is the waiting! Why the delay?

The rising orchestra found power and inspiration from the singers, and they played fully and richly. Demetrius watched, also happy that the evening's performance was soon to be completed.

The operatic tension grew with each building note. The Maestro swept his arms to the players, pulling long elegant lines from the core of their musical hearts.

Enzo was still, standing in his position for the final scene of the opera. All he had to do now was fall, collapse to the ground, and complete Puccini's great tragedy. Enzo looked up. He looked to his Tosca, singing as an angel above him.

"Soon, Gwen, I'll come to find you," the tenor said in his mind.

Tosca sang, bringing the moment closer still.

The two down-stage soldiers wrapped their arms around their rifles, checking the chambers again. The leader wrapped his left hand under the long barrel, propping the gun on his hand, not holding the gun, but guiding it. The backside of his left hand faced Enzo.

Tosca swept into melody.

Gia sorge il sole. Perche indugiano ancor?
Already rises the sun. Why the delay?

E una commedia, lo so, ma questo angoscia eterna pare!
It is a comedy, I know, but this anguish seems endless

Burrows searched his mind. Why would the man who injured him, and who had killed Frank Stanza, reveal himself to Enzo in this opera?

The moment approached. The great brass joined the enclave of instruments. The humongous sound again shook the building.

Burrows' head looked at the deadly man. His answer had been found.

The general director stood, helpless, choking and childlike before this, another horror.

Tosca sang.

Ecco! Apprestano l'armi—
There! The soldiers raise there rifles—

The captain of the guard raised his sword to prepare the soldiers for their shot. Enzo looked at the friend raising his hand with the sword, comforted by the familiar face. He looked down the line of soldiers, arms raised, rifles aimed, ready for their cue to execute him. One after another faces of these dedicated friends met the tenor's eye with familiarity.

Sam Wheaton winked to him. Sam was the third soldier.

It was ironic. His friend pointed this rifle at him, one who in life would never harm him.

The next to last super was unfamiliar to him. He was partially hidden under his soldier's garb.

The trumpets and trombones blasted their six huge chords, full and forceful, seeming overpowering to Enzo. He closed his eyes a moment and looked upon the last of the eight soldiers.

The artists' dressing rooms were deserted. Most of the dressers had gone to the wings of the stage to watch the historic performance. Jeff Mallory decided to clean up after his singers now, instead of waiting until later. He walked into Enzo's dressing room and looked at the rack of clothes to the right, just inside the door.

From the shelf above the costume rack, a bulletproof vest, heavy and solid, hung over the shelf's edge. Jeff pulled it from the shelf, shook it open, and knew what it was. He took a hanger and hung the vest next to Enzo's street clothes.

Tosca sang.

Come e bello il mio Mario!
How handsome is my Mario!

Again, Enzo looked at the eighth soldier. Enzo searched his mind. He knew this man. He looked more closely in the single flash of a moment. The sneer on this man's face pained Enzo. From where did he know him? The man winked, not as Sam, in friendship, but in spite and in harm.

The man whispered over the great orchestral sound.

"You're dead."

Enzo panicked. He was confused. He stared at the man.

This last soldier slowly released and regripped the barrel of his gun again. Enzo looked upon the barrel, and upon the moving left hand of this man.

There it was. Outlined in black, filled in red, and stung with yellow. There, upon this man, was the hideous mark of death, brought to Frank, and witnessed by him.

Enzo screamed out and took a step forward. He reached up to the man, pointing at him. The orchestra wailed its huge chords, swept into the onslaught by the intensity of the moment.

The sword dropped.

BANG! A horrible blast of gunfire penetrated the motionless hall.

Tosca sang.

La, Muori! Muori! Ecco un artista!
There, Die! He is such an artist!

The orchestra, swelling to greater volume, in greater threat, pounced upon Tosca's line and finished the march of death.

"No!" yelled Burrows, trying to cut through the huge brass. He was unheard.

BANG! Enzo stared at this demon, pointing to the offender and accusing this vile man of murder. But his body was thrown back. The kick of bullets and powder to his chest slammed his frame back six feet into the set wall. Enzo's head crashed in ricochet to the wall, whipped as the force of his body gave way to the hard wooden surface.

Enzo felt the heat of flying lead enter his body. He felt his own blood flow down his shirt. He stared at the man, the killer, who had now killed him.

Enzo's body slid down the wall, his arm still raised, grasping to place judgment upon the one now fleeing the stage. The blood upon his back dragged a crimson streak down the gray surface behind him.

Enzo felt consciousness leaving him as he collapsed onto the floor.

BANG! Demetrius's ears pinged with the huge blast of gunfire. It was louder than he had expected and he winced with the ignition. He looked around to the opera people who were in a similar state of agitation.

"Who the hell changed the rifle charge?" screamed the stage right assistant manager. "That shot was a lot louder than the other night."

One of the backstage technicians watched the television monitor of the stage and also spoke up.

"When did they add the blood bag to the scene?" The assistant looked to the technician and was perplexed. "I don't remember using a blood bag in the execution before now."

Demetrius listened to the comments and listened to his heart. Dread grew within his chest.

Demetrius ran to the stage. Two assistants grabbed his arms, seeing him attempting to dash past them, onto the stage.

"Hey, buddy, what the hell you doin'?" they yelled. The orchestra slowly decrescendoed from the march of death. Demetrius watched the stage, trying to see his friend only twenty feet away. A shock of black hair was all Demetrius could see around the huge set wall.

Demetrius looked for solutions. There, on the stage, two soldiers fled. The other six men, finished with their task, marched slowly off, but these two men ran off the stage, fleeing the discovery of their act.

Demetrius pulled away from the two men gripping him and bolted backstage, around the set, toward stage right, hoping to apprehend the two fleeing soldiers.

BANG!

"No!" William Burrows yelled in a weak suffocated voice.

It was too late. He watched the young tenor, Enzo Santi, slam into the set wall and slide down, reaching out to the fleeing man. Burrows ran out of his box and headed backstage.

Tosca tried to awaken her lover for their final escape. Valencia touched Enzo's shoulder and blood stained her hand. Blood had never been present before. She was startled, but she continued.

Presto su, Mario, Mario, su presto! Andiam
Quickly up, Mario, Mario, quickly! We must go!

Ah! Morto! Morto! O Mario...Morto!
Ah! Dead! Dead! Oh Mario...You are dead!

The final orchestral measures flew into motion. Tosca fled up the steps to the castle turret and turned to her hated rivals.

Demetrius ran to stage right.

"Where did they go?" Demetrius asked. Gary Moore answered, somehow knowing the question.

"Those idiot supers? They missed their exit cue and took off down the hall." Gary spoke into his stage microphone. "Ready final entrance of soldiers, ready final curtain. Go supers."

Demetrius ran to the side stage exit and looked down the hallway, just off stage right. There was no one there. The men had gone. It was too late.

Supers flocked onto the stage, Tosca's murder of Scarpia having been discovered. Demetrius looked at the fifteen men running on-stage. He ran after them.

"Wait!" screamed Gary. "You son of a bitch!" Demetrius ran up the stairs, on-stage, and straight over to his friend, slumped on the hard cold castle floor.

Tosca sang her final vow.

O Scarpia, Avanti a Dio!
O Scarpia, we shall meet before God!

The orchestra overwhelmed the hall with the opera's tragic love theme as Tosca flung herself off the castle top to her death.

"Curtain, go." Gary Moore yelled into the stage microphone.

The great gold curtain came crashing in, over the prison, over the entourage, ending the great performance of the great opera.

The curtain also closed upon Demetrius, leaning over Enzo, supporting the head of his dying friend.

"Enzo!" cried Demetrius, "Enzo, talk to me, please!" Enzo's eyes opened in exhaustion. "Hold on, Enzo. You can't die, you can't die!" The tenor's blood stained the detective's jacket. Demetrius hugged the dying man to himself.

The tenor inhaled, summoning all the strength that remained in his stricken body. The evening, the opera, and now his execution at the hands of the man who had initiated all this bloodshed; all this pain was nothing compared to the love Enzo was losing. If he must die for his wife to live, so be it. He had offered himself in his wife's stead, and his offering had been accepted.

Enzo looked up at Demetrius. Enzo was desperate, yet powerless.

"Save Gwen, Demetrius," Enzo choked as the words caught in his constricting throat. "Find her and save her."

"I will, Enzo. I promise." Enzo convulsed as the molten object sapped his life away. He spoke softly now.

"Tell Gwen I love her with all my heart..."

All the power, all the vibrance, the enormous voice, the consummate drama, all the beauty of self-sacrifice and the adoring love he offered, they all fell silent as Enzo Santi surrendered his life to an assassin's bullet.

The audience erupted, overwhelming the final forte chords of the orchestra in applause. They screamed frenzied screams, eager to greet their singers. The public was adamant, offering its gratitude to those who had selflessly given their inmost being in this superb performance.

They waited, applause never weakening. Five minutes, ten minutes… Finally, the great curtain spotlights were illuminated and the great gold curtain pulled apart. William Burrows walked onto the stage, microphone in hand, putting his hands up, silencing the raucous crowd.

As the din subsided, Burrows put the microphone to his mouth.

"Ladies and gentlemen, if you would please be seated. The performers apologize. They will be unable to receive your kind appreciation this evening."

Disappointment fell over the theatre. Burrows again silenced the great enclave. He swallowed, cleared his choked throat, and again raised the microphone to his mouth.

"There has been a terrible accident..."

Forty-Two

The evening passed slowly for Gwen. The threats to her husband hit her very hard. The cruelty of these men to force Enzo into performing seemed to no end except more torture.

As the sun set, the green glow of her trailer prison became fainter. She settled and sat, having been given more food by her captors.

Her body clock told her of the start of the opera. She worried all throughout the eve. She could picture her husband taking the stage, singing of Tosca, but directing his love to her.

She could hear the power in his voice, the passion in his drama, and the sincerity in his art. The opera played in her mind almost as perfectly as it had on the stage of the Illinois State Theatre that night.

She saw his anguish as, in the final act, as Enzo sang of his fleeting life and how, in those final moments, life was more precious to him than ever before. Gwen sang this great aria with her husband, not in its music, but with its perfect adoring sentiment.

But it was now late, and the evil eyes outside had promised horrible things. As the night progressed, Gwen found herself more in prayer. No matter what these men would do, she was forever dedicated to only one man: Enzo Santi.

She sipped on the water allowed her and used the faint warehouse light to check her store of glass, sawdust, and wood chips, still sitting in the hidden corner of the trailer doorway.

As she sipped, a gurgle rolled through her stomach. She looked at her water bottle. Could they have drugged her? Her stomach ached again, this time accompanied by a sharp pain. She doubled over to try and ease the hurt. The pressure seemed to relieve the discomfort.

The pain subsided. She put the water bottle down and would not drink any more. She would not eat anything else they gave her. They had said tonight would be the last of their plot, so she prepared herself for what was to come.

BRAD GARVIN

By her best guess it was about midnight. She was not certain, as the lonely hours she spent trapped were not a reliable indicator, but she knew the opera was over and the long night was approaching.

She decided to move to her hidden corner and wait for the horrible eyes to appear. This man had been silent for a long while, but that would not last. He would be back to claim his reward and take full advantage of his possession.

Gwen heard the two men through the walls of the trailer. They were not next to the trailer, but several yards off.

"A little longer, then she's yours," the older man said to the man who would claim her. Gwen overheard the men.

One man's footsteps approached the trailer and the familiar voice spoke to the silent man sitting, guarding Gwen.

"You can take off," said the eyes to his cohort. "I've got her the rest of the night." Gwen did not move and did not breathe. She heard a radio fading in and out of static, and finally being tuned to a station.

The metal window inched open; the creak of metal on metal pulled like nails on a blackboard. Gwen grabbed a hand full of the powdered projectile in her hand, ready to cast the debris into the man's face as the door opened.

Light streamed in the trailer as the window opened. The radio blared, held down alongside the man's body. Gwen watched the cast of light in the trailer. Finally, a shadow broke the stream of illumination. Gwen pressed into the trailer corner, averting the eyes. The voice came now, taunting and teasing.

"Gwenny?" he sang in harsh, horrible tones. "Where are you?"

He peered into the dark, searching for his captive object of lust.

"I have a surprise for you," he intoned again.

Gwen turned her head and looked towards the opening, pulling her dangling chemise back to her body.

"We'll be together soon, honey. Just listen to this."

The radio had been tuned to a twenty-four hour news station. The reporter confirmed the time as 12:30, Thursday morning. The deep resonant speaking voice began the newscast with a breaking story.

"Tragedy struck this evening at the Illinois State Theatre. While performing the role of Mario Cavaradossi, the rising young opera superstar, Enzo Santi, was shot and killed. Chicago Grande Opera General Director William Burrows has just finished speaking to reporters about this tragedy from Cook County Hospital, where doctors worked to save the life of the man, but were unable to do so. Let's go live to the press room and William Burrows."

Burrows' voice came over the radio via the press conference.

"I must sadly inform you of the death of Enzo Santi. Doctors confirm his death at 11:22 p.m.—a shot to the chest by an improperly loaded rifle. During the last scene of the opera *Tosca*, in which Mr. Santi was performing, his character, Mario Cavaradossi, is executed. Apparently, one of the rifles used in the execution was improperly loaded with its blank cartridge, and Mr. Santi was actually shot."

Reporters clamored for more information. Burrows continued.

"Police are still investigating this tragedy, so that is all I can say at this time about the investigation. I do want to extend my deepest sympathies to the friends and family of Mr. Santi. He was a great artist, a great friend, and most importantly, a giving and caring person." Burrows' voice broke as he finished his speech. "He was trained at the Chicago Grande Opera, and he was one of Chicago's own. We will miss him..." the director left the microphone. The reporter again took over the newscast.

"In tragedy at the Chicago Grande Opera tonight, Enzo Santi is killed. Mr. Santi was 38 and leaves behind his wife, Gwen, who has not yet to be reached for comment. Again, ladies and gentlemen, Enzo Santi, dead at 38."

Gwen slid down the side of the trailer, tears pouring from her soul, drenching her body. Enzo had been taken. The one intimate, spiritual love of her life had been killed in some horrible masquerade of an accident. She began to weep audibly, the pain of her loss filling her mind and being. Enzo was dead. These evil men had tortured her with the worst possible crime. They had crucified her love, murdered her lovely innocent husband.

She convulsed in torment, falling to the ground, her hand full of debris clutched in pain. Her body contracted into itself, fighting off death, pushing reality away, but the wails and sobs from this gentle woman had heard the reality. The man for whom she would gladly give her life had given his life for her. Her dear love had died, cruelly shot, unsuspecting and unaware.

"Please, dear God, no!" she cried, falling onto her knees. Her hands came to her head, mixing debris with tears. Gwen's heart felt only desolation.

The man at the little metal window delighted in the view he had. She had been hiding in the corner, but now had fallen into his sightlines. Her wails were music to him. Her screams were calls of encouragement to his decadent heart. Her body was stained with the debris of the opera, fallen into the trailer. Her silken chemise fell on her convulsing form, caressing her buttocks, and outlining her breasts.

The eyes that sought to defile her moved to see her completely, sliding to the far right of the little window. His delight at her defenselessness produced laughter in his heart. These inward chuckles soon erupted from his mouth. The volume of his incessant cackles grew with her sobs.

To his warped mind, he saw her now as depraved. She was now deprived of her love, deprived of her heart, and deprived of her senses. She was in pain, inflicted by him, and he now saw her as all the more tempting. His laughter rose.

Gwen, through her pain, through her sobs, heard his laughter, and wanted vengeance. She wanted her pain to be felt by the one who had forced death on her husband. She did not care about what happened to herself now. She wanted the men responsible for Enzo's death to feel the hurt they had caused.

She looked over at the face, still in the little window, rocking back and forth in laughter. Her tears did not ebb, but her weeping did. Gwen stood. The eyes in the window slowed in their rocking, and again peered intently, yet darkly, into the trailer. She sprang to her feet.

With one swipe of her hand Gwen threw the witch's brew of debris at the open three-inch window. She plunged her fingers through the slot, digging into the face of her tormentor. She felt his eyes and scraped her fingernails deeply, clawing at these windows to his wretched soul.

She felt the glass cut into her fingertips, the chunks of wood bumped over his flesh, and she felt his skin give way to her claws.

The man screamed in pain, blinded by the dust, shards, and wood. The fingernails drew his blood as they ripped at his face. He dropped the radio and grabbed for the fingers protruding through the little crack. He clutched at them, but they slithered away, into the safety of their imposed fiberglass den.

"You goddam bitch!" he screamed, reeling from the assault. "I'm gonna fuck the life right out of you." He stumbled backwards, temporarily blinded by the projectiles. He dug at his eyes, blinking to remove the glass. Each wink of his eyelids cut deeper into his delicate membrane.

He fell to the ground, groping for the bottle of water next to the chair on which he had been sitting. His hands fell to the side of the trailer, and he felt along the bottom edge. The water was found and doused over his face and eyes. The great portion of debris was washed away. He blinked painfully several more times and climbed to his feet, screaming with each wink from the shards and splinters.

He squinted into the metal window and saw the woman right before him, staring back.

"You're gonna die, bitch, and I'm gonna fuck your dead body!"

Gwen no longer feared for her life, for her life had already been taken from her. "Come on, you stupid bastard," she taunted her aggressor. She threw more debris at the window. The eyes turned away, avoiding the second offensive. He stared back at her, anger seeping out of his bleeding eyes and cheeks. She continued her taunt.

"You get all your women by drugging them, you bastard?" she screamed at the pervert. "Is that the only way you can get off?! You son-of-a-goddamned bitch!"

Gwen was white with rage, shrieking at the man she knew would kill her.

"If you're so tough, come on and take me. Or are you happy out there, playin' with yourself? Come on you, you murderer!"

Gwen felt the stream of assault coming out of her mouth. Her verbal barrage felt horrible, but it was the only thing with which she could provoke this man. And these were the words that she felt in her heart for this contemptible assassin.

She looked through the window at the eyes peering back at her.

"Come on, asshole!" she screamed again, her arms flailing in antagonism.

Gwen watched as the man looked down at the door. A steady stream of obscenity flowed from his mouth in response to her provocation.

"All right, bitch, you've got it!" he yelled back.

Gwen heard the "clink" of a latch, and the squeal of metal on rusted metal. The huge metal seam that sealed the two doors of the trailer cracked ajar. Light peeked in through the crack. The door was opening. The man outside unlatched a second lock and the trail of light doubled in size. With the final swing of the door handle and a thrust of the huge fiberglass door the man would be in the room for his final assault.

Gwen scrambled to grab more debris in the ridges of the fiberglass floor. Her finger found something. She grabbed it and clutched it in her right hand.

It was a thin strip of steel, the size of a ballpoint pen. It had fallen from a prop that had been loaded in this trailer. The galvanized steel rod came to a sharp tip, and Gwen held the tip out. This would now be her weapon. She would not submit to the atrocities of this man. She would plunge this makeshift knife into his evil eyes; she would thrust it into this cold soul, and she would drive it deep into his black heart.

The door creaked and started to open.

"What the hell is goin' on?" yelled another man approaching. The voice was familiar. "What the hell do you think you're doin'?" Again he yelled.

Gwen jumped over to the little window and stood watching the proceedings through the open metal slit. It was the older man who had assisted this young vile one, about to open the trailer door.

The young man turned to his partner. Blood stained his face, claw marks seeped drops down his cheeks. The old man shook his head.

"I told ya ta leave her alone. Now close that trailer up and sit down." He yelled instructions to the scarred apprentice. Gwen peered through the window, still open, and stared at the two men standing there.

"But she nearly blinded me," claimed the younger.

"I don't care what she did," came the answer. "We've got to keep her until the detective is taken care of." The older man walked to the trailer door. Gwen peered out as long as she could, taking in her surroundings, looking for possibilities, and storing the knowledge of these two faces— one old and Italian, the other bloody and scarred. She ducked down as the older man grabbed at the outside of the door and sealed the trailer again. The stream of light thinned and disappeared as her tomb was again made tight. The thin metal window was slammed shut with a whisk. She listened to the muffled voices.

"Now sit down and listen to the radio and leave her alone until you're given the word."

There was silence. Gwen listened. She heard the chair legs scratch the ground as the young one sat down.

"I'm goin' back upstairs. Just wait, kid. She'll be yours as soon as we have the tape," footsteps led the old voice away from the trailer, "and as soon as we have the detective." The steps disappeared in the distance. The metal window opened again, and the bloody young man looked in.

"He can't save you every time, Gwen, and as soon as we have your nigger friend, you're all mine." The man smacked his lips audibly, sucking a gouged stream of blood into his mouth.

"I hope you like the taste of blood, Gwen," he sneered over his smacking lips, "'cause now that you've given me a taste for it, I love it." The man laughed again and shut the metal window.

Gwen sat still in her corner. They had killed Enzo, forcing him to do what he should not, and now these men were luring Demetrius into a trap under the same pretense.

She looked down and found it difficult to pray. If the Almighty could not keep Enzo safe, how would he keep Demetrius safe?

Gwen did not know what to do. She did not know who to turn to, or who to trust. She felt forsaken in her time of need, and taunted by the power of darkness.

"Demetrius, forget about me; go to the police." Her stomach pained her again. She crouched over and tried to ease the discomfort.

"Figure it out, Demetrius. Figure it out."

Forty-Three

Demetrius had accompanied Enzo to the hospital, riding in the ambulance. Detective John McGrail was waiting outside when the ambulance pulled away from the Illinois State Theatre. The Chicago cop followed Demetrius to Cook County. Brick also followed the ambulance, at Demetrius's request.

A huge entourage had congregated at the hospital, but the only thing that anyone was able to do was to speak to the press. William Burrows, assisted by Emil Walker, delivered the news quickly.

The arts world entered a state of mourning. Enzo Santi was to carry opera into the new millennium, thrilling audiences with his beautiful voice and winning new patrons to a community dominated by older folks. But Enzo had been killed in a horrific accident at the conclusion of his most thrilling performance ever. Death in the theatre is not uncommon, but the potential snuffed out with the drop of a sword ripped a hole into the heart of Chicago, and grieved the world of artisans everywhere. Opera in Chicago would never be the same again.

Demetrius met his friend, Detective McGrail, outside the hospital emergency room twenty minutes after the ambulance arrived.

"D," spoke the cop, "if you want to call it a night, I certainly understand."

Demetrius was composed, but shaky. He declined.

"Enzo's wife is still being held, and if I can do anything to help her out, now is the time to do it."

The cop nodded.

"Did the APB come up with anything?" Demetrius continued.

The Chicago cop handed Demetrius the information he had written down. Demetrius took the paper and read the cop's information.

> Black limo, license plate
> 2BO-R2DI
> Location: Calumet City-docks

"How recent is this?" asked Demetrius.

"Hot off the presses," smiled John, betraying the tragedy of the moment.

"Let me get some stuff." Demetrius walked over to the dark blue limo that Brick had rented and opened the trunk. He pulled out his handguns and strapped the holsters on his shoulder. One gun went in his belt, the other in the shoulder strap.

"Go home, Brick. I'll call you later," Demetrius told the fine young helper. "Thanks for all your help." Demetrius shook his hand.

"But Mr. McDiess," Brick asked, "isn't there anything I can do?"

Demetrius turned to the young man, defeated.

"Enzo is dead, Brick. There's nothin' left for you to do. We're hoping to find his wife before she's dead too."

"All right, Mr. McDiess," the young man responded. "I'm sorry, Mr. McDiess," Brick offered in simple condolence.

Demetrius turned and walked to McGrail's car. His eyes were weary, his body shaken and sapped of energy. As he climbed in the passenger seat of the car he thought back to Enzo. He saw his friend lying there, blood streaming down his chest, in front of four thousand people, not one soul knowing he was truly dying.

John started the car and drove away from the hospital. Demetrius closed his eyes and again saw Enzo, with his last breath, look up at him.

"Find Gwen, D," he had choked. "Save Gwen."

The car headed south to Calumet City. He would do as Enzo asked and he would save Gwen, even at the cost of his own life.

Demetrius looked over to Detective McGrail and stared.

"What?" John asked.

"Let's just get these bastards."

John hit the gas pedal.

"You got it, D."

John drove through the city, knowing exactly where he was going. He looked over at Demetrius and felt sorry for him, one who had lost a close friend. *But now*, the cop thought, *it is time to take care of business.*

Sitting in the dark blue Town Car, Brick watched the other car pull away, whisking cop and investigator to their appointed destiny. He waited until the auto was at a distance to open his hand. There was a wad of paper. Demetrius had passed him a note.

Brick opened the small slip of white paper and read it. The short message was clear and obvious. He would wait with the car as the note said. He would not retire for the evening. He would wait in the blue Town Car.

Before Detective McGrail and Demetrius were out of sight, Emil Walker came to the blue Town Car and knocked at the window. Brick lowered the window.

"Are you Brick Youngblood?" Emil asked.

"Yessir," responded the boy.

"Start your car and be ready to do whatever I say," Emil ordered. "There isn't much time."

Forty-Four

Warehouse District
Calumet City
Chicago South Side

The detective's sedan crept through the warehouses along the docks that bordered the Great Lake. It was almost two o'clock in the morning, and not a creature was stirring. The car weaved down alleys and along huge, block-long warehouses, many abandoned due to the recession that dwelled within the economic centers of the country.

Calumet City had once been a huge hub of mighty industrial commerce. Ocean-going ships hauled iron ore to docks along this coast, all the way down the end of the lake to places like East Chicago and Gary, Indiana.

With the shake-up of the steel industry, conglomerates had swallowed small steel companies and absorbed them into their grand schemes, leaving huge tracts of industrial buildings desolate.

This is where Chicago Police Detective John McGrail and Investigator Demetrius McDiess were headed, into desolation, filth, and emptiness.

This emptiness is perfect for the men with whom we are dealing, Demetrius thought as the two men rode slowly along the access roads. *With the recession, the land and warehouse are almost free, and there is little to no activity in the area. This is the perfect isolated place to store your opera sets, to transport your smuggled merchandise, or to keep your human baggage.*

The sedan slowed as it approached the corner of one of the huge warehouses. The detective had turned off the lights of the car to increase the car's covertness.

Huge spotlights illuminated the abandoned area. The men looked across the expanse of road to the spot that the police APB had located.

There was indeed several cars parked in front of the building that they faced. Demetrius whipped out the binoculars that John had brought along.

The end car, the Black Lincoln Town Car, had the license plate of 2BO-R2DI. This warehouse was where Demetrius believed Gwen would be held captive, and where he hoped to apprehend the men behind the killings and this narcotics trade.

"You ready to head in?" Demetrius asked his friend. John nodded. "You want a vest, John?"

"No, D," he replied. "I've got my own protection." John reached into the back seat of the sedan and pulled from the floor a huge, loaded shotgun, ready to serve and protect. Demetrius eyed the double-barreled equalizer.

"That should do it," Demetrius said.

"What about you, D?" John asked his friend.

"I don't need one," Demetrius said. "It'll just get in the way."

The two men stepped out of the car and ran across the open space to the front of the warehouse. On the count of three they sprang through the small door and began their sweep of the colossal, almost completely desolate factory building.

Car tires crackled on the gravel of the alleyway from where the two detectives had just run. A car crept up behind the detective's sedan and parked there. The windows were dark and the occupants ready for combat. They climbed out of their vehicle and followed the two previous men into the warehouse without a sound.

The warehouse was two square city blocks long. Above Demetrius and John, three stories high, was the great machinery used to lift and position semi-trailers. It was used very little. As more sets arrived in Chicago from Mexico City, the warehouse would fill up, but as of this moment within the enormous building there sat only three fiberglass trailers. The containers were empty, their contents having been unloaded at the CGO. These were the containers that held the operas presently being performed.

Two containers sat side by side, a third sat alone at the far end of the warehouse. In front of the lone green container at the far end of the building, snuggled up to the offices to the west, a man sat guarding this huge emerald prize. He cared only for what was inside this cask.

Demetrius led the way. He and John sneaked along the first floor and came to a stairwell, halfway down the warehouse. There appeared to be offices up this flight of stairs, and since there was obviously nothing below, they would investigate above.

The old wooden stairs sagged and moaned with every step. Demetrius walked as lightly as he could, but the wood would not stop its moaning. John started up the stairs, scanning the room for aggressors. All was quiet and all was black.

As they ascended the stairs, light from the outside flood lamps poured into the second-story windows, illuminating the two men. The gray of light helped their eyes, but revealed their presence to whoever was in the warehouse.

Demetrius was at the top of the stairs. John hopped up to the top and spun north, searching for problems. In front of the men was an open area, a lunchroom most likely, but to either side of this open area were offices, lined up side by side. A five-foot hallway with a wooden banister overlooked the warehouse and provided access to the rooms.

"Which way?" asked the cop.

"Let's try this way," Demetrius pointed south, above and towards the lone guarded trailer.

"What about him?" asked John, seeing the young guard, and worried about being discovered.

"I don't think he's gonna bother us," Demetrius replied. John shook his head, confused.

"Well, if he does move," whispered the cop, "I'm gonna blow him away." Demetrius nodded.

The slow walk south began. The men felt exposed. The lights from the outside were cast on them, walking down this five-foot wide hallway, just above the supposed henchman. This did not seem like the smartest way to proceed, but John went along with his friend and his friend's instincts.

Each room had four big windows in it, overlooking the warehouse. Dividing the four windows of each office was the office door. The floor no longer creaked, so the men crouched down and looked into each dark office. Their search was going slowly, but safely, and the offices seemed completely unoccupied.

Demetrius looked up, past several more offices. A faint light streamed out one of the office windows. With each step down the hallway, the voices grew stronger.

The two arrived at the office, crouched down. Demetrius glanced into the office and quickly pulled his head back again. There were four men: two fairly young, mid-thirties, one a bit older-forties, and one sitting at a desk, smoking a cigar, obviously the leader and about sixty-five.

Demetrius squatted on the floor; John pulled up next to him.

"This is it, John," Demetrius said solemnly. "You get the door, I'll go first."

"You sure, babe?"

"I'm sure." They crept under the two windows to the north of the office door. John leaned into the door, his backside pressed against it. Demetrius crouched like a cat, just to John's side, ready to pounce and capture his prey.

"On three," John said. "One, two, *three!*"

John flung the door open and Demetrius jumped into the office.

"Freeze! Nobody move!" Demetrius screamed.

With his handgun drawn, he eyed each man. His grip tightened as he slowly aimed at each man, letting them know he was in control and had them all in his sights.

The four men were crowded around the desk, talking to the boss. The two youngest were to the front, their backs turned, as Demetrius sprang through the door. The young men slowly turned towards the middle of the room and backed away from the desk.

There sat the fat old man, leaning back at this filthy desk. Next to him stood his sidekick, thick and strong, arms folded.

"Let me see your hands," Demetrius screamed at them, still bouncing from target to target with his gun, ready to fire at their slightest provocation.

The four men looked back at Demetrius. The boss eyed the men who had just busted into his meeting, and he started to laugh. The other men joined in the laughter.

Demetrius looked at their faces. What was happening? He had caught these men dead to rights. He had evidence of their conspiracy to commit murder, of the narcotics ring that they had formed, and of their intent to continue doing so, and they were laughing.

Demetrius kept his eye on each of the four men. He scanned and discriminated the scene, confused by their relaxation.

Then Demetrius heard a click from the shotgun behind him, its rounds being locked into place, ready to fire.

"Demetrius," John said, "put down your gun."

The dark car that had pulled up behind the detective's sedan was empty now. Its two occupants had entered the warehouse also, following quietly, but closely behind the previous two men. They also feared discovery, both from the man guarding the container and from the men lurking just ahead and above them. As they reached the second floor staircase, which the previous men had ascended, they slipped behind and under the stairs, hoping for a more complete, hidden approach.

Behind the front stairway and its adjoining offices they discovered a backside hallway, behind the offices, both on the first and second floors. This space was completely desolate, and more fully safeguarded their approach. They made their way down the hallway quickly and quietly, came to the end of the building, and curled around to the front of the offices. They were prepared to spring their trap.

John took Demetrius's gun and put it into his pant's waistband, sticking the muzzle down, secure. One of the young henchmen came over and searched the strong black man and pulled a videocassette from his inside jacket pocket. The man threw it to the tattooed helper standing next to the boss.

"I think this is mine," said the tattooed man to Demetrius.

Demetrius looked back to his supposed friend John.

"So, all my evidence from the opera house?" he asked the obvious question.

"I got rid of it, D," he responded. "I was still workin' on the opera house beat when these guys started their little operation. They offered me a little cut, and it paid better than bein' a cop, so I took the money and turned my head."

"Do you even know what they're doin'?" Contempt for this traitor seeped though every word. "They're selling death."

John was uncomfortable with the attitude, but he responded in classic denial.

"No, I don't know what they're doin'. They're payin' me not to know. Besides," John exonerated himself, "they're not sellin' it to my kids, babe. And, the extra money gets *my* kids into private school. They're just doin' business with scum who don't have a life anyway."

Demetrius was furious as his friend excused his treacherous crime. John tried to spin the conversation into a lighter mode.

"You unconscionable bastard," Demetrius cursed his friend.

"Enough," said the boss, puffing on the stogie. Demetrius turned to the boss and his tattooed sidekick.

"You've got your tape," declared the unarmed man. "Let the woman go."

Smiles filled the faces of the four men in control.

"She doesn't know anything, I promise you," Demetrius said.

"You know we can't take that chance, Mr. McDiess," spoke the boss, polite in this deadly transaction. Demetrius fought for time.

"There's too many people who know about your little scam, and there's too much evidence lying around. Burrows knows everything and he's going to the police."

The number one, the tattooed man, the man who shot Enzo, spoke.

"There is no more evidence. Burrows is a total imbecile and he will do whatever we say," he proudly refuted Demetrius, "and there were four people who knew about our little business who we couldn't control. You, the opera couple, and your little shit friend in the van." The evil man smiled. "He sure did glow in the dark, didn't he?"

Demetrius stared directly at the man who spoke. Demetrius was filled with righteous indignation at this man, these men, and his own friend. They had valued this life so little, and fattened themselves on the misery of others. *They all should die*, he thought, *for they have all killed the innocent. And they should face their eternal damnation in a hot fiery hell.*

"We've eliminated two of the four problems," the tattooed man continued, "and now we have in our possession the other two problems." The evil man beamed confidence. "You see, all our problems have been taken care of."

John spoke up, trying to add to the conversation.

"You've screwed everything up, Demetrius. Now our whole game plan has to change."

The boss railed at his bribed police officer.

"We're not changing a thing, you stupid ass. Why do you think we risked killing that tenor in front of four thousand people? We've got a great set-up here, and too much to lose."

The boss leaned back in his chair, confident in his decision. "Everything stays in place as it is. Besides, our partners in Mexico are counting on us keeping this outpost open." The boss continued his speech, addressing his number one. "Robert, tell the kid downstairs he can have the woman." The number one nodded.

"And McGrail, take care of your friend."

The man outside the plastic container had been quiet for a while. He played the radio for about an hour, but then turned it off as the batteries wore down. To unnerve Gwen, he would pound on the sides of the plastic container from time to time, using his chair and even his fists.

Gwen never became acclimated to the sensory horror, but at least she was grateful that he no long was leering at her. His eyes no longer tore at her and fondled her. The sliding metal window had stayed shut for several hours now, and for this small favor she was grateful.

She spent the moments thinking about her husband, about her beloved Enzo. She had been snatched away from him in the dead of night, and now he had been taken from her, in the lonely chill of this October night.

She cried deeply, pain returning to her stomach. She clenched her gut and bobbed up and down, sensorily depraved of the man who had given her hope, happiness, life, and love. Enzo was forever gone. She would never touch his sweet lips, feel his warm breath, or stroke his gentle hand again.

She had never felt this kind of encompassing pain before. Its unrelenting hollowness pulled her into its black hole of depression. How could she and her husband have been so forsaken?

Questions filled her head, while their apparent answers defeated her more. It had not rained on the just and the unjust. The wages of sin were not death. Life had raged, thunder had pounded, and the storms of turmoil had swept away the righteous, while those unrighteous had not suffered. The corrupt held to life, defying purity and purging righteousness from its midst.

Would justice ever come to these vile men? Gwen fumed, her mind racing in confusion, and her heart lost in desperation. She felt intensely alone.

Let the world go to hell, and let evil rage. All she wanted, all she loved, and all she lived for, was Enzo Santi. But, her love had been slain. What the slayer did not know, what he could not comprehend, was that in the moment Enzo Santi was slain, this assassin had slain her also. With the death of Enzo Santi came the death of Gwendolyn Silva.

Gwen was quiet, lost in her sorrow. In the stillness, she heard a creak at the far end of her prison. The chill of night had sent the container into wails as it contracted under the cool air. This little sound was nothing she had not heard before.

There was another sound, this tiny creak squealed from midway down the container. Again, a click met her ears, closer to her still. It was nothing.

The young man guarding her had not moved, but sat there, tapping his foot. He was fidgety, having been seated for an hour now. It was time to torment his captive again. His fists pounded into the plastic doors at the front of the container.

Gwen did not move. She was now acclimated to the periodic disturbances from this putrid human being.

There was another "click" from right beside her, outside the container. The creaking began to annoy Gwen. More fists pounded into the door.

"You awake, Gwenny?" asked his horrible voice. "You know you're my bitch, don't ya?"

The young man did not hear anything from within the container. He became irate. He pounded harder on the door, kicking it for added disruption. He yelled at the door, not opening the sliding metal window.

"Do I have to come in there and wake you up, honey?"

Gwen found the sliver of steel she had laid next to her. If he were to enter, she would be ready.

"I bet you miss your man right about now, don't ya?"

The young, evil-eyed man was whipping himself into a frenzy.

"I'll give you a man you'll never forget." He pounded on the door again.

Gwen heard the latches and handle of the door start to open. He was coming for her. She stood up in her corner, ready to pounce on him before he pounced upon her. The metal spike was in her hand, cocked back, ready to inflict pain.

There was another sound just outside the container, the fiberglass rumbled under the weight of being struck.

The man outside pounded on the door again, but he did not rail as he had before. The walls of the container moaned with impact, bending with each blow.

What was happening? Had the older man come to silence this young upstart?

There was a scrape on the ground outside the doors to the container. Gwen grew more fearful as the storm of noise had been suddenly silenced.

The doors scraped and rasped as they were forced open. He was coming to take her. He was coming to rape her.

"Give me strength, Enzo," she prayed to her dead husband. "Give me strength, my love."

The door opposite to her hidden corner position was pulled open. The reflection from the lights outside filled the opening. The form of a man walked into the dim shadow. The man did not speak, he was silent.

Gwen pulled back the steel spike, knowing that surprise was a vital weapon against this one. She slipped closer to the door opening. The time had come. It was time to die.

She found the thought a relief. She would be with her only love again, united in glory, and bonded in eternal peace.

The shadow grew larger as it approached the door, only now he did not shout, and he no longer railed against her.

Then the man stopped. There was no movement. All was silent. The shadow stood large in the door, but it did not enter. It stopped just outside the open fiberglass door. The man's arm moved and his head lowered.

There was a voice. Gwen heard a whisper from outside the container. She could not understand the words, but the man in shadow turned to the voice, and then quickly turned again to the open door.

Another whisper fell upon her ears, and she understood.

"Gwen?"

Then there was silence. The shadow stepped into the doorway of the container.

"Gwen, are you there?"

It was Demetrius. She heard his voice. He had come to save her. He had not given up, and he had come to free her from these captors.

The steel spike fell from her hand and she walked to the door, her eyes now full of joy. She turned to the opening and looked up to throw herself into Demetrius's arms.

"Demetrius!"

She hugged him and pulled herself to him, blinded by her wet eyes. He hugged her also, clutching her tight to his breast. The joy of salvation was theirs; they were safe in the arms of friendship.

Gwen pulled back from the embrace to thank Demetrius for saving her.

"Thank you, Demetrius..." her speech stopped as she looking upon this man.

Gwen jumped back from him, afraid of this one in shadow. She stared up at the man before her. The light streaming through the doorway cast an aura about him. What was he? Was he an angel? Her heart leapt in her chest as she staggered. She stumbled and fell to her knees before the face of this seraph.

Light streamed through the dark curls upon his head, radiance pouring from his countenance. She did not know if he were flesh or angel. She did not know if this were truth or deception. He had been taken from her and murdered. But there, just in her arms a moment ago, holding her hands, touching her face, was her husband, Enzo.

Was he alive?

There he stood, arms outstetched, welcoming her to cast off her burden and stand safe in the arms of love.

Gwen could not breathe.

"Gwen, it's me...Enzo! Don't be afraid, honey, I'm here to save you."

She could not move. She fell to the floor, sobbing, her face down before him, her tears washing his feet and her hair mingling therein.

Enzo knelt down, taking his wife's precious face in his hands and kissing her heaving lips.

"My love," he whispered in passion, "I'm here and you're safe."

Enzo took his wife in his arms, himself lost in weeping, and pulled her fragile, terror stricken body up to his.

"My love," Gwen said over and over, convulsing in sobs. "You've risen from the dead—and you've come to save me."

Gwen fell onto his shoulder, heaving in relief and love. Enzo clutched her to his breast in the most passionate embrace the two had ever shared. The bond between them had experienced death, and its foundation had not cracked. Its strength held fast. The deeds of evil men could not sever their union.

They touched one another as never before, in gratitude, in compassion, in tenderness, and in consummate, self-sacrificing adoration.

"My love, we must go," Enzo spoke through his tears. "There isn't much time."

She clung to him, glued to his chest, her heart in his hands, and his heart unified with hers.

"Please, Gwen, we must go."

She stood with him, sobbing, and stepped out of her plastic sarcophagus. Through the doorway, Gwen saw Brick Youngblood. The young man straddled a body. Below Brick was her tormentor, now unconscious. Brick had pounced upon this man, disabled him, and now stood on watch, a baseball bat in one hand and a handgun in the other.

Brick watched Gwen and Enzo step out of the container. She was unharmed. Brick continued to scan the warehouse for potential problems. All seemed quiet, except for the men in the office upstairs.

Enzo led his wife back around the outside of the huge green container, and into the backside hallway. Brick dragged the unconscious man, scratched face and bloody eyes, into the plastic container, dropped him there, and closed the doors, swinging the latch back into place. He set the man's chair upright so as to avoid suspicion from others.

Brick followed the reunited couple back around the hidden side of the container and into the backside hallway. As he hugged the container wall he looked up, saw the lit office, and heard the men arguing.

"Take care of him?" asked the Chicago cop. "What do you mean, take care of him?" The boss responded to the suddenly ignorant officer.

"You know what I mean, dumb ass," the boss snarled. John was stunned. His face screwed up in protest.

"You never said I'd have to do somethin' like this," he spoke, pleading his case. The boss's number one spoke up to the idiot cop.

"Didn't you know," he sneered, "when you make a deal with the devil, the devil always gets your soul?" The four men surrounding the desk laughed. "Now get out of here and kill this fuckin' asshole."

"I can't!" John protested further. "I'm a cop!"

Great roars of laughter came from the group of four. John's face strained to keep composure. Even Demetrius looked at his friend.

"Did you really think they were gonna let me live, John?" Demetrius asked.

The cop searched his lost soul and found nothing but a wasteland. These men wanted him to take the final steps to become one of them.

The cop looked around the room. The faces across from him, these four men, now all appeared to him as demonic. Their temptation had been so easy, so non-threatening. But now, they asked for his heart, a blood sacrifice in their dastardly fraternity. Demetrius saw the pain on his friend's face.

"If it makes you feel any better," Demetrius whispered to his deceived friend, unheard by the others, "I've known since yesterday."

John looked up at Demetrius.

"How?" John asked. Demetrius looked at his friend, clamoring for his humanity.

"Since the van blew up," Demetrius explained. "You were the only one I told about the van. And the license plate I gave you this morning, you brought me to the location of a totally different car."

John looked into Demetrius's eyes, confused.

"You brought me here, gave me this location, but I gave you a license plate to a different car. They ordered you to bring me here, and so you gave me the information necessary to get me here."

"If you knew, D," John asked, "then why did you come?" The cop searched for answers.

"I came here to distract these guys from a rescue operation." Demetrius smiled in sympathy. "I knew you would lead me here, and I knew you would turn me over to these guys, John." Demetrius paused. "But I had to rescue my friends."

John listened to Demetrius. He was sacrificing his safety for the other two people. But why? Why would he put himself into harm's way to help those around him? Demetrius could read the scared, confused man's mind, and he answered the unspoken question.

"Because I love them, John."

John looked into Demetrius's eyes. There was no hatred there. There was no contempt for the actions he had taken. There was no malice for him, the man who had betrayed a friend's trust and life for personal gain.

But there was pity. Pity for one who made the wrong choices and was sending his friend to certain death. And there was something else in those soft brown eyes, something that ate at John's tender, ignorant heart.

There was forgiveness. Demetrius was the lamb, mute and merciful, led before the men who would slaughter him.

"And John," Demetrius spoke. The officer looked up to him.

"I love *you*."

McGrail's mind was a flurry, running back and forth, trying to collect all the information his friend had just offered him. He had walked his friend into a trap, and that friend returned no malice. Instead, his friend offered him compassion.

A millstone of guilt fell upon his shoulders. He wished he had been cast into the great lake.

The Chicago detective finally shook his head and roused himself.

"O.K.," shouted the cop, "I'll get rid of him."

The boss was leery of the indecisive cop now and changed his mind.

"No, you won't," the boss spoke up.

The plump man looked at one of the two young henchmen and threw his head towards Demetrius.

"I don't trust you, McGrail," the boss said. "Tommy, you take care of him."

The strapping young man, proud to be called upon, started to walk toward John and Demetrius.

"And don't leave any traces," the boss finished.

John turned his back to the four men at the desk and faced Demetrius. He looked into his friend's brown eyes.

"Take care, Demetrius," McGrail spoke. "It was nice knowin' ya."

Demetrius looked into John's eyes. The detective's eyes met Demetrius's, then the cop looked down to his own belt. Demetrius looked at him again.

"Take your gun," John whispered.

Demetrius saw his opportunity, and, hidden by his friend's body, took the gun from John's belt. As he pulled it from his friend's belt, Demetrius looked again at John.

"I'll cover you, babe." The cop winked to his longtime friend. "And D, thanks.'"

The young wiseguy walked up to the two men. With a heave, John thrust the butt of his shotgun into the stomach of the unsuspecting man. Demetrius squatted and moved backwards to the door of the office, looking for guns from the remaining three men.

The boss ducked down, and in a flash the tattooed man, the boss's number one, threw himself over the old man and simultaneously pulled out his gun. The other young wiseguy pulled his gun out, intent on killing the cop, but John, with the element of surprise on his side, cocked and fired the huge shotgun at the young man. The man's body flew back into the corner of the office, blood spraying from his chest.

Demetrius looked to fire, but John, by turning and firing upon the one man, had blocked his sight lines.

The second young wiseguy, recovered from the blow to his stomach, pulled a gun from his shoulder strap and drew to kill John. The handgun went off and the bullet struck John in the shoulder. John reeled to the right.

Demetrius fired at the man on the floor, striking him in the chest. As he sprawled from the impact of the bullet, the man's gun flew out of his hands, landing on the floor next to the desk. The boss picked up the gun, his number one still hunched over him. The boss began to fire towards the door.

John, spun sideways from the second man's shot and with his shoulder impaired, struggled to cock his shotgun again. The huge gun finally clicked into position, and in the wink of an eye John turned to the desk.

He was hit again and flew backwards. As his body was penetrated, his shotgun discharged, the shower of metal blowing through the hung office ceiling. Styrofoam exploded from the spraying impact and cascaded into the room. The fluorescent light above rocked with the force of the blast, flickering on and off. Demetrius retreated into the hallway, firing at will, emptying his clip towards the desk.

As Demetrius ran down the hall, through the glass windows, he saw John repeatedly shot by the two men behind the desk. John screamed in pain as each molten lead charge struck his body.

The glass windows of the office shattered as the bullets headed for Demetrius. The man raced down the hallway and slid down the stairs to safety. He prayed that the other two had found Gwen. If they had not, this sacrifice would be in vain. Demetrius ran out of the building and to the waiting blue Town Car, parked behind the Chicago cop's sedan.

In the warehouse office, the two remaining men took survey of the damage. The boss pulled himself up from his hunched position, and his number one checked the two young wiseguys.

"Well, are they alive?" the boss barked at his assistant.

The man shook his head. The boss stood and walked around to the front of the desk.

Lying in the middle of the floor before them, still alive, John struggled to reach his shotgun, which had fallen to his right. He winced in pain as he desperately lurched his paralyzed body towards his lost firearm.

The assistant walked over to the traitor twice over, and as John's hand grabbed the shotgun, the assistant stepped on the gun. John's fingers were wedged under the gun and pressed into the floor by the man's weight.

The assistant looked down on the cop and aimed at the man's chest.

"You son of a bitch!"

The gun fired.

Brick drove the dark blue car into the Chicago night. The friends were reunited. Enzo and Gwen clung to one another in the back seat. Demetrius turned and hugged the two of them as best he could. There was no joy on their faces, for hell had burst into their lives and had held them in its grip. But now they were all safe, out of hell's infliction. And now, Demetrius was in a position to end the misdeeds of the Chicago Grande Opera.

Enzo looked at Demetrius.

"Your friend?" Enzo asked.

Demetrius shook his head.

"He's dead," Demetrius said, turning back to the front, "but he saved my life."

Chicago Police Detective John McGrail was dead. He had been selfish and foolhardy, yielding to evil and living life solely for personal gain. When confronted with evil, he had buckled. When offered the unholy, he ravenously partook. He had crossed over the bridge of morality and stepped into the land of regret.

But this corrupt cop had been saved. This flawed man had found truth in his friend's love. And his redemption had come at the hour of his death, in his final earthly act. He had laid down his life for his friend.

Forty-Five

Patricia was waiting for the group as they pulled into the alley. Gwen was shivering, suffering from exposure and the psychic trauma of the last few days. But she was safe!

The Latino woman brought out a blanket and wrapped Gwen in it. She helped Gwen up the stairs to her apartment, hugging her from the side opposite Enzo.

Brick was on constant watch, scanning and looking. He had let these people down once, and he would not let his guard down again. He turned his back to the stairs as the others went up, checking the alley for intruders. Everything seemed safe and quiet.

The group entered the apartment and Patricia whisked Gwen and Enzo into the bedroom. Patricia offered herself to Gwen in whatever capacity she could be of help.

"I think I'm fine," said Gwen.

Patricia took no chances, got out her medical kit and began checking the traumatized woman for physical disparities.

Enzo closed the bedroom door and walked over to his wife. He hugged her and wrapped himself around her while Patricia checked Gwen's blood pressure. It was slightly elevated, but still within normal range.

Enzo broached the subject he knew that Patricia would understand.

"Gwen, I want to ask you something."

Gwen stared to her husband, completely trusting him, fully loving him.

"They told me you were dead, Enzo," Gwen quietly uttered. "They played the radio, and the news said that you had been killed."

"I'm sorry for tormenting you, Gwen," Enzo apologized. "I didn't know what to do. They said I had to perform or they would kill you,"

Enzo looked down. "I had to, Gwen. I didn't want to, but I had to," he paused, "so that I could come back and save you."

Patricia pulled back, finished with her cursory examination.

"I'm sorry I had to put you through that, my love. I didn't know that you would be told."

Gwen shook her head and refused the apology.

"Enzo, my love, you came for me. You gave up your life for mine, and now heaven has given you back to me."

Gwen put her cut hand upon Enzo's cheek and moved her head to his. The couple shared a kiss, reuniting their hearts and consecrating their love. Enzo looked again to his wife.

"My love, I must ask this, did these men..."

"No, Enzo, they didn't. I think I'm bruised on my left side," Gwen smiled in pride, "but you rescued me before they could get their hands on me."

Patricia took over the nursing duties again and asked permission to see the bruise Gwen spoke about.

Gwen unbuttoned her torn chemise and pulled it off. Enzo looked at his wife's breast and was aghast at the black and blue marks that lined his wife's side. Patricia received permission to examine the area by touch, and slowly pressed Gwen's left breast.

Gwen winced in pain as Patricia poked and prodded, moving down her side, but the pain was not unbearable.

"To be safe we should get you x-rayed, but I think it can wait." Patricia left and got two aspirins and a tiny muscle relaxant.

"The aspirin will help the pain and the bruising, and this will help you relax."

Gwen swallowed the pills all at once, downing them with the water Patricia had brought along.

"Can I take a shower, Patricia?" Gwen remembered Patricia from the pizza parlor ten years ago.

"Of course. I'll get some towels. But after the shower, you need to sleep."

Gwen nodded.

Enzo helped his wife stand. He would not leave her now until she fell to sleep. The couple walked into the bathroom and Enzo helped Gwen finish disrobing.

"How about a bath, Gwen?" Enzo asked.

She nodded again and Enzo drew the water. It was very warm, just the way his wife liked it. As the tub filled, he caressed her, holding every inch of her that he possibly could.

"I thought I had lost you forever," Enzo said, his chin quivering, "and now I have you in my arms again. I love you, Gwendolyn Silva."

The lovers held each other in the glorious moment of gratitude. Nothing would ever tear them apart again. Time, distance, even death had stood in their way, but through Enzo's hideous death on the stage of the Chicago Grande Opera came the glorious resurrection of the man the world assumed to be dead.

Enzo helped Gwen into the tub. She relaxed into the warmth, her body shivering at its first touch of heat in several days. Enzo ran his hands over her body, cleansing his wife. He let the water cascade down her back; he softly washed her injured side, and lathered her soiled hair. Gwen lay in the bathtub, tears cascading down her face, dropping into the water. Those tears, poured out for her husband, poured out in turmoil, and offered in sacrifice, had been the holy water that wafted her prayers to heaven.

Enzo let his wife soak in the water a while, undisturbed. She whispered his name and he appeared at her side. He helped her up, dried her off, and carried her to the bed. He covered her body with the soft downy cover, then he sat next to her until sleep befell her.

Enzo kissed her forehead, stood, and closed the bedroom door behind him. He saw Demetrius standing in the main room, the remote control in his hand.

Demetrius looked at his friend. Patricia was sitting in front of the television, with Demetrius.

"Is Gwen asleep?" Patricia asked Enzo.

Enzo nodded. Demetrius looked solemnly at his friend.

"You should be in there too."

"I don't need to, Demetrius," Enzo explained. "I'm dead, remember?" Demetrius was very serious, but so was Enzo.

"The element of surprise is gone, Enzo. They know you're alive, and they're still gonna be after us."

"Who knows I'm alive, Demetrius? Only *we* know that I'm still alive." Enzo was correct. "Emil, Brick, and Patricia know, but Brick and I got into the warehouse without being seen, and Brick disabled the man guarding Gwen."

Demetrius followed Enzo's line of thought. It was true. The friends in their group were the only ones who had knowledge of Enzo's resurrection.

Enzo winced in pain, cupping his left shoulder in his right hand. Patricia stood and addressed the pain. Blood oozed from the bullet hole in Enzo's shoulder. One of the two real bullets fired at him in the execution had penetrated the fleshy lower part of his shoulder. It had passed in and out, and gave him some pain, but it did not disable him. He also did not want

Gwen to know of the bullet wound in his shoulder until this whole ordeal was over.

The bulletproof vest he had asked Emil to retrieve from the Town Car outside the State Theatre had saved his life. The one rifle shot hit directly over his heart, slamming into the kevlar, and slamming him into the opera set wall. The other shot had burned the hole in his shoulder, passing through just below the bones.

Enzo continued talking while Patricia checked the injury.

"Demetrius, I know you're going after these guys, and no matter what you say, I'm coming along. I don't need sleep, and I don't need rest."

"I have found freedom in my assassination last night. I was freed in death. It doesn't hold any sting for me," Enzo declared. "These guys, this tattooed guy, they've killed Frank and they've killed Harris, and they were gonna kill you and Gwen," Enzo explained.

"And they killed me! You said they're shipping drugs into Chicago, so who knows how many others are dying because of these guys?" Enzo's sincerity grew with each phrase.

"They need to pay for their transgressions, Demetrius, and I want to be there when justice is done."

Demetrius knew that Enzo was coming along, no matter what stood in his way.

"O.K., Enzo. When we go, you're with me."

The ride to the downtown office was an abusive one for the number one man. Neither he nor the boss was injured in the gunfire but, three men had been killed, and the opera star's wife had escaped. The boss was livid, and he harassed his number one without ceasing.

The one consolation to the evening was their possession of the surveillance videotape. With this videotape in their possession there was no hard evidence to implicate them or their associates in any wrongdoing. The entire smuggling network was still in place, and more products would continue to arrive. But two of the four snoops were still alive: the investigator and the wife. At least the tenor was dead, annihilated under the handiwork of the number one.

The number one pushed the videotape into the video player. The two men wanted to see the evidence the investigator had possessed.

The boss sat at his desk, weary and angry, the former exacerbating the latter. They had to get rid of these problems and they had to do it fast. The boss barked at his man.

"We have to pressure Burrows hard," he said. "He may know where those two are hiding. After that, it may be time to eliminate that son of a bitch!"

The office television was turned on and the videotape began to roll. Several gray lines crossed the screen, then up popped the image. The boss squinted, assuring himself that he was seeing what he thought he was seeing.

"Is this some kind of fuckin' joke?" he screamed.

A Warner Brothers cartoon began to play on the television screen.

The number one hit the fast forward button on the VCR and scrolled through the tape. He hit the "play" button again. Elmer Fudd began to sing his rendition of the famous operatic music, and Bugs Bunny appeared, fully regaled as Brunnhilde, to meet his knight in his shining, magic helmet.

They had been duped. The investigator had given them the wrong videotape.

"God damn it, fuckin' shit!" screamed the boss, slamming his fist to the desk. "You totally incompetent piece of shit! Can't you fuckin' do any fuckin little thing right, you asshole?"

The boss raised himself to the edge of his huge chair, his arms pushing up and off the desktop.

"We are up shit creek if we don't kill those fuckin' bastards, you understand me?" The boss flailed his arms in disdain at the man he now viewed as his greatest liability.

"Now get the fuck out of here and kill those sons of bitches, you little piece of dog shit!"

The number one pushed the "stop" button and turned the television and video tape player off. He pushed the rolling set of electronic equipment back into the corner from where it had originated.

The boss was right. It was time to end all this pussyfooting around and take matters into his own hands. The boss was beet red, his blood pressure raising to extreme heights, and still cursing. The continued barrage released the anger that was ruining his health.

He cursed at everything—the opera, the singers, the deal this evening, the cop who turned on them, the escaped wife, and the clever friend who had given them this cute operatic cartoon—but mostly, the stream of obscenities focused on his number one, Robert Anarino.

It was his blood lust, his incompetence those two weeks ago in the murder of that little piss ant of a props man, which had led to this cataclysm.

The boss would not move. He would stew in that chair all night, pondering this challenge from without, seeking an escape from this quagmire.

"Get me a god damn fucking drink!"

The number one walked to the bar, silently obeying, and made a drink for the boss. He walked over to the man and placed the liquor on the desk next to him. The number one opened the cigar case and cut a cigar for his boss.

The boss thought this was a good idea, but he cursed him anyway.

"Hurry up, you stupid fuck!"

The cigar was lit, and the intoxicating draw of nicotine slowed the boss's pulse. He sat back, grabbed his drink, and slugged a mouthful.

"Now get the fuck out of here," the boss ordered. "I need to think." The number one did not move from the boss's side, but wanted to stay and think through these problems with the man, his mentor. The boss would not have it.

"I said, get the fuck out of here!"

Demetrius stepped over to the little rack of videotapes Patricia had stacked next to the television and pulled a video from its colorfully painted cover. It was a Loony Tunes video box. Demetrius pushed the video into Patricia's VCR. Patricia was confused.

"What are you doing, D?" she asked quietly, not wanting to disturb the sleeping woman in the next room.

"I wanted to watch a little Bugs Bunny," he responded coyly. The tape began to roll and the henchmen appeared on the CGO's truck docks. "I gave Emil Walker a note to mail to you, Patrice," Demetrius explained. "You can ignore it now."

"What did it say?" the unsuspecting friend asked the investigator.

"The letter said that we were all dead, and to take this video tape to the FBI." Demetrius corrected himself. "Or to a cop you could trust with your life."

Enzo looked on as Demetrius revealed the treachery he had perpetrated on the mobsters.

"You never intended on giving them the tape, did you?" Enzo asked.

"No, Enzo," Demetrius said. "As you said, they're killing our kids for money, and I won't let 'em get away with it."

Enzo smiled back at the man.

"Even if it meant your own life?" Enzo asked, knowing the answer.

"Even if it meant my life," Demetrius responded.

Enzo and Patricia watched as Demetrius checked and watched, focused and examined, trying to find some clue that might tell him how to proceed.

"What are you looking for?" Enzo asked.

"This is the shipment that came in to the opera house the other night. I'm hoping that there's some clue here that will tell me what these guys are gonna do next."

"Why don't we go to the cops now?" asked Patricia. "Or the FBI?" Demetrius looked at Patricia quickly.

"I don't trust the cops right now, especially if these guys got to John."

"Why not the FBI?" Enzo continued.

"For one thing, we'd have to go into protective custody. With their investigation, *we* will be the prisoners, not these bastards," Demetrius pointed to the television screen. "And if this cartel is connected in Mexico City, then this investigation is gonna be long and arduous."

Demetrius then thought of John, the friend who had betrayed him, then given his life for him. Maybe John did not actually destroy the evidence he had given him. Maybe he had just stored it.

"What are you lookin' for on the tape, D?" Patricia asked.

"Anything peculiar, just something that will give me a hint to what they might do."

The tape rolled, the video scrolled. The product was torn out of the scenery, coffee and pellets pouring out.

"What's he doin'?" asked the observant nurse. She had noticed the leader on the docks—the tattooed man, the tuxedoed man Enzo had seen kill Frank. She had noticed him setting something aside.

Periodically, one of the henchmen would partially fill the nylon satchel, first with what was believed to be narcotics, then later, as Demetrius scrolled through the tape, several stacks of wrapped bills.

"I don't get it," Enzo said, watching with the group.

"He's takin' care of himself," Demetrius said. "He's taking his cut."

"I don't understand, either." Patricia spoke this time.

"All the other satchels are being kept together. My guess is that the one satchel is for the leader. It's his personal bag. He can do whatever he wants with it."

Brick walked into the little living room, the alley completely quiet and clear. He joined the inspectors.

"It's his 401-K distribution," Demetrius said. Brick understood, but everyone else was still confused. "He's skimming off the top and keeping all that for himself." Demetrius pointed to the black bag set off to the side of the dock. "I bet there is so much profit coming in from this operation that nobody even cares. It's his reward for being in charge of all the dirty work."

Enzo and Patricia finally understood.

Demetrius had to get on top of the situation. He had been playing defense for the last two days. Now, maybe a little offense would do some good.

There was a "coo" from the bedroom. Patricia started to get up, but Enzo walked into the bedroom to attend to his wife.

"Brick, you want to go with me?" Demetrius asked. The young man nodded enthusiastically.

"Demetrius," whispered Patricia in a harsh tone. "You told Enzo he would be involved in all this."

"He needs to stay with Gwen. You know that as well as I do," explained the investigator. "Besides, we're just gonna go sit on these guys' lair for a bit. See how badly we've upset things." Patricia still did not like the deceptive move.

"What do I tell Enzo?" she asked darkly, upset with her friend.

"Tell him the truth," Demetrius said, "or tell him nothing. He needs to be with Gwen, and he needs to stay safe. These guys are gonna be out of control now, and I need counter their moves, then stop them."

Demetrius took Patricia by the shoulders and kissed her forehead. Her arms had crossed in front of her, just as her attitude towards Demetrius had.

The two men left the apartment, got in the big blue Town Car, and started on their journey.

Gwen awakened from her short slumber and feared that Enzo was gone again. To her relief, Enzo came through the door, light once again streaming around him, the angel of deliverance that had rescued her.

She put out her hand to him, and he took it. She rolled onto her right side and pulled him onto the bed with her. He spooned into her covered body and with her arm guiding, wrapped his left arm over her side and around her waist. Gwen breathed deeply, secure in his arms. She snuggled into the pillows again.

Enzo did not say a word, but stroked her hair with his right hand. Gwen quickly fell into sleep again, wrapped in the consummate love of her husband.

Patricia peeked into the room and saw that everything was fine. The couple was quiet and serene. She closed the door without a sound and moved to the television set. Demetrius had activated the pause button on the VCR. In the picture were the henchmen, frozen, unmoving in their work. In the background was the one satchel, aside and alone, full of drugs and money. Stacks of other satchels were already full, put off to the south end of the dock.

Patricia stopped the player and turned the television off. She was unhappy with Demetrius and his decision to go find these men alone. His arrogance and ego had never gotten him into life-threatening trouble before; that was, not until last night.

Patricia ejected the videotape. If Demetrius had been killed last night, the note that would come to her in the mail would have directed her to inform the FBI with the contents of this video.

She took the video and walked to her kitchen, taking the phone book from a drawer.

"How would the FBI be listed in the phone book?" she asked herself.

She thumbed through the listings of government agencies, and found the Federal Bureau of Investigation's main phone number. She dialed the number.

What would she say? How would she get these men to take her seriously about the information that Demetrius was uncovering? She placed the receiver back on the phone cradle, unsure of how to proceed.

How could she keep her friends safe?

The boss was quiet and settled now. Robert was just leaving the office. Robert had never before seen the boss so vehement in his condemnation of anyone, especially himself. And he did not like the discipline meted out by the boss, as he had not liked it before.

The car ride to the office had been littered with insult. The private elevator ride up to their office had been a tortured rise, spiked with scorn. Indignity rolled upon indignity, affront piled upon affront. Robert received each blow in silence, graciously accepting each aggression, all the while plotting his wrath upon those who had deceived him.

He had decided what he would do while the boss railed against him within the office. He made the drink for the old man and cut the cigar for the chairman as he sat in his chair.

"Chairman" was not actually correct. The boss was a dictator. His word was law. There were no votes; there was to be no dissent. He was ruler and power, authority and king, and untimately, judge and jury to the crime family that obeyed his every word.

But whether dictator or corporate head, within this business, hostile takeover would be the only means of transposing power. Robert was next in line, poised for election, awaiting this old man's blessing, a blessing that after tonight's mishap would never come.

The boss sat quietly now in his chair, his drink cradled in his right hand. His bulbous lips, hanging off his face, were wet with the bitter alcohol of his choice. His cigar smoldered in his left hand, ashes growing as the man sat in his soft leather recliner.

There was work to be done. Robert was out the great oak doors, off to his duties, and off to correct the mistakes of recent hours. The boss did not object. The problems must be fixed. The wife and investigator must be killed, and Burrows must be addressed in a vehement manner.

The office door languidly returned to its framed home. The warm glow of the Chicago morning could be seen through the southern office windows directly behind the boss. The man did not look out onto the city.

The old man's head slumped down onto his chest as he fell to sleep. His cradled drink fell to the floor as his arm fell to his side. The cigar burned into the varnished desk, the weight of the boss's hand pushing the tobacco into the antique.

His lips were wet and beads of sweat grew cold upon his head.

The Chicago sunrise glowed bright amber behind the man, sitting silently in his favorite chair. The boss did not move. His eyes were closed, looking down upon the drops of blood seeping from his heart, soaking into his perfectly pressed white shirt.

His lips were wet with liquor; his lungs still held the inhaled smoke from his last puff of Cuban cigar. He was asleep to the world, asleep to life. The boss was as still as the grave, and soundless as the dark tomb that would soon receive him.

Forty-Six

Enzo emerged from Patricia's bedroom to an empty apartment. Demetrius was gone, Brick was gone, and Patricia was gone. Only he and Gwen were in the little home above the pizza parlor.

Where had everyone disappeared? Enzo looked about, searching for clues as to their disappearance. There was nothing in the little living room. He walked into the kitchen, lights still on, and the back door open.

There was a note on the kitchen table.

> Enzo,
> Demetrius left without you to try and end this thing.
> The young kid went with him. I have taken the videotape to the FBI,
> like Demetrius told me to do in his letter. I'll be back as soon as possible.
> If there is anything you need, please tell Mama next door. I am sure
> she is awake, so feel free to knock. Back soon.
>
> Patricia

Enzo was upset with Demetrius. He had said he would wait for him. But where could Demetrius be? What could he be looking for?

Enzo realized that everything had started at the opera house. He decided to go to the Illinois State Theatre and search for Demetrius. They had been through too much for Demetrius to go running off on his own now.

Enzo ran next door and knocked on the door to Patricia's parents' apartment. Her mother answered the door. The old woman opened the door and hugged the man for whom her prayers had been answered. Enzo received the affection, but he also needed a favor from the woman.

Spanish was the more fluent of the languages between the two people, so Enzo quickly asked the elderly woman to watch Gwen as she slept. He must look for the friends who had deserted him.

Of course she agreed. She would attend to his wife. She would keep Gwen as one of her own. Mama came straight over and Enzo grabbed a taxi to the opera house. As Gwen slept, Mama read, prayed, and cooked. The sleeping woman would need food to recover from her ordeal.

The smell of breakfast filled the apartment as Enzo left to find those who were again lost, but hopefully, safe from danger, and soon to be found.

Demetrius and Brick were both carrying guns, but they kept them concealed. They approached the office building where Demetrius had photographed the leader and his henchmen. At this early hour they might be able to access the keyed floor and take a look around the cartel's environs.

The clock was swinging up to 6:00 a.m. as they drove up to the building. The city was still drowsy, trying to find its way out of bed, so the men were quite alone on the streets and in the building. The night guard at the bank of elevators looked like he needed to get right to bed.

Demetrius did not want to mess around with getting thrown off the trail by a snoopy guard, so he only asked a simple question.

"What floor does the private elevator stop at, sir?"

"Forty-fifth," answered the guard, before thinking. Demetrius and Brick entered the elevator next to the private one. Brick added his two-cents worth.

"I just lost a bet. Thanks man." The elevator closed and the men pressed "44" on the glowing white keypad. There were no stops, no passengers other than themselves. The lifts whisked them to the forty-fourth floor.

They quickly left the elevator and walked to the emergency stairwell and up one flight to the forty-fifth floor. Demetrius knew the exit stairwell door would be locked, but he had prepared for this contingency.

He slid the metal bar into place, slipped a pick into the keyhole and pushed. The door popped open and the men were on the forty-fifth floor.

Demetrius and Brick drew their guns. They looked in opposite directions. Demetrius glanced back at Brick. The college kid was shaking, but in control.

"Brick, breathe, son—breathe. There isn't anybody up here, so relax," he reiterated, "and breathe."

Brick cleared his lungs.

"And Brick, switch the safety on your gun off. If I need ya, I want you to be ready." The men smiled at each other, both believing the guns would be unnecessary.

The hall was perfect and pristine, immaculate in appointments and spangling in its cleanliness. At the end of the hallway was a reception desk, empty for the night. On either side of the desk were huge oak doorways, bedecked with polished brass fixtures. Demetrius signaled to the young man that they would enter the office to the south.

Ever the student, Brick was curious as to the investigator's rationale. Demetrius pointed to the stream of light coming from under the door. The other office was dark.

The men walked to the door. Demetrius pushed slowly. It seemed empty. There was the smell of cigars, and another burning smell, unlike the cigar.

The door gave way to Demetrius's continued push and he peeked into the room. It was indeed lifeless. There was a smoldering paper on the desk thirty feet away, and behind the desk sat the man he had met just five hours earlier. His blood-stained shirt told of his demise.

Brick entered behind Demetrius. The huge office was smoky. Demetrius walked to the boss, sitting lifeless at the desk. He smothered the paper that had ignited from the cigar embers, filling the room with a slight haze. Brick was confused.

"What happened, Mr. McDiess?"

"There's been a coup d'etat, a violent overthrow of power. The former CEO lost favor with his workforce, and the workers forced a change." Demetrius tried to put the overthrow into the young man's language. "In this business, there is nothing but hostile takeovers. This way his successor can consolidate all his power," Demetrius pointed to the dead boss and spoke to Brick, "then he'll crush his competitors. The new man doesn't want any retiree giving advice to new lieutenants."

Demetrius walked around the desk to feel for the man's pulse, just to be sure. He was certainly dead. Demetrius looked at the old man, fat and pitiful. He had died a quick, painless death. That was not justice, he thought. Considering the people he had killed, the innocent men he had tortured, and the good people he had manipulated, why should a man like this die without enduring the pain he had inflicted on others?

Life was not equitable in all its dealings with mankind, but Demetrius believed that the future of this man would be punishment—engulfing and eternal.

The torture the boss was now enduring would surely make him wish that death, like life, were unjust as well, but he was now realizing that death was the great equalizer, respecting neither persons nor powers, and the boss would now know that damnation for some would be as vile as salvation would be joyous for others.

Demetrius left the body alone and walked back to his apprentice.

"Help me think, Brick," he ordered the young man. "What do you need when you start a business?"

The college kid thought the question obvious.

"Really?"

"Yeah," replied Demetrius.

"Well, you need a product to sell."

"What else?"

"And you need working capital. You need cash."

Demetrius pointed to his young friend.

"Right. But why do you need working capital?"

Brick looked around the room as if searching for the answer within the office.

"To pay debts, to pay employees, you need to have a little cash to guarantee the workers' efforts."

"So what is our new CEO doing right now?"

"Collecting capital?" asked Brick. Demetrius nodded as the boy continued his thoughts. "And scrounging up his product."

The men flew out of the office door, talking and thinking at the same time.

"And the last time we saw him with his capital and his product was at the opera house," Demetrius concluded.

The men hustled down the single flight of stairs and onto the elevator. Demetrius would once again go to the Illinois State Theatre. He believed somewhere within its hallowed musical walls, somewhere lurking in the crevasse between art and business, there was an enterprising evil ready to attain the throne, a throne he himself had emptied. He would ascend, annex the business, and without question he would rule with an iron fist.

Demetrius walked over to the opera house while Brick watched the comings and goings at the office building. If anything happened, he would call Demetrius immediately.

Demetrius walked in through the stage door of the opera house and went to the security office. The door was locked. Randall Scott would not be in for a least an hour.

Demetrius needed an overall view of the opera house. He still had his lock-picking kit. He decided to jimmy the lock to the monitoring office, just down the hall from the security office.

The guard watching the stage door was no problem; he was an old friend and a trusted comrade. Demetrius walked down the little hall and quickly unlocked the door to the room.

The room was warm from the constant heat of the electronic devices within. The monitors had been turned off for the night, but the cameras and recorders still captured overnight images. Management did not want to take any chances with intruders

Demetrius flipped on every switch on every monitor. The blue-gray of the eight blinked with their surge of electricity, and images spread across the screen.

One screen was nothing but snow. The tiny plaque at the bottom of the monitor identified its location: loading dock. The men running the CGO did not want anyone to capture them or their work on camera.

Demetrius sat on the little stool before the monitors. His man had to come through the stage door entrance. It was the only open entrance to the opera house this time of day. Demetrius found this monitor and watched intently. From time to time he would scan the other monitors, but only cursorily.

Half an hour passed. It was nearly 6:30. Demetrius yawned. He checked his gun several times. He ejected and reinserted the clip time after time. He finally shoved the gun back into his shoulder holster.

As he shoved, he looked across the other monitors. There was a man walking around backstage. The camera could not capture him. He was too far away. The wide lens of the back stage surveillance camera took in the entire stage from a stage right point of view.

"Damn it," the investigator cursed himself, believing he had let the man slip by the stage door entrance without seeing him. The man must have used another entrance to the opera house.

The faint nightlights increased the difficulty of identifying the man. He walked directly below the camera. His face was still hidden. He marched towards the back of the stage. He reached up and rubbed his face with his left hand. As he glanced to the left, Demetrius saw the one thing that ensured the man's identity.

The tattooed left hand showed clearly and hideously in the camera. It was him. It was the man who had killed time and time again, and who now, after eliminating his competition and his mentor, was on the cusp of ruling the narcotics traffic in Chicago.

Demetrius watched as the man walked backstage, up stage right, and into the theatre's rear corridor.

He had to follow his movements so as to locate and disable him. Demetrius looked over the bank of monitors, seeking the correct one. It was found. Demetrius watched the man disappear into the doorway that led into the corridor. He twisted his head to the next monitor—the corridor monitor—and stared, waiting for the appearance.

The man never came through the door. Demetrius was confused. His head twisted to the backstage monitor. There was nothing there. The path into the backstage corridor was clear. Again, he checked the other monitor. There was not a soul around. The clean white walls of the outer corridor were undisturbed.

What in the world had just happened? Demetrius bolted out of the room.

"Is there anything between the back stage right hallway and the corridor to the rear of the stage?" he asked the guard at the security desk.

"No," answered the guard, "just some lighting equipment." Demetrius looked more perplexed than ever. The guard added to his previous statement. "The elevator's there too."

"The elevator?"

"Yeah, the elevator up to the winches and the grid. Ya know, that's where the opera hangs the scenery, pulls it up and down. I think you can even get onto the roof from up there."

"Thanks."

Demetrius was off to stage right. His long legs strode across the empty stage and the darkened theatre. As he galloped across the stage from left to right, he looked into the darkened auditorium. Red exit lights cast an ether over the hall, and the night lights electrified the stale air.

Behind him stood the set for *Tosca*. It had not been moved so that the death of Enzo Santi, slain during last night's performance, could be investigated more thoroughly.

The open stage and darkened theatre were haunting. The buzz and colored cast shimmered off the red seats and reflected off the walls. Demons lurked in every corner. Demetrius slowed his gallop halfway across the stage. He looked up to the great set behind him. The huge seraph stood atop the great prison Castle Saint Angelo, wings spread, ready for flight, ready to mount battle, and ready for salvation. By theatrical night she had cast her protective wings over Rome, guarding and guiding the great Italian City under the throes of Scarpia.

But now, her transposed presence watched Demetrius, the good man lurking in darkness, searching for his phantom within the opera.

Demetrius walked up the stage right corridor and reached the elevator just before he got to the backstage exit door. He had to take the elevator if he were to pursue the man. He would be trapped in the elevator for the eleven floors he needed to travel, and then, when the elevator doors opened upon that darkness, they could quite possibly open upon the killer.

He had to go. The button was pressed, and the gears swung into motion. Each mechanical jolt sounded like a gong in a silent symphony, jarring all that would listen.

Demetrius stood to the side as the elevator door opened. If the lift were occupied, he hoped surprise would be on his side.

The doors slid apart. It was dark within. The elevator light had been broken.

He stepped into the nothingness. As soon as he stepped in, the doors shut, sealing the light out and trapping him within.

Blind, Demetrius felt along the elevator panel. There were eight buttons protruding from the metal face. He pressed the top button, hoping his choice would land him in proper pursuit.

The small elevator jerked into motion, pressing Demetrius down and buckling his knees.

It was the longest elevator ride he had ever taken. As the vehicle ascended, he pulled his gun from its holster, ready to use it if pounced upon. The elevator motor spun up into blackness, transporting him to heaven.

The eerie, high-pitched whine of the motor glissandoed, and Demetrius knew the elevator was coming to a stop. He again hid to the side, pressing himself against the black wall. The doors parted and the phantasmal glow again filled the hall outside the elevator. There was no one there. His exit was empty.

Demetrius held the doors of the elevator and quickly peeked into the open walkway. Both directions were dark and quiet. The elevator doors pressed against his hands and he released them. As he stepped out of the lift, its doors closed behind him.

It was unsettling. He was on the grid of the opera house, the open, catwalk-lined ceiling above the stage. It was here that all the flying mechanisms on stage had their origin. Tied to winches and anchored to motors, ropes and cables ran up, down, across, and alongside every angle. The metal slats that covered the open expanse before him gave no feeling of security. There was no possible way to fall through the slats, but when one sees no support, ones senses react despite the facts.

This was the highest opera house grid in the world, the limited side space necessitating the enormous hanging space.

Demetrius stepped onto the catwalk that lined the outer rim of the grid, feeling uneasy. He decided not to look down, only sideways, horizontally, along his own level.

He peered towards the back of the theatre. The catwalk abutted a cinderblock wall. Demetrius looked to his right, towards the front of the stage. There was a faint light that did not come from the catwalk, but from a hallway to the right.

Demetrius walked towards the light. The sound of his footsteps bothered him. He lifted and placed each foot on the metal walkway, but he could not avoid the scrape he produced with each lift. The walkway creaked under his weight.

The light grew more intense as he approached it. He again peeked around the corner, into the little hallway to the right. There was a five-foot corridor, then the hallway turned back upon itself.

Demetrius crossed the five feet with one bound, and peeked right again, around another small corridor. The concrete walls extended twenty feet and led to a five-step staircase. Light filled the hallway, pouring in through the metal door at the top of the steps. The door had been wedged open, and an open padlock was hung in the latch.

Demetrius stepped slowly up the metal staircase and looked through the slit of the open door into the faint morning light. He looked northeast into the light and saw the huge air conditioning unit that sat atop the roof. The motors hummed and the enormous fans spun, sucking in the air to cool the theatre below.

The roof was littered with cinder blocks and paper debris, blown by the mighty wind, whipping about the rooftops on this autumn morn.

Demetrius heard footsteps on the gravel roof, on the other side of the metal door. The sound traveled through the unsealed frame. Each footstep of the man scratched the stones, digging and twisting in response to their master.

Demetrius pushed the door away from the frame. It moved silently. His gun was in his right hand, ready to battle the fearsome foe ahead. He pushed the door further, slowly and silently.

He glanced to his right and saw nothing. The scrapes were to the left. Demetrius slid through the door and leaned into the wall through which he had come.

There was a clack of stones past the encased stairwell. The beast was to the left of the outer stairway wall.

The wind kicked up the detective's coat and it flapped in the breeze.

He let the door settle back into its frame. Demetrius was happy with his silent approach, and the closing door did not utter a sound as it settled into its frame.

Several more rocks clacked to the far left of the roof. The detective inched his way along the door, letting his feet touch the gravel below them, but not allowing noise.

It was time to apprehend this man, to surprise him and to prevent any more killing. The evil deeds would stop now, with his capture and his prosecution.

Demetrius breathed, just as he had told Brick to breathe. He counted to himself, "One, two, three…"

Demetrius wheeled out from behind the staircase and spun into the open roof of the Illinois State Theatre. He looked left and right, ready to yell "freeze" to the unsuspecting criminal.

There was no one there. He looked West upon the city, seeing across from him Union Station and the Northwestern Center, but there was no criminal here, only cinderblocks stacked in the corner, against the roof's retaining wall.

In the far southwest corner was a black nylon satchel, pushed up against the retaining wall.

Where could he have gone?

There was another crackle of gravel, then another. Demetrius, this strong determined man, gun drawn, ready to apprehend evil, grew frightened.

Then he saw it. From over his head Demetrius saw two pieces of stone fly through the air and crash back to the gravel roof.

"Behind me!" he shouted to himself as he jerked to turn.

"Don't fuckin' move, or I'll blow your god damn head off."

Demetrius heard a stream of gravel drop back to the roof, falling out of the hands of the man behind him. The prey had doubled back behind the stairway's outer walls and had pounced upon the hunter.

"Drop the gun, asshole!" shouted the man. Demetrius had no choice but to obey. The gun fell to the gravel. "Step out into the open roof." Demetrius stepped away from the cover of the stairway walls, onto the huge expanse of roof.

"Turn around," was the final order from the tattooed man.

Demetrius heard the shuffle of gravel as the man retrieved the gun he had just dropped.

"You son of a bitch. Won't ever give up, will ya?" the man sneered.

"Not when you're killing my friends," Demetrius replied.

The man snorted at what he found as a preposterous statement.

"Friends? You stupid fucker. People aren't worth shit. They're just a means to an end, and when they fuck up, you gotta replace 'em."

"And Frank Stanza 'fucked' up?" was Demetrius' vulgar question. The man slid Demetrius's gun into his waistband with his left hand, keeping his own gun aimed perfectly at his captive.

"It was real simple. Do your job and obey your orders. That stupid idiot went snoopin' around when he should have been takin' care of his job." The man became more irate as he spoke.

"None of these stupid fuckers would even have jobs if we hadn't come along, so they shoulda been kissin' my ass from day one."

"What did the old man do to piss you off?"

Demetrius tried to occupy the man's mind while he looked for an escape.

"Nobody slaps me around for too long without gettin' the shit kicked out of 'em. The old man was a good teacher, but it was time for new blood, and time for him to quit screwin' with me."

"I can see why the boss abused you," Demetrius said, taunting the man in his own vile language. "You are a stupid fucker!"

Immediately, the man fired his gun and struck Demetrius in the left leg. Demetrius shouted in pain and fell to the gravel. He pushed backwards, away from the assassin, but even through the searing pain, he continued his taunt.

"They're gonna be after you."

The villain stared at Demetrius, walking towards him, forcing Demetrius towards the west edge of the roof.

"You don't just kill the chairman. He's protected. The leaders are gonna want your head on a platter."

Demetrius scooted backwards, regaining his feet and limping on his good leg. The gravel scattered across the roof, and the wind whipped violently in the Chicago morning.

"You're wrong," Robert shouted over the mounting wind. "There's a new mob order, and might makes right."

Adrenaline surged through the killer's entire being. He was receiving that rush he loved, that thrill of the kill, that jolt of electricity for which he lived.

"And I am mighty," he yelled, firing the gun again at the detective, striking him in the right leg.

Demetrius yelled in pain, collapsing onto the retaining wall. The villain continued. "I have attained power," he screamed, his eyes wide and thirsty for the demise of this man, prostrate before him. "I hold the keys to life and death," he said, "and you—you are deserving of death."

The man took his gun, lifted it high into his line of sight, held his arm out straight, and aimed at Demetrius's bowed head.

Demetrius peered up at the man who was about to take his life.

"But you can't kill someone who's come back to life."

The man looked at Demetrius, understanding the words, but not comprehending the meaning. He defied the crippled Demetrius.

"Fuck you!"

The man fired the gun.

Pain buckled the arm that fired at Demetrius. The gunshot flew high into the air. A softball bat had swung down onto the man's arm, and his right side crumpled under the force. His gun flew into the air.

The villain turned to see from whence came Demetrius's salvation. The man was startled. There, before him, stood a ghost. His eyes grew larger than before, shocked at the sight. The man he had assassinated within the opera stood over him, pummeling him.

Enzo pulled the bat from the man's crippled arm and swung again, driving all his strength into the villain's chest. The head of the bat flew through the air. The villain ducked as best he could to avoid the oncoming club.

The bat struck the man across his crippled arm as he fell to the left. The bat deflected up his arm onto his brow, cracking as no "crack of a bat" should.

The villain reeled onto the gravel, rocking into a crumpled position, still looking up at Enzo.

Enzo followed his hit, pouncing on top of the man, knees to his chest, and in a final blow he whipped the fat of the bat up and across the fallen man's chin. The wood scraped up, breaking the man's chin and smashing into the villain's nose.

Enzo straddled the man, waiting for signs of life, but the man did not move. His chest still heaved in breath, but his head rested upon the gravel rooftop, blood oozing from his nose and mouth. Robert Anarino lay silent, sprawled upon the roof where he had disposed of his victims, one after another, and where he intended to dispose of Demetrius McDiess.

Enzo climbed off of the man and moved to Demetrius.

"Are you all right, Demetrius?" asked Enzo. Demetrius winced in pain.

"Yeah, I'm all right," he answered, "but these things burn like fire," referring to his wounded legs.

"Can you walk?"

"I think so." Demetrius pulled himself higher up, supported by Enzo and the retaining wall. The men looked to the west, out over the city. And the friends were silent a moment. There would be no more fury surrounding them, and no more clutching in the dark for clues. The men stood there, peering out over the beautiful city of Chicago, Enzo to Demetrius's left, and they sighed a huge breath of relief, for it was finally over.

Enzo finally took Demetrius's arm and pulled it over his head. He would carry his friend to safety.

In the flash of the moment, something slammed into Enzo from behind and arms clutched him around the waist. Enzo felt himself hoisted upward from behind and shoved into Demetrius. Demetrius fell backwards onto the gravel, for his injured legs could not steady him. He scrambled to the retaining wall, pulling his body with his arms. He reached up to the top of the retaining wall to pull himself up. Enzo turned his head to see what was happening.

This villain, this murderer, had recovered from Enzo's attack and was lifting Enzo up from the waist. And now, Robert Anarino meant to throw him over the edge of the roof, down to the Chicago River below, and once again to his death.

Enzo grabbed at the villain's arms around his waist, lifting him up. His own arms seemed useless, having been grabbed from behind. So he fought with his legs, pushing back from the retaining wall with his knees and feet, thrusting his body back onto the roof, but the man had too quickly surprised him. His legs could not get the leverage they needed to hold his body back from the precipice.

The river grew large and the retaining wall small, as Enzo found his body cresting the four feet of cinderblock. He dug in his heels, but the top of the wall had no grip. His feet slid off the edge quickly. He was going over. His mind raced to try and save himself.

Then, as Enzo fell over the edge of the wall, he twisted his body to the right, spinning and jumping up, off of the top of the retaining wall as violently as possible. His right arm, useless until now, grabbed the backside belt of the man thrusting him over the edge.

This old maneuver, remembered from his soccer playing youth, worked to perfection.

The violent twist diverted the killer's energy, and with Enzo's right arm now wrapped around the man's backside pulling the killer over with him, the killer stared over the edge of the wall as well, down upon the riverfront embankment.

Enzo screamed for strength, exerting every muscle within his body. He held to the backside of this horrible man, pulling and gripping the belt of the man who had earlier assassinated him.

In a flash of thought, Enzo knew that if he were to die again, then he would not allow this killer to go on tormenting the living and threatening the people whom he loved. He had once offered his life in sacrifice for his wife, and he would gladly offer it again, not only for his wife, Gwen, but also for his friend, Demetrius.

The killer lunged over the wall, pulled from behind by Enzo and pushed by his own diverted energy. As he tumbled over the edge, his crippled right arm reached for the twelve inches of hope at the top of the retaining wall.

Enzo threw his left arm out, praying that his injured shoulder would hold the wall and not collapse under the weight of his body.

Demetrius got to his feet and clamored to the falling men.

Enzo's left arm hooked the top of the retaining wall, as did the killer's right arm. Enzo released the grip he had kept on the man's belt, and slammed his right fist onto the top of the killer's hand.

Bones crackled under the blow as the twisting, sliding killer released the top of the retaining wall with his right hand. As his right hand gave way, his legs toppled over the edge of the wall, but the man still held on to Enzo tightly, grabbing him around the waist.

Enzo quickly grabbed at the retaining wall with his right arm. Both of his arms were hooked over the retaining wall. The killer held on to Enzo with his left arm and grabbed at his clothing with his wilting right arm.

The two bodies, twisted together, crashed into the outside of the theatre's retaining wall. Enzo screamed in pain, his arms weakening under the stress of his and the killer's combined weights.

The killer's body swung down, flopping onto Enzo's body. Robert Anarino clung to life, a life that was now dependent upon the strength of the man he had wanted to kill.

Anarino's right arm could not aid him, and his left arm, wrapped around Enzo's waist, slowly lost its grip. He slid down Enzo's body, his feet digging into the outer wall of the Illinois State Theatre. He screamed.

Enzo could not hold himself and the other man. His body jerked down under the weight, his forearms scraping into the concrete of the top of the wall. Enzo felt his grip on the inside of the retaining wall give way. His fingers slipped further to the edge. They could not hold on at this angle any longer. His fingers released. His hands and forearms slid to the outside edge of the twelve-inch retaining wall.

Enzo looked down at the man who had fallen over the wall behind him, now grappling with his legs. Anarino's hold around Enzo's waist was loosening, but Enzo's own grip was also giving way.

Enzo watched the man's left hand fall from around his waist. He watched that hideous tattoo slide down his leg, still holding to life. The hand landed on the singer's foot, digging in to Enzo's flesh, holding the foot, clutching Enzo's leg for his own life.

If this was how it was to end, then so be it. The evidence was clear, and the evidence was in hand. And this man below him would never hurt anyone again.

It was time to give his life, again. Enzo's fingers were weak. He could hold on no longer. He looked down at the villain.

"We're gonna die. Eternity is upon us. You better save your soul."

Anarino, defiant to the last, looked up at the singer and spit.

"Fuck you!"

Enzo ignored the man and looked to the heavens.

"Forgive me."

Enzo let go of the wall.

Demetrius reached up and grabbed Enzo's hands before they released the wall. Demetrius was not going to let Enzo die. He laid claim to Enzo's hands and held them with all of his might.

"I don't know if I can hold you," Demetrius screamed, looking over the edge at the two men. Enzo concentrated on keeping his fingers locked. He looked down at the killer, and Enzo offered him life.

"Climb up me," Enzo cried. "I think I can hold on."

Anarino sneered back, for still nestled in his waistband was Demetrius's gun. He hung there from Enzo's left foot, by his hideous, tattooed, left hand, groping for that gun. His crippled right hand would not grip it as he wished. But he was intent on that one thing, and Enzo watched the man struggle to pull the gun out from his waist.

"Drop the gun and climb up," Enzo screamed. Anarino refused. He held onto the gun and turned it upwards to fire upon Enzo.

Enzo watched as the man refused life, both present and eternal, and again looked toward heaven.

"Forgive me."

The gun turned upwards. Enzo's strength was gone.

Anarino pulled to fire.

With the little energy left within him, Enzo lifted his right foot and thrust his heel down onto the hideous image burned onto Anarino's left hand, this hand that gripped Enzo's left foot, that had brought death to all those around it, and that cursed the very joy of life. And that hand lost its grip.

Anarino screamed in pain, but still held fast. He moved the gun into position.

Enzo stomped into his own foot again, crushing the foul demon below his heel.

Robert Anarino screamed as his hand released Enzo's foot. And the man fell. His body tumbled down the side of the building, careening off the cinderblock wall and heading for the Chicago River.

Robert Anarino became the living embodiment of his own carnage, of his own grisly disposal, but this man's body never reached its river grave.

Twisting and screaming as he fell, the demons of hell clutching at his half-dead body, he fell headlong into the concrete river embankment behind the Illinois State Theatre. The falling force of his two hundred pounds shattered his frail shell of humanity, killing him instantly.

His corpse fractured, spilling into the Chicago River and tumbling onto the river walkway. The red and black demon burned upon the killer's hand, severed from its body at impact, toppling onto the ten feet of space behind the Illinois State Theatre.

The hand that had wielded destruction was now destroyed. The arm that had punished innocence was now paralyzed. The demon burned upon that hand no longer held any power. It lay limp, palm down, revealing its intent and its purpose.

Within the flared shield of the beast, stained in nicotine, and burned in blood, were the words, *"Lasciate ogne speranze,"*—*"*Abandon all hope." Dante's signpost above the gates of hell had been emblazoned on Robert Anarino's hand.

Anarino had found the Latin phrase fitting. He was ruler and enforcer, and those who betrayed him had indeed forsaken hope and suffered his personal wrath. But Dante's signpost was incomplete, and Anarino had been ignorant of hell's final statement. *"Lasciate ogne speranze, voi ch'intrate"*— "Abandon all hope, ye who enter here."

For years, Robert Anarino had ushered men through the gates of the damned, screaming and wailing, their cries forever silenced in the din of corruption, but now Robert Anarino walked through these very gates. And he was not ushered, but thrust into the essence of darkness.

As he entered, his soul felt the truth of the words written upon his flesh. Hope left his soul, cast off in the throws of a gruesome death, and he was immediately acquainted with the timeless tortures that would be his only and forever future.

Enzo hung by his fingertips, his strength being sapped with each second. Demetrius reached over the edge of the retaining wall and latched onto the arms of the tenor.

"Come on, Enzo, pull!" Demetrius shouted, forcing the man to lift with all his might. Enzo's shoes slipped on the brick surface of the wall, but his left foot caught on a notch.

Demetrius wedged the tenor up with the leverage in his elbows. Enzo pulled and his head appeared above the wall. He hoisted his right arm onto the rail and pushed from his shoulder. Demetrius continued pulling his friend, not about to let him misstep.

Enzo's torso scraped along the top of the wall and he rolled onto the roof of the Illinois State Theatre. Demetrius also fell over, yanking his friend to safety, unsupported by his legs, and sprawling backwards.

The men breathed heavily as they recovered from their dance with death. Demetrius was in great pain; his legs needed immediate medical attention. The men moaned as oxygen again filled their muscles, reviving their attacked limbs and clearing their cluttered minds.

But the man who had sought them out as the angel of death, seeping into their lives with unrelenting malice, was now dead. Even in his last moments of life, he remained unrepentant, unforgiving, and hideous, unwilling to ask for help, and unable to receive pardon. And just as Wormwood was rewarded for his failed earthly deceptions, so too would this man be devoured by the demons that provoked his earthly iniquities.

Robert Anarino had fallen from the heights of his depraved earthly power, and now descended into the vile hell that had created him.

Forty-Seven

Just as a house divided cannot stand, the organization built to smuggle illicit drugs to the Midwest crumbled. In the instant when Robert Anarino murdered his mentor, Anthony Guarino, he cracked the foundation of the Chicago narcotics ring, then, with his own death on the riverfront behind the Illinois State Theatre, the would-be successor doomed the covert operation.

Anarino's body was partially recovered from the queue, but divers had to submerge beneath the murky river water to recover the dismembered portions of his remains. The divers were dismayed at their findings.

Anarino's body was fully accounted for, but as the divers searched below the waves, evidence mounted and woven nylon netting revealed body part after body part. The length of the opera house was searched, and the remains of five corpses were found. The dead man was blamed for these atrocities. He held the only key to the padlocked roof, and he had the only motivation to commit such crimes.

The evidence Demetrius had collected and given to Detective John McGrail was recovered from his police desk. In addition, Demetrius's photographs of Anarino and his henchmen, Frank Stanza's loading dock photos, the surveillance video tape, and Anarino's personal cache of drugs and money recovered from the opera house roof all placed guilt upon the conspiracy within the Chicago Grande Opera. The ignition switch and pencil tip dabbed with Frank Stanza's blood again confirmed the crimes.

Patricia had notified the FBI, who, with Chicago Police Department support, immediately descended upon the CGO's new warehouse. Four dead bodies were recovered: three underlings within the syndicate, and Chicago Police Detective John McGrail. Also on the premises, huge stores of cash and narcotics were recovered. With Demetrius's statements, the Chicago police also combed the remains of his surveillance van, finding evidence of the same trigger and explosive that was used in the original opera warehouse fire almost a year ago. The cartel would soon be out of business.

The FBI took control of the investigation, rounding up those hoodlums identified in the videotape and photographs. As their house of deception crumbled around them, the rats fled the city as quickly as they could. These "not-so-wise" guys turned up in Florida and Las Vegas, but were quickly returned to Chicago for indictment.

The FBI worked with William Burrows and the Mexican government in an effort to seek out the cartel connection south of the border. Crushing the drug pipeline was a daunting task, but if the two governments could extinguish the source of the cartel within the Mexico City Opera Theatre, then ultimate eradication could occur.

The government also decided that the public should be kept in the dark about the dealings within the Chicago Grande Opera. Their continued surveillance and investigation would lead to further and more significant arrests in the ongoing "Drug War."

William Burrows was viewed as a pawn, unknowingly helping the cartel. Burrows spun fabrication after fabrication. He had believed the money granted the CGO to be legitimate; his lawyers had sworn so. The productions the CGO was receiving were legitimate and of the highest quality. He never had reason to believe there were any problems south of the border.

The feds allowed Burrows to continue his directorship of the CGO. They would be watching his finances now, and, with their discriminating governmental eye upon him, Burrows could do what he did best—run the Chicago Grande Opera. The FBI also believed Burrows' presence would leave in place a visible and significant member of the charade that had been passed off during the past twelve months. The cartel members south of the border would want this stability, but they too would be apprehended soon enough.

The drug money was so thoroughly "laundered" within the CGO that the opera company was allowed to continue using the hundred million within its coffers. The cash and drugs recovered were clearly illegal, but the money that had been laid within the CGO could not be proven illegitimate.

With all pressure relieved of him and all intimidation eradicated, William Burrows smiled as never before, sealing his personal deception deep within his heart. He did run the CGO more effectively than ever, swearing to himself, under plaster-casted arm, never to let men like those use him again.

"I was ignorant of their treachery and blind to their deception," was one of his notable quotes. "These men came to me in good faith, in apparent honesty, and I was trusting. Chicago is my home and my life. She does not deserve these men of betrayal and deception. Yes, I am guilty—guilty of ignorance, for which I hope the people of our great land will forgive me…"

But William Burrows' clean exterior would not appease the Santis or Demetrius McDiess. Upon hearing of Burrows' statement, Enzo finished his obligation to the Chicago Grande Opera through the end of the run of *Tosca*, but furious at the arrogance and continued deception, Enzo terminated all future performances with the company.

Free of terror and free of obligation, Enzo sang the final four performances of Mario Cavaradossi with a fervor that filled his soul and a confidence that had come from being refined in the fires of life. Passion filled each moment; fire from within burned through each phrase, engulfing every high note. Each show took on new, exciting vocal and emotional dimensions, thrilling the Chicagoans deep to their enormous hearts. Audiences flocked to him, cheered him, and worshipped at the feet of the operatic "god," proud to proclaim him as one of their own.

The short news conference after his final performance explained his intentions. Gwen joined him, as did an unsuspecting William Burrows. The coward snuggled up to the couple in artistic pandering.

"I regret to inform my beloved Chicago that I cannot accept any further engagements with the Chicago Grande Opera after tonight. I love this city and her people, but I cannot be associated with a company that allows deception and dishonesty to reign, even to the highest ranks.

"I am proud to say that my wife and I are becoming permanent members of this great community, and we are ecstatic to be nurtured by this great heartland, but until there are dramatic changes within the structure of this company, we must regretfully decline any offer of employment." Disappointment filled the press conference.

"Please realize, my friends, this gives me no pleasure. I love this city and look forward to raising my family here, but when elements within this opera house endanger my wife and my family, I will not tolerate this treachery.

"Thank you for your support in all my recent and unnamed trials, and until that time when the Chicago Grande Opera again belongs to the people of Chicago, I beg your understanding, and I beg your forgiveness."

Journalists speculated the performance mishap of several weeks before, nearly ending his life, was to blame for Mr. Santi's remarks. They were wrong. The city would not know the truth until the Federal investigation into the currently clandestine matter was made public.

"Mr. Santi," one arts reporter asked, "does your performance restriction include all Chicago performing arts groups, or solely the CGO?"

"I would love to sing with other groups within the Chicago area, but I cannot, and will not perform for the CGO again until changes are made. Changes from the top down. Thank you."

Enzo and Gwen walked out of the room and raced to their place of refuge.

William Burrows sat down, stunned by the revelation. Reporters pounced upon him.

"Mr. Burrows, would you like to comment on Mr. Santi's declaration of *Opera non grata* towards the CGO?"

The man pushed his face into a smile.

"We at the CGO will do whatever it takes to have Mr. Santi back in our theatre. He was bred here, and we want him to be happy here. We will do whatever it takes to make him feel at home."

Emil Walker had slipped into the back of the room and listened to Enzo declare his intentions. The young assistant lowered his head as he heard his boss weasel his way out of another jam. Emil realized that William Burrows could not be trusted, for his employer, William Burrows, was a liar and would forever remain a coward.

The best surgeons in Chicago treated Demetrius's legs. His left leg was a fairly simple bullet removal, but his right leg suffered more extensively. The bullet had gone to the man's bone. Four hours of surgery were needed to remove the bullet and insert screws to hold the shattered femur together. He would have a considerable limp for a while, but once the leg healed and the screws were removed he would be good as new.

Enzo and Gwen visited him every day, as did Patricia.

"Why did you take the tape to the FBI after I told you to ignore that letter?" asked the patient.

"I thought you were gonna get yourself killed, running out like that without any help," Patricia answered, "and I was hoping the FBI would get to the opera house and lend you a hand. I didn't think an opera singer would end up being the hero."

The two people smiled. Demetrius clasped Patricia's hand.

"Thank you."

Demetrius decided that Chicago was calling him home. Family, friends, and now a woman with whom he wanted to share life drew him back to the city, and Chicago welcomed him back with open arms and "Big Shoulders."

He could set up an investigative practice here in the city quite easily, and with his convalescence in the tony River Forest home of the Santis he could rest and relax for a good while. He would even offer a bright young college kid a position, if he so desired.

Adagio molto e cantabile:

la vita ed essere innamorato

Any time that is not spent in love is wasted

— Tasso —

Forty-Eight

8:30 a.m.
Saturday, November 4th
1246 Park Street
River Forest, Illinois

Enzo canceled all of his performances for the next several months. The opera companies would understand, once the full story of his ordeal was revealed, and after his tremendous performances with the CGO, the opera companies would wait. Enzo also told his manager to assure the companies that the personal crisis would not hinder him in the future.

He and Gwen stayed with each other, loved each other and poured their lives into each other as never before. The trauma of the last month was over and the couple could resume their relatively normal lives, but neither one of them would forget the feeling of emptiness that they had endured when faced with the death of the other.

Not a day went by that they were not in each other's arms, thanking God for their deliverance, and pleading forgiveness for their doubts in the midst of trial.

The couple had bought their dream house, and this was the day on which they were to occupy their new home. Gwen's mother would be arriving at O'Hare Airport later that day to help the couple settle in. Gwen had just recently told her mother of the events of the last month and her mother wanted to see her daughter in person, to verify her well-being.

The movers were supposed to be at the house at 8:00 a.m. They were late, and nowhere to be found. That was fine with the couple. They wandered around the house, planning their layout. Enzo let Gwen run this show. He did not care how things were arranged, as long as she was there and she was with him.

They bounced down the stairs, having inspected the master bedroom, and deciding where her mother would sleep, and, when more fully recovered, where Demetrius would stay.

Enzo stepped into the front hall at the bottom of the stairs, and Gwen stopped on the first stair, elevating herself to her husband's height.

"E, I think we had better buy a couple more beds. We've got our king size for the master bedroom, and the queen for Mom, but we really need to get a better bed for Demetrius," she said, "or at least a better one than that old clunker we have."

"O.K., sweetheart." Enzo looked at his watch, wondering about the movers. "Do you want to go out and get one, or call one of those services? They could get it here today and move it right in."

"That's a great idea," Gwen said. "I'll order a queen sized one." Then she paused and added, "and I'll check to see if they sell baby beds too."

"O.K.," Enzo said, looking out the front door window, without really hearing his wife. His mind played her statement again. He spun in his sneakers.

"What?" he shouted tenorally, the operatic delivery reverberating in the empty house. "Baby beds?"

He jumped to his wife, still standing on the first step, seeing a smile growing on her face. Enzo jumped up and down, playing like a little boy about to get an ice cream cone.

"Tell me, tell me, tell me."

Gwen giggled at her husband's enthusiasm. She put up her hands to halt his bounding, and he settled.

"When I was locked in, you know..."

"Yeah, honey," Enzo finished, understanding her thoughts.

"I started getting stomach cramps. Well, I thought I'd been drugged."Gwen looked down, took her husband's hand, and slid it under her sweatshirt, placing his open palm on the silken skin of her abdomen.

Enzo's smile was huge, his eyes glowing as his wife told her tale.

"I wasn't drugged, Enzo. I wasn't injured. Just the first sign that I had some company." Gwen smiled. "Enzo, we're going to have a baby."

Enzo looked deep into his wife's eyes.

"I love you so much, Gwen," he said, "and I love our baby."

Enzo wrapped his arms around his wife, and Gwen leaned in to her husband. The adoring husband lifted his precious wife into the air, spun her around, kicking and yelping all the way, and then placed her back on the first stair step. They looked at each other with the fullness of love, and kissed.

And in that kiss, in that surrender of life and love, Enzo and Gwen, husband and wife, dedicated their home and their child to the love, laughter and happiness that they shared with one another. The Madonna in the backyard smiled as the husband and wife were fully united in the glory of passionate, spiritual love.

The pair cradled down onto the stairs, physically expressing their dedication and passion for one another, enjoying the freedom of union, and the expression of intimacy.

There was a knock at the front door. The lovers looked at each other, caught in their passion, on their very first day in their new house. They began to laugh, trying to stand, but stumbling over each other.

Gwen grabbed her clothes and, laughing riotously, ran upstairs to straighten herself. Enzo sat on the stairs for a moment, giggling, then stood, straightened his clothes, and walked to the front door. He swung the door open, wide as the smile on his face.

"Good morning, gentlemen. Welcome to the Santi Home."